I0788551

VOLUME III OF
E THREE-FOLD MIMESIS OF LIFE

The Representation of the Human Reality

Your Mimesis is your Reality
Mimesis evolves.
You do not have to stay where you start

DR. RONALD BARNES

ISBN: 978-1-961677-12-8 (Paperback)
ISBN: 978-1-961677-16-6 (Hardback)
ISBN: 978-1-961677-19-7 (E-book)

Library of Congress Control Number: 2025924716

Printed in the United States of America

Published by:

THE
QUIPPY™
QUILL

info@thequippyquill.com
(302) 295-2278

Table of Contents

Disclaimer

The lived experiences and profiles of the individuals in this book are from public information. Much of the information is verbatim because the only use of the information is to present their lived experiences and phenomena encountered in their lives as accurately as possible. Their lived experiences present, their life encounters, decisions, and response to their lived experiences, and their Mimesis construction resulting thereof. Insights presented both individually and compared with other individuals reveal their reality. The author believes that presenting the concept of Mimesis in the context of well-known individuals will help the reader understand Mimesis and apply the concept of Mimesis to their own lived experiences.

This author does not have first-hand knowledge about the individuals profiled in this book. The comments about their lived experiences and relationships were taken from books written about them, media articles, interviews, and research studies on the topics of psychology, developmental theories, relationships, infidelity, forgiveness, repentance, reconciliation, personality, and behavioral response to lived experiences and environmental phenomena.

Preface

Volume III of *the Three-Fold Mimesis of Life* is dedicated to the individuals profiled in this Volume III and to their families. The profiles examined in this Volume are a presentation and representation of the reality of the individuals profiled, as documented in various cited sources.

Dr. Martin Luther King, Jr., Muhammad Ali, Oprah Winfrey, Barack Hussein Obama, Billy Graham, Queen Elizabeth II, Richard Nixon, Malcolm X, Stanley "Tookie" Williams, Donald Trump, Jay-Z, Tupac Shakur, Elvis Presley, Beyonce, Marilyn Monroe.

Stress, poverty, and the desire to achieve in life are often motivators in life that stimulate individuals' will to achieve and attain success. In Muhammad Ali's case, his will to become a boxer was motivated because his bicycle was stolen, and he wanted to find the thief and beat him up. In 1954, a twelve-year-old then known as Cassius Clay approached a police officer, Joe Martin, to report that his bicycle had been stolen and told Martin that he wanted to "whup" the thief. Martin offered to teach him how to box and guided his career for the next six years. As a 1960 Olympic coach, Martin accompanied the champion to the Olympic Games in Rome, Italy, where Ali won a gold medal.[1]

Oprah Winfrey was born poor and experienced hardship became wealthy because she syndicated her television show. The late movie critic Roger Ebert, a friend of Winfrey's who said he persuaded her to enter syndication, put it this way: She made the decision to syndicate her show immediately after he jotted down her potential earnings on a napkin.[2] Winfrey's empathy and concern for the plight of others were a motivating factor in her rise to prominence. One can argue that reflecting on her own life instilled in Ms. Winfrey a sense of caring for the welfare of others.

Queen Elizabeth was motivated to achieve because of duty. One can argue Donald Trump was motivated because of selfish Greed, ego, and because he was advantaged to have a wealthy father. Dr. Martin Luther King, Jr. and Malcolm X were motivated because of their faith and duty to God. Also, Martin Luther King, Jr. and Malcolm X were not only motivated by their faith in their God but also because of their commitment to remedy the inequalities in society. Billy Graham, who was also a religious man, seemed to be motivated by his faith in God. Graham's religious beliefs did not have the tone of equality for all people as did King's and Malcolm's. Graham's religious sermons focused mainly on human devotion to God. King, Malcolm, and Graham all garnered the support of millions of people who supported them. The point is that each of the individuals profiled in this Volume III was motivated to achieve by circumstances in their life that involved other people who opened doors for them and who cared about them. While many of the individuals experienced childhood poverty, they still managed to overcome the hardship of their childhood (*Richard Nixon, Malcolm X, Stanley "Tookie" Williams, Jay-Z, Tupac Shakur, Elvis Presley, and Marilyn Monroe*). Even "Tookie" Williams, who murdered 4 people, was tried, convicted, condemned to death, and executed, eventually was rehabilitated and became a person dedicated to helping youth. With his new outlook on life, he started writing books just two years later in 1996. His first book was written with the help of Barbara Cottman Becnel, who was the co-author. Williams published twelve books in collaboration with Becnel. These books were for children and spoke against gang violence and the gang life that he once led.

The point is that all of these individuals were motivated to change the path they started on, to achieve greater success, and to change their initial social location and lifestyle because they wanted more. The trajectory of their lives was changed because they were influenced by people who cared about them and/or because they became committed to duty or a cause. The significant factor about Mimesis is that when people experience positive influence in their lives, it can become a transformational experience, regardless of past influences in their lives.

Individuals are confronted with a myriad of choices and decisions during their lifetime. The decisions they make about the choices they face factor into the Mimesis.

Volume III of the *Three-Fold Mimesis of Life* is devoted to reviewing the Mimesis evolution of the following individual:

> *Dr. Martin Luther King, Jr., Muhammad Ali, Oprah Winfrey, Barack Hussein Obama, Billy Graham, Queen Elizabeth II, Richard Nixon, Malcolm X, Stanley "Tookie" Williams, Donald Trump, Jay-Z, Tupac Shakur, Elvis Presley, Beyonce, Marilyn Monroe.*

Understanding the choices they were confronted with and the decisions they made regarding those choices will give insight into their Mimesis. The result of their choices, and the response others had to the choices they made, will help the reader to understand their Mimesis. Hopefully, this will also give the reader insight using aforethought into how to construct their own Mimesis.

How to read Volume III of the Three-Fold Mimesis of Life

Volume III, alone of Three-Fold Mimesis of Life, is 500 pages. The readable text in the entire book (all four volumes) is almost 900 pages. The author recognizes this is a healthy read. Chapters 1 and 2 of Volume III review and profile the Mimesis of individuals for the purpose of giving the reader a clear understanding of the concept of Mimesis as it applies to real Life. Reader understanding is accomplished by presenting the lived experiences of noteworthy individuals the reader may have familiarity. Insight into the Mimesis of familiar individuals, their lived experiences, and how they responded to experiences and phenomena they encountered, how others responded to the individuals' Mimesis, and how the individual's environment influenced their Mimesis, will give the reader clarity on Mimesis. This will allow the reader to understand how Mimesis relates to their own personal situation. The reader will also gain insight into how Mimesis constructs represent the human reality. Insight into individual differences and the different paths life's journey can take us on.

Volumes I, II, and IV capture and present the essence of the author's purpose. The primary purpose of the author is to give the reader insight and understanding that you have the ability to construct their own Mimesis of Life, and the individual has agency over how their life turns out. The individual needs to learn how to navigate the environment they are in, the society, the government, and their day-to-day experiences. This author presents an obvious truism that an individual's life develops and turns out according to the Mimesis they construct. Individuals are catalysts for their lived experiences.

Volume I explains and gives an understanding of the concept of the Mimesis of Life and insight into the Theories of Psychology that establish the foundation for Mimesis construction. Volume II takes the reader through the stages of Mimesis construction and addresses challenges and obstacles to functional Mimesis constructs. Volume IV connects the construct of the Three-Fold Mimesis of Life to the Development Theories and summarizes *"the Three-Fold Mimesis of Life."*

Chapter 1 of Volume III gives the reader insight into the Mimesis of people the reader may be familiar. The reader should read the text on select individuals to understand how their lived experiences relate to their Mimesis construct and to relate the profiles of the individuals to the concept of Mimesis described in Volume 1, II, and IV. The reader should read at least two of the Mimesis descriptions of the individuals profiled in Chapter 1. When the reader reads the Individual's Mimesis, they should also read the comparative Mimesis descriptions in Chapter 2. The reader should read the descriptions of individuals in Chapter 1 that correspond with the comparative descriptions in Chapter 2. For example, in Chapter 2, Dr. Martin Luther King, Jr. and Reverend Billy Graham are compared to each other. The reader should read the individual Mimesis description of both Dr. King and Reverend Graham in Chapter 1. Then read the comparative Mimesis comparisons in Chapter 2 on Dr. King and Billy Graham.

The four volumes of *"the Three-Fold Mimesis of Life"* are also excellent as a reference resource to refer to throughout your life. The concepts and theories in these four volumes are universal, time-proven, and have empirical value to the lives of the readers.

Introduction

Volume III discusses the lived experiences of the following individuals:

Dr. Martin Luther King, Jr., Muhammad Ali, Oprah Winfrey, Barack Hussein Obama, Billy Graham, Queen Elizabeth II, Richard Nixon, Malcolm X, Stanley "Tookie" Williams, Donald Trump, Jay-Z, Tupac Shakur, Elvis Presley, Beyonce, Marilyn Monroe.

The lived experiences of each individual mentioned are reviewed in Chapter 1 of Volume III. The information on the individuals comes from public records. The comments on how these individuals response and responded to their environment, to the phenomena they encountered and how they responded to their lived experiences is referenced from books written about them, media articles, interviews, and expert peer reviewed research studies on the topics of psychology, developmental theories, relationships, infidelity, forgiveness, repentance, reconciliation personality, and behavioral response to lived experiences and environmental phenomena.

In Chapter 2 of Volume III, comparisons are made between the individuals profiled. The comparisons are meant to unveil the dilemmas in society that influence, impact, and challenge Mimesis' construction. Each of the individuals mentioned has experienced relatively widespread publicity at one time or another in their lives. At least enough publicity and media coverage such that the general public should have an idea of who they are. There is a possibility that Generational differentiation may make some individuals more aware of the individuals and some individuals less aware. Baby boomers, born from 1946 to 1964, and Generation X, born from 1965 to 1980, should have more awareness of the individuals profiled. However, Millennials, born from 1981 to 1996, and Generation Z, born from 1997 to 2012, should have some general knowledge of the individuals. Chapters 1 and 2 of this Volume III should fill in the details on the lived experiences of these individuals.

The individuals mentioned herein this Volume have experienced a range of differences in their Stage 1 Mimesis influence. Both Queen Elizabeth and Donald Trump were born with "silver spoons", so to speak. Muhammad Ali and Beyoncé were born into a relatively normal, stable childhood with both parents and a middle-class to lower-middle-class upbringing. Barack Obama was born into an unstable family environment, but thanks to his extended family and his mother, he did not appear to suffer a deficiency in the area of attachment and security of being loved, even though he grew up without his father. Oprah Winfrey, Billy Graham, Richard Nixon, Malcolm X, Stanley "Tookie" Williams, Jay-Z, Tupac Shakur, Elvis Presley, and Marilyn Monroe all grew up poor. With the exception of Richard Nixon, Billy Graham, and Elvis Presley, all of the individuals mentioned who grew up poor also experienced broken homes, raised by one parent, in all cases, their mother. For most of them, being poor seemed to motivate them to achieve success in terms of material values and money. With the Exception of Malcolm X and Tookie Williams, everyone else achieved a considerable degree of financial and monetary success.

Dr. Martin Luther King Jr., Malcolm X, Tookie Williams, Elvis Presley, Tupac Shakur, and Marilyn Monroe all died prematurely. They did not experience Stage 3 Mimesis. They only experienced the Final Mimesis. This author wants the reader to consider the reasons these individuals died prematurely, in Stage 2 Mimesis. What was it about their Mimesis construct that caused their lives to be cut short in Stage 2? What is it about the environment they engaged that influenced their fate? What is it about the associations of the individuals that influenced their Mimesis? What is it about the decisions they made that influenced their Mimesis? In short, why did some of these individuals experience a premature death, while the others survived through Stage 3 Mimesis, and as of 2023, some are still relishing in Stage 2 Mimesis? Consider these issues as you read Chapters 1 and 2 of this Volume. By reviewing, investigating, and analyzing the lives of the individuals profiled, the reader should be able to understand the concept of Mimesis as it applies to the reality of an individual's life, of your own life. Ideally, the reader will gain an understanding and insight into how they can construct their own Mimesis and, more so, influence the Mimesis of those to whom they are responsible for giving care and advice.

CHAPTER 1

The Reality of the Human Mimesis in Lived Experiences

Reality vs. Illusion

The human mind in the developmental process constructs a concept of reality. However, practically, Yacobi (2013) advances that conscious experiences for different individuals create different concepts of reality. Having a common environmental development experience allows individuals to internalize common perceptions of reality. Identifying the boundaries of an individual's perception of reality is essential. If boundaries and limits of an individual's concept of reality are not well defined, the ideologies, theories, and behaviors an individual exhibit can manifest their internalization of dogmas that only give illusions of understanding.

"Concepts and theories cannot fully describe the ultimate reality due to the inaccessibility to all the elements of emergent reality, and due to the inherent unknowability of all that remains to be discovered and understood. Thus, some disconnect from reality is inevitable, and humans are caught between illusion and reality. The fundamental problem of illusions seizing the individual's awareness is the resulting reluctance to see things as they are and to be seen without illusions."[3]

> **Surreal** is an escape from the world, you can see in front of you and connecting with imaginary, fantasy, or dream-like ideas within your own head.

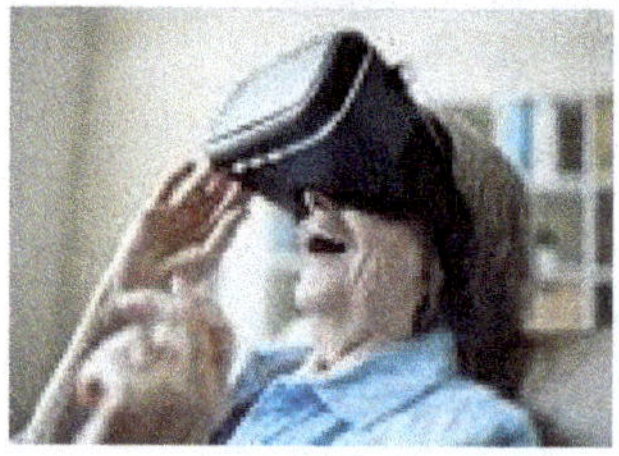

back
WELCOME TO
REALITY

The individuals reviewed herein led lives that are unrealistic to most of us. They had experiences that most people don't encounter. Their lives are magnifications of our realities and normalcies; however, they are also real lived experiences for the individuals reviewed herein. That their lived experiences are magnifications of our own will allow us to understand their Mimesis development and outcomes with more clarity.

In this Chapter, the lived experiences of some high-profile individuals are examined. The reason we review the lives of well-known people is that many of their lived experiences are public information. Framing their life experiences in the context of the Three-Fold Mimesis of their lives will give the reader clarity on the concept of the Three-Fold Mimesis of Life and the objective of this book.

> *Dr. Martin L. King, Jr., Muhammad Ali, Oprah Winfrey, Richard Nixon, Barack Obama, Queen Elizabeth II, Billy Graham, Stanley "Tookie" Williams, Malcolm X, Donald Trump, Jay-Z, Tupac Shakur, Elvis Presley, Beyonce, and Marilyn Monroe.*

Reviewing the lives of these individuals, understanding their evolution through Mimesis Stages 1, 2, and 3, hopefully, will give clarity to the concept of the Three-Fold Mimesis. The lives of each of these individuals took different paths in life. The life experiences of each of these individuals can be examined and evaluated in terms of outcomes. Looking at the lived experiences of each individual, one can gain insight into how their perceptions of real and surreal caused them to believe in the dogma created by how they perceived the reality of their lived life experiences.

Who individuals become is seeded in their Stage 1 Mimesis. Stage 1 Mimesis influences their transition into Stage 2 Mimesis. How they respond to the phenomena that confront them throughout Stage 2 Mimesis determines who they become. At birth, individuals are in the formation stage. A parent's perspective should perceive infants as blank slates to be molded and guided into a masterpiece. Infants are fertile ground to plant seeds of greatness, normalcy, or failure. They have no influence or control over their social location when they enter into consciousness. The influence and guidance of parents, caregivers, or guardians set the stage for the direction individuals will take in life. Which roads in life will they travel? The decisions they will make. The lived experiences they will encounter. Their life will turn out based on how they respond to the lived experiences they encounter, which determines who they will become. The becoming of an individual takes shape when they become agents of their own life decisions. This process continues when the child responds to experiences outside of the home and outside of the jurisdiction of their parents or guardian. When they go to school, nursery, or kindergarten, and begin to develop friendships and associations. When they interact with teachers or teachers' aides (new influences in their lives) in nursery school or kindergarten, their perspectives are enlarged and introduced to new influences. The ongoing process of emplotments throughout their Stage 2 Mimesis contributes to an individual's becoming. An individual's "becoming" is always in formation during Stage 2 of Mimesis. During stage 2, individuals will continuously encounter phenomena, experiences, and influences that will present a variety of situations. The way they respond to the experiences they encounter will determine their path in life or reinforce the path they are on. Their response to the experiences encountered will construct the narrative of their Mimesis. Some will go from a positive direction to a negative direction. Some will go from a negative direction to a positive direction. Some will stay on a negative course, and some will stay on a positive course. The "becoming" of an individual stabilizes when the individual has become who they will be; when the way a person perceives themselves aligns with the way others perceive them. These perceptions are reinforced in Stage 2 Mimesis and become a source of reflection, stability, and their reality. Stage 3 Mimesis is the reflection stage of life. Stage 3 is when the individual looks back on their life and evaluates themselves, and when others look through their life and evaluate them, as well. Stage 3 ends when life ends (the Final Mimesis), and when the final memory of the deceased individual no longer exists.

Can dysfunction in society be significantly reduced or eliminated? Elimination of dysfunction might idealistically be stretching the reality of human nature, wishful thinking. However, the reduction of dysfunction is a realistic achievement if individuals are cognitively directed to value positive behavior and if the environment/society reinforces said positive behavior. The weight of internalizing positive behavior in society is placed on the individual, as it should be, but the support of positive behaviors in the American environment is very narrow and weak in reinforcement. This is what needs to change. The environment/society (American Society) needs to become more committed to supporting the positive behaviors of its population. The support for positive behavior in America is legal or judicial intervention, or incarceration. If an individual does not conform, then they will be punished. American society is reactive instead of proactive in terms of constructing a society focused on positive human development. There are many who believe law enforcement, legal, and judicial intervention are abusive in their exercise of power, especially against minorities.[4] There are also others who think deterrence from dysfunction can be handled in a different manner, proactively. [5]

Positive Mimesis best flourishes in a positive, supportive environment. Limitations/inhibitors/barriers to the type of environment in a society that supports a positive Mimesis are racism/prejudice, neglect, fear, and greed.

- **Racism** causes the majority of individuals to make overt efforts and establish social, political, and economic protocols that discriminate and limit opportunity for minority individuals.

- **Prejudice** results in limited opportunity for individuals because of an unfavorable opinion or feeling formed beforehand or without knowledge, thought, or reason. Prejudice also results from a preconceived opinion or feeling, either favorable or unfavorable. Unreasonable feelings, opinions, or attitudes, especially of a hostile nature, regarding an ethnic, racial, social, or religious group, are considered prejudicial. Prejudice in the law enforcement and legal system is considered to have different standards for arresting and incarcerating minorities and people of color than they do for White people.

- **Neglect** is an incompetence to meet the needs of a person or people in a society, and a disregard for the needs of the people in a society.

- **Fear** is a normal human response to isolation from and ignorance about others who are not carbon copies of oneself. Lack of education, knowledge, misunderstanding, and no interaction with others who are different can cause individuals to be afraid and feel threatened by their ignorance. It is their ignorance that causes their fear; however, too often, the other individuals are viewed as the agency/catalyst of one's fear. A common belief is that White people fear Black men.[6]

- **Greed** is a self-centered focus on the needs of an individual without consideration for others. The accompanying attitude of greed is: No one else matters but me.

Individual responsibility is taught. A supportive society is a socialization developmental, and even political process, requiring collaboration. A problem is that American society has no positive agenda for disenfranchised people. American society is so fragmented and divided that it is a challenge to develop and maintain a universal reinforced positive Mimesis. There is division in America between Republican and Democrat; between Rich and Poor; between Minorities and White; and between religions. The primary institutions in America lack the ability, determination, will, or moral value to establish and reinforce a positive environment to construct Mimesis for all citizens. America, being a heterogeneous, melting pot country, with a variety of individual differences, has been a country of incompatibilities since the first White settlers came to America from England and landed on Plymouth Rock. It has historically been a significant challenge for Americans to get along with each other. Especially disenfranchised are people who are not white or not socially, economically connected or connected through nepotism. The homeless on the streets of America are one example. A great country would remove the scar of homelessness and help these people, as a government cause. As of January 2024, **771,480 people** in America experienced homelessness, an 18% increase from the previous year. This figure, based on the Department of Housing and Urban Development's (HUD) annual "point-in-time" count, is the highest recorded since data collection began in 2007. The count includes people in emergency shelters, transitional housing, and those unsheltered.[7]

The number of Americans living in poverty is another example. America has a culture that discriminates and manipulates minorities, poor people, uneducated people, and those who are not "sanctioned (chosen)" by White society (often referred to as he "Old Boys Club"). Some people who are in the discriminated class do have the ability or knowledge to mitigate their underprivileged status. A major problem with discrimination and prejudice is that inadequate, less qualified, and less intelligent White people are prioritized over others, who are more qualified, more capable, and minorities that are more intelligent. A simple explanation, in addition to racism, discrimination, and prejudice, is that White people are just more comfortable with other White people. Educational institutions (High School, College/University) give evidence that Black and White people can intermingle and relate to each other on a human being-to-human being basis, giving some slight hope for the future. [8]

Examining the lived experiences and Mimesis of high-profile individuals, understanding the variation in their Mimesis and the diversities of outcome in their lives will give the reader insight into their own Mimesis. The individual is responsible for constructing their Mimesis.

This applies to each of the following:

> Dr. Martin Luther King Jr., a minister and civil rights leader
> Muhammad Ali, a great boxer, and champion of social justice
> Oprah Winfrey, television personality, business entrepreneur and philanthropist
> Barack Obama, 44th President of the United States of America

Rev. Billy Graham, an evangelist, minister, and moral leader

Queen Elizabeth II, Queen of England and the UK Commonwealth

Malcom X, Minister of the Nation of Islam and civil rights leader

Richard Nixon, 37th President of the United States of America

Stanley "Tookie" Williams, founder and leader of the Crips street gang

Donald Trump, businessperson, TV personality, and 45th President of the United States of America

Shawn Carter (Jay-Z), rapper and businessperson

Tupac Shakur, rapper

Elvis Presley, singer, King of Rock and Roll

Beyonce, singer and entertainer

Marilyn Monroe, model and actor.

Again, the purpose of examining the lived experiences and Mimesis of these notable individuals is to show the reader how lived experiences influence and impact Mimesis and outcomes in life. To give the reader insight in how to construct their own Mimesis so they can achieve positive outcomes in their own lives. Overcoming challenges is important to a positive Mimesis. Understanding the lived experiences of these individuals will inform the reader to the fact that regardless of the social location you inherit, you can construct a life worth living, a life of self-esteem and a life appreciated by others.

Because they are individuals who have lived their lives in high profile, significant narrative is available and a matter of public record regarding their lived experiences. This makes it possible to understand their Mimesis from the extensive narrative of their life. The information used to examine the lived experiences and Mimesis of these high-profile individuals is public information. It is from the information made public that the emplotments in their lives allow us to understand their Mimesis. The author's intent is for the audience to understand the various outcomes produced from their lived experiences and how they emplot to produce the Three-Fold Mimesis of the Life of these individuals. The one most important concept the author wants to convey is that any individual can construct their lived experiences and their Mimesis. Most youth live their lives in the moment without giving much thought to the future until they accumulate live experiences. However, decisions made in early childhood and adolescence impact the choices you have in the future. It is the intent of this author to convey the understanding that when positive choices in the formative and adolescent stages of life, gives you more abundant and positive options in life. The experiences you attract and encounter are less encumbered. Environmental circumstances also influences Mimesis.

Some people consider human life as both a gift and an ordeal, full of wonderful moments, memories, and experiences to balance the dark background of pain, suffering, and the dread of uncertainty and then death. "The uncertainties and ambiguities of life may result in existential angst".[9] Life experiences are characterized by constant comparisons and differences; the opposites and choices, highs and lows; ups and downs; happiness and sadness; having and wanton; laughter and crying; the dichotomy characterized by these juxtaposed states of experience create the emotion range between content and discontent and often the nagging feeling that something is missing in life. The ultimate challenge in life is to discover the key to manage the dualities in human experience such that they manifest as an aligned construct of marriage between human Realities. Yacobi (2013) insightfully understands the concept of the influence human reality and human illusion manifesting in human behavior and the illusion of uncertainty dualities can impress on the human understanding of who they are.   However, humans do not have to experience unresolved dilemmas, or feelings the absurdities of life have no resolution. Yacobi (2013) suggest that at the end of life, after enduring the endless series of changes, and dichotomies one is left with the understanding that there is no definitive answer to the absurdity of life. Unresolved dilemmas in stage three is a result of a Mimesis that is incomplete in its development, or unfortunately did not reconcile the life experiences they encountered. In the case of this human drama, individuals are actors looking either for a role, or the original author, or for the primary source of it all. It does not have to be this way if the human has a positive Mimesis construction or is able to reconcile difficult lived experiences in the construction of their Mimesis.

The lived experiences of well-known individuals profiled in this book were taken from public information. Much of the information was taken verbatim because the only use of the information was to give the reader a perception of their lived experiences and phenomena they encountered in their lived experience.

Understanding how the concept of The Mimesis of Life applies to the lived experiences of well-known individuals will enable the reader to better understand the concept of The Mimesis of Life and how it applies to their own lived experiences.

The Life Mimesis comparison between the individuals mentioned herein will also give the reader a better understanding of how Mimesis varies from one individual to another, keeping in mind that a purpose of this book is to enable the reader to understand that they can create and construct their own Mimesis in life with forethought.

Mimesis of Life for Dr. Martin Luther King, Jr. (1929-1934)

Dr. King was a Baptist minister. He was also a prominent national leader of a nonviolent movement during the late 1950s and 1960s to achieve equality for Black and minority Americans, both legally and in their daily life experiences. Dr. Martin Luther King, Jr. was born on January 15, 1929, in Atlanta, Georgia, to the Reverend Martin Luther King Sr. and Alberta Williams King. He died on April 4th, 1968, from an assassin's bullet. Like his father, he became a Baptist minister. King did not hide the fact that his father whipped him until the age of 15. King noticed firsthand his father's rebellion and protest against segregation.[10] King was not always the non-violent, tempered man defined by his legacy. Initially, he had a deep resentment against White people because of racial humiliation, prejudice, and discrimination suffered by him, his family, and his neighbors. He witnessed racism, first-hand, in the segregated South.[11] In 1948, King graduated from Morehouse College in Atlanta, Georgia, and then graduated from Crozer Theological Seminary in Chester, Pennsylvania, in 1951 with a Divinity degree. Then, in 1955 graduated from Boston College with a PhD in theology.[12] Even as an accomplished, educated American, Dr. King was humiliated, jailed numerous times, and ridiculed by White Americans because of his activities to end discrimination and prejudice against Black people in America. Even some Black Americans condemned his non-violent approach to the civil rights movement. His house was bombed by racist Whites attempting to change his life direction against civil rights. Yet in the face of constant and considerable opposition to his life direction, Dr. King was unwavering and stood firm in his ethical and moral convictions to do what he thought was right and just.

Mimesis Stage 1 for Dr. Martin Luther King, Jr. [13]

Martin Luther King Jr. was born on Tuesday, January 15, 1929, to Reverend Martin Luther King Sr. and Alberta Williams King. Martin had two siblings: a sister, Willie Christine, and a brother, Alfred Daniel Williams. He lived in a household with his parents, his grandparents, and his brother and sister.

Dr. King grew up in Atlanta, Georgia, the South.

Dr. King grew up in a strict household.

Dr. King was born into a religious family.

His grandfather was a Baptist minister for Ebenezer Baptist Church.

His father was a Baptist minister for Ebenezer Baptist Church.

Martin Luther King's childhood was a normal, happy upbringing. He and his siblings learned to play the piano from their mom and were guided by the spiritual teachings from their dad and grandfather. But the family was quickly schooled on the harsh reality of the racial segregation of the South.

Martin Luther King came from a comfortable middle-class family steeped in the tradition of the Southern Black ministry: both his father and maternal grandfather were Baptist preachers. His parents were college-educated, and King's father had succeeded his father-in-law as pastor of the prestigious Ebenezer Baptist Church in Atlanta.

Mimesis Stage 2 for Dr. Martin Luther King, Jr.

1934 At the age of five, Martin Luther King Jr. began school at Yonge Street Elementary School in Atlanta. This, however, was before the legal school entrance age of six; thus, Martin was sent home and not allowed to continue his education until he turned six years old. The tightly knit extended family in which King, Jr., was raised had a profound influence on his worldview. "It is quite easy for me to think of a God of love mainly because I grew up in a family where love was central and where lovely relationships were ever present."

Martin was a paper boy and wanted to be a fireman when he grew up. He learned early about southern segregation. If a black family wanted to eat at a restaurant, they had to sit in a separate section of the restaurant. They had to sit in the back of the movie theater and even use separate restroom facilities. He did not understand this. The laws that kept black people and white people apart were called Jim Crow laws. One day, Martin and his father went to buy some new shoes. The clerk told them to go to the back of the store. "We do not serve colored people in the front of the store," he said. Martin and his father proceeded to leave the store, as they knew that this was not respectful treatment. Martin's mother told him, "Even though some people make you feel bad or angry, you should not show it. You are as good as anyone else."

1942   Following his education at Yonge Street Elementary School, he attended David T. Howard Elementary School. He also attended the Atlanta University Laboratory School and Booker T. Washington High School. He scored so high on his college entrance exam at Booker High School that he did not formally finish high school; he went on to college in his junior year of high school.

1944   King enrolled in Morehouse College in Atlanta 1944. He wasn't planning to enter the ministry, but then he met Dr. Benjamin Mays, a scholar whose manner and bearing convinced him that a religious career could be intellectually satisfying. Dr. Mays became a mentor to Martin Luther King.

The prejudice Dr. King experienced at the behest of Whites caused him to develop a hatred for White people. Living in the south, he had firsthand experience with racism.

As he became more educated and learned about Mahatma Gandhi, his views changed, and he understood the strength in and of non-violence.

1948   After receiving his bachelor's, King attended Crozer Theological Seminary in Chester, Pa., winning the Plafker Award as the outstanding student of the graduating class, and the J. Lewis Crozer Fellowship as well. He went on to become a minister

1953 Dr. King attended Boston College to earn a PhD and became a Doctor of Theology (PhD).

1953 King married Coretta Scott on June 18, on the lawn of her parents' house in her hometown of Heiberger, Alabama. They became the parents of four children: Yolanda King (1955–2007),

Martin Luther King III (b. 1957), Dexter Scott King (b. 1961), and Bernice King (b. 1963). During their marriage, King limited Coretta's role in the civil rights movement, expecting her to be a housewife and mother.

1955 King became the pastor of the Dexter Avenue

Baptist Church in Montgomery, Alabama. There, he made his first mark on the civil-rights movement by

mobilizing the black community during a 382-day boycott of the city's bus lines. King helped organize the first major protest of the African American civil rights movement: the successful Montgomery Bus Boycott. Influenced by Mohandas Gandhi, he advocated restraint from civil disobedience and nonviolent resistance to segregation in the South.

Dr. King got involved in a bus boycott because  Ms. Rosa Parks (Pictured left with Dr. King) refused to sit in the back of the bus, which was the southern Jim Crow segregation policy. Black people refused to ride the bus in Montgomery, which caused the White city officials to succumb to Black demands.

1956 Dr. King became the most visible civil rights leader of his era. The peaceful protests he led throughout the American South were often met with violence, but King and his followers persisted, and the movement gained momentum. On January 30, 1956, a White supremacist terrorist bombed the Montgomery home of Dr. Martin Luther King, Jr. No one was injured. This incident of terrorism did not deter King. It actually strengthened his resolve. King overcame arrest and other violent harassment, including the bombing of his home. Ultimately, the U.S. Supreme Court declared bus segregation unconstitutional.

1957 A national hero and a civil-rights figure of growing importance, King summoned together a number of black leaders in 1957 and laid the groundwork for the organization now known as the Southern Christian Leadership Conference (SCLC). King was elected its president, and he soon began helping other communities organize their own protests against discrimination.

1958 King survived a knife attack. On September 20, 1958, King was signing copies of his book "*Stride Toward Freedom*" in Blumstein's department store in Harlem when he narrowly escaped death. Izola Curry, a mentally ill black woman who thought that King was conspiring against her with communists, stabbed him in the chest with a letter opener, which nearly impinged on his aorta. King received first aid from police officers Al Howard and Philip Romano.

1960 Dr. Martin Luther King, Jr. returned to Atlanta to be co-pastor, with his father, of Ebenezer Baptist Church.

1963 Three years later, King's nonviolent tactics were put to their most severe test in Birmingham, during a mass protest for fair hiring practices and the desegregation of department-store facilities. Birmingham, Alabama, at the time, was described as the "most segregated city in America." Police brutality used against the marchers and shown on national television, dramatized the plight of blacks to the nation at large, with enormous impact. King was arrested, but his voice was not silenced: He wrote "Letter from a Birmingham Jail" to refute his critics.

1963 Later in 1963, Dr. King was one of the driving forces behind the March for Jobs and Freedom, more commonly known as the "March on Washington," which drew over a quarter-million people to the National Mall. King was a principal speaker at the historic March on Washington, where he delivered one of the most passionate addresses of his career, the "I have a dream" speech (Appendix II).

1963 Time magazine designated him as its Person of the Year for 1963. King took on new challenges. In Selma, Ala., he led a voter-registration campaign that ended in the Selma-to-Montgomery Freedom March.

1964 At 35 years old, Martin Luther King, Jr. became the youngest person to win the Nobel Peace Prize. Martin Luther King, Jr. was awarded the Nobel Peace Prize for his dynamic leadership of the Civil Rights movement and steadfast commitment to achieving racial justice through nonviolent action. Even after becoming a civil rights leader and a Nobel Peace Prize winner, in the "quiet recesses" of his heart, Martin Luther King, Jr., remained a Baptist preacher. "This is my being and my heritage," he once explained, "for I am also the son of a Baptist preacher, the grandson of a Baptist preacher, and the great-grandson of a Baptist preacher".

Dr. King peacefully demonstrated against the injustice, unfair treatment, and racism against minorities.

Dr. King was loved by the majority of African Americans. He was respected by many White people. He was hated by many White people.

      Some Black people did not believe in his non-violent approach to peacefully demonstrating.

1964   Partly due to the March on Washington, Congress passed the landmark Civil Rights Act. The civil rights movement achieved two of its greatest successes: the ratification of the 24th Amendment, which abolished the poll tax, and the Civil Rights Act of 1964, which prohibited any form of American legalized racial discrimination in employment and education. The bill also outlawed racial segregation in public facilities.

1965   Congress went on to pass the Voting Rights Act, which was an equally important set of laws that eliminated the remaining barriers to voting for African Americans, who in some locales had been almost completely disenfranchised. This legislation resulted directly from the Selma to Montgomery, AL March for Voting Rights lead by Dr. King.

1965   King next brought his crusade to Chicago, where he launched programs to rehabilitate the slums and provide housing.

Civil rights leader Dr. Martin Luther King, Jr. (center, bottom) marches along State Street in 1966 as part of the Chicago Freedom Movement.

Although he was trying to create a new coalition based on equal support for peace and civil rights, it caused an immediate rift. The National Association for the Advancement of Colored People (NAACP) saw King's shift of emphasis as "a serious tactical mistake." The Urban League warned that the "limited resources" of the civil-rights movement would be spread too thin. In the North, young and angry blacks did not care for his preaching and even less for his non-violent pleas for peaceful protest. Their disenchantment with Dr. King was one of the reasons he rallied behind a new cause: the war in Vietnam.

Between 1965 and 1968, Dr. King shifted his focus toward economic justice, which he highlighted by leading several campaigns in Chicago, Illinois. He was also an advocate for international peace, which he championed by speaking out strongly against the Vietnam War.

1968	King gave his support to the Memphis sanitation men's strike. He wanted to discourage violence, and he wanted to focus national attention on the plight of the poor, unorganized workers of the city. The men were bargaining for basic union representation and long-overdue raises.

Final Mimesis for Dr. Martin Luther King, Jr.

On April 4th, 1968, Dr. Martin Luther King, Jr. leadership ended abruptly and tragically when he was assassinated at the Lorraine Motel in Memphis, Tennessee. Dr. King's body was returned to his hometown of Atlanta, Georgia, where high-level leaders of all races and political stripes attended his funeral ceremony.

The Final Mimesis for Dr. Martin Luther King, Jr.

- Dr. King was posthumously awarded the Presidential Medal of Freedom and the Congressional Gold Medal.

- Martin Luther King Jr. Day was established as a holiday in numerous cities and states beginning in 1971; the holiday was enacted at the federal level by legislation signed by President Ronald Reagan in 1986.

- Hundreds of streets in the U.S. have been renamed in his honor, and a county in Washington State was also rededicated for him.

- The Martin Luther King Jr. Memorial on the National Mall in Washington, D.C., was dedicated in 2011.

- For his stand and outspokenness against racism in America, Dr. King was assassinated in 1968 by a White assassin.

- Numerous people mourned the death of Dr. King. Almost every major city in America has a street named after him.

- Dr. King is memorialized in the United States capital and in Washington, D.C.

- Dr. King's birthday, January 17, is celebrated as a national holiday.

Mimesis of Life Summary for
Dr. Martin Luther King, Jr.

Martin Luther King Jr. was born on Tuesday, January 15, 1929, to Reverend Martin Luther King Sr. and Alberta Williams King. Martin had two siblings: a sister, Willie Christine, and a brother, Alfred Daniel Williams. He lived and grew up in Atlanta, Georgia, in a household with his parents, his grandparents, and his brother and sister. Dr. King was born into a religious family. His father and grandfather were Baptist ministers. Dr. King grew up in a loving and strict household.

Martin Luther King's childhood was normal, happy, and comfortable. He and his siblings learned to play the piano from their mom and were guided by the spiritual teachings from their dad and grandfather. But the family was quickly schooled on the harsh reality of the racial segregation of the South.

The early childhood experiences of Martin King are full of love and family values. He was raised in an extended family with his parents, grandparents, and siblings. The closeness and tight-knit family experience established valuable and purposeful character and security in his life.

There is a possibility that Dr. King was conflicted. The conflict was between the confidence, security, and love he experienced as a child and the segregation and racism he was confronted with in society when he walked out of his front door. Martin was smart. Evidently, the conflict he experienced caused him to resolve the issue in a way his life experience and background prepared him for, the Christian Ministry. The guidance he received at home prepared him to achieve ahead of his years and ahead of his peers. While racism is a negative influence on Mimesis construction, Dr. King was able to overcome the negativity of racism in his environment and the negative feelings he held toward Whites. Dr. King's lived experiences as a child, an adolescent, a young adult, and an adult all contributed to his disdain for injustice and racism. Dr. King was called to fight against racism and injustice. The general racist and unjust condition of the society, the social environment, challenged Martin. Who knows how great American society would have become if Dr. King's contributions had been actualized in longevity? However, it seems that when Dr. King was assassinated, American society's racism remained rooted in American society. It was inevitable that Dr. King would have rebelled against racism and injustice in America. That his father and grandfather were ministers gave him a pulpit from which to express his ideology. His charisma drew thousands of people to his cause. However, the most important and significant factor Dr. Martin King, Jr. had on his side was, he was right and he spoke for the majority of people in America, White and Minority. He was a voice for the frustration many Black Americans felt and likewise for the White people, who themselves were against racism but afraid to speak out. That is why when he spoke or led demonstrations, he got the support of thousands of people. Because thousands and millions of Black Americans and White Americans identified with the civil rights cause. White people know they are racist and that White America is a racist culture. Many wanted to be racist because it put blinders on their inadequacy as human beings and their insecurity as below-average individuals. The Constitution of the United States and the Holy Bible tell us that all people are created equal. The only people who don't believe that are people who are not equal. If they were equal, they would adhere to the dogma that respects human beings.

Being born into a religious environment, Dr. King followed the same path as his grandfather and father.

Being born in the racist South and encountering racist life experiences characteristic of that environment, at the time, influenced Dr. King's life direction and the decisions he made. All of which led to the way people and society perceived and responded to him as a man and contributed to the legacy he left behind. During the less than 13 years of Dr. Martin Luther King, Jr.'s leadership of the modern American Civil Rights Movement, from December 1955 until April 4, 1968, African Americans achieved more genuine progress toward racial equality in America than the previous 350 years had produced. Dr. King is widely regarded as America's pre-eminent advocate of nonviolence and one of the greatest civil rights leaders in world history. Dr. King is often compared on a par basis with Mahatma Gandhi.[14]

His house was bombed. He was stabbed by a woman with a letter opener. He was hit in the head with a brick while demonstrating in Chicago, Illinois. He was beaten and jailed on numerous occasions. Dr. King's resolve, determination, willpower, and commitment to

civil rights were unrivaled. The civil rights movement was marked by violent attacks by whites in the midst of non-violent demonstrations by Black people.

The attacks by police, the beatings, and the use of attack dogs to brutalize people who were demonstrating peacefully and exercising their rights as American citizens, only present the reality of racism in America. Dr. King, as a minister, a man of God, a Christian, and an American citizen, could not do anything but fight against injustice, which indicates how true to his cause Dr. King was. Jesus was the same.

Dr. Martin Luther King, Jr. was assassinated and died on April 4, 1968. The racist environment and racist individuals in America are catalysts and agents of his assassination. White culture has to shoulder responsibility for the assassination of this great man. If the moral, ethical elements in White culture, at any time over the last 400 years, dealt with racism the same way they dealt with terrorists, then America would be a much better country. The truth is that White culture supports racists and racism; otherwise, Dr. King might still be alive today. Dr. King received numerous death threats. The FBI had him under constant surveillance. Dr. King sensed the danger that was ever-present in his life. Not only from the United States Government but from the sick, fanatical, White racist who hated him. Evidence of his thoughts of danger was expressed in his "I've been to the Mountaintop" speech delivered on April 3, 1968, in Memphis, Tennessee. The city in which he was killed. The speech was delivered the day before he was killed. He stated in his speech:[15]

"And then I got into Memphis. And some began to say the threats, or talk about the threats that were out there. What would happen to me from some of our sick white brothers? Well, I don't know what will happen now. We've got some difficult days ahead. But it really doesn't matter with me now, because I've been to the mountaintop.

And I don't mind.

Like anybody, I would like to live a long life. Longevity has its place. But I'm not concerned about that now. I just want to do God's will. And He's allowed me to go up to the mountain. And I've looked over. And I've seen the Promised Land. I may not get there with you. But I want you to know tonight that we, as a people, will get to the Promised Land!"

Here's a question everyone should ask themselves: Was Dr. Martin Luther King, Jr. a good man? What did Dr. King do that was illegal? Was he acting in terms of an ethical and moral society construction? If your answer to these questions is yes, he was a good man acting for the betterment of society, then ask yourself, why was he killed? If your answer to that question is because there are racists in America who do not want America to be a country that treats all people equally, then does the environment in America need to change? To make America a country that treats all of its citizens fairly, as the Constitution says, the type of people with the mentality of those who killed Dr. King are the ones who are unjust and should be targets of American justice. An America that was true to itself would avenge Dr. King's death. Dr. King did not live a full life. He was assassinated at 39 years old. He knew the possibilities of his being killed were very real, yet he did not retreat from his calling. Dr. King is considered a martyr, along with the likenesses of Jesus Christ and Mahatma Gandhi. Each of these people attracted powerful enemies during their lifetimes, but when they were killed, the whole world loved them. Ironic. The components of being a Black man in America, fighting for equality and justice for all American citizens, within the American Society environmental construct, were two of the factors that caused Dr. King to be killed. What does this say about America?

There is no question that Dr. King was not only a good man but a great man. The response to Dr. King's legacy by American citizens, both Black and White was overwhelming. The irony is that America loved Dr. King after he was dead. Acknowledgement of his contribution to America and the world is as follows:

He was awarded the Nobel Peace Prize.

Almost every major city has a street named after him.

He is memorialized in the nation's capital, in the House of Representatives, with a bronze bust.

The Martin Luther King, Jr. Memorial is a national memorial located in West Potomac Park next to the National Mall in Washington, D.C., United States. It covers four acres (1.6 ha) and includes the Stone of Hope, a granite statue of Civil Rights Movement leader Martin Luther King Jr., A rare honor in the vein of the Lincoln Memorial, the Jefferson Memorial, and the Washington Monument.

A national holiday is established in honor of Dr. Martin Luther King, Jr.

Although Dr. King's birthday is January 15th, the holiday is celebrated on the third Monday of January to align with the Uniform Monday Holiday Act. It is designated as a National Day of Service, encouraging volunteerism and community service across the country.[16]

To keep his dream alive, 50 identical statues of Martin Luther King were placed from Washington to Amsterdam, Netherlands, on locations that refer to slavery and places that let us remember how important it is to end racism and fight for equality, regardless of gender, religion, and race.[17]

This praise of the Mimesis of Dr. Martin Luther King, Jr., in no way suggests that martyrdom is acceptable to achieve greatness. Dr. King's assassination is an American tragedy that will stain this country's history forever. It tells how racist America is and that America has too many deplorable people in the White culture. America also has many good and decent White people. Deplorable people exist in all cultures, but Dr. King's lived experiences magnified the brutality and dysfunction in White culture as well as their inability to get along with other non-White Americans. A legacy of Dr. Martin Luther King, Jr. is his dedication to rid America of racism and injustice, and for all Americans to live together in peace and harmony. In the opinion of this author, the deplorability in White culture will only be eliminated when White people want it to be. The dysfunction in America was especially evident during this era (1960's). Leaders who wanted to build a better, more inclusive, America were eliminated (assassinated). Dr. King (1968), Malcolm X (1965), President John F. Kennedy 1963), Senator Robert Kennedy (1968), and Medgar Evers (1963) were all assassinated during that era.

An irony of the aftermath to the assassination of Dr. King is that no one was prepared or willing to fill his shoes. Of all the individuals surrounding him, closely participating with him in the civil rights movement and standing by his side, none of them rose to take over the mantle of Dr. King. While many of his close associates continued the civil rights struggle in their own way, after Dr. King's assassination the movement was severely weakened. This is an example of why Dr. King was a great human being. That no one else could do or did do what he did.

The only thing Dr. Martin Luther King Jr. asked of America was that America be true to the dogma America professed to be governed by. The dogma America declares to follow, and that is written on paper (The Constitution of the United States of America, The Declaration of Independence, The Emancipation

Proclamation, and The Holy Bible). America (White America) has not been true to what America professes to believe. America has never been true to American dogma since Europeans came to America in 1619. This is the environment in which the Mimesis of Dr. Martin Luther King, Jr. was constructed. It is also the environment in which the Mimesis of all Americans is constructed: White, Black, Minority, Hispanic, Asian, LGBTQ, and religious Christians and religious others than Christians. As Dr. King evolved, his views became more closely aligned with those of Malcolm X. At the same time, Malcolm X evolved, and his views became more aligned with those of Dr. King. One might say the growth of both men evolved such that they met each other in the middle. Dr. King stated, "That dream I had that day has in many points turned into a nightmare".[18] This statement was made in reflection on the status of American society after his "*I had a dream*"

speech. Reflecting on the Environment in America in which the Mimesis of Americans is constructed, both for White and Black Americans, Dr. King acknowledged that there are two Americas: one White and one Black. In a country where everyone is an American citizen and where all American citizens under the Constitution have equal rights, Mimesis construction among Americans does not reflect the reality of American dogma. American reality represents a hypocritical America, according to Dr. Martin Luther King, Malcolm X, and the truth. Dr. King evolved to strengthen his realization that White America is racist and discriminates against everyone who is not White.

The Martin Luther King, Jr. Memorial is a national memorial located in West Potomac Park next to the National Mall in Washington, D.C., United States. It covers four acres and includes the *Stone of Hope*, a granite statue of Civil Rights Movement leader Martin Luther King Jr. The inspiration for the memorial design is a line from King's "I Have a Dream" speech: "Out of the mountain of despair, a stone of hope." The memorial opened to the public on August 22, 2011, after more than two decades of planning, fundraising, and construction.

The Martin Luther King Jr. statue is a public monument of civil rights activist Martin Luther King Jr. in Atlanta, Georgia. The statue stands on the grounds of the Georgia State Capitol, overlooking Liberty Plaza.

In 1968, after he was assassinated, Dr. Martin Luther King, Jr. was carried upon a farm wagon drawn by mules to Southview Cemetery. In 1970, Dr. King's remains were removed from Southview Cemetery to what is the current King Center campus, and in 2006. His crypt was rebuilt to also include the remains of Mrs. Coretta Scott King.

Dr. & Mrs. King's crypt is constructed of Georgia marble, a timeless acknowledgment of his southern roots.

The irony and truly unfortunate tragedy in the assassination of Dr. Martin Luther King, Jr. is that he was a great man who was killed by an individual or individuals. A Black American citizen was killed by White Americans, all citizens of the United States of America. The honors Dr. King received after his death are a testament to his greatness and the quality of his character. He was demonstrating and campaigning for just and right causes, and not only for African Americans but for all Americans who are disenfranchised, as citizens of the "so-called' best country in the world. The Mimesis construct of Dr. King's ontology was obviously different and in conflict with the Mimesis ontology of those who killed him.

What does that say about the Mimesis construction and ontology of the individual or individuals who are responsible for Dr. King's death? Americans killing Americans. Comparing the Mimesis of Dr. King and those others who killed him is clear evidence that individuals have different Mimesis constructs. Dr. King was non-violent and he was killed by violence (violent people). It also is an indication that even good people become victims of bad people. It is a reinforcement that focus on Mimesis construction, especially in the Stage 1 thru Stage 2 adolescent is critical. It is an American tragedy that a man like Dr. King was killed and those who killed him are alive.

> **One of the ironic dilemmas about America is how the American Government can seek to destroy and discredit a human during their lifetime then Honor and Revere that same individual in their death.**

Mimesis of Life for Muhammad Ali (1942-2016)

Muhammad Ali, born as Cassius Marcellus Clay, Jr. in Louisville, Kentucky on January 17, 1942, died on June 3rd, 2016. He was an American, a professional heavyweight boxer, a three-time heavyweight champion, a civil rights leader, and a minister of the Islamic faith. There are many dynamic aspects of Muhammad Ali's life and lived experiences that give his Mimesis a wonderfully unique quality. His Boxing Career, his personal life, his religious and spiritual life, and his civil rights activism; each is a lifetime of experiences for the normal individual.

Cassius Clay changed his name to Muhammad Ali on March 6, 1964, after converting to Islam and joining the Nation of Islam. He viewed his birth name as a "slave name" and chose Muhammad Ali as a new, free name. Cassius Clay was born into a family whose father was a sign painter in Louisville, Kentucky. His mother was a homemaker. A family not of great wealth whose name legacy was from a southern white abolitionist. He rose to become one of the greatest, most well-known, and most recognized individuals of the 20th century. Ali encountered great obstacles to his life direction and overcame them, not without great cost, personal and financial. In spite of the obstacles, he became one of the most decorated and recognized individuals in history. The circumstances in life he encountered were but phases in his life that did not encumber his success or greatness as a human being. Actually, it was the manner in which he responded to life challenges he encountered that reinforced his greatness. The phenomena and life experiences he confronted, the decisions he made dealing with his lived experiences, culminated in a legacy of one of the greatest individuals in history.

He grew up in a time when the South was segregated, separated by race, and he experienced some discrimination in his childhood. Ali started boxing at the age of 12 in a random way. His bike was stolen, and he told a police officer that he wanted to beat up the person who stole it. Police officer Joe E. Martin encountered young Clay and found the 12-year-old in a rage over having his bicycle stolen. He told the officer he was going to "whup" the thief. The officer told Clay he had better learn how to box first, but it was a black trainer named Fred Stoner who taught Ali the science of boxing. Stoner taught him to move with the grace of a dancer and impressed upon him the subtle skills necessary to move beyond good and into the realm of great. When young Clay got in the gym, the rest is history. Ali began boxing when he was 12 years old and won the Golden Gloves championship at the age of 18.[19]

In 1964, at the age of 22, he defeated Sonny Liston to become the professional boxing heavyweight champion of the world. Soon thereafter, he changed his name from Cassius Clay, Jr., which he referred to as his "slave name," and took on the name of Muhammad Ali, given to him by Elijah Muhammad, the leader of the Black Muslim, Islamic religion in America. Ali became a symbol of racial pride for African Americans by his motives to resist white racial prejudice, discrimination, and domination during the civil rights era.

Ali set an example of racial pride for African Americans and resistance to white domination during the Civil Rights Movement.[20] [21] In 1966, Ali refused to be drafted into the United States of America military, indicating that his religious beliefs were in opposition to the American war in Vietnam. He was a conscientious objector to participating in the military. He was arrested, found guilty of draft evasion, and stripped of his boxing title in the prime of his career. Ali appealed his case to the United States Supreme Court, which overturned his

1971 conviction and allowed him to be a free man and resume his career as a professional boxer. During the four years of fighting the American legal system in the courts, he was not allowed to fight opponents in the ring. He was deprived of making a living from his chosen profession. However, his stand as a conscientious objector, the decision he made to stand up for his convictions and his beliefs, made him an icon to both black and white people in his generation. The position he took did not exclude him from the racist hatred and prejudiced characteristics of the white racist in American society.[22] [23] His communications and movements were monitored by the FBI and law enforcement even after his exoneration. However, even in the face of government harassment, Ali became one of the greatest professional athletes in history, and according to many, The Greatest.

Due to years of boxing and punches suffered in the ring, Ali was diagnosed with Parkinson's disease in 1984. This did not stop him from pursuing his religious, Philanthropic, humanitarian, and political endeavors.

Muhammad Ali's Lived Experiences

Mimesis 1 for Cassius Marcellus Clay, Jr. Stage 1 Mimesis

1942   Muhammad Ali, born as Cassius Marcellus Clay, Jr., was born on January 17, 1942, in Louisville, Kentucky, to Cassius Marcellus Clay, Sr. and Odessa O'Grady Clay. Cassius, Jr. had one brother named Rudolph Valentino Clay, who was born in 1944. Cassius Senior and Junior were named after a 19th-century abolitionist

Republican politician named Cassius Marcellus Clay. The grandparents of Cassius Jr. were descendants of slaves in the antebellum South.

Cassius Sr. was a sign and billboard painter. Odessa Clay, the wife and mother of Cassius Jr., was a domestic who worked in White homes. [24] Cassius Jr.'s mother raised him in the Methodist religious faith. Cassius Jr. grew up in the mist of racial segregation. One childhood experience he had was being denied a drink of water because of his color.

Mimesis Stage 2 for Muhammad Ali - Personal Life

Ali was married four times and had seven daughters and two sons.

1964 Ali was introduced to cocktail waitress Sonji Roi by Herbert Muhammad and asked her to marry him after their first date. They married approximately one month later on August 14, 1964

They quarreled over Sonji's refusal to join the Nation of Islam. According to Ali, "She wouldn't do what she was supposed to do. She wore lipstick; she went into bars; she dressed in clothes that were revealing and didn't look right." The marriage was childless, and they divorced on January 10, 1966. Just before the divorce was finalized, Ali sent Sonji a note: "You traded heaven for hell, baby."

1967 On August 17, Ali married Belinda Boyd. Born into a Chicago family that had converted to the

Nation of Islam, she later changed her name to Khalilah Ali, though she was still called Belinda by old friends and family. They had four children: author and rapper Maryum "May May" (born 1968); twins Jamillah and Rasheda (born 1970), who married Robert Walsh and have a son, Biaggio Ali, born in 1998; and Muhammad Ali Jr. (born 1972). Rasheda's son Nico, is a professional boxer.

1972 He had another daughter, Miya (born 1972), from an extramarital relationship with Patricia Harvell.

1974 Ali began an extramarital relationship with 16-year-old Wanda Bolton (who subsequently changed her name to Aaisha Ali), with whom he fathered another daughter, Khaliah (born 1974). While still married to Belinda, Ali married Aaisha in an Islamic ceremony that was not legally recognized.

1977 By the summer of 1977, his second marriage ended due to Ali's repeated infidelity, and he had married actress and model Veronica Porché. At the time of their marriage, they had a daughter, Hana, and Veronica was pregnant with their second child. Their second daughter, Laila Ali, was born in December 1977. By 1986, Ali and Porché were divorced due to Ali's continuous infidelity.

1986 On November 19, 1986, Ali married Yolanda "Lonnie" Williams. Lonnie first met Ali at the age of 6 when her family moved to Louisville in 1963. In 1982, she became Ali's primary caregiver, and in return, he paid for her to attend graduate school at UCLA. Together they adopted a son, Asaad Amin (born 1986), when Asaad was five months old.

2006   Ali sold his name and image for $50 million, after which *Forbes* estimated his net worth to be $55 million in 2006. Following his death in 2016, his fortune was estimated to be between $50 million and $80 million

It is estimated that by 1978, Ali's total fight purse earnings were estimated to be nearly $60 million (inflation-adjusted $322 million), including an estimated $47.45 million grossed between 1970 and 1978. By 1980, his total fight purse earnings were estimated to be up to $70 million.

Stage 2 Mimesis Muhammad Ali's Religion and Political Beliefs

1961   Muhammad Ali, then Cassius Clay, attended his first Nation of Islam meeting.

1962   Cassius Clay met Malcolm X, who became his spiritual and political mentor. Clay initially wanted to join the Nation of Islam (then known as Black Muslims) in 1960. However, he was refused entry because he was a boxer.

1964   After Clay defeated Sonny Liston, he announced to the world that his name was Muhammad Ali and he was a member of the Nation of Islam. When Cassius Clay defeated Liston and became the Heavyweight Champion of the world, the Nation of Islam became more receptive to his membership. As a boxer, they rejected him. As the Heavyweight Champion of the World, they accepted him. Still a boxer!

1964   Elijah Muhammad, the leader of the Nation of Islam, renamed Cassius Clay Muhammad Ali.

The American public, journalists, and other boxers did not accept or respect the fact that Ali joined the Nation of Islam and changed his name to Muhammad Ali. Ali rejected the name Cassius Clay, referring to it as his "slave name." The White establishment was antagonized considerably. Ali's braggadocio, his ability to back it up, his pride, and his self-respect angered the White establishment in America, as well as numerous White people. White people are more comfortable and accepting of humble Black individuals. Ali often spoke out against racial injustice and White racism. Labeling the white race as the perpetrator of genocide against African Americans made Ali a target of hostile White reaction. Stating that his enemy is the white people, not Vietcong or the Chinese or the Japanese, when he refused to join the Army during the Vietnam War. His stance on the war attracted White condemnation. In relation to integration, he said: "We who follow the teachings of Elijah Muhammad don't want to be forced to integrate. Integration is wrong. We don't want to live with the white man; that's all." Ali did not believe in integration or Black / White marriage.

In spite of his devotion to the Islamic religion, Ali believed that good Christians or good Jews can receive God's blessing and enter heaven as he stated, "God created all people, no matter what their religion". He also stated, "If you're against someone because he's a Muslim that's wrong. If you're against someone because he's a Christian or a Jew, that's wrong".

1972 Ali left the religious following of Elijah Muhammed and became a follower of the Sunni Islamic sect.

1972 Ali had gone on the Hajj pilgrimage to Mecca in 1972, which inspired him in a similar manner to Malcolm X, meeting people of different colors from all over the world giving him a different outlook and greater spiritual awareness of the Islamic faith.

1984 Ali announced his support for the re-election of United States President Ronald Reagan. When asked to elaborate on his endorsement of Reagan, Ali told reporters, "He's keeping God in schools and that's enough.

1985 Ali visited Israel to request the release of Muslim prisoners at the Atlit detainee camp, which Israel declined.

1988 Ali went on another Pilgrimage to Mecca.

1990 Ali traveled to Iraq prior to the Gulf War and met with Saddam Hussein in an attempt to negotiate the release of American hostages. Ali secured the release of the hostages in exchange for promising Hussein that he would bring America "an honest account" of Iraq.

1996 Ali lit the flame at the 1996 Summer Olympics in Atlanta, Georgia. It was watched by an estimated 3.5 billion viewers worldwide

1999   The Muhammad Ali Boxing Reform Act was introduced in 1999 and passed in 2000, to protect the rights and welfare of boxers in the United States.

The **September 11, 2001,** bombing of the World Trade Center buildings alarmed Ali.

He stated that "Islam is a religion of peace" and "does not promote terrorism or killing people", and that he was "angry that the world sees a certain group of Islamic followers who caused this destruction, but they are not real Muslims. They are racist fanatics who call themselves Muslims.

After retiring from boxing, Ali became a student of the Quran and a dedicated Muslim. Ali received counsel from Islamic scholars. In accord with the tenants of the Islamic faith, Ali was a man of considerable generosity, a dedicated humanitarian and philanthropist. He focused on practicing his Islamic duty of charity and good deeds, donating millions to charity organizations and disadvantaged people of all religious backgrounds. It is estimated that Ali helped to feed more than 22 million people afflicted by hunger across the world. Ali was the largest single Black donor to the United Negro College Fund in 1967.

Ali visited Africa, Palestine, Bangladesh, Sudan, Iraq, and Ireland, the home of his great-grandfather.

On **January 19, 1981**, in Los Angeles, Ali talked a suicidal man down from jumping off a ninth-floor ledge, an event that made national news.

2002   Ali went to Afghanistan as the "U.N. Messenger of Peace."

2012 Ali was a titular bearer of the Olympic flag during the opening ceremonies of the 2012 Summer Olympics in London.

Stage 2 Mimesis, Cassius Clay/Muhammad Ali Boxing Career (professional life)

1955 The murder of Emmitt Till had a devastating effect on young Cassius. He was also strongly affected by the 1955 murder of Emmett Till, which led to young Clay and a friend taking out their frustration by vandalizing a local rail yard.

1954 Young Cassius had his bike stolen. Angered that someone stole his bike, He told a police officer he was going to "whup the thief." The police officer replied that "You had better learn how to box first".

Cassius Clay's motivation to become a boxer was activated because his bicycle was stolen, and he wanted to find the thief and beat him up. In 1954, a twelve-year-old then known as Cassius Clay approached police officer Joe Martin to report that his bicycle had been stolen and told Martin that he wanted to "whup" the thief. Martin offered to teach him how to box and guided his career for the next six years.

With the idea of boxing planted in his head, Cassius, after watching amateur boxers, decided to learn. He began to work with trainer Fred Stoner, who gave him "real training", molded his style, developed his stamina, and taught him the "system" of boxing.

As a 1960 Olympic coach, Martin accompanied the champion to the Olympic Games in Rome, Italy, where Ali won a gold medal. [25]

1954   Cassius had his amateur boxing debut against a local boxer, Ronnie O'Keefe, and won by a split decision.

Subsequently, he went on to win six Kentucky Golden Gloves titles, two national Golden Gloves titles, and an Amateur Athletic Union national title.

1960   Clay won the light heavyweight gold medal in the 1960 Summer Olympics in Rome, Italy.

Clay's amateur record was 100 wins with five losses.

Allegedly, shortly after his return from the Rome Olympics, he threw his gold medal into the Ohio River after he and a friend were refused service at a "whites-only" restaurant and fought with a white gang.

Ali made his professional debut, winning a six-round bout against Tunney Hunsaker.

1960-1962   Clay accumulated a record of 19–0 with 15 wins by knockout. He defeated boxers including Tony Esperti, Jim Robinson, Donnie

Fleeman, Alonzo Johnson, George Logan, Willi Besmanoff, LaMar Clark, Doug Jones, and Henry Cooper. Clay also beat his former trainer and veteran boxer Archie Moore in a 1962 match.

Watching the Clay / Doug Jones fight on TV, Sonny Liston commented that, if he fought Clay, he might get locked up for murder. The fight between Clay and Liston was later named "Fight of the Year" by *The Ring* magazine.

It was during these fights that Clay developed the "art of trash talk". In each of these fights, Clay vocally belittled his opponents and bragged about his abilities. He called Jones "an ugly little man" and Cooper a "bum". He said he was embarrassed to get in the ring with Alex Miteff and claimed that Madison Square Garden was "too small for me".

1961 Cassius trash-talk was inspired by professional wrestler "Gorgeous George" after he saw George's talking ability attract huge crowds to events. Cassius met with George in Las Vegas in 1961, when George told him that talking a big game would earn paying fans who either wanted to see him win or wanted to see him lose, thus Ali transformed himself into a self-described "big-mouth and a bragger."

1960 Clay hired Angelo Dundee to be his trainer. Clay had met Dundee in **February 1957** during Clay's amateur career. Around this time, Clay sought longtime idol Sugar Ray Robinson to be his manager, but was rebuffed. So he signed up with Angelo Dundee.

1964 The Sonny Liston/Cassius Clay fight was set for **February 25, 1964**, in Miami Beach. Liston was an intimidating personality, a dominating fighter with a criminal past and alleged ties to the mob. Based on Clay's uninspired performance against Jones and Cooper in his previous two fights, and Liston's destruction of former heavyweight champion Floyd Patterson in two first-round knockouts, Clay was a 7–1 underdog. Despite this, Clay taunted Liston during the pre-fight buildup, calling him "the big ugly bear", saying "Liston even smells like a bear," and claiming "After I beat him, I'm going to donate him to the zoo."Clay turned the pre-fight weigh-in into a circus, shouting at Liston that "someone is going to die at ringside tonight." Clay's pulse rate was measured at 120, more than double his normal 54. Many of those in attendance thought Clay's behavior stemmed from fear, and some commentators wondered if he would show up for the bout.

The outcome of the fight was a major upset. At the opening bell, Liston rushed at Clay, seemingly angry and looking for a quick knockout. However, Clay's superior speed and mobility enabled him to elude Liston, making the champion miss and look awkward. In round 7 Liston did not come out at the bell. The victory went to Clay as a defeat against Liston to become the Heavyweight Champion of the World.

1964   Soon after the Liston fight, Clay changed his name to Cassius X, and then later to Muhammad Ali and converting to Islam and becoming a member of the Nation of Islam led by Elijah Muhammad.

1965   Muhammad Ali won the rematch with Sonny Liston by knocking him out in the first round.

1965-1967   Muhammad Ali, aka Ali, defeated Floyd Patterson on November 22, 1965, Ernie Terrell (WBA Heavyweight Champ), George Chuvalo, Henry Cooper, Brian London, Karl Mildenberger, Cleveland Williams, and Zora Folley.

1966   Ali was classified as 1-A by the U.S. Army draft board. When notified of this status, Ali declared that he would refuse to serve in the army and publicly considered himself a conscientious objector.

1967   Ali was drafted, reported to the draft board in Houston, Texas, and refused to step forward to be inducted into the United States Army, in spite of the threats that it was a felony to refuse induction, punishable by 5 years in prison and a fine of $10,000. In addition to conscientiously objecting, Ali stated, "Why should they ask me to put on a uniform and go ten thousand miles from home and drop bombs and bullets on brown people in Vietnam while so-called Negro people in Louisville are treated like dogs and denied simple human rights?" "No Viet Cong ever called me Nigger."

1967   Ali was found guilty of refusing induction by court trial. The Court of Appeals upheld the verdict, and the case was scheduled to go before the Supreme Court of the United States.

Ali's boxing license was revoked by the boxing commission, denying him the right to earn a living. Ali did not box for 3 years while his case was scheduled to go before the Supreme Court of the United States.

1970   With his case still on appeal, Ali was granted a license by the New York State Boxing Commission to fight Oscar Bonavena. They fought, and Ali won.

1971   On June 28, the Supreme Court of the United States in *Clay v. United States* overturned Ali's conviction by a unanimous 8–0 decision (Justice Thurgood Marshall, a Black justice, recused himself, as he had been the U.S. Solicitor General at the time of Ali's conviction). The 3 years layoff from boxing robbed him of his best years, his prime years, according to Angelo Dundee.

In a secret operation code-named "Minaret", the National Security Agency (NSA) intercepted the communications of leading

Americans, including **Ali**, Senators Frank Church and Howard Baker, **Dr. Martin Luther King Jr.**, prominent U.S. journalists, and others who criticized the U.S. war in Vietnam.

1971   Ali fought Jimmy Ellis, his one-time sparring partner, and won

1971   Labeled the fight of the Century, Ali fought Joe Frazier (then Heavyweight Champion of the World) and lost in a comeback on the quest to regain his title.

1972-1973   After the loss to Frazier, Ali fought Jerry Quarry, had a second bout with Floyd Patterson, and faced Bob Foster in 1972, winning a total of six fights that year. In 1973, Ken Norton broke Ali's jaw while giving him the second loss of his career. After initially considering retirement, Ali won a controversial decision against Norton in their second bout. This led to a rematch with Joe Frazier at Madison Square Garden on January 28, 1974; Frazier had recently lost his title to George Foreman. Ali beat Frazier in their second match.

1974   The defeat of Frazier set the stage for a title fight against heavyweight champion George Foreman in Kinshasa, Zaire, on October 30, 1974—a bout nicknamed *The Rumble in the Jungle*. Foreman was considered one of the hardest punchers in heavyweight history. In assessing the fight, analysts pointed out that Joe Frazier and Ken Norton, who had given Ali four tough battles and won two of them, had both been devastated by Foreman in second-round knockouts. Ali was 32 years old and had clearly lost speed and reflexes since his twenties. Contrary to his later persona, Foreman was at the time a brooding and intimidating presence. Almost no one associated with the sport, not even Ali's long-time supporter Howard Cosell, gave the former champion a chance of winning. Ali knocked Foreman out in the 8th round to win the heavyweight title for the second time.

1975 On October 1, a third Ali and Joe Frazier match was held in Manila, Philippines. The bout, known as the "*Thrilla in Manila*". Ali won the fight. **BUT**

An ailing Ali said afterward that the fight "was the closest thing to dying that I know", and, when later asked if he had viewed the fight on videotape, reportedly said, "Why would I want to go back and see Hell?" After the fight, he cited Frazier as "the greatest fighter of all time next to me."

After this fight, Ali considered retirement. He should have. There is something about great athletes. Rarely do they don't know when to quit. Many participate in sports far beyond their prime and into their waning years.

1978 In February, Ali fought Leon Spinks and lost. In September of the same year, Ali won in a rematch with Spinks. This made Ali the first Heavyweight Champion to win the title three times.

1980 Announcing a comeback, Ali fought Larry Holmes and took a terrible beating. Holmes did not want to fight Ali. After the Holmes fight, Ali began to show signs of slurred speech and trembling hands.

1981 Ali, stubborn to retire, fought Trevor Berbick in Nassau, Bahamas, and lost a 10-round decision. This match marked the end of Ali's boxing career.

It is estimated that Ali had absorbed an estimated 200,000 hits

1984 After checking himself into Columbia Presbyterian Hospital, Ali was given a devastating diagnosis: Parkinson's disease.

Awards and Accolades given to Muhammad Ali

- Practicing his Islamic duty of charity and good deeds, Ali donated millions to charity, organizations, and disadvantaged people of all religious backgrounds. It is estimated that Ali helped to feed more than 22 million people afflicted by hunger across the world.[26][27]
- "In 1980, Ali was recruited by President Jimmy Carter for a diplomatic mission to Africa, in an effort to persuade a number of African governments to join the US-led boycott of the

Moscow Olympics (in response to the Soviet Invasion of Afghanistan)."

- On January 19, 1981, in Los Angeles, Ali talked a suicidal man down from jumping off a ninth-floor ledge, an event that made national news.[28]
- Around 1987, the California Bicentennial Foundation for the U.S. Constitution selected Ali to personify the vitality of the U.S. Constitution and Bill of Rights. Ali rode on a float at the following year's Tournament of Roses Parade, launching the U.S. Constitution's 200th birthday commemoration.[29]
- Ali received the Liberty Medal in a public ceremony on Thursday, September 13, 2012, at 7:00 p.m. at the National Constitution Center on Independence Mall in Historic Philadelphia.[30]
- In 1998, Ali began working with actor Michael J Fox, who has Parkinson's disease, to raise awareness and fund research for a cure. They made a joint appearance before Congress to push the case in 2002. In 2000, Ali worked with the Michael J Fox Foundation for Parkinson's disease to raise awareness and encourage donations for research. [31]

More accolades and honors awarded to Ali (Lived Experiences).[32]

- Ali was honored with the annual Martin Luther King Award in 1970 by civil rights leader Ralph Abernathy, who called him "a living example of soul power, the March on Washington in two fists." Coretta Scott King added that Ali was "a champion of justice and peace and unity.

- Muhammad Ali defeated every top heavyweight in his era, which has been called the golden age of heavyweight boxing. Ali was named "Fighter of the Year" by *The Ring* magazine more times than any other fighter, and was involved in more *Ring* "Fight of the Year" bouts than any other fighter. He was an inductee into the International Boxing Hall of Fame and held wins over seven other Hall of Fame inductees. He was one of only three boxers to be named "Sportsman of the Year" by *Sports Illustrated*.

- In 1978, three years before Ali's permanent retirement, the Louisville Board of Aldermen in his hometown of Louisville, Kentucky, voted 6–5 to rename Walnut Street to Muhammad Ali Boulevard.

- In 1993, the Associated Press reported that Ali was tied with Babe Ruth as the most recognized athlete, out of over 800 dead or living athletes, in America. The study found that over 97% of Americans over 12 years of age identified both Ali and Ruth. He was the recipient of the 1997 Arthur Ashe Courage Award.

- In 1999, *Time* magazine named Ali one of the 100 Most Important People of the 20th Century. He was crowned Sportsman of the Century by *Sports Illustrated*.[279] Named Sports Personality of the Century in a BBC poll, he received more votes than the other contenders (which included Pelé, Jesse Owens, and Jack Nicklaus) combined.[280] On September 13, 1999, Ali was named "Kentucky Athlete of the Century" by the

Kentucky Athletic Hall of Fame in ceremonies at the Galt House East.

- On January 8, 2001, Muhammad Ali was presented with the Presidential Citizens Medal by President Bill Clinton. In November 2005, he received the Presidential Medal of Freedom from President George W. Bush, followed by the Otto Hahn Peace Medal in Gold of the UN Association of Germany (DGVN) in Berlin for his work with the civil rights movement and the United Nations, which he received on December 17, 2005.

- On November 19, 2005, the $60 million non-profit Muhammad Ali Center opened in downtown Louisville. In addition to displaying his boxing memorabilia, the center focuses on core themes of peace, social responsibility, respect, and personal growth. On June 5, 2007, he received an honorary doctorate of humanities at Princeton University's 260th graduation ceremony.

- Ali Mall, located in Araneta Center, Quezon City, Philippines, is named after him. The mall opened in 1976 with Ali attending its opening.

- The Muhammad Ali Boxing Reform Act was introduced in 1999 and passed in 2000 to protect the rights and welfare of boxers in the United States. In June 2016, U.S. Senator Rand Paul proposed an amendment to the US draft laws named after Ali, a proposal to eliminate the Selective Service System.

- In 2015, *Sports Illustrated* renamed its Sportsman Legacy Award to the *Sports Illustrated* Muhammad Ali Legacy Award. The annual award was originally created in 2008 and honors former "sports figures who embody the ideals of sportsmanship, leadership, and philanthropy as vehicles for changing the world." Ali first appeared on the magazine's cover in 1963 and went on to be featured on numerous covers during his storied career.

- On July 27, 2012, Ali was a titular bearer of the Olympic flag during the opening ceremonies of the 2012 Summer Olympics in London.[33]

- Muhammad Ali defeated every top heavyweight in his era, which has been called the golden age of heavyweight boxing. Ali was named "Fighter of the Year" by The Ring magazine more times than any other fighter, and was involved in more Ring "Fight of the Year" bouts than any other fighter. He was an inductee into the International Boxing Hall of Fame and held wins over seven other Hall of Fame inductees. He was one of only three boxers to be named "Sportsman of the Year" by Sports Illustrated.

- In 1978, three years before Ali's permanent retirement, the Louisville Board of Aldermen in his hometown of Louisville, Kentucky, voted 6–5 to rename Walnut Street to Muhammad Ali Boulevard. This was controversial at the time, as within a week, 12 of the 70 street signs were stolen.

- In 1993, the Associated Press reported that Ali was tied with Babe Ruth as the most recognized athlete, out of over 800 dead or living athletes, in America. The study found that over 97% of Americans over 12 years of age identified both Ali and Ruth.[274][34] He was the recipient of the 1997 Arthur Ashe Courage Award.

- In 1999, Time magazine named Ali one of the 100 Most Important People of the 20th Century.[35] He was crowned Sportsman of the Century by Sports Illustrated.[36] Named Sports Personality of the Century in a BBC poll, he received more votes than the other contenders (which included Pelé, Jesse Owens, and Jack Nicklaus) combined.[37] On September 13, 1999, Ali was named "Kentucky Athlete of the Century" by the Kentucky Athletic Hall of Fame in ceremonies at the Galt House East.[38]

- In 2015, Sports Illustrated renamed its Sportsman Legacy Award to the Sports Illustrated Muhammad Ali Legacy Award. The annual award was originally created in 2008 and honors former "sports figures who embody the ideals of sportsmanship, leadership, and philanthropy as vehicles for changing the world." Ali first appeared on the magazine's cover in 1963 and went on to be featured on numerous covers during his storied career.[39]

- Citations for Recipients of the 2005 Presidential Medal of Freedom: President George W. Bush Honors Recipients of the Presidential Medal of Freedom. The President today awarded the Presidential Medal of Freedom. The text of each citation reads as follows:

"Muhammad Ali is one of the greatest athletes of all time. He produced some of America's most memorable and lasting sports memories, from winning the Gold Medal at the 1960 Summer Olympics to carrying the Olympic torch at the 1996 Summer  Olympics. As the first three-time heavyweight boxing champion of the world, he thrilled, entertained, and inspired us. His deep commitment to equal justice and peace has touched people around the world. The United States honored Muhammad Ali for his lifetime of achievements and for his principled service to mankind," with the Medal of Freedom.[40] The Medal of Freedom is the highest honor that the United States Government can bestow upon a civilian American citizen.

Stage 3 Mimesis of Muhammad Ali

- Ali's bout with Parkinson's Syndrome led to a gradual decline in his health, though he was still active into the early years of the millennium,

- In February 2013, Ali's brother, Rahman Ali, said Muhammad could no longer speak and could be dead within days

- In his waning years, Ali became more loved by the people of the world.

Final Mimesis of Muhammad Ali

Ali was hospitalized in Scottsdale, Arizona, on June 2, 2016, with a respiratory illness. Though his condition was initially described as fair, it worsened, and he died the following day at the age of 74 from septic shock.

Following Ali's death, he was the number one trending topic on Twitter for over 12 hours and on Facebook for several days. BET played their documentary *Muhammad Ali: Made in Miami*. ESPN played four hours of non-stop, commercial-free coverage of Ali. News networks, such as ABC News, BBC, CNN, and Fox News, also covered him extensively.

He was mourned globally, and a family spokesman said the family "certainly believes that Muhammad was a citizen of the world ... and they know that the world grieves with him.

Mimesis of Life Summary for Muhammad Ali [41]

Muhammad Ali was born in Louisville, Kentucky. His Father was a painter, and his mother was a domestic. He was born Cassius Marcellus Clay. He had a younger brother named Rudolph Valentino Clay (Rahman Ali).

Young Cassius Clay was not a good student, graduating near the bottom of a class of 382. He was a good athlete and well-liked by his classmates. Ali started boxing at the age of 12. He traveled to Rome, Italy, and won the light heavyweight gold medal in the 1960 Summer Olympics. Upon his return from Rome, he encountered a racist incident(s) that caused him to throw his gold medal into the Ohio River, believing it was a meaningless relic.

At 22, Clay became the heavyweight champion of the world, defeating Sonny Liston in 1964. After the victory, Clay changed his name to Muhammad Ali and announced he was a member of the Nation of Islam. Ali defended his title on eight occasions after defeating Liston a second time. In the midst of the Vietnam War, Ali was drafted into the Army. He showed up for induction and refused to step forward, refusing to be inducted into the U.S. Armed Forces on April 28, 1967. Citing his religious beliefs, he refused to serve. Ali was arrested, the New York State Athletic Commission suspended his boxing license, and revoked his heavyweight belt. Convicted of draft evasion, Ali was sentenced to the maximum of five years in prison and a $10,000 fine, but he remained free while the conviction was appealed to the Supreme Court.

As public opinion turned against the war, support for Ali grew. In 1970, the New York State Supreme Court ordered his boxing license reinstated, and the following year, the U.S. Supreme Court overturned his conviction in a unanimous decision.

In his first return bout to regain the title, Ali was defeated by Joe Frazier. Ali returned to boxing and won his next 10 matches. Frazier, as the heavyweight champion, was defeated by George Foreman. Ali fought

Foreman and regained the title a second time. On October 30, 1974, in Kinshasa, Zaire, the fight was named the "Rumble in the Jungle." On February 15, 1978, an aging Ali lost his title to Leon Spinks in a 15-round split decision. Seven months later, Ali defeated Spinks in a unanimous 15-round decision to reclaim the heavyweight crown and become the first fighter to win the world heavyweight boxing title three times.

Ali was renowned and loved worldwide. Ali adhered to the Muslim faith and gave considerable millions of dollars to charity. Many White people did not like Ali early in his career, throughout his avoidance of serving in the army, and after his comeback, people (mostly white) came to his matches to see him lose (according to Ali).

As Ali aged, he came down with Parkinson's disease, and his detractors softened. Ali became known as a national treasure, a hero, and loved by both Black and White Americans. Ali has been married four times and has seven daughters and two sons. He married his fourth wife, Yolanda, in 1986.

Ali had the honor of lighting the cauldron during the opening ceremonies of the 1996 Summer Olympics in Atlanta.

In 1999, Ali was voted the BBC's "Sporting Personality of the Century," and Sports Illustrated named him "Sportsman of the Century." Ali was awarded the Presidential Medal of Freedom by President Ronald Regan in a 2005 White House ceremony, and in the same year, the $60 million Muhammad Ali Center, a nonprofit museum and cultural center focusing on peace and social responsibility, opened in Louisville.

Ring Magazine named Ali "Fighter of the Year" five times, more than any other boxer, and he was inducted into the International Boxing Hall of Fame in 1990.

Ali died at the age of 74 on June 3, 2016. Ali's funeral had been pre-planned by himself and others for several years prior to his actual death. The services began in Louisville on June 9, 2016, with an Islamic Janazah prayer service at Freedom Hall on the grounds of the Kentucky Exposition Center. On June 10, 2016, the funeral procession passed through the streets of Louisville, ending at Cave Hill Cemetery, where his body was interred during a private ceremony. A public memorial service for Ali at downtown Louisville's KFC Yum! The center was held during the afternoon of June 10. The pallbearers included Will Smith, Lennox Lewis, and Mike Tyson, with honorary pallbearers including George Chuvalo, Larry Holmes, and George Foreman. Ali's memorial was watched by an estimated 1 billion viewers worldwide.

During his Stage 2 Mimesis, Muhammad Ali was loved by the liberals, anti-Vietnam faction of society, Black people, and college students, but hated by the White establishment and racist White people. Ali was anti-establishment, anti-integration, anti-mixed marriage, and anti-racist. Muhammad Ali has the distinction of being loved by millions of people and hated by millions of people. Ali confronted and successfully overcame many challenges in his life. Aging has a way of bringing an individual to reflect on their life and focus on the important areas of life and their lived experiences. When Ali retired from boxing and no longer needed to promote himself, he showed the real qualities he possessed as an individual, a man, a caring human being. The people who loved him loved him more, and the people who hated him grew to love him. Ali's lived experiences gave him a full personal life, a full career, and a full spiritual life. Muhammad Ali was not only a great boxer. He was a great human being.

Muhammad Ali won the Heavyweight Boxing Championship of the world, defeating Sonny Liston on February 25, 1964.

Heavyweight Championship Muhammad Ali beats Sonny Liston again in their rematch on May 25, 1965.

Muhammad Ali beat George Foreman to capture his second Heavyweight Championship in a victory over George Foreman on October 30, 1974. The fight was promoted as the Rumble in the Jungle in Kinshasa, Zaire, Africa.

Muhammad Ali defeats Leon Spinks to regain his title he lost to Spinks on February 15, 1978. Ali regained the title in a rematch on September 15, 1978. It was Ali's third Heavyweight Championship title.

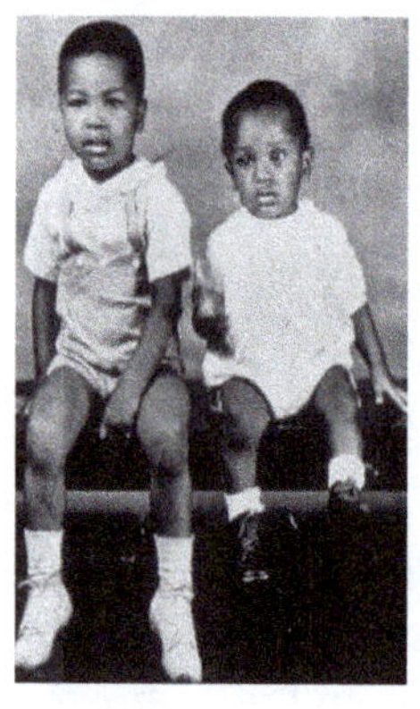 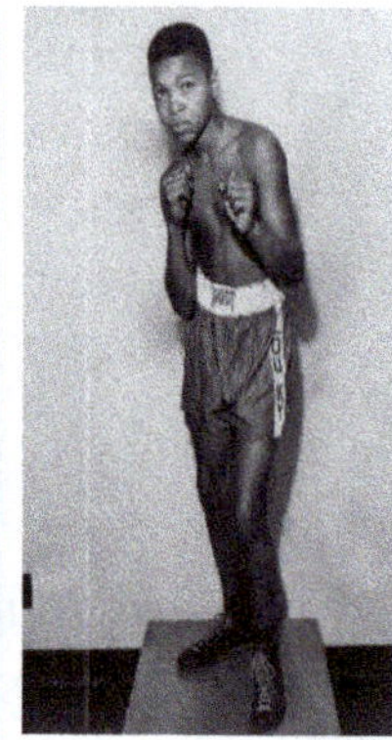

Cassius and his brother Rudolph Valentino Clay (later renamed Rahman Ali)

Young Cassius is becoming a boxer

Cassius Clay

Olympic Gold Metal Champion.

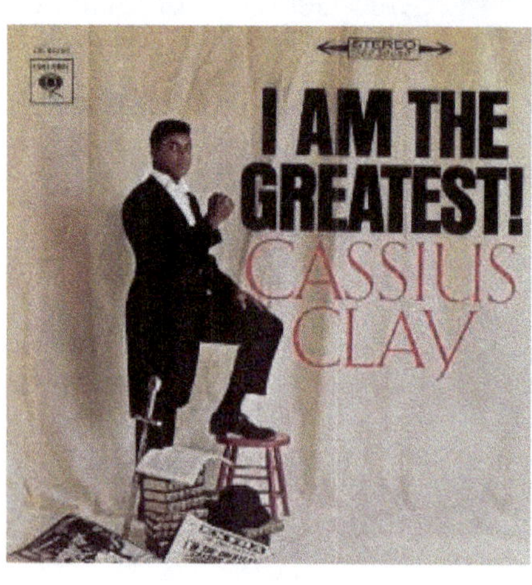

Muhammad Ali

ALI
"SERVICE TO OTHERS
IS THE RENT YOU
PAY FOR YOUR ROOM
IN HEAVEN"

Mimesis of Life for Oprah Winfrey

Raised by a single teenage mother in Mississippi, between being shuffled to live with her father in Tennessee, Oprah's ambition, determination, and talent helped her make her way through the difficulties of life and become one of the most influential people in the world in the 21st century. She's now a billionaire and one of America's most generous philanthropists.

Oprah Gail Winfrey was born on January 29, 1954. She is an American media executive, actress, talk show host, television producer, author, and philanthropist. She is best known for her talk show "The Oprah Winfrey Show," which was the highest-rated television program of its kind in history and was nationally syndicated from 1986 to 2011 in Chicago.[42] Ms. Winfrey was the richest African American of the 20th century[43] and North America's first black multi-billionaire.[44] She has been ranked as the most influential woman in the world.[45]

Oprah Winfrey was born into poverty in rural Mississippi to a teenage single mother and was later raised in an inner-city Milwaukee neighborhood. She has stated that she was molested during her childhood and early teens and became pregnant at 14; her son died in infancy.[46] She was sent to live with the man she calls her father, Vernon Winfrey, a barber in Tennessee. Her childhood is blighted by sexual abuse and rape. She is sent to a juvenile detention home at 13.

However, despite her early childhood experiences,[47] she got a job in radio while still in high school and co-anchored the local evening news at the age of 19. Her emotional ad-lib delivery eventually got her transferred to the daytime talk show arena, and after boosting a third-rated local Chicago talk show to first place,[48] she launched her own production company and became internationally syndicated. Dubbed the "Queen of All Media," she was the richest African American of the 20th century, was once the world's only black billionaire, and the greatest black philanthropist in U.S. history. By 2007, she was sometimes ranked as the most influential woman in the world."[49]

Oprah Winfrey's Lived Experiences. [50]

Stage 1 Mimesis for Oprah Winfrey

1954 Born to a poor, unwed couple in Kosciusko, Mississippi, she was raised by her grandmother. Her given name, Orpah, is misspelled on her birth certificate as Oprah. Her mother, Vernita Lee (1935–2018), was a housemaid. Vernon Winfrey (born c. 1933) is considered Winfrey's biological father. He was in the Armed Forces when she was born. He was a coal miner turned barber turned city councilman. However, Mississippi farmer and World War II Veteran

Noah Robinson Sr. (born c. 1925) has claimed to be her biological father.

After Winfrey's birth, her mother traveled north, and Winfrey spent her first six years living in rural poverty with her maternal grandmother, Hattie Mae (Presley) Lee (April 15, 1900 – February 27, 1963). Her grandmother was so poor that Winfrey often wore dresses made of potato sacks, for which other children made fun of her. Her grandmother taught her to read before the age of three and took her to the local church, where she was nicknamed "The Preacher" for her ability to recite Bible verses. When Winfrey was a child, her grandmother was reportedly abusive.

Stage 2 Mimesis for Oprah Winfrey

1960 At age six, Winfrey moved to an inner-city neighborhood in Milwaukee, Wisconsin, with her mother, who was less supportive and encouraging than her grandmother had been, largely as a result of the long hours she worked as a maid. During this time, Oprah's mother had another daughter, Patricia, Oprah's half-sister, who died in 2003.

1962 Oprah was sent to live with her father, Vernon, in Nashville, Tennessee.

1963 Oprah returned to live with her mother.

1962 Oprah was baptized in a Baptist Church.

Oprah has stated that she was molested on several occasions by an uncle, a cousin, and a family friend, beginning when she was nine years old. Years later, when Winfrey mentioned the abuse to family members, they did not believe her.

1967   Oprah ran away from home at 13 years old because of the abuse she suffered.

1968   At age 14, Oprah got pregnant, but her child died shortly after birth.

Winfrey attended Lincoln High School in Milwaukee, but after early success in the Upward Bound program, was transferred to the affluent suburban Nicolet High School. Upon transferring, she said she was continually reminded of her poverty as she rode the bus to school with fellow African-Americans, some of whom were servants of her classmates' families. She began to rebel and steal money from her mother in an effort to keep up with her free-spending peers. As a result, her mother once again sent her to live with Vernon in Nashville, although this time she did not take her back. Vernon was strict but encouraging, and made her education a priority. Winfrey became an honors student, was voted Most Popular Girl, and joined her high school speech team at East Nashville High School, placing second in the nation in dramatic interpretation.

1971   At the age of 17, Winfrey won the Miss Black Tennessee beauty pageant.[53] She also attracted the attention of the local black radio station, WVOL, which hired her to do the news part-time.[41] She worked there during her senior year of high school and in her first two years of college. Oprah won an oratory contest and received a full scholarship to Tennessee State University, where she majored in communications. Oprah credits her grandmother for being an influence in her media endeavor and a fluent public speaker. Oprah states that her grandmother influenced her to have a positive image of herself. Working in local media, Winfrey was both the youngest news anchor and the first black female news anchor at Nashville's WLAC-TV (now WTVF-TV),

1972 Oprah switches from performing arts to media at Tennessee State University. She leaves her first broadcasting job, as a reporter for a Nashville radio station, to become the first African American anchor on the city's WTVF-TV station.

1976 Oprah moved to Baltimore's WJZ-TV to co-anchor the six o'clock news.

1977 Ms. Winfrey moves to Baltimore to co-anchor the six o'clock news, but is head-hunted to co-host a local TV talk show, *People Are Talking*. She also hosted the local version of *Dialing for Dollars*

1984 **Ms. Winfrey** moves to Chicago to host WLS-TV's morning talk show, *"AM"*. It becomes the number one talk show just one month later. The show is renamed *"The Oprah Winfrey Show"*.

1985 Winfrey co-starred in Steven Spielberg's *The Color Purple*, as distraught housewife Sofia. She was nominated for an Academy Award for Best Supporting Actress for her performance

1986   Her show is the number one talk show and will be for 14 seasons. It receives 34 Emmys - seven of those are for the host.

On the advice of movie critic Roger Ebert, Oprah was persuaded to sign a syndication deal with King World. The syndicated show was named the *"Oprah Winfrey Show."*

1989   In addition to her talk show, Winfrey also produced and co-starred in the drama miniseries *The Women of Brewster Place*

1991   Oprah initiated the National Child Protection Act. She testifies in front of the US Senate Judiciary Committee in a bid to establish a national database of convicted child abusers.

1992    She is engaged to Stedman Graham, a former basketball player and public relations executive. They are engaged but remain unmarried.

1993   President Clinton signed the 'Oprah Bill' into law, establishing a national database of convicted child abusers.

1996   Oprah's Book Club begins - all the club selections to date become instant bestsellers. Her show is aired in 132 countries.

1997   Oprah was named Newsweek's most important person in books and media. She launches the Angel Network, a campaign encouraging people to help those in need.

1998   She is named one of the 100 Most Influential People of the 20th Century by Time magazine.

1999   Oprah becomes Professor Winfrey, teaching at Northwestern University's J.L. Kellogg Graduate School of Management.

2000   Oprah's Angel Network began presenting the $100,000 'Use Your Life Award' every Monday to people who are using their lives to improve the lives of others. *O Magazine* is launched as 'a personal growth guide' for women between the ages of 25-49.

2000   Ms. Winfrey was awarded the Spingarn Medal from the NAACP

2001   O sells an average of 2.5 million copies monthly. The magazine is 'an extension of Oprah's personal vision' and features sections like: Oprah To Go, The O List, Oprah's favorite things (fluffy pajamas, Fendi sunglasses, Ralph Lauren mules), recipes by Oprah's personal chef, tips from Oprah's trainer, a picture of Oprah's dog, and ads for Oprah Personal Growth Summits.

2002   Sales of O fell by a third. Oprah shelves her famous 'Book Club', saying it has become harder to find books that I feel absolutely compelled to share,' – the publishing industry braces itself for a $150 million plunge in revenue.

2004   Winfrey became the first black person to rank among the 50 most generous Americans, and she remained among the top 50 until 2010. By 2012, she had given away about $400 million to educational causes.

2002-2006   Winfrey co-founded the women's cable television network Oxygen, which was the initial network for her *"Oprah After the Show"* program from 2002 to 2006, before moving to Oprah.com when Winfrey sold her stake in the network.

She is also the president of Harpo Productions (*Oprah* spelled backward), a film and TV production company. Oprah is considered the catalyst responsible for the success of the careers of Dr. Phil, Rachael Ray, The Dr. Oz Show, Nate Berkus, Iyanla Vanzant, and many others. She also moderated three *ABC Afterschool Special*s from 1992 to 1994.

2006   Winfrey and Discovery Communications announced plans to change the Discovery Health Channel into a new channel called *OWN: Oprah Winfrey Network*. It was scheduled to launch in 2009 but was delayed, and actually launched on January 1, 2011

2007   Ms. Winfrey opened the *Oprah Winfrey Leadership Academy for Girls.*

The school is set over 22 acres, opened in January 2007 with an enrollment of 150 pupils (increasing to 450) and features state-of-the-art classrooms, computer and science laboratories, a library, theatre, and beauty salon. Nelson Mandela praised Winfrey for overcoming her own disadvantaged youth to become a benefactor for others.

2011   The series finale of *The Oprah Winfrey Show* airs on May 25.

2011   The OWN network launches.

2013   Winfrey was awarded the Presidential Medal of Freedom by President Obama.

Ms. Winfrey was instrumental in launching the careers of Phil McGraw, known as Dr. Phil, a psychologist who has his own television show.

Ms. Winfrey was also instrumental in launching the career of Dr. Mehmet Oz, who also had a television show, until he decided to enter politics and run for the U.S. Senate in 2022.

2017   CBS announced that Winfrey would join *60 Minutes* as a special contributor on the Sunday evening news magazine program starting in September 2017. Winfrey left *60 Minutes* by the end of 2018.

2018   The National Museum of African American History and Culture. A special exhibit on Winfrey's cultural influence through television was opened.

2018   Apple announced a multi-year content partnership with Winfrey. They agreed that Winfrey would create new original programs exclusively for Apple's streaming service.

Ms. Winfrey received honorary doctorate degrees from Duke and Harvard.

Stage 3 Mimesis (Not yet)

Oprah Winfrey is still in Stage 2 Mimesis. However, there is no reason to doubt that she will receive the same honor, respect, and love in her Stage 3 Mimesis as she has accumulated during her Stage 2 Mimesis. Most likely even more.

Mimesis of Life Summary for Oprah Winfrey

Oprah Winfrey has encountered some devastating hardships in her early life. Being born into poverty, taken advantage of as a youth, and experiencing an unstable home life. Oprah Winfrey has experienced phenomena that would direct some people in a dysfunctional, negative life direction. Two people in Oprah's life who seemed to throw her a lifeline, in the early years of her life, were her grandmother and her father, Vernon.

Amazingly, Winfrey reconstructed her life and set a path for herself that made her one of the most popular, recognized, loved, and wealthiest people in America. The public reception and approval for Ms. Winfrey is positive, and she has become a role model for women and people around the world. Ms. Winfrey represents an individual who, although having inherited poor circumstances at birth, rose above her inherited circumstances and became the quality human being she is today. She was obviously smart, having won a college scholarship. She was definitely articulate. How else could she be a television anchor and host? However, the most important quality Oprah seemed to have was positive resilience. She was able to overcome the negative experiences in her early life and maintain an attitude that others responded to with respect and confidence in her ability. It is a special human being who can overcome the experiences Oprah encountered and do so without showing any apparent scars from her early childhood experiences.

The opportunities that came her way were not wasted. While Oprah had negative experiences, when she encountered positive opportunities, the negative experiences seemed to go into her absent-minded subconscious. Not many people could accomplish this without extensive counseling and therapy. It is not known if Oprah experienced therapy sessions, but the Wall Street Journal coined an expression from her approach to life. It is called "*Oprahfication.*" The intended meaning of "Oprahfication" is *public* confession as a form of therapy. By confessing intimate details about her weight problems, tumultuous love life, and sexual abuse, and crying alongside her guests, Winfrey has been credited by *Time* magazine with creating a new form of media communication known as "rapport talk" as distinguished from the "report talk." Winfrey recognized television's power to blend public and private; that links strangers, sharing their problems, creating a synergy between people, over public airwaves, that comforts them. She makes people care because she cares. That is Winfrey's genius, and will be her legacy.

Oprah is intimately connected with her long-time beau, Steadman Graham. Their relationship has been solid for many years, yet they have not married. While their relationship appears strong and mutually supportive, one cannot help but wonder if Oprah's inability to commit to marriage is a residue from her childhood upbringing.

Few people would have bet on Oprah Winfrey's swift rise to host of the most popular talk show on TV in a field dominated by white males. Conventional wisdom would say that because she is a black female, she can't compete. Not only did she compete, but she won, and kept winning for years. Oprah connected with her audience. They saw her as addressing issues and concerns that connected to their everyday lives. The Oprah Show was a form of Cognitive Group Therapy (CGT) for many women and men in America. She demonstrated a plainspoken curiosity, robust humor, and, above all, empathy. "Guests with sad stories to tell are apt to rouse a tear in Oprah's eye..." They, in turn, often find themselves revealing things they would not imagine telling anyone, much less a national TV audience. Viewers and guests saw Oprah as one of them.

"Oprah became a millionaire at the age of 32 when her talk show received national syndication. Oprah negotiated ownership rights to the television program and started her own production company. At the age of 41, Oprah had a net worth of $340 million and was the only African American on the Forbes 400. By 2000, with a net worth of $800 million, Oprah was believed to have been the richest African American of the 20th century. There has been a course taught at the University of Illinois focusing on Oprah's business acumen, namely: "History 298: Oprah Winfrey, the Tycoon". Oprah was the highest-paid television entertainer in the United States in 2006, earning an estimated $260 million during the year, five times the sum earned by second-place music executive Simon Cowell. By 2008, her yearly income had increased to $275 million".

"Forbes' list of The World's Billionaires has listed Oprah as the world's only black billionaire from 2004 to 2006 and as the first black woman billionaire in the world, which was achieved in 2003. As of 2014, Oprah had a net worth in excess of 2.9 billion dollars and had overtaken former eBay

CEO Meg Whitman as the richest self-made woman in America".

Winfrey was called *"arguably the world's most powerful woman"* by CNN and *TIME*, *"arguably the most influential woman in the world"* by *The American Spectator*, *"one of the 100 people who most influenced the 20th Century"* and *"one of the most influential people"* from 2004 to 2011 by *TIME*. Winfrey is the only person to have appeared in the latter list on ten occasions.

Ms. Winfrey is still going strong. She is among the most admired people in the world. Certainly, Oprah is an individual who was able to overcome problematic early life circumstances that would have sent many other people on a dysfunctional life path. Ms. Winfrey is one of those rare few individuals who has an internal consciousness to overcome adversity. Having a light brought into her life by her initial experience with media set her on a path to discover her life's calling. Few people are fortunate enough to discover their life calling. The world is fortunate that Ms. Winfrey discovered hers. For the most part, the perception, image, and character of Ms. Winfrey is set in stone for the people who know who she is, the millions nationally and internationally. What could possibly happen to change the Stage 3 Mimesis for Ms. Winfrey? Most likely nothing. People already know her as a good lady with a good heart. A smart, successful lady who cares about others, and they love her.

Audience feedback on how Oprah is received among Americans is evident in the following statistics:

- Viewership for *The Oprah Winfrey Show* was highest during the 1991–92 season, when about

13.1 million U.S. viewers were watching each day.

- By 2003, ratings declined to 7.4 million daily viewers.

- Ratings briefly rebounded to approximately 9 million in 2005 and then declined again to around 7.3 million viewers in 2008, though it remained the highest-rated talk show.

- In 2008, Winfrey's show was airing in 140 countries internationally and was seen by an estimated 46 million people in the US weekly.

- According to the Harris poll, Winfrey was America's favorite television personality in 1998, 2000, 2002–06, and 2009.

- Winfrey was especially popular among women, Democrats, political moderates, Baby Boomers, Generation X, Southern Americans, and East Coast Americans.

- In 2004, Winfrey became the first black person to rank among the 50 most generous Americans, and she remained among the top 50 until 2010.

- By 2012, she had given away about $400 million to educational causes.

Oprah's Angel Network

In 1998, Winfrey created Oprah's Angel Network, a charity that supported charitable projects and provided grants to nonprofit organizations around the world.

Oprah's Angel Network raised more than $80 million. Winfrey personally covered all administrative costs associated with the charity, so 100% of all funds raised went to charity programs. In May 2010, with Oprah's show ending, the charity stopped accepting donations and was shut down.

In the wake of Hurricane Katrina, Oprah created the Oprah Angel Network Katrina registry, which raised more than $11 million for relief efforts. Winfrey personally gave $10 million to the cause. Homes were built in Texas, Mississippi, Louisiana, and Alabama before the one-year anniversary of Hurricanes Katrina and Rita.

God bestows the privilege on a rare few people to be able to touch the lives of others. It is a blessing God bestows on the privileged few. Some abuse the blessing and value selfishness over generosity. Oprah is an example of the concept that *"the more generous you are, the more you are blessed."*

Mimesis of Life for Barack Hussein Obama

"Coming from a fairly modest family, one cannot help but stop and admire Barack Obama's determination and path to success, which culminated in 2008 when he became the first African American to be elected as President of the United States".

Barack Hussein Obama II was born August 4, 1961, in Honolulu, Hawaii. He is an attorney and politician, having served as the 44th president of the United States and elected for two terms from 2009-2013 and from 2014-2017. A member of the Democratic Party, he was the first African American to be elected to the presidency. He previously served as a United States senator from Illinois from 2005 to 2008. He also served as an Illinois State Senator from 1997 to 2004.

Barack Obama was born to a white mother and a black father. His mother, Ann Dunham (1942–1995), was born in Wichita, Kansas; she was mostly of English descent with German, Irish, Scottish, Swiss, and Welsh ancestry. His father, Barack Obama Sr. (1936–1982), was a Luo Kenyan man from Nyang'oma Kogelo. Kenya.[51] Barack Obama's parents divorced in March 1964. Obama Sr. returned to Kenya in 1964. He visited his son in Hawaii only once, before he was killed in an automobile accident in 1982, when Obama was 21 years old. Recalling his early childhood, Obama said, "That my father looked nothing like the people around me, that he was black as pitch, my mother white as milk, barely registered in my mind." He described his struggles as a young adult to reconcile social perceptions of his multiracial heritage.[52][53] He would joke that he had relatives who looked like Bernie Mac and Margaret Thatcher.[54]

In 1965, Ann Dunham married Lolo Soetoro, an Indonesian man. Barack and his mother moved to Indonesia. From the age of six to ten, Obama attended two Indonesian-language schools, a state elementary school, and was home-schooled by his mother. He learned to speak Indonesian. In 1971, he moved to Hawaii to live with his maternal grandparents. He attended high school in Hawaii. In 1980, his mother divorced her second husband. In 1992, she earned her PhD, then unfortunately passed away in 1995. While in Hawaii, Barack experimented with marijuana and "hung out" with the "choom gang."[55] After graduating from high school in 1979, Obama attended Occidental College in Los Angeles, California. In 1981, he transferred to Columbia University in New York as a junior, majoring in political science,[56] and graduating in 1983 with a BA Degree. He worked for about a year at the Business International Corporation, where he was a financial researcher and writer, then as a project coordinator for the New York Public Interest Research Group on the City College of New York campus for three months in 1985.[57] In 1983, he moved to Chicago and worked as a community organizer. In 1988, he enrolled in Harvard Law School, becoming the first Black president of the Harvard Law Review. After graduating from Harvard, he became a civil rights attorney and a professor, teaching constitutional law at the University of Chicago Law School from 1992 to 2004. He represented the 13th district for three terms in the Illinois Senate from 1997 to 2004, when he ran for the U.S. Senate. He received national attention in 2004 with his March primary win, his well-received July Democratic National Convention keynote address, and his landslide November election to the Senate. In 2008, he was nominated for president a year after his campaign began and after a close primary campaign against Hillary Clinton. He was elected over Republican John McCain and was inaugurated on January 20, 2009. Nine months later, he was named the 2009 Nobel Peace Prize laureate.

In June 1989, Obama met Michelle Robinson when he was employed as a summer associate at the Chicago law firm of Sidley Austin. Robinson was assigned for three months as Obama's adviser at the firm, and she joined him at several group social functions but declined his initial requests to date. They began dating later that summer, became engaged in 1991, and were married on October 3, 1992. The couple's first daughter, Malia Ann, was born in 1998, followed by a second daughter, Natasha ("Sasha"), in 2001. The Obama daughters attended the University of Chicago Laboratory Schools.[58 59 60 61]

President Obama is a Protestant Christian whose religious views did not develop until his adult life. He wrote in *The Audacity of Hope* that he "was not raised in a religious household". He described his mother, raised by non-religious parents, as being detached from religion, yet "in many ways the most spiritually awakened person that I have ever known." He described his father as a "confirmed atheist" by the time his parents met, and his stepfather as "a man who saw religion as not particularly useful." Obama explained how, through working with black churches as a community organizer while in his twenties, he came to understand "the power of the African-American religious tradition to spur social change."[62] [63]

He was frequently accused by his political opponents of being a Muslim and of not being a citizen of the United States, having been born in Africa, causing him to issue the following statement to *Christian Today* in January 2008: "I am a Christian, and I am a devout Christian. I believe in the redemptive death and resurrection of Jesus Christ. I believe that faith gives me a path to be cleansed of sin and have eternal life."[64] One can conclude that Barack Obama had a keen ability to overcome any negative criticism stemming from his multicultural heritage, and especially his namesake (Barack Hussein Obama). America had experienced the September 11, 2001, bombing of the United Trade Center in New York. Islamic terrorists were behind the United Trade Center bombing and are still at the top of America's enemy list. That Obama overcame this phenomenon, given his name is Islamic, was no small task.

On September 27, 2010, Obama released a statement commenting on his religious views, stating, "I'm a Christian by choice. My family... they weren't folks who went to church every week. And my mother was one of the most spiritual people I knew, but she didn't raise me in the church. So I came to my Christian faith later in life, and it was because the precepts of Jesus

Christ spoke to me in terms of the kind of life that I would want to lead, being my brothers' and sisters' keeper, treating others as they would treat me."[65] Obama met Trinity United Church of Christ pastor Rev. Jeremiah Wright in October 1987 and became a member of Trinity in 1992. During Obama's first presidential campaign in May 2008, he resigned from Trinity after some of Wright's statements were criticized. Since moving to Washington, D.C., in 2009, the Obama family has attended several Protestant churches, including Shiloh Baptist Church and St. John's Episcopal Church, as well as Evergreen Chapel at Camp David, but the members of the family do not attend church on a regular basis.[66][67][68][69]

President Barack Obama is a great example of a person who confronted life experiences and phenomena early in life that could have led him in multiple directions. He was born into a unique situation that gave him multiple and numerous models to define himself. There was the potential that his inherited situation could have confused his life; however, the combination of life experiences he encountered gave him the advantage of embracing his heritage and understanding the positive influence of multicultural heritage and exposure. While opponents and racists in America made attempts to hinder his progress, he handled controversy with dignity and intelligence.

Gallup Poll has named President Barack Obama and First Lady Michelle Obama the most admired man and woman of 2018.[70] This honor indicates how the public responds to not only him as a person and her as a person but to them both as a couple. In addition, President Obama was named "the most admired man" for the 11th consecutive year in a row.[71]

By all accounts, President Barack Obama had a challenging life. He was a mixed-race individual, born of a White mother and a Nigerian Black father. His father left him and his mother during his formative years. He barely knew his father. His mother remarried an Indonesian man, causing him to embrace an additional culturally diverse experience. A significant part of his upbringing was done by his grandparents. His father and mother passed away when he was a young man. There are many who encounter life experiences much less unstable than that of President Obama. However, despite his unstable lived experiences in his childhood, in his adolescence, the formative years of his life, and in his young adult stage, he managed to become somebody, somebody significant in our American history.

The question to ask President Barack Hussein Obama is: how did you become the great man that you are, considering the unstable and challenging life experiences in your developmental years, childhood, and adolescence?

Lived Experiences of Barack Obama

Stage 1 Mimesis for Barack Obama

1961   Barack Obama was born in Honolulu, Hawaii.

His mother (Ann Dunham) was a Caucasian American, and his father was a Black man (Barack Obama Sr.) from Kenya.

Stage 2 Mimesis for Barack Obama

1962 Barack's father earned a Master's degree in economics from Harvard University.

1963 Barack Graduated from Columbia University.

1964 His parents divorced, and his father returned to Kenya.

1965 Barak's mother married a second time to Lolo Soetore and moved to Indonesia in 1970. Barak lived there from age 6 – 10.

Having spent 4 years in Indonesia, Barak learned to speak the Indonesian language.

1971 Obama returned to Hawaii to live with his mother's parents, his grandparents.

1971 The only time Obama saw his father after the divorce.

1979 Barack graduated from high school and moved to Los Angeles to attend Occidental College.

1980 Barack's mother divorces her Indonesian husband.

1981 Barack transferred to Columbia University in New York and majored in political science.

1982 Barack Obama Sr. was killed in an automobile accident.

Barack Attended Harvard Law School.

Became the first Black President of the Harvard Law Review.

1988 Barack worked as a community organizer in Chicago, Illinois.

1989 Obama worked for the Sidney Austin law firm as a civil rights attorney, where he met Michelle Robinson.

1992 Barak's mother earned a PhD degree.

1992 Barak and Michelle Robinson married.

1998 Daughter Malia was born.

2001 Daughter Sasha was born.

1992-2004 Taught Constitutional Law at the University of Chicago Law School.

1997-2004 Represented the 13th district in the Illinois Senate

2004 Elected to the Illinois State Senate.

2004 Gave the Democratic National Convention keynote address.

2008 Nominated by the Democratic Party to run for President, defeating Hilary Clinton.

2008-2012 Defeated John McCain in the Presidential race to become the first Black President of the United States of America.

2009 Received the Nobel Peace Prize.

While President Obama was responsible for signing into law the following: the Affordable Health Care Act, Enacted the Dodd-Frank Wall Street Reform and Consumer Protection Act, Re-enacted the Don't Ask –Don't Tell Act, Repeal Act of 2010, American Recovery and Investment Act, and the Job Creation Act.

2009 Obama signed into law the National Defense Authorization Act for Fiscal Year 2010, which contained the Matthew Shepard and James Byrd Jr. Hate Crimes Prevention Act.

2011   President Obama ordered the military operation that killed Osama Bin Laden.

2013-2017   President Obama was elected to a second term by defeating Republican candidate Mitt Romney.

Reversed the same-sex marriage ban.

Oversaw the United States' process in joining the Paris Agreement for climate control.

His Administration negotiated the Iran Agreement, preventing Iran from developing nuclear weapons.

Under Obama's presidency, relations with Cuba softened.

2018   President Obama's second term ended, and he retired into life as a private citizen.

Mimesis of Life Summary for President Barack Obama

Barack Obama is an unusually gifted individual. He was born into non-traditional circumstances. His mother was white. His father was African. As a mixed-race child, he does not appear to have confusion about his identity or any inhibition or insecurity regarding his life direction. Despite his unstable upbringing, divorced parents, his mother remarried, living in Indonesia, and living with his grandparents, these experiences seemed to contribute to his diversity and open-mindedness, rather than confuse his identity.

In addition, a male who lacks a male role model in his developmental stages can become confused about life. Possibly, his grandfather filled this role. The point is that even though Barak did not have the stable benefit of a male role model in his developmental years, his life direction, on observation, does not appear to have been damaged. Possibly his own lack of a father image contributed to him being a great father and positively contributing to the development of his daughters.

A broken home can be a problem for most kids; however, the stability he experienced in living with his grandparents may have contributed to his adjustment as well as allowed him to keep his focus. The fact that both of his parents were highly educated gave him a value for education. Possibly these factors in to his own desire to accomplish educationally and academically.

"Of his years in Honolulu, Obama wrote: "The opportunity that Hawaii offered — to experience a variety of cultures in a climate of mutual respect — became an integral part of my world view, and a basis for the values that I hold most dear." Obama has also written and talked about using alcohol, marijuana, and cocaine during his teenage years to stating that his experience "push questions of who I was, out of my mind." Obama was also a member of the "choom gang", a self-named group of friends who spent time together and occasionally smoked marijuana."[72] Admittedly, Barak experimented with drugs, marijuana, and cocaine. The surprising aspect of this experimentation is not that he experimented, but that the experimentation did not take him off on a negative life path. It appears Barak had a focus to achieve.

During Obama's terms as president, the United States' reputation abroad, as well as the American economy, significantly improved. Obama's presidency has generally been regarded favorably, and evaluations of his presidency among historians, political scientists, and the general public frequently place him among the upper tier of American presidents.[73] As President Obama is still active in politics and a post-retirement author, the jury is still out on his stage 3 Mimesis. However, all indices point to the fact that he is respected and a role model for many young people, both Black and White. His legacy in American history is carved in stone.

Senator Barack Obama

Achieving goals is an accomplishment that gives the individual a sense of well-being. It's a happy feeling.

President Barack Obama

Time and stress take their toll.

Being President is not a stroll in the park, Natural evolution ages everyone. But the Presidency of the United States of America speeds up the evolution process.

Mimesis of Life for Billy Graham

William Franklin Graham Jr., born on November 7, 1918, and died on February 21, 2018. Billy Graham was a prominent American evangelical Christian figure and an ordained Southern Baptist minister who became well-known internationally in the late 1940s. One of his biographers indicated he was "among the most influential Christian leaders of the 20th century.[74] Billy Graham was of Scottish-Irish ancestry. Billy Graham was known worldwide. He had an audience with every President

from Dwight Eisenhower to Bill Clinton. Billy Graham. Graham also met with many world leaders. Billy Graham's reputation as a world Evangelical leader was well known and well respected.

What is Evangelicalism? [75]

*"**Evangelicalism**, also called **evangelical Christianity** or **evangelical Protestantism**, is a worldwide interdenominational movement within Protestant Christianity that affirms the centrality of being 'born again', in which an individual experiences personal conversion; the authority of the Bible as God's revelation to humanity (biblical inerrancy); and spreading the Christian message. The word evangelical comes from the Greek (euangelion) word for "good news".*

Its origins are usually traced to 1738, with various theological streams contributing to its foundation, including Pietism and Radical Pietism, Puritanism, Quakerism, Presbyterianism, and Moravianism (in particular, its bishop Nicolaus Zinzendorf and his community at Herrnhut). Preeminently, John Wesley and other early Methodists were at the root of sparking this new movement during the First Great Awakening. Today, evangelicals are found across many Protestant branches, as well as in various denominations around the world, not subsumed to a specific branch. Among leaders and major figures of the evangelical Protestant movement were Nicolaus Zinzendorf, George Fox, John Wesley, George Whitefield, Jonathan Edwards, Billy Graham, Bill Bright, Harold Ockenga, Gudina Tumsa, John Stott, Francisco Olazábal, William J. Seymour, and Martyn Lloyd-Jones.

The movement has long had a presence in the Anglosphere before spreading further afield in the 19th, 20th, and early 21st centuries. The movement gained great momentum during the 18th and 19th centuries with the Great Awakenings in Great Britain and the United States.

In 2016, there were an estimated 619 million evangelicals in the world, meaning that one in four Christians would be classified as evangelical. The United States has the largest proportion of evangelicals in the world. American evangelicals are a quarter of that nation's population and its single largest religious group. As a transdenominational coalition, evangelicals can be found in nearly every Protestant denomination and tradition, particularly within the Calvinist (Continental Reformed, Presbyterian, Congregational), Arminian, Plymouth Brethren, Baptist, Methodist (Wesleyan, Holiness), Lutheran, Moravian, Free Church, Mennonite, Quaker, Pentecostal, Charismatic, and non-denominational churches.

Graham was raised on the family dairy farm with two younger sisters and a younger brother. His parents were Associate Reformed Presbyterians, which is the religion he inherited. Albert McMakin, an employee on the Graham farm, convinced Billy to meet evangelist Mordecai Ham, who, according to Graham, converted him in 1934 at the age of 16.[76] After graduating from Sharon High School in May 1936, Graham attended Bob Jones College, then located in Cleveland, Tennessee, then dropped out after one year. He became influenced and inspired by Pastor Charley Young from Eastport Bible Church. He was almost expelled, but Bob Jones Sr. warned him not to throw his life away: "At best, all you could amount to would be a poor country Baptist preacher somewhere out in the sticks ...You have a voice that pulls. God can use that voice of yours. He can use it mightily."[77]

Lived Experiences for Reverend Billy Graham

Stage 1 Mimesis for Reverend Billy Graham

1918   William (Billy) Franklin Graham was born in North Carolina in the downstairs bedroom of a farmhouse. He was the elder of 4 children. Raised on a farm with two sisters, a brother and parents who were dairy farmers.

Stage 2 Mimesis for Reverend Billy Graham

Graham was raised in the Reformed Presbyterian Church. He read books at an early age. One of his favorites was Tarzan.

1933   When Graham was 15. Prohibition ended. His father forced him and his sister to drink beer until they became sick. This caused them to dislike alcohol so that they never drank.

1934   Graham was converted to Christianity after attending revival meetings in Charlotte, N.C.

1936   Graham graduated from Sharon High School.

1936   Graham attended one semester at Bob Jones College. Instead of being expelled, he was encouraged by Pastor Charley Young to pursue a career in the ministry.

1937   Graham transferred to Florida Bible Institute in Temple Terrace Florida.

As a student Graham preached his first sermon

According to Graham, he received his calling to the ministry on the 18th hole of the Temple Terrace Golf and Country Club.

1939   Graham was ordained by a group of Southern Baptist clergy at Peniel Baptist Church in Palatka, Florida.

1940   Graham graduated with a Bachelor of Theology degree.

Graham enrolled in Wheaton College in Illinois after graduation.

1941   While attending Wheaton in 1941, Graham was invited to preach one Sunday at the United Gospel Tabernacle church. After that, the congregation asked Graham to preach at their church again, then subsequently he was asked to become the pastor. He accepted.

It was during his time at Wheaton College that Graham decided to accept the Bible as the infallible word of God.

1943   Graham graduated from Wheaton College with a degree in anthropology. Graham Married Ruth Bell.

Graham and his wife had five children together.

His Children are:

> **Virginia Leftwich (Gigi) Graham** (b. 1945), an inspirational speaker and author.

> **Anne Graham Lotz** (b. 1948), leader of AnGeL ministries.

> **Ruth Graham** (b. 1950), founder and president of Ruth Graham & Friends and leader of conferences throughout the US and Canada.

> **Franklin Graham** (b. 1952), president and CEO of the Billy Graham Evangelistic Association and president and CEO of international relief organization Samaritan's Purse.

> **Nelson Edman Graham** (b. 1958), a pastor who runs East Gates

1944 Graham was sponsored by his congregation to take over a radio program, *Songs in the Night*. Graham recruited the bass-baritone George Beverly Shea as his director of radio ministry.

1948 In a hotel room in Modesto, California, Graham and his evangelistic team established the Modesto Manifesto, a code of ethics for life and work to protect against accusations of financial, sexual, and power abuse.

1948 At 29, Graham became president of Northwestern Bible College in Minneapolis; he was the youngest president of a college or university in the country and held the position for four years before he resigned in 1952.

1949 Graham scheduled a series of revival meetings in Los Angeles, for which he erected circus tents in a parking lot.

From the time his ministry began in 1947, Graham conducted worldwide crusades.

1950 Graham founded the Billy Graham Evangelistic Association (BGEA) with its headquarters in Minneapolis. The association relocated to Charlotte, North Carolina, in 1999, and maintains a number of international offices, such as in Hong Kong, Tokyo, and Buenos Aires.

BGEA ministries included:

Hour of Decision, a weekly radio program broadcast around the world for 66 years (1950-2016).

Mission television specials are broadcast in almost every market in the US and Canada.

A syndicated newspaper column, *My Answer*, is carried by newspapers across the United States and distributed by Tribune Content Agency.

Decision magazine, the official publication of the association.

Christianity Today was started in 1956 with Carl F. H. Henry as its first editor.

Passageway.org, the website for a youth discipleship program created by BGEA.

World Wide Pictures which has produced and distributed more than 130 films.

1950s Graham's early crusades were segregated, but he began adjusting his approach in the 1950s.[59] During a 1953 rally in Chattanooga, Tennessee, Graham tore down the ropes that organizers had erected in order to segregate the audience into racial sections. In his memoirs, he recounted that he told two ushers to leave the barriers down "or you can go on and have the revival without me."[60] He warned a white audience, "We have been proud and thought we were better than any other race, any other people. Ladies and gentlemen, we are going to stumble into hell because of our pride." [78]

1957 Graham's stance towards integration became more publicly shown when he allowed black ministers Thomas Kilgore and Gardner C. Taylor to serve as members of his New York Crusade's executive committee.

Dr. Martin Luther King, Jr. and Reverend Billy Graham had tensions, but the two still remained friends, and King told a Canadian television audience the following year that Graham had taken a "very strong stance against segregation.

Graham advised King and other members of the Southern Christian Leadership Conference (SCLC).

1960s King and Graham traveled together to the Tenth Baptist World Congress of the Baptist World Alliance.

1963 According to some, Graham posted bail for King to be released from jail during the Birmingham campaign.

Graham was considered the minister to Presidents, having had an audience with 12 consecutive presidents, beginning with Harry Truman, Dwight Eisenhower, John F. Kennedy, Lyndon B. Johnson, Richard Nixon, Gerald Ford, Jimmy Carter, Ronald Regan, George H. Bush, Bill Clinton, George W. Bush, and Barack Obama.

Graham leaned toward the Republicans during the presidency of Richard Nixon, whom he had met and befriended. Nixon was vice president under Dwight D. Eisenhower. He did not completely ally himself with the later religious right, saying that "Jesus did not have a political party". He gave his support to various political candidates over the years.

Graham had a friendly relationship with Queen Elizabeth II and was frequently invited by the Royal Family to special events.

During his life, Billy Graham received numerous awards, among them are:

Greatest Living American.

He consistently ranked among the most admired persons in the United States and the world.

He appeared most frequently on Gallup's list of most admired people.

In 1983, he was awarded the Presidential Medal of Freedom by US President Ronald Reagan.

In 2001, Queen Elizabeth II awarded him an honorary knighthood.

The movie *Billy: The Early Years* officially premiered in theaters on October 10, 2008.

1996 Congressional Gold Medal shows Ruth and Billy Graham in profile (front); the Ruth and Billy Graham Children's Health Center in Asheville, North Carolina (rear).

These are only a slight few of the honors and awards Billy Graham received. One lived experience after another reinforced Billy's life direction, creating and reinforcing his Mimesis.

2007   Ruth Graham dies.

Ruth Graham had been in frail health since suffering spinal meningitis in 1995. This was exacerbated by a degenerative osteoarthritis of the back and neck that began with a fall while testing a swing she made for her grandchildren in 1974, which resulted in chronic back pain for many years. During the final months of her life, she was bedridden and had contracted pneumonia. The day before Ruth Graham's death, Billy Graham released a statement through the Billy Graham Evangelistic Association stating, "Ruth is my soul mate and best friend, and I cannot imagine living a single day without her by my side. I am more and more in love with her today than when we first met over 65 years ago as students at Wheaton College.

2013   The Billy Graham Evangelistic Association started "My Hope With Billy Graham", the largest outreach in its history, encouraging church members to spread the gospel in small group meetings after showing a video message by Graham.

Other honors[79]

1996 Congressional Gold Medal shows Ruth and Billy Graham in profile (obverse); the Ruth and Billy Graham Children's Health Center in Asheville, North Carolina (reverse).

- The Salvation Army's Distinguished Service Medal

- Who's Who in America listing annually since 1954

- Freedoms Foundation Distinguished Persons Award (several years)

- Gold Medal Award, National Institute of Social Science, New York, 1957

- Annual Gutenberg Award of the Chicago Bible Society, 1962

- Gold Award of the George Washington Carver Memorial Institute, 1964, for contribution to race relations, presented by Senator Javits (NY)

- Speaker of the Year Award, awarded by Delta Sigma Rho-Tau Kappa Alpha, 1965

- The American Academy of Achievement's Golden Plate Award, 1965

- Horatio Alger Award, 1965

- National Citizenship Award by the Military Chaplains Association of the United States of America, 1965

- Wisdom Award of Honor, 1965

- The Torch of Liberty Plaque by the Anti-Defamation League of B'nai B'rith, 1969

- George Washington Honor Medal from Freedoms Foundation of Valley Forge, Pennsylvania, for his sermon "The Violent Society", 1969 (also in 1974)

- Honored by Morality in Media for "fostering the principles of truth, taste, inspiration, and love in media", 1969

- International Brotherhood Award from the National Conference of Christians and Jews, 1971

- Distinguished Service Award from the National Association of Broadcasters, 1972

- Franciscan International Award, 1972

- Sylvanus Thayer Award from United States Military Academy Association of Graduates at West Point (The most prestigious award the United States Military Academy gives to a US citizen), 1972

- Direct Selling Association's Salesman of the Decade award, 1975

- Philip Award from the Association of United Methodist Evangelists, 1976

- American Jewish Committee's First National Interreligious Award, 1977

- Southern Baptist Radio and Television Commission's Distinguished Communications Medal, 1977

- Jabotinsky Centennial Medal presented by The Jabotinsky Foundation, 1980

- Religious Broadcasting Hall of Fame award, 1981

- Templeton Foundation Prize for Progress in Religion award, 1982

- Presidential Medal of Freedom, the nation's highest civilian award, 1983

- National Religious Broadcasters Award of Merit, 1986

- North Carolina Award in Public Service, 1986

- Good Housekeeping Most Admired Men Poll, 1997, No. 1 for five years in a row and 16th time in top 10

- Congressional Gold Medal (along with wife Ruth), the highest honor Congress can bestow on a private citizen, 1996

- Ronald Reagan Presidential Foundation Freedom Award, for monumental and lasting contributions to the cause of freedom, 2000

- Honorary Knight Commander of the Order of the British Empire (KBE) for his international contribution to civic and religious life over 60 years, 2001

- Many honorary degrees including University of Northwestern – St. Paul, Minnesota, where Graham was once president, named its newest campus building the Billy Graham Community Life Commons. He also received honorary Doctor of Divinity degrees

As a Christian Evangelist, Billy Graham filled stadiums. People were thirsty to hear him preach the Gospel. One can speculate that it was more the Graham style of preaching that drew crowds to hear him because the majority of his followers were White. While Graham did denounce racism, he was moderate in the way he criticized racism and racists.

Stage 3 Mimesis for Reverend Billy Graham

As he aged, Graham approached his death with a direct realism.

When he preached, he said that death was inevitable. He stated, "Christ would return", he said, "everyone should think instead about the sure thing they did know: the certainty of their own death". Graham repeatedly insisted that death fell on everyone.

Graham noted elsewhere that many people tried to avoid this inescapable reality by playing word games, by changing the title of a cemetery to a memorial park, for example. But he left them no loopholes. First, he said, "accept the fact that you will die." Second, "make arrangements." Third, "make provision for those you are leaving behind." And finally, "make an appointment with God.".[80]

Graham's failing health caused him to retire. He had suffered from a disease diagnosed as "hydrocephalus", which was actually Parkinson' from 1992 on. In August 2005.[81] Graham appeared at the groundbreaking for his library in Charlotte, North Carolina. Then 86, he used a walker during the ceremony. On July 9, 2006, he spoke at the Metro

Maryland Franklin Graham Festival, held in Baltimore, Maryland, at Oriole Park at Camden Yards.

In April 2010, Graham was 91 and experiencing substantial vision, hearing, and balance loss when he made a rare public appearance at the re-dedication of the renovated Billy Graham Library.

There was controversy within his family over Graham's proposed burial place. He announced in June 2007 that he and his wife would be buried alongside each other at the Billy Graham Library in his hometown of Charlotte. Graham's younger son Ned argued with older son Franklin about whether burial at a library would be appropriate. Ruth Graham had said that she wanted to be buried in the mountains at the Billy Graham Training Center at The Cove near Asheville, North Carolina, where she had lived for many years; Ned supported his mother's choice.[82] Novelist Patricia Cornwell, a family friend, also opposed burial at the library, calling it a tourist attraction. Franklin wanted his parents to be buried at the library site.[83] When Ruth Graham died, it was announced that they would be buried at the library site. At the time of his death at age 99 in 2018, Graham was survived by 5 children, 19 grandchildren (including

Will Graham and Tullian Tchividjian), 41 great-grandchildren, and 6 great-great-grandchildren.

Graham died in his sleep at his North Carolina home. The only person with him was the attendant nurse. Graham's body laid in repose at the Graham family home for two days before his internment.

Graham's body was buried at a cross-shaped brick walkway in the northeast side of the Billy Graham Library, next to his wife Ruth, who was buried in 2007. The interment will be private and family-only.

The final Mimesis of Billy Graham among people in the world was abundant with respect and love for a man who contribute so much love, kindness and good into the world. While many of his followers were from the Jim Crow South, he came to reject their viewpoints on racism. One can truly say, Billy Graham was a man of God, a good man.

Mimesis of Life Summary for Billy Graham

Billy Graham was born in a farmhouse near Charlotte, North Carolina, on November 7, 1918. He was of Scottish and Irish descent. He was the eldest of four children born to Morrow and William Franklin Graham Sr., a dairy farmer.

Billy Graham attended college, receiving degrees in Theology and anthropology. His ability to preach and reach the hearts and minds of large groups of people, coupled with his belief in God, set his life direction. Billy Graham dedicated his life to preaching the word of God.

From all accounts, he was a good man, a good husband, a good father, a good friend, a good human being, and a good Christian.

Graham received numerous rewards during his lifetime, which indicates how people from all walks of life felt about and perceived him. Graham died of natural causes on February 21, 2018, at his home in Montreat, North Carolina, at the age of 99. On February 28 and March 1, 2018, Graham became the fourth private citizen in United States history to lie in honor at the United States Capitol rotunda in Washington, D.C. Graham has been referred to as "America's pastor" and "an ambassador for Christ."

Billy Graham was honored and revered in death as he was in his life. No doubt Graham was a gifted and blessed human being, an asset to the world. While he was not perfect and did have controversial life experiences. Harry Truman thought he was a phony. Dr.

Martin Luther King, Jr. was disappointed by the way Graham responded to his "Letter from a Birmingham jail." Dr. King was also disappointed that Graham did not show an urgency to resolve the civil rights problem in America. However, for the most part, Billy Graham was one of the most respected individuals of his era. He was a moral icon for White culture as well as having the respect of many common and prominent Black people.

The journey through life is over before we know it.

Billy Graham, being a religious man, found solace in his religion.

Going from young to old presents a dilemma for many people.

The ability to accept the inevitable is critical to well-being.

Reflective moments for Reverend Graham. He has much to be proud of. However, the twilight years of the human lived experience are mixed with emotions, thoughts, feelings, and anticipation of what is to come, variable to each individual.

Mimesis of Life for Queen Elizabeth II

Her birth name is Elizabeth Alexandrea Mary Windsor (Born April 21, 1926, Died September 8, 2022). Elizabeth II was the Queen of the United Kingdom and 15 other Commonwealth realms. Elizabeth, named after her mother, was born in Mayfair, London. She was the first born of the Duke and Duchess of York on April 21, 1926. Her father ascended the throne when his brother King Edward VIII abdicated the throne in 1936. The abdication of Edward VIII made Elizabeth the next in line to the throne; she was the heir presumptive. Her father was King George VI and her mother the wife of King George VI, Queen Elizabeth, The Queen Mother, Elizabeth Angela Marguerite Bowes-Lyon (Pictured left)…

When her father died in February 1952, Elizabeth, then 25 years old, became the Queen of England and of seven independent Commonwealth countries: the United Kingdom, Canada, Australia, New Zealand, South Africa, Pakistan, and Ceylon (known today as Sri Lanka), as well as head of the Commonwealth.

Queen Elizabeth II was the longest-serving monarch in the history of England. She was married to Philip Mountbatten in 1947, who died in 2021 at the age of 99. His titles include Philip, Prince of Greece and Denmark, Prince Philip, Duke of Edinburgh, Earl of Merioneth, and Baron Greenwich. Queen Elizabeth has four children: Charles, Prince of Wales, Princess and York, and Prince Edward Duke of Edinburgh. Queen Elizabeth had eight Grandchildren: Prince William, Duke

of Cambridge, Prince Harry, Duke of Sussex, Princess Beatrice, Princess Eugenie, Peter Philips, Zara Tindall, Lady Louise Windsor and James Viscount Severn.

Elizabeth was born into royalty. Most would think her life began and continued to be a fairy tale. According to normal standards her situation is among the most fortunate in the world. However, one has to understand that regardless of your status in life there is not existence without challenges. No one escapes the challenges and hardships in life. Elizabeth has had her share. The most exceptional phenomenon about

Elizabeth is that she has demonstrated her personal sacrificed to conduct her duties to her country and fulfill her role as the Queen of England. She has subscribed to a role in life that was not of her making but her birthright. Even as the Queen of England, Elizabeth made a significant sacrifice. She sacrificed Elizabeth for the Queen. In addition, Queen Elizabeth has honored her country by conducting herself with dignity for over 9 decades. The reality in the way Elizabeth has conducted her life and represented her subjects is the real fairy tale.

Elizabeth's Lived Experiences

Stage 1 Mimesis of Princess Elizabeth

1926   Elizabeth Alexandra Mary Windsor was born in Mayfair, London to King George VI and Queen Elizabeth (the Queen Mother) on April 21, 1926.

Elizabeth was named Elizabeth after her mother; Alexandra after her paternal great-grandmother, who had died six months earlier; and Mary after her paternal grandmother. She was also called Lilibet, as a nickname.

Her father ascended to the throne when his brother, King Edward VIII, the rightful heir, abdicated. This sequence of events made Elizabeth Alexandra the presumptive heir to the English throne.

Elizabeth was home schooled and educated privately.

1930 Princess Margaret was born, Elizabeth's only sibling.

Both Princess Elizabeth and Princess Margaret had their early lives and education supervised by their mother and governess, Marion Crawford.

Elizabeth on the cover of Time Magazine. How many kids get this kind of worldwide exposure?

Elizabeth's stage 1 Mimesis lasted longer than normal for most children. She was tutored by her mother, Queen Elizabeth, and her governess, Marion Crawford. Therefore, Elizabeth's exposure outside of her family oversight was limited to servants, tutors, and family. Her life was heavily scrutinized and sheltered in preparation for her to become the Queen of England. Elizabeth spent most of her early childhood with her sister Margaret (August 21, 1930 – February 9, 2002) as her closest companion. Margaret was Elizabeth's only sibling. The two princesses were educated at home under the supervision of their mother and their governess, Marion Crawford. Sheltered from the outside world, the focus of Elizabeth's

Stage 1 Mimesis was to educate and train Elizabeth on how to become the Queen of England, the Commonwealth, and its territories.

Stage 2 Mimesis of Princess Elizabeth

- Elizabeth grew up with a love for horses and dogs. According to her governess, Elizabeth had a character of orderliness and an attitude of responsibility.

- Winston Churchill described Elizabeth when she was two years old as "a character. She has an air of authority and reflectiveness astonishing in an infant." Her cousin Margaret Rhodes described her as "a jolly little girl, but fundamentally sensible and well-behaved"

- A Girl Guides company, the 1st Buckingham Palace Company, was formed specifically so she could socialize with girls her own age

- During her grandfather's reign, Elizabeth was third in the line of succession to the British throne, behind her uncle Edward and her father. Although her birth generated public interest, she was not expected to become queen, as Edward was still young and likely to marry and have children of his own, who would precede Elizabeth in the line of succession

- When her grandfather died in 1936 and her uncle succeeded as Edward VIII, she became second in line to the throne, after her father. Later that year, Edward abdicated, after his proposed marriage to divorced socialite Wallis Simpson provoked a constitutional crisis. Consequently, Elizabeth's father became king, taking the regnal name George VI. Since Elizabeth had no brothers, she became heir presumptive.

1934 Elizabeth met her future husband, Prince Philip of Greece and Denmark

They were second cousins once removed through King Christian IX of Denmark and third cousins through Queen Victoria. After another meeting at the Royal Naval College in Dartmouth in July 1939, Elizabeth, though only 13 years old, said she fell in love with Philip, and they began to exchange letters. She was 21 when their engagement was officially announced on July 9, 1947.

1939 The first transatlantic telephone call was made between Elizabeth and her parents when they toured North America, and she stayed in England.

1939 England entered World War 2

In September 1939, Britain entered World War II. Lord Hailsham suggested that Princess Elizabeth and Princess Margaret should leave England and go to Canada to avoid the aerial bombings of London by Germany. This suggestion was rejected by their mother, who stated, "The children won't go without me. I won't leave without the King. And the King will never leave". [84]

1940 14-year-old Elizabeth made her first radio broadcast during the BBC's *Children's Hour*, addressing other children who had been evacuated from the cities. She stated: "We are trying to do all we can to help our gallant sailors, soldiers, and airmen, and we are trying, too, to bear our own share of the danger and sadness of war. We know, every one of us, that in the end all will be well.

1943 Elizabeth undertook her first solo public appearance on a visit to the Grenadier Guards, of which she had been appointed colonel the previous year. As she approached her 18th birthday, parliament changed the law so she could act as one of five Counselors of State in the event of her father's incapacity or absence abroad, such as his visit to Italy in July 1944.

1945  Elizabeth was appointed as an honorary second subaltern in the Auxiliary Territorial Service. She trained as a driver and mechanic and was given the rank of honorary junior commander (female equivalent of captain at the time) five months later.

1945 World War II ended. Wanting to celebrate Victory in Europe Day, Elizabeth and Margaret mingled incognito with the celebrating crowds in the streets of London.

1947 Princess Elizabeth went on her first overseas tour 1947, accompanying her parents through southern Africa. During the tour, in a broadcast to the British Commonwealth on her 21st birthday, she made the following pledge: "I declare before you all that my whole life, whether it be long or short, shall be devoted to your service and the service of our great imperial family to which we all belong".[85]

1947 Elizabeth and Philip became engaged on July 9. However, there were concerns. Philip had no financial standing. He was foreign-born (though a British subject who had served in the Royal Navy throughout the Second World War). Through marriage and relations, Philip was a Prince of Greece and Denmark. Philip had sisters who had married German noblemen with Nazi ties. Elizabeth's mother had reservations about the union initially and teased Philip as "The Hun". In later life, however, the Queen Mother said that Philip was "an English gentleman".[86]

1947 Elizabeth and Philip were married on 20 November 1947 at Westminster Abbey. Before the wedding, Philip renounced his Greek and Danish titles.[87]

1948 Elizabeth gave birth to her first child, Prince Charles, on 14 November

1950 A second child, Princess Anne, was born

1952 King Edward VIII died, and Elizabeth, at 25, became the Queen of England and queen regnant of seven independent Commonwealth countries: The United Kingdom, Canada, Australia, New Zealand, South Africa, Pakistan, and Ceylon. Elizabeth is no longer the constitutional monarch of Ireland, and over the years, as countries have vied for independence, the territories she controls have diminished. [88]

1952

The coronation of Elizabeth took place on June 2 and was televised for the first time.

1952 Elizabeth issued a declaration that *Windsor* would continue to be the name of the royal house. This was a disappointment to Prince Philip, who declared, "I am the only man in the country not allowed to give his name to his own children."[89]

1953 On March 24, Elizabeth's Grandmother, Queen Mary, died.

1953 Queen Elizabeth and Prince Philip embarked on a seven-month around-the-world tour, visiting 13 countries, under her reign, as well as a State visit to the United States.

1957   Queen Elizabeth made a state visit to the United States, where she addressed the United Nations General Assembly on behalf of the Commonwealth

1959   Prince Andrew was born to Queen Elizabeth and Prince Philip.

1963   Prince Edward was born to Queen Elizabeth and Prince Philip.

1960 – 1970 During the 1960s and 1970s decolonization of Africa and countries in the Caribbean increased. More than 20 countries gained independence from Britain as part of a planned transition to self-government.

1972   Elizabeth toured Yugoslavia in October 1972, becoming the first British monarch to visit a communist country.[90]

1974 - 1975 Elizabeth was confronted with a Constitutional crisis both at home in Britain and in Australia, where she is the ruling head of state. In February 1974, the British prime minister, Edward Heath, advised Elizabeth to call a general election in the middle of her tour of the Austronesian Pacific Rim, requiring her to fly back to Britain. The election resulted in a hung parliament; Heath's Conservatives were not the largest party but could stay in office if they formed a coalition with the Liberals. When discussions on forming a coalition failed, Heath resigned as prime minister, and Elizabeth asked the Leader of the opposition, Labor party's, Harold Wilson, to form a government.

A year later, at the height of the 1975 Australian constitutional crisis, the Australian prime minister, Gough Whitlam, was dismissed from his post by Governor-General Sir John Kerr, after the Opposition-controlled Senate rejected Whitlam's budget proposals. As Whitlam had a majority in the House of Representatives, Speaker Gordon Scholes appealed to Elizabeth to reverse Kerr's decision. She declined, saying she would not interfere in decisions reserved by the Constitution of Australia for the Governor-General. The crisis fueled Australian republicanism. [91]

1977 Elizabeth celebrated the Silver Jubilee of her reign. The celebrations throughout Britain reaffirmed Elizabeth's popularity.

1978 Elizabeth suffered disappointment and sadness: one was the unmasking of Anthony Blunt, former Surveyor of the Queen's Pictures, as a communist spy; the other was the assassination of her relative and in-law Lord Mountbatten by the Provisional Irish Republican Army.[92]

1981 Six shots were fired at the Queen from close range. The shots were blanks. Marcus Sarjeant, the 17-year-old assailant, was sentenced to five years in prison and released after three.

1981 During the 1981 Trooping the Color ceremony, six weeks before the wedding of Prince Charles and Lady Diana Spencer, six shots were fired at Elizabeth from close range as she rode down the

London Mall on her horse, Burmese. Police later discovered the shots were blanks. A 17-year-old assailant who fired the shots, Marcus Sarjeant, was sentenced to five years in prison and released after three.[115] Elizabeth's composure and skill in controlling her mount were widely praised.

In October, the Queen was the subject of another attack while on a visit to Dunedin, New Zealand. New Zealand Security Intelligence Service documents, declassified in 2018, revealed that 17-year-old Christopher John Lewis fired a shot with a .22 rifle from the fifth floor of a building overlooking the parade, but missed.[93]

1982   On 9 July, Queen Elizabeth awoke in her bedroom at Buckingham Palace to find an intruder, Michael Fagan, in the room with her. This was a serious lapse of security. Assistance only arrived after two calls to the Palace police switchboard.[94]

1986   The Queen made a six-day state visit to China, becoming the first British monarch to visit the country. The visit also signified the acceptance of both countries that sovereignty over Hong Kong would be transferred from the United Kingdom to China in 1997.[95]

1991   In the wake of coalition victory in the Gulf War, the Queen became the first British monarch to address a joint meeting of the United States Congress.

1992   The Queen considered 1992 a horrible year for her and the monarchy.

- Republican feeling in Britain had risen because of press estimates of the Queen's private wealth, which the Palace contradicted.

- Reports of affairs and strained marriages among her extended family.

- In March, her second son, Prince Andrew, and his wife, Sarah, separated. The country of Mauritius removed Elizabeth as head of state.

- In April, her daughter, Princess Anne, divorced Captain Mark Phillips.

- During a state visit to Germany in October, angry demonstrators in Dresden threw eggs at her.

- In November, a large fire broke out at Windsor Castle, one of her official residences.

The monarchy came under increased criticism and public scrutiny. In an unusually personal speech, the Queen said that any institution must expect criticism, but suggested it be done with "a touch of humor, gentleness and understanding". Two days later, Prime Minister John Major announced reforms to the royal finances planned since the previous year, including the Queen paying income tax from 1993 onwards, and a reduction in the civil list.

- In December, Prince Charles and his wife, Diana, formally separated.

-      The year ended with a lawsuit, as the Queen sued *The Sun* newspaper for breach of copyright when it published the text of her annual Christmas message two days before it was broadcast. Courts forced the newspaper to pay her legal fees and donate £200,000 to charity. The Queen's lawyers had taken action against *The Sun* five years earlier for breach of copyright, after it published a photograph of the Duchess of York and Princess Beatrice. The case was solved with an out-of-court settlement that made the newspaper pay $180,000.

1996 Charles and Diana divorced.

1997 Diana was killed in a car crash in Paris.

1997 Diana was loved by the English people. The Queen suffered negative feedback because she did not express immediate sentiment for Diana. The day before Diana's funeral, the Queen gave a speech expressing admiration for Diana, and the hostility waned.

2002 Elizabeth marked her Golden Jubilee, the 50th anniversary of her accession.

Her sister and mother died in February and March, respectively.

2007 In November, Elizabeth became the first British monarch to celebrate a diamond wedding anniversary.

Elizabeth surpassed her great-great-grandmother, Queen Victoria, to become the longest-lived British monarch on December 21.

2015   She became the longest-reigning British monarch and longest-reigning queen regnant and female head of state in the world on September 9. She became the oldest current monarch after King Abdullah of Saudi Arabia died on January 24.

2016   She later became the longest-reigning current monarch and the longest-serving current head of state following the death of King Bhumibol of Thailand on October 13.

2017   Queen Elizabeth became the oldest current head of state on the resignation of Robert Mugabe of Zimbabwe on November 21.

On February 6, she became the first British monarch to commemorate a sapphire jubilee.

On November 20, she was the first British monarch to celebrate a platinum wedding anniversary. Philip had retired from his official duties as the Queen's consort in August. [96]

2020   On March 19, as the COVID-19 pandemic hit the United Kingdom, Elizabeth moved to Windsor Castle and sequestered there as a precaution. Public engagements were cancelled and Windsor Castle followed a strict sanitary protocol nicknamed "HMS Bubble"

2021   Prince Philip died on April 9, after 73 years of marriage, making Elizabeth the first British monarch to reign as a widow or widower since Queen Victoria. She was at her husband's bedside when he died, and remarked in private that his death had "left a huge void". [97]

On Christmas Day 2021, while she was staying at Windsor Castle, 19-year-old Jaswant Singh Chail broke into the gardens using a rope ladder and carrying a crossbow with the intention of assassinating Elizabeth in revenge for the Amritsar massacre. Before he could enter any buildings, he was arrested and detained under the Mental Health Act. In 2023, he pled guilty to attempting to injure or alarm the sovereign. [98]

2022 On February 6. Elizabeth celebrated her Platinum Jubilee, marking 70 years since she acceded to the throne after the death of her father.

Elizabeth rarely gives interviews, therefore little is known about her personal feelings. She has not explicitly expressed her own political opinions in a public forum, and it is against convention to ask or reveal her views. Elizabeth has a deep sense of religious and civic duty, and takes her Coronation Oath seriously. Aside from her official religious role as Supreme Governor of the established Church of England, she is a member of that church and also of the national Church of Scotland. She has demonstrated support for inter-faith relations and has met with leaders of other churches and religions, including five popes: Pius XII, John XXIII, John Paul II, Benedict XVI and Francis. She is patron of over 600 organizations and charities. The Charities Aid Foundation estimated that Elizabeth has helped raised over £1.4 billion for her patronages during her reign. Polls in Britain in 2006 and 2007 revealed strong support for Elizabeth, and in 2012, her Diamond Jubilee year, and approval ratings hit 90 percent.[99]

Her family came under scrutiny again in 2019 and the early 2020s due to her son Andrew's association with convicted sex offenders Jeffrey Epstein and Ghislaine Maxwell, his lawsuit with Virginia Giuffre amidst accusations of sexual impropriety, and her grandson Harry and his wife Meghan's exit from the monarchy and subsequent move to the United States.

Elizabeth's personal fortune has been the subject of speculation for many years. In 1971, Jock Colville, her former private secretary and a director of her bank, Coutts, estimated her wealth at £2 million (equivalent to about £29 million in 2020). In 1993, Buckingham Palace called estimates of £100 million "grossly overstated". In 2002, she inherited an estate worth an estimated £70 million from her mother. The *Sunday Times Rich List 2020* estimated her personal wealth at £350 million, making her the 372nd richest person in the UK. She was number one on the list when it began in the *Sunday Times Rich List 1989*, with a reported wealth of £5.2 billion, which included state assets that were not hers personally, (approximately £13.2 billion in today's value). The Royal Collection, which includes thousands of historic works of art and the British Crown Jewels, is not owned personally but is held in trust by the Queen, as are her official residences, such as Buckingham Palace and

Windsor Castle, and the Duchy of Lancaster, a property portfolio valued at £472 million in 2015. (The Paradise Papers, leaked in 2017, show that the Duchy of Lancaster held investments in two tax haven overseas territories, the Cayman Islands and Bermuda). Sandringham House and Balmoral Castle are personally owned by the Queen. The British Crown Estate – with holdings of £14.3 billion in 2019 – is held in trust and cannot be sold or owned by her in a personal capacity.

Mimesis 3 of the Three-Fold Mimesis for Queen Elizabeth

2022 On 8 September 2022, Buckingham Palace released a statement which read: "Following further evaluation this morning, the Queen's doctors are concerned for Her Majesty's health and have recommended she remain under medical supervision. The Queen remains comfortable and at Balmoral." Her immediate family rushed to Balmoral to be by her side.[257][258] She died peacefully at 15:10 BST at the age of 96, with two of her children, Charles and Anne, by her side. Her death was announced to the public at 18:30, setting in motion Operation London Bridge and, because she died in Scotland, Operation Unicorn. Elizabeth was the first monarch to die in Scotland since James V in 1542. Her death certificate recorded her cause of death as "old age".[100]

Elizabeth's coffin escorted by the Royal Navy.

Queen Elizabeth II was the longest reigning monarch in the history of the United Kingdom. She sat on her throne for over 70 years and 214 days, from February 6, 1952, until September 8, 2022. Queen Elizabeth is highly popular in England and around the world. She is admired and respected worldwide. There are a handful of people who believe the monarchy is outdated, irrelevant, and should be disbanded. The majority of England believe it is part of their heritage. Their love for the Queen reinforces their sentiment about the monarchy. Prince Charles is next in line to the throne. Elizabeth's humility, grace, and dedication to public service is her trademark and reasons she is so widely loved. Elizabeth is the longest-lived and longest-reigning British monarch, the longest-serving female head of state in history, the oldest living and longest-reigning current monarch, and the oldest and longest-serving incumbent head of state.

The Queen's 90th birthday celebration which happened all over the UK on the weekend of June, 10-12, 2016.

In addition to her 90th birthday celebration, Queen Elizabeth has celebrated the following Jubilee's marking the years of service to the people of England and the years she has reigned as Queen over the Commonwealth.

1977   The Queen's Silver Jubilee

1992   The Queen's Ruby Jubilee

2002   The Queen's Golden Jubilee

2012   The Queen's Diamond Jubilee

2022   The Queens Platinum Jubilee

Mimesis of Life Summary for Queen Elizabeth

Elizabeth Alexandra Mary Windsor was born on April 21, 1926. Elizabeth was the first child of the Duke and Duchess of York (later King George VI and Queen Elizabeth, The Queen Mother). Her social location is defined by being born into the royal family of England. Her early childhood experiences were highly scrutinized. She did not venture outside of the influence of her father and mother until her late adolescent years. Her primary relationships during the stage 1 Mimesis were her parents, Princess Margaret (her sister), her nanny (Marion Crawford), her tutor (Henry Marten) and the numerous house servants and help. Elizabeth was sheltered from the wider outside world for her protection.

Elizabeth did not experience a significant development of her Stage 2 Mimesis until she participated in WWII as an auto mechanic and truck driver. It is ironic for the Queen of England to be imagined as an auto mechanic. However, one can assume, it was this experience that put her in touch with the nature of commoners. One can also assume this experience as a truck driver influenced her perspective such that she appeared humbled to the common people of England. Though Elizabeth was a "Royal" the people of England loved her and accepted her as their Queen. Elizabeth had a quality that allowed her to bridge the gap between herself, as a royal, and the common people.

Elizabeth became the Queen of England because of circumstances that broke the order of succession to the throne. When her grandfather King George VI died, the next in line to the throne was her uncle, Prince Edward. Prince Edward later called King Edward VIII upon his ascension to the throne. However Edward VIII abdicated the throne which put her father (Albert Frederick Arthur George Windsor), who became King George VI upon his ascension to the throne. This event put Elizabeth, as the first born of King George VI, next in line to the throne. King George VI died on February 6, 1952. Upon his death Elizabeth, thereafter called Elizabeth II, ascended to the throne and became the Queen of England, Queen of the commonwealth of the United Kingdom and Queen over all of England's territories throughout the world.

Elizabeth was the longest ruling monarch in England's history. During her reign she encountered many challenges but maneuvered through them with thoughtful intelligent dignity.

One would assume that the life of a royal is privileged, easy and without difficult life challenges. It is true, that being born into privilege does come with many advantages. However, no one gets through life without challenges. Consider the case of her uncle, King Edward VIII, who abdicated the throne.

In her twilight years, Elizabeth remained the Queen up until her death on September 8, 2022. Elizabeth had a deep sense of religious and civic duty, and took her Coronation Oath seriously. Aside from her official religious role as Supreme Governor of the established Church of England, she worshipped with that church and also the national Church of Scotland. She demonstrated support for inter-faith relations and met with leaders of other churches and religions, including five popes: Pius XII, John XXIII, John Paul II, Benedict XVI and Francis. A personal note about her faith often featured in her annual Christmas Message broadcast to the Commonwealth. In 2000, she said: [101]

"To many of us, our beliefs are of fundamental importance. For me the teachings of Christ and my own personal accountability before God provide a framework in which I try to lead my life. I, like so many of you, have drawn great comfort in difficult times from Christ's words and example."

Queen Elizabeth II

Elizabeth supported more than 600 organizations and charities. The Charities Aid Foundation estimated that Elizabeth helped raise over £1.4 billion for her patronages during her reign. Her main leisure interests included equestrianism and dogs, especially her Pembroke Welsh Corgis. Her lifelong love of corgis began in 1933 with" Dookie", the first corgi owned by her family. Occasionally she and her family, from time to time, prepared a meal together and washed the dishes afterwards. [102]

Throughout her reign Queen Elizabeth had to deal with numerous challenges

Challenges in her own government regarding political issues and misogynistic issues.

Challenges in the Commonwealth, including the war with Ireland and issues resolving their differences

Territories under her rule that issued declarations of independence

Political challenges from other territories that accepted her as their Queen.

However, there is reason to believe that the challenges that took the greatest toll on the Queen were family Challenges that confronted her.

The dysfunctional relationship between her son Prince Andrew and Sarah Ferguson.

The affairs of King Charles and his dysfunctional relationship with Princess Diana

The marriage ending in divorce between Prince Charles (now called King Charles) and Princess Diana.

The death of her daughter-in-law, Princess Diana.

The association of her son, Prince Andrew with child molester Jeffrey Epstein.

The marriage of her grandson Prince Harry to Megan Markle, a black woman.

The Death of her husband, Prince Philip.

The dissociation of her grandson, Prince Harry from the Royal Family.

While there has been talk of abolishing the monarchy. The widespread outpour of grief following the death of Queen Elizabeth II, indicates the British people are loyal and are royalist in their support of the monarchy. It is not uncommon for Anti-monarchy protested to be arrested for voicing their sentiments in public. The duties of the royal family are primary ceremonial. They have no significant or controlling role in the operation of government operations but that is not to say they have no influence. The major objection to the monarchy is that the anti-monarchy English Taxpayers complain that the money the government pays to the royal family is a waste and should be spent otherwise.[103]

In the fiscal year 2020-2021 the English taxpayers paid the royal family £86.3 million - The total taxpayer-funded Sovereign Grant, made up of £51.8 million for the "core" funding and an extra £34.5 million for the re-servicing of Buckingham Palace.

In the fiscal year 2022-2023 the Sovereign Grant is around £86 million a year but can exceed £369 million if the palace urgently requires 30 more clocks. This money comes from HM Treasury and is funded by the taxpayer.

The fact remains, that the vast majority of the English population favor the monarchy because of the dignity and professionalism in which Queen Elizabeth shaped and molded the monarchy to compliment the English people and the English government

If there was any significant support to eliminate the monarchy, it would have been done before the 70 years of the reign of Queen Elizabeth. Support for the Royal Monarchy grew with each milestone of the Queen's reign

1977 The Queen's Silver Jubilee

1992 The Queen's Ruby Jubilee

2002 The Queen's Golden Jubilee

2012 The Queen's Diamond Jubilee

2022 The Queens Platinum Jubilee

Queen Elizabeth on her throne with husband, Prince Philip.

Queen Elizabeth on her throne with her son, Prince Charles, now King Charles.

Mimesis of Life for Richard Nixon
(1913 – 1994)

Richard Milhous Nixon born January 9, 1913 and died April 22, 1994. He was a member of the Republican political party and the 37th president of the United States from 1969 until 1974 and the only president to resign from the position. He had previously served as the 36th vice president of the United States from 1953 to 1961, and prior to that, as both a U.S. representative and senator from California.

Nixon served as President for five years. He ended America's involvement in the Vietnam War. He negotiated détente with the Soviet Union and China. Nixon established the Environmental Protection Agency (EPA). Nixon's second term ended early, when he became the only president to resign from office, following the Watergate scandal.

Nixon was born in to a poor family in Yorba Linda, California. He graduated from Whittier College, then attended Duke University and graduated from Duke University School of Law in 1937. Nixon was offered a scholarship to Harvard, but decided to attend Whittier College in his hometown so he could help his ill father continue to run the family store.[104] After returning to California to practice law, he and his wife Pat moved to Washington in 1942 to work for the federal government. He served on active duty in the U.S. Navy Reserve during

World War II. Nixon was elected to the House of Representatives in 1946 and to the Senate in 1950. His participation and leadership in the Hiss Case established his reputation as a leading anti-communist and elevated him to national prominence. Dwight D. Eisenhower, the Republican Party presidential nominee in the 1952 election, selection Nixon as his running mate for Vice-President. Nixon served for eight years as Vice President, becoming the second-youngest vice president in history at age 40. In 1960 he unsuccessfully ran for president of the United States and narrowly lost to John F. Kennedy. Nixon lost a race for Governor of California to Pat Brown in 1962. In 1968, he ran for the presidency again and was elected, defeating incumbent Vice President Hubert Humphrey.

His mother was a Quaker, and his father converted from Methodism to the Quaker faith. Nixon was a descendant of the early American settler, Thomas Cornell, who was also an ancestor of Ezra Cornell, the founder of Cornell University. Jimmy Carter and Bill Gates were decedents of the same line. As a Quaker, Richard Nixon's upbringing was characterized by evangelical Quaker observances, such as refraining from alcohol, dancing, and swearing. While his family was of modest means, Nixon was quoted as saying to Eisenhower, "We were poor, but the glory of it was we didn't know it".[105] Richard Nixon's father, Frank, owned a grocery store and gas station. Richard's younger brother, Arthur died in 1925 at the age of seven. At the age of twelve, a spot was found on Richard's lung, and, with a family history of tuberculosis, he was restricted from participating in sports. The spot was later found to be scar tissue from an early bout of pneumonia.[106]

Richard Nixon was an astute politician and instituted significant accomplishments during his tenure in office. At the time of his election as President, Nixon was the only modern president to have previously worked as a practicing attorney. The following information overviews the Stage 1 Stage 2 and Stage 3 Mimesis of Richard Milhous Nixon.[107]

Stage 1 Mimesis for Richard Nixon

1913   Richard Nixon was born on January 9th to Hannah and Francis (Frank) Nixon on a ranch in Yorba Linda, California. He grew up poor. His mother was a Quaker, and his father converted from Methodism to the Quaker faith. Through his mother, Nixon was a descendant of the early English settler Thomas Cornell, who was also an ancestor of Ezra Cornell, the founder of Cornell University. His upbringing was influenced by the Quaker religion. Abstinence from alcohol, dancing, and swearing were part of his observances. Nixon had four brothers: Harold (1909–1933), Donald (1914–1987), Arthur (1918–1925), and Edward (1930–2019).

Stage 2 Mimesis for Richard Nixon

1922   The Nixon family ranch failed in 1922, and the family moved to Whittier, California, in an area inhabited with Quakers. Frank Nixon opened a grocery store and gas station.

    Richard attended East Whittier Elementary School, where he was president of his eighth-grade class.

1925 Richard's younger brother Arthur died in 1925 at the age of seven after a short illness. Richard was twelve years old when a spot was found on his lung, and with a family history of tuberculosis, he was forbidden to play sports. The spot turned out to be scar tissue from an early bout of pneumonia.

1928 Richard transferred to Whittier High School. At Whittier, Nixon suffered his first election defeat when he lost his bid for student body president. He often rose at 4 a.m., to drive the family truck into Los Angeles and purchase vegetables at the market. He then drove to the store to wash and display them before going to school.

- Richard's brother Harold was diagnosed with tuberculosis and their mother took him to Arizona hoping to improve his health. The demands on Richard increased, causing him to give up football. Nevertheless, Richard graduated from Whittier High third in his class of 207.

1933 His older brother Harold had attended Whittier High School, which his parents thought resulted in Harold's dissolute lifestyle, before he contracted tuberculosis (that killed him in 1933).

After this this incident Richard's parents sent him to Fullerton Union High School.

- He lived with an aunt in the Fullerton school district during the week because during his first year he had to ride a school bus an hour each way. Nevertheless, .he received excellent grades Nixon played junior varsity football, and seldom missed a practice, though he rarely played. He had better success as a debater, winning a number of championships and taking his only formal tutelage in public speaking from Fullerton's Head of English, H. Lynn Sheller.

1934 Richard graduated *summa cum laude* with a Bachelor of Arts degree in history from Whittier, Nixon was accepted at the new Duke University School of Law. He received a scholarship and was elected president of the Duke Bar Association

1937 He was inducted into the Order of the Coif, an honor society for United States Law graduates, Nixon graduated third in his class in June 1937.

After graduating from Duke, Nixon initially hoped to join the FBI. He received no response to his letter of application, and learned years later that he had been hired, but his appointment had been canceled at the last minute due to budget cuts.

Returning to California, he was admitted to the California bar. He practiced in Whittier in the Law Firm of Wingert and Bewley, focusing on commercial litigation for petroleum companies and other corporations.

- As a side note according to reliable sources … Nixon was reluctant to work on divorce cases, disliking frank sexual talk from women.

1938 He opened up his own branch of Wingert and Bewley in La Habra, California, and became a full partner in the firm the following year (1939).

1938   Nixon was cast in the Whittier Community Players production of *The Dark Tower*. There he played opposite a high school teacher named Thelma "Pat" Ryan. Nixon described it in his memoirs as "a case of love at first sight. She turned him down several times before agreeing to date him.

1940   Once they began their courtship, Pat was reluctant to marry Nixon; they dated for two years before she accepted his proposal. They wed in a small ceremony on June 21, 1940. After a honeymoon in Mexico, they began their married life in Whittier. They had two daughters, Tricia (born 1946) and Julie (born 1948).

1942   Nixon and his wife Pat moved to Washington D. C. to work for the federal government.

- Nixon Applied for a commission in the Navy. His application was approved, and he was appointed a lieutenant junior grade in the United States Naval Reserve on June 15, 1942.

- Nixon was assigned as aide to the commander of the Naval Air Station Ottumwa in Iowa until May 1943

1943   Nixon was assigned to Marine Aircraft Group 25 and the South Pacific Combat Air Transport Command (SCAT), supporting the logistics of operations in the South Pacific Theater.

- Nixon was promoted to lieutenant

- Nixon commanded the SCAT forward detachments at Vella Lavella, Bougainville, and finally at Green Island (Nissan Island).[43][47] His unit prepared manifests and flight plans for R4D/C-47 operations and supervised the loading and unloading of the transport aircraft. For this service, he received a Navy Letter of Commendation (awarded a Navy Commendation Ribbon, which was later updated to the Navy and Marine Corps Commendation Medal) from his commanding officer for "meritorious and efficient performance of duty as Officer in Charge of the South Pacific Combat Air Transport Command". Upon his return to the U.S., Nixon was appointed the administrative officer of the Alameda Naval Air Station in California.

1945 In January 1945 he was transferred to the Bureau of Aeronautics office in Philadelphia to help negotiate the termination of war contracts, and received his second letter of commendation, from the Secretary of the Navy

1946 On March 10, 1946, he was relieved of active duty

- After active duty in the Naval Reserve during World War II, he was elected to the House of Representatives in 1946.

1947-1950 Nixon ran for a Congressional representative seat in Whittier, California and won the election, receiving 65,586 votes to his opponents 49,994 votes.

- In June 1947, Nixon supported the Taft–Hartley Act, a federal law that monitors the activities and power of labor unions.

- He served on the Education and Labor Committee.

- In August 1947, he became one of 19 House members to serve on the Herter Committee, which went to Europe to report on the need for U.S. foreign aid. Nixon was the youngest member of the committee and the only Westerner. Advocacy by Herter Committee members, including Nixon, led to congressional passage of the Marshall Plan

1948 Nixon had co-sponsored a "Mundt–Nixon Bill" to implement "a new approach to the complicated problem of internal communist subversion. It provided for registration of all Communist Party members and required a statement of the source of all printed and broadcast material issued by organizations that were found to be Communist fronts.

- Nixon first gained national attention in August 1948, when his persistence as a HUAC member helped break the Alger Hiss spy case. While many doubted Whittaker Chambers's allegations that Hiss, a former State Department official, had been a Soviet spy, Nixon believed them to be true and pressed for the committee to continue its investigation

- Nixon was reelected to congress

1950 Nixon won the election by almost twenty percentage points. During the campaign, Nixon was first called "Tricky Dick" by his opponents for his campaign tactics.

- In the Senate, Nixon took a prominent position in opposing global communism,

- He maintained friendly relations with his fellow anti-communist, controversial Wisconsin senator Joseph McCarthy, but was careful to keep some distance between himself and McCarthy's allegations.

- Nixon criticized President Harry S. Truman's handling of the Korean War.

- He supported statehood for Alaska and Hawaii.

- Nixon voted in favor of civil rights for minorities.

- He supported federal disaster relief for India and Yugoslavia.

- He voted against price controls and other monetary restrictions, benefits for illegal immigrants, and public power.

1950 His work on the Alger Hiss Case established his reputation as a leading anti-Communist, which elevated him to national prominence, and in 1950, he was elected to the Senate.

1952 Nixon was the running mate of Dwight D. Eisenhower, the Republican Party's presidential nominee in the 1952 election, and served for eight years as the vice president.

1953 On June 1, 1953, he was promoted to commander in the U.S. Naval Reserve, from which he retired in the U.S. Naval Reserve on June 6, 1966.

1953-1961 General Dwight D. Eisenhower was nominated for president by the Republicans in 1952. He had no strong preference for a vice-presidential candidate. Nixon was recommended Nixon to the general, who agreed to the senator's selection.

- Nixon was 39. He stood strongly against communism, He had a political base in California—one of the largest states—were all seen as campaign strengths and vote winners by Republicans.

- Nixon served for eight years as Vice President, becoming the second-youngest vice president in history at age 40.

- Eisenhower gave Nixon more responsibilities during his term than any previous vice president

- In early 1957, Nixon took a trip to Africa. On his return, he helped shepherd the Civil Rights Act of 1957 through Congress. The bill was weakened in the Senate, and civil rights leaders were divided over whether Eisenhower should sign it. Nixon advised the President to sign the bill, which he did.

- Richard and Pat Nixon reluctantly went on a goodwill tour of South America.

- In July 1959 President Eisenhower sent Nixon to the Soviet Union for the opening of the American National Exhibition in Moscow.

1960   Nixon served for eight years as Vice President, becoming the second-youngest vice president in history at age 40. As Vice-President he gained national attention for his famous "kitchen debate" with Soviet leader Nikita Khrushchev.

1960   He ran for president in 1960. He faced little opposition in the Republican primaries and chose former Massachusetts Senator Henry Cabot Lodge Jr. as his running mate. His Democratic opponent was John F. Kennedy. The race remained close for the duration. Nixon campaigned on his experience but Kennedy ran on a platform of the need for "new blood", claiming the Eisenhower–Nixon administration had allowed the Soviet Union to overtake the U.S. in ballistic missiles (the "missile gap"). Nixon narrowly lost the election by a narrow margin. Kennedy won the popular vote by only 112,827 votes (0.2 percent).

1962   Nixon ran for governor of California and lost.

1968   Nixon made another run for the presidency and was elected, defeating Hubert Humphrey and George Wallace in a close contest.

1972   He was reelected in one of the largest electoral landslides in U.S. history when he defeated George McGovern.

1972   Nixon's visit to China opened up diplomatic relations.

1972   Nixon negotiated the Anti-Ballistic Missile Treaty with the Soviet Union.

1972   He also endorsed the Equal Rights Amendment after it passed both houses of Congress in 1972 and went to the states for ratification.

1973   Nixon ended American involvement in the Vietnam War and brought the American POWs home.

1973   Nixon ended the draft into the military armed service.

- His administration generally transferred power from Washington D.C. to the states.
- He imposed wage and price controls for ninety days, enforced desegregation of Southern schools.
- President Nixon established the Environmental Protection Agency.

- He began the War on Cancer.
- Nixon also presided over the Apollo 11 moon landing, which signaled the end of the moon race.
- Nixon implemented the Philadelphia Plan in 1970—the first significant federal affirmative action program.
- He also pushed for African American civil rights and economic equity through a concept known as black capitalism.
- Nixon had campaigned as an ERA supporter in 1968, though feminists criticized him for doing little to help the ERA or their cause after his election. Nevertheless, he appointed more women to administration positions than Lyndon Johnson had.
- While Nixon received a number of complaints from both African-Americans and Women that his support for equal rights was nothing more than empty promises and political bantering, on the record he supported these causes.

Watergate

Watergate was Nixon's Waterloo, his downfall. Having won the Presidency in 1968, defeating Hubert Humphrey and being re-elected in in 1972, defeating South Dakota Senator, George McGovern by one of the largest victories in presidential history, both in electoral and popular votes, his election soon became in jeopardy because it was discovered Republican party members in the executive branch of government supported a break-in at the Democratic National Committee offices in the Watergate office complex in Washington, D.C. Media and official investigations soon uncovered a broader pattern of abuse of power by the Nixon administration. The break-in was engineered by members of his immediate circle and his re-election committee. When the courts ruled, Nixon had to turn over tape recordings that contained conversations of the conspiracy to break-in to the Democratic offices, it became evident that President Nixon was directly involved in the conspiracy. These revelations overshadowed his noteworthy accomplishments as President. Facing impeachment and removal from office, President Nixon resigned from office in front of the American people by a nationally televised speech on August 8, 1974. His resignation became effective at noon the next day, August 9, 1974. Vice President Ford took over as president of the United States. On September 8, 1974. Ford pardoned Nixon for "all offenses against the United States" which Nixon "has committed or may have committed or taken part in" during his presidency.

The tragedy of this situation is that Richard Nixon, before Watergate led a life dedicated to his family, his country and his party. He rose from humble beginnings to become a successful American, realizing the "American dream." His political beliefs may have been different from the Democratic Party but there is no doubt Nixon was responsible to his country and a good American citizen. Nevertheless, in spite of the accumulation of life experiences that he responded in a relative positive manner, the one mistake, bad decision, he made caused his entire life to change. He was humiliated and shamed because of one wrong decision among a multitude of acceptable responses he made regarding life experiences and phenomena that he encountered up to that point in his life. His position as President of the United States of America, the esteem in which he was held by the American public and the irony of his direct participation in Watergate was a considerable diversion from his perceived image. This caused people to realize they were deceived, people felt they misjudged his character. Naturally, his enemies were supportive of Nixon's downfall, but the deception become so disappointing to Nixon's supporters, it caused the American people and his colleagues to turn against him, some in order to save their own political careers. The result being, Nixon became the first ever President to resign from office.

1973 By late 1973, the Nixon administration's involvement in Watergate eroded his support in Congress and the country.

1974 Facing almost certain impeachment and removal from office, Nixon resigned the presidency on August 9th. Afterwards, he was issued a full and complete pardon by his successor, Gerald Ford.

1974 After his resignation from office Nixon and his wife returned to their home, La Casa Pacifica in San Clemente, California.

In October, Nixon became ill with phlebitis. Doctors gave him the option of dying or having an operation. He chose the operation.

1976 Nixon was disbarred by the New York State Bar Association for obstruction of justice in the Watergate scandal.

1980 Throughout the 1980's Nixon kept a busy schedule of speaking engagements.

1990 On July 19, the Richard Nixon library opened in Yorba Linda, California.

1993 Pat Nixon died of emphysema and lung cancer.

1994 On April 18, Nixon suffered a stroke while eating dinner at his home. A blood clot ensued and traveled to his brain. He went into a coma and died on April 22. Richard Nixon was 81 years old when he died.

Stage 3 Mimesis of Richard Nixon

There is no doubt that Richard Nixon was an American patriot. He was misdirected in his lust for power. A psychologist might assess his fear of loss, having loss elections, led to his overzealous need to hold on to power, once he got it. The irony is that he won the 1972 presidential election and Watergate was bad judgement. In his post-presidential years Nixon worked on rehabilitating his image. In the nearly 20 years of his retirement, Nixon wrote his memoirs and nine other books. He made foreign trips in the role of elder statesman. On April 18, 1994, he suffered a severe stroke and died four days later at age 81. Mourners waited in line for up to eight hours in chilly, wet weather to pay their respects. At its peak, the line to pass by Nixon's casket was three miles long with an estimated 42,000 people waiting.

Nixon was a skillful politician and served America with a strong sense of dedication. Unfortunately, because of his shortcomings, especially the branding of his reputation due to the Watergate scandal, historians and political scientists rank Nixon as a below-average president. Watergate was Nixon's Achilles heel, the anchor that stained his reputation. Additionally, evaluations of him are tainted by the circumstances of his departure from office. Richard Nixon reached the pinnacle of the American dream. A poor boy who rose to become president of the United States of America. Then became the tragic hero who lost the respect of the American people because of his tragic flaws, the lust for power, and his fear of loss. Nixon's life Mimesis is comparable to that of a Shakespearean tragic hero. An individual in a heroic life position, whose lived experiences are noble except for the tragic flaw that causes their downfall. They suffer a catharsis of emotion that eventually leads to their downfall and their casts a shadow over their legacy.

Mimesis of Life Summary for
President Richard M. Nixon

Richard Nixon's life story can be described as an individual who pulled himself up by the bootstraps and made something out of his life, until he suffered from his tragic flaws, distrust, insecurity, and fear of loss. Nixon was inaugurated as president on January 20, 1969. The Nixon administration transferred significant power from federal control to state control. He imposed wage and price controls for 90 days, enforced desegregation of Southern schools, established the Environmental Protection Agency, and began the War on Cancer. He also presided over the Apollo 11 moon landing, which signaled the end of the Space Race. He was re-elected in one of the largest electoral landslides in American history in 1972 when he defeated George McGovern. The Nixon presidency witnessed the first large-scale integration of public schools in the South. Nixon sought a middle way between the segregationist Wallace and liberal Democrats, whose support of integration was alienating some Southern whites. Hopeful of doing well in the South in 1972, he sought to dispose of desegregation as a political issue before then. Soon after his inauguration, he appointed Vice President Agnew to lead a task force, which worked with local leaders, both white and black, to determine how to integrate local schools. Agnew had little interest in the work, and most of it was done by Labor Secretary George Shultz. Federal aid was available, and a meeting with President Nixon was a possible reward for compliant committees. By September 1970, less than ten percent of black children were attending segregated schools. By 1971, however, tensions over desegregation surfaced in Northern cities, with angry protests over the busing of children to schools outside their neighborhood to achieve racial balance. Nixon opposed busing personally but enforced court orders requiring its use. [108]

Nixon ended American involvement in Vietnam in 1973, ending the military draft that same year. Nixon's visit to China in 1972 eventually led to diplomatic relations between the two nations, and he gained the Anti-Ballistic Missile Treaty with the Soviet Union the same year. Some scholars, such as James Morton Turner and John Isenberg, believe that Nixon, who had advocated for civil rights in his 1960 campaign, slowed down desegregation as president, appealing to the racial conservatism of Southern whites, who were angered by the civil rights movement. This, he hoped, would boost his election chances in 1972. In addition to desegregating public schools, Nixon implemented the Philadelphia Plan in 1970—the first significant federal affirmative action program. He also endorsed the Equal Rights Amendment after it passed both houses of Congress in 1972 and went to the states for ratification. He also pushed for African American civil rights and economic equity through a concept known as black capitalism.[109] While his efforts on integration can be seen as token and politically motivated, nevertheless, his position was contrary to the traditional Republican platform.

The legacy of Richard Nixon is clouded by his resignation over the Watergate scandal. Many people see him as a "crook". Some people see him as a competent statesman. The point is that a single mistake in an individual's life can ruin them and neutralize the many good deeds they accomplish. There is a saying that it takes one thousand good deeds to build trust and only one negative deed to destroy all the trust that was built.

Historian Keith W. Olson has written that Nixon left a legacy of fundamental mistrust of government, rooted in Vietnam and Watergate. In surveys of

historians and political scientists, Nixon is generally ranked as a below-average president. [110]

Photo Images of Richard Nixon expanding over his life can be found at:

https://www.cnn.com/2013/01/08/politics/gallery/nixon/index.html

Mimesis of Life for Malcolm X (1925 – 1965)

Born Malcolm Little on May 19, 1925. Died on February 21, 1965. Malcolm X. was an African American minister of and spokesman for the Nation of Islam religion and a civil rights activist. As an adolescent, Malcolm lived in a number of foster homes. He did not have a stable growing up process. His father died when he was six years old. His mother got involved with a man who abused her and she had a nervous breakdown when he was twelve years. He lived with relatives after his father's death and his mother's hospitalization. Without parental direction, Malcolm got involved in a number of illicit activities. Eventually he was caught committing crimes and was sentenced to 10 years in prison in 1946 for larceny and breaking and entering.

While in prison Malcolm became a member of the Nation of Islam (taking the name Malcolm X to symbolize his unknown African ancestral surname). After his parole in 1952, Malcolm became one of the Nation's most influential leaders. He was the public face of the Nation of Islam for a dozen years, advocating for black empowerment and separation of black and white Americans. He criticized Martin Luther King Jr. and the mainstream civil rights movement for its emphasis on nonviolence and racial integration. The Nation of Islam was actively involved in social welfare and drug rehabilitation programs for the prison inmates. The Nation of Islam is noted for rehabilitating the lives of numerous Black men. Throughout his life, beginning in the 1950s, Malcolm X was under surveillance by the Federal Bureau of Investigation (FBI) because of his connection with the Nation of Islam and outspoken activity against injustice and racism [111]

"In the 1960s, Malcolm X began to grow disillusioned with the Nation of Islam, as well as with its leader Elijah Muhammad. He subsequently embraced Sunni Islam and the civil rights movement after completing the Hajj to Mecca, and became known as "el-Hajj Malik el-Shabazz". After a brief period of travel across Africa, he publicly renounced the Nation of Islam and founded the Islamic Muslim Mosque, Inc. (MMI) and the Pan-African Organization of Afro-American Unity (OAAU). Throughout 1964, his conflict with the Nation of Islam intensified, and he was repeatedly sent death threats. On February 21, 1965, he was assassinated in New York City. Three Nation members were charged with the murder and given indeterminate life sentences; in 2021 two of the convictions were vacated. Speculation about the assassination and whether it was conceived or aided by leading members of the Nation, or with law enforcement agencies, have persisted for decades after the shooting". [112]

Malcolm X was one of the most controversial figures of his era. He was accused of preaching racism and violence. Many believe he was speaking the truth. Within the African American and Muslim American communities Malcolm X is highly revered and respected. The speeches Malcolm delivered expressed his relentless pursuit of racial justice are revered by African Americans of every persuasion. His delivery was mixed with passion and anger about the plight of African

American people, historically and in contemporary times. Although Malcolm did give expressive speeches inferring that Black people achieve freedom "by any means necessary", it should be noted that Malcolm, himself, never participated any acts of violence as a member of the Nation of Islam or after he rejected the Nation.

He was posthumously honored with Malcolm X Day, on which he is commemorated in various cities across the United States. Hundreds of streets and schools in the U.S. have been renamed in his honor. The Audubon Ballroom, the site of his assassination, was partly redeveloped in 2005 to accommodate the Malcolm X and Dr. Betty Shabazz Memorial and Educational Center.

Mimesis 1 for Malcolm Little

1925   Born Malcolm Little in Omaha Nebraska. Malcolm was the 4th of 7 children born to Louise Helen Little and Earl Little. Earl was a preacher who adopted the Pan African philosophy of Marcus Garvey, believing Black people should vacate the US and return to Africa. Earl was the leader of the Universal Negro Improvement Association (UNIA). Louise was a secretary. Malcolm stated that White violence killed four of his uncles.

1926   Earl, because of his civil rights activity, incurred the wrath of the Ku Klux Klan. This caused the family to move to Milwaukee Wisconsin and soon after, to Lansing Michigan.

1929 In Lansing, Malcolm's family was harassed by the Black Legion, a White racist organization. Their house was burned down.

1931 Malcolm's father, Earl, died when he was 6 years old.. His death was ruled an accident but it was believed Earl was killed by the White racist group, Black Legion. The family had insurance on Earl. Louise received a life insurance benefit (nominally $1,000 —about $18,000 in 2022 adjustment) in payments of $18 per month. The issuer of another, larger policy refused to pay, claiming her husband Earl had committed suicide.

Stage 2 Mimesis for Malcolm Little

1937 A man Louise had been dating and hoped to marry, vanished from her life when she became pregnant with his child.

1938 Louise had a nervous breakdown and was committed to Kalamazoo State Hospital. The children were separated and sent to foster homes. Malcolm and his siblings secured her release 24 years later.

1941 Malcolm attended West Junior High School in Lansing and then Mason High School in Mason, Michigan, but left high school in 1941, before graduating. He excelled in junior high school but dropped out of high school after a white teacher told him that practicing law, his aspiration at the time, was "no realistic goal for a nigger". Later, Malcolm X recalled feeling that the white world offered no place for a career-oriented black man, regardless of talent. [113]

From age 14 to 21, Malcolm held a variety of jobs while living with his half-sister Ella Little-Collins in Roxbury, a largely African-American neighborhood of Boston.[114]

1943 After a short time in Flint, Michigan, he moved to New York City's Harlem neighborhood in 1943, where he found employment on the New Haven Railroad and engaged in drug dealing, gambling, racketeering, robbery, and pimping.[23] According to recent biographies, Malcolm also occasionally had sex with other men, usually for money, though this conjecture has been disputed by those who knew him. He befriended John Elroy Sanford, a fellow dishwasher at Jimmy's Chicken Shack in Harlem who aspired to be a professional comedian. Both men had reddish hair, so Sanford was called "Chicago Red" after his hometown and Malcolm was known as "Detroit Red". Years later, Sanford became famous as comedian and actor Redd Foxx. [115]

Summoned by the local draft board for military service in World War II, he feigned mental disturbance by declaring: "I want to be sent down South. Organize them nigger soldiers... steal us some guns, and kill us [some] crackers". He was declared "mentally disqualified for military service". [116]

1945 Malcolm returned to Boston. He and four accomplices committed a series of burglaries targeting wealthy white families. In 1946, he was arrested while picking up a stolen watch he had left at a shop for repairs. In February he began serving an eight-to-ten-year sentence at Charlestown State Prison for larceny and breaking and entering. Two years later, Malcolm was transferred to Norfolk Prison Colony in Massachusetts.[117]

Prison

A Boston police mug shot of Malcolm, following his arrest for larceny, (1946).[118]

1946   In prison Malcolm a fellow convict named John Bembry. Bembry is self-educated. Malcolm described Bembry as the first man he ever met who commanded total respect. Bembry motivated Malcolm's interest in reading. [119]

Malcolm's siblings wrote him about the Nation of Islam, religious organization, teaching Black independence, a return to Africa and separation from Whites. Malcolm's brother, Reginald, wrote him to stop eating pork, stop smoking and to stop drinking. Malcolm followed the advice of his brother. Reginald made a prison visit to see Malcolm, describing the teachings of the Nation of Islam. Reginald instilled in Malcolm that White people were devils and reflecting back on his life, Malcolm viewed all of his interactions with Whites were tainted with dishonesty, injustice, greed, and hatred. [120]

1948   Malcolm wrote to Elijah Muhammad, the leader of the Nation of Islam. Muhammad (NOI) advised him to renounce his past, humbly bow in prayer to God, and promise never to engage in destructive behavior again. Though he later recalled the inner struggle he had before bending his knees to pray. Malcolm soon became a member of the Nation of Islam, maintaining a regular correspondence with Muhammad. [121]

1950   The FBI opened a file on Malcolm after he wrote a letter from prison to President Truman expressing opposition to the Korean War and declaring himself a communist. That year, he also began signing his name "Malcolm X." Muhammad instructed his followers to leave their family names behind when they joined the Nation of Islam (NOI) and use "X" instead. When the time was right, after they had proven their sincerity, he said, he would reveal the Muslim's "original name." In his autobiography, Malcolm X explained that the "X" symbolized the true African family name that he could never know. "For me, my 'X' replaced the White slave master name of 'Little' which some blue-eyed devil named "Little" had imposed upon my paternal forebears."[122]

1952   Malcolm was paroled in August and went to visit Elijah Muhammed in Chicago.[123]

1953   In June Malcolm was named assistant minister of the Nations Temple Number One in Detroit.

Malcolm established Temple Number 11 in Boston.

Becoming more visible as a member of the Nation of Islam, the FBI began to run surveillance on Malcolm. [124]

1954   Malcolm grew the congregation of Philadelphia Temple Number 12 in March.

In May Malcolm was chosen to lead Temple Number 7 in Harlem, New York. [125]

1955   Malcolm was successful and the primary instrument in the growth of the Nation of Islam. He established Temples in Springfield, MA (#13), I Hartford, Connecticut (#14) and in Atlanta, GA. (# 15). [126]

Malcolm possessed an imposing physical stature, which made him more impressive as a speaker. He was 6 ft. 3 in. tall and weighed 180 pounds. Malcolm was always well dressed which added to his presence and authority as an influential persona.

1955 Malcolm met Betty Sanders. His future wife.

1958 Malcolm proposed to Betty Sanders, later called Betty Shabazz. They married two days later and had six daughters born from their union.

1957   Malcolm gained notoriety with the American public when Hinton Johnson, a member of the NOI, was beaten by two New York City police officers, on April 26. Johnson with two other onlookers saw police beating an African American man and commented "You're not in Alabama". The police then turned on Johnson, beating him severely causing a concussion and brain damage. [127]

When Malcolm went to see Johnson at the police station he was accompanied by 500 people. Malcolm demanded that Johnson be taken to Harlem Hospital. One police commented, "No one should have that much power The New York police department assigned undercover officers to infiltrate the NOI. [128]

1959   Malcolm adopted the name Malcolm Shabazz or Malik el-Shabazz but most people still referred to him as Malcolm X.

1960   The United Nations General Assembly in New York invited Malcolm X to the official functions of several African nations. He met Gamal Abdel Nasser of Egypt, Ahmed Sékou Touré of Guinea, and Kenneth Kaunda of the Zambian African National Congress. Fidel Castro also attended the Assembly, and Malcolm X met publicly with him as part of a welcoming committee of Harlem community leaders. Castro was sufficiently impressed with Malcolm X to suggest a private meeting, and after two hours of talking, Castro invited Malcolm X to visit Cuba. [129]

Malcolm's teachings basically revolved around 5 issues while he was associated with the NOI:[130]

That Black people are the original people of the world

That White people are "devils"

That the demise of the White race is imminent

Separation of Black and White people.

And "freedom by any means necessary".

Many people, especially Whites and many Blacks did not understand or agree with Malcolm's teachings. Whites and Blacks labeled him as a racist and as a hate teacher, or as being anti-White or as teaching Black Supremacy". A primary objective of the civil rights movement was to integrate and end disenfranchisement of African Americans, but the Nation of Islam forbade its members from participating in the voting and other aspects of the political process. The NAACP and other civil rights organizations denounced him and the Nation of Islam as irresponsible extremists whose views did not represent the common interests of African Americans. [131] The civil rights organizations fought against racial segregation and the NOI advocated separation of African Americans from Whites. Malcolm and the NOI rejected the non-violent strategy of civil rights organizations. [132]

Malcolm X was widely criticized for being anti-Semitic Malcolm X believed that the fabricated anti-Semitic text "*Protocols of the Elders of Zion*", was authentic and introduced it to NOI members, but he also blamed Jewish people for "perfecting the modern evil" of neo-colonialism because of the their financial culture and values and because of the Zionist movement. [133]

Neocolonialism is the continuation or reposition of imperialist rule by a state (usually, a former colonial power) over another nominally independent state (usually, a former colony). Neocolonialism takes the form of economic imperialism, globalization, cultural imperialism and conditional aid to influence or control a developing country instead of the previous colonial methods of direct military control or indirect political control (hegemony).

Malcolm X was considered as the second most influential leader of the Nation of Islam after Elijah Muhammad. He was responsible for the NOI's increase in membership between the early 1950s and early 1960s (from 500 to 25,000 by one estimate; from 1,200 to 50,000 or 75,000 by another). [134]

He influenced Muhammad Ali to join the Nation, and the two became close. When Malcolm X left the Nation of Islam, he tried to convince Ali (who had just been renamed by Elijah Muhammad) to join him in converting to Sunni Islam, but Ali instead broke ties with him, later describing the break as one of his greatest regrets.[135] Stating:

"Turning my back on Malcolm was one of the mistakes that I regret most in my life. I wish I'd been able to tell Malcolm that I was sorry, that he was right about so many things. But he was killed before I got the chance... I might never have become a Muslim if it hadn't been for Malcolm. If I could go back and do it over again, I would never have turned my back on him."

Malcolm X mentored and guided Louis X (later known as Louis Farrakhan), who eventually became the leader of the Nation of Islam. Malcolm X also served as a mentor and confidant to Elijah Muhammad's son, Wallace D. Muhammad; the son told Malcolm X about his skepticism toward his father's "unorthodox approach" to Islam. Wallace Muhammad was excommunicated from the Nation of Islam several times, although he was eventually re-admitted. [136]

1961   Police in Los Angeles attacked Muslims in a unprovoked incident, killed one Muslim, paralyzed another and desecrated Mosque Number 27. Malcolm sought Elijah Muhammed's approval to take revenge against the police, and was denied. Malcolm also sought the approval of Elijah Muhammed to work with other Black politicians and civil rights organizations and was denied. This is considered a turning point in the relationship between Malcolm X and the NOI.[137]

1962-1963   Malcolm reevaluates his relationship with the NOI and Elijah Muhammed.

1963   Malcolm discovers that Elijah Muhammed was having extramarital affairs with young secretaries of the NOI. When Malcolm confronted Elijah Muhammed about these incidents Elijah Muhammed confirmed the incidents. At least seven of the girls became pregnant. Elijah Muhammed was seen as a child rapist. [138]

1964-1965   In a series of TV interviews, Malcolm recounted the child molesting claims against Elijah Muhammed. Revealing the truth about

Elijah Muhammed's extramarital affairs cause Malcolm to receive death threats. He also discovered a bomb placed under his car.

1963 President John F. Kennedy was assassinated and Malcolm commented, "The chickens have come home to roost", essentially meaning he got what he deserved. Malcolm cited the incidents of Black people being killed by Whites (Patrice Lumumba, Medgar Evers and the church bombing, killing Black girls in Birmingham, Alabama). [139]

These comments cause the NOI to censure Malcolm for 90 days. [140]

1964 Media attention grew over Malcolm's conflict with Elijah Muhammed and the NOI. Rumors started that Elijah Muhammed was jealous of Malcolm's growing media attention.

In March, Malcolm publicly announces his break from the NOI. He still remained a Muslim but stated the NOI was rigid and had gone as far as it can grow. Malcolm stated his plan to organize a Black Nationalism movement and announced his plan to work with other civil rights organizations. [141]

Malcolm founded Muslim Mosque, Inc. (MMI) and the Organization of Afro-American Unity (OAAU), advocating Pan-Africanism. [142]

Malcolm converts to the Sunni Muslim sect of Islam. [143]

1964 Malcolm takes a pilgrimage to Mecca. He completes his Hajj rituals and the next day had met with Prince Faisal of Saudi Arabia.

Pan-Africanism is a worldwide movement that aims to encourage and strengthen bonds of solidarity between all Indigenous and diaspora peoples of African ancestry. Based on a common goal dating back to the Atlantic slave trade, the movement extends beyond continental Africans with a substantial support base among the African diaspora in the Americas and Europe.

During his pilgrimage Malcolm saw that Muslims were of all colors from blue eyed blonds to Black skinned Africans. Integrating and relating as equals, Malcolm envisioned that Islam was a vehicle for solving racial problems.[144]

After his pilgrimage Malcolm visited Africa and spoke at the University of Ibadan, the Nigerian Muslim Students Association bestowed him the Yoruba name *Omowale* ('the son who has come home'). He later commented this was his greatest honor. [145]

1964 Upon his return to the United States Malcolm became in high demand as a speaker, especially on college campuses.

Throughout 1964 Malcolm's death threats continued.

Elijah Muhammed commented that "hypocrites like Malcolm should have their heads cut off". [146]

1964 Malcolm's house was destroyed by fire.

1965 On February 19th Malcolm told Gordon Parks in an interview that the NOI of trying to kill him. On February 21st, while addressing an audience at the Audubon Ballroom in New York, a yell was

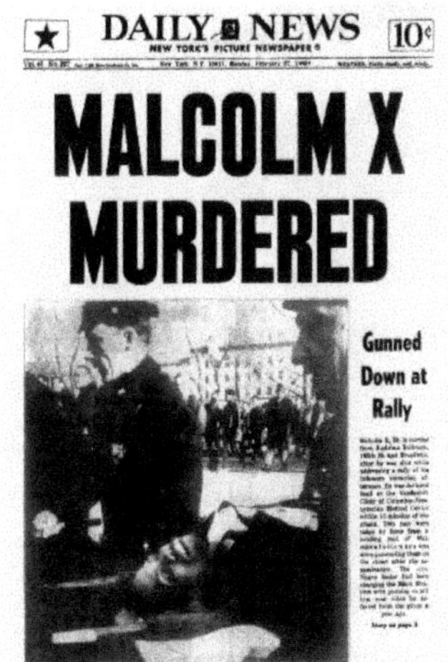

heard, "Nigger, Get your hand out of my pocket". A man then charged the stage and shot Malcolm once in the chest with a sawed-off shotgun. Two other men charged the stage firing semi-automatic handguns. Malcolm X was pronounced dead at 3:30 pm, shortly after arriving at Columbia Presbyterian Hospital. An autopsy revealed 21 gunshot wounds to the chest, left shoulder, arms and legs, including ten buckshot wounds from the initial shotgun blast.[147]

Malcolm X is taken away from the Audubon Ballroom on a stretcher after being shot.

The Final Mimesis for Malcolm X

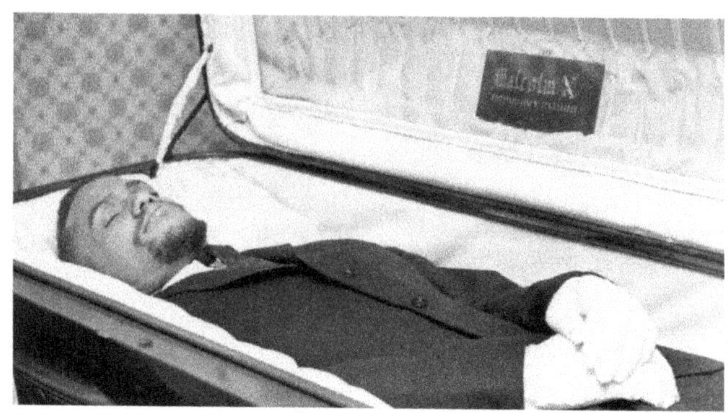

1965 Public viewing of Malcolm's remains was held at Unity Funeral Home was for four days, February 23 – February 26. Between 14,000 and 30,000 people viewed his body. Malcolm's funeral was held on February 27th. Malcolm's obituary was delivered by famed actor Ossie Davis. [148]

Actor and activist Ruby Dee, wife of Ossie Davis, and Juanita Poitier, wife of Sidney Poitier, raised money for a home for Malcolm's family and his children's education. [149]

Dr. Martin Luther King Jr. sent a telegram to Malcolm's wife, Betty Shabazz stating: [150]

While we did not always see eye to eye on methods to solve the race problem, I always had a deep affection for Malcolm and felt that he had a great ability to put his finger on the existence and root of the problem. He was an eloquent spokesman for his point of view and no one can honestly doubt that Malcolm had a great concern for the problems that we face as a race.

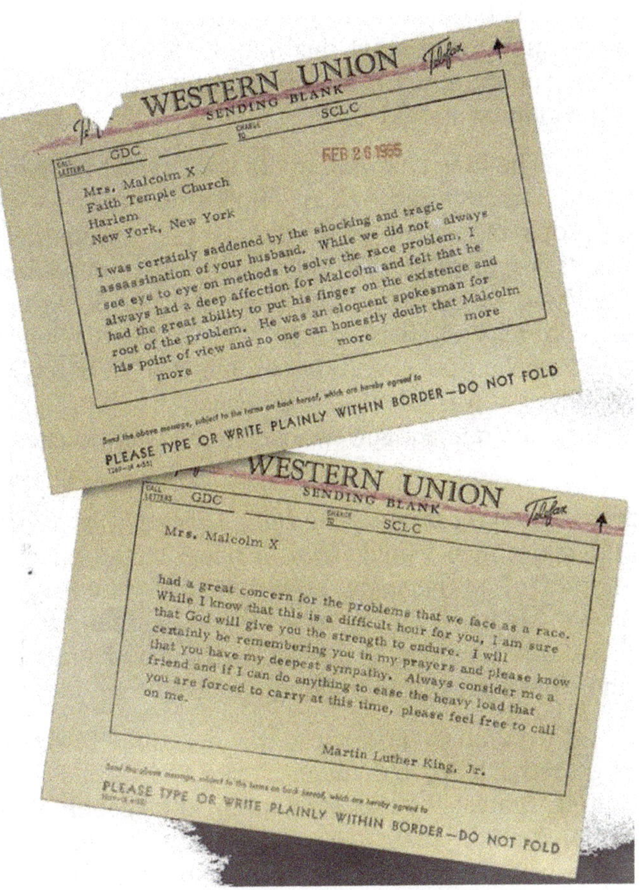
WESTERN UNION
SENDING BLANK
GDC
SCLC
FEB 26 1965

Mrs. Malcolm X
Faith Temple Church
Harlem
New York, New York

I was certainly saddened by the shocking and tragic
assassination of your husband. While we did not always
see eye to eye on methods to solve the race problem, I
always had a deep affection for Malcolm and felt that he
had the great ability to put his finger on the existence and
root of the problem. He was an eloquent spokesman for
his point of view and no one can honestly doubt that Malcolm
more
more
more

PLEASE TYPE OR WRITE PLAINLY WITHIN BORDER—DO NOT FOLD

WESTERN UNION
SENDING BLANK
GDC
SCLC

Mrs. Malcolm X

had a great concern for the problems that we face as a race.
While I know that this is a difficult hour for you, I am sure
that God will give you the strength to endure. I will
certainly be remembering you in my prayers and please know
that you have my deepest sympathy. Always consider me a
friend and if I can do anything to ease the heavy load that
you are forced to carry at this time, please feel free to call
on me.

Martin Luther King, Jr.

PLEASE TYPE OR WRITE PLAINLY WITHIN BORDER—DO NOT FOLD

Writer James Baldwin, who had been a friend of Malcolm X's, was in London when he heard the news of the assassination. He responded with indignation towards the reporters interviewing him, shouting, "You did it! It is because of you—the men that created this White supremacy—that this man is dead. You are not guilty, but you did it.... Your mills, your cities, your rape of a continent started all this." [151]

The *New York Post* wrote that "even his sharpest critics recognized his brilliance—often wild, unpredictable and eccentric, but nevertheless possessing promise that must now remain unrealized." *The New York Times* wrote that Malcolm X was "an extraordinary and twisted man" who "turn[ed] many true gifts to evil purpose" and that his life was "strangely and pitifully wasted." *Time* called him "an unashamed demagogue" whose "creed was violence."

Outside of the U.S., particularly in Africa, the press was sympathetic. The *Daily Times of Nigeria* wrote that Malcolm X would "have a place in the palace of martyrs" The *Ghanaian Times* likened him to John Brown, Medgar Evers, and Patrice Lumumba, and counted him among "a host of Africans and Americans who were martyred in freedom's cause."

In China, the *People's Daily* described Malcolm X as a martyr killed by "ruling circles and racists" in the United States; his assassination, the paper wrote, demonstrated that "in dealing with imperialist oppressors, violence must be met with violence." The *Guangming Daily*, also published in Beijing, stated that "Malcolm was murdered because he fought for freedom and equal rights." In Cuba, *El Mundo* described the assassination as "another racist crime to eradicate by violence the struggle against discrimination." [152]

Mimesis of Life Summary for Malcolm X

Malcolm had a dysfunctional upbringing. His childhood was unstable. He lost his father at an early age. His mother was committed to a mental institution. He committed crimes and spent time in Jail. One can affirmatively argue, that Malcolm was rehabilitated in Jail. It was during the time Malcolm spent in jail that he became influenced by the Islamic religion under the followers of the NOI and the philosophy of Elijah Muhammed.

Malcolm was a gifted orator and became spokesman for the NOI, gaining the favor of its leader, Elijah Muhammed. Under the NOI Malcolm found purpose in his life. This provokes a significant thought, that finding purpose in one's life gives a positive direction, a functional direction creating functional lived experiences. Malcolm's troubles did not start until he became conflictive with Elijah Muhammed. When he began to speak out negatively against the Nation of Islam. It is not proven that the NOI was responsible for Malcolm's death but it is a fact that members of the NOI, including Elijah Muhammed made defamatory and threating remarks about Malcolm. Then again, one can argue that Malcolm did not exercise good strategic judgement in attacking the NOI and Elijah Muhammed. This author can argue that Malcolm experienced "repentance syndrome". [153] While Malcolm spent his younger years involved in criminal activity, when he found direction being associated with the NOI, his tolerance level for "wrong doing", inequity and racism was low, intolerant. As a result, when he became disenchanted with the NOI his widespread vocalization of the problems he witnessed with the NOI caused conflict, which some believe led to his assassination.

Would things have turned out different if Malcolm merely separated from the NOI and kept his personal reasons and opinions to himself? We will never know but one thing we do know is that Malcolm, in taking the ethical and moral ground and being vocal about it, brought negative response into his environment and lived experiences.

Malcolm X has been described as one of the greatest and most significant influences in to African Americans and in African American history. He is credited with raising the self-esteem of Black Americans and reconnecting them with their African heritage. He is largely responsible for the spread of Islam in the Black community in the United States. Many African Americans, especially those who lived in cities in the Northern and Western United States, felt that Malcolm X conveyed their complaints, concerning, and issues with inequality better than did the mainstream civil rights movement. One biographer says that by giving expression to their frustration, Malcolm X "made clear the price that White America would have to pay if it did not accede to Black America's legitimate demands." [154]

In the late 1960s, increasingly radical Black activists based their movements largely on Malcolm X and his teachings. The Black Power movement, the Black Arts Movement, and the widespread adoption of the slogan "Black is beautiful" can all trace their roots to Malcolm X. In 1963, Malcolm X began a collaboration with Alex Haley on his life story, *The Autobiography of Malcolm X*. He told Haley, "If I'm alive when this book comes out, it will be a miracle." Haley completed and published it some months after the assassination. [155]

During the late 1980s and early 1990s, there was a resurgence of interest in his life among young people. Hip-hop groups such as Public Enemy adopted Malcolm X as an icon, and his image was displayed in hundreds of thousands of homes, offices, and schools, as well as on T-shirts and jackets. In 1986 Ella Little-Collins merged the Organization of Afro-American Unity with the African American Defense League. In 1992 the film *Malcolm X* was released, an adaptation of *The Autobiography of Malcolm X*. In 1998, *Time* named *The Autobiography of Malcolm X* one of the ten most influential nonfiction books of the 20th century. [156]

Malcolm X was an inspiration for several fictional characters. The Marvel Comics writer Chris Claremont confirmed that Malcolm X was an inspiration for the *X-Men* character Magneto, while Martin Luther King was an inspiration for Professor X. Malcolm X also inspired the character Erik Killmonger in the film *Black Panther*. [157]

The house that once stood at 3448 Pinkney Street in North Omaha, Nebraska, was the first home of Malcolm Little, with his birth family. The house was torn down in 1965 by new owners who did not know of its connection with Malcolm X, However, the site was listed on the National Register of Historic Places in 1984. [158]

Malcolm X House Site (added 1984-#84002463)

3448 Pinkney St., Omaha, NE.

In Lansing, Michigan, a Michigan Historical Marker was erected in 1975 on Malcolm Little's childhood home. [159]

Malcolm X Boulevard in New York City

Many cities have renamed streets after Malcolm X. In 1987, New York mayor Ed Koch proclaimed Lenox Avenue in Harlem to be Malcolm X Boulevard.[160]

Dozens of schools have been named after Malcolm X, including. Malcolm X Shabazz High School in Newark, New Jersey, Malcolm Shabazz City High School in Madison, Wisconsin, Malcolm X College in Chicago, Illinois, and El-Hajj Malik El-Shabazz Academy in Lansing, Michigan. Malcolm X Liberation University, based on the Pan-Africanist ideas of Malcolm X, was founded in 1969 in North Carolina. [161]

In 1996, the first library named after Malcolm X was opened It was called, the Malcolm X Branch Library and Performing Arts Center of the San Diego Public Library system. [162]

Like others of his generation who were assassinated, including Dr. Martin L. King Jr., President John F. Kennedy, and Senator Robert Kennedy, Malcolm was appreciated and loved much more in death then in life. In death Malcolm's ideology was referred to as truth and honorable, but when he was alive his ideology was considered, racist and radical. However, the real dilemma is,: what is the problem with a country that kills its leaders? Who are the real criminals?

Mimesis of Life for Stanley "Tookie" Williams (1953 – 2005)

Stanley "Tookie" Williams III is known as the original co-founder and leader of the Crips street gang originating in South Central Los Angeles. He was born on December 29, 1953 and died by a court ordered lethal injection on December 13, 2005. Williams was arrested in 1979 and convicted for murder of four people in 1981.

Mimesis 1 for Stanley "Tookie" Williams III

1953 Williams was born in Shreveport Louisiana. His father abandoned the family when Williams was one year old. In 1959, Williams moved with his mother, Louisiana Williams, to Los Angeles, California to the South Central area. Tookie's mother was 17 years old when she gave birth to him. [163]

1959 Williams and his mother relocate to the South-Central Los Angeles

Mimesis 2 for Stanley "Tookie" Williams III

Williams Mother worked several jobs to support the family and Tookie essentially grew up as a latch key kid. This gave him opportunity to spend many hours on the streets of South Central Los Angeles. Williams spent a lot of time with adults watching them get drunk, abuse drugs, gambling and engage in dog fighting. They would make the children, including Tookie, fight each other. The adults would bet on him and give him part of the proceeds for winning his fights. Often a target of older kids and thugs in his neighborhood, Tookie, by the age of twelve, began carrying a switchblade to protect himself. Tookie did not finished high school.

As a teenager, Williams gained a reputation in South Central's West Side as a vicious street fighter. He was expelled from George Washington Preparatory High School and denied entry by several other high schools in the South Central area for fighting. The rejections from attending high school allowed Tookie to spend more time in the streets. It is said that, "an idle mind is the devils workshop." Hanging out in the streets gave Tookie opportunity to engage criminal activity, and he did. As a result he spent time doing stints in L.A. Central Juvenile Hall.

1968   Older gangs disbanded to join the Black Power Movement, most notably as part of the Black Panther Party, to protect black people from police brutality and corruption in the Los Angeles Police Department. Juvenile crime increased in South Central as violent youth gangs filled the vacuum left by older gang members. Williams despised any of the newer gangs that formed because he viewed them as predatory. Williams earned the respect of many gangsters because of his viciousness and willingness to fight older youths, These gangs were mostly small-time neighborhood cliques that operated independently from each other and therefore leadership was not chosen but determined naturally. At age fifteen, Williams was invited into a small West Side clique after he befriended a local teenager, Donald, Doc Sweetback, Archie. Williams earned the clique's respect after beating up one of their members for insulting his mother. Williams became the unofficial leader of this clique as his reputation for violent spread across South Central.

1969   At age 15, Williams was arrested in Inglewood for car theft and was sent to the Los Padrinos Juvenile Hall in Downey. While doing time at the detention center, Williams was introduced to Olympic weightlifting by the facility's gym coach, which would spark an interest in bodybuilding. By his release from custody in early 1971, aged 17, Williams was physically bigger and stronger. According to Williams, upon his release from custody the review board asked him what he planned to do after being released, to which he replied "being the leader of the biggest gang in the world."

After his release from prison, Raymond Washington at Washington Preparatory High School, approached Williams, after hearing about him from a mutual friend. The friend had informed Washington of Williams' toughness and his willingness to fight members of larger, more established street gangs such as the L.A. Brims and the Chain Gang. Washington and Williams seemed to have much in common. Washington proposed they use their influence in their respective regions to form the larger Crips street gang. Initially, the purpose for creating the larger gang was to eliminate all street gangs and create a neighborhood watch in South Central LA. According to Williams: "We started out, at least my intent was to, in a sense, address all of the so-called neighboring gangs in the area and to put, in a sense—I thought 'I can cleanse the neighborhood of all these, you know, marauding gangs.' But I was totally wrong. And eventually, we morphed into the monster we were addressing." [164]

1971 Williams co-found and joins the Crips street gang at the age 18 years old. The Crips were originally called the Cribs. The Cribs, formed by high school friend, Raymond Washington was renamed to the Crips when Williams joined.[165]

1973 Raymond Washington was arrested for 2nd degree robbery and went to prison for 5 years. After his release from prison, Washington was murdered.

Curtis "Buddha" Morrow was shot to death in South Central following a petty argument. Mac Thomas was murdered under mysterious circumstances in the mid-1970s. Many other Crips were murdered in conflicts with rival gang members. Williams began to live an ironic double life in which he worked in a legal job as an anti-gang youth counselor in Compton while also serving as the over boss for one of the largest gangs in Los Angeles. Williams would work as a counselor and study Sociology at Compton College during working hours, then spend his free time participating in numerous violent attacks against the Bloods.[166]

1974   Williams becomes the leader of the Crips gang throughout LA.

1976   Williams was wounded in a drive-by shooting while sitting on the porch of his house in Compton. The shooting was committed by members of the Bloods rival street gang. To avoid getting hit, Williams dove to the ground from the porch but was shot in both of his legs. Williams was told by doctors that he would never walk again, but after a nearly year-long process of physical rehabilitation and an intense workout regimen, he regained his ability to walk. After the shooting, Williams re-developed a substance abuse problem when he began smoking PCP. Williams had begun dabbling in street drugs around the age of twelve, and as a preteen befriended a neighborhood pimp who, in return for performing errands for him, would reward Williams with money and drugs, Quaaludes, barbiturates (then known as "Red Devils") or marijuana. Williams' personal life began to unravel when his maternal grandmother, with whom he was very close, died in 1976.

1977   He lost his counseling job after being implicated in a robbery that was committed by two youths from a group home that Williams supervised. He was denied an opportunity to compete in an amateur bodybuilding contest after it was discovered that he was a gang leader (Williams would later appear on the 1970s variety show *The Gong Show* performing a bump dance routine). Eventually his gangster lifestyle was beginning to take a mental toll on him, which included a brief stay in the psychiatric ward of a hospital after Williams experienced a bad trip while high on PCP. With each of these setbacks Williams increasingly found himself using PCP and supported his drug habit by intimidating and robbing drug dealers in South Central LA.

1979 Williams allegedly committed four counts of murder. One involved killing a cashier while robbing a convenience store. The other murder was the killing of three immigrants from Taiwan, owners of a motel.in South Central LA.

1981 Williams was convicted of all four murders even though he maintained his innocence.[167] He was sentenced to death. When his appeals to higher courts and to the California governor, exhausted and all were denied, his death conviction held. The United States Court of Appeals for the Ninth Circuit, the lower federal court, the appellate court denied Williams' appeal in 2002, but noted that the federal courts were not the only forum for relief and that he could request clemency from Arnold Schwarzenegger, Governor of California. [168]

Protestors argued on both sides of the issue. Some wanted clemency and a stay of execution for Tookie. Others wanted him to be put to death.

Stanley "Tookie" Williams III married Bonnie Williams-Taylor. They had 3 children from this union.

2005 Governor of California, Arnold Schwarzenegger, on December 12, denied clemency for Williams.

Williams was the 12th person to be executed by the state of California following the 1976 U.S. Supreme Court decision of *Gregg v. Georgia*.to reinstate the death penalty after the death penalty was suspended in 1976. [169]

The Final Mimesis for Stanley "Tookie" Williams III

2005 On December 13, sixteen days away from his 52nd birthday, after exhausting all appeals, Stanley "Tookie" Williams III was executed by lethal injection at San Quentin State Prison. Newsweek reported thousands of protesters outside, most of whom were seeking Williams' clemency. He was the 12th person to be executed by the state of California following the 1976 U.S. Supreme Court decision of Gregg v.

Georgia. Williams provided no last words to the prison warden, but in an interview on WBAI Pacifica radio hours before the execution, he stated:[170]

My lack of fear of this barbaric methodology of death, I rely upon my faith. It has nothing to do with machismo, with manhood, or with some pseudo former gang street code. This is pure faith, and predicated on my redemption. So, therefore, I just stand strong and continue to tell you, your audience, and the world that I am innocent and, yes, I have been a wretched person, but I have redeemed myself. And I say to you and all those who can listen and will listen that redemption is tailor-made for the wretched, and that's what I used to be ... That's what I would like the world to remember me. That's how I would like my legacy to be remembered as: a redemptive transition, something that I believe is not exclusive just for the so-called sanctimonious, the elitists. And it doesn't—is not predicated on color or race or social stratum or one's religious background. It's accessible for everybody. That's the beauty about it. And whether others choose to believe that I have redeemed myself or not, I worry not, because I know and God knows, and you can believe that all of the youths that I continue to help, they know, too. So with that, I am grateful... I say to you and everyone else, God bless. So take care.

2005 Williams' body was laid out for viewing on December 19, 2005, and drew 2,000 mourners. A memorial service was held in Los Angeles on December 20, 2005, where Barbara Becnel, his spokesperson and co-author of book collaboration with Tookie, read his final wishes. Williams' funeral filled the 1,500-seat Bethel AME Church and drew a wide variety of people from current gang members to celebrities and religious leaders.

At his funeral, the last words of Williams were played from a tape to mourners, whom he asked to spread a message to loved ones:

> "The war within me is over. I battled my demons and I was triumphant. Teach them how to avoid our destructive footsteps. Teach them to strive for higher education. Teach them to promote peace and teach them to focus on rebuilding the neighborhoods that you, others, and I helped to destroy."

2006 On June 25, Barbara Becnel and Williams' longtime friend, Shirley Neal, sprinkled his ashes into a lake in Thokoza Park in the city of Soweto, South Africa as Williams had wished. [171]

In prison Stanley "Tookie" Williams by all counts, appeared to be rehabilitated. His consistent efforts and writings to inform youth on the wrongs of gang activity and his attempts to give them positive life direction did not go unnoticed. Stanley "Tookie" Williams wrote numerous books on gangs and redemption, all of which spread a positive message to youth.

Swiss Parliamentarian Mario Fehr nominated Williams for the prize after learning about his anti-gang activity and positive messages to young people, being distributed on his website. The fact that Somali youth immigrants in Zurich were using the site. The Web site links anti-gang counselors and youth in at least five countries.

How much ironic dichotomy can there be in life when an individual in prison, on death row, is nominated for the Nobel Peace Prize

He has been nominated for the Nobel peace prize four times for his anti-gang initiatives

He's been nominated for the *Nobel Peace Prize* five times and for the Nobel Prize for literature once. [172]

Books by Tookie Williams

Blue Rage, Black Redemption: A Memoir (Quality Trade) by Stanley Tookie Williams, foreword by Tavis Smiley, epilogue by Barbara Becnel, 2007, (QT) ISBN 978-1-4165-4449-4

Blue Rage, Black Redemption: A Memoir (paperback) by Stanley Tookie Williams, 2005, (PB) ISBN 0-9753584-0-5

Gangs and Drugs (Williams, Stanley. Tookie Speaks Out Against Gang Violence,) by Stanley Williams, Barbara Cottman Becnel, 1997, (PB) ISBN 1-56838-135-2, 24 pages, Reading level: Ages 9–12

Gangs and Self-Esteem: Tookie Speaks Out Against Gang Violence (Tookie Speaks Out Against Gang Violence) by Stanley Williams, Barbara Cottman Becnel, 1999, (PB) ISBN 0-613-02690-X, 24 pages, Reading level: Ages 4–8

Gangs and the Abuse of Power (Williams, Stanley. Tookie Speaks Out Against Gang Violence.) by Stanley Williams, Barbara Cottman Becnel, 1997, ISBN 1-56838-130-1, 24 pages, Reading level: Ages 9–12

Gangs and Violence (Williams, Stanley. Tookie Speaks Out Against Gangs.) by Stanley Williams, Barbara Cottman Becnel, 1997, (PB) ISBN 1-56838-134-4 (HB) ISBN 0-8239-2345-2, 24 pages, Reading level: Ages 4–8

Gangs and Wanting to Belong (Williams, Stanley. Tookie Speaks Out Against Gang Violence.) by Stanley Williams, Barbara Cottman Becnel, 1997, (PB) ISBN 1-56838-131-X, 24 pages, Reading level: Ages 9–12

Gangs and Weapons (Tookie Speaks Out Against Gang Violence) by Stanley Tookie Williams, Barbara Cottman Becnel, 1997, (PB) ISBN 1-56838-132-8, 24 pages, Reading level: Ages 9–12

Gangs and Your Friends (Williams, Stanley. Tookie Speaks Out Against Gangs.) by Stanley Williams, Barbara Cottman Becnel, 1997, (PB) ISBN 1-56838-136-0, 24 pages, Reading level: Ages 4–8

Gangs and Your Neighborhood (Williams, Stanley. Tookie Speaks Out Against Gang Violence.) by Stanley Williams, Barbara Cottman Becnel, 1997, (PB) ISBN 1-56838-137-9, 24 pages, Reading level: Ages 4–8

Life in Prison by Stanley Tookie Williams, Barbara Cottman Becnel, 1998, (PB) ISBN 1-58717-094-9, 80 pages, Reading level: Ages 4–8 (royalties donated to the Institute for the Prevention of Youth Violence)

Redemption: From Original Gangster to Nobel Prize Nominee - The Extraordinary Life Story of Stanley Tookie Williams paperback) by Stanley Williams, 2004, (HB) ISBN 1-903854-34-2. https://audiobookstore.com/authors/stanley-%E2%80%9Ctookie%E2%80%9D-williams-audiobooks/

Mimesis of Life Summary for
Stanley "Tookie" Williams

Tookie Williams grew up without a father. His mother spent a lot of time working, which gave him time to spend in the streets. Tookie grew up in a life of crime early in his youth. His entire life consisted of criminal influence, except for the time he was an anti-gang counselor and during the time he spent in jail. The environment Tookie grew up in and created did not give him much influence to change. His change occurred when he went to prison, looked into what his life meant (reflected and experienced a catharsis), then changed. The books he wrote are examples of his change into a good human being. The problem is that the crimes he is alleged to have committed and was convicted of were grave. His positive transformation could not resolve or give clemency to his criminal life. Therefore, he was executed by lethal injection. This is a lesson all people should learn. That no matter what you do, there are some situations that have no recourse.

However, with his dysfunctional life experiences, Tookie eventually came to realize that he put himself in the position of being incarcerated and realized the problems he made for himself. In reflection, he saw the light and changed. Tookie's change was genuine enough for him to gain a number of people who wanted him to have his sentence converted from death to life. Many felt he could do a lot of good to dissuade youth from gangs, drugs and criminal activity. But his crimes were too overbearing and his positive contributions could not compensate for his past lived experiences.

Mimesis of Life for Donald J. Trump

Donald John Trump was born June 14, 1946 to Fred and Mary Anne Macleod Trump. Donald was the fouth of five children. His siblings were Maryanne, Fred Jr., and Elizabeth, and younger brother Robert. In 2017-2021, Donald Trump became the one term President of the United States of America. Fred Trump's parents were German immigrants who migrated to America. Trumps mother was an immigrant from Scotland. It is ironic that as president Donald Trump took such an anti-immigration stand when his own grandparents and mother were immigrants. Trumps third wife, Melania was an immigrant from Slovakia and Melania's parents immigrated to America from Slovakia. However, the truth is that Trump was not actually anti-immigration, as long as the immigrants were White (Caucasian).

Trump graduated with a bachelor degree from the Wharton School of the University of Pennsylvania in 1968. He was named president of his father's real estate business in 1971 and changed the name to "The Trump Organization". He expanded the company's operations to building and renovating skyscrapers, hotels, casinos, and golf courses and later started side ventures, mostly by licensing his name. From 2004 to 2015, he co-produced and hosted the reality television series *The Apprentice*. Trump and his businesses have been involved in more than 4,000 state dand federal legal actions, including six bankruptcies.

Trump's political positions have been described as populist, protectionist, isolationist, and nationalist. He won the 2016 United States presidential election as the Republican nominee against Democratic nominee Hillary Clinton despite losing the national popular vote.[a] He became the first U.S. president with no prior military or government service. His election and policies sparked numerous protests. The 2017–2019 special counsel investigation established that Russia interfered in the 2016 election to favor the election of Trump. Trump promoted conspiracy theories and made many false and misleading statements during his campaigns and presidency, to a degree unprecedented in American politics. Many of his comments and actions have been characterized as racially charged or racist, and many as misogynistic.

Trump ordered a travel ban on citizens from several Muslim-majority countries, diverted military funding towards building a wall on the U.S.–Mexico border, and implemented a policy of family separations for apprehended migrants from the Southern Latin countries. He rolled back more than 100 environmental policies and regulations in an aggressive attempt to weaken environmental protections. Trump signed the Tax Cuts and Jobs Act of 2017, which cut taxes for individuals and businesses and rescinded the individual health insurance mandate penalty of the Affordable Care Act. He appointed 54 federal appellate judges and three United States Supreme Court justices. Trump initiated a trade war with China and withdrew the U.S. from the proposed Trans-Pacific Partnership trade agreement, the Paris Agreement on climate change, and the Iran nuclear deal. Trump met with North Korean leader Kim Jong-un three times, but made no progress on denuclearization. He reacted slowly to the COVID-19 pandemic, ignored or contradicted many recommendations from health officials in his messaging, and promoted misinformation about unproven treatments and the need for testing.

Trump lost the 2020 presidential election to Joe Biden but refused to concede defeat He falsely claiming widespread electoral fraud and attempting to overturn the results by pressuring government officials, conducting numerous unsuccessful legal challenges. He refused to insure a smooth transition of power and with unprecedented action obstructed Joe Biden from gaining access to information and government departments in a timely manner. On January 6, 2021, Trump urged his supporters to march to the United States Capitol, which many of them then attacked, resulting in multiple deaths and interrupting the electoral vote count.

Trump is the only American president to have been impeached twice. After he tried to pressure Ukraine in 2019 to investigate Biden, he was impeached in December by the House of Representatives for abuse of power and obstruction of Congress and acquitted by the Republican majority Senate in February 2020. The House impeached Trump a second time in January 2021, for incitement of insurrection, and the Republican Senate acquitted him again in February. Since leaving office, Trump has remained heavily involved in the Republican Party. In November 2022, he announced his candidacy for the Republican nomination in the 2024 presidential election. In December 2022, the House January 6 Committee recommended criminal charges against Trump for obstructing an official proceeding, conspiracy to defraud the United States, and inciting or assisting an insurrection. Scholars and historians rank

Trump as one of the worst presidents in American history. [173]

Mimesis 1 for Donald John Trump

1946   Donald Trump was born

1951 – 1958   Donald attended Kew-Forest School private school from kindergarten through seventh grade.

Mimesis 2 for Donald John Trump

1959

Trump was enrolled at age 13, he was enrolled at the New York Military Academy, a private boarding school. Trump's parents sent him to a military school because they thought he was unruly and needed discipline in his life.

Trump was confirmed at the First Presbyterian Church in Jamaica, N.Y.

1964   Donald Trump enrolled at Fordham University.

1966   Donald transfers to the Wharton School of the University of Pennsylvania,

1968   Donald graduates in May with a B.S. in economics from Wharton.

While in college, Trump obtained four student draft deferments during the Vietnam War era. In 1966, he was deemed fit for military service based upon a medical examination, and in July 1968, a local draft board classified him as eligible to serve. In October 1968, he was classified 1-Y, a conditional medical deferment, and in 1972, he was reclassified 4-F due to bone spurs, permanently disqualifying him from service. Allegedly, Trump's deferment based on medical conditions are false claims. With good reason, some think Trump's medical claims were false and his intentions were merely to dodge the draft.

In 2015, Trump's lawyer Michael Cohen threatened Trump's colleges, high school, and the College Board with legal action if they released Trump's academic records.[174] Why would an individual not want their grades released to the public if they were running for president of America, unless the grades show the individual is academically weak or intellectually inept?

1970 The Trump family joined Marble Collegiate Church, pastored by Norman Vincent Peale Trump described Dr. Peale as a mentor to him. In 2015, Church records stated that Trump was not an active member.

2019 While President, Trump appointed his personal pastor, televangelist Paula White, to the White House Office of Public Liaison. In 2020, he said he identified as a non-denominational Christian. There is speculation that in politics, religion, personal life, business, and marriage, Donald Trump has no loyalty or allegiance. Motives for his beliefs are strictly based on what is in his best interest.[175] He demands/requires loyalty but does not give it, which is the presumption many people have of Trump.[176]

Mimesis 2 for Donald John Trump – Wealth

How did Donald Trump get rich? Inheritance from his parents gave him enough money to fail and fail and fail enough that the law of averages finally kicks in. He finally won. Failure however, is a learning experience. One doesn't just learn what to do. One also learns what not to do. Trump dealt with people who were weak for money. Like him, they would do anything for money.

1982 Trump made the Forbes list of the wealthiest people in America. The shares he owned in the Trump Family business are estimated to be worth $200 million ($521 million in 2021 dollars).

2015 Trump announced his net worth is $10 billion. Forbes, however, estimated his net worth at $4.5 billion, after subtracting liabilities.

2018 Journalist Jonathan Greenberg reported 2018 that Trump used the pseudonym "John Barron" and claimed to be a Trump Organization official. Trump called him in 1984 to falsely assert that he owned more than 90% of the Trump family's business, to gain a higher ranking on the *Forbes* 400 list of wealthy Americans. Greenberg also wrote that Forbes had significantly overestimated Trump's wealth and wrongly included him on the *Forbes* 400 rankings of 1982, 1983, and 1984.[177]

2021 Trumps ranking was $2.4 billion.

Trump has often said he began his career with "a small loan of one million dollars" from his father, and that he had to pay it back with interest. He was a millionaire by age eight.

The truth is that Donald Trump borrowed at least $60 million from his father, largely failed to repay those loans, and received another $413 million (adjusted for inflation) from his father's company. In 2018, he and his family were reported to have committed tax fraud, and the New York State Department of Taxation and Finance began investigating. His investments underperformed the stock and New York property markets. *Forbes* estimated in October 2018 that his net worth declined from $4.5 billion in 2015 to $3.1 billion in 2017, and his product licensing income from $23 million to $3 million.[178]

Over a period of 20 years, Trump lost hundreds of millions of dollars and deferred payments, declaring $287 million in forgiven debt as taxable income. His income mainly came from his share in *The Apprentice* and businesses in which he was a minority partner, and his losses mainly came from majority-owned businesses. He had significant income labeled as tax credits for his losses, which allowed him to avoid annual income tax payments or lowered them to $750. In the last decade, he balanced his businesses' losses by selling and borrowing against assets, including a $100 million mortgage on Trump Tower (due in 2022) and the liquidation of over $200 million in stocks and bonds. He personally guaranteed $421 million in debt, most of which is due by 2024.[179]

Contrary to his claims of financial health and business acumen, Trump's tax returns from 1985 to 1994 show net losses totaling $1.17 billion. The losses were higher than those of almost every other American taxpayer. The losses in 1990 and 1991, more than $250 million each year, were more than double those of the nearest losers. In 1995, his reported losses were $915.7 million (equivalent to $1.63 billion in 2021).[180]

As of October 2020, Trump had over $1 billion in debts, secured by his assets. He owed $640 million to banks and trust organizations, including Bank of China, Deutsche Bank, and UBS, and approximately $450 million to unknown creditors. The value of his assets does, however, exceed his debt.[181]

Mimesis 2 for Donald John Trump – Business Career

Starting in 1968, Trump was employed at his father Fred's real estate company, Trump Management, which owned middle-class rental housing in

New York City's outer boroughs in 1971, he became president of the company and began using the Trump Organization as an umbrella brand.[182]

Umbrella branding *(also known as **family branding**) is a marketing practice involving the use of a single brand name for the sale of two or more related products. Umbrella branding is mainly used by companies with a positive brand equity (value of a brand in a certain marketplace). All products use the same means of identification and lack additional brand names or symbols, etc. This marketing practice differs from brand extension in that umbrella branding involves the marketing of similar products, rather than differentiated* *products, under one brand name. Hence, umbrella branding may be considered as a type of brand extension. The practice of umbrella branding does not disallow a firm to implement different branding approaches for different product lines (e.g., brand extension).*

1970's – 1980's   Fixer Roy Cohn served as Trump's lawyer and mentor for 13 years

1973   Cohn helped Trump countersue the United States government for $100 million (equivalent to $610 million in 2021) over the government's charges that Trump's properties had racially discriminatory practices. Trump and Cohn lost that case when the countersuit was dismissed and the government's case went forward.

1975   An agreement was struck requiring Trump's properties to furnish the New York Urban League with a list of all apartment vacancies, every week for two years, among other things. Cohn introduced political consultant Roger Stone to Trump, who enlisted Stone's services to deal with the federal government.

Cohn introduced Donald Trump to Roger Stone, who helped Trump deal with the federal government.

As of November 2016, Trump and his businesses had been involved in more than 4,000 state and federal legal actions, according to a running tally by USA Today.

While Trump has not filed for personal bankruptcy, his over-leveraged hotel and casino businesses in Atlantic City and New York filed for Chapter 11 bankruptcy protection six times between 1991 and 2009. They continued to operate while the banks restructured debt and reduced Trump's shares in the properties.

During the 1980s, more than 70 banks had lent Trump $4 billion, but in the aftermath of his corporate bankruptcies of the early 1990s, most major banks declined to lend to him, with only Deutsche Bank still willing to lend money. After the January 6 United States Capitol attack, the bank decided not to do business with Trump or his company in the future. [183]

1978   Trump's profile came gained public attention with the purchase and renovation of his family's first Manhattan venture, the Commodore Hotel, next to Grand Central Terminal. The financing was facilitated by a $400 million city property tax abatement arranged by Fred Trump, who also, jointly with Hyatt, guaranteed a $70 million in bank construction financing. The hotel reopened in 1980 as the Grand Hyatt Hotel, and that same year, Trump obtained rights to develop Trump Tower, a mixed-use skyscraper in Midtown Manhattan. The building houses the headquarters of the Trump Corporation and Trump's PAC and was Trump's primary residence until 2019.[184]

1988   Trump acquired the Plaza Hotel in Manhattan with a loan of $425 million (equivalent to $974 million in 2021) from a consortium of banks. Two years later, the hotel filed for bankruptcy protection, and a reorganization plan was approved in 1992. In 1995, Trump sold the Plaza Hotel along with most of his properties to pay down his debts, including personally guaranteed loans, allowing him to avoid personal insolvency.[185]

1996 Trump acquired the mostly vacant 71-story skyscraper at 40 Wall Street, later rebranded as the Trump Building, and renovated it. In the early 1990s, Trump won the right to develop a 70-acre tract in the Lincoln Square neighborhood near the Hudson River. Burdened with debt from other ventures in 1994, Trump sold most of his interest in the project to Asian investors, who were able to finance the completion of the project, Riverside South.[186]

1984 Trump opens Harrah's at Trump Plaza, a hotel and casino in Atlantic City, New Jersey, with financing and management help from the Holiday Corporation. It was unprofitable, and Trump paid Holiday $70 million in May 1986 to take sole control.

1984 Trump bought a hotel and casino in Atlantic City from the Hilton Corporation for $320 million. When renovation was completed in 1985, it became Trump Castle.

1985 Trump acquires Mar-a-Lago.

1988 Trump bought a third Atlantic City Casino called the Trump Taj Mahal. It was financed with $675 million in junk bonds and completed for $1.1 billion.

1990 The Taj Mahal opens in April. It went bankrupt in 1989.

Reorganizing left him with half his initial stake and required him to personally guarantee future performance. To reduce his $900 million of personal debt, he sold the Trump Shuttle airline and his mega-yacht, the Trump Princess.[187]

1995 In 1995, Trump founded "Trump Hotels & Casino Resorts" (THCR), which took ownership of Trump Plaza, Trump Castle, and the Trump Casino in Gary, Indiana. THCR purchased the Taj Mahal in 1996 and went bankrupt in 2004, 2009, and 2014, leaving Trump with 10 percent ownership. He remained chairman until 2009.[188]

1999 The Trump Organization began building and buying golf courses. It owns fourteen and manages another three Trump-branded courses worldwide.[189]

The Trump name has been licensed for various consumer products and services, including foodstuffs, apparel, adult learning courses, and home furnishings. According to reports by The Washington Post, there are more than 50 licensing or management deals involving Trump's name, which have generated at least $59 million in revenue for his companies. By 2018, only two consumer goods companies continued to license his name.[190]

1983 Trump purchased the New Jersey Generals, a team in the United States Football League. After the **1985** season, the league folded, largely due to Trump's strategy of moving games to a fall schedule (when they competed with the NFL for audience) and trying to force a merger with the NFL by bringing an antitrust suit against the organization.[191]

1988 Trump purchased the Eastern Air Lines Shuttle, with 21 planes and landing rights in New York City, Boston, and Washington, D.C. He financed the purchase with $380 million (equivalent to $871 million in 2021) from 22 banks, rebranded the operation the Trump Shuttle, and operated it until 1992. Trump failed to earn a profit with the airline and sold it to USAir.[192]

The Donald J. Trump Foundation was established. In the foundation's final years, its funds mostly came from donors other than Trump. Trump did not donate any personal funds to the charity from **2009** until **2014**. The foundation gave to health care and sports-related charities, as well as conservative groups. [193]

1992   Trump, his siblings Maryanne, Elizabeth, and Robert, and his cousin John W. Walter, each with a 20 percent share, formed All County Building Supply & Maintenance Corp. The company had no offices and is alleged to have been a shell company for paying the vendors providing services and supplies for Trump's rental units, then billing those services and supplies to Trump Management with markups of 20–50 percent and more. The owners shared the proceeds generated by the markups. The increased costs were used as justification to get state approval for increasing the rents of Trump's rent-stabilized units.[194]

1996-2015   Trump purchased the Miss Universe pageants, including Miss USA and Miss Teen USA. Due to disagreements with CBS about scheduling, he moved the pageants to NBC in **2002**.

2007   Trump received a star on the Hollywood Walk of Fame for his work as the producer of Miss

Universe. NBC and Univision dropped the pageants from their broadcasting lineups in June 2015.[195]

2004 In 2004, Trump co-founded Trump University, a company that sold real estate training courses priced from $1,500 to $35,000. After New York State authorities notified the company that its use of the word "university" violated state law (as it was not an academic institution), its name was changed to Trump Entrepreneur Initiative in 2010.[196]

2013 The State of New York filed a $40 million civil suit against Trump University, alleging that the company made false statements and defrauded consumers. In addition, two class actions were filed in federal court against Trump and his companies. Internal documents revealed that employees were instructed to use a hard-sell approach, and former employees testified that Trump University had defrauded or lied to its students. Shortly after he won the 2016 presidential election, Trump agreed to pay a total of $25 million to settle the three cases.[197]

2016 *The Washington Post* reported that the charity had committed several potential legal and ethical violations, including alleged self-dealing and possible tax evasion. Also in 2016, the New York State Attorney General's office said the foundation appeared to be in violation of New York laws regarding charities and ordered it to immediately cease its fundraising activities in New York. Trump's team announced in December 2016 that the foundation would be dissolved.[198]

2018 In June, the New York Attorney General's office filed a civil suit against the foundation, Trump, and his adult children, seeking $2.8 million in restitution and additional penalties. In December, the foundation ceased operation and disbursed all its assets to other charities. [199]

2019 In November, a New York state judge ordered Trump to pay $2 million to a group of charities for misusing the foundation's funds, in part to finance his presidential campaign. [200]

Mimesis 2 for Donald John Trump – Family

Donald Trump has been married three times. His first wife and mother of three of his five children (Donald, Jr., Ivanka, and Eric) was Ivana (Zelnickova) Trump, born in 1949. She was a fashion model and businesswoman who became a naturalized U.S. citizen in 1988. They were married for 17 years from 1977 to 1990. Ivanna Trump died at her home in New York City at age 73 on July 14, 2022.

Ivana Trump was vice president of interior design for the Trump Organization, leading the signature design of Trump Tower. Afterwards, her then-husband appointed her to head up the Trump Castle Hotel and Casino as president. She remained with the Trump Organization until the divorce from Donald, at which time it is reported she received a $25,000,000.00 settlement from the divorce. [201]

Donald Trump's second wife was Marla Maples, born on October 27, 1963. Marla (Maples) Trump. They were married for 7 years from 1993 to 1999. They had one daughter, Tiffany, from this union. Maples was an American actress, television personality, model, singer, and presenter.

Donald Trump's third wife is Melania (Knauss) Trump, born April 26, 1970. They married in 2005 and still remained married to date. Melania Trump was born in Slovenia. Melania Trump grew up in Slovenia (then part of Yugoslavia), and worked as a fashion model through agencies in the European fashion capitals of Milan and Paris before moving to New York City in 1996. She served as the First Lady of the United States of America as the wife of President Donald Trump from 2017 to 2021.

2006 Donald and Melanie have one child born from this marriage. His name is Baron Trump.

Later that year, she became an American naturalized citizen. She is the second naturalized woman to become First Lady and the first non-native English speaker

The first American naturalized first lady was Louisa Adams, wife of the sixth President of the United States John Quincy Adams,

Donald Trump's three wives Ivana, Marla and Melania

Donald Trump's five Children from his three marriages, left to right: Eric (Ivanna), Tiffany (Marla), Baron (Melania), Ivanka (Ivana) and Donald, Jr. (Ivana)

Mimesis Stage 2 for Donald John Trump – Racist Accusations [202]

Donald Trump is often referred to as a racist. While he denies being a racist, there are other people who cite his racist beliefs as being socialized into him by his father and reinforced by Roy Cohn. There is, however, an abundance of information on Donald Trump and statements he has made that give people the impression he is a racist. However, University of California, Berkeley Professor Ian Haney López raises the issue that Donald Trump is not only racist, but he uses racism as a strategy to divide the country for the benefit of himself, other wealthy Americans, and not to alienate the right-wing voters, even the extreme right-wing. [203]

Examples and Incidents of Donald Trump's racist behaviors are as follows: [204]

1) During his presidential campaign, he called Mexican immigrants criminals and rapists.

2) He proposed a ban on all Muslims entering the US.

3) He suggested a judge should recuse himself from a case solely because of the judge's Mexican heritage.

4) During a news reporting session at the White House, April Ryan, a Black reporter with American Urban Radio Networks in Baltimore, asked Trump if he plans to meet and work with the Congressional Black Caucus. Trump's response to her Indicated that he views "black people as a monolithic "other" — a group of people who work and

behave in exactly similar ways. Not only does this seem to define an entire group of people down to a lowest common denominator, but it's also simply dehumanizing to treat individuals as only part of a bigger group."

"He repeatedly referred to black people with a "the" before he mentioned them — saying "the African Americans" and "the blacks." As linguist Lynne Murphy of the University of Sussex explained at Quartz, there is a purpose, albeit one Trump may not be totally aware of, to this".

In one of his presidential campaign speeches to black voters during the campaign, for instance, Trump said, "You're living in poverty, your schools are no good, you have no jobs, and fifty-eight percent (58%) of your youth is unemployed. What the hell do you have to lose?" [205]

5) Trump has called the SARS-CoV-2 coronavirus the "Chinese virus" and "kung flu" — racist terms that reference a stereotype Asian image and stirs xenophobia. He coupled this terminology onto during his 2016 presidential campaign;

6) Trump insinuated that Sen. Kamala Harris, who's Black, "doesn't meet the requirements" to run for vice president. This is ironic considering Trump, himself, never held government office. Has no government experience. He never served in the military (he dodged the draft) and his behavior insinuates his commitment is not to America but to himself. Trumps motto seems to be:

> Ask not what I can do for my country, but what my country can do for ME.

Trump has a long history of racist controversies

Here's a breakdown of Trump's history, taken largely from Dara Lind's list for Vox and an op-ed by Nicholas Kristof in the New York Times:[206]

1973 The US Department of Justice — under the Nixon administration, out of all administrations — **sued** the Trump Management Corporation for violating the Fair Housing Act. Federal officials found **evidence** that Trump had refused to rent to Black tenants and lied to Black applicants about whether apartments were available, among other accusations. Trump said the federal government was trying to get him to rent to welfare recipients. In the aftermath, he signed an agreement in 1975 agreeing not to discriminate to renters of color without admitting to previous discrimination.

1980 Kip Brown, a former employee at Trump's Castle, accused another one of Trump's businesses of discrimination. "When Donald and Ivana came to the casino, the bosses would order all the black people off the floor," Brown **said**. "It was the eighties, I was a teenager, but I remember it: They put us all in the back."

1989 In a controversial case that's been characterized as a modern-day lynching, four Black teenagers and one Latino teenager, the "Central Park Five", were accused of attacking and raping a White female jogger in New York City, Central Park. Trump immediately took charge in the case, running an ad in local papers demanding, "BRING BACK THE DEATH PENALTY. BRING BACK OUR POLICE!" The teens were found to be innocent, and their convictions were later vacated after they spent seven to 13 years in prison, and the city paid $41 million in a settlement to the teens. But Trump, in October 2016, said he still believes they're guilty, despite the DNA evidence to the contrary. [207]

The Central Park Five, when they were convicted and went to prison (left). The Central Park Five, when they were exonerated and released from prison (right).

Next is the full-page ad Donald Trump took out in the New York Times and other News media in and around New York.

BRING BACK THE DEATH PENALTY.

BRING BACK OUR POLICE!

What has happened to our City over the past ten years? What has happened to law and order, to the neighborhood cop we all trusted to safeguard our homes and families, the cop who had the power under the law to help us in times of danger, keep us safe from those who would prey on innocent lives to fulfill some distorted inner need. What has happened to the respect for authority, the fear of retribution by the courts, society and the police for those who break the law, who wantonly trespass on the right of others? What has happened is the complete breakdown of life as we knew it.

Many New York families — White, Black, Hispanic and Asian — have had to give up the pleasure of a leisurely stroll in the Park at dusk, the Saturday visit to the playground with their families, the bike ride at dawn, or just sitting on their stoops — given them up as hostages to a world ruled by the law of the streets, as roving bands of wild criminals roam our neighborhoods, dispensing their own vicious brand of twisted hatred on whomever they encounter. At what point did we cross the line from the fine and noble pursuit of genuine civil liberties to the reckless and dangerously permissive atmosphere which allows criminals of every age to beat and rape a helpless woman and then laugh at her family's anguish? And why do they laugh? They laugh because they know that soon, very soon, they will be returned to the streets to rape and maim and kill once again — and yet face no great personal risk to themselves.

Mayor Koch has stated that hate and rancor should be removed from our hearts. I do not think so. I want to hate these muggers and murderers. They should be forced to suffer and, when they kill, they should be executed for their crimes. They must serve as examples so that others will think long and hard before committing a crime or an act of violence. Yes, Mayor Koch, I want to hate these murderers and I always will. I am not looking to psychoanalyze or understand them. I am looking to punish them. If the punishment is strong, the attacks on innocent people will stop. I recently watched a newscast trying to explain the "anger in these young men". I no longer want to understand their anger. I want them to understand our anger. I want them to be afraid.

How can our great society tolerate the continued brutalization of its citizens by crazed misfits? Criminals must be told that their CIVIL LIBERTIES END WHEN AN ATTACK ON OUR SAFETY BEGINS!

When I was young, I sat in a diner with my father and witnessed two young bullies cursing and threatening a very frightened waitress. Two cops rushed in, lifted up the thugs and threw them out the door, warning them never to cause trouble again. I miss the feeling of security New York's finest once gave to the citizens of this City.

Let our politicians give back our police department's power to keep us safe. Unshackle them from the constant chant of "police brutality" which every petty criminal hurls immediately at an officer who has just risked his or her life to save another's. We must cease our continuous pandering to the criminal population of this City. Give New York back to the citizens who have earned the right to be New Yorkers. Send a message loud and clear to those who would murder our citizens and terrorize New York— BRING BACK THE DEATH PENALTY AND BRING BACK OUR POLICE!

Donald J. Trump

1991   A book by John O'Donnell, former president of Trump Plaza Hotel and Casino in Atlantic City, quoted Trump's criticism of a Black accountant: "Black guys counting my money! I hate it. The only kind of people I want counting my money are short guys who wear yarmulkes every day. … I think that the guy is lazy. And it's probably not his fault, because laziness is a trait in blacks. It really is, I believe that. It's not anything they can control." Trump later said in a 1997 Playboy interview that "the stuff O'Donnell wrote about me is probably true."

1992   The Trump Plaza Hotel and Casino had to pay a $200,000 fine because it transferred Black and women dealers off tables to accommodate a big-time gambler's prejudices.

1993   In congressional testimony, Trump said that some Native American reservations operating casinos shouldn't be allowed because "they don't look like Indians to me."

2000   In opposition to a casino proposed by the St. Regis Mohawk tribe, which he saw as a financial threat to his casinos in Atlantic City, Trump secretly ran a series of ads suggesting the tribe had a "record of criminal activity [that] is well documented."

2004:   In season two of *The Apprentice*, Trump fired Kevin Allen, a Black contestant, for being overeducated. "You're an unbelievably talented guy in terms of education, and you haven't done anything," Trump said on the show. "At some point you have to say, 'That's enough.'"

2005 Trump publicly pitched what was essentially *The Apprentice: White People vs. Black People*. He said he "wasn't particularly happy" with the most recent season of his show, so he was considering "an idea that is fairly controversial — creating a team of successful African Americans versus a team of successful whites. Whether people like that idea or not, it is somewhat reflective of our very vicious world."

2010 In 2010, there was a huge national controversy over the "Ground Zero Mosque" — a proposal to build a Muslim community center in Lower Manhattan, near the site of the 9/11 attacks. Trump opposed the project, calling it "insensitive," and offered to buy out one of the investors in the project. On *The Late Show With David Letterman*, Trump argued, referring to Muslims, "Well, somebody's blowing us up. Somebody's blowing up buildings, and somebody's doing lots of bad stuff."

2011 Trump played a big role in pushing false rumors that Obama — the country's first Black president — was not born in the US. He claimed to send investigators to Hawaii to look into Obama's birth certificate. Obama later released his birth certificate, calling Trump a "carnival barker." The research has found a strong correlation between birtherism, as the conspiracy theory is called, and racism. But Trump has reportedly continued pushing this conspiracy theory in private.

2011 While Trump suggested that Obama wasn't born in the US, he also argued that maybe Obama wasn't a good enough student to have gotten into

Columbia or Harvard Law School, and demanded Obama release his university transcripts. Trump claimed, "I heard he was a terrible student. Terrible. How does a bad student go to Columbia and then to Harvard?" This is an ironic request for President Obama to produce his grades because Trump ordered the University of Pennsylvania, not to release his grades from the Warton School of Business. It is a thought that the reason Trump does not want his grades released is because he was at the bottom of his class. Listening to him talk it is evident his vocabulary is limited. The information listed in this section alone, indicates his mentality is antiquated and reflects ignorance, yet Trump suggest Harvard graduate, editor of the Harvard Business Review, Barack Obama has low grades.

It is reported that Trump's intelligence quotient was discovered after threats by Trump to sue schools that released his grades to the public. Trump's intelligence score was found to be 73. That is a couple of points away from "intellectually disabled" and far below the average IQ score of 100.[208] However, Trump has denied having a low IQ, calling this report "fake". He states he has a high IQ without providing any proof of his elementary, high school, or college academic performance. Some findings cite his IQ as high as 156. It can be assumed that, by his actions and speaking patterns that Donald Trump does not have a high IQ, average at best. With reasonable support, Donald Trump does not have a high IQ (Intelligence Quotient), but he also has a low EQ (Emotional Quotient). Examples of his emotional immaturity are examples of his vindictive and revengeful personality, his belief in the position to "never apologize". Even after the Central Park Five were exonerated and found innocent, Trump displayed no remorse, nor did he apologize. Trump demands complete loyalty from people who work for or associate with him, yet he makes no reciprocal commitment of loyalty. The Measurement of an individual's IQ or EQ is difficult to measure without testing and diagnosis. In Trump's case, is not available, nor is it reasonable to think he will assist in making that knowledge available to the public.

EQ is a complex combination of personal emotional abilities or traits. EQ is considered an important character trait for working with people and for leadership. According to experts, Trump's EQ evaluation is based on observation and is as follows: [209]

- **Low emotional awareness**

    He often speaks slowly in a highly controlled way and puts his right-hand thumb and forefinger together to enforce his belief systems on others.

    Trump seems neither to care nor to be open to adapting his view to become more congruent with what may be commonly accepted.

- **Emotional expression**

    He focuses on strong negative emotions such as anger and fear in order to communicate and persuade.

    Some see Trump as impulsive. Others see him as making poor judgments and poor expressions.

- **Impulse control**

  Trump's control of emotions seems high much of the time as he rarely demonstrates outbursts of uncontrolled emotion.

- **Lower authenticity**

  Beliefs filter our reality and skew awareness.

- **Very high self-regard**

  There seems little chink in Trump's 'self-regard' amour.

  Trump's demonstrable absence of shame and guilt are his most worrying attributes.

- **High assertiveness with low empathy**

  Mr Trump exhibits very low empathy. He seems not to notice or care about the feelings of others.

  High self-actualization acts like another accelerator for Trump's self-motivation.

- **The bombast and bully**

  *Strong assertion and low **empathy** reflect a powerful, bombastic quality that makes engaging with this type very difficult.*

- **Power from charismatic opportunism**

  Trump motivates through his wide use of fear and fear-based language – 'crooked Hillary', 'build a wall', 'taking your jobs'.

- **Emotional intelligence is about balance**

  Great leadership rests on one's ability to know their true value and appreciate others' value.

Emotions are ultimately a feedback mechanism delivering messages to us in order to enable us to adapt to constant change.

Composite Areas EQ-I® 2.0	Weaker skills	Average	Strong skills
EQ Profile			
SELF-PERCEPTION			
Self-Regard (SR)			X
Self-Actualisation (SA)			X
Emotional Self-Awareness (ES)	X		
SELF-EXPRESSION			
Emotional Expression (EE)	X		
Assertiveness (AS)			X
Independence (IN)			X
INTERPERSONAL			
Empathy (EM)	X		
Interpersonal Relationships (IR)	X		
Social Responsibility (RE)	X		
DECISION-MAKING			
Problem Solving (PS)		X	
Reality Testing (RT)		X	
Impulse Control (IC)		X	
STRESS MANAGEMENT			
Flexibility (FL)	X		
Stress Tolerance (ST):			X
Optimism (OP)		X	

Mean =100

Mimesis Stage 2 for Donald John Trump – Extra Marital Affairs and Sexual Misconduct Allegations

Normally an individual's indiscretions should be private affairs, but in the case of Donald Trump they should be discussed because they are a significant part of his lived experience, Mimesis and character. He is being sued by the New York Attorney General for making "hush" payments to Stormy Daniels, a woman who he is accused of having an affair. The accusation is that he made the "hush" payment during his run for President of the United States and tried to cover it up. Questions remain did he make the payment with campaign money? Nevertheless, he is accused of lying about the affair. This is the same accusation made against Bill Clinton, the 42nd President of the United

States, during his impeachment trial in 1998 for lying under oath about his affair. Donald Trump was not under oath to Congress, but he has frequently denied the affair, while his counterparts to the affair and numerous others admitted the affairs took place.

It is alleged, with verifiable information, that Donald Trump had affairs with two women, Stormy Daniels (Stefanie Clifford) and Karen McDougal, during his marriage to Melania.

Stormy Daniels (her stage Name) is an established adult-entertainment actress and a director with several awards and credits to her name.

Karen McDougal was a Playboy model when she met Donald Trump in 2006. Trump allegedly paid off both women to be quiet and to deny the affairs. Daniels was paid $130,000.00 and McDougal was paid $150,000.00 according to news sources. [210]

According to these sources the hush money payment was made to Stormy Daniels by Trump lawyer and fixer Michael Cohen. The hush money payment was made to Karen McDougal by Trump friend and National Enquirer publisher, David Pecker. Trump is allegedly to have had a sexual encounter with former adult film star Stormy Daniels just four months after Melania gave birth to his 5th child, Baron. In 2006. Playboy model Karen McDougal allegedly started an affair with Trump even closer to the birth of Barron, in June 2006.

In September 2005, Trump was caught on tape telling "Access Hollywood" host Billy Bush that he was able to "grab" women "by the pussy" because "when you're a star they let you do it." The real irony about this statement is that he said it but more so, that is was aired on public media, heard by the voting public, by women across America and they still voted for Donald Trump in the 2016 Presidential Election. One can't blame Trump for the public's mental state of mind.

Donald Trump could soon become the first U.S. president in history (sitting or former) to face criminal charges amid new momentum in a Manhattan district attorney's probe into a hush money payment to adult film star Stormy Daniels. [211]

The criminal lawsuit against Donald Trump is focused on the hush-money payments made to two women who alleged they had extramarital encounters with Donald Trump in 2016. Trump has denied the accusations. The criminal case revolves around how the payments were made. If they were made from The Trump Organization accounts, how were they accounted for? If they were made from campaign contributions, how were they accounted for? The New York District Attorney Alvin Bragg and the New York Federal justice system question Trump's integrity and honesty; therefore, they are investigating him. [212]

Sexual Misconduct Allegations against Donald J. Trump

Donald Trump has been accused of rape, sexual assault, and sexual harassment. At least 25 women since 1970 have accused Donald Trump of sexual misconduct. Even his own wife accused him of rape during their 1969 divorce proceedings, but later recanted her story. [213]

Other sexual misconduct accusations against Trump are:

Jill Harth (1992) alleged that Trump assaulted her several times. [214]

E. Jean Carroll (1995) filed a lawsuit against Trump, accusing him of defamation by claiming she lied about him raping her in 1995 or 1996. [215] As a result, a Manhattan federal jury found that Donald Trump sexually abused E. Jean Carroll in a luxury department store dressing room in the spring of 1996 and awarded her $5 million for battery and defamation. Trump has indicated he will appeal the ruling. [216]

Summer Zervos (2007) was a contestant on the fifth season of *The Apprentice*, which filmed in 2005 and aired in 2006. Subsequently, she contacted Trump in 2007 about a job after the show's completion, and he invited her to meet him at The Beverly Hills Hotel. Zervos has said that Trump was sexually suggestive during their meeting, kissing her open-mouthed, groping her breasts, and thrusting his genitals on her. She also has said that his behavior was aggressive and not consensual.[217]

Alva Johnson (2019) filed a lawsuit against Trump, alleging he had forcibly kissed her at a rally in Florida in August 2016 while she was working on his 2016 presidential campaign. [218]

Jessica Leeds (1980) was a businesswoman at a paper company on a flight from the Midwest, returning to New York. A flight attendant offered her an empty seat in the first-class cabin next to Trump. Leeds alleged that about 45 minutes after takeoff, Trump lifted the armrest and began touching her, grabbing her breasts, and tried to put his hand up her skirt.[219]

Kristin Anderson (1990) On October 14, 2016, reported to the *Washington Post* an allegation that Trump groped her beneath her skirt in a Manhattan nightclub in the early 1990s. She was an aspiring model at the time of the alleged incident. [220]

Lisa Boyne (1996) reported to the *Huffington Post* that in October, Sonja Morgan (then Sonja Tremont) invited her to a dinner with Trump, modeling agent John Casablanca, and five or six other models. Boyne alleged that Trump made the models walk across the table, looked under their skirts, and described whether they were wearing underwear. [221]

Cathy Heller (1997) on October 15, 2016, Cathy Heller reported to *The Guardian* an allegation that she was grabbed and kissed by Donald Trump two decades earlier. Heller said that, in 1997, she met Trump when she attended a Mother's Day brunch with her children, her husband, and her husband's parents at his Mar-a-Lago estate. Her parents-in-law were members of Mar-a-Lago. Heller was introduced to Trump, who became angry when she avoided a kiss. He then "grabbed" her and, when he tried to kiss her, she turned her head. Trump kissed her on the side of the mouth "for a little too long," and then he left her. [222]

Temple Taggart McDowell (1997). In May 2016, *The New York Times* reported allegations by Temple Taggart McDowell. McDowell, who was Miss Utah USA in 1997, accused Trump of unwanted kisses and embraces that left McDowell and one of her chaperones so uncomfortable, according to McDowell, that she claimed she was instructed not to be left in a room alone with him again. According to McDowell, a chaperone had accompanied her to Trump's office. At the time, McDowell was 21 and was known as Temple Taggart. This incident occurred in Trump's first year of ownership of the Miss USA contest. [223]

Amy Dorris (1997). Former model Amy Dorris said in September 2020 that she and her boyfriend, Jason Binn, attended the 1997 U.S. Open with Donald Trump, who Binn had described as his best friend. She alleges that Trump groped and kissed her without her consent at the event. *The Guardian* confirmed that she told her mother and a friend in New York immediately after the incident and that she had told her therapist and several other friends about it over the years. [224]

Karena Virginia (1998). At an October 2016 press conference with attorney Gloria Allred, yoga instructor and life coach Karena Virginia said that in 1998, Trump grabbed her arm and touched her breast. Virginia, who was 27 years old at the time, was waiting for a ride after the US Open in Queens, New York. She said Trump, whom she had not met previously, approached her with a small group of other men, while commenting on her legs, then he grabbed her right arm. Virginia continued, "Then his hand touched the right side of my breast. I was in shock. I flinched. 'Don't you know who I am? Don't you know who I am?'—that's what he said to me. I felt intimidated, and I felt powerless.[225]

Karen Johnson (early 2000s). In Barry Levine and Monique El-Faizy's book *All the President's Women: Donald Trump and the Making of a Predator*, Karen Johnson alleged that she attended a New Year's Eve party at Trump's Mar-a-Lago estate, where Trump grabbed her by her genitals, pulled her behind a tapestry, and forcibly kissed her. Johnson also alleged that days after the incident, Trump repeatedly called her (without her giving him the phone number), offering to fly her to meet him, which she rejected.[226]

Mindy McGillivray (2003). In an October 2016 article by *The Palm Beach Post*, Mindy McGillivray stated that in January 2003, when she was 23 years old, she was groped by Trump at his Mar-a-Lago estate. She said, "All of a sudden, I felt a grab, a little nudge. I think it's [my friend Ken Davidoff's] camera bag that was my first instinct. I turn around and there's Donald. He sort of looked away quickly." [227]

Rachel Crooks (2005). In 2005, Rachel Crooks was a 22-year-old receptionist at Bayrock Group, a real estate investment and development company in Trump Tower in Manhattan. She says she encountered Trump in an elevator in the building one morning and turned to introduce herself. They shook hands, but Trump would not let go. Instead, he began kissing her cheeks, then directly on the mouth. "It was so inappropriate," Crooks recalled in an interview. "I was so upset that he thought I was so insignificant that he could do that." Her story was printed by *The New York Times* in October 2016, along with that of Jessica Leeds. Trump has disputed Crooks' claims, writing on Twitter, "Who would do this in a public space with live security cameras running?" Crooks is a public supporter and donor to Hillary Clinton's presidential campaign.[228]

Natasha Stoynoff (2005), Canadian author and journalist Natasha Stoynoff, who wrote for *People* magazine and, previously, the *Toronto Star* and *Toronto Sun*, went to Trump's Florida estate in December 2005 to interview him and his wife, Melania. While there, Trump gave Stoynoff a tour of the Mar-a-Lago estate. She says that during this tour, he pushed her against a wall and forced his tongue into her mouth.[229]

Juliet Huddy (2005 or 2006). In early December 2017, the reporter Juliet Huddy said Trump kissed her on the lips while they were on an elevator in Trump Tower with Trump's security guard in 2005 or 2006. Regarding this incident, Huddy said, "I was surprised that he went for the lips. But I didn't feel threatened ... Whatever, everything was fine. It was a weird moment. He never tried anything after that, and I was never alone with him.[230]

Jessica Drake (2006). On October 22, 2016, Jessica Drake and attorney Gloria Allred held a news conference in which Drake accused Trump of having sexually assaulted her by tightly in a hug and kissing her and two acquaintances nearly ten years prior. Drake, an adult film actress and sex education advocate, said she met Trump at her company's booth during a charity golf tournament at Lake Tahoe in 2006. Drake claims she was invited to meet with Trump, who was married at the time, at his hotel suite; she was "uncomfortable going alone" and brought two friends. Describing the meeting with Trump, Drake recounted that "He grabbed each of us tightly, in a hug, and kissed each one of us without asking permission." Drake said she and her friends left the suite after 30–45 minutes. Shortly thereafter, Drake claims she received phone calls from Trump or his associate, requesting that she join him in his suite for $10,000, and offering to fly her on his jet back to Los Angeles. She said she declined his offers.[231]

Ninni Laaksonen (2006). On October 27, 2016, a local Finnish tabloid, *Ilta-Sanomat*, reported an allegation by Ninni Laaksonen, Miss Finland 2006. Laaksonen appeared with Trump on The *Late Show with David Letterman* on July 26, 2006. Laaksonen claims that before they went on the air, Trump grabbed her buttocks. As Laaksonen describes the interaction: "He really grabbed my butt. I don't think anybody saw it, but I flinched and thought: "What is happening?" Someone later told Laaksonen that Trump liked her because she looked like his wife, Melania, when she was younger. [232]

Cassandra Searles (2013). In October 2016, *Rolling Stone* and NPR reported that Trump fondled Cassandra Searles, Miss Washington USA of 2013, without her consent during the Miss USA pageant of that year. In June 2016, Searles wrote that Trump invited her to his hotel room. Yahoo! News published an article in June 2016 stating that Searles had made Facebook postings that accused Trump of making unwanted advances. She said he was "continually" groping her buttocks and had asked her to go "to his hotel room". Searles also asserted that Trump had "treated us like cattle".[233]

Mariah Billado, Victoria Hughes, and three other Miss Teen USA contestants (1997). Mariah Billado, Miss Vermont Teen USA, is one of five women to mention such a dressing room visit incident in 1997. Billado said of the visit: "I remember putting on my dress really quick, because I was like, 'Oh my god, there's a man in here.' Trump, she recalled, said something like, 'Don't worry, ladies, I've seen it all before.' "Billado recalled talking to Ivanka, Trump's daughter, who responded, "Yeah, he does that." Victoria Hughes, Miss New Mexico Teen USA, also said Trump did conduct a dressing room visit, and that the youngest contestant there was 15. The dressing room had 51 contestants, each with their own stations.[234]

Bridget Sullivan (2000) in 2000, Bridget Sullivan was Miss New Hampshire USA. As she prepared for a television broadcast, Trump allegedly walked into the dressing room. She told *BuzzFeed* he was coming to wish the contestants good luck, but they "were all naked".[235]

In 1992, Trump appeared on NBC News' show *A Closer Look*, hosted by **Faith Daniels.** During the show, Daniels said Trump (divorced at the time) agreed to make an appearance because: "You kissed me on the lips in front of the paparazzi, and I said, 'That'll cost you. I'm booking you on the show.'" Trump replied that the kiss was "so open and nice", and that he thought Daniels' husband "had his back turned at the time". Trump had invited NBC News to film a party he threw for himself and Jeffrey Epstein at Mar-a-Lago, where they joined various NFL cheerleaders; the kiss incident occurred there. NBC News revealed footage of the party in July 2019, showing Trump, Epstein and the cheerleaders. At one point during the video, Trump grabbed a woman around her waist, pulled her against his body, and patted her buttocks. At another point, Trump appears to tell Epstein: "Look at her, back there... She's hot".[236]

Donald Trump has denied all of the sexual misconduct allegations made against him. The conclusions one can draw are that all 20-plus women who accused Donald Trump are lying or that Donald Trump is the liar. What do you think?

Shaun R. Harper, executive director of the Penn Graduate Center for Education, has said that "many men talk like Donald Trump," objectifying women and saying offensive things about them. He puts Trump in a class of men whose behavior sometimes includes sexual assault and degrading women. *The Economist* drew similar parallels, pointing to research that objectifying women can make sexual assault more likely. NPR reported that Trump has exhibited questionable behavior in his treatment of women for some time, using offensive language to describe women, including Megyn Kelly, Rosie O'Donnell, and former Miss Universe Alicia

Machado. Arwa Mahdawi of *The Guardian* called his past remarks a "masterclass in rape culture", pointing to statements such as "26,000 unreported sexual assaults in the military—only 238 convictions. What did these geniuses expect when they put men and women together?" and "women, you have to treat 'em like shit."[237]

Considering all of the accusations made against Donald Trump, he did a news conference and claimed, "I have no idea who these women are".[238] If the accusations from the 20-plus women are true, this causes one to wonder about the following:

Why would women want to marry a man like Donald Trump?

Why would people, especially women, vote for a man like Donald Trump?

Why is Donald Trump still walking around as a free man?

Harvey Weinstein is in Jail.

Jeffrey Epstein was jailed and hanged himself in his cell.

Why were these men jailed, and Donald Trump's sexual misconduct was ignored by law enforcement?

If these accusations are true, and we have no reason to believe 20 or more women would lie or misrepresent the incidents they recount, then Donald John Trump is a sick, perverted criminal. He either needs professional psychological help or he needs to be put in jail as a menace to the general public, especially women. Furthermore, what is the problem with the American people who support his candidacy for the 2024 President? This is an insight into the mentality and dysfunctional perspective of a significant number of American citizens, but in America, they have the freedom to be stupid, ignorant, and have a preference for a sexual deviant as president. After all, America is the bastion of Democracy, equality, and freedom, except for Asians, Hispanics, Blacks, Jews, and LGBTQ and all others who are non-White.

Mimesis Stage 2 for Donald John Trump – Politics

Trump's political party affiliation has changed many times. He registered as a Republican in 1987, a member of the Independence Party, the New York state affiliate of the Reform Party, in 1999, a Democrat in 2001, a Republican in 2009, unaffiliated in 2011, and a Republican in 2012. One has to wonder what Donald Trump's political views. Understanding the personality of Trump, one would believe he has no stable political views. He follows the platform of: What is best for Donald Trump.[239]

For years, Trump has been courting a run for political office. In 1987, Trump took out a full-page ad in three newspapers stating his viewpoints on foreign policy.[240] In 1988, he approached Lee Atwater requesting to be considered as the  Republican Vice President Nominee running mate with George H. W. Bush.[241]

In 2000, Trump started a run in the California and Michigan primaries for nomination as the Reform Party candidate for the 2000 United States presidential election. However, he withdrew from the race in February 2000. A July 1999 poll citing Trump running against Republican nominee George W. Bush and Democratic nominee Al Gore showed Trump with only seven percent support. He decided not to run.[242]

In 2011, Trump thought about running against President Barack Obama in the 2012 election. He made his first speech at the Conservative Political Action Conference (CPAC) in February 2011.[243] In May 2011, he announced he would not run. Instead, he endorsed Mitt Romney in February 2012, who lost to Barack Obama.[244]

In 2016, Trump decided to run for President after Barack Obama served two terms as president. Trump ran against Hilary Clinton, the wife of Bill Clinton, the 42nd two-term President of the United States of America.

Trump's fame and controversial rhetoric gained him an unprecedented amount of free media coverage, contributing to gaining him standing in the Republican primaries.[245] He adopted the phrase "truthful hyperbole", coined by his ghostwriter Tony Schwartz, to describe his public speaking style.

Hyperbole is an exaggerated statement or claim, not meant to be taken literally.

The term "truthful hyperbole" is spin for confusing the public, a contradiction of terms, BS.

His campaign statements were often opaque and suggestive, insulting, and an unprecedented number of them were false. The *Los Angeles Times* wrote, "Never in modern presidential politics has a major candidate made false statements as routinely as Trump has."[246] Trump said he disdained political correctness and frequently made claims of media bias. He was alienating opponents and people who did not agree with him and who criticized his viewpoints. [247]

Trump announced his candidacy in June 2015. He quickly rose to the top of opinion polls. He became the front-runner in March 2016 and was declared the presumptive Republican nominee in May. Hillary Clinton led Trump in national polling throughout the campaign, but in early July, her lead narrowed. In mid-July, Trump selected Indiana governor Mike Pence as his vice presidential running mate, and the two were officially nominated at the 2016 Republican National Convention. Trump and Clinton faced off in three presidential debates in September and October 2016. Trump twice refused to say whether he would accept the result of the election if he lost.[248] Trump's political ideology was right-wing populist. [249]

Trumps campaign platform consisted of the following: [250]

Renegotiation of U.S.–China relations.

Free trade agreements such as NAFTA and the Trans-Pacific Partnership.

Strongly enforcing immigration laws.

Build a wall along the U.S.–Mexico border.

Pursue energy independence.

Opposed climate change regulations such as the Clean Power Plan.

Withdrawal from the Paris Agreement.

Modernization and expansion of services for veterans.

Repealing and replacing the Affordable Care Act.

Abolish Common Core education standards.

Invest in America's infrastructure,

Simplify the tax code and reduce taxes for all economic classes.

Impose tariffs on imports by companies that offshore jobs.

A non-interventionist approach to foreign policy.

Increase military spending.

Extreme vetting or banning immigrants from Muslim-majority countries·

Pre-empt domestic Islamic terrorism,

Aggressive military action against the Islamic State of Iraq and the Levant.

NATO is obsolete, withdraw.

During his campaign and during his presidency, Trump was a facilitator for the far-right ideologies, ideas, beliefs, and organizations to have voice and be brought into the mainstream. Trump was slow to disavow an endorsement from David Duke or any other far-right racist, after he was questioned about it during a *CNN* interview on **February 28, 2016**. Duke supported Trump and said he and like-minded people voted for Trump because of his promises to "take our country back". The phrase "take our country back" is rhetoric for restoring White supremacy. In **August 2016**, Trump hired Steve Bannon, the executive chairman of *Breitbart News*—described by Bannon as "the platform for the alt-right"—as his campaign CEO. Bannon is known as an avowed racist. The alt-right movement coalesced around and supported Trump's candidacy, due in part to its opposition to multiculturalism and immigration.[251]

Contrary to the practice of every individual running for president since 1976, Trump did not release his tax returns, and reneged on his promises to do so in 2014 and 2015 if he ran for office. He said his tax returns were being audited, and his lawyers had advised him against releasing them, which was a lie. After a lengthy court battle to block the release of his tax returns and other records to the Manhattan district attorney for a criminal investigation, including two appeals by Trump to the United States Supreme Court, in February 2021, the high court allowed the records to be released to the prosecutor for review by a grand jury.[252] In October 2016, portions of Trump's state filings for **1995** were leaked to a reporter from *The New York Times*. They show that Trump had declared a loss of $916 million that year, which could have let him avoid taxes for up to 18 years.[253]

Mimesis Stage 2 for Donald John Trump – The President of the United States of America

On November 8, 2016, Donald Trump became President of the United States of America and was inaugurated on January 20, 2017. He won an upset victory over Hilary Clinton. Trump received 306 pledged electoral votes versus 232 for Clinton. The official counts were 304 and 227, respectively, after adjustments on both sides. Trump received almost 2.9 million fewer popular votes than Clinton, which made him the fifth person to be elected president while losing the popular vote. Trump is the only president who did not serve in the military or hold any government office before becoming president.[254] On the day after Trump's inauguration, an estimated 2.6 million people worldwide, including an estimated half million in Washington, D.C., protested against Trump in the Women's Marches. [255]

Trump was elected despite claims of Russian interference in the 2016 election. In January 2017, American intelligence agencies (the CIA, the FBI, and the NSA) jointly stated with "high confidence" that the Russian government interfered in the 2016 presidential election to favor the election of Trump. In March 2017, FBI Director James Comey told Congress, the FBI, as part of our counterintelligence mission, is investigating the Russian government's efforts to interfere in the 2016 presidential election. That includes investigating the nature of any links between individuals associated with the Trump campaign and the Russian government, and whether there was any coordination between the campaign and Russia's interference. [256]

Trump was viewed to have conflicts of interest while serving as president. While in office, Trump was accused of being a "grafter" in the United States Government. He owned a Washington hotel that people coming to do business in Washington thought it strategically beneficial to stay at. He owned Golf courses and hotels throughout the United States that he, along with his secret service detail, stayed at during his travels. The government was charged with these accommodations. He rarely used Camp David, the retreat away from Washington, as most other Presidents but rather Trump chose to use Mar-a-lago, his Florida resort, as a substitute for Camp David, at a cost to the

United States government. When Trump and his entourage stayed at his properties, prices were increased.

Before his inauguration, Trump moved his businesses into a revocable trust run by his sons, Eric and Donald Jr, and a business associate. He continued to profit from his businesses and to know how his administration's policies affected his businesses. Though Trump said he would eschew "new foreign deals", the Trump Organization pursued expansions of its operations in Dubai, Scotland, and the Dominican Republic.

Trump was sued for violating the Domestic and Foreign Emoluments Clauses of the U.S. Constitution, marking the first time that the clauses had been substantively litigated. The plaintiffs said that Trump's business interests could allow foreign governments to influence him. After Trump's term had ended, the U.S. Supreme Court dismissed the cases as moot. [257]

Mimesis 2 for Donald John Trump as President of the United States – The Economy

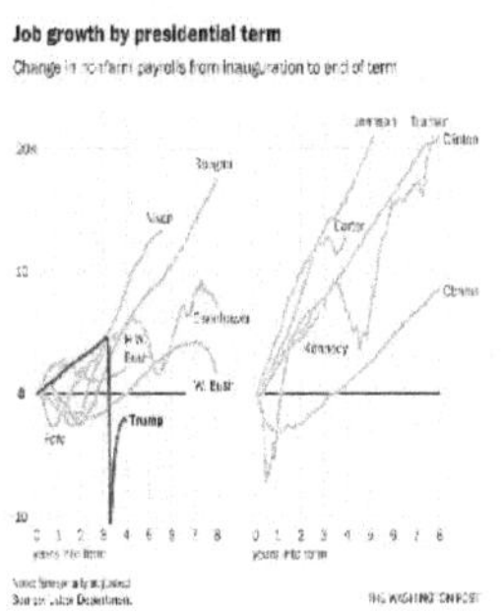

President Trump took office at the crest of the longest economic expansion in U.S. history, inherited from the Obama administration. He leaves presiding over the worst labor market in modern U.S. history, as an already-sputtering economic recovery has turned negative.[258]

Job growth by presidential term

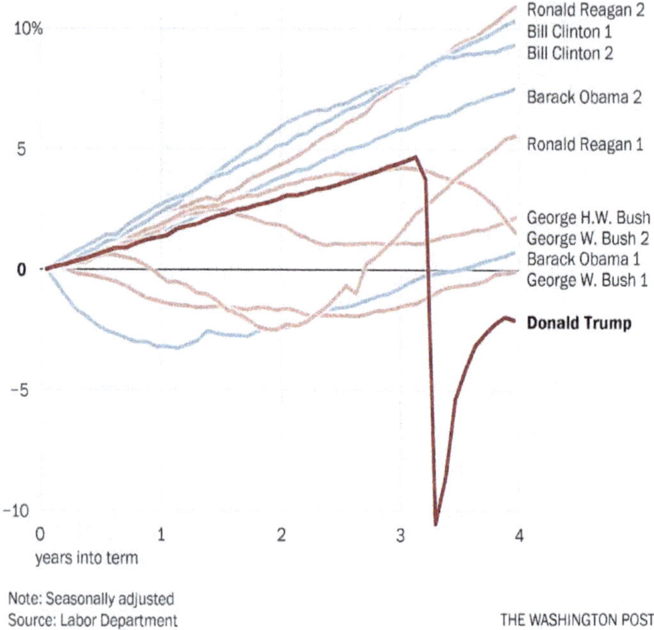

The only category where President Trump does not lag behind his predecessors is Transportation and warehousing. That sector, which pays less than either manufacturing or mining, has added more than half a million jobs since Trump took office, thanks to the boom in online retail during the lockdown era of Covid-19. In all fairness to Donald Trump, his administration was plagued by the COVID-19 pandemic. Otherwise, maybe he would not have compared so poorly (See the next Chart).[259] Who knows,

Trump against all other modern presidents, by industry

Change in jobs by industry, from inauguration to end of term

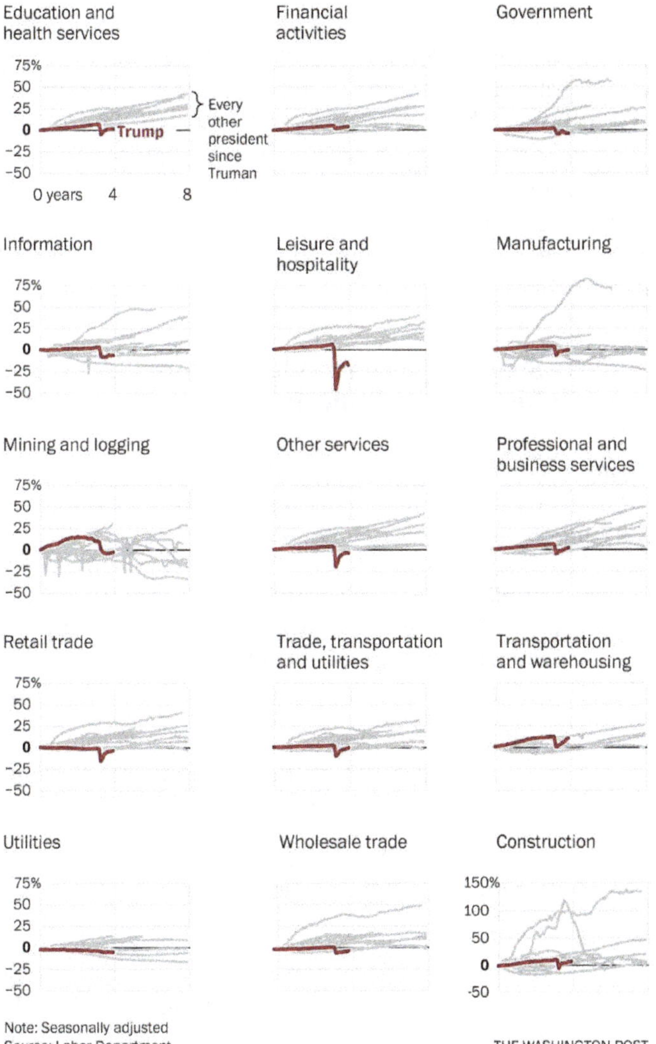

Note: Seasonally adjusted
Source: Labor Department

THE WASHINGTON POST

Despite a campaign promise to eliminate the national debt in eight years, Trump approved large increases in government spending and the 2017 tax cut. As a result, the federal budget deficit increased by almost 50%, to nearly $1 trillion in 2019. Under Trump, the U.S. national debt increased by 39 percent, reaching $27.75 trillion by the end of his term; the U.S. debt-to-GDP ratio also hit a post-World War II high. Trump also failed to deliver the $1 trillion infrastructure spending plan on which he had campaigned. Trump is the only modern U.S. president to leave office with a smaller workforce than when he took office, by 3 million people.[260]

Mimesis Stage 2 for Donald John Trump, President of the United States – Policies

During his administration, Trump took the following positions on issues that were controversial and heavily debated among the American public.

> Trump stated that he was committed to appointing "pro-life" justices, pledging to appoint justices who would "automatically" overturn *Roe v. Wade.*

> He also said he supported "traditional marriage" but considered the nationwide legality of same-sex marriage a "settled" issue.

> Trump said he is opposed to gun control in general, although his views have shifted over time.

> Trump is a long-time advocate of capital punishment. Under his administration, the federal government executed 13 prisoners, more

than in the previous 56 years combined, and after a 17-year moratorium in 2016.

Trump said he supported the use of interrogation torture methods such as waterboarding, but later appeared to recant this due to the opposition of Defense Secretary James Mattis.

In March 2017, his administration rolled back key components of the Obama administration's workplace protections against discrimination against LGBT people.

After several mass shootings during his term, he said he would propose legislation to curtail gun violence, but this was abandoned in November 2019.

His administration took an anti-marijuana position, revoking Obama-era policies that provided protections for states that legalized marijuana.

One of the most disturbing policies of the Trump administration was the separation of more than 5,400 children of migrant families from their parents at the U.S.–Mexico border while the immigrants were attempting to enter the U.S. A sharp increase in the number of family separations at the border starting from the summer of 2017. In April 2018, the Trump administration announced a "zero tolerance" policy. Every adult suspected of illegal entry would be criminally prosecuted. This resulted in family separations, as the migrant adults were put in criminal detention for prosecution, while their children were separated as unaccompanied alien minors. Administration officials described the policy as a way to deter illegal immigration.[261] In reality, the policy of separating children from their parents was insensitive and racist.

Donald Trump took an anti-American position in his interaction with Russia and North Korea. He showed the American people how weak he really was and displayed an admiration for dictators. While every intelligence agency in America claimed with a high degree of certainty that Russia interfered in the 2016 election, Trump repeatedly took the position of Vladimir Putin and denied that Russia interfered in the election. Trump repeatedly praised and rarely criticized Russian President Vladimir Putin, and at their Helsinki Conference, Trump did everything but get on his knees and shine Putin's shoes. [262]

In 2017, when North Korea's nuclear weapons were increasingly seen as a serious threat, Trump escalated his rhetoric, warning that North Korean aggression would be met with "fire and fury like the world has never seen". In 2017, Trump declared that he wanted North Korea's "complete denuclearization" and engaged in name-calling with leader Kim Jong-un.

After this period of tension, Trump and Kim exchanged at least 27 letters in which the two men described a warm personal friendship. Trump met Kim three times: in Singapore in 2018, in Hanoi in 2019, and in the Korean Demilitarized Zone in 2019. Trump became the first sitting U.S. president to meet a North Korean leader or to set foot on North Korean soil

Trump appointed 226 Article III judges, including 54 to the courts of appeals and three to the Supreme Court: Neil Gorsuch, Brett Kavanaugh, and Amy Coney Barrett. As president, Trump criticized courts and judges with whom he disagreed, often in personal terms, and questioned the judiciary's constitutional authority. Trump's attacks on the courts have drawn disdain from others, including sitting federal judges, who are concerned about the effect of Trump's statements on judicial independence and public confidence in the judiciary. Many of the judges appointed by Trump were surrounded in controversy (sexual harassment charges) or considered incompetent.[263]

Mimesis Stage 2 for Donald John Trump – The COVID-19 Pandemic

It is important to review the events and decisions that took place during the COVID-19 pandemic. That was a significant time in the Trump administration because more people died during that period. According to the Centers for Disease Control (CDC), between the outbreak of COVID-19 in January 2020 to February 2023, 1,125,366 people died from the Covid-16 virus.[264]

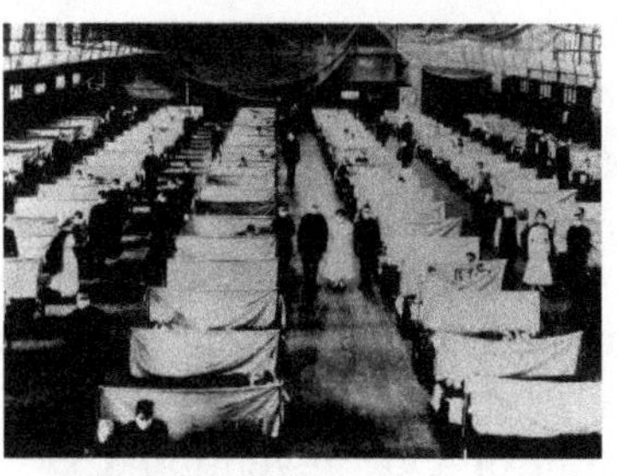

The Influenza (Casualty scene left) virus only killed 441,000 people. This makes the COVID-19 pandemic one of the worst in American history. Therefore, it is important to understand the circumstances surrounding the COVID-19 pandemic and how it was handled. [265] The total number of Americans who died from COVID-19 (1,125,366) is more than twice the number of Americans who died in World War II (405,399) and the Civil War (655,000). Therefore, is important to look at this phenomenon as an evaluation factor in the Trump administration.[266]

Allegedly, in December 2019, COVID-19 was developed in Wuhan, China. The SARS-CoV-2 virus spread worldwide within weeks. The first confirmed case in the U.S. was reported on January 20, 2020. The outbreak was officially declared a public health emergency by Health and Human Services (HHS) Secretary Alex Azar on January 31, 2020.[267] Trump's public statements on COVID-19 were in conflict with his private statements. In February 2020, Trump publicly asserted that the outbreak in the U.S. "was less deadly than influenza, and very much under control, and would soon be over". At the same time, he acknowledged the opposite in a private conversation with Bob Woodward. In March 2020, Trump privately told Woodward that he deliberately "played it down" in public so as not to create panic.[268] Trump was slow to address the spread of the disease, initially dismissing the threat and ignoring repeated public health warnings and calls for action from health officials within his own administration, including Health Secretary Azar. Trump's focus during January and February was on the economic and political impact of COVID-19. For the most part, he ignored the danger of the disease. By mid-March, most global financial markets had severely contracted in response to the emerging pandemic.[269] Trump continued to claim that a vaccine was less than a year away, although HHS and Centers for Disease Control and Prevention (CDC) officials had repeatedly told him that vaccine development would take 12–18 months. Trump falsely claimed that "anybody who wants a test can get a test," despite the limited availability of tests.[270]

On March 6, Trump signed the Coronavirus Preparedness and Response Supplemental Appropriations Act into law, which provided $8.3 billion in emergency funding for federal agencies. On March 11, the World Health Organization (WHO) recognized the spread of COVID-19 as a pandemic, and Trump announced partial travel restrictions for most of Europe, effective March 13 That same day, he gave his first serious assessment of the virus in a nationwide Oval Office address, calling the outbreak "horrible" but "a temporary moment" and saying there was no financial crisis. On March 13, he declared a national emergency, freeing up federal resources. [271]

In September 2019, the Trump administration terminated the United States Agency for International Development's PREDICT program, a $200 million epidemiological research program initiated in 2009 to provide early warning of pandemics abroad. The program trained scientists in sixty foreign laboratories to detect and respond to viruses that have the potential to cause pandemics. One such laboratory was the Wuhan lab that first identified the virus that causes COVID-19. After revival in April 2020, the program was given two 6-month extensions to help fight COVID-19 in the U.S. and other countries. [272]

On April 22, Trump signed an executive order restricting some forms of immigration to the United States. In late spring and early summer, with infections and death counts continuing to rise, he adopted a strategy of blaming the states for the growing pandemic, rather than accepting that his initial assessments of the course of the pandemic were overly optimistic or his failure to provide presidential leadership. [273]

Trump established the White House Coronavirus Task Force on January 29, 2020. Beginning in mid-March, Trump held a daily task force press conference, joined by medical experts and other administration officials, sometimes disagreeing with them by promoting unproven treatments. Trump was the main speaker at the briefings, where he praised his own response to the pandemic, frequently criticized rival presidential candidate Joe Biden, and denounced the press. On March 16, he acknowledged for the first time that the pandemic was not under control and that months of disruption to daily lives and a recession might occur. His repeated use of the terms "Chinese virus" and "China virus" to describe COVID-19 drew criticism from health experts. [274]

By early April, as the pandemic worsened and amid criticism of his administration's response, Trump refused to admit any mistakes in his handling of the outbreak, instead blaming the media, Democratic state governors, the previous administration, China, and the World Health Organization (WHO). The daily coronavirus task force briefings ended in late April, after a briefing at which Trump suggested the dangerous idea of injecting disinfectant to treat COVID-19; the comment was widely condemned by medical professionals.[275]

In early May, Trump proposed the phase-out of the coronavirus task force and its replacement with another group centered on reopening the economy. Amid a backlash, Trump said the task force would "indefinitely" continue. By the end of May, the coronavirus task force's meetings were sharply reduced.[276]

Prior to the pandemic, Trump criticized the World Health Organization (WHO) and other international bodies, which he stated were taking advantage of U.S. aid. His administration's proposed 2021 federal budget reductions for the WHO by more than half. In May and April, Trump accused the WHO of "severely mismanaging and covering up the spread of the coronavirus" and alleged without evidence that the organization was under Chinese control and had enabled the Chinese government's concealment of the origins of the pandemic. He then announced that he was withdrawing funding for the organization. Trump's criticisms and actions regarding the WHO were seen as attempts to distract attention from his own mishandling of the pandemic. In July 2020, Trump announced the formal withdrawal of the United States from the WHO effective July 2021. The decision was widely condemned by health and government officials as "short-sighted", "senseless", and "dangerous".[277]

In June and July, Trump said several times that the U.S. would have fewer cases of coronavirus if it did less testing, that having a large number of reported cases "makes us look bad". The CDC guideline at the time was that any person exposed to the virus should be "quickly identified and tested," even if they are not showing symptoms, because asymptomatic people can still spread the virus. In August 2020, the CDC quietly lowered its recommendation for testing, advising that people who have been exposed to the virus, but are not showing symptoms, "do not necessarily need a test". The change in guidelines was made by HHS political appointees under Trump administration, against the wishes of CDC scientists. The day after this political interference was reported, the testing guideline was changed back to its original recommendation, stressing that anyone who has been in contact with an infected person should be tested. [278]

In April 2020, Republican-connected groups organized anti-lockdown protests against the measures state governments were taking to combat the pandemic; Trump encouraged the protests on Twitter, even though the targeted states did not meet the Trump administration's own guidelines for reopening. In April 2020, he first supported, then later criticized, Georgia Governor Brian Kemp's plan to reopen some nonessential businesses. Throughout spring, he increasingly pushed for ending the restrictions as a way to reverse the damage to the country's economy. [279]

Trump often refused to wear a face mask at public events, contrary to his own administration's April 2020 guidance that Americans should wear masks in public and despite nearly unanimous medical consensus that masks are important to preventing the spread of the virus. By June, Trump had said masks were a "double-edged sword"; ridiculed Biden for wearing masks; continually emphasized that mask-wearing was optional; and suggested that wearing a mask was a political statement against him personally. Trump's contradiction of medical recommendations weakened national efforts to mitigate the pandemic.[280] Despite record numbers of COVID-19 cases in the U.S. from mid-June onward and an increasing percentage of positive test results, Trump largely continued to downplay the pandemic, including his false claim in July 2020 that 99 percent of COVID-19 cases are "totally harmless". He also began insisting that all states should open schools to in-person education in the fall despite a July increase in reported cases. [281]

Trump repeatedly pressured federal health agencies to take actions he favored, such as approving unproven treatments or speeding up the approval of vaccines. Trump administration political appointees at HHS sought to control CDC communications to the public that undermined Trump's claims that the pandemic was under control. CDC resisted many of the changes but increasingly allowed HHS personnel to review articles and suggest changes before publication. Trump alleged without evidence that FDA scientists were part of a "deep state" opposing him, and delaying approval of vaccines and treatments to hurt him politically.[282]

Then came the irony of all ironies. COVID-19 broke out at the White House, and Donald Trump, his wife, Melania Trump, and his son Baron Trump all contracted the COVID-19 virus. Many staff members and visitors to the White House also became infected. In October 2020, Trump was hospitalized at Walter Reed National Military Medical Center, reportedly due to labored breathing and a fever. He was treated with antiviral and experimental antibody drugs and a steroid. He returned to the White House on October 5 with the disease. During and after his treatment, he continued to downplay the virus. In 2021, it was revealed that his condition had been far more serious; he had dangerously low blood oxygen levels, a high fever, and lung infiltrates, indicating a severe case of the disease. [283]

The voting public realized that Trump's handling of the COVID-19 pandemic cost lives, as reported based on numerous false claims, lies, and deceptions. His successor, Joe Biden, made the pandemic a campaign issue, and the facts spoke for themselves. Trump lost the 2020 Presidential election to Joe Biden.

It is generally, if not widely, acknowledged that Donald Trump and his administration did a poor job of handling the pandemic. They did not listen to experts, and as a result, lives were lost. More lives were lost than needed to be had the Trump administration followed the advice of medical experts. At one point, Donald Trump suggested that disinfectant should be taken (ingested) as a way to remedy COVID-19. Now, how stupid is that?

Mimesis Stage 2 for Donald John Trump Investigations [284]

Donald Trump is the only President in history to be charged with and put on trial for criminal behavior before being in office, while in office after leaving office. Depending on the results of the follow crimes he is charged with, he may become the only President in United States history to be convicted of crime (s).[285]

Manhattan Criminal Case

The Manhattan district attorney, Alvin L. Bragg, brought the case over Mr. Trump's role, when he was running for president, in a hush-money payment to a porn star, Stormy Daniels, who then agreed to keep quiet about her story of an affair with him. He is scheduled to be arraigned on Tuesday, April 4, 2023.

Classified Documents Inquiry

A special counsel appointed by the Justice Department, Jack Smith, is conducting a criminal investigation into Mr. Trump's handling of sensitive government documents after he left office. After Trump left office, the FBI investigated his residence at Mar-a-Lago and found numerous documents marked Classified, Trump failed to turn in when he left office, even after he was requested and warned to do so.

New York State Civil Inquiry

In a September lawsuit, the New York attorney general, Letitia James, accused Mr. Trump in a September lawsuit of lying to lenders and insurers by fraudulently overvaluing his assets by billions of dollars. The case is now being taken over by District Attorney Alvin Bragg. Trump is formally charged with falsifying records and misleading the American public by paying off and hush payments to people who had knowledge of his indiscretions. The motivation was to prevent negative information on Trump from getting out to the public, which might have harmed his chances of becoming president. How Trump handled the payoffs is the issue. Evidently, the District Attorney has information that Trump handled the payoffs fraudulently. [286]

Georgia Criminal Inquiry

Prosecutors in Georgia are expected to make a decision soon on whether to seek indictments in their investigation of Mr. Trump and some of his allies over their efforts to interfere with the results of the 2020 presidential election in the state. The Georgia Criminal case is based on a tape-recorded phone call where Donald Trump appealed to the Georgia Secretary of State to "find him" enough votes to overturn the Georgia election results.

Donald Trump is alleged to have attempted to overturn the 2020 election. It was his efforts to overturn the election that led to the insurrection at the Capitol when Trump urged to crowd to move to the Capitol and demonstrate against the House of Representatives' final vote to approve Joe Biden as President of the United States. Alabama Republican Mo Brooks made a public statement that former President Donald Trump raised the idea to him, on many occasions, to conduct an effort to rescind the 2020 election results and reinstall him as president.[287] A bipartisan committee was convened to investigate the actions of Donald Trump in instigating the January 6, 2020, insurrection at the United States Capitol building by Donald Trump supporters. The committee findings are now before the Justice Department to determine what, if any, action should be taken.

These cases do not count the case brought against Trump by E. Jean Carroll who is suing him for battery and defamation based on her claim that he raped her.[288]

Mimesis Stage 2 for Donald John Trump President of the United States - Impeachments

Donald Trump has a natural way of cutting corners, doing things under the table, getting with he wants without concern for methodology (right way or wrong way, doesn't matter). These are things he is teaching his kids. However, as a result of this personality trait he is the only President in history to be impeached twice.

In August 2019, a whistleblower filed a complaint with the Inspector General of the Intelligence Community about a July 25 phone call between Trump and President of Ukraine Volodymyr Zelenskyy, during which Trump had pressured Zelenskyy to investigate Crowd Strike, Democratic presidential candidate Biden and his son Hunter Biden. He pressured Zelenskyy to pursue the investigation based on the funding the United States provided to Ukraine. The whistleblower indicated that the release of funding to the Ukraine was contingent on Zelenskyy's pursuit of the investigations. The White House tried to cover-up the incident. The whistleblower stated that the call was part of a wider campaign by the Trump administration and his attorney Rudy Giuliani that may have included withholding financial aid from Ukraine in July 2019 and canceling Pence's May 2019 Ukraine trip. [289]

House Speaker Nancy Pelosi initiated a formal impeachment inquiry on September 24. Trump then confirmed that he withheld military aid from Ukraine, offering contradictory reasons for the decision. On September 25, the Trump administration released a memorandum of the phone call which confirmed that, after Zelenskyy mentioned purchasing American anti-tank missiles, Trump asked him to discuss investigating Biden and his son with Giuliani and Barr.[290] Trump was cleared of impeachment charges when the case went before the Republican majority United States Senate.[291]

Trump was impeached a second time for insurrection. He was accused of contributing to the insurrection of a riot and break into the United States Capital on the January 6, 2020.

On January 11, 2021, an article of impeachment charging Trump with incitement of insurrection against the U.S. government was introduced to the House. The House voted 232–197 to impeach Trump on January 13, making him the first U.S. president to be impeached twice. When the Articles of Impeachment went to the Senate for ruling that would strip Trump of his powers and duties via Section 4 of the 25th Amendment. On February 13, following a five-day Senate trial, Trump was acquitted when the Senate voted 57–43 for conviction, falling ten votes short of the two-thirds majority required to convict; Every Democrat voted to impeach and seven Republicans joined in voting to convict.[292]

A Congressional Committee was established to investigate Donald Trump's role in the Capitol riots. As a result of the House Congressional Committee investigation, a report was sent to the FBI recommending that Donald Trump be investigated and held accountable for his role in the Capitol riot. [293]

Mimesis Stage 2 for Donald John Trump – A man is known by the company he keeps [294]

Casualties of supporting Donald Trump

There is a saying: "A man is known by the company he keeps". In the case of Donald Trump, at least 11 people and 1 news company that were involved in Trump's presidential campaigns or his administration have been charged with crimes or sued for false claims. Tom Barrack, who chaired Trump's inaugural committee and has been a longtime friend, was accused of illegal foreign lobbying on behalf of the United Arab Emirates. In addition, others who operated in Trump's orbit have also been charged and/or convicted of crimes. Most have spent time in jail. In addition, Fox News, a major supporter of Donald Trump, was sued by Dominion Voting Systems for network promotion of misinformation and false claims in support of Donald Trump's lies about his 2020 election loss.

1. Steve Bannon: Trump's political Svengali was charged with fraud in August 2020 for a fundraising scam tied to raising dollars to build Trump's much-ballyhooed border wall. The allegation, which Bannon has denied, was that he and others involved in the We Build The Wall group used money raised to pay for lavish personal expenses.

2. Tom Barrack: Barrack was charged on seven counts on Tuesday. The allegations, according to the indictment, center on the idea that Barrack used his closeness to Trump to "advance the interests of and provide intelligence to the UAE while simultaneously failing to notify the Attorney General that their actions were taken at the direction of senior UAE officials." Following Trump's 2016 victory, Barrack asked UAE officials to provide him with a "wish list" they hoped for from the administration over the first 100 days of Trump's presidency. "The defendant is charged with acting under the direction or control of the most senior leaders of the U.A.E. over a course of years," wrote the prosecutors of Barrack.

3. Elliott Broidy: Broidy, a top fundraiser for Trump's 2016 presidential campaign, pleaded guilty in October 2020 to conducting a secret lobbying campaign in exchange for millions of dollars. As CNN's Kara Scannell wrote at the time of his Broidy's guilty plea: "Broidy was charged earlier this month with conspiracy for failing to register and disclose his role in a lobbying effort aimed at stopping a criminal investigation into massive fraud at a Malaysian investment fund and advocating for the removal of a Chinese billionaire living in the US."

4. Michael Cohen: The one-time fixer for Trump, Cohen was sentenced to three years in prison for a series of crimes, most notably secret hush-money payments made during the final months of the 2016 presidential campaign to two women alleging affairs with Trump. The sentencing judge said that Cohen had pleaded guilty to "a veritable smorgasbord" of crimes. Cohen turned informant on Trump and, in sworn testimony in front of Congress in 2019, Cohen called Trump "a racist," "a conman," and "a cheat" – and insisted that the president was fully aware of the hush-money payments.

5. Michael Flynn: Flynn spent a brief stint as Trump's national security adviser before being forced to resign after he failed to disclose the depth and breadth of his contacts with Russian officials during the transition. Later that year, Flynn admitted that he had lied to the FBI about his contact with Russia and had also done work for Turkey as an unauthorized lobbyist. In early 2020, Flynn and his legal team sought to have his conviction overturned. That effort was rendered moot when Trump pardoned him in November 2020.

6. Rick Gates: Gates, deputy to the campaign chairman of Trump's 2016 campaign, pleaded guilty to aiding and abetting Paul Manafort in concealing $75 million in foreign bank accounts. Gates turned informant for the government as part of the broader probe into Russian meddling in the 2016 election and was sentenced to 45 days in jail.

7. Paul Manafort: Trump's campaign manager for part of the 2016 presidential campaign, Manafort pleaded guilty in 2018 to one count of conspiracy against the US and one count of conspiracy to obstruct justice due to attempts to tamper with witnesses, and agreed to cooperate with the ongoing Russia probe. Manafort was sentenced to 47 months in prison in 2019. Trump pardoned Manafort, who wound up serving just under two years in prison, in the final weeks of his presidency.

8. George Nader: An informal foreign policy adviser to Trump's 2016 campaign, Nader cooperated heavily with special counsel Robert Mueller's probe into Russian interference in the 2016 election. In early 2020, he pleaded guilty to two counts of sex crimes involving minors.

9. George Papadopoulos: Papadopoulos, a relatively junior adviser to Trump's campaign, was sentenced to 12 days in prison for lying to investigators about his contacts with individuals tied to Russia. Papadopoulos was defiant about his innocence; "The truth will all be out," he tweeted the night before reporting to prison. "Not even a prison sentence can stop that momentum." Trump pardoned Papadopoulos in December 2020.

10. Roger Stone: Stone spent years advising Trump, although he was only formally affiliated with the 2016 campaign very briefly. He was convicted in November 2019 for lying to Congress and threatening a witness regarding his efforts for Trump's campaign. According to the judge, Stone's actions "led to an inaccurate, incorrect and incomplete report" from the House on Russia, WikiLeaks and the Trump campaign. Stone, and stop me if you've heard this one before, was pardoned by Trump in December 2020.

11. Allen Weisselberg: Earlier this month, the longtime chief financial officer for the Trump Organization was charged with tax crimes tied to perks he was given in lieu of salary. "All told, the indictment alleged, Weisselberg evaded taxes on $1.76 million in income over a period beginning in 2005 and concealed for years that he was a resident of New York City, thereby avoiding paying city income taxes," wrote CNN s Erica Orden, Kara Scannell and Sonia Moghe. Weisselberg pleaded not guilty. The Trump Organization, which was also indicted and has pleaded not guilty, called Weisselberg a "pawn in a scorched earth attempt to harm the former president."

12. Fox News: [295]

Fox News agreed Tuesday to pay Dominion Voting Systems nearly $800 million ($787.5 million) to avert a trial in the voting machine company's lawsuit that would have exposed how the network promoted lies, in support of Donald Trump's false claims about election fraud. in the 2020 presidential election.

The company argues that Fox News broadcast a series of blatant lies in support of Trump's stolen election conspiracy theory and that hosts and guests broadcast 100 false statements: among them, that Smartmatic was involved in 2020 election counts in six battleground states when, in fact, it was present only at the count in Los Angeles County.

13. Tucker Carlson, Fox News' highest-rated host and their number 1 news anchor, was fired. Because Carlson acted as a trumpet player playing to the tunes of Donald Trump, his Fox News firing listed him as a casualty of the Donald Trump brigade. Carlson backed Donald Trump's claims that the election was stolen. While the exact reason for Carlson's firing at Fox News remains unclear, a lawsuit against the network stemming from Dominion Voting Systems' defamation case appears to have been a central factor.[296]

14. The Proud Boys on May 4th, 2023, a jury in the District of Columbia returned guilty verdicts on multiple felonies against five members of the Proud Boys, finding four of the defendants guilty of seditious conspiracy for their actions before and during the breach of the U.S. Capitol on Jan. 6, 2021.

Henry "Enrique" Tarrio, 39, of Miami, the former national chairman of the Proud Boys; Ethan Nordean, 32, of Auburn, Washington; Joseph Biggs, 39, of Ormond Beach, Florida; Zachary Rehl, 37, of Philadelphia, were found guilty of seditious conspiracy and conspiracy to obstruct an official proceeding. The four defendants and co-defendant Dominic Pezzola, 45, of Rochester, New York, were also found guilty of obstruction of an official proceeding, conspiracy to prevent Members of Congress and federal law enforcement officers from discharging their duties, civil disorder, and destruction of government property. Pezzola was also found guilty of assaulting, resisting, or impeding certain officers and robbery involving government property.

In the 27 months since Jan. 6, 2021, more than 1,000 individuals have been arrested in nearly all 50 states for crimes related to the breach of the U.S. Capitol, including more than 320 individuals charged with assaulting or impeding law enforcement. The investigation remains ongoing.[297]

According to the Proud Boys, they were following the directives they believed came from Donald Trump himself.

The foundation of the government's case was hundreds of messages exchanged by Proud Boys in the days leading up to Jan. 6 that show the far-right extremist group supporting Trump's false claims of a stolen election and trading fears over what would happen when Biden took office. [298]

Mimesis 2 for Donald John Trump – Personal and Public Opinion

What do people think about Donald Trump? The final Mimesis for Donald Trump is still outstanding. He has been a controversial figure for years. There are people who "hate" him, and there are people who "love" him. In the presidential election that Trump lost, 74 million people voted for him, approximately 1/3 of the total American population. However, he lost because 84 million people voted for Joe Biden. Trump is an alienating force among liberals and Democrats. He is also an alienating force among many republicans. However, he is a solidifying force among hard-core conservatives, White racists, and many in the upper-class business community. Among minorities, he is for the most part held in disdain.

Mimesis Stage 2 for Donald John Trump - Relationship with the press

Donald Trump has sought after and craved media attention throughout his career. He constantly refers to "ratings" as an indicator of popularity and support. For the most part, he is right. However, he fails to realize that not everyone follows him in the media because they support him. Muhammad Ali once stated that some people come to see him fight because they want him to win. Some people come to his fights because they want to see him lose. It does not matter to Ali why they come because they all pay for the seats.

Trump maintains a "love–hate" relationship with the press. In the 2016 campaign, Trump benefited from a record amount of free media coverage, elevating his standing in the Republican primaries. *The New York Times* writer Amy Chozick wrote in 2018 that Trump's media dominance enthralled the public and created "must-see TV". Trump's media savvy is a result of his time spent hosting *The Apprentice* television show. It was a popular show. People saw Trump as a Reality Show host, not necessarily as a President of the United States material. However, his experience as host of the Apprentice TV Reality Show drew attention to him, and people across America became Apprentice and Trump followers, in that they watched his show diligently. As a TV personality, people became enthralled with Donald Trump. As a result, when Trump ran for president, he received a considerable amount of free news coverage, simply because he was Donald Trump running for President of the United States of America. Some people might confuse curiosity about Trump in place of Support for Trump. The graph below indicates how Trump received more free media coverage than his competition. Some cite this as a reason for his 2016 primary victory and his presidential victory.

As a candidate and as president, Trump often accused the press of bias, calling it the "fake news media" and "the enemy of the people". Trump has a strategy for criticizing the press. **In 2018**, journalist Lesley Stahl recounted Trump's saying he intentionally demeaned and discredited the media "so when you write negative stories about me no one will believe you". In other words Trump himself is aware of his alienating personality and his disagreeable ideologies,

Figure 1: Ad-Equivalent Value of Republican Candidates' Coverage

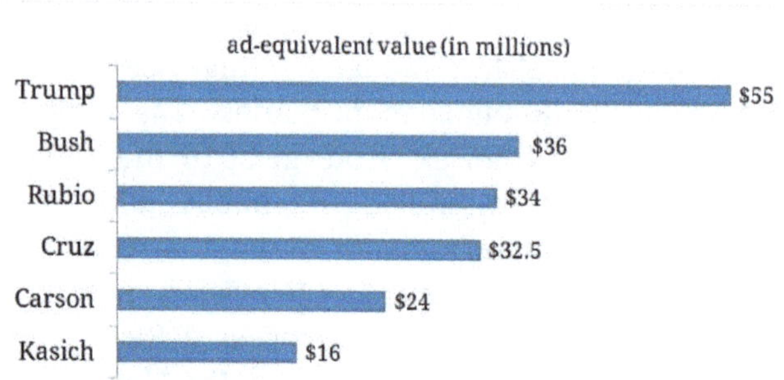

Source: Media Tenor. Based on amount of positive and neutral news coverage in eight news outlets—CBS, Fox, the Los Angeles Times, NBC, The New York Times, USA Today, The Wall Street Journal, and The Washington Post— for the period January 1-December 31, 2015.

As president, Trump privately and publicly mused about revoking the press credentials of journalists he viewed as critical. His administration moved to revoke the press passes of two White House reporters, which were restored by the courts. In **2019**, a member of the foreign press reported many of the same concerns as those of media in the U.S., expressing concern that a normalization process by reporters and media results in an inaccurate characterization of Trump. The Trump White House held about a hundred formal press briefings in 2017, declining by half during **2018** and to two in **2019**.

Trump also used the legal system to intimidate the press. In early 2020, the Trump campaign sued *The New York Times*, *The Washington Post*, and CNN for defamation in opinion pieces about Russian election interference. Legal experts said that the lawsuits lacked merit and were not likely to succeed. By March **2021**, the lawsuits against *The New York Times* and CNN had been dismissed.[299] However, not all of the national media drew the ire of Donald Trump. Fox news were the promoters of Trump positive propaganda. One his primary supporters was Fox News commentator Sean Hannity. However, even Fox news on occasion drew the ire of Trump because not even Fox news could spin a blatant non-truth about Donald Trump.

Mimesis Stage 2 for Donald John Trump - False or misleading statements made by Donald Trump

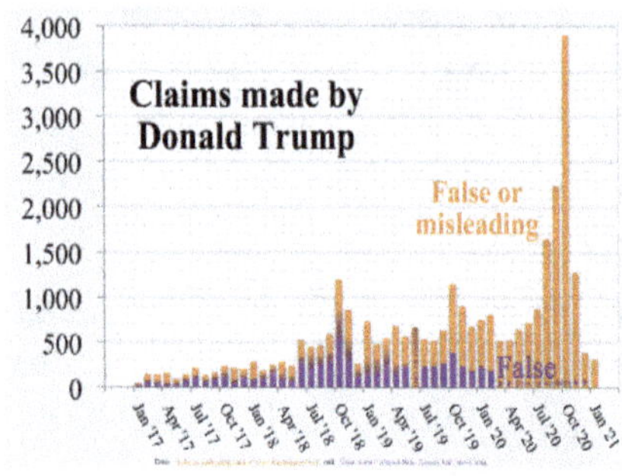

One thing Donald Trump is NOT known for is telling the truth. Not even his supporters believe everything he says. Their support for Trump is not necessarily based on the truth. It is a common fact that Donald Trump lies and at the minimum distorts and exaggerates the truth. The graph above indicates the false or misleading claims made by Donald Trump. Fact-checkers from *The Washington Post*, the *Toronto Star*, and CNN compiled data on "false or misleading claims" (orange background), and "false claims" (violet foreground), respectively. The FackCheck.org calls Donald Trump the "King of Whoppers, having documented more than 5,000 inaccurate statements made by Donald Trump. [300]

The prognosis has to be that Donald Trump does not care whether he tells the truth or not because he continues to make false, misleading statements and lies. Seems that it is in his DNA to lie. Another hypothesis is that he believes people are stupid to believe his false statements. His ratings continue to be higher than other republicans despite the lies he tells. What incentive does he have to tell the truth? Obviously, ethics and morality are not motivating incentives to tell the truth.

According to fact checkers at the Washington Post, Trump averaged about six claims a day in his first year as president, 16 claims a day in his second year, 22 claims a day in his third year, and 39 claims a day in his final year. Put another way, it took him 27 months to reach 10,000 claims and an additional 14 months to reach 20,000. He then exceeded the 30,000 mark less than five months later. Over the period of four years as president, Donald Trump has totaled 30,573 false of misleading claims.[301] One reason Donald Trump was conflictive with the news media is that they held him accountable. He was not used to being held accountable for his actions. He has gotten away with every obstacle he encountered, bankruptcies, sexual harassment, Military draft dodging, sexual harassment and rape accusations, divorces, debt responsibilities, and more. It is no wonder that when he became accountable for his actions, he gave considerable pushback to scrutiny.

According to a 2019 Gallup poll, Trump is viewed marginally as an effective leader but not honest.[302]

The following chart shows the results of the Gallup polling on the views Americans have about Donald Trump's Characteristics and Qualities.

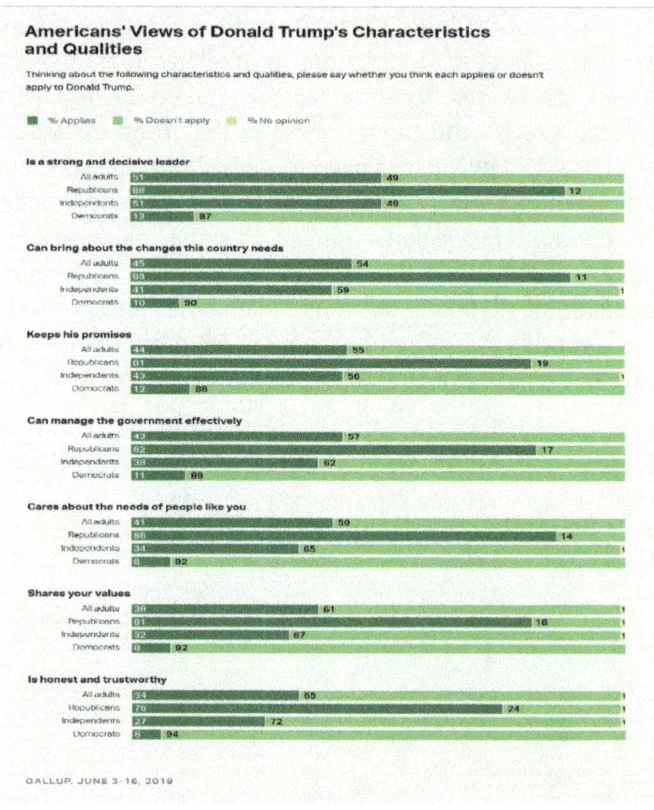

Comparison of Americans' Views of Personal Qualities of Recent Presidents

% saying each quality applies to each president [303]

	Trump 2019	Obama 2011	Bush 2003	Clinton 1995
	%	%	%	%
Is a strong and decisive leader	51	52	75	N/A
Shares your values	38	51	54	45
Is honest and trustworthy	34	61	65	46

Based on polls conducted in the first half of each year

GALLUP

Mimesis 2 for Donald John Trump - Approval ratings and scholar surveys

The approval ratings reported here are based on Gallup Daily tracking averages for President Donald Trump in 2017 and 2018, and periodic multiday polls for Trump starting in 2019. [304]

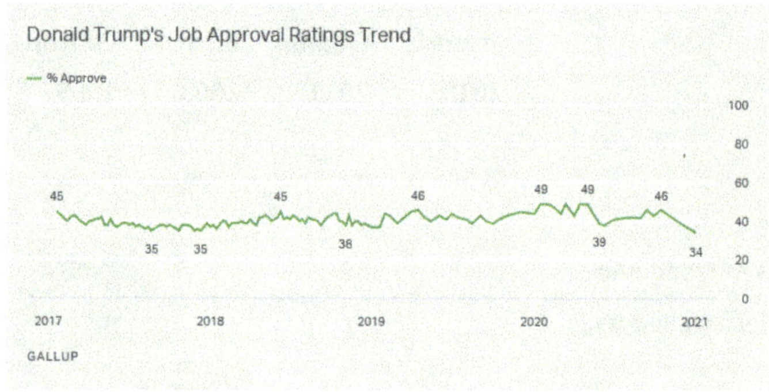

The following data is from the Gallup Poll and includes only presidents inaugurated following the election. Based on this data, Donald Trump has the lowest approval rating in the first 100 days of all elected presidents in modern history and the highest disapproval rating. [305]

Year	Inter-view Dates	President	% Approval	% Dis-approval	% No Opinion	Initial Appro-val	% Change
1953	Apr. 19-24	Dwight D. Eisenhower	73	10	17	68	5
1961	Apr. 28-May 3	John Kennedy	83	5	12	72	11
1969	May 1-6	Richard Nixon	62	15	23	59	3
1977	Apr. 29-May 2	Jimmy Carter	63	18	19	66	-3
1981	May 8-11	Ronald Reagan	68	21	11	51	17
1989	May 4-7	George Bush	56	22	22	51	5

Year	Inter-view Dates	President	% Approval	% Dis-approval	% No Opinion	Initial Appro-val	% Change
1993	Apr. 22-24	William J. Clinton	55	37	8	58	-3
2001	Apr. 20-22	George W. Bush	62	29	9	57	5
2009	Apr. 28-30	Barack Obama	65	29	6	68	-3
2017	Apr. 24-30	Donald Trump	41	54	5	45	-4
2021	Apr. 1-21	Joseph R. Biden	57	40	3	57	0

The majority of Americans do not view Donald Trump as being honest. As a matter of fact, Americans believe Trump is reckless and thin-skinned. Not honest. Not compassionate. Not stable.[306]

Considering all accounts, Donald Trump, even at age 76, born in 1946, has not entered into his third stage of Mimesis yet. He is still going strong. He is planning his next run for the White House in 2024, for his second term as President of the United States. He is a controversial figure, and many others have reflected on him. Some good, some bad. Obviously, there are more Americans who do not support Donald Trump than Americans who support Donald Trump. After all, he lost the 2020 Presidential election.

Does _ apply to Trump?	Yes	No
Strong leader	39%	50%
Trustworthy	33%	53%
Knowledgable	42%	46%
Too liberal	12%	67%
Too conservative	26%	52%
Sexist	50%	35%
Racist	45%	40%
Keeps his promises	34%	50%
Reckless	56%	31%
Honest	35%	51%
Cares about people like me	34%	53%
Thin-skinned	52%	33%
Compassionate	33%	54%
Stable	33%	54%

Mimesis of Life Summary for Donald John Trump

Donald Trump was born into privilege. His father was a stern businessman, and his mother was a housewife. Donald was an unruly child growing up, and his parents sent him to a military school so he would develop discipline. However, in Donald's formative year's one thing that was missing in his hierarchy of needs was LOVE. Donald's father never showed much love or compassion toward him. This could contribute to his rebellious and self-centered nature that followed him throughout his life up until the present. Trump was narcissistic, self-centered, misogynistic, and dishonest; he was and is a liar. Donald Trump never showed much compassion toward others, just as his father did not show compassion to him. Concern for others, in more than a superficial/shallow way that fed his own ego, did not exist in Donald Trump's nature. He never apologized, even when he was wrong. In addition to his stern father, Donald looked up to Roy Cohn, his lawyer and mentor, who like Trump, was cold-hearted and believed in getting his way at any cost, even lying and bending the rules. Roy Cohn could not deal with the reality of his own truth. Although Cohn always denied his homosexuality in public, he had a few known boyfriends over the course of his life, including his assistant Russell Eldridge, who died from AIDS in 1984, and Peter Fraser, Cohn's partner for the last two years of his life, who was 30 years his junior. Roy Cohn could not deal with his own truth, and Donald Trump inherited this characteristic from Cohn.[307]

However, Donald Trump cannot be discounted as a significant figure. He is a billionaire. He was President of the United States of America. He does have significant following among republican supporters.

However, no one can ignore what is right for long and not be held accountable. As many of his adversaries have stated, "no one is above the law", as stated by Senator Elizabeth Warren and many others. [308] The saying, "the chickens have come home to roost," is applicable to Trump's present-day experiences. The phrase, "the chickens have come home to roost," is used to mean that the bad things that someone has done in the past have come back to bite or haunt the individual.[309]

Examples of how Trump's past, his conditioned behavior, his attitude of entitlement, his ego, his misogyny, his narcissism, his lies, and his disregard for other people have come back to haunt him are evident in the many criminal investigations into his political and personal behaviors. However, if the allegation against Trump is true, then the most despicable indication of Trump's pathetic self-concept is the charge of rape brought against him by E. Jean Carroll (shown below with Donald Trump as she currently looks. The picture to the right is how she looked at the time she says Trump raped her). Ironically, when Trump was shown the younger picture of E. Jean Carroll, he mistook her for his second wife, Marla Maples. [310]

Rape is the ultimate disrespect of a woman. That a man is even accused of raping a woman is demeaning and indicates the questionable ways in which Trump conducts his life.

On June 21, 2019, prior to the release of her book *What Do We Need Men For?: A Modest Proposal*, Carroll wrote in *New York* magazine that Donald Trump had sexually assaulted her in late 1995 or early 1996 in the Bergdorf Goodman department store in New York City. Her book contains details of the alleged incident. Carroll said that on her way out of the store, she ran into Trump, and he asked for help buying a gift for a woman. After suggesting a handbag or a hat, the two reputedly moved on to the lingerie section and joked about the other trying some on. Carroll said they ended up in a dressing room together, the door of which was shut, and Trump forcefully kissed her, pulled down her tights, and raped her before she was able to escape. She stated that the alleged incident lasted less than three minutes. Lisa Birnbach and Carol Martin told *New York* magazine that Carroll had confided in them after the alleged assault. Trump denied the allegations and also claimed that he had never met her, although Carroll provided *New York* with a photograph of her socializing with Trump in 1987. Trump dismissed the photograph's significance. Carroll initially chose not to describe the alleged sexual assault as rape, instead describing it as a fight. "My word is fight. My word is not the victim word... I fought." [311]

While the Mimesis 3 verdict is still out on Donald Trump, one has to wonder how his trials will turn out. What will be his Mimesis 3 outcome? How will others view Donald Trump in his stage 3 Mimesis? How will he reflect on his past lived experiences? When all is said and done, one has to conclude that Donald Trump gives us a clear, exaggerated image of the White supremacy myth in America. Trump's behavior reflects the false mythological concept of White privilege and White supremacy in America. Donald Trump supports these White racist groups because he is reluctant to disavow them. Donald Trump identifies the image so profoundly that he gives it a cartoon character persona.

Mimesis of life for Shawn Carter, professionally known as Jay-Z

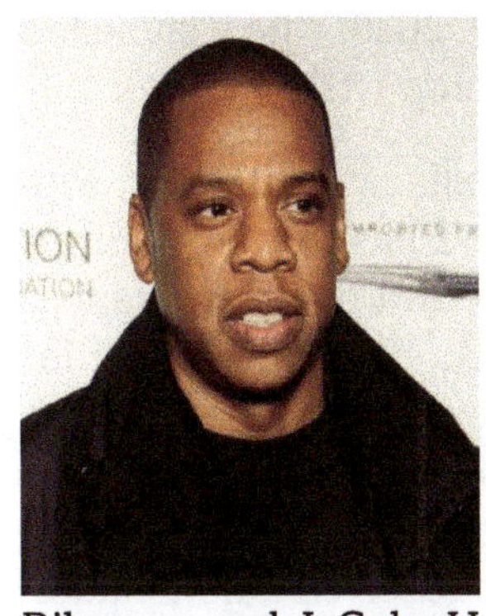

Shawn Corey Carter aka Jay-Z was born on December 4, 1969. Jay-Z is an American rapper, record producer, and entrepreneur. Jay-Z is often considered as the greatest rapper of all time. He has been crucial to the creative and commercial success of artists including Kanye West, Rihanna, and J. Cole. He is the founder and chairman of the entertainment company Roc Nation, and was the president and chief executive officer of Def Jam Recordings from 2004 to 2007. [312]

Jay-Z was born and raised in New York City. He began his musical career in the late 1980s. He co-founded the record label Roc-A-Fella Records in 1995 and released his debut studio album *Reasonable Doubt* in 1996. The album was released to widespread critical success and solidified his standing in the music industry. He went on to release twelve additional albums, including the acclaimed albums *The Blueprint* (2001), *The Black Album* (2003), *American Gangster* (2007), and *4:44* (2017). He also released the full-length collaborative albums *Watch the Throne* (2011) with Kanye West and *Everything Is Love* (2018) with his wife, Beyoncé.

Jay-Z became the first hip-hop billionaire. In 1999, he founded the clothing retailer Rocawear, and in 2003, he founded the luxury sports bar chain 40/40

Club. Both businesses have grown to become multi-million-dollar corporations, and have allowed him to start up Roc Nation in 2008. In 2015, he acquired the tech company Aspiro and took charge of their media streaming service Tidal. In 2020, he launched "Monogram", a line of cannabis products. [313]

One of the world's best-selling music artists, with over 140 million records sold, Jay-Z has won 24 Grammy Awards, the joint-most Grammy awards of any rapper along with Kanye West. Jay-Z also holds the record for the most number-one albums by a solo artist on the *Billboard* 200 (14). The recipient of the NAACP's President's Award, a Primetime Emmy Award, and a Sports Emmy Award, he has also received a nomination for a Tony Award. Ranked by *Billboard* and *Rolling Stone* as one of the 100 Greatest Artists of All Time, Jay-Z was the first rapper honored in the Songwriters Hall of Fame, and the first solo living rapper inducted in the Rock and Roll Hall of Fame. In 2013, *Time* named him one of the 100 most influential people in the world. [314]

Mimesis 1 for Shawn Corey Carter

1969

Shawn Corey Carter was born in Brooklyn, New York. He was raised in the Marcy House Projects in the Bedford Stuyvesant neighborhood. Shawn and his three siblings (Eric Carter, Andrea Carter and Michelle Carter) were raised by their mother, Gloria Carter, after his father abandoned the family.

Mimesis 2 for Shawn Corey Carter – Music

1982   At 13 years old, Shawn shot his brother in the shoulder for stealing his jewelry.

He attended Eli Whitney High School. When Eli Whitney closed, he attended

George Westinghouse Career and Technical Education High School with rappers The Notorious B.I.G. and Busta Rhymes. He briefly attended Trenton Central High School in Trenton, New Jersey, but did not graduate, dropping out during his sophomore year. Taking to street life, he sold crack cocaine and was shot at three times during his endeavors in the drug business. [315]

Shawn's mother noticed his interest in music. He would wake up the household at night, banging out drum patterns on the kitchen table. His mother bought him a boom box for his birthday, which further sparked his interest in music. He began freestyling and writing lyrics.[316]

As Shawn began to write lyrics and freestyle through the neighborhood, he became known as "Jazzy". He later adopted the stage name "Jay-Z" in recognition to his mentor Jaz-O. Jay-Z became embroiled in several battles with rapper LL Cool J in the early 1990s.

1995   Jay-Z released his first official rap single called "In My Lifetime", for which he also released a music video. An unreleased music video was also produced for the B-side "I Can't Get with That."[317]

1998-2000   Jay-Z released *Vol. 2... Hard Knock Life* which launched the biggest hit of his career at the time, "Hard Knock Life (Ghetto Anthem)". He relied more on flow and wordplay, and he continued with his penchant for mining beats

from the popular producers of the day such as Swizz Beatz, an upstart in-house producer for Ruff Ryders, and Timbaland. Other producers included DJ Premier, Erick Sermon, The 45 King, and Kid Capri. Charting hits from this album included "Can I Get A...", featuring Ja Rule and Amil, and "Nigga What, Nigga Who", featuring Amil and Jaz-O. *Vol. 2* would eventually become Jay-Z's most commercially successful album; it was certified 5× Platinum in the United States and has to date sold over five million copies. The album went on to win a Grammy Award, although Jay-Z boycotted the ceremony, protesting DMX's failure to garner a Grammy nomination and the academy's decision not to broadcast urban music categories.[318]

1999

Jay-Z collaborated with Mariah Carey on "Heartbreaker", a song from her seventh album, *Rainbow*. The song became Jay-Z's first chart-topper in the US, spending two weeks atop the *Billboard* Hot 100. In that same year,

Jay-Z released *Vol. 3... Life and Times of S. Carter*. The album proved successful and sold over 3 million copies. *Vol. 3*'s most successful single was "Big Pimpin", featuring UGK. [319]

2000 Jay-Z released *The Dynasty: Roc La Familia*, which was originally intended to become a compilation album for Roc-A-Fella artists, but Def Jam turned it into a Jay-Z album. The album helped to introduce newcomer producers The Neptunes, Just Blaze, Kanye West, and Bink, who have all gone on to achieve notable success. This is also the first album where Jay-Z utilizes a more soulful sound than on his previous albums. *The Dynasty* sold over two million units in the U.S. alone.[320]

2001-2002 The Rap Music for some reason inspired what they called, "beefs", or conflicts with other Rappers. Jay-Z had his share. Jay-Z spoke our

against Prodigy after he took an issue with a Jay-Z line from "Money, Cash, Hoes" that he felt alluded disparagingly to Mobb Deep and Prodigy's dispute with Tupac Shakur, Snoop Dogg, and Death Row Records.

He later performed the song "Takeover", at Summer Jam 2001, which initially attacked Prodigy and revealed photos of Prodigy dressed like Michael Jackson.

A line at the end of "Takeover" referred to Nas, who criticized him on "We Will Survive". Nas responded with a diss track called

"Ether" and Jay-Z straightaway added a verse to "Takeover," which dissed Nas and would start a feud between the two rappers. The feud had ended by 2005, Jay-Z stated Mark Pitts had helped them settle the feud.[321]

2001   On September 11, Jay-Z released his sixth studio album, *The Blueprint*, which received a coveted five-mic review from hip-hop magazine *The Source*. Written in just two days, the album sold more than 427,000 copies, debuted at number one on the *Billboard* 200, and reached 2× Platinum status in the U.S It was lauded for its production and its balance of "mainstream" and "hardcore" rap. Eminem was the only guest rapper on the album, producing and rapping on the song "Renegade". Four tracks were produced by Kanye West and the album represents one of West's first major breaks in the industry. [322]

2001   In October, Jay-Z pleaded guilty to aggravated assault for stabbing record producer Lance Rivera at the Kit Kat Klub in New York City in 1999. For this second-degree felony, Jay-Z was sentenced to three years' probation.

2002   Jay-Z continued to prolifically produce music.

2012    As of February, the album had sold 2.7 million copies worldwide. In 2019, *The Blueprint* was selected by the Library of Congress for preservation in the National Recording Registry for being culturally, historically, or aesthetically significant.[323]

A primary focus of Jay-Z's throughout the years, from the time his mother gave him a boom box until the present, has been music. According to Jay-Z, his earliest exposure to music was through his parents' record collection. He mostly listened to soul artists such as Marvin Gaye and Donny Hathaway. He says "I grew up around music, listening to all types of people... I'm into music that has soul in it, whether it be rap, R&B, or pop music, whatever. As long as I can feel their soul through the wax, that's what I really listen to." He often uses excerpts from these artists as samples in his work. 324

People often overlook the genius in rap music. The ability to rhyme words and phrases. The spontaneity in which rappers can put together thoughts, phrases, rhymes and meaningful lyrics. Rap is a creative musical style. While rap incurred early criticism because its lyrics focused on the hardship Black people encountered in their neighborhoods. Rap music expressed the frustration of Black lived experiences. Rap music was demeaning and disrespectful to women. Early rap music expressed the harsh reality of Black life. Poverty, Police conflict, violence, and drugs were all part of Black life that was referenced in rap music. Because of the subject matter, rap music got, "a bad rap". However, in time and with some influence by Jay-Z rap music still talked about Black life but with a different tone. Less emphasis was on demeaning women and violence than on the creativity with which Black people adopted to their environment. Rap music became less confrontational and more insightful. Jay-Z was responsible for much of the rap music evolution.

Jay-Z learned the music business with astute intelligence uncommon for someone who, according to establishmentarians, did not finish or graduate from high school. That is a phenomenon internalized by many Black people, the ability to survive and adopt to their environment. Slavery extracted Black people from their native environment. Black people have had to adopt to White America since they came to America. Often adopting to America leads people down dark and criminal paths, however, Jay-Z was astute to instinctively find a path in the American culture that allowed him to successfully combine his learned experiences in the Black, White and Business worlds and create a metamorphosed Jay-Z, while staying true to his roots. One can conclude that music was not just music to Jay-Z. Jay-Z learned the business of music as well as the art of music. It was the skills learned in the business of music that Jay-Z applied to other endeavors.

Mimesis 2 for Jay-Z - Business Career

Jay-Z did not limit himself to the business of music. He ventured out into other areas of entrepreneurship. Jay-Z established himself as a successful entrepreneur with a business empire spanning a variety of industries, from clothing lines, beverages, real estate, sports teams, and record labels.[325]

Jay-Z and Damon Dash are the founders of the urban clothing brand Rocawear. Rocawear has clothing lines and accessories for men, women, and children. The line was taken over by Jay-Z in early 2006 following a falling out with Dash. In March 2007, Jay-Z sold the rights to the Rocawear brand to Iconix Brand Group for $204 million. He retains his stake in the company and continues to oversee marketing, licensing, and product development. [326]

2003 Jay-Z became the first rapper in Reebok's history to endorse the company's footwear. He signed a three-year endorsement deal. He appeared in commercials advertising the S. Carter Reebok Collection. Later that year, he and 50 Cent appeared in a commercial to promote their S. Carter and G-Unit footwear for the company, with a Just Blaze-produced song made for it. [327]

2006 Jay-Z's deal with Reebok expired with no renewal.

2014 Jay-Z invested $200 million in Armand de Brignac champagne—owned at the time by Sovereign Brands, a New York–based wine and spirits company—for a 100 percent stake, making it the second alcoholic product acquisition in his financial investment portfolio. The brand is known for its popularity with high-profile artists, as the gold bottles are often referred to in the media. His ties to the company date back to 2006, and he received millions of dollars per year for his association with Armand de Brignac before he bought the entire company.

Jay-Z serves as co-brand director for Budweiser Select and collaborates with the company on strategic marketing programs and creative ad development. He provides direction on brand programs and ads that appear on TV, radio, print, and high-profile events. [328]

2015 In March, Jay-Z completed the $56 million acquisition of Aspiro, a Norwegian media technology company that operates the subscription-based music streaming service

Tidal, which has been in operation since October 2014. The music service was acquired through his company, Project Panther Bidco Ltd. (an entity indirectly owned by Jay-Z's S. Carter Enterprises, a company holding interests in leading international music, media, and entertainment companies). The music service combines audio and music videos with curated editorial. The main idea of the service is to bring major revenue streams back to the music artists themselves as the idea of an artist-owned streaming platform was stated as to "restore the value to music by launching a service owned by artists." Jay-Z is currently a major shareholder in the company. [329]

In July, Carter made a significant investment in JetSmarter, an app helping people book private executive plane flights. The app was built by Sergey Petrossov. [330]

2005-2008   Jay-Z was president of Def Jam Records. Under Jay-Z's leadership, Def Jam launched the successful careers of contemporary R&B singers Rihanna and Ne-Yo. At the end of 2007, after he released *American Gangster*, Jay-Z decided not to renew his contract as the president and CEO of Def Jam in order to start his new Live Nation venture, Roc Nation.

In April 2011, it was reported that Jay-Z had outbid executives at Universal Music and Jive Records to acquire independent record label Block Starz Music.[331]

2011   On April 5, Jay-Z launched the popular culture and lifestyle online magazine *Life + Times*. It features content that showcases his high-end tastes in clothing, appliances, and cars. The site design is aesthetically aimed at the upwardly mobile young male demographic, with sports and music-related posts accompanying those about fashion and design.[332]

2003–2013   For ten years, Jay-Z enjoyed his role as a part-owner of the Brooklyn Nets NBA team, having paid a reported $1 million for his share, which declined in value to $350,000 in April 2013, based on *Forbes* magazine's valuation of the team. He encouraged the team's relocation to Brooklyn's Barclays Center (from New Jersey) in the 2012–2013 season, at which point the team took on the Brooklyn Nets moniker. [333]

2013   On April 18, Jay-Z officially announced through his Life + Times website in a press release that he would be relinquishing his ownership in the Brooklyn Nets. The shares were eventually sold to singer, rapper, actor and entrepreneur Will Pan, making Pan the first American of Taiwanese descent to own a U.S. professional sports franchise.

In September, his stake in Barclays Center was sold for $1.5 million. [334]

2013   On April 2, ESPN reported Jay-Z's plans to launch his own sports agency, Roc Nation Sports, with a focus on the representation of various professional athletes. The sport management group is a partnership with Creative Artists Agency. In conjunction with the agency's launch, New York Yankees' second baseman Robinson Canó left agent Scott Boras to sign with the company. ESPN also mentioned that Jay-Z himself was planning to be a certified sports agent, first in baseball and eventually in basketball and football. In order to represent clients in basketball, he would have to give up his small share of the Brooklyn Nets. [335]

Mimesis 2 for Jay-Z - Other Business Ventures – Diversification [336]

Jay-Z also co-owns the 40/40 Club, an upscale sports bar that started in New York City, and has since expanded to Atlantic City and Chicago. In 2008, the 40/40 Club in Las Vegas was closed down and bought back by the hotel after attendance steadily declined. In 2005, Jay-Z became an investor in Carol's Daughter, a line of beauty products, including products for hair, skin, and hands.

In 2010, he announced plans to expand his 40/40 Club sports bar chain into as many as 20 airports, joining his Roc Nation business partners, husband and wife Juan and Desiree Perez, in a deal with Delaware North.

Parlux fragrances sued Jay-Z for $18 million for the failure of his cologne, *Gold*. They claim the cologne's failure is due to Jay-Z not doing social media posts and interviews about the cologne. Parlux claims they projected selling $15 million the first year, and $35 million the second, and subsequent years after the launch. The fragrance sold $14 million the first year and $6.1 million the second. Parlux lost money on the venture and have had constant returns of unsold inventory.

Jay-Z collaborated with Cohiba to launch his own cigars.

In August **2020**, Jay-Z's Roc Nation partnered with Brooklyn's Long Island University to establish the Roc Nation School of Music, Sports & Entertainment.

In November **2020**, it was announced that Jay-Z would be join TPCO Holding Corp., a newly formed cannabis products company, in the role of "Chief Visionary Officer".

Mimesis 2 for Jay Z – Personal Life [337]

In 2002, Jay-Z and singer Beyoncé collaborated on the song "'03 Bonnie & Clyde". He also appeared on Beyoncé's hit single "Crazy in Love" as well as "That's How You Like It" from her debut album *Dangerously in Love*. On her second album, *B'Day*, he made appearances on the hits "Déjà Vu" and "Upgrade U". In the video for the latter song, she comically imitates his appearance. They kept a low profile while dating and were married on April 4, 2008. Their relationship became a matter of public record on April 22, 2008, but Beyoncé did not publicly debut her $5 million Lorraine Schwartz-designed wedding ring until the Fashion Rocks concert on September 5, 2008. They reside in an $88 million home in the Bel Air neighborhood of Los Angeles. They generally avoid discussing their relationship, and Beyoncé has stated her belief that this has helped them, while Jay-Z agreed in a *People* article that they do not "play with [their] relationship".

Beyoncé and Jay-Z were listed as the most powerful couple for *Time* magazine's 100 most influential people of 2006. In January 2009, *Forbes* ranked them as Hollywood's top-earning couple, with a combined total of $162 million. They made it to the top of the list the following year, with a combined total of $122 million between June 2008 and June 2009.

At the 2011 MTV Video Music Awards, Beyoncé revealed that she was pregnant with their first child. Their daughter, Blue Ivy, was born at New York's Lenox Hill Hospital on January 7, 2012. Jay-Z released "Glory", a song dedicated to their child, through his website on January 9, 2012. The song detailed the couple's pregnancy struggles, including a miscarriage Beyoncé had suffered. Because Blue's cries were included at the end of the song and she was officially credited on the song as "B.I.C.", she became the youngest person ever (at two days old) to appear on a *Billboard* chart when "Glory" debuted at No. 74 on Hot R&B / Hip-Hop Songs. On June 18, 2017, Beyoncé's father Mathew Knowles confirmed that she and Jay-Z had welcomed twins: a daughter named Rumi and a son named Sir.

Mimesis of Life Summary for Jay-Z
aka Shawn Corey Carter

Shawn Corey Carter was born into a disadvantaged household. He is the youngest of four siblings raised by his Gloria Carter. The ideology that people born into disadvantaged environments and situations are likely to fail in life is an adage that Jay-Z proves is not a rule. It is a handicap to be born into a disadvantaged situation; however, many people encounter disadvantage. Individuals are considered disadvantaged if they are Black; if they are uneducated; if they are fat; if they are female; if they have a criminal record; if they are handicapped; if they don't come from the "right bloodline" or frankly if they are not White Anglo Saxon Protestant. However, this is America, and while challenges exist, they are not impossible to overcome. Jay-Z is a prime example of this adage; challenges can be overcome in America.

The final catharsis and evaluation on the life of Shawn Corey Carter aka Jay-Z is still out. Jay-Z is going strong on all cylinders of his life, family, professional, and business, and from all accounts, he appears to be happy. Although happiness is a factor that cannot be evaluated from the outside.

Jay-Z came from humble beginnings and put things together in his life to make something out of his life. His childhood / adolescent environment was such that he could have gone in other life directions. Black youth growing up in broken homes, in poverty, have a higher incidence of being incarcerated than White youth. The system of mass incarceration particularly targets Black people, who are 13 percent of the U.S. population but are 38 percent of the people in jails and prisons. May 19, 2022. [338] While Jay-Z did encounter incidents in his life that could have caused him devastating repercussions, he managed to avoid the severities that could have impacted his life with dysfunctional results. Alternatively, Jay-Z kept a laser focus on his music. Learning the skills of rap lyrics and melodies, but more importantly, Jay-Z learned the business of music, which carried him further into a life of success, financial security, and as a role model for many youth. A major contribution Jay-Z has made to rap music, which was born out of the African American culture and lived experience, is that he helped position rap music into the mainstream of the music industry. He helped establish rap music as a cultural icon in the arts.

Jay-Z is an example that smart does not always equate to educated, and educated does not always mean college-educated. Jay-Z is a genius in life and dealing with other people. "Ole boy knows how to deal". Jay-Z has much to accomplish in his remaining years on earth. Unless the odds are broken, Jay-Z has much more to accomplish that quite possibly will be more astonishing than what he has already achieved. With Beyoncé as his partner, the sky is the limit.

Mimesis of Life for Tupac Shakur
(1971 – 1996)

Tupac Amaru Shakur; born Lesane Parish Crooks (**Born June 16, 1971 – Died September 13, 1996**) Tupac was also known by his stage names 2Pac and Makaveli. He was an American rapper and actor. He is widely considered one of the most influential rappers of all time. Shakur is among the best-selling music artists, having sold more than 75 million records worldwide. Much of Shakur's music has been noted for addressing contemporary social issues that plagued inner cities, and he is considered a symbol of activism against inequality.[339] Tupac was born in New York City to parents who were both political activists and Black Panther Party members.

Raised by his mother, Afeni Shakur, he relocated to Baltimore in 1984 and to the San Francisco Bay Area in 1988. With the release of his debut album, *2Pacalypse Now*, in 1991, he became a central figure in West Coast hip hop for his conscious rap lyrics. Tupac achieved further critical and commercial success with his follow-up albums, *Strictly 4 My N.I.G.G.A.Z...*(1993) and *Me Against the World* (1995). His

Diamond-certified album *All Eyez on Me* (1996), the first double-length album in hip-hop history, abandoned his introspective lyrics for volatile gangsta rap. In addition to his music career, Shakur also found considerable success as an actor, with his starring roles in *Juice* (1992), *Poetic Justice* (1993), *Above the Rim* (1994), *Bullet* (1996), *Gridlock'd* (1997), and *Gang Related* (1997).

In 1994, Tupac was shot five times in the lobby of a New York recording studio and experienced legal troubles, including incarceration. In 1995, Shakur served eight months in prison on sexual abuse charges, but was released pending an appeal of his conviction. Following his release, he signed to Marion "Suge" Knight's label Death Row Records and became heavily involved in the growing East Coast–West Coast hip hop rivalry. On September 7, 1996, Tupac was shot four times by an unidentified assailant in a drive-by shooting in Las Vegas; he died six days later. Following his murder, Shakur's friend-turned-rival, the Notorious B.I.G., was at first considered a suspect due to their public feud. Notorious B.I.G. was also murdered in another drive-by shooting six months later, in March 1997, while visiting Los Angeles. [340]

Tupac's double-length posthumous album *Greatest Hits* (1998) is one of his two releases—and one of only nine hip hop albums—to have been certified Diamond in the United States. Five more albums have been released since Shakur's death, including his critically acclaimed posthumous album *The Don Killuminati: The 7 Day Theory* (1996) under his stage name Makaveli, all of which have been certified Platinum in the United States. In 2002, Shakur was inducted into the Hip-Hop Hall of Fame. In 2017, he was inducted into the Rock and Roll Hall of Fame in his first year of eligibility. *Rolling Stone* ranked Shakur among the 100 Greatest Artists of All Time. [341]

Mimesis 1 for Lesane Parish Crooks, aka Tupac Shakur

1971   Tupac Shakur was born on June 16, 1971, in the East Harlem section of Upper Manhattan, New York City. Born Lesane Parish Crooks, at age one, he was renamed Tupac Amaru Shakur. He was named after Túpac Amaru II, the descendant of the last Incan ruler, who was executed in Peru in 1781 after his failed revolt against Spanish rule. Tupac's mother, Afeni Shakur, explained, "I wanted him to have the name of revolutionary, indigenous people in the world. I wanted him to know he was part of a world culture and not just from a neighborhood."[342]

Tupac had an older stepbrother, Mopreme "Komani" Shakur, and a half-sister, Sekyiwa Shakur, two years his junior.

1960's – 1970's   Shakur's parents, Afeni Shakur—born Alice Faye Williams in North Carolina—and his biological father, Billy Garland, had been active Black Panther Party members in New York in the late 1960s and early 1970s. A month before Shakur's birth, his mother was tried in New York City as part of the Panther 21 criminal trial. She was acquitted of over 150 charges. Other family members who were involved in the Black Panthers' Black Liberation Army were convicted of serious crimes and imprisoned, including Shakur's stepfather, Mutulu Shakur, who spent four years among the FBI's Ten Most Wanted Fugitives. Mutulu Shakur was apprehended in 1986 and subsequently convicted for a 1981 robbery of a Brinks armored truck, during which police officers and a guard were killed. Shakur's godfather, Elmer "Geronimo" Pratt, a high-ranking Black Panther, was convicted of murdering a school teacher during a 1968 robbery. After spending 27 years in prison, his conviction was overturned due to the prosecution's having concealed evidence that proved his innocence.

Shakur's godmother, Assata Shakur, is a former member of the Black Liberation Army, who was convicted of the first-degree murder of a New Jersey State Trooper and is still wanted by the FBI.[343]

Mimesis Stage 2 for Tupac Shakur

In the 1980s, Shakur's mother found it difficult to find work because she was addicted to drugs.

1984 The family moved from New York City to Baltimore, Maryland. Tupac attended eighth grade at Roland Park Middle School, then ninth grade at Paul Laurence Dunbar High School. He transferred to the Baltimore School for the Arts in the tenth grade, where he studied acting, poetry, jazz, and ballet. He performed in Shakespeare's plays.

At the Baltimore School for the Arts, Tupac befriended actress Jada Pinkett, who became a subject of some of his poems. With his friend Dana "Mouse" Smith as beatbox, he won

competitions as reputedly the school's best rapper. Also known for his humor, he could mix with all crowds. He listened to a diverse range of music that included Kate Bush, Culture Club, Sinéad O'Connor, and U2.

Upon connecting with the Baltimore Young Communist League USA, Shakur dated Mary Baldridge, who was the daughter of the director of the local chapter of the Communist Party USA. Baldridge, who was white, was described as an attractive young woman who was raised to look past color.

In 1988, Shakur moved to Marin City, California, an impoverished community in the San Francisco Bay Area. In nearby Mill Valley, he attended Tamalpais High School where he performed in several theater productions. Shakur did not graduate from high school, but he later earned his GED. [344]

1989 Tupac recorded under the stage name MC.[345]

Tupac attended the poetry classes taught by Leila Steinberg, who became his manager. [346]

Mimesis Stage 2 for Tupac Shakur – Professional Life / His Music

1991 Tupac debuted under the stage name 2Pac on Digital Underground, under a new record label, Interscope Records, on the group's January 1991 single "Same Song". The song was featured on the soundtrack of the 1991 film *Nothing but Trouble*, starring Dan Aykroyd, John Candy, Chevy Chase, and Demi Moore.

1993 Shakur's second album, *Strictly 4 My N.I.G.G.A.Z...*, was released in February.

1993, Shakur formed the group Thug Life with Tyrus "Big Syke" Himes, Diron "Macadoshis" Rivers, his stepbrother Mopreme Shakur, and Walter "Rated R" Burns. Thug Life released its only album, *Thug Life: Volume 1*, on October 11, 1994, which is certified Gold. It carries the single "Pour Out a Little Liquor", produced by Johnny "J" Jackson, who would also produce much of Shakur's album *All Eyez on Me*.

1993 While visiting Los Angeles, the Notorious B.I.G. asked a local drug dealer to introduce him to Shakur, and they quickly became friends. The pair would socialize when Tupac was in New York or when B.I.G. was in Los Angeles. At his live shows, Tupac would call B.I.G. onto the stage to rap with him and Stretch. Together, they recorded the songs "Runnin' from tha Police" and "House of Pain".[347]

Rumor has it that B.I.G. asked Tupac to manage him. Tupac advised him that Sean Combs would make him a star. Yet in the meantime, Tupac's lifestyle was comparatively lavish compared to B.I.G., who had not yet established himself. Tupac welcomed B.I.G. to join his side group Thug Life, but he would instead form his own side group, the Junior M.A.F.I.A., with his Brooklyn friends Lil' Cease and Lil' Kim.

The lyrics of Tupac and other rappers got the attention of US Vice President Dan Quayle and other White establishment politicians. Quayle said, "There's no reason for a record like this to be released. It has no place in our society." Tupac, finding himself misunderstood, explained, in part… "I just wanted to rap about things that affected young Black males. When I said that, I didn't know that I was gonna tie myself down to just take all the blunts and hits for all the young Black males, to be the media's kicking post for young Black males."[348]

1994   Tupac had a falling out with B.I.G. after he was shot at Quad Studios.[349]

1995   In March, Tupac released his third album, *Me Against the World*, while he was incarcerated.

1995   While Shakur was imprisoned in his mother was about to lose her house. Shakur had his wife Keisha Morris contact Death Row Records founder Suge Knight in Los Angeles. Reportedly, Shakur's mother promptly received $15,000. After an August visit to Clinton Correctional Facility in northern New York State, Knight traveled southward to New York City to attend the 2nd Annual Source Awards ceremony. Meanwhile, an East Coast–West Coast hip hop rivalry was brewing between Death Row and Bad Boy Records. In October 1995, Knight visited Shakur in prison again and posted $1.4 million bond under the terms that Tupac join Death Row Records and produce three albums. Shakur returned to Los Angeles and joined Death Row with the appeal of his December 1994 conviction pending.[350]

1996   Tupac's fourth album, *All Eyez on Me*, came out on February 13. It was rap's first double album—meeting two of the three albums due in Shakur's contract with Death Row—and bore five singles. The album shows Shakur rapping about the gangsta lifestyle, leaving behind his previous political messages. With standout production, the album has more party tracks and often a triumphant tone. Music journalist Kevin Powell noted that Shakur, once released from prison, became more aggressive and "seemed like a completely transformed person".

When Tupac was released from prison and came under the influence of Death Row Records and Shug Knight, he appeared to adopt his lyrics more to the gangster rap genre. Tupac's antics and lyrics also fueled the feud between the West Coast – East Coast rap rivalry.

Tupac's second album to hit No. 1 on both the Top R&B / Hip-Hop Albums chart and the pop albums chart, the *Billboard* 200, it sold 566,000 copies in its first week and was it was certified 5× Multi-Platinum in April. The singles "How Do U Want It" and "California Love"

reached No. 1 on the *Billboard* Hot 100. Death Row released Shakur's diss track "Hit 'Em Up" as the non-album B-side to "How Do U Want It." In this venomous tirade, the proclaimed "Bad Boy killer" threatens violent payback on all things Bad Boy — B.I.G., Sean Combs, Junior M.A.F.I.A., the company — and on any in the East Coast rap scene, like rap duo Mobb Deep and rapper Chino XL, who allegedly had commented against Shakur about the dispute. *All Eyez on Me* won R&B/Soul or Rap Album of the Year at the 1997 Soul Train Music Awards. At the 1997 American Music Awards, Tupac won Favorite Rap / Hip-Hop Artist. The album was certified 9× Multi-Platinum in June 1998, and 10× in July 2014.[351]

Mimesis Stage 2 for Tupac Shakur – Film Career [352]

1991 Tupac made his first film appearance in the film *Nothing but Trouble*, a cameo by the Digital Underground.

1992 Tupac starred in *Juice*, where he plays the fictional Roland Bishop, a militant and haunting individual. *Rolling Stone*'s Peter Travers calls him "the film's most magnetic figure".

1993 Tupac starred alongside Janet Jackson in John Singleton's romance film, *Poetic Justice*. Singleton later fired Shakur from the 1995 film *Higher Learning* because the studio would not finance the film following his arrest. For the lead role in the eventual 2001 film *Baby Boy*, a role played by Tyrese Gibson, Singleton originally had Tupac in mind. Ultimately, the set design includes a Tupac mural in the protagonist's bedroom, and the film's score includes Tupac's song "Hail Mary".

1993 Director Allen Hughes had cast Shakur as Sharif in the 1993 film *Menace II Society*, but replaced him when Tupac assaulted him on set due to a discrepancy with the script. Nonetheless, in 2013, Hughes appraises that Shakur would have outshone the other actors "because he was bigger than the movie".

1994 Shakur played a gangster called Birdie in the 1994 film *Above the Rim*. By some accounts, that character had been modeled after former New York drug dealer Jacques "Haitian Jack" Agnant, who managed and promoted rappers. Shakur was introduced to him at a Queens nightclub. Reportedly, B.I.G. advised Shakur to avoid him, but Shakur disregarded the warning. Through Haitian Jack, Shakur met James "Jimmy Henchman" Rosemond, also a drug dealer who doubled as music manager.

1996 Soon after Shakur's death, three more films starring him were

1997 released, *Bullet* (1996), *Gridlock'd* (1997), and *Gang Related* (1997).

Mimesis Stage 2 for Tupac Shakur - Sexual assault case, prison sentence, appeal and release

Previously, it was stated that Tupac was jailed in 1995.

1993 In November Tupac and two other men were charged in New York with sodomizing a woman in Tupac's hotel room. The woman, Ayanna Jackson, alleged that after she performed a simulation of oral sex on Tupac on the public dance floor of a Manhattan nightclub. Later, she went to the hotel room with Tupac, record executive Jacques "Haitian Jack" Agnant, Shakur's road manager Charles Fuller, and an unidentified fourth man. According to her testimony, they forced her to perform non-consensual oral sex on each of them. Shakur was also charged with illegal possession of a firearm, as two guns were found in the hotel room. When he was interviewed on *The Arsenio Hall Show*, Tupac said he was hurt that "a woman would accuse me of taking something from her", as he had been raised in a female household and surrounded by women his whole life. [353]

1994   On December 1, Tupac was acquitted of three counts of sodomy and the associated gun charges but convicted of two counts of first-degree sexual abuse for "forcibly touching the woman's buttocks" in his hotel room. Jurors have said the lack of evidence negated a sodomy conviction.

1995   In February, he was sentenced to 18 months to $4+\frac{1}{2}$ years in prison by a judge who decried "an act of brutal violence against a helpless woman". Tupac's lawyer characterized the sentence as "out of line" with the groping conviction and the setting of bail at $3 million as "inhumane". Tupac's accuser later filed a civil suit against Tupac seeking $10 million for punitive damages, which was subsequently settled.[354]

After Tupac had been convicted of sexual abuse, Jacques Agnant's case was separated and closed via misdemeanor plea without incarceration. A. J. Benza reported in *New York Daily News,* Tupac's disdain for Agnant, who Tupac theorized had set him up. Tupac reportedly believed his accuser was connected to and had sexual relations with Agnant and James Rosemond in association with his 1994 Quad Studios shooting.[355]

1995 On February 14, Tupac began serving his prison sentence on sexual abuse charges at Clinton Correctional Facility. He spent a few months at Rikers Island. While imprisoned, he began reading again, which he had been unable to do as his career progressed due to his marijuana and alcohol habits. Works such as *The Prince* by Italian philosopher Niccolò Machiavelli and *The Art of War* by Chinese military strategist Sun Tzu sparked Shakur's interest in philosophy, philosophy of war, and military strategy.[356]

1995 On April 4, Shakur married his girlfriend Keisha Morris; the marriage was later annulled. While in prison, Shakur exchanged letters with celebrities such as Jim Carrey and Tony Danza, among others. He was also visited by Al Sharpton, who helped Shakur get released from solitary confinement.

1995 By October pending a judicial appeal, Shakur was incarcerated in New York. On October 12, he bonded out of the maximum security Dannemora Clinton Correctional Facility in the process of appealing his conviction, once Suge Knight, CEO of Death Row Records, arranged for the posting of his $1.4 million bond.[357]

It was during his incarceration that Tupac became beholding to, and under the influence of, Shug Knight and took on the Death Row Records persona, including gangsta rap lyrics and gangster persona. Suge came to the rescue of Tupac's mother, giving her $15,000.00 to save her house from foreclosure. Suge Knight also put up $1.4 million to bail Tupac out of jail. The cost to Tupac was going into business with Suge Knight. Tupac's personable, sentimental, sensitive nature was not suppressed outside of the Death Row environment, but when he was under the influence of Death Row, Tupac displayed a harder, more aggressive persona, his version of a gangsta.

Mimesis Stage 2 for Tupac Shakur – More Trouble

1993   Shooting in Atlanta

1994   Quad Studious Shooting,

Setup accusations involving the Notorious B.I.G.

1991   Oakland Police Department lawsuit

Misdemeanor assault convictions

Concealed weapon case and Concealed weapon case

1995   wrongful death suit

1993   On October 31, Tupac was arrested in Atlanta for shooting two off-duty police officers, Brothers Mark Whitwell and Scott Whitwell. The Atlanta police claimed the shooting occurred after the brothers were almost struck by a car carrying Shakur while they were crossing the street with their wives. As they argued with the driver, Tupac's car pulled up, and he shot the Whitwells in the buttocks and the abdomen. However, there are conflicting accounts that the Whitwells were harassing a black motorist and uttered racial slurs. According to some witnesses, Shakur and his entourage had fired in self-defense as Mark Whitwell shot at them first.

Tupac was charged with two counts of aggravated assault. Mark Whitwell was charged with firing at Shakur's car and later with making false statements to investigators. Scott Whitwell admitted to possessing a gun he had taken from a Henry County police evidence room. Prosecutors ultimately dropped all charges against both parties. Mark Whitwell resigned from the force seven months after the shooting. Both brothers filed civil suits against Tupac; Mark Whitwell's suit was settled out of court, while Scott Whitwell's $2 million lawsuit resulted in a default judgment entered against the rapper's estate in 1998.[358]

1994 On November 30, while in New York recording verses for a mixtape of Ron G, Tupac was repeatedly distracted by his beeper. Music manager James "Jimmy Henchman" Rosemond reportedly offered Tupac $7,000 to stop by Quad Studios in Times Square that night to record a verse for his client Little Shawn. Tupac was unsure but agreed to the session as he needed the cash to offset legal costs. He arrived with Stretch and one or two others. In the lobby, three men robbed and beat him at gunpoint; Tupac resisted and was shot. Tupac speculated that the shooting had been a setup.

Against the doctor's advice, Shakur checked out of Metropolitan Hospital Center a few hours after surgery and secretly went to the house of the actress Jasmine Guy to recuperate. The next day, Tupac arrived at a Manhattan courthouse bandaged in a wheelchair to receive the jury's verdict for his sexual abuse case. Shakur posted a $25,000 bond and spent the next few weeks being cared for by his mother and a private doctor at Guy's home. The Fruit of Islam and former members of the Black Panther Party stood guard to protect him.[359]

1995  In an interview with *Vibe Magazine*, Tupac accused Sean Combs, Jimmy Henchman, and the Notorious B.I.G., who were at Quad Studios at the time, among others, of setting up or being privy to the November 1994 robbery and shooting. *Vibe* alerted the names of the accused. The accusations were significant to the East-West Coast rivalry in hip-hop; in 1995, months after the robbery, Combs and B.I.G. released the track "Who Shot Ya?", which Shakur took as a mockery of his shooting and thought they could be responsible, so he released a diss song, "Hit 'Em Up", in which he targeted B.I.G., Combs, their record label, Junior M.A.F.I.A., and at the end of "Hit 'Em Up", he mentions rivals Mobb Deep and Chino XL.[360]

1991   In October, one month before the release of *2Pacalypse Now*, two Oakland Police Department officers stopped Tupac for jaywalking. The officers allegedly asked for his name since it did not sound American. He answered them, and they brutalized him, scratching his face over the street. Shakur filed a $10 million lawsuit against the Oakland Police Department. The case was settled for about $43,000.[361]

1993   On April 5, Tupac was charged with felonious assault. He allegedly threw a microphone and swung a baseball bat at rapper Chauncey Wynn, of the group M.A.D., at a concert at Michigan State University. Shakur claimed the bat was a part of his show, and there was no criminal intent. Nonetheless, on September 14, 1994, Shakur pleaded guilty to a misdemeanor and was sentenced to 30 days in jail, twenty of them suspended, and ordered to 35 hours of community service.

Slated to star as Sharif in the 1993 Hughes Brothers' film *Menace II Society*, Shakur was replaced by actor Vonte Sweet after allegedly assaulting one of the film's directors, Allen Hughes. In early 1994, Shakur served 15 days in jail after being found guilty of the assault. The prosecution's evidence included a *Yo! MTV Raps* interview where Shakur boasts that he had "beat up the director of *Menace II Society*". [362]

1994   Tupac was arrested in Los Angeles, when he was stopped by police on suspicion of speeding. Police found a concealed semiautomatic pistol in the car, a felony offense because of a prior conviction in 1993 in Los Angeles for carrying a concealed firearm.[363]

1996,   Tupac was sentenced to 120 days in jail for violating his release terms for the 1994 gun possession charge and failing to appear for a road cleanup job but was allowed to remain free awaiting appeal. On June 7, his sentence was deferred via appeals pending in other cases.

1992   On August 22, in Marin City, Shakur performed outdoors at a festival. For about an hour after the performance, he signed autographs and posed for photos. A conflict broke out and Tupac allegedly drew a legally carried Colt Mustang but dropped it on the ground. Shakur claimed that someone with him picked it up when it accidentally discharged.

About 100 yards (90 meters) away in a schoolyard, Qa'id Walker-Teal, a boy aged 6 on his bicycle, was fatally shot in the forehead. Police matched the bullet to a .38-caliber pistol registered to Tupac. His stepbrother Maurice Harding was arrested on suspicion of having fired the gun, but no charges were filed. Lack of witnesses stymied the prosecution. In 1995, Qa'id's mother filed a wrongful death suit against Tupacr, which was settled for about $300,000 to $500,000. [364]

Mimesis Stage 2 for Tupac Shakur – Personal Life

1993   In an interview published in *The Source*, Shakur criticized record producer Quincy Jones for his interracial marriage to actress Peggy Lipton. Their daughter Rashida Jones responded with an irate open letter. Shakur later apologized to her sister Kidada Jones, whom he began dating in 1996. Shakur and Jones attended Men's Fashion Week in Milan and walked the runway together for a Versace fashion show. Jones was at their hotel in Las Vegas when Tupac was shot.

1995   In an interview with *Vibe* magazine, Shakur listed Jada Pinkett, Jasmine Guy, Treach, and Mickey Rourke among the people who were looking out for him while he was in prison. Shakur also mentioned that Madonna was a supportive friend. Madonna later revealed that they had dated in 1994.

1995   On April 29, Tupac married his then-girlfriend Keisha Morris, a pre-law student. Their marriage was annulled ten months later.

Shakur met Jada Pinkett while attending the Baltimore School for the Arts. She appeared in his music videos "Keep Ya Head Up" and "Temptations." She also came up with the concept for his "California Love" music video and had intended to direct it, but she removed herself from the project. In 1995, Pinkett contributed $100,000 towards Shakur's bail as he awaited an appeal on his sexual abuse conviction. Tupac stated: "Jada is my heart. She will be my friend for my whole life"; and Pinkett said he was "one of my best friends. He was like a brother. It was beyond friendship for us. The type of relationship we had, you only get that once in a lifetime."

After Shakur was shot in 1994, he recuperated at Jasmine Guy's home. They had met during his guest appearance on the sitcom *A Different World* in 1993. Guy appeared in his music video "Temptations" and later wrote his mother's 2004 biography, *Afeni Shakur: Evolution of a Revolutionary*.

Shakur befriended Treach when they were both roadies on Public Enemy's tour in 1990. He made a cameo in Naughty by Nature's music video "Uptown Anthem" in 1992. Treach collaborated with Shakur on his song "5 Deadly Venomz" and appeared in his music video "Temptations." Treach was also a speaker at a public memorial service for Shakur in 1996.

Shakur and Mickey Rourke formed a bond while filming the movie *Bullet* in 1994. Rourke recalled that Shakur "was there for me during some very hard times." Shakur had friendships with other celebrities, including Mike Tyson Chuck D, Jim Carrey, and Alanis Morissette.

The Final Mimesis for Tupac Shakur

Tupac Shakur, despite his conflictive and volatile lifestyle, was loved by millions of people. Tupac was a talented genius who engaged in a gangster world he was not skilled to navigate. Tupac declared himself, "I am not a gangster". While Tupac might have shown a hard exterior, he had a sensitive and compassionate inner core. Tupac did not have time to reflect on his life. He was killed while living his life.

On the night of September 7, 1996, Shakur was in Las Vegas, Nevada, to celebrate his business partner Tracy Danielle Robinson's birthday and attended the Bruce Seldon vs. Mike Tyson boxing match with Suge Knight at the MGM Grand. Afterward, in the lobby, someone in their group spotted Orlando "Baby Lane" Anderson, an alleged Southside Compton Crip, whom the individual accused of having recently tried to snatch his neck chain with a Death Row Records medallion in a shopping mall. The hotel's surveillance footage shows the ensuing assault on Anderson. Shakur soon stopped by his hotel room and then headed with Knight to his Death Row nightclub, Club 662, in a black BMW 750iL sedan, part of a larger convoy.

At about 11 pm on Las Vegas Boulevard, bicycle-mounted police stopped the car for its loud music and lack of license plates. The plates were found in the trunk, and the car was released without a ticket. At about 11:15 pm at a stoplight, a white, four-door, late-model Cadillac sedan pulled up to the passenger side, and an occupant rapidly fired into the car. Shakur was struck four times: once in the arm, once in the thigh, and twice in the chest with one bullet entering his right lung. Shards hit Knight's head. Frank Alexander, Shakur's bodyguard, was not in the car at the time. He would say he had been tasked to drive the car of Tupac's girlfriend, Kidada Jones.

Tupac was taken to the University Medical Center of Southern Nevada, where he was heavily sedated and put on life support. In the intensive-care unit on the afternoon of September 13, 1996, Shakur died from internal bleeding. He was pronounced dead at 4:03 pm. The official causes of death are respiratory failure and cardiopulmonary arrest associated with multiple gunshot wounds. Shakur's body was cremated the next day. Members of the Outlawz, recalling a line in his song "Black Jesus", (although uncertain of the artist's attempt at a literal meaning chose to interpret the request seriously) smoked some of his body's ashes after mixing them with marijuana.[365]

Tupac's body was cremated the next day. Members of the Outlawz, recalling a line in his song "Black Jesus" (although uncertain of the artist's attempt at a literal meaning, chose to interpret the request seriously) smoked some of his body's ashes after mixing them with marijuana.[366]

In 2002, investigative journalist Chuck Philips, after a year of work, reported in the *Los Angeles Times* that Anderson, a Southside Compton Crip, having been attacked by Suge and Shakur's entourage at the MGM Hotel after the boxing match, had fired the fatal gunshots, but that Las Vegas police had interviewed him only once, briefly, before his death in an unrelated shooting. Philips's 2002 article also alleges the involvement of Christopher "Notorious B.I.G." Wallace and several within New York City's criminal underworld. Both Anderson and Wallace denied involvement, while Wallace offered a confirmed alibi. Music journalist John Leland, in *The New York Times*, called the evidence "inconclusive".

In 2011, via the Freedom of Information Act, the FBI released documents related to its investigation, which described an extortion scheme by the Jewish Defense League (classified as "a right-wing terrorist group" by the FBI) that included making death threats against Shakur and other rappers, but did not indicate a direct connection to his murder.[367]

The Final Mimesis for Tupac Shakur - Legacy and remembrance

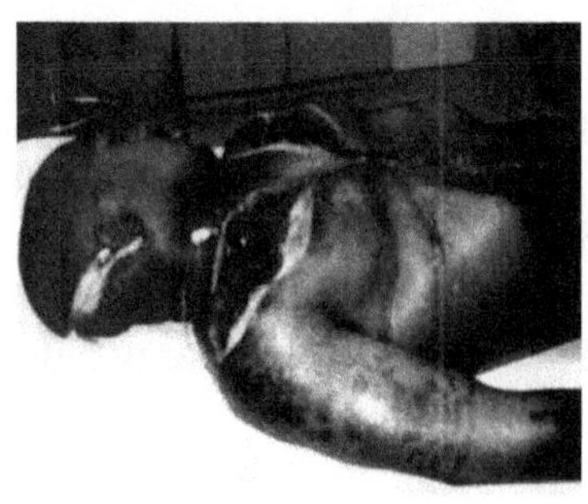

Tupac was loved and his music touched people not only in the America but internationally. Tupac is considered one of the most influential rappers of all time. He is widely credited as an important figure in hip hop culture, and his prominence in pop culture in general has been noted. Dotdash, formerly About.com, while ranking him fifth among the greatest rappers, notes, "Tupac Shakur is the most influential hip-hop artist of all time. Even in death, 2Pac remains a transcendental rap figure." Yet to some, he was a "father figure" who, said rapper YG, "makes you want to be better—at every level." Among many, Tupac Shakur has achieved iconic status.

A statue of Tupac Shakur at the MARTa museum in Herford, Germany

AllMusic's Stephen Thomas Erlewine described Shakur as "the unlikely martyr of gangsta rap", with Tupac paying the ultimate price of a criminal lifestyle. Shakur was described as one of the top two American rappers in the 1990s, along with Snoop Dogg. The online rap magazine *AllHipHop* held a 2007 roundtable at which New York rappers Cormega, citing tour experience with New York rap duo Mobb Deep, commented that B.I.G. ran New York, but Tupac ran America.

In 2010, writing *Rolling Stone* magazine's entry on Tupac at No. 86 among the "100 greatest artists", New York rapper 50 Cent appraised;

"Every rapper who grew up in the Nineties owes something to Tupac. He didn't sound like anyone who came before him."

According to music journalist Chuck Philips, Tupac "had helped elevate rap from a crude street fad to a complex art form, setting the stage for the current global hip-hop phenomenon." Philips writes, "The slaying silenced one of modern music's most eloquent voices—a ghetto poet whose tales of urban alienation captivated young people of all races and backgrounds." Via numerous fans perceiving him, despite his questionable conduct, as a martyr, "the downsizing of martyrdom cheapens its use", Michael Eric Dyson concedes. But Dyson adds, "Some, or even most, of that criticism can be conceded without doing damage to Tupac's martyrdom in the eyes of those disappointed by more traditional martyrs."

In 2014, BET explained that "his confounding mixture of ladies' man, thug, revolutionary and poet has forever altered our perception of what a rapper should look like, sound like and act like. In 50 Cent, Ja Rule, Lil Wayne, newcomers like Freddie Gibbs, and even his friend-turned-rival B.I.G., it's easy to see that Pac is the most copied MC of all time. There are murals bearing his likeness in New York, Brazil, Sierra Leone, Bulgaria, and countless other places; he even has statues in Atlanta and Germany. Quite simply, no other rapper has captured the world's attention the way Tupac did and still does." His writings, published after his death, inspired rapper YG to return to school and get his GED. In 2020, former California Senator and current Vice-president Kamala Harris called Shakur the "best rapper alive", which she explained because "West Coast girls think 2Pac lives on". [368]

The Final Mimesis for Tupac Shakur - The Amaru Shakur Foundation

In 1997, Shakur's mother founded the Shakur Family Foundation. Later renamed the Tupac Amaru Shakur Foundation, or TASF, it launched with a stated mission to "provide training and support for students who aspire to enhance their creative talents." The TASF sponsors essay contests, charity events, a performing arts day camp for teenagers, and undergraduate scholarships. In June 2005, the TASF opened the Tupac Amaru Shakur Center for the Arts, or TASCA, in Stone Mountain, Georgia. It closed in 2015.

The Final Mimesis for Tupac Shakur – Posthumous Lawsuit

Even in death Tupac could not rest in peace from controversy. Civil rights activist and fierce rap critic C. Delores Tucker sued Shakur's estate in federal court, claiming that lyrics in "How Do U Want It" and "Wonda Why They Call U Bitch" inflicted emotional distress, were slanderous, and invaded her privacy. The case was later dismissed.

The Final Mimesis for Tupac Shakur – Posthumous Albums

One of the testaments of a true artist is the longevity of his music. Some artist create music that lives long beyond their lives. Tupac Shakur was such an artist. At the time of his death, a fifth and final solo album was already finished, *The Don Killuminati: The 7 Day Theory*, under the stage name Makaveli. It had been recorded in one week in August 1996 and released that year. The lyrics were written and recorded in three days, and mixing took another four days. In 2005, MTV.com ranked *The 7 Day Theory* at No. 9 among hip hop's greatest albums ever, and by 2006 a classic album. Its singular poignance, through hurt and rage, contemplation and vendetta, resonates with many fans.

According to George "Papa G" Pryce, Death Row Records' then director of public relations, the album was meant to be "underground" and was not intended for release before the artist was murdered. It peaked at No. 1 on *Billboard*'s Top R&B / Hip-Hop Albums chart and on the *Billboard* 200, with the second-highest debut-week sales total of any album that year. On June 15, 1999, it was certified 4× multi-Platinum.

Later posthumous albums are archival productions; these albums are:

- *R U Still Down?* (1997)

- *Greatest Hits* (1998)

- *Still I Rise* (1999)

- *Until the End of Time* (2001)

- *Better Dayz* (2002)

- *Loyal to the Game* (2004)

- *Pac's Life* (2006)

Mimesis of Life Summary for Tupac Shakur

Tupac experienced childhood challenges. That his mother and father were members of the Black Panthers did not make Tupac's early childhood uneventful. His mother and caregiver had a drug addiction that contributed to an unstable element in Tupac's early childhood life experiences. Nevertheless, despite his early childhood dysfunction, Tupac still managed to find the calling of his talent. Possibly, it was the dysfunction in Tupac's life that led him to pursue areas that gave him peace and solace to counter the chaos in areas of his life. Whatever it was that connected with Tupac and led him to discover his artistic genius put him on a path to make his mark on the rap/hip hop culture. Tupac is considered one of the most genius and talented artists of his era, in the genre of rap/ hip hop; if not the most talented artist of all time, by some. One can wonder how such a genius gets integrated with such dysfunction? Tupac was killed in the prime of his life. Tupac got mixed up with a gangsta mentality and gangsta environment when he joined Death Row Records. The decisions individuals make in life determine the paths their lives take. Tupac made decisions that caused his life to spiral into an environment he was not totally conditioned or experienced to relate with. Tupac has a soft, sensitive, and compassionate inner core. His relationships and friendships with other people support the depth and quality of how Tupac touched others. The hard toughness of thug-life was not natural to Tupac. Frankly, one can raise the issue that Tupac was outside of his natural element during the time he spent with Death Row Records. The gangsta persona Tupac attempted to assume was not natural to him. The misalignment of his true nature and the gangsta influence in his life led him into scenarios that got him killed. It is ironic that Suge Knight, a real gangsta, is alive. Although he is incarcerated, he is alive. Suge is a true gangsta. Suge has gangsta instincts that Tupac did not have.

Nevertheless, Tupac was one of the greatest artists of his time, if not one of the greatest artists of all time. Tupac is an example of a common legacy among many individuals who came out of poverty and rose to successful heights. Tupac exemplifies how an individual who grows up in relative poverty, encounters dysfunctional challenges in their early life, finds their niche, and proceeds to become successful, overcoming the disadvantages of their prior life experiences. Tupac managed this. Unfortunately, Tupac is not alone in having his life cut short in his prime. Many other individuals have encountered the same unfortunate fate ...Elvis Presley, Marilyn Monroe, Martin L. King, Malcolm X, Sam Cooke, Robin Williams, Anna Nicole Smith, Selena Quintanilla, Jimi Hendrix, Chadwick Boseman, Aaliyah, Princess Diana, Anne Heche, Jim Morrison, Paul Walker, Philip Seymour Hoffman, Whitney Houston, John Belushi, James Dean, Janis Joplin, River Phoenix, Prince, Michael Jackson, Kobe Bryantm Kurt Cobain, Amy Winehouse, John Lennon and so many other individuals in life who died before the normal expectancy of life. With every one of these individuals, including Tupac Shakur, it is the decisions they made that led to the experiences they encountered, in their case, the life-ending experience they encountered.

Mimesis of Life for Elvis Aron Presley (1935 – 1977)

Elvis Aron Presley, Born January 8, 1935 – Died August 16, 1977. He is often referred to simply as Elvis, and people immediately know who that is. Elvis was an American singer, actor, and sergeant in the United States Army. Dubbed the "King of Rock and Roll", he is regarded as one of the most significant cultural figures of the 20th century. His energized interpretations of songs and sexually provocative performance style, combined with a singularly potent mix of influences across color lines during a transformative era in race relations, led him to both great success and initial controversy.

Presley was born in Tupelo, Mississippi, and relocated to Memphis, Tennessee, with his family when he was 13 years old. His music career began there in 1954, recording at Sun Records with producer Sam Phillips, who wanted to bring the sound of African-American music to a wider audience. Presley, on rhythm acoustic guitar, and accompanied by lead guitarist Scotty Moore and bassist Bill Black, was a pioneer of rockabilly, an uptempo, backbeat-driven fusion of country music and rhythm and blues. In 1955, drummer

D. J. Fontana joined to complete the lineup of Presley's classic quartet, and RCA Victor acquired his contract in a deal arranged by Colonel Tom Parker, who would manage him for more than two decades. Presley's first RCA Victor single, "Heartbreak Hotel", was released in January 1956 and became a number-one hit in the United States. Within a year, RCA would sell ten million Presley singles. With a series of successful network television appearances and chart-topping records, Presley became the leading figure of the newly popular sound of rock and roll; though his performative style and promotion of the then-marginalized sound of African Americans led to him being widely considered a threat to the moral well-being of the White American youth.

In November 1956, Presley made his film debut in *Love Me Tender*. Drafted into military service in 1958, Presley relaunched his recording career two years later with some of his most commercially successful work. He held few concerts, however, and guided by Parker, proceeded to devote much of the 1960s to making Hollywood films and soundtrack albums, most of them critically derided. Some of his most famous films included *Jailhouse Rock* (1957), *Blue Hawaii* (1961), and *Viva Las Vegas* (1964). In 1968, following a seven-year break from live performances, he returned to the stage in the acclaimed television comeback special *Elvis*, which led to an extended Las Vegas concert residency and a string of highly profitable tours. In 1973, Presley gave the first concert by a solo artist to be broadcast around the world, *aloha from Hawaii*. Years of prescription drug abuse and unhealthy eating habits severely compromised his health, and he died suddenly in 1977 at his Graceland estate at the age of 42.

Having sold roughly 500 million records worldwide, Presley is one of the best-selling music artists of all time. He was commercially successful in many genres, including pop, country, rhythm & blues, adult contemporary, and gospel. Presley won three Grammy Awards, received the Grammy Lifetime Achievement Award at age 36, and has been inducted into multiple music halls of fame. He holds several records, including the most RIAA-certified gold and platinum albums, the most albums charted on the *Billboard* 200, the most number-one albums by a solo artist on the UK Albums Chart, and the most number-one singles by any act on the UK Singles Chart. In 2018, Presley was posthumously awarded the Presidential Medal of Freedom.[369]

Mimesis Stage 1 for Elvis Aron Presley

1935

Elvis Aron Presley was born on January 8, 1935, in Tupelo, Mississippi, to Vernon Elvis and Gladys Love Presley in a two-room shotgun house. Vernon built the house for the special occasion of the arrival of their twin boys. However, Elvis's identical twin brother, Jesse Garon Presley, was delivered stillborn, 35 minutes before Elvis. Elvis became close to both parents and formed an especially close bond with his mother. The family attended an Assembly of God church, where he found his initial musical inspiration.[370]

Vernon Presley was of German, Scottish, and English descent. Elvis' mother, Gladys, was Scottish / Irish with some French Norman ancestry. Gladys and other members of the family believed their great-great-grandmother, Morning Dove White, was Cherokee. [371]

Vernon moved from one odd job to the next, showing little ambition. The family often relied on help from neighbors and government food assistance.

1938 They lost their home after Vernon was found guilty of altering a check written by his landowner and sometime-employer. He was jailed for eight months, while Gladys and Elvis moved in with relatives. [372]

Mimesis Stage 2 for Elvis Aron Presley

1941 In September, Elvis entered first grade at East Tupelo Consolidated, where his teachers regarded him as "average".

1945 He was encouraged to enter a singing contest after impressing his schoolteacher with a rendition of Red Foley's country song "Old Shep" during morning prayers. The contest, held at the Mississippi–Alabama Fair and Dairy Show on October 3. This was his first public performance. Elvis, just 10 years old, stood on a chair to reach the microphone and sang "Old Shep". He recalled placing fifth. A few months later, Presley received his first guitar for his birthday; he had hoped for something else—by different accounts, either a bicycle or a rifle. Over the following year, he received basic guitar lessons from two of his uncles and the new pastor at the family's church. Presley recalled, "I took the guitar, and I watched people, and I learned to play a little bit. But I would never sing in public. I was very shy about it."

In September 1946, Presley entered a new school, Milam, for sixth grade; he was regarded as a loner. The following year, he began bringing his guitar to school on a daily basis. He played and sang during lunchtime and was often teased as a "trashy" kid who played hillbilly music. By then, the family was living in a largely black neighborhood. Presley was a devotee of Mississippi Slim's show on the Tupelo radio station WELO. He was described as "crazy about music" by Slim's younger brother, who was one of Presley's classmates and often took him into the station. Slim supplemented Presley's guitar instruction by demonstrating chord techniques. When Elvis was 12 years old, Slim scheduled him for two on-air performances. Elvis was overcome by stage fright the first time, but did perform the following week.[373]

Mimesis Stage 2 for Elvis Aron Presley – Teenage Years in Memphis

1948 In November, the family moved to Memphis, Tennessee. After residing for nearly a year in rooming houses, they were granted a two-bedroom apartment in the public housing complex known as the Lauderdale Courts. Enrolled at L. C. Humes High School, Presley received only a C in music in eighth grade. When his music teacher told him that he had no aptitude for singing, he brought in his guitar the next day and sang a recent hit, "Keep Them Cold Icy Fingers Off Me", to prove otherwise. A classmate later recalled that the teacher "agreed that Elvis was right when he said that she didn't appreciate his kind of singing". He was usually too shy to perform openly and was occasionally bullied by classmates who viewed him as a "mama's boy". [374]

1950   Elvis began practicing guitar regularly under the tutelage of Lee Denson, a neighbor two and a half years his senior. They and three other boys—including two future rockabilly pioneers, brothers Dorsey and Johnny Burnette—formed a loose musical collective that played frequently around the Courts. That September, he began working as an usher at Loew's State Theater. Other jobs followed at Precision Tool, Loew's again, and MARL Metal Products. Presley also helped Jewish neighbors, the Fruchters, by being their shabbos goy.

During his junior year, Presley began to stand out more among his classmates, largely because of his appearance: he grew his sideburns and styled his hair with rose oil and Vaseline. In his free time, he would head down to Beale Street, the heart of Memphis's thriving blues scene, and gaze longingly at the wild, flashy clothes in the windows of Lansky Brothers. By his senior year, he was wearing those clothes.[375]

1953   Overcoming his reluctance to perform. In April, Elvis competed in Humes' Annual "Minstrel" show. Singing and playing guitar, he opened with "Till I Waltz Again with You", a recent hit for Teresa Brewer. Presley recalled that the performance did much for his reputation: "I wasn't popular in school ... I failed music—the only thing I ever failed. And then they entered me in this talent show ... when I came onstage, I heard people kind of rumbling and whispering and so forth, 'cause nobody knew I even sang. It was amazing how popular I became in school after that."[376]

Elvis had no formal music training and could not read music; he studied and played by ear. He also visited record stores that provided jukeboxes and listening booths to customers. He knew all of Hank Snow's songs, and he loved records by other country singers such as Roy Acuff, Ernest Tubb, Ted Daffan, Jimmie Rodgers, Jimmie Davis, and Bob Wills. The Southern gospel singer Jake Hess, one of his favorite performers, was a significant influence on his ballad-singing style. He was a regular audience member at the monthly All-Night Singings downtown, where many of the white gospel groups that performed reflected the influence of African-American spiritual music. He adored the music of black gospel singer Sister Rosetta Tharpe.[377]

Elvis listened to regional radio stations, such as WDIA-AM, that played "race records": spirituals, blues, and the modern, backbeatheavy sound of rhythm and blues. Like some of his peers, he may have attended blues venues only on nights designated for exclusively white audiences — a necessity in the segregated South. Many of his future recordings were inspired by local African-American musicians such as Arthur Crudup and Rufus Thomas. B.B. King recalled that he had known Presley before he was popular when they both used to frequent Beale Street. By the time he graduated from high school in June 1953, Presley had already decided music was his future.[378]

Mimesis Stage 2 for Elvis Aron Presley – First Recordings (1953-1956)

1953  In August Elvis visited the offices of Memphis Recording Service, run by Sam Phillips before he started Sun Records. Elvis only wanted to buy a few minutes of studio time to record a two-sided acetate disc: "My Happiness" and "That's When Your Heartaches Begin". He later claimed that he intended the record as a birthday gift for his mother, or that he was merely interested in what he "sounded like", although there was a much cheaper, amateur record-making service at a nearby general store. Biographer Peter Guralnick argued that he chose Sun in the hope of being discovered. Marion Keisker, studio receptionist asked Elvis, what kind of singer he was, Presley responded, "I sing all kinds." When she pressed him on who he sounded like, he repeatedly answered, "I don't sound like nobody." After he recorded, Sun boss Sam Phillips asked Keisker to note down the young man's name, which she did along with her own commentary: "Good ballad singer. Hold."

1954   In January, Elvis cut a second record at Sun Records—"I'll Never Stand in Your Way" and "It Wouldn't Be the Same Without You", but again nothing came of it. Not long after, he failed an audition for a local vocal quartet, the Songfellows. He explained to his father, "They told me I couldn't sing." Songfellow Jim Hamill later claimed that he was turned down because he did not demonstrate an ear for harmony at the time.

In April, Elvis began working for the Crown Electric Company as a truck driver. His friend Ronnie Smith, after playing a few local gigs with him, suggested he contact Eddie Bond, leader of Smith's professional band, which had an opening for a vocalist. Bond rejected him after a tryout, advising Presley to stick to truck driving "because you're never going to make it as a singer". [379]

Phillips, meanwhile, was always on the lookout for someone who could bring to a broader audience the sound of the black musicians on whom Sun focused. As Keisker reported, "Over and over I remember Sam saying, 'If I could find a white man who had the Negro sound and the Negro feel, I could make a billion dollars.' "In June, he acquired a demo recording by Jimmy Sweeney of a ballad, "Without You", that he thought might suit the teenage singer. Presley came by the studio but was unable to do it justice. Despite this, Phillips asked Elvis to sing as many numbers as he knew. He was sufficiently affected by what he heard to invite two local musicians, guitarist Winfield "Scotty" Moore and upright bass player Bill Black, to work something up with Presley for a recording session. Presley transformed not only the sound but the emotion of the song, turning what had been written as a "lament for a lost love into a satisfied declaration of independence."[380]

The session held the evening of July 5, proved entirely unfruitful until late in the night. As they were about to abort and go home, Presley took his guitar and launched into a 1946 blues number, Arthur Crudup's "That's All Right". Moore recalled, "All of a sudden, Elvis just started singing this song, jumping around and acting the fool, and then Bill picked up his bass, and he started acting the fool, too, and I started playing with them. Sam, I think, had the door to the control booth open... he stuck his head out and said, 'What are you doing?' And we said, 'We don't know.' 'Well, back up,' he said, 'try to find a place to start, and do it again.'" Phillips quickly began taping; this was the sound he had been looking for.[381]

Three days later, popular Memphis DJ Dewey Phillips played "That's All Right" on his *Red, Hot, and Blue* show. Listeners began phoning in, eager to find out who the singer was.

The interest was such that Phillips played the record repeatedly during the remaining two hours of his show. Interviewing Presley on-air, Phillips asked him what high school he attended to clarify his color for the many callers who had assumed that he was black. During the next few days, the trio recorded a bluegrass song, Bill Monroe's "Blue Moon of Kentucky", again in a distinctive style and employing a jury-rigged echo effect that Sam Phillips dubbed "slapback". A single was pressed with "That's All Right" on the A-side and "Blue Moon of Kentucky" on side B.[382]

The trio of Elvis Presley lead singer, guitarist Winfield "Scotty" Moore and upright bass player Bill Black played publicly for the first time on July 17 at the Bon Air club. At the end of July, they appeared at the Overton Park Shell, with Slim Whitman headlining. Here Elvis pioneered 'Rubber Legs', his signature style dance movement that he is best known for. A combination of his strong response to rhythm  and nervousness at playing before a large crowd led Presley to shake his legs as he performed: his wide-cut pants emphasized his movements, causing young women in the audience to start screaming. Moore recalled, "During the instrumental parts, he would back off from the mike and be playing and shaking, and the crowd would just go wild".[383]

Soon after, Moore and Black left their old band, the Starlite Wranglers, to play with Presley regularly, and DJ/promoter Bob Neal became the trio's manager. From August through October, they played frequently at the Eagle's Nest club and returned to Sun Studio for more recording sessions, and Presley quickly grew more confident on stage. According to Moore, "His movement was a natural thing, but he was also very conscious of what got a reaction. He'd do something one time and then he would expand on it real quick." Presley made what would be his only appearance on Nashville's *Grand Ole Opry* stage on October 2; after a polite audience response, *Opry* manager Jim Denny told Phillips that his singer was "not bad" but did not suit the program.[384]

1954 In November, Presley performed on *Louisiana Hayride*—the *Opry*'s chief, and more adventurous, rival. The Shreveport-based show was broadcast to 198 radio stations in 28 states. He had another attack of nerves during the first set, which drew a muted reaction. A more composed and energetic second set inspired an enthusiastic response. House drummer D. J. Fontana brought a new element, complementing Presley's movements with accented beats that he had mastered playing in strip clubs. Soon after the show, the *Hayride* engaged Presley for a year's worth of Saturday-night appearances. Trading in his old guitar for $8 (and seeing it promptly dispatched to the garbage), he purchased a Martin instrument for $175 (equivalent to $1,800 in 2021), and his trio began playing in new locales, including Houston, Texas, and Texarkana, Arkansas. [385]

Presley made his first television appearance on the KSLA-TV broadcast of *Louisiana Hayride*. Soon after, he failed an audition for *Arthur Godfrey's Talent Scouts* on the CBS television network.

1955　Elvis's regular *Hayride* appearances, constant touring, and well-received record releases made him a regional star, from Tennessee to West Texas.

In January, Neal signed a formal management contract with Presley and introduced him to Colonel Tom Parker. Neal considered Parker the best promoter in the music business. Parker, born in the Netherlands, had immigrated illegally to the United States and claimed to be from West Virginia. Parker received an honorary colonel's commission from the Louisiana governor and country singer Jimmie Davis. Parker successfully managed the top country star Eddy Arnold. Parker was working with the new number-one country singer, Hank Snow and booked Presley on Snow's February tour. When the tour reached Odessa, Texas, a 19-year-old Roy Orbison saw Presley for the first time: "His energy was incredible, his instinct was just amazing. ... I just didn't know what to make of it. There was just no reference point in the culture to compare it."[386]

By August, Sun had released ten sides credited to "Elvis Presley, Scotty and Bill"; on the latest recordings, the trio were joined by a drummer. Some of the songs, like "That's All Right", were what one Memphis journalist described as the "R&B genre of negro field jazz"; others, like "Blue Moon of Kentucky", were "more in the country genre", "but Elvis presented a blending of the two different music styles". This blend of styles made it difficult for Elvis's music to find radio airplay. According to Neal, many country-music disc jockeys would not play it because he sounded too much like a black artist and none of the rhythm-and-blues stations would touch him because "he sounded too much like a hillbilly." The blend came to be known as rockabilly. At the time, Presley was billed as "The King of Western Bop", "The Hillbilly Cat", and "The Memphis Flash".

1955   In August, Elvis renewed Neal's management contract, and appointed Parker as his special adviser. The group maintained an extensive touring schedule throughout the second half of the year. Neal recalled, "It was almost frightening, the reaction that came to Elvis from the teenaged boys. So many of them, through some sort of jealousy, would practically hate him. There were occasions in some towns in Texas when we'd have to be sure to have a police guard because somebody'd always try to take a

crack at him. They'd get a gang and try to waylay him or something." However, the teenage girls loved Elvis with a trance fixed devotion. The trio became a quartet when *Hayride* drummer Fontana joined as a full member. In mid-October, they played a few shows in support of Bill Haley, whose "Rock Around the Clock" track had been a number-one hit the previous year. Haley observed that Presley had a natural feel for rhythm and advised him to sing fewer ballads.[387]

In early November, at the Country Disc Jockey Convention, Presley was voted the year's most promising male artist. Several record companies had shown interest in signing him. After three major labels made offers of up to $25,000, Parker and Phillips struck a deal with RCA Victor on November 21 to acquire Presley's Sun contract for an unprecedented $40,000. Presley, at 20, was still a minor, so his father signed the contract. Parker arranged with the owners of Hill & Range Publishing, Jean and Julian Aberbach, to create two entities, Elvis Presley Music and Gladys Music, to handle all the new material recorded by Presley. Songwriters were obliged to forgo one-third of their customary royalties in exchange for having him perform their compositions. By December, RCA Victor had begun to heavily promote its new singer, and before the month's end had reissued many of his Sun recordings.[388]

1956 On January 10, Elvis made his first recordings for RCA Victor in Nashville. Additions were made to the group, including mainstays of Moore, Black, and Fontana, added *Hayride* pianist Floyd Cramer, who had been performing at live club dates with Presley. Also, RCA Victor added guitarist Chet Atkins and three background singers, including Gordon Stoker of the popular Jordanaires quartet, to fill in the sound. The session produced the moody, unusual "Heartbreak Hotel", released as a single on January 27.

Parker finally brought Elvis to national television, booking him on CBS's *Stage Show* for six appearances over two months. The program, produced in New York, was hosted on alternate weeks by big band leaders and brothers Tommy and Jimmy Dorsey. After his first appearance on January 28, Presley stayed in town to record at the RCA Victor New York studio. The sessions yielded eight songs, including a cover of Carl Perkins' rockabilly anthem "Blue Suede Shoes". In February, Presley's "I Forgot to Remember to Forget", a Sun recording initially released the previous August, reached the top of the *Billboard* country chart. Neal's contract was terminated, and on March 2, Parker became Presley's manager.[389]

1956 On April 3, Presley made the first of two appearances on NBC's *Milton Berle Show*. His performance, on the deck of the USS *Hancock* in San Diego, California, prompted cheers and screams from an audience of sailors and their dates. A few days later, a flight taking Presley and his band to Nashville for a recording session left all three badly shaken when an engine died and the plane almost went down over Arkansas. Twelve weeks after its original release, "Heartbreak Hotel" became Elvis's first number-one pop hit. In late April, Presley began a two-week residency at the New Frontier Hotel and Casino on the Las Vegas Strip. The shows were poorly received by the conservative, middle-aged hotel guests—"like a jug of corn liquor at a champagne party", wrote a critic for *Newsweek*. Amid his Vegas tenure, Presley, who had serious acting ambitions, signed a seven-year contract with Paramount Pictures. He began a tour of the Midwest in mid-May, taking in 15 cities in as many days. He had attended several shows by Freddie Bell and the Bellboys in Vegas and was struck by their cover of "Hound Dog", a hit in 1953 for blues singer Big Mama Thornton by songwriters Jerry Leiber and Mike Stoller. It became the new closing number of his act. After a show in La Crosse, Wisconsin, an urgent message on the letterhead of the local Catholic diocese's newspaper was sent to FBI director J. Edgar Hoover. It warned that "Presley is a definite danger to the security of the United States... [His] actions and motions were such as to rouse the sexual passions of teenage youth...

After the show, more than 1,000 teenagers tried to gang into Elvis's room at the auditorium... Indications of the harm Presley did just in La Crosse were the two high school girls... whose abdomen and thigh had Presley's autograph."[390]

The second *Milton Berle Show* appearance came on June 5 at NBC's Hollywood studio. Berle persuaded Elvis to leave his guitar backstage, advising, "Let 'em see you, son." During the performance, Presley abruptly halted an uptempo rendition of "Hound Dog" with a wave of his arm and launched into a slow, grinding version accentuated with energetic, exaggerated body movements. Elvis's gyrations created a storm of controversy. Television critics were outraged: Jack Gould of *The New York Times* wrote, "Mr. Presley has no discernible singing ability... His phrasing, if it can be called that, consists of the stereotyped variations that go with a beginner's aria in a bathtub... His one specialty is an accented movement of the body ... primarily identified with the repertoire of the blond bombshells of the burlesque runway." Ben Gross of the New York *Daily News* opined that popular music "has reached its lowest depths in the 'grunt and groin' antics of one Elvis Presley. ... Elvis, who rotates his pelvis ... gave an exhibition that was suggestive and vulgar, tinged with the kind of animalism that should be confined to dives and bordellos". The Ed Sullivan Show, the most popular American variety show at the time, declared Elvis "unfit for family viewing". To Elvis's displeasure, he soon found himself being referred to as "Elvis the Pelvis", which he called "one of the most childish expressions I ever heard, comin' from an adult".[391]

1956   The Berle shows drew such high ratings that Elvis was booked for a July 1 appearance on NBC's *Steve Allen Show* in New York. Allen, no fan of rock and roll, introduced a "new Elvis" in a white bow tie and black tails. Presley sang "Hound Dog" for less than a minute to a basset hound wearing a top hat and bow tie. As described by television historian Jake Austen, "Allen thought Presley was talentless and absurd ... [he] set things up so that Presley would show his contrition,"[392] Elvis told a reporter, "I'm holding down on this show. I do not want to do anything to make people dislike me. I think TV is important, so I'm going to go along, but I won't be able to give the kind of show I do in a personal appearance." Elvis would refer back to the Allen show as the most ridiculous performance of his career.[393]

The next day, Presley recorded "Hound Dog", along with "Any Way You Want Me" and "Don't Be Cruel". The Jordanaires sang harmony, as they had on *The Steve Allen Show*; they would work with Presley through the 1960s. A few days later, Presley made an outdoor concert appearance in Memphis, where he announced, "You know, those people in New York are not gonna change me none. I'm gonna show you what the real Elvis is like tonight." In August, a judge in Jacksonville, Florida, ordered

Presley to tame his act. Throughout the following performance, he largely kept still, except for wiggling his little finger suggestively in mockery of the order. The single pairing "Don't Be Cruel" with "Hound Dog" ruled the top of the charts for 11 weeks—a mark that would not be surpassed for 36 years. Recording sessions for Presley's second album took place in Hollywood during the first week of September. Leiber and Stoller, the writers of "Hound Dog", contributed "Love Me". [394]

Allen's show with Presley, for the first time, beat CBS's *Ed Sullivan Show* in the ratings. Sullivan, despite his June pronouncement, booked Presley for three appearances for an unprecedented $50,000. The first, on September 9, 1956, was seen by approximately 60 million viewers—a record 82.6 percent of the television audience. Actor Charles Laughton hosted the show, filling in while Sullivan was recovering from a car accident. Presley appeared in two segments that night from CBS Television City in Los Angeles. According to Elvis legend, Presley was shot only from the waist up. Watching clips of the Allen and Berle shows with his producer, Sullivan had opined that Presley "got some kind of device hanging down below the crotch of his pants—so when he moves his legs back and forth you can see the outline of his cock... I think it's a Coke bottle... We just can't have this on a Sunday night. This is a family show!" Sullivan publicly told *TV Guide*, "As for his gyrations, the whole thing can be controlled with camera shots." In fact, Presley was shown head-to-toe in the first and second shows. Though the camerawork was relatively discreet during his debut, with leg-concealing close-ups when he danced, the studio audience reacted in customary style: screaming. Presley's performance of his forthcoming single, the ballad "Love Me Tender", prompted a record-shattering million advance orders. More than any other single event, it was this first appearance on *The Ed Sullivan Show* that made Elvis a national celebrity.

Accompanying Elvis's rise to fame, a cultural shift was taking place that he both helped inspire and came to symbolize. The historian Marty Jezer wrote that Presley began the "biggest pop craze" since Glenn Miller and Frank Sinatra and brought rock and roll to mainstream culture: "As Presley set the artistic pace, other artists followed... Presley, more than anyone else, gave the young a belief in themselves as a distinct and somehow unified generation—the first in America ever to feel the power of an integrated youth culture."[395]

The audience response at Presley's live shows became increasingly fevered. Moore recalled, "He'd start out, 'You ain't nothin' but a Hound Dog,' and they'd just go to pieces. They'd always react the same way. There would be a riot every time." At the two concerts he performed in September at the Mississippi–Alabama Fair and Dairy Show, 50 National Guardsmen were added to the police security to ensure that the crowd would not cause a riot. *Elvis*, Presley's second RCA Victor album, was released in October and quickly rose to number one on the billboard. The album includes "Old Shep", which he sang at the talent show in 1945, and which now marked the first time he played piano on an RCA Victor session. According to Guralnick, one can hear "in the halting chords and the somewhat stumbling rhythm both the unmistakable emotion and the equally unmistakable valuing of emotion over technique." Assessing the musical and cultural impact of Presley's recordings from "That's All Right" through *Elvis*, rock critic Dave Marsh wrote that "these records, more than any others, contain the seeds of what rock & roll was, has been and most likely what it may foreseeably become."

1956   Presley returned to the Sullivan show at its main studio in New York, hosted this time by its namesake, on October 28. After the performance, crowds in Nashville and St. Louis burned him in effigy. His first motion picture, *Love Me Tender*, was released on November 21. Though he was not top-billed, the film's original title—*The Reno Brothers*—was changed to capitalize on his latest number-one record: "Love Me Tender" had hit the top of the charts earlier that month. To further take advantage of Presley's popularity, four musical numbers were added to what was originally a straight acting role. The film was panned by critics but did very well at the box office. Presley would receive top billing on every subsequent film he made.

1956 On December 4, Presley dropped into Sun Records where Carl Perkins and Jerry Lee Lewis were recording and had an impromptu jam session along with Johnny Cash. Though Phillips no longer had the right to release any Presley material, he made sure that the session was captured on tape. The results, none officially released for 25 years, became known as the "Million Dollar Quartet" recordings. The year ended with a front-page story in *The Wall Street Journal* reporting that Presley merchandise had brought in $22 million on top of his record sales, and *Billboard*'s declaration that he had placed more songs in the top 100 than any other artist since records were first charted. In his first full year at RCA Victor, then the record industry's largest company, Presley had accounted for over 50 percent of the label's singles sales.[396]

Mimesis 2 for Elvis Aron Presley – Military Service

1958 On March 24, 1958, Presley was drafted into the United States Army at Fort Chaffee, Arkansas. His arrival was a major media event. Hundreds of people descended on Presley as he stepped from the bus; photographers then accompanied him into the installation. Presley announced that he was looking forward to his military stint, saying that he did not want to be treated any differently from anyone else: "The Army can do anything it wants with me."[397]

On October 1, 1958, Presley was assigned to the 1st Medium Tank Battalion, 32d Armor, 3d Armored Division, at Ray Barracks, Germany, where he served as an armor intelligence specialist.[1] On November 27, he was promoted to private first class.[398]

Elvis was drafted and joined the Army in 1958. Like Muhammad Ali, who was drafted in 1966, Elvis was drafted at the brink of his fame and with a budding future ahead. The difference between Ali rejecting military service and Elvis embracing military service is as simple as Black and White, literally. American society responded differently to Black Americans than it did to White Americans. Black Americans had to deal with racism on a constant basis, whereas White Americans did not. Even though Elvis owes much of his success to Black influence, musically and soulfully, he still toed the line on the side of his White heritage.

1959   On June 1, 1959, to a specialist fourth class. While on maneuvers, Presley was introduced to amphetamines by another soldier. He became "practically evangelical about their benefits", not only for energy but for "strength" and weight loss, and many of his friends in the outfit joined him in indulging. The Army also introduced Presley to karate, which he studied seriously, training with Jürgen Seydel. It became a lifelong interest, which he later included in his live performances. Fellow soldiers have attested to Presley's wish to be seen as an able, ordinary soldier, despite his fame, and to his generosity.

He donated his Army pay to charity, purchased TV sets, and bought an extra set of fatigues for everyone in his outfit.

1960 Presley was promoted to sergeant on February 11.[399]

Mimesis 2 for Elvis Aron Presley – The Death of his Mother, Gladys

1958 In early August, his mother was diagnosed with hepatitis, and her condition rapidly worsened. Presley was granted emergency leave to visit her and arrived in Memphis on August 12. Two days later, she died of heart failure at age 46. Presley was devastated and never the same; their relationship had remained extremely close— even into his adulthood, they would use baby talk with each other and Presley would address her with pet names. [400]

Mimesis 2 for Elvis Aron Presley – Priscilla Beaulieu

1960 While in Bad Nauheim, Germany, Presley, 24 at the time, met 14-year-old Priscilla Beaulieu. Priscilla said that due to their age difference, when they met, he told her: "Why, you're just a baby." They would eventually marry after a seven-and-a-half-year courtship. In her autobiography, Priscilla said that Presley was concerned that his 24-month spell as a G.I. would ruin his career. In Special Services, he would have been able to give musical performances and remain in touch with the public, but Parker had convinced him that to gain popular respect, he should serve his country as a regular soldier. Media reports echoed Presley's concerns about his career, but RCA Victor producer Steve Sholes and Freddy Bienstock of Hill and Range had carefully prepared for his two-year hiatus. Armed with a substantial amount of unreleased material, they kept up a regular stream of successful releases. Between his induction and discharge, Presley had ten top 40 hits, including "Wear My Ring Around Your Neck", the bestselling "Hard Headed Woman", and "One Night" in 1958, and "(Now and Then There's) A Fool Such as I" and the number-one "A Big Hunk o' Love" in 1959. RCA Victor also generated four albums compiling previously issued material during this period, most successfully *Elvis' Golden Records* (1958), which hit number three on the LP chart.[401]

Mimesis 2 for Elvis Aron Presley – Return to the United States

1960 Elvis returned to the United States on March 2, and was honorably discharged three days later. The train that carried him from New Jersey to Tennessee was mobbed all the way, and Presley was called upon to appear at scheduled stops to please his fans. On the night of March 20, he entered RCA Victor's Nashville studio to cut tracks for a new album along with a single, "Stuck on You", which was rushed into release and swiftly became a number-one hit. Another Nashville session two weeks later yielded a pair of his bestselling singles, the ballads "It's Now or

Never" and "Are You Lonesome Tonight?", along with the rest of *Elvis Is Back!* The album features several songs described by Greil Marcus as full of Chicago blues "menace, driven by Presley's own super-miked acoustic guitar, brilliant playing by Scotty Moore, and demonic sax work from Boots Randolph. Elvis' singing wasn't sexy, it was pornographic." As a whole, the record "conjured up the vision of a performer who could be all things", according to music historian John Robertson: "a flirtatious teenage idol with a heart of gold; a tempestuous, dangerous lover; a gutbucket blues singer; a sophisticated nightclub entertainer; [a] raucous rocker". Released only days after the recording was complete, it reached number two on the album chart.[402]

Elvis returned to television on May 12 as a guest on *The Frank Sinatra Timex Special*—ironic for both stars, given Sinatra's earlier excoriation of rock and roll. Also known as *Welcome Home Elvis*, the show had been taped in late March, the only time all year Presley performed in front of an audience. Parker secured an unheard-of $125,000 fee for eight minutes of singing. The broadcast drew an enormous viewership.[403]

1960 Colonel Tom Parker guided Elvis' career into a heavy filmmaking schedule. The focus was on modest budgeted musical comedies. Presley, at first, insisted on pursuing higher roles, but when two films in a more dramatic vein—*Flaming Star* (1960) and *Wild in the Country* (1961)—were less commercially successful, he reverted to the formula. Among the 27 films he made during the 1960s, there were a few further exceptions. His films were almost universally panned; critic Andrew Caine dismissed them as a "pantheon of bad taste". Nonetheless, they were virtually all profitable. Hal Wallis, who produced nine of them, declared, "A Presley picture is the only sure thing in Hollywood.[404]

Along with the films Elvis made he often recorded the soundtracks as well.

Three of Presley's soundtrack albums were ranked number one on the pop charts, and a few of his most popular songs came from his films, such as "Can't Help Falling in Love" (1961) and "Return to Sender" (1962). ("Viva Las Vegas", the title track to the 1964 film, was a minor hit as a B-side, and later became popular.) But, as with artistic merit, the commercial returns steadily diminished. During a five-year span—1964 through 1968—Presley had only one top-ten hit: "Crying in the Chapel" (1965), a gospel number recorded back in 1960. As for non-film albums, between the June 1962 release of *Pot Luck* and the November 1968 release of the soundtrack to the television special that signaled his comeback, only one LP of new material by Presley was issued: the gospel album *How Great Thou Art* (1967). It won him his first Grammy Award, for Best Sacred Performance. As Marsh described, Presley was "arguably the greatest white gospel singer of his time [and] really the last rock & roll artist to make gospel as vital a component of his musical personality as his secular songs". [405]

1968 Presley's only child, Lisa Marie, was born on February 1. During this period, Elvis became unhappy with his career. Of the eight Elvis singles released between January 1967 and May 1968, only two charted in the top 40, and none higher than number 28. His forthcoming soundtrack album, *Speedway*, would rank at number 82 on the *Billboard* chart. Parker had already shifted his plans to television, where Elvis had not appeared since the Sinatra Timex show in 1960. He maneuvered a deal with NBC that committed the network to both financing a theatrical feature and broadcasting a Christmas special.[406]

1968  The Christmas special, simply called *Elvis*, aired on December 3. Later known as the *'68 Comeback Special*, the show featured lavishly staged studio productions as well as songs performed with a band in front of a small audience—Elvis's first live performances since 1961. The live segments saw Elvis dressed in tight black leather, singing and playing guitar in an uninhibited style reminiscent of his early rock and roll days. Director and co-producer Steve Binder had worked hard to produce a show that was far from the hour of Christmas songs Parker had originally planned. The show, NBC's highest-rated that season, captured 42 percent of the total viewing audience.   Jon Landau of *Eye* magazine remarked, "There is something magical about watching a man who has lost himself find his way back home. He sang with the kind of power people no longer expect of rock 'n' roll singers. He moved his body with a lack of pretension and effort that must have made Jim Morrison green with envy." Dave Marsh calls the performance one of "emotional grandeur and historical resonance".[407]

The special reminded Elvis of what he had not been able to do for years, being able to choose the people; being able to choose what songs and not being told what had to be on the soundtrack. ... He felt like he was out of prison, man. Binder said of Presley's reaction, "I played Elvis the 60-minute show, and he told me in the screening room, 'Steve, it's the greatest thing I've ever done in my life. I give you my word, I will never sing a song I don't believe in.'"[408]

1969   The success of the Comeback Special gave Elvis an open door to go back into the studio and record a series of songs. Recording at the American Sound Studio, led to the acclaimed *From Elvis in Memphis*. Released in June, it was his first secular, non-soundtrack album from a dedicated period in the studio in eight years. As described by Dave Marsh, it is "a masterpiece in which Presley immediately catches up with pop music trends that had seemed to pass him by during the movie years. He sings country songs, soul songs and rockers with real conviction, a stunning achievement." The album featured the hit single "In the Ghetto", issued in April, which reached number three on the pop chart—Presley's first non-gospel top ten hit since "Bossa Nova Baby" in 1963. Further hit singles were culled from the American Sound sessions: "Suspicious Minds", "Don't Cry Daddy", and "Kentucky Rain". [409]

Elvis was anxious to perform live again. The success of the Comeback Special caused offers to come from around the world. The London Palladium offered Parker $28,000 (equivalent to $207,000 in 2021) for a one-week engagement. He responded, "That's fine for me, now how much can you get for Elvis?" In May, the brand-new International Hotel in Las Vegas, boasting the largest showroom in the city, announced that it had booked Presley. He was scheduled to perform 57 shows over four weeks, beginning July 31. His group, Moore, Fontana, and the Jordanaires, declined to participate, afraid of losing the lucrative session work they had in Nashville. Presley assembled new, top-notch accompaniment, led by guitarist James Burton and including two gospel groups, The Imperials and Sweet Inspirations. Costume designer Bill Belew, responsible for the intense leather styling of the Comeback Special, created a new stage look for Presley, inspired by Presley's passion for karate. Nonetheless, he was nervous: his only previous Las Vegas engagement, in 1956, had been dismal. Parker, who intended to make Presley's return the show business event of the year, oversaw a major promotional push. For his part, International Hotel owner Kirk Kerkorian arranged to send his own plane to New York to fly in rock journalists for the debut performance. [410]

Elvis took to the stage without introduction. The audience of 2,200, including many celebrities, gave him a standing ovation before he sang a note and another after his performance. A third followed his encore, "Can't Help Falling in Love" (a song that would be his closing number for much of his remaining life). At a press conference after the show, when a journalist referred to him as Elvis, "The King", he gestured toward Fats Domino, who was taking in the scene. "No," Elvis said, "that's the real king of rock and roll," referring to Domino. The next day, Parker's negotiations with the hotel resulted in a five-year contract for Presley to play each February and August, at an annual salary of $1 million. *Newsweek* commented, "There are several unbelievable things about Elvis, but the most incredible is his staying power in a world where meteoric careers fade like shooting stars." *Rolling Stone* called Presley "supernatural, his own resurrection." In November, Presley's final non-concert film, *Change of Habit*, opened. The double album *From Memphis to Vegas/From Vegas to Memphis* came out the same month; the first LP consisted of live performances from the International, the second of more cuts from the American Sound sessions. "Suspicious Minds" reached the top of the charts—Elvis's first US pop number-one in over seven years, and his last. [411]

Mimesis Stage 2 for Elvis Aron Presley - Women

Of all the things in his life, Elvis lacked, women  were not one of them. Women flocked to Elvis. He was handsome. He was a gentleman, and his southern boyish charm was irresistible to women, especially those who were used to the aggressive, arrogant male persona. Priscilla Beaulieu Presley, the only woman to get Elvis to the altar. They had a daughter, Lisa Marie, born on February 1, 1968, and died on January 12, 2023. Priscilla described herself during her time with Elvis as "crazed with worry" about other women. According to Priscilla, they did not sleep together until their wedding night. The one woman who particularly caused Priscilla worry was Ann-Margret, who became involved with Elvis after he had proposed to Priscilla.

Other celebrities linked with Presley include Natalie Wood, Connie Stevens, Monique Van Vooren, and Nancy Sinatra, who was rumored to be seeing him during his wife's pregnancy. Bookstores practically have a subsection under Presley for memoirs by women who claim to have had affairs with him.

Cybill Shepherd has confirmed in interviews that she dated him in 1972, when his marriage to Priscilla was in its final stage. A friend who knew Shepherd from Memphis called and said the singer wanted to meet her and invited her to a private screening. When the movie started, everyone on one side of her slid down a seat, and Presley, dressed all in white, plopped down next to her.[412] These women who were drawn to Elvis do not even include the ones among his millions of female fans who were seduced by his boyish charm.

Mimesis 2 for Elvis Aron Presley – Back on Tour

1970 Elvis returned to International touring, performing two shows a night. Recordings from these shows were issued on the album *On Stage*. In late February, Elvis performed six attendance-record–breaking shows at the Houston Astrodome. In April, the single "The Wonder of You" was issued—a number one hit in the UK, it topped the US adult contemporary chart, as well. Metro-Goldwyn-Mayer filmed rehearsal and concert footage at the International during August for the documentary *Elvis: That's the Way It Is*. Presley was performing in a jumpsuit, which would become a trademark of his live act. During this engagement, he was threatened with murder unless US$50,000 (equivalent to $349,000 in 2021) was paid. Elvis had been the target of many threats since the 1950s, often without his knowledge. The FBI took the threat seriously and security was stepped up for the next two shows. Presley went onstage with a Derringer in his right boot and a .45 pistol in his waistband, but the concerts succeeded without any incidents. [413]

Elvis's expanded his musical style. Country was put on the back burner, and soul and R&B was left in Memphis. Elvis adopted a classy, very clean white pop—perfect for the Las Vegas crowd, but a definite retrograde step for Elvis." After the end of his International engagement on September 7, Elvis embarked on a week-long concert tour, largely of the South, his first since 1958. Another week-long tour, of the West Coast, followed in November. [414]

1970  Elvis meets US President Richard Nixon in the White House Oval Office on December 21. Elvis arranged a meeting with President Richard Nixon at the White House, where he expressed his patriotism and explained how he believed he could reach out to the hippies to help combat the drug culture he and the president abhorred. He asked Nixon for a Bureau of Narcotics and Dangerous Drugs badge, to add to similar items he had begun collecting and to signify official sanction of his patriotic efforts. Nixon, who apparently found the encounter awkward, expressed a belief that Presley could send a positive message to young people and that it was, therefore, important that he "retain his credibility". Elvis told Nixon that the Beatles, whose songs he regularly performed in concert during the era, exemplified what he saw as a trend of anti-Americanism. Elvis and his friends previously had a four-hour get-together with the Beatles at his home in Bel Air, California, in August 1965. On hearing reports of the meeting, Paul McCartney later said that he "felt a bit betrayed... The great joke was that we were taking [illegal] drugs, and look what happened to him", a reference to Elvis's early death, linked to prescription drug abuse. [415]

1971   The US Junior Chamber of Commerce named Elvis one of its annual Ten Most Outstanding Young Men of the Nation on January 16. Not long after, the City of Memphis named the stretch of Highway 51 South on which Graceland is located "Elvis Presley Boulevard". The same year, Presley became the first rock and roll singer to be awarded the Lifetime Achievement Award (then known as the Bing Crosby Award) by the National Academy of Recording Arts and Sciences, the Grammy Award organization. Three new, non-film Presley studio albums were released in 1971, as many as had come out over the previous eight years. The biggest seller was *Elvis Sings The Wonderful World of Christmas*, "the truest statement of all", according to Greil Marcus. "In the midst of ten painfully genteel Christmas songs, every one sung with appalling sincerity and humility, one could find Elvis tom-catting his way through six blazing minutes of "Merry Christmas Baby", a raunchy old Charles Brown blues... If [Presley's] sin was his lifelessness, it was his sinfulness that brought him to life".[416]

Mimesis Stage 2 for Elvis Aron Presley – Marriage Problems

1971   Presley and his wife, meanwhile, had become increasingly distant, barely cohabiting. In 1971, an affair he had with Joyce Bova resulted—unbeknownst to him—in her pregnancy and an abortion. He often raised the possibility of her moving into Graceland, saying that he was likely to leave Priscilla.[247] The Presleys separated on

February 23, 1972, after Priscilla disclosed her relationship with Mike Stone, a karate instructor Presley had recommended to her. Priscilla related that when she told him, Presley "grabbed ... and forcefully made love to" her, declaring, "This is how a real man makes love to his woman".[248] She later stated in an interview that she regretted her choice of words in describing the incident, and said it had been an overstatement. Five months later, Presley's new girlfriend, Linda Thompson, a songwriter and one-time Memphis beauty queen, moved in with him. Presley and his wife filed for divorce on August 18. According to Joe Moscheo of the Imperials, the failure of Presley's marriage "was a blow from which he never recovered". At a rare press conference that June, a reporter had asked Presley whether he was satisfied with his image. Presley replied, "Well, the image is one thing and the human being another ... it's very hard to live up to an image. [417]

Mimesis Stage 2 for Elvis Aron Presley – Health Deterioration

1973-1977   Elvis's divorce was finalized on October 9, 1973. By then, his health was in serious decline. Twice during the year, he overdosed on barbiturates, spending three days in a coma in his hotel suite after the first incident. Towards the end of 1973, he was hospitalized, semi-comatose from the effects of a pethidine addiction. According to his primary care physician, Dr. George C. Nichopoulos, Presley "felt that by getting drugs from a doctor, he wasn't the common everyday junkie getting something off the street".[265] Since his comeback, he had staged more live shows with each passing year, and 1973 saw 168 concerts, his busiest schedule ever. Despite his failing health, in 1974, he undertook another intensive touring schedule.[418]

1974 Elvis's condition declined in September. Keyboardist Tony Brown remembered Presley's arrival at a University of Maryland concert: "He fell out of the limousine, to his knees. People jumped to help, and he pushed them away like, 'Don't help me.' He walked on stage and held onto the mic for the first thirty minutes like it was a post. Everybody's looking at each other like, 'Is the tour gonna happen? '" Guitarist John Wilkinson recalled, "He was all gut. He was slurring. He was so fucked up... It was obvious he was drugged. It was obvious there was something terribly wrong with his body. It was so bad the words to the songs were barely intelligible... I remember crying. He could barely get through the introductions." [419]

Wilkinson recounted that a few nights later in Detroit, "I watched him in his dressing room, just draped over a chair, unable to move. So often I thought, 'Boss, why don't you just cancel this tour and take a year off...?' I mentioned something once in a guarded moment. He patted me on the back and said, 'It'll be all right. Don't you worry about it.'" Elvis continued to play to sellout crowds. Cultural critic Marjorie Garber wrote that he was now widely seen as a garish pop crooner: "In effect, he had become Liberace. Even his fans were now middle-aged matrons and blue-haired grandmothers." [420]

Presley made no official studio recordings in 1974.

1976 On July 13, Elvis's father—who had become deeply involved in his financial affairs—fired "Memphis Mafia" bodyguards Red West (Presley's friend since the 1950s), Sonny West, and David Hebler, citing the need to "cut back on expenses". Elvis was in Palm Springs at the time, and some suggested that he was too cowardly to face the three himself. Another associate of Presley's, John O'Grady, argued that the bodyguards were dropped because their rough treatment of fans had prompted too many lawsuits. However, Presley's stepbrother, David Stanley, claimed that the bodyguards were fired because they were becoming more outspoken about Presley's drug dependency. [421]

1976 RCA sent a mobile recording unit to Graceland, which made possible two full-scale recording sessions at Presley's home. However, the recording process had become a struggle for him. Parker's attempts to arrange another session toward the end of the year were unsuccessful. [422] Greil Marcus described Elvis's performances that year as his "apocalyptic attack" on the soul classic "Hurt". Dave Marsh wrote of Presley's performance: "If he felt the way he sounded, the wonder isn't that he had only a year left to live but that he managed to survive that long."[423]

1976   Elvis and Linda Thompson split in November 1976, and Presley took up with a new girlfriend, Ginger Alden. He proposed to Alden and gave her an engagement ring two months later, though several of his friends later said he had no serious intention of marrying again. [424]

Mimesis Stage 2 for Elvis Aron Presley - Final months

1977   The journalist Tony Scherman wrote that, "Elvis had become a grotesque caricature of his sleek, energetic former self. Grossly overweight, his mind dulled by the pharmacopia he daily ingested, he was barely able to pull himself through his abbreviated concerts." According to Andy Greene of *Rolling Stone*, Presley's final performances were mostly "sad, sloppy affairs where a bloated, drugged Presley struggled to remember his lyrics and get through the night without collapsing ... Most everything from the final three years of his life is sad and hard to watch." In Alexandria, Louisiana, he was on stage for less than an hour and "was impossible to understand". On March 31, Presley canceled a performance in Baton Rouge, unable to get out of his hotel bed; four shows had to be canceled and rescheduled.[425] However, despite the increasing deterioration of his health, Presley fulfilled most of his touring commitments. According to Guralnick, fans were becoming disappointed in his performances, but Elvis seemed to ignore it. He was becoming increasingly reclusive; he mostly remained confined to his room between performances and read his spiritualism books. Presley's cousin. [426]

Presley's final concert was held in Indianapolis at Market Square Arena on June 26.

The book *Elvis: What Happened?*, co-written by the three bodyguards who were fired the previous year, was published on August 1. It was the first exposé to reveal Presley's years of drug abuse. He was devastated by the book and tried unsuccessfully to halt its publication by offering money to the publishers. By now, Elvis suffered from glaucoma, hypertension, liver damage, and an enlarged colon, each probably caused by drug abuse. [427]

The Final Mimesis for Elvis Aron Presley – Death

1977 On the evening of August 16, Presley was scheduled to fly out of Memphis to begin another tour. That afternoon, Ginger Alden discovered him in an unresponsive state on the bathroom floor of his Graceland mansion. "For some reason, possibly involving a reaction to the codeine and attempts to move his bowels, Elvis experienced pain while sitting on the toilet. Alarmed, he stood up ... and fell face down in the fetal position." Drooling on the rug and unable to breathe, he died." Attempts to revive him failed, and he was pronounced dead at Baptist Memorial Hospital at 3:30 p.m. He was 42 years old. [428]

President Jimmy Carter issued a statement that credited Presley with having "permanently changed the face of American popular culture". Thousands of people gathered outside Graceland to view the open casket. One of Presley's cousins, Billy Mann, accepted US$18,000 (equivalent to $80,000 in 2021) to secretly photograph the body; the picture appeared on the cover of the *National Enquirer*'s biggest-selling issue ever. Alden struck a $105,000 (equivalent to $470,000 in 2021) deal with the *Enquirer* for her story, but settled for less when she broke her exclusivity agreement. Presley left her nothing in his will. [429]

Presley's funeral was held at Graceland on Thursday, August 18. Outside the gates, a car plowed into a group of fans, killing two young women and critically injuring a third. About 80,000 people lined the processional route to Forest Hill Cemetery, where Presley was buried next to his mother. Within a few weeks, "Way Down" topped the country and UK singles  charts. Following an attempt to steal Presley's body in late August, the remains of both Presley and his mother were exhumed and reburied in Graceland's Meditation Garden on October 2. Presley is buried alongside his parents, daughter, grandson, and his paternal grandmother in the Meditation Garden at Graceland. [430]

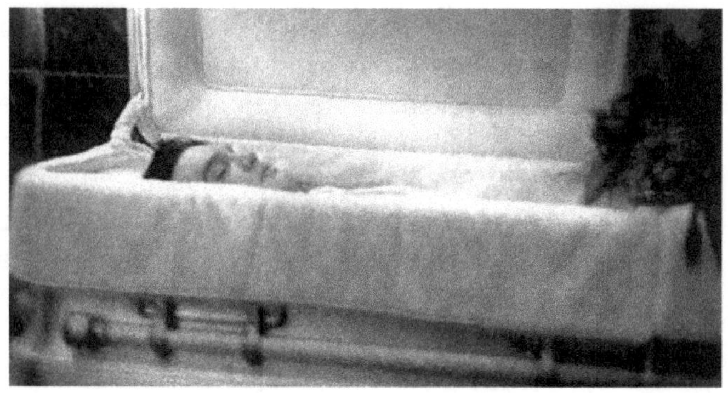

An autopsy was taken the same day Presley died. Memphis medical examiner Jerry Francisco announced that the immediate cause of death was cardiac arrest. Asked if drugs were involved, he declared that "drugs played no role in Presley's death". The fact is, however, that "drug use was heavily implicated" in Presley's death, writes Guralnick. The pathologists conducting the autopsy thought it possible, for instance, that he had suffered "anaphylactic shock brought on by the codeine pills he had gotten from his dentist, to which he was known to have had a mild allergy". A pair of lab reports filed two months later strongly suggested that polypharmacy was the primary cause of death; one reported "fourteen drugs in Elvis' system, ten in significant quantity". In 1979, forensic pathologist Cyril Wecht conducted a review of the reports and concluded that a combination of central nervous system depressants had resulted in Presley's accidental death. Forensic historian and pathologist Michael Baden viewed the situation as complicated: "Elvis had had an enlarged heart for a long time. That, together with his drug habit, caused his death. But he was difficult to diagnose; it was a judgment call."[431]

The competence and ethics of two of the centrally involved medical professionals were seriously questioned. Jerry Francisco had offered a cause of death before the autopsy was complete, claiming the underlying ailment was cardiac arrhythmia, a condition that can be determined only in someone who is still alive. Francisco denied that drugs played any part in Presley's death before the toxicology results were known. Allegations of a cover-up were widespread. A 1981 trial of Elvis's main physician, George C. Nichopoulos, exonerated him of criminal liability for his death. "In the first eight months of 1977 alone, he had [prescribed] more than 10,000 doses of sedatives, amphetamines, and narcotics: all in Elvis' name." His license was suspended for three months. It was permanently revoked in the 1990s after the Tennessee Medical Board brought new charges of over-prescription. [432]

In 1994, the Presley autopsy report was reopened. Joseph Davis, who had conducted thousands of autopsies as Miami-Dade County coroner, declared at its completion, "There is nothing in any of the data that supports a death from drugs. In fact, everything points to a sudden, violent heart attack." More recent research has revealed that Francisco did not speak for the entire pathology team. Other staff "could say nothing with confidence until they got the results back from the laboratories, if then. That would be a matter of weeks." One of the examiners, E. Eric Muirhead, "could not believe his ears. Francisco had not only presumed to speak for the hospital's team of pathologists, but he had announced a conclusion that they had not reached... A dissection of the body... confirmed [that] Elvis was chronically ill with diabetes, glaucoma, and constipation. As they proceeded, the doctors saw evidence that his body had been wracked over a span of years by a large and constant stream of drugs. They had also studied his hospital records, which included two admissions for drug detoxification and methadone treatments." Writer Frank Coffey thought Presley's death was due to "a phenomenon called the Valsalva maneuver (essentially straining on the toilet leading to heart stoppage. This is plausible because Elvis suffered constipation, a common reaction to drug use)". In similar terms, Dan Warlick, who was present at the autopsy, "believes Presley's chronic constipation—the result of years of prescription drug abuse and high-fat, high-cholesterol gorging caused Elvis to suffer from Valsalva's maneuver, the strain of attempting to defecate compressed the singer's abdominal aorta, shutting down his heart." [433]

The Final Mimesis for Elvis Aron Presley – Legacy

One of the most significant tributes to the legacy of Elvis is the numerous impersonators that have sprung up, keeping his memory alive. Thanks to Elvis's legion of impersonators, his name, image, and voice are recognized around the world. In polls and surveys, Elvis is recognized as one of the most important popular music artists and influential Americans. American composer and conductor Leonard Bernstein said, "Elvis Presley is the greatest cultural force in the twentieth century. He introduced the beat to everything, and he changed everything—music, language, clothes. It's a whole new social revolution—the sixties came from it." John Lennon said that "Nothing really affected me until Elvis." Bob Dylan described the sensation of first hearing Presley as "like busting out of jail". [434]

Elvis has sold 500 million records worldwide and is one of the best-selling music artists of all time. Presley holds the records for most songs charting in *Billboard*'s top 40 (115) and top 100 (152), according to chart statistician Joel Whitburn, 139 according to Presley historian Adam Victor. Presley's rankings for top ten and number-one hits vary depending on how the double-sided "Hound Dog/Don't Be Cruel" and "Don't/I Beg of You" singles, which precede the inception of *Billboard*'s unified Hot 100 chart, are analyzed. According to Whitburn's analysis, Presley holds the record with 38, tying with Madonna; per *Billboard*'s current assessment, he ranks second with 36. Whitburn and *Billboard* concur that the Beatles hold the record for most number-one hits with 20, and that Mariah Carey is second with 19. Whitburn has Presley with 18; *Billboard* has him third with 17.[472] According to *Billboard*, Presley has 79 cumulative weeks at number one: alone at 80, according to Whitburn and the Rock and Roll Hall of Fame, with only Mariah Carey having more with 91 weeks. He holds the record for the most number-one singles on the UK chart with 21 and singles reaching the top ten with 76. [435]

As of 2023, the Recording Industry Association of America (RIAA) credits Presley with 146.5 million certified album sales in the US, third all-time behind the Beatles and Garth Brooks. He holds the records for most gold albums (101, nearly twice as many as second-place Barbra Streisand's 51) and most platinum albums (57). His 25 multi-platinum albums are second behind the Beatles' 26. His total of 197 album certification awards (including one diamond award) far outpaces the Beatles' second-best 122. He has the 9th-most gold singles (54, tied with Justin Bieber), and the 16th-most platinum singles (27). [436]

In 2018, President Donald Trump awarded Presley the Presidential Medal of Freedom posthumously.

Mimesis of Life Summary for Elvis Aron Presley

There is something magical about the career of Elvis. Everything he touched during his professional life turned to gold. For much of his adult life, Presley, with his rise from poverty to riches and fame, had seemed to epitomize the American Dream. In his final years and following the revelations about his circumstances after his death, he became a symbol of excess and gluttony. Increasing attention was paid to his appetite for the rich, heavy Southern cooking of his upbringing, foods such as chicken-fried steak and biscuits, and gravy. In particular, his love of fried peanut butter, banana, and (sometimes) bacon sandwiches, now known as "Elvis sandwiches", came to symbolize this characteristic. According to the media scholar Robert Thompson, the sandwich also signified Presley's enduring all-American appeal: "He wasn't only the king, he was one of us."[437]

However, the question has to be raised that questions Elvis's ability to handle the fame that was thrust upon him. The Svengali control Colonel Parker had over his life. Was Elvis so hungry for fame and success that he was willing to achieve it at all costs? Once Elvis was in the grasp of fame and fortune, did he control the fame and fortune, or did it control him? The fact remains that of all of Elvis's wonderful fortune and life experiences, he died at 42 years old, in the prime of his life. Elvis could be considered a tragic hero. Evaluating the life of Elvis Presley, like everyone else, it is the decisions he made and his response to phenomena he encountered that determined his Mimesis.

The King of Rock and Roll, Elvis Presley, has a star on the Hollywood Walk of Fame at 7080 Hollywood Boulevard. He was awarded the 2,602nd star on the Walk of Fame on February 8, 1960.[438] Elvis impacts the lives of his fans so profoundly that even today, there are people who believe he is alive and not dead. [439]

ELVIS PRESLEY

Mimesis of Life for Beyoncé Giselle Knowles-Carter

Beyoncé Giselle Knowles was born on September 4, 1981, and is an American singer, songwriter, record producer, dancer, and actress. Regarded as one of the most successful performers of her generation, she is known for her boundary-pushing artistry and vocal abilities. Her success earned her the nickname "Queen Bey" and led her to become a pop icon of the 21st century.

Beyoncé started performing in various singing and dancing competitions as a child. She rose to fame in the late 1990s as a member of the R&B girl group Destiny's Child, one of the best-selling girl groups of all time. Their hiatus saw the release of her debut album *Dangerously in Love* (2003), which featured the US *Billboard* Hot 100 number-one singles "Crazy in Love" and "Baby Boy." Following the 2006 disbanding of Destiny's Child, Beyoncé released a series of successful solo albums, including *B'Day* (2006), *I Am... Sasha Fierce* (2008), *4* (2011), *Beyoncé* (2013), *Lemonade* (2016), and *Renaissance* (2022), and became the first solo artist to have their first seven studio albums debut at number one on the *Billboard* 200.[440]

After professionally splitting from her manager and father, Mathew Knowles, in 2010, Beyoncé's artistry achieved wider critical acclaim for releasing sonically experimental visual albums and exploring societal themes such as infidelity, feminism, womanism, escapism, and hedonism. In 2018, she released *Everything Is Love*, a collaborative album with her husband, Jay-Z, as the Carters. In 2020, she released the musical film *Black Is King*, inspired by the music of the film soundtrack *The Lion King: The Gift* (2019), with praise from critics. Beyoncé also starred in multiple films such as *Austin Powers in Goldmember* (2002), *The Pink Panther* (2006), *Dreamgirls* (2006), *Cadillac Records* (2008), *Obsessed* (2009), and *The Lion King* (2019).[441]

Having sold 200 million records worldwide, Beyoncé is one of the world's best-selling recording artists. Throughout her career, she has amassed multiple chart-topping singles, including "Check on It," "Irreplaceable," "Single Ladies," and "Break My Soul." As a featured artist, Beyoncé topped the *Billboard* Hot 100 with the remixes of "Perfect" by Ed Sheeran and "Savage" by Megan Thee Stallion. With 31 career top ten singles on the *Billboard* Hot 100, she became the first female artist and third overall to achieve at least twenty as a solo artist and ten as a group member. [442]

Beyoncé's accolades include 32 Grammy Awards, 26 MTV Video Music Awards (including the Michael Jackson Video Vanguard Award in 2014), 24 NAACP Image Awards, 31 BET Awards, and 17 Soul Train Music Awards, all of which are more than any other artist. Her success during the 2000s earned her recognition as the Recording Industry Association of America (RIAA)'s Top Certified Artist of the Decade and *Billboard*'s Top Female Artist of the Decade. In 2014, *Billboard* named her the highest-earning black musician of all time. In 2020, *Time* magazine featured her among a list of 100 women who defined the last century. [443]

Mimesis 1 for Beyonce Giselle Knowles

1981 Beyonce Giselle Knowles was born on September 4 in Houston Texas to Celestine "Tina" and Matthew Knowles. Tina was a hairdresser and salon owner. Matthew was a Xerox company sales manager. Beyoncé has a younger sister, Solange.

Beyoncé's maternal grandparents, Lumas Beyoncé and Agnez Dereon (daughter of Odilia Broussard and Eugene DeRouen), were French-speaking Louisiana Creoles, with roots in New Iberia. Beyoncé is considered a Creole, passed on to her by her grandparents. Through her mother, Beyoncé is a descendant of many French aristocrats from the southwest of France, including the family of the Viscounts *de* Béarn since the 9th century, and the Viscounts *de* Belzunce. She is a descendant of Acadian militia officer Joseph Broussard, who was exiled to French Louisiana after the expulsion of the Acadians. [444]

Her fourth great-grandmother, Marie-Françoise Trahan, was born in 1774 in Bangor, located on Belle Île, France. Trahan was a daughter of Acadians who had taken refuge on Belle Île after the Acadian expulsion. The Estates of Brittany had divided the lands of Belle Île to distribute them among 78 other Acadian families and the already settled inhabitants. The Trahan family lived on Belle Île for over ten years before immigrating to Louisiana, where she married a Broussard descendant. Beyoncé researched her ancestry and discovered that she is descended from a slave owner who married his slave. Her mother is also of distant Jewish, Spanish, Chinese, and Indonesian ancestry.

Beyoncé was raised Catholic and attended St. Mary's Montessori School in Houston, where she enrolled in dance classes. Her singing was discovered when dance instructor Darlette Johnson began humming a song, and she finished it, able to hit the high-pitched notes. Beyoncé's interest in music and performing continued after winning a school talent show at age seven, singing John Lennon's "Imagine" to beat 15/16-year-olds.[445]

1990 In the fall, Beyoncé enrolled in Parker Elementary School, a music magnet school in Houston, where she would perform with the school's choir. She also attended the High School for the Performing and Visual Arts and later Alief Elsik High School. Beyoncé was also a member of the choir at St. John's United Methodist Church as a soloist for two years.[446]

Mimesis 2 for Beyonce Giselle Knowles – Discovering her Talent

1989 When Beyoncé was eight, she met LaTavia Roberson at an audition for an all-girl entertainment group. They formed a group called Girl's Tyme with three other girls, and rapped and danced on the talent show circuit in Houston. After seeing the group, R&B producer Arne Frager brought them to his Northern California studio and placed them in *Star Search*, the largest talent show on national TV at the time. Girl's Tyme failed to win, and Beyoncé later said the song they performed was not good. In 1995, Beyoncé's father resigned from his job to manage the group. The move reduced Beyoncé's family's income by half, and her parents were forced to sell their house and cars and move into separate apartments. [447]

Mathew cut the original line-up to four, and the group continued performing as an opening act for other established R&B girl groups. The girls auditioned before record labels and were finally signed to Elektra Records, moving to Atlanta Records briefly to work on their first recording, only to be cut by the company. This put further strain on the family, and Beyoncé's parents separated.

1995   On October 5, Dwayne Wiggins's Grass Roots Entertainment signed the group.

1996   The girls began recording their debut album under an agreement with Sony Music, the Knowles family reunited, and shortly after, the group got a contract with Columbia Records with the assistance of Columbia talent scout Teresa LaBarbera Whites.[448]

Mimesis 2 for Beyonce Giselle Knowles – Destiny's Child

1997-2002   The group changed their name to Destiny's Child in 1996, based upon a passage in the Book of Isaiah. In 1997, Destiny's Child released their major label debut song "Killing Time" on the soundtrack to the 1997 film *Men in Black*. In November, the group released their debut single and first major hit, "No, No, No". They released their self-titled debut album in February 1998, which established the group as a viable act in the music industry, with moderate sales and winning the group three Soul Train Lady of Soul Awards for Best R&B/Soul Album of the Year, Best R&B/Soul or Rap New Artist, and Best R&B/Soul Single for "No, No, No". [449]

1999 

The group released their Multi-Platinum second album, *The Writing's on the Wall*, in 1999. The record features some of the group's most widely known songs, such as "Bills, Bills, Bills", the group's first number-one single, "Jumpin' Jumpin'", and "Say My Name", which became their most successful song at the time, and would remain one of their signature songs. "Say My Name" won the Best R&B Performance by a Duo or Group with Vocals and the Best R&B Song at the 43rd Annual Grammy Awards. *The Writing's on the Wall* sold more than eight million copies worldwide. During this time, Beyoncé recorded a duet with Marc Nelson, an original member of Boyz II Men, on the song "After All Is Said and Done" for the soundtrack to the 1999 film, *The Best Man.* [450]

LeToya Luckett and Roberson became unhappy with Mathew's management of the band and eventually were replaced by Farrah Franklin and Michelle Williams. Beyoncé experienced depression following the split with Luckett and Roberson after being publicly blamed by the media, critics, and blogs for the cause of their departure. Her long-standing boyfriend left her at this time. The depression was so severe that it lasted for a couple of years, during which she occasionally kept herself in her bedroom for days and refused to eat anything. Beyoncé stated that she struggled to speak about her depression because Destiny's Child had just won their first Grammy Award, and she feared no one would take her seriously. Beyoncé would later speak of her mother as the person who helped her fight it. Franklin was then dismissed, leaving just Beyoncé, Rowland, and Williams.[451]

Beyoncé landed a major role in the MTV made-for-television film, *Carmen: A Hip Hopera*, starring alongside American actor Mekhi Phifer. Set in Philadelphia, the film is a modern interpretation of the 19th-century opera *Carmen* by French composer Georges Bizet.[53] When the third album *Survivor* was released in May 2001, Luckett and Roberson filed a lawsuit claiming that the songs were aimed at them. The album debuted at number one on the U.S. *Billboard* 200, with first-week sales of 663,000 copies sold.[452]

2002   Beyoncé made her theatrical film debut, playing Foxxy Cleopatra alongside Mike Myers in the comedy film *Austin Powers in Goldmember*, which grossed $73 million in its first weekend. Beyoncé released "Work It Out" as the lead single from its soundtrack album, which entered the top ten in the UK, Norway, and Belgium. In 2003, Beyoncé starred opposite Cuba Gooding, Jr., in the musical comedy *The Fighting Temptations* as Lilly, a single mother with whom Gooding's character falls in love. The film received mixed reviews from critics but grossed $30 million in the U.S. Beyoncé released "Fighting Temptation" as the lead single from the film's soundtrack album, with Missy Elliott, MC Lyte, and Free, which was also used to promote the film. Another of Beyoncé's contributions to the soundtrack, "Summertime", fared better on the U.S. charts.

Mimesis 2 for Beyonce Giselle Knowles -   Meeting Jay-Z

2003-2005   Beyoncé's first solo recording was a feature on Jay-Z's song "'03 Bonnie & Clyde" that was released in October 2002, peaking at number four on the U.S. *Billboard* Hot 100 chart. On June 14, 2003, Beyoncé premiered songs from her first solo album, *Dangerously in Love*, during her first solo concert and the pay-per-view television special, "Ford Presents Beyoncé Knowles, Friends & Family, and Live from Ford's 100th Anniversary Celebration in Dearborn, Michigan". The album was released on June 24, 2003, after Michelle Williams and Kelly Rowland had released their solo efforts. The album sold 317,000 copies in its first week, debuted atop the *Billboard* 200, and has since sold 11 million copies worldwide. [453]

The album's lead single, "Crazy in Love", featuring Jay-Z, became Beyoncé's first number-one single as a solo artist in the US. The single "Baby Boy" also reached number one, and singles "Me, Myself and I" and "Naughty Girl" both reached the top five. The album earned Beyoncé a then record-tying five awards at the 46th Annual Grammy Awards; Best Contemporary R&B Album, Best Female R&B Vocal Performance for "Dangerously in Love 2", Best R&B Song and Best Rap/Sung Collaboration for "Crazy in Love", and Best R&B Performance by a Duo or Group with Vocals for "The Closer I Get to You" with Luther Vandross. During the ceremony, she performed with Prince. [454]

2003   In November, Beyoncé went on the Dangerously in Love Tour in Europe and later toured alongside Missy Elliott and Alicia Keys for the Verizon Ladies First Tour in North America.

2004   On February 1, Beyoncé performed the American national anthem at Super Bowl XXXVIII at the Reliant Stadium in Houston, Texas. After the release of *Dangerously in Love*, Beyoncé had planned to produce a follow-up album using several of the leftover tracks. However, this was put on hold so she could concentrate on recording *Destiny Fulfilled*, the final studio album by Destiny's Child. Released on November 15 in the US and peaking at number two on the *Billboard* 200, *Destiny Fulfilled* included the singles "Lose My Breath" and "Soldier", which reached the top five on the *Billboard* Hot 100 chart. [455]

Destiny's Child embarked on a worldwide concert tour, Destiny Fulfilled... and Lovin' It", sponsored by McDonald's Corporation, and performed hits such as "No, No, No", "Survivor", "Say My Name", "Independent Women", and "Lose My Breath". In addition to renditions of the group's recorded material, they also performed songs from each singer's solo careers, most notably numbers from *Dangerously in Love*, and during the last stop of their European tour, in Barcelona on June 11, 2005, Rowland announced that Destiny's Child would disband following the North American leg of the tour. The group released their first compilation album *Number 1's* , on October 25, 2005, in the US, and accepted a star on the Hollywood Walk of Fame in March 2006. The group has sold 60 million records worldwide.

Beyoncé's younger sister, Solange Knowles, is also a singer and a former backup dancer for Destiny's Child. Solange and Beyoncé are the first sisters to have number-one solo albums.[456]

Mimesis 2 for Beyonce Giselle Knowles – 2006-2007[457]

Beyoncé's second solo album, *B'Day*, was released on September 4, 2006, in the US, to coincide with her twenty-fifth birthday. It sold 541,000 copies in its first week and debuted atop the *Billboard* 200, becoming Beyoncé's second consecutive number one album in the United States. The album's lead single, "Déjà Vu", featuring Jay-Z, reached the top five on the *Billboard* Hot 100 chart. The second international single, "Irreplaceable," was a commercial success worldwide, reaching number one in Australia, Hungary, Ireland, New Zealand, and the United States. *B'Day* also produced three other singles: "Ring the

Alarm", "Get Me Bodied", and "Green Light" (released in the United Kingdom only).

At the 49th Annual Grammy Awards (2007), *B'Day* was nominated for five Grammy Awards, including Best Contemporary R&B Album, Best Female R&B Vocal Performance for "Ring the Alarm" and Best R&B Song and Best Rap/Sung Collaboration" for "Déjà Vu"; the Freemasons club mix of "Déjà Vu" without the rap was put forward in the Best Remixed Recording, Non-Classical category. *B'Day* won the award for Best Contemporary R&B Album. The following year, *B'Day* received two nominations – for Record of the Year for "Irreplaceable" and Best Pop Collaboration with Vocals for "Beautiful Liar" (with Shakira), also receiving a nomination for Best Compilation Soundtrack Album for Motion Pictures, Television or Other Visual Media for her appearance on *Dreamgirls: Music from the Motion Picture* (2006).

Her first acting role of 2006 was in the comedy film *The Pink Panther,* starring opposite Steve Martin, which grossed $158.8 million at the box office worldwide. Her second film, *Dreamgirls,* the film version of the 1981 Broadway musical loosely based on The Supremes, received acclaim from critics and grossed $154 million internationally. In it, she starred opposite Jennifer Hudson, Jamie Foxx, and Eddie Murphy playing a pop singer based on Diana Ross. To promote the film, Beyoncé released "Listen" as the lead single from the soundtrack album. In April 2007, Beyoncé embarked on The Beyoncé Experience, her first worldwide concert tour, visiting 97 venues and grossing over $24 million. Beyoncé conducted pre-concert food donation drives during six major stops in conjunction with her pastor at St. John's and America's Second

Harvest. At the same time, *B'Day* was re-released with five additional songs, including her duet with Shakira, "Beautiful Liar".

Mimesis Stage 2 for Beyonce Giselle Knowles – 2008-2010 [458] - Alter Ego "Sasha Fierce"

Beyonce is "sexy, seductive and provocative" when performing on stage. She created the alter ego "Sasha Fierce" to keep that stage persona separate from who she really is. She described Sasha as being "too aggressive, too strong, too sassy [and] too sexy", stating, "I'm not like her in real life at all." Sasha was conceived during the making of "Crazy in Love", and Beyoncé introduced her with the release of her 2008 album, *I Am... Sasha Fierce*. In **February 2010**, she announced in an interview with *Allure* magazine that she was comfortable enough with herself to no longer need Sasha Fierce. However, Beyoncé announced in **May 2012** that she would bring her back for her *Revel Presents: Beyoncé Live* shows later that month.[

I Am... Sasha Fierce was released on November 18, 2008, in the United States. The album formally introduces Beyoncé's alter ego, Sasha Fierce, conceived during the making of her 2003 single "Crazy in Love". It sold 482,000 copies in its first week, debuting atop the *Billboard* 200, and giving Beyoncé her third consecutive number one album in the US. The album featured the number-one song "Single Ladies (Put a Ring on It)" and the top-five songs "If I Were a Boy" and "Halo". She achieved the accomplishment of becoming her longest-running Hot 100 single in her career.

2008   Beyoncé further expanded her acting career, starring as blues singer Etta James in the musical biopic *Cadillac Records*. Her performance in the film received praise from critics, and she garnered several nominations for her portrayal of James, including a Satellite Award nomination for Best Supporting Actress and a NAACP Image Award nomination for Outstanding Supporting Actress. Beyoncé donated her entire salary from the film to Phoenix House, an organization of rehabilitation centers for heroin addicts around the country.

2009   On January 20, Beyoncé performed Etta James' "At Last" at the First Couple Barack and Michelle Obama's first inaugural ball.

"Halo's success in the U.S. helped Beyoncé attain more top-ten singles on the list than any other woman during the 2000s. It also included the successful "Sweet Dreams", and singles "Diva", "Ego", "Broken-Hearted Girl", and "Video Phone". The music video for "Single Ladies" has been parodied and imitated around the world, spawning the "first major dance craze" of the Internet age, according to the *Toronto Star*. The video has won several awards, including Best Video at the 2009 MTV Europe Music Awards, the 2009 Scottish MOBO Awards, and the 2009 BET Awards.

At the 2009 MTV Video Music Awards, the video was nominated for nine awards, ultimately winning three, including Video of the Year. Its failure to win the Best Female Video category, which went to American singer-songwriter Taylor Swift's "You Belong with Me", led to Kanye West interrupting the ceremony and Beyoncé improvising a re-presentation of Swift's award during her own acceptance speech. In March 2009, Beyoncé embarked on the "I Am... World Tour", her second headlining worldwide concert tour, consisting of 108 shows, grossing $119.5 million.

Beyoncé starred opposite Ali Larter and Idris Elba in the thriller, *Obsessed*. She played Sharon Charles, a mother and wife whose family is threatened by her husband's stalker. Although the film received negative reviews from critics, the movie did well at the U.S. box office, grossing $68 million – $60 million more than *Cadillac Records* – on a budget of $20 million. The fight scene finale between Sharon and the character played by Ali Larter also won the 2010 MTV Movie Award for Best Fight.

At the 52nd Annual Grammy Awards, Beyoncé received ten nominations, including Album of the Year for *I Am... Sasha Fierce*, Record of the Year for "Halo", and Song of the Year for "Single Ladies (Put a Ring on It)", among others. She tied with Lauryn Hill for the most Grammy nominations in a single year by a female artist. Beyoncé went on to win six of those nominations, breaking a record she previously tied in 2004 for the most Grammy awards won in a single night by a female artist with six. In 2010, Beyoncé was featured on Lady Gaga's single "Telephone" and appeared in its music video. The song topped the U.S. Pop Songs chart, becoming the sixth number-one for both Beyoncé and Gaga, tying them with Mariah Carey for most number-ones since the Nielsen Top 40 airplay chart launched in 1992. "Telephone" received a Grammy Award nomination for Best Pop Collaboration with Vocals.

Beyoncé announced a hiatus from her music career in January 2010, heeding her mother's advice, "to live life, to be inspired by things again". During the break, she and her father parted ways as business partners. Beyoncé's musical break lasted nine months and saw her visit multiple European cities, the Great Wall of China, the Egyptian pyramids, Australia, English music festivals and various museums and ballet performances.

Mimesis Stage 2 for Beyonce Giselle Knowles – 2011-2013[459]

2011

On June 26, Beyoncé became the first solo female artist to headline the main Pyramid stage at the 2011 Glastonbury Festival in Her released two days later in the US. *4* sold 310,000 copies in its first week and debuted atop the *Billboard* 200 chart, giving Beyoncé her fourth consecutive number one album in the US. The album was preceded by two of its singles, "Run the World (Girls)" and "Best Thing I Never Had". The fourth single, "Love on Top," spent seven consecutive weeks at number one on the Hot R&B/Hip-Hop Songs chart, while peaking at number 20 on the *Billboard* Hot 100, the highest peak from the album. *4* produced four other singles: "Party", "Countdown", "I Care", and "End of Time". "Eat, Play, Love", a cover story written by Beyoncé for *Essence* that detailed her 2010 career break, won her a writing award from the New York Association of Black Journalists.

In late 2011, she took the stage at New York's Roseland Ballroom for four nights of special performances: he 4 Intimate Nights with Beyoncé concerts saw the performance of her *4* album to a standing room only. On August 1, 2011, the album was certified platinum by the Recording Industry Association of America (RIAA), having shipped 1 million copies to retail stores. By December 2015, it reached sales of 1.5 million copies in the US. The album reached one billion Spotify streams on February 5, 2018, making Beyoncé the first female artist to have three of their albums surpass one billion streams on the platform.

2012   In June she performed for four nights at Revel Atlantic City's Ovation Hall to celebrate the resort's opening, her first performances since giving birth to her daughter.

2013   In January, Destiny's Child released *Love Songs*, a compilation album of the romance-themed songs from their previous albums and a newly recorded track, "Nuclear". Beyoncé performed the American national anthem singing along with a pre-recorded track at President Obama's second inauguration in Washington, D.C. The following month, Beyoncé performed at the Super Bowl XLVII halftime show, held at the

Mercedes-Benz Superdome in New Orleans. The performance stands as the second most tweeted about moment in history at 268,000 tweets per minute. At the 55th Annual Grammy Awards, Beyoncé won for Best Traditional R&B Performance for "Love on Top".Her feature-length documentary film, *Life Is*.

Mimesis Stage 2 for Beyonce Giselle Knowles – 2013-2015[460]

2013

Beyoncé embarked on The Mrs. Carter Show World Tour on April 15 in Belgrade, Serbia; the tour included 132 dates that ran through to March 2014. It became the most successful tour of her career and one of the most successful tours of all time. In May, Beyoncé's cover of Amy Winehouse's "Back to Black" with André 3000 on *The Great Gatsby* soundtrack was released.[160] Beyoncé voiced Queen Tara in the 3D CGI animated film, *Epic*, released by 20th Century Fox on May 24, and recorded an original song for the film, "Rise Up", co-written with Sia.

On December 13, 2013, Beyoncé unexpectedly released her eponymous fifth studio album on the iTunes Store without any prior announcement or promotion. The album debuted atop the *Billboard* 200 chart, giving Beyoncé her fifth consecutive number one album in the US. This made her the first woman in the chart's history to have her first five studio albums debut at number one. *Beyoncé* received critical acclaim and commercial success, selling one million digital copies worldwide in six days; Musically, an electro-R&B album, it concerns darker themes previously unexplored in her work, such as "bulimia, postnatal depression [and] the fears and insecurities of marriage and motherhood". The single "Drunk in Love", featuring Jay-Z, peaked at number two on the *Billboard* Hot 100 chart.

2014   In April, Beyoncé and Jay-Z officially announced their On the Run Tour. It served as the couple's first co-headlining stadium tour together. On August 24, 2014, she received the Michael Jackson Video Vanguard Award at the 2014 MTV Video Music Awards. Beyoncé also won three competitive awards: Best Video with a Social Message and Best Cinematography for "Pretty Hurts", as well as Best Collaboration for "Drunk in Love". In November, *Forbes* reported that Beyoncé was the top-earning woman in music for the second year in a row – earning $115 million in the year, more than double her earnings in 2013.

Beyoncé was reissued with new material as part of a platinum edition box set. According to the International Federation of the Phonographic Industry (IFPI), in the last 19 days of 2013, the album sold 2.3 million units worldwide, becoming the tenth best-selling album of 2013. The album also went on to become the twentieth best-selling album of 2014. As of November 2014, *Beyoncé* has sold over 5 million copies worldwide and has generated over 1 billion streams, as of March 2015.

2015 In February, at the 57th Annual Grammy Awards, Beyoncé was nominated for six awards, ultimately winning three: Best R&B Performance and Best R&B Song for "Drunk in Love", and Best Surround Sound Album for *Beyoncé*. She was nominated for Album of the Year, but the award went to Beck for his album *Morning Phase*.

Mimesis Stage 2 for Beyonce Giselle Knowles – 2016-2018[461]

Beyoncé performing during The Formation World Tour In 2016. The tour grossed

On February 6, 2016, Beyoncé released "Formation" and its accompanying music video exclusively on the music streaming platform Tidal; the song was made available to download for free. She performed "Formation" live for the first time during the NFL Super Bowl 50 halftime show. The appearance was considered controversial as it appeared to reference the 50th anniversary of the Black Panther Party, and the NFL forbids political statements in its performances. Immediately following the performance, Beyoncé announced The Formation World Tour, which highlighted stops in both North America and Europe. It ended on October 7, with Beyoncé bringing out her husband Jay-Z, Kendrick Lamar, and Serena Williams for the last show. The tour went on to win Tour of the Year at the 44th American Music Awards.

In April 2016, Beyoncé released a teaser clip for a project called *Lemonade*. A one-hour film which aired on HBO on April 23, a corresponding album with the same title was released on the same day exclusively on Tidal. *Lemonade* debuted at number one on the U.S. *Billboard* 200, making Beyoncé the first act in *Billboard* history to have their first six studio albums debut atop the chart; she broke a record previously tied with DMX in 2013. With all 12 tracks of *Lemonade* debuting on the *Billboard* Hot 100 chart, Beyoncé also became the first female act to chart 12 or more songs at the same time.

Lemonade was streamed 115 million times through Tidal, setting a record for the most-streamed album in a single week by a female artist in history. It was 2016's third highest-selling album in the U.S. with 1.554 million copies sold in that time period within the country well as the best-selling album worldwide with global sales of 2.5 million throughout the year. In June 2019, *Lemonade* was certified 3× Platinum, having sold up to 3 million album-equivalent units in the United States alone.

Lemonade became her most critically acclaimed work to date, receiving universal acclaim according to Metacritic, a website collecting reviews from professional music critics. Several music publications included the album among the best of 2016, including *Rolling Stone*, which listed *Lemonade* at number one. The album's visuals were nominated in 11 categories at the 2016 MTV Video Music Awards, the most ever received by Beyoncé in a single year, and went on to win 8 awards, including Video of the Year for "Formation". The eight wins made Beyoncé the most-awarded artist in the history of the VMAs (24), surpassing Madonna (20). Beyoncé occupied the sixth place for *Time* magazine's 2016 Person of the Year.

In January 2017, it was announced that Beyoncé would headline the Coachella Music and Arts Festival. This would make Beyoncé only the second female headliner of the festival since it was founded in 1999. It was later announced on February 23, 2017, that Beyoncé would no longer be able to perform at the festival due to doctors' concerns regarding her pregnancy. The festival owners announced that she will instead headline the 2018 festival. Upon the announcement of Beyoncé's departure from the festival lineup, ticket prices dropped by 12%. At the 59th Grammy Awards in February 2017, *Lemonade* led the nominations with nine, including Album, Record, and Song of the Year for *Lemonade* and "Formation" respectively. and ultimately won two, Best Urban Contemporary Album for *Lemonade* and Best Music Video for "Formation". Adele, upon winning her Grammy for Album of the Year, stated *Lemonade* was monumental and more deserving.

In September 2017, Beyoncé collaborated with J Balvin and Willy William to release a remix of the song "Mi Gente". Beyoncé donated all proceeds from the song to hurricane charities for those affected by Hurricane Harvey and Hurricane Irma in Texas, Mexico, Puerto Rico, and other Caribbean Islands.[205] On November 10, Eminem released "Walk on Water" featuring Beyoncé as the lead single from his album *Revival*. On November 30, Ed Sheeran announced that Beyoncé would feature on the remix to his song "Perfect".[206] "Perfect Duet" was released on December 1, 2017. The song reached number one in the United States, becoming Beyoncé's sixth song of her solo career to do so.

On January 4, 2018, the music video of Beyoncé and Jay-Z's *4:44* collaboration, "Family Feud," was released. It was directed by Ava DuVernay. On March 1, 2018, DJ Khaled released "Top Off" as the first single from his forthcoming album *Father of Asahd*, featuring Beyoncé, husband Jay-Z, and Future. On March 5, 2018, a joint tour with Knowles's husband Jay-Z was leaked on Facebook. Information about the tour was later taken down. The couple announced the joint tour officially as the On the Run II Tour on March 12 and simultaneously released a trailer for the tour on YouTube.

On April 14, 2018, Beyoncé played the first of two weekends as the headlining act of the Coachella Music Festival. Her performance on April 14, attended by 125,000 festival-goers, was immediately praised, with multiple media outlets describing it as historic. The performance became the most-tweeted-about performance of weekend one, as well as the most-watched live Coachella performance and the most-watched live performance on YouTube of all time. The show paid tribute to black culture, specifically historically black colleges and universities, and featured a live band with over 100 dancers. Destiny's Child also reunited during the show.

On June 6, 2018, Beyoncé and husband Jay-Z kicked off the On the Run II Tour in Cardiff, United Kingdom. Ten days later, at their final London performance, the pair unveiled *Everything Is Love*, their joint studio album, credited under the name The Carters, and initially available exclusively on Tidal. The pair also released the video for the album's lead single, "Apeshit", on Beyoncé's official YouTube channel. *Everything Is Love* received generally positive reviews and debuted at number two on the U.S. *Billboard* 200, with 123,000 album-equivalent units, of which 70,000 were pure album sales. On December 2, 2018, Beyoncé, alongside Jay-Z, headlined the Global Citizen Festival: Mandela 100, which was held at FNB Stadium in Johannesburg, South Africa. Their 2-hour performance had concepts similar to the On the Run II Tour, and Beyoncé was praised for her outfits, which paid tribute to Africa's diversity.

Mimesis Stage 2 for Beyonce Giselle Knowles – 2019-2021[462]

Homecoming, a documentary and concert film focusing on Beyoncé's historic 2018 Coachella performances, was released by Netflix on April 17, 2019. The film was accompanied by the surprise live album *Homecoming: The Live Album*. It was later reported that Beyoncé and Netflix had signed a $60 million deal to produce three different projects, one of which is *Homecoming*. *Homecoming* received six nominations at the 71st Primetime Creative Arts Emmy Awards.

Beyoncé starred as the voice of Nala in the remake *of The Lion King*, which was released in July 2019. Beyoncé is featured on the film's soundtrack, released on July 11, 2019, with a remake of the song "Can You Feel the Love Tonight" alongside Donald Glover, Billy Eichner, and Seth Rogen, which was originally composed by Elton John. An original song from the film by Beyoncé, "Spirit", was released as the lead single from both the soundtrack and *The Lion King: The Gift* – a companion album released alongside the film, produced and curated by Beyoncé.

Beyoncé called *The Lion King: The Gift* a "sonic cinema". She stated that the album is influenced by everything from R&B, pop, hip hop, and Afrobeat. The songs were produced by African producers, which Beyoncé said was because "authenticity and heart were important to [her]", since the film is set in Africa. In September of the same year, a documentary chronicling the development, production, and early music video filming of *The Lion King: The Gift,* entitled "Beyoncé Presents: Making The Gift," was aired on ABC.

In April 2020, Beyoncé was featured on the remix of Megan Thee Stallion's song "Savage", marking her first musical material of music for the year. The song peaked at number one on the *Billboard* Hot 100, marking

Beyoncé's eleventh song to do so across all acts. On June 19, 2020, Beyoncé released the nonprofit charity single "Black Parade". On June 23, she followed up the release of its studio version with an a cappella version exclusively on Tidal. *Black Is King*, a visual album based on the music of *The Lion King: The Gift,* premiered globally on Disney+ on July 31, 2020. Produced by

Disney and Parkwood Entertainment, the film was written, directed, and executive-produced by Beyoncé. The film was described by Disney as "a celebratory memoir for the world on the Black experience". Beyoncé received the most nominations (9) at the 63rd Annual Grammy Awards and the most awards (4), which made her the most-awarded singer, most-awarded female artist, and second-most-awarded artist in Grammy history.

Beyoncé wrote and recorded a song titled "Be Alive" for the biographical drama film *King Richard*.[236] She received her first Academy Award nomination for Best Original Song at the 94th Academy Awards for the song, alongside co-writer DIXSON.

Mimesis Stage 2 for Beyonce Giselle Knowles – 2022-Quarter 1 of 2023[463]

On June 9, 2022, Beyoncé removed her profile pictures across various social media platforms, causing speculation that she would be releasing new music. Days later, Beyoncé caused further speculation via her nonprofit BeyGood's Twitter account, hinting at her upcoming seventh studio album. On June 15, 2022, Beyoncé officially announced her seventh studio album, titled *Renaissance*. The album was released on July 29, 2022. The first single from *Renaissance*, "Break My Soul", was released on June 20, 2022. The song became Beyoncé's 20th top ten single on the *Billboard* Hot 100, and in doing so, Beyoncé joined Paul McCartney and Michael Jackson as the only artists in Hot 100 history to achieve at least twenty top ten as a solo artist and ten as a member of a group.

Upon release, *Renaissance* received universal acclaim from critics. *Renaissance* debuted at number one on the *Billboard* 200 chart, and in doing so, Beyoncé became the first female artist to have her first seven studio albums debut at number one in the United States. "Break My Soul" concurrently rose to number 1 on the Billboard Hot 100, becoming the twelfth song to do so across her career discography.

The song "Heated," which was co-written with Canadian rapper Drake, originally included the lyrics Spazzin' on that a-- / spazz on that a--". Critics, including a number of disability charities and activists, argued that the word "spaz" represented a derogatory term for spastic diplegia, a form of cerebral palsy. In response, in August 2022, a representative for Beyoncé issued a statement and explained that "The word not used intentionally in a harmful way, will be replaced".

On January 21, 2023, Beyoncé performed in Dubai at a private show. The performance, which was her first full concert in more than four years, was delivered to an audience of influencers and journalists. Beyoncé was reportedly paid $24 million to perform. Beyoncé faced criticism for her decision to perform in the United Arab Emirates, where homosexuality is illegal. On February 1, Beyoncé announced the Renaissance World Tour with dates in North America and Europe.

Mimesis Stage 2 for Beyonce Giselle Knowles Carter – Influences[464]

Beyoncé's major influences include Michael Jackson (*left*) and Tina Turner (*right*).

Beyoncé names Michael Jackson as her major musical influence. Aged five, Beyoncé attended her first ever concert where Jackson performed, and she claims to have realized her purpose. When she presented him with a tribute award at the World Music Awards in 2006, Beyoncé said, "If it wasn't for Michael Jackson, I would never ever have performed." Beyoncé was heavily influenced by Tina Turner, who she said, "Tina Turner is someone that I admire, because she made her strength feminine and sexy".

She admires Diana Ross as an "all-around entertainer" and Whitney Houston, who she said "inspired me to get up there and do what she did." Beyoncé cited Madonna as an influence "not only for her musical style, but also for her business sense", saying that she wanted to "follow in the footsteps of Madonna and be a powerhouse and have my own empire." She also credits Mariah Carey's singing and her song "Vision of Love" as influencing her to begin practicing vocal runs as a child. Her other musical influences include Rachelle Ferrell, Aaliyah, Janet Jackson, TLC, Prince, Shakira, Lauryn Hill, Sade Adu, Donna Summer, Mary J. Blige, Anita Baker, and Toni Braxton.

The feminism and female empowerment themes on Beyoncé's second solo album *B'Day*, were inspired by her role in *Dreamgirls* and by singer Josephine Baker. Beyoncé paid homage to Baker by performing "Déjà Vu" at the 2006 Fashion Rocks concert, wearing Baker's trademark mini-hula skirt embellished with fake bananas. Beyoncé's third solo album, *I Am... Sasha Fierce* was inspired by Jay-Z and especially by Etta James, whose "boldness" inspired Beyoncé to explore other musical genres and styles. Her fourth solo album, *4*, was inspired by Fela Kuti, 1990s R&B, Earth, Wind & Fire,

DeBarge, Lionel Richie, Teena Marie, The Jackson 5, New Edition, Adele, Florence and the Machine, and Prince.

Beyoncé has stated that she is personally inspired by Michelle Obama (the 44th First Lady of the United States), saying "she proves you can do it all", and has described Oprah Winfrey as "the definition of inspiration and a strong woman." She has also discussed how Jay-Z is a continuing inspiration to her, both with what she describes as his lyrical genius and in the obstacles he has overcome in his life. Beyoncé has expressed admiration for the artist Jean-Michel Basquiat, posting in a letter, "what I find in the work of Jean-Michel Basquiat, I search for in every day in music... he is lyrical and raw". Beyoncé also cited Cher as a fashion inspiration.

People who have influenced Beyonce [465]

How we think, how we behave, how we find interests, how interests are developed and shaped are influenced by the phenomena and people we encounter in life.

Mimesis Stage 2 for Beyonce Giselle Knowles-Carter –Beyonce and Jay-Z Relationship, Marriage, Children[466]

2000

Beyoncé told Seventeen that she met Jay-Z when she was 18, but they began dating about a year and a half later (2001), when she was 19 years old. The rapper is 12 years older than his wife. "We were friends first for a year and a half before we went on any dates," the pop icon told Oprah Winfrey in an OWN interview.

2008 They secretly wed on April 4. To date, Beyoncé and Jay-Z are parents to three children, Blue Ivy, born in 2012, and twins Sir and Rumi, born in 2017.

In 2002, Beyoncé and Jay-Z collaborated on the song "'03 Bonnie & Clyde", which appeared on his seventh album, *The Blueprint 2: The Gift & The Curse* (2002). Beyoncé appeared as Jay-Z's girlfriend in the music video for the song, fueling speculation about their relationship. On April 4, 2008, Beyoncé and Jay-Z married without publicity. As of April 2014, the couple had sold a combined 300 million records together. They are known for their private relationship, although they have appeared to have become more relaxed since 2013. Both have acknowledged the difficulty that arose in their marriage after Jay-Z had an affair.

Beyoncé miscarried around 2010 or 2011, describing it as "the saddest thing" she had ever endured. She returned to the studio and wrote music to cope with the loss. In April 2011, Beyoncé and Jay-Z traveled to Paris to shoot the album cover for *4*, and she unexpectedly became pregnant in Paris. In August, the couple attended the 2011 MTV Video Music Awards, at which Beyoncé performed "Love on Top" and ended the performance by revealing she was pregnant. Her appearance helped that year's MTV Video Music Awards become the most-watched broadcast in MTV history, pulling in 12.4 million viewers; the announcement was listed in *Guinness World Records* for "most tweets per second recorded for a single event" on Twitter, receiving 8,868 tweets per second, and "Beyonce pregnant" was the most Googled phrase the week of August 29, 2011. On January 7, 2012, Beyoncé gave birth to a daughter, Blue Ivy, at Lenox Hill Hospital in New York City.

Following the release of *Lemonade*, which included the single "Sorry", in 2016, speculations arose about Jay-Z's alleged infidelity with a mistress referred to as "Becky". Jon Pareles in *The New York Times* pointed out that many of the accusations were "aimed specifically and recognizably" at him. Similarly, Rob Sheffield of *Rolling Stone* magazine noted the lines "Suck on my balls, I've had enough" were an "unmistakable hint" that the lyrics revolve around Jay-Z.

On February 1, 2017, she revealed on her Instagram account that she was expecting twins. Her announcement gained over 6.3 million likes within eight hours, breaking the world record for the most liked image on the website at the time. On July 13, 2017, Beyoncé uploaded the first image of herself and the twins onto her Instagram account, confirming their birth date as a month prior, on June 13, 2017, with the post becoming the second most liked on Instagram, behind her own pregnancy announcement. The twins, a daughter named Rumi and a son named Sir, were born at Ronald Reagan UCLA Medical Center in California. She wrote of her pregnancy and its aftermath in the September 2018 issue of *Vogue*, in which she had full control of the cover, shot at Hammerwood Park by photographer Tyler Mitchell.

Mimesis Stage 2 for Beyonce Giselle Knowles – Carter - Jay-Z Infidelity[467]

Normally, I would not be interested in the private life indiscretions of individuals. I consider that personal and private between the individuals involved, but in the case of Beyoncé and Jay-Z, there is a significant and valuable message to be learned. They are public figures, and news of this incident was front-page news. The incident was widely covered, but what was not exposed was the underlying outcome and character-building growth both parties seem to have experienced. A lesson in character and growth underlies this story. A lesson in being an adult.

2014   The perfect couple, Beyonce and Jay Z faced issues in their marriage after the latter allegedly cheated on his wife. The cracks in their married life began in the year 2014 as there were rumours of cheating. Bey's bombshell album Lemonade confirmed the rumors of infidelity, and then Jay Z broke the silence on it & admitted that the reports were true.

The duo got married in the year 2008 and are proud parents of three children. The duo has been together for over 20 years and have proved you need to constantly work on your marriage to make it work.

Jay-Z has admitted cheating on Beyoncé for the first time in an interview about his life.

He told The New York Times Style Magazine that he'd built up walls due to issues from his childhood, which led to him shutting down and infidelity.

"The hardest thing is seeing pain on someone's face that you caused, and then having to deal with yourself," he said.

The couple had both hinted about it in their music.

"You have to survive," he said. "So you go into survival mode, and when you go into survival mode, what happens? You shut down all emotions.

He hinted that they could have gotten divorced, but he'd had therapy to help him deal with his past experiences.

"You know, most people walk away, and, like, divorce rate is like 50% or something 'cause most people can't see themselves."

2013   Rumours came out that the rapper had been cheating and then there was #elevatorgate when Solange Knowles attacked Jay-Z, while sister Beyonce stayed silent.

More recently, Jay-Z's album, 4:44, alluded to him being unfaithful.

He wrote: "Look, I apologize / Often womanize / Took for my child to be born to see through a woman's eyes."

The most significant thing about Jay-Z cheating is not that he cheated. The most significant thing is how infidelity was handled. How it impacted their relationship. How it caused them to rebound and grow as human beings. In all appearances, their relationship is stronger than ever. While it is noble that Jay-Z admitted his indiscretion and apologized, the most wonderful aspect of the entire incident was that Beyonce appears to have overcome the hurt, the trauma, and the embarrassment to forgive and get on with their life …. Apparently, better than ever. Hopefully, both Beyoncé and Jay-Z are better human beings, and their love for each other is stronger than ever. Beyonce was strong enough to forgive, and Jay-Z was strong enough to repent. In the case of Beyoncé and Jay-Z, there is a significant and valuable message to be learned. A lesson in character and growth. A lesson in being an adult.

It is easier to forgive a spouse for being late than it is to forgive a spouse for infidelity. Forgiveness is a characteristic of character and the quality of an individual. That Beyoncé appears to have forgiven Jay-Z and that they are still together speaks volumes to the quality of Beyoncé's character and her spirit of forgiveness. It also speaks to her love for Jay-Z. Possibly Jay-Z was insecure about being loved and about loving because of his childhood and not having a positive perspective on husband/wife relationships. He was raised in a single-parent home with his mother raising him and his siblings. Maybe Jay-Z needs the reinforcement that Beyonce truly loved him. Maybe the potential of loss confronted Jay-Z with the importance of Beyoncé to his life. All of this is personal to them. What we do know is that despite the infidelity, they are still together and appear to be going strong. Congratulations, Jay-Z and Beyonce. That they overcame this most difficult of life experiences may make other experiences they encounter seem like a "walk in the park. It takes a mature adult to overcome adversity and forgive their spouse. It takes character and an awakening that is a growth experience.

Music has a spiritual quality that touches the individual beneath the exterior of their being. Jay-Z is not the only one to consider music as a healing and positive energy force influencing lived experiences. Music is also an important part of spiritual and religious worship that gives an additional emphasis and reinforcement to the wonderment of God, Jesus, and the power of living an ethical and moral life. Allen Bergin addresses the healing and positive power of music, stating, "I feel close to him (God), and the music has enhanced that feeling".[468]

There is a significant life lesson inherent in the relationship between Jay-Z and Beyoncé. A number of themes come to mind. "Love conquers all," " forgiveness, and repentance all play important roles in the re-bonding of the relationship between Jay-Z and Beyonce. Again, I want to reiterate the quality in the character of Beyoncé to have such a forgiving spirit. Jay-Z is also to be commended for admitting his mistake, being honest and forthright, and then redevoting himself to his family with a much greater commitment. One that I believe will serve them for a lifetime (their lifetime).

One of the most challenging things for an individual to accomplish is "Change", repent, make amends for their mistake, and maintain their re-constructed behavior. There is a psychology to repentance. One has to consider that Jay-Z and Beyoncé were socialized in a different family structure. Beyonce, in her formative developmental years, grew up with a mother, father, and sister, in a family setting that reinforced traditional values of marriage, fidelity, and family. Jay-Z, on the other hand, grew up in a broken home. His mother was his caregiver. In his formative developmental years, he did not have a father / male role model. One might say that Beyonce taught Jay-Z about the value and quality of bonding between a husband and wife, how to maintain the security of the family. There is a school of thought that a husband or a wife cheats because they are insecure about their own security. Why do people cheat? A wide variety of factors can bring out some type of affair. A study of 495 people revealed eight key reasons: anger, low self-esteem, lack of love, low or lack of commitment, need for variety, neglect, sexual desire, and circumstance. [469] Infidelity can be a complicated phenomenon, especially when one is unfaithful to someone they love. The most important takeaway from this incident is that Beyoncé and Jay-Z appeared to have worked out their issues and are stronger than ever. That in itself is an accomplishment many people are not capable of making. The factors in both of their characters could be likewise factors in their mutual and separate success, as well as the success they accomplish together. Often, people don't communicate openly and honestly to understand the alignment of their values and expectations in a relationship. This is a critical factor in rejecting (not engaging), developing, or abandoning a relationship. It is also a critical factor in maintaining and sustaining a relationship.

In order for an individual to forgive, the other individual has to repent, become worthy of forgiveness. There is a psychology to repentance that requires the transformation of an individual's thinking and behavior. Based on the semantic functions of repentance, we could consider at least four psychological functions for repentance: a) "making and improving the meaning of life", b) "reducing psycho-spiritual struggles and conflicts", c) "increased mental health", and d) "increased spiritual development".[470]

Anyone who has ever been victimized—and that includes survivors of crime, accidents, childhood abuse, political imprisonment, warfare, and individuals who are victims of infidelity- must decide whether or not to forgive the perpetrator. There can be no middle ground to this decision: either you decide to forgive the person who hurt you, or you hold on to bitterness and anger. Holding on to bitterness and anger can cause problems of their own, so if you have ever been victimized, being able to forgive your victimizer is a crucial part of your healing. If one person is injured by another, we could say that the two persons are "pushed apart" by the injury, and so, if they are to become friendly again, this gap between them must be repaired; they must be reconciled. Reconciliation comes from the Latin words *re-*, meaning "again," and *conciliare*, which means "to bring together," so reconciliation means "to bring together—or to make friendly—again." The act of reconciliation involves two parts: forgiveness and penance.

> **First is the act of *confession*:** admitting the act ("We broke your window"). The act has to be admitted, aloud, to the person offended, or the entire process stops and no one gets anywhere.

> **Second is the act of *repentance*:** asking for forgiveness ("We're sorry"). Remember, if the children had run away, they would have avoided their responsibility to repair the damage they caused, and so they would have prevented the process of penance from getting started.

And third is the act of *penalty*: accepting the punishment ("OK"). After all, a broken window is a broken window, and it has to be fixed. If the children do not pay to fix it, their confession and repentance are really worthless. (For those of you still thinking about the issue of homeowner's insurance, let's say that Mrs. Smith's insurance pays the damages, and the children help Mrs. Smith clean up the mess in her living room. In this case, their work would serve to fulfill the function of the penalty.)

The concept of forgiveness is elusive for some people. Forgiveness by itself is still psychologically preferable to holding a grudge. Because the bitterness of a grudge works like a mental poison that doesn't hurt anyone but yourself. Seeking revenge or wishing harm to another will, at the minimum, deplete your strength and prevent your wounds from healing. In the worst case, the cold hunger for revenge will make you into a victimizer yourself. Lacking forgiveness, you and your victimizer will be locked together in the hell of eternal revenge.

Real forgiveness and reconciliation take time. Premature forgiveness may not remove the residue of anger and hostility. There will be an imbalance in the relationship. Time that involves reinforcing acts and behavior that demonstrate sincerity in repentance and restore the security of the injured party is developed over time, if both parties are willing to commit to a reconciliation effort.[471]

The incident of infidelity between Jay-Z and Beyoncé was made public and discussed in a number of media interviews. The incident of infidelity is normally a private matter between two adults. Discussing it in open forums, numerous times, can make the incident public and open the door to unwanted and unnecessary comments from irrelevant people. This is not to mention how Beyoncé and Jay-Z felt about having their personal lives open to the public. Nevertheless, if talking about it helped them to resolve the matter, then great. That they were able to address and resolve the matter in the midst of public scrutiny is all the more a positive insight into their intestinal fortitude, quality of character, maturity, and real love they have for each other.

What if the shoe were on the other foot?[1]

Would Jay-Z have been able to forgive Beyoncé?

Mimesis Stage 2 for Beyonce Giselle Knowles-Carter

Beyoncé is still a young lady in the prime of her career. As of 2023, Beyoncé is 41 years old. She has developed a professionalism and a mastery of her craft. Beyoncé has the respect of her peers and critics. She was fortunate to have discovered her calling early in life and to have been surrounded by people and influences who supported her dream. This is usually a challenge in adolescent years: discovering one's passion/interest, pursuing one's interest to the point of developing a future perspective, having supportive influences, and in many cases having the resources to pursue one's area of interest. The reflection Beyonce has on her lived experiences, at this point, is reflection that fuels and feeds her progress in the future.

---

[1] Disclaimer – This author does not have first-hand knowledge of the relationship between Jay-Z and Beyonce. The comments about their relationship are based on media articles. Interviews by Jay-Z, research studies on the topics of psychology, relationships, infidelity, forgiveness, repentance, reconciliation and the experience and knowledge of the author.

Mimesis of Life Summary for Beyonce Giselle Knowles-Carter [472]

Beyoncé's success has led to her becoming a cultural icon and earning her the nickname "Queen Bey". Constance Grady wrote for *Vox*, "The transformation of Beyoncé from well-liked pop star to cultural icon came in three phases, punctuated by the self-titled *Beyoncé* album of 2013, 2016's *Lemonade*, and 2018's *Homecoming* concert at Coachella." In *The New Yorker*, music critic Jody Rosen described Beyoncé as "the most important and compelling popular musician of the twenty-first century... the result, the logical end point, of a century-plus of pop." She topped NPR list of the "21st Century's Most Influential Women Musicians".James Clear, in his book *Atomic Habits* (2018), draws a parallel between Beyoncé's success and the dramatic transformations in modern society: "In the last one hundred years, we have seen the rise of the car, the airplane, the television, the personal computer, the internet, the smartphone, and Beyoncé." *The Observer* named her Artist of the Decade (2000s) in 2009.

Writing for *Entertainment Weekly*, Alex Suskind noticed how Beyoncé was the decade's (2010s) defining pop star, stating that "no one dominated music in the 2010s like Queen Bey", explaining that her "songs, album rollouts, stage presence, social justice initiatives, and disruptive public relations strategy have influenced the way we've viewed music since 2010." British publication *NME* also shared similar thoughts on her impact in the 2010s, including Beyoncé, on their list of the "10 Artists Who Defined The Decade". In 2018, *Rolling Stone* included her on its Millennial 100 list.

Music critics have often credited Beyoncé with the invention of the staccato rap-singing style that has since dominated pop, R&B, and rap music. Lakin Starling of *The Fader* wrote that Beyoncé's innovative implementation of the delivery style on Destiny's Child's 1999 album *The Writing's on the Wall* invented a new form of R&B. Beyoncé's new style subsequently changed the nature of music, revolutionizing both singing in urban music and rapping in pop music, and becoming the dominant sound of both genres. The style helped to redefine both the breadth of commercial R&B and the sound of hip hop, with artists such as Kanye West and Drake implementing Beyoncé's cadence in the late 2000s and early 2010s. The staccato rap-singing style continued to be used in the music industry in the late 2010s and early 2020s; Aron Williams of *Uproxx* described Beyoncé as the "primary pioneer" of the rapping style that dominates the music industry today, with many contemporary rappers implementing Beyoncé's rap-singing. Michael Eric Dyson agrees, saying that Beyoncé "changed the whole genre" and has become the "godmother" of mumble rappers, who use the staccato rap-singing cadence. Dyson added: "She doesn't get credit for the remarkable way in which she changed the musical vocabulary of contemporary art."

Beyoncé has been credited with reviving the album as an art form in an era dominated by singles and streaming. This started with her 2011 album *4*; while mainstream R&B artists were forgoing album-led R&B in favor of singles-led EDM, Beyoncé aimed to place the focus back on albums as an art form and re-establish R&B as a mainstream concern. This remained a focus of Beyoncé's, and in 2013, she made her eponymous album only available to purchase as a full album on iTunes, rather than being able to purchase individual tracks or consume the album via streaming. Kaitlin Menza of *Marie Claire* wrote that this made listeners "experience the album as one whole sonic experience, the way people used to, noting the musical and lyrical themes".

Jamieson Cox for *The Verge* described how Beyoncé's 2013 album initiated a gradual trend of albums becoming more cohesive and self-referential, and this phenomenon reached its endpoint with *Lemonade*, which set "a new standard for pop storytelling at the highest possible scale".Megan Carpentier of *The Guardian* wrote that with *Lemonade*, Beyoncé has "almost revived the album format" by releasing an album that can only be listened to in its entirety. Myf Warhurst on *Double J*'s "Lunch With Myf" explained that while most artists' albums consist of a few singles plus filler songs, Beyoncé "brought the album back", changing the art form of the album "to a narrative with an arc and a story, and you have to listen to the entire thing to get the concept".

She is known for coining popular phrases such as "put a ring on it", a euphemism for a marriage proposal, "I woke up like this", which started a trend of posting morning selfies with the hashtag #iwokeuplikethis, and "boy, bye", which was used as part of the Democratic National Committee's campaign for the 2020 election. Similarly, she also came up with the phrase "visual album" following the release of her fifth studio album, which had a video for every song. This has been recreated by many other artists since, such as Frank Ocean and Melanie Martinez.[443] The album also popularized surprise releases, with many artists releasing songs, videos, or albums with no prior announcement, such as Taylor Swift, Nicki Minaj, Eminem, Frank Ocean, Jay-Z, and Drake.

In January 2012, research scientist Bryan Lessard named *Scaptia beyonceae*, a species of horse-fly found in Northern Queensland, Australia, after Beyoncé due to the fly's unique golden hairs on its abdomen.

Various recording artists and celebrities have cited Beyoncé as their influence. Lady Gaga explained how Beyoncé gave her the determination to become a musician, recalling seeing her in Destiny's Child's music video and saying: "Oh, she's a star. I want that." Rihanna was inspired to start her singing career after watching Beyoncé, telling *etalk* that after Beyoncé released *Dangerously In Love* (2003), "I was like 'wow, I want to be just like that.' She's huge and just an inspiration." Lizzo was first inspired by Beyoncé to start singing after watching her perform at a Destiny's Child concert. Lizzo taught herself to sing by copying Beyoncé's *B'Day* (2006).

Ariana Grande said she learned to sing by mimicking Beyoncé. Adele cited Beyoncé as her inspiration and favorite artist, telling *Vogue*: "She's been a huge and constant part of my life as an artist since I was about ten or eleven... I think she's inspiring. She's beautiful. She's ridiculously talented, and she is one of the kindest people I've ever met... She makes me want to do things with my life." Both Paul McCartney and Garth Brooks said they watch Beyoncé's performances to get inspiration for their shows, with Brooks saying that when watching one of her performances, "take out your notebook and take notes. No matter how long you've been on the stage – take notes on that one." Beyoncé was also cited as an influence by several other mainstream artists. It will be exciting, not only for Beyonce, but for her fans as well to witness how her career develops from the pinnacle it is already on.

Mimesis of Life for Marilyn Monroe aka Norma Jeane Mortenson (1926 – 1962)

Marilyn Monroe was born Norma Jeane Mortenson; (June 1, 1926 – died: August 4, 1962). Ms. Monroe was an American actress, model, and singer. Famous for playing comic "blonde bombshell" characters, she became one of the most popular sex symbols of the 1950s and early 1960s, as well as an emblem of the era's sexual revolution. She was a top-billed actress for a decade, and her films grossed $200 million (equivalent to $2 billion in 2021) by the time of her death in 1962. Long after her death, Monroe remains a major icon of pop culture. In 1999, the American Film Institute ranked her sixth on their list of the greatest female screen legends from the Golden Age of Hollywood.

Born and raised in Los Angeles, Monroe spent most of her childhood in a total of 12 foster homes and an orphanage before marrying James Dougherty at age sixteen. She was working in a factory during World War II when she met a photographer from the First Motion Picture Unit and began a successful pin-up modeling career, which led to short-lived film contracts with 20th Century Fox and Columbia Pictures. After a series of minor film roles, she signed a new contract with Fox in late 1950. Over the next two years, she became a popular actress with roles in several comedies, including *As*

Young as You Feel and *Monkey Business*, and in the dramas *Clash by Night* and *Don't Bother to Knock*. Monroe faced a scandal when it was revealed that she had posed for nude photographs prior to becoming a star, but the story did not damage her career and instead resulted in increased interest in her films.

By 1953, Monroe was one of the most marketable Hollywood stars. She had leading roles in the film noir *Niagara*, which overtly relied on her sex appeal, and the comedies *Gentlemen Prefer Blondes* and *How to Marry a Millionaire*, which established her star image as a "dumb blonde". The same year, her nude images were used as the centerfold and on the cover of the first issue of *Playboy*. Monroe played a significant role in the creation and management of her public image throughout her career, but felt disappointed when she was typecast and underpaid by the studio. She was briefly suspended in early 1954 for refusing a film project but returned to star in *The Seven Year Itch* (1955), one of the biggest box office successes of her career.

When the studio was still reluctant to change Monroe's contract, she founded her own film production company in 1954. She dedicated 1955 to building the company and began studying method acting under Lee Strasberg at the Actors Studio. Later that year, Fox awarded her a new contract, which gave her more control and a larger salary. Her subsequent roles included a critically acclaimed performance in *Bus Stop* (1956) and her first independent production in *The Prince and the Showgirl* (1957). She won a Golden Globe for Best Actress for her role in *Some Like It Hot* (1959), a critical and commercial success. Her last completed film was the drama *The Misfits* (1961).

Monroe's troubled private life received much attention. She struggled with addiction and mood disorders. Her marriages to retired baseball star Joe DiMaggio and to playwright Arthur Miller were highly publicized but ended in divorce. On August 4, 1962, she died at age 36 from an overdose of barbiturates at her Los Angeles home. Her death was ruled a probable suicide. [473]

Mimesis Stage 1 for Norma Jeane Mortenson aka Marilyn Monroe – Childhood

1926-1934   Marilyn Monroe was born Norma Jeane

Mortenson on June 1, in Los Angeles, California. Her mother, Gladys Pearl Baker (1902–1984), was born in Piedras Negras, Coahuila, Mexico[7] to a poor Midwestern family who migrated to California at the turn of the century. At age 15, Gladys married John Newton Baker, an abusive man nine years her senior. They had two children, Robert (1918–1933) and Berniece (1919–2014). She successfully filed for divorce and sole custody in 1923, but Baker kidnapped the children soon after and moved with them to his native Kentucky. Marilyn did not know she had a sister until she was 12 years old. They eventually met when Marilyn was 17 or 18 years old. [474]

After Glady's the divorce, Gladys worked as a film negative cutter at Consolidated Film Industries. In 1924, she married Martin Edward Mortensen, but they separated just months later and divorced in 1928. In 2022, DNA testing indicated that Monroe's father was Charles Stanley Gifford (1898–1965), a co-worker of Gladys, with whom she had an affair in 1925. Monroe also had two other half-siblings from Gifford's marriage with his first wife, a sister, Doris (1920–1933), and a brother, Charles (1922–2015). [475]

Although Gladys was mentally and financially unprepared for a child, Monroe's early childhood was stable and happy. Gladys placed her daughter with an Evangelical Christian foster family, Albert and Ida Bolender in the rural town of Hawthorne. She also lived there for six months, until she was forced to move back to the city for employment. She then began visiting her daughter on weekends. In the summer of 1933, Gladys bought a small house in Hollywood with a loan from the Home Owners' Loan Corporation and moved seven-year-old Monroe in with her. They shared the house with lodgers, actors George and Maude Atkinson and their daughter, Nellie. [476]

1934 Gladys had a mental breakdown and was diagnosed with paranoid schizophrenia. After several months in a rest home, she was committed to the Metropolitan State Hospital. She spent the rest of her life in and out of hospitals and was rarely in contact with Monroe.

Monroe became a ward of the state, and her mother's friend Grace Goddard took responsibility over her and her mother's affairs.[477]

Over the next four years, Monroe's living situation changed often. For the first 16 months, she continued living with the Atkinsons, and may have been sexually abused during this time. [478]

Mimesis Stage 2 for Norma Jean Mortensen 1935-1943 – Adolescence and First Marriage

1935   Marilyn was always shy. She developed a stutter and became withdrawn. In the summer of 1935, she briefly stayed with Grace Goddard and her husband Erwin "Doc" Goddard and two other families. In September 1935, Grace placed her in the Los Angeles Orphans Home. The orphanage was "a model institution" and was described in positive terms by her peers, but Monroe felt abandoned.

Encouraged by the orphanage staff, who thought that Monroe would be happier living in a family, Grace became her legal guardian in 1936, but did not take her out of the orphanage until the summer of 1937.

1937   Monroe's second stay with the Goddards lasted only a few months because Doc molested her. She then lived for brief periods with her relatives and Grace's friends and relatives in Los Angeles and Compton.

Monroe's childhood experiences first made her want to become an actress: "I didn't like the world around me because it was kind of grim ... When I heard that this was acting, I said that's what I want to be ... Some of my foster families used to send me to the movies to get me out of the house and there I'd sit all day and way into the night. Up in front, there with the screen so big, a little kid all alone, and I loved it."

1938   Monroe found a more permanent home in September, when she began living with Grace's aunt Ana Lower in the west-side district of Sawtelle. She was enrolled at Emerson Junior High School and went to weekly Christian Science services with Lower. She excelled in writing and contributed to the school newspaper but was otherwise a mediocre student. Owing to the elderly Lower's health problems.

1941   Monroe returned to live with the Goddards in Van Nuys in early 1941.

1942    The same year, she began attending Van Nuys High School. In 1942, the company that employed Doc Goddard relocated him to West Virginia. California child protection laws prevented the Goddards from taking Monroe out of state, and she faced having to return to the orphanage. As a solution, she married their neighbors' 21-year-old son, factory worker James Dougherty, on June 19, 1942, just after her 16th birthday. Monroe subsequently dropped out of high school and became a housewife. She found herself and Dougherty mismatched, and later said she was "dying of boredom" during the marriage. In 1943, Dougherty enlisted in the Merchant Marine and was stationed on Santa Catalina Island, where Monroe moved with him.[479]

Mimesis Stage 2 for Norma Jeane Mortensen 1944–1948: Modeling and first film roles

In April 1944, Dougherty was shipped out to the Pacific, where he remained for most of the next two years. Monroe moved in with her in-laws and began a job at the Radioplane Company, a munitions factory in Van Nuys. In late 1944, she met photographer David Conover, who had been sent by the U.S. Army Air Forces First Motion Picture Unit to the factory to shoot morale-boosting pictures of female workers. Although none of her pictures were used, she quit working at the factory in January 1945 and began modeling for Conover and his friends. Defying her deployed husband, she moved on her own and signed a contract with the Blue Book Model Agency in August 1945.

Monroe posing as a pin-up model for a postcard

The agency deemed Monroe's figure more suitable for pin-up than high fashion modeling. She was featured to make herself more employable, she straightened her hair and dyed it blonde. According to Emmeline Snively, the agency's owner, Monroe quickly became one of its most ambitious and hard-working models; by early 1946, she had appeared on 33 magazine covers for publications such as *Pageant*, *U.S. Camera*, *Laff*, and *Peek*. As a model, Monroe occasionally used the pseudonym Jean Norman.

Through Snively, Monroe signed a contract with an acting agency in June 1946. After an unsuccessful interview at Paramount Pictures, she was given a screen test by Ben Lyon, a 20th Century-Fox executive. Head executive Darryl F. Zanuck was unenthusiastic about it, but he gave her a standard six-month contract to avoid her being signed by rival studio RKO Pictures. Monroe's contract began in August 1946, and she and Lyon selected the stage name "Marilyn Monroe". The first name was picked by Lyon, who was reminded of Broadway star Marilyn Miller; the surname was Monroe's mother's maiden name. In September 1946, she divorced Dougherty, who opposed her career.

Monroe spent her first six months at Fox learning acting, singing, and dancing, and observing the film-making process. Her contract was renewed in February 1947, and she was given her first film roles, bit parts in *Dangerous Years* (1947) and *Scudda Hoo! Scudda Hay!* (1948). The studio also enrolled her in the Actors' Laboratory Theatre, an acting school teaching the techniques of the Group Theatre; she later stated that it was "my first taste of what real acting in a real drama could be, and I was hooked". Despite her enthusiasm, her teachers thought her too shy and insecure to have a future in acting, and Fox did not renew her contract in August 1947. She returned to modeling while also doing occasional odd jobs at film studios, such as working as a dancing "pacer" behind the scenes to keep the leads on point at musical sets.

Monroe was determined to make it as an actress, and continued studying at the Actors' Lab. She had a small role in the play *Glamour Preferred* at the Bliss-Hayden Theater, but it ended after a couple of performances. To network, she frequented producers' offices, befriended gossip columnist Sidney Skolsky, and entertained influential male guests at studio functions, a practice she had begun at Fox. She also became a friend and occasional sex partner of Fox executive Joseph M. Schenck, who persuaded his friend Harry Cohn, the head executive of Columbia Pictures, to sign her in March 1948.

At Columbia, Monroe's look was modeled after Rita Hayworth, and her hair was bleached platinum blonde. She began working with the studio's head drama coach, Natasha Lytess, who would remain her mentor until 1955. Her only film at the studio was the low-budget musical *Ladies of the Chorus* (1948), in which she had her first starring role as a chorus girl courted by a wealthy man. She also screen-tested for the lead role in *Born Yesterday* (1950), but her contract was not renewed in September 1948. *Ladies of the Chorus* was released the following month and was not a success. [480]

Mimesis Stage 2 for Marilyn Monroe 1949–1952: Breakthrough years

When her contract at Columbia ended, Monroe returned again to modeling. She shot a commercial for Pabst beer and posed for artistic nude photographs by Tom Kelley for John Baumgarth calendars, using the name 'Mona Monroe'. Monroe had previously posed topless or clad in a bikini for other artists including Earl Moran, and felt comfortable with nudity. Shortly after leaving Columbia, she also met and became the protégée and mistress of Johnny Hyde, the vice president of the William Morris Agency.

Through Hyde, Monroe landed small roles in several films, including two critically acclaimed works: Joseph Mankiewicz's drama *All About Eve* (1950) and John Huston's film noir *The Asphalt Jungle* (1950). Despite her screen time being only a few minutes in the latter, she gained a mention in *Photoplay* and according to biographer Donald Spoto "moved effectively from movie model to serious actress". In December 1950, Hyde negotiated a seven-year contract for Monroe with 20th Century-Fox. According to its terms, Fox could opt to not renew the contract after each year. Hyde died of a heart attack only days later, which left Monroe devastated. In 1951, Monroe had supporting roles in three moderately successful Fox comedies: *As Young as You Feel*, *Love Nest*, and *Let's Make It Legal*. According to Spoto all three films featured her "essentially [as] a sexy ornament", but she received some praise from critics: Bosley Crowther of *The New York Times* described her as "superb" in *As Young As You Feel* and Ezra Goodman of the *Los Angeles Daily News* called her "one of the brightest up-and-coming [actresses]" for *Love Nest*.

Her popularity with audiences was also growing: she received several thousand fan letters a week, and was declared "Miss Cheesecake of 1951" by the army newspaper *Stars and Stripes*, reflecting the preferences of soldiers in the Korean War. In February 1952, the Hollywood Foreign Press Association named Monroe the "best young box office personality".In her private life, Monroe had a short relationship with director Elia Kazan and also briefly dated several other men, including director Nicholas Ray and actors Yul Brynner and Peter Lawford. In early 1952, she began a highly publicized romance with retired New York Yankees baseball star Joe DiMaggio, one of the most famous sports personalities of the era.

Monroe found herself at the center of a scandal in March 1952, when she revealed publicly that she had posed for a nude calendar in 1949. The studio had learned about the photos and that she was publicly rumored to be the model some weeks prior, and together with Monroe decided that to prevent damaging her career it was best to admit to them while stressing that she had been broke at the time. The strategy gained her public sympathy and increased interest in her films, for which she was now receiving top billing. In the wake of the scandal, Monroe was featured on the cover of *Life* magazine as the "Talk of Hollywood", and gossip columnist Hedda Hopper declared her the "cheesecake queen" turned "box office smash". Three of Monroe's films —*Clash by Night, Don't Bother to Knock* and *We're Not Married!*— were released soon after to capitalize on the public interest.

Despite her newfound popularity as a sex symbol, Monroe also wished to showcase more of her acting range. She had begun taking acting classes with Michael Chekhov and mime Lotte Goslar soon after beginning the Fox contract, and *Clash by Night* and *Don't Bother to Knock*, showed her in different roles. In the former, a drama starring Barbara Stanwyck and directed by Fritz Lang, she played a fish cannery worker; to prepare, she spent time in a fish cannery in Monterey. She received positive reviews for her performance: *The Hollywood Reporter* stated that "she deserves starring status with her excellent interpretation", and *Variety* wrote that she "has an ease of delivery which makes her a cinch for popularity". The latter was a thriller in which Monroe starred as a mentally disturbed babysitter and which Zanuck used to test her abilities in a heavier dramatic role.[1] It received mixed reviews from critics, with Crowther deeming her too inexperienced for the difficult role and *Variety* blaming the script for the film's problems.

Monroe's three other films in 1952 continued with her typecasting in comedic roles that highlighted her sex appeal. In *We're Not Married!* Her role as a beauty pageant contestant was created solely to "present Marilyn in two bathing suits", according to its writer Nunnally Johnson. In Howard Hawks's *Monkey Business*, in which she acted opposite Cary Grant, she played a secretary who is a "dumb, childish blonde, innocently unaware of the havoc her sexiness causes around her". In *O. Henry's Full House*, with Charles Laughton, she appeared in a passing *vignette* as a nineteenth-century street walker. Monroe added to her reputation as a new sex symbol with publicity stunts that year: she wore a revealing dress when acting as Grand Marshal at the Miss America Pageant parade, and told gossip columnist Earl Wilson that she usually wore no underwear. By the end of the year, gossip columnist Florabel Muir named Monroe the "it girl" of 1952.

During this period, Monroe gained a reputation for being difficult to work with, which would worsen as her career progressed. She was often late or did not show up at all, did not remember her lines, and would demand several re-takes before she was satisfied with her performance. Her dependence on her acting coaches—Natasha Lytess and then Paula Strasberg—also irritated directors. Monroe's problems have been attributed to a combination of perfectionism, low self-esteem, and stage fright. She disliked her lack of control on film sets and never experienced similar problems during photo shoots, in which she had more say over her performance and could be more spontaneous instead of following a script. To alleviate her anxiety and chronic insomnia, she began to use barbiturates, amphetamines, and alcohol, which also exacerbated her problems, although she did not become severely addicted until 1956. According to Sarah Churchwell, some of Monroe's behavior, especially later in her career, was also in response to the condescension and sexism of her male co-stars and directors. Biographer Lois Banner said that she was bullied by many of her directors.

Mimesis Stage 2 for Marilyn Monroe - 1953: Rising star[481]

Niagara

Diamonds are a girl's best friend.

1953 The studio released three of Marilyn's movies in the same year. The three movies she starred in were *Niagara, Gentlemen Prefer Blondes and How to Marry a Millionaire*. The first was the Technicolor film noir *Niagara*, in which she played a *femme fatale* scheming to murder her husband, played by Joseph Cotten . By then, Monroe and her make-up artist Allan "Whitey" Snyder had developed her "trademark" make-up look: dark arched brows, pale skin, "glistening" red lips, and a beauty mark. According to Sarah Churchwell, *Niagara* was one of the most overtly sexual films of Monroe's career. In some scenes, Monroe's body was covered only by a sheet or a towel, considered shocking by contemporary audiences. *Niagara*'s most famous scene is a 30-second long shot behind Monroe where she is seen walking with her hips swaying, which was used heavily in the film's marketing. When *Niagara* was released in January 1953, women's clubs protested it as immoral, but it proved popular with audiences. While *Variety* deemed it "clichéd" and "morbid", *The New York Times* commented that "the falls and Miss Monroe are something to see", as although Monroe may not be "the perfect actress at this point ... she can be seductive—even when she walks".

1953   Monroe continued to attract attention by wearing revealing outfits, most famously at the *Photoplay* Awards in January, where she won the "Fastest Rising Star" award. A pleated "sunburst" waist-tight, deep decolleté gold lamé dress designed by William Travilla for *Gentlemen Prefer Blondes*, but barely seen at all in the film, was to become a sensation. Prompted by such imagery, veteran star Joan Crawford publicly called the behavior "unbecoming an actress and a lady".

Niagara made Monroe a sex symbol and established her "look".

1953   Her second film, the satirical musical comedy *Gentlemen Prefer Blondes*, cemented her screen persona as a "blonde". Based on Anita Loos' novel and its Broadway version, the film focuses on two "gold-digging" showgirls played by Monroe and Jane Russell. Monroe's role was originally intended for Betty Grable, who had been 20th Century-Fox's most popular "blonde bombshell" in the 1940s; Monroe was fast eclipsing her as a star who could appeal to both male and female audiences. As part of the film's publicity campaign, she and Russell pressed their hand and footprints in wet concrete outside Grauman's Chinese Theatre in June.[132] *Gentlemen Prefer Blondes* was released shortly after and became one of the biggest box office successes of the year. Crowther of *The New York Times* and William Brogdon of *Variety* both commented favorably on Monroe, especially noting her performance of "Diamonds Are a Girl's Best Friend"; according to the latter, she demonstrated the "ability to sex a song as well as point up the eye values of a scene by her presence".

1953 In September, Monroe made her television debut in the *Jack Benny Show*, playing Jack's fantasy woman in the episode "Honolulu Trip". She co-starred with Betty Grable and Lauren Bacall in her third movie of the year, *How to Marry a Millionaire*, released in November. It featured Monroe as a naïve model who teams up with her friends to find rich husbands, repeating the successful formula of *Gentlemen Prefer Blondes*. It was the second film ever released in CinemaScope, a widescreen format that Fox hoped would draw audiences back to theaters as television was beginning to cause losses to film studios. Despite mixed reviews, the film was Monroe's biggest box office success at that point in her career.

1953-1954 Monroe was listed in the annual Top Ten Money Making Stars Poll, and according to Fox historian Aubrey Solomon, became the studio's "greatest asset" alongside CinemaScope. Monroe's position as a leading sex symbol was confirmed in December 1953, when Hugh Hefner featured her on the cover and as centerfold in the first issue of *Playboy*; Monroe did not consent to the publication The cover image was a photograph taken of her at the Miss America Pageant parade in 1952, and the centerfold featured one of her 1949 nude photographs.

Marilyn's starring roles, her talent and public acceptance by both men and women caused her to emerged as a major sex symbol and one of Hollywood's most bankable performers.

Mimesis Stage 2 for Marilyn Monroe - 1954–1955: Conflicts with 20th Century-Fox and Marriage to Joe DiMaggio [482]

Monroe had become one of 20th Century-Fox's biggest stars, but her contract had not changed since 1950, so that she was paid far less than other stars of her stature and could not choose her projects Her attempts to appear in films that would not focus on her as a pin-up had been thwarted by the studio head executive, Darryl F. Zanuck, who had a strong personal dislike of her and did not think she would earn the studio as much revenue in other types of roles Under pressure from the studio's owner, Spyros Skouras, Zanuck had also decided that Fox should focus exclusively on entertainment to maximize profits and canceled the production of any "serious films".

1954

In January, Zanuck suspended Monroe when she refused to begin shooting yet another musical comedy, *The Girl in Pink Tights*. This was front-page news, and Monroe immediately took action to counter negative publicity. On January 14, she and Joe DiMaggio were married at the San Francisco City Hall. They then traveled by carto to San Luis Obispo, then honeymooned outside Idyllwild, California, in the mountain lodge of Monroe's lawyer Lloyd Wright. On January 29, 1954, fifteen days later] they flew to Japan, combining a "honeymoon" with his commitment to his former San Francisco Seals coach Lefty O'Doul, to help train Japanese baseball teams. From Tokyo, she traveled with Jean O'Doul, Lefty's wife, to Korea, where she participated in a USO show, singing songs from her films for over 60,000 U.S. Marines over a four-day period. After returning to the U.S., she was awarded *Photoplay*'s "Most Popular Female Star" prize. Monroe settled with Fox in March, with the promise of a new contract, a bonus of $100,000, and a starring role in the film adaptation of the Broadway success *The Seven Year Itch*.

1954 In April, Marilyn filmed Otto Preminger's western *River of No Return*, the last film that Monroe had filmed prior to the suspension, was released. She called it a "Z-grade cowboy movie in which the acting finished second to the scenery and the CinemaScope process", but it was popular with audiences. The first film she made after the suspension was the musical *There's No Business Like Show Business*, which she strongly disliked but the studio required her to do for dropping *The Girl in Pink Tights*. It was unsuccessful upon its release in late 1954, with Monroe's performance considered vulgar by many critics.

1954 In September, Monroe began filming Billy Wilder's comedy *The Seven Year Itch*, starring opposite Tom Ewell as a woman who becomes the object of her married neighbor's sexual fantasies. Although the film was shot in  Hollywood, the studio decided to generate advance publicity by staging the filming of a scene in which Monroe is standing on a subway grate with the air blowing up the skirt of her white dress on Lexington Avenue in Manhattan. The shoot lasted for several hours and attracted nearly 2,000 spectators. The "subway grate scene" became one of Monroe's most famous, and *The Seven Year Itch* became one of the biggest commercial successes of the year after its release in June 1955.

The publicity stunt placed Monroe on international front pages, and it also marked the end of her marriage to DiMaggio, who was infuriated by it. The union had been troubled from the start by his jealousy and controlling attitude; he was also physically abusive. After returning from NYC to Hollywood in October 1954, Monroe filed for divorce, after only nine months of marriage.

1954 *The Seven Year Itch* wrapped up in November, Monroe left Hollywood for the East Coast, where she and photographer Milton Greene founded their own production company, Marilyn Monroe Productions (MMP)—an action that has later been called "instrumental" in the collapse of the studio system. Monroe stated that she was "tired of the same old sex roles" and asserted that she was no longer under contract to Fox, as it had not fulfilled its duties, such as paying her the promised bonus. This began a year-long legal battle between her and Fox in **January 1955**. The press largely ridiculed Monroe, and she was parodied in the Broadway play *Will Success Spoil Rock Hunter?* (1955), in which her lookalike Jayne Mansfield played a dumb actress who starts her own production company.

1955 After founding MMP, Monroe moved to Manhattan and spent the year studying acting. She took classes with Constance Collier and attended workshops on method acting at the Actors Studio, run by Lee Strasberg. She grew close to Strasberg and his wife Paula, receiving private lessons at their home due to her shyness, and soon became a family member. She replaced her old acting coach, Natasha Lytess, with Paula; the Strasbergs remained an important influence for the rest of her career. Monroe also started undergoing psychoanalysis, as Strasberg believed that an actor must confront their emotional traumas and use them in their performances.

Monroe continued her relationship with DiMaggio despite the ongoing divorce process; she also dated actor Marlon Brando and playwright Arthur Miller. She had first been introduced to Miller by Elia Kazan in the early 1950s. The affair between Marilyn and Miller became increasingly serious after October 1955, when her divorce was finalized and Miller separated from his wife. The studio urged her to end it, as Miller was being investigated by the FBI for allegations of communism and had been subpoenaed by the House Un-American Activities Committee, but Monroe refused. The relationship led to the FBI opening a file on her.

1955 By the end of the year, Monroe and Fox signed a new seven-year contract, as MMP would not be able to finance films alone, and the studio was eager to have Monroe working for them again. Fox would pay her $400,000 to make four films and granted her the right to choose her own projects, directors, and cinematographers. She would also be free to make one film with MMP for a completed film for Fox.

Mimesis Stage 2 for Marilyn Monroe 1956–1959: Critical acclaim and marriage to Arthur Miller

1956

Marilyn decided to legally change her name to *Marilyn Monroe.* [483]

Ben Lyon, her agent, suggested Marilyn change her name

> The Photo inscription reads:
>
> *"Dear Ben, You found me, named me and believed in me when no one else did. My thanks and love forever.   Marilyn"*

1956 Marilyn announced her reconciliation (some considered it a victory) with 20th Century-Fox. The press wrote favorably about her decision to fight the studio; *Time* called her a "shrewd businesswoman" and *Look* predicted that the win would be "an example of the individual against the herd for years to come". In contrast, Monroe's relationship with Miller prompted some negative comments, such as Walter Winchell's statement that "America's best-known blonde moving picture star is now the darling of the left-wing intelligentsia."

In March, Monroe began filming the drama *Bus Stop*, her first film under the new contract. She played Chérie, a saloon singer whose dreams of stardom are complicated by a naïve cowboy who falls in love with her. For the role, she learned an Ozark accent, chose costumes and makeup that lacked the glamor of her earlier films, and provided deliberately mediocre singing and dancing. Broadway director Joshua Logan agreed to direct, despite initially doubting Monroe's acting abilities and knowing of her difficult reputation.

The filming took place in Idaho and Arizona, with Monroe "technically in charge" as the head of MMP, occasionally making decisions on cinematography and with Logan adapting to her chronic lateness and perfectionism. The experience changed Logan's opinion of Monroe, and he later compared her to Charlie Chaplin in her ability to blend comedy and tragedy.

1956

On June 29, Monroe and Miller were married at the Westchester County Court in White Plains, New York; two days later they had a Jewish ceremony at the home of Kay Brown, Miller's literary agent, in Waccabuc, New York. With the marriage, Monroe converted to Judaism, which led Egypt to ban all of her films. Due to Monroe's status as a sex symbol and Miller's image as an intellectual, the media saw the union as a mismatch, as evidenced by *Variety*'s headline, "Egghead Weds Hourglass".

1956 *Bus Stop* was released in August and became a critical and commercial success. *The Saturday Review of Literature* wrote that Monroe's performance "effectively dispels once and for all the notion that she is merely a glamour personality" and Crowther proclaimed: "Hold on to your chairs, everybody, and get set for a rattling surprise. Marilyn Monroe has finally proved herself an actress." She also received a Golden Globe nomination for Best Actress for her performance.

1956 In August, Monroe also began filming MMP's first independent production, *The Prince and the Showgirl*, at Pinewood Studios in England. Based on a 1953 stage play by Terence Rattigan, it was to be directed and co-produced by, and to co-star, Laurence Olivier. The production was complicated by conflicts between him and Marilyn. Olivier, who had also directed and starred in the stage play, angered her with the patronizing statement "All you have to do is be sexy", and with his demand she replicate Vivien Leigh's stage interpretation of the character. He also disliked the constant presence of Paula Strasberg, Monroe's acting coach, on set. In retaliation, Marilyn became uncooperative and began to deliberately arrive late, later saying, "if you don't respect your artists, they can't work well."

Monroe also experienced other problems during production. Her dependence on pharmaceuticals escalated and, according to Spoto, she had a miscarriage. She and Greene also argued over how MMP should be run. Despite the difficulties, filming was completed on schedule by the end of 1956.

1957 *The Prince and the Showgirl* was released to mixed reviews in June and proved unpopular with American audiences. It was better received in Europe, where she was awarded the Italian David di Donatello and the French Crystal Star awards and nominated for a BAFTA.

After returning from England, Monroe took an 18-month hiatus to concentrate on family life. She and Miller split their time between NYC, Connecticut, and Long Island. She had an ectopic pregnancy in mid-1957 and a miscarriage a year later; these problems were most likely linked to her endometriosis. Monroe was also briefly hospitalized due to a barbiturate overdose. As she and Greene could not settle their disagreements over MMP, Monroe bought his share of the company.

1958  Marilyn returned to Hollywood in July to act opposite Jack Lemmon and Tony Curtis in Billy Wilder's comedy on gender roles, *Some Like It Hot*. She considered the role of Sugar Kane another "dumb blonde" but accepted it due to Miller's encouragement and the offer of 10% of the film's profits on top of her standard pay. The film's difficult production has become "legendary". Monroe demanded dozens of retakes and did not remember her lines or act as directed. Curtis famously said that kissing her was "like kissing Hitler" due to the number of retakes.

Monroe privately likened the production to a sinking ship and commented on her co-stars and director saying, "[but] why should I worry, I have no phallic symbol to lose." Many of the problems stemmed from her and Wilder—who also had a reputation for being difficult—disagreeing on how she should play the role. She angered him by asking to alter many of her scenes, which in turn made her stage fright worse, and it is suggested that she deliberately ruined several scenes to act them her way.

In the end, Wilder was happy with Monroe's performance, saying: "Anyone can remember lines, but it takes a real artist to come on the set and not know her lines and yet give the performance she did!"

1959 *"Some Like It Hot"* was a critical and commercial success when it was released in March. Marilyn won a Golden Globe for her performance as Best Actress. *Variety Magazine* called her "a comedienne with that combination of sex appeal and timing that just can't be beat". The film was voted one of the best films ever made in polls by the BBC, the American Film Institute, and *Sight & Sound.*

Mimesis Stage 2 for Marilyn Monroe 1960–1962: Career decline and personal difficulties

After *Some Like It Hot*, Monroe took another hiatus until late 1959, when she starred in the musical comedy *Let's Make Love*. She chose George Cukor to direct, and Miller rewrote some of the script, which she considered weak. She accepted the part solely because she was behind on her contract with Fox. The film's production was delayed by her frequent absences from the set. During the shoot, Monroe had an affair with co-star Yves Montand that was widely reported by the press and used in the film's publicity campaign. *Let's Make Love* was unsuccessful upon its release in September 1960. Crowther described Monroe as appearing "rather untidy" and "lacking ... the old Monroe dynamism", and Hedda Hopper called the film "the most vulgar picture she's ever done". Truman Capote lobbied for Monroe to play Holly Golightly in a film adaptation of *Breakfast at Tiffany's*, but the role went to Audrey Hepburn as its producers feared that Monroe would complicate the production.

The last film Monroe completed was John Huston's *The Misfits*, which Miller had written to provide her with a dramatic role. She played a recently divorced woman who becomes friends with three aging cowboys, played by Clark Gable, Eli Wallach and Montgomery Clift. The filming in the Nevada desert between July and November 1960 was again difficult. Monroe's and Miller's marriage was effectively over, and he began a new relationship with set photographer Inge Morath.

The Misfits was the last completed film for Monroe and Gable, who both died within two years. Marilyn disliked that he had based her role partly on her life and thought it inferior to the male roles. She also struggled with Miller's habit of rewriting scenes the night before filming. Her health was also failing: she was in pain from gallstones, and her drug addiction was so severe that her makeup usually had to be applied while she was still asleep under the influence of barbiturates. In August, filming was halted for her to spend a week in a hospital detox. Despite her problems, Huston said that when Monroe was acting, she "was not pretending to an emotion. It was the real thing. She would go deep down within herself and find it and bring it up into consciousness."

1961 Monroe and Miller separated after filming wrapped, and she obtained a Mexican divorce in January. *The Misfits* was released the following month, failing at the box office. Its reviews were mixed, with *Variety* complaining of frequently "choppy" character development, and Bosley Crowther calling Monroe "completely blank and unfathomable" and writing that "unfortunately for the film's structure, everything turns upon her". It has received more favorable reviews in the 21st century. Geoff Andrew of the British Film Institute has called it a classic, Huston scholar Tony Tracy called Monroe's performance the "most mature interpretation of her career". Geoffrey McNab of *The Independent* praised her "extraordinary" portrayal of the character's "power of empathy".

Monroe was next to star in a television adaptation of W. Somerset Maugham's *Rain* for NBC, but the project fell through as the network did not want to hire her choice of director, Lee Strasberg.

1961 Instead of working, she spent the first six months preoccupied by health problems. She underwent a cholecystectomy and surgery for her endometriosis, and spent four weeks hospitalized for depression. She was helped by

DiMaggio, with whom she rekindled a friendship, and dated his friend Frank Sinatra for several months. Monroe also moved permanently back to California in 1961, purchasing a house at 12305 Fifth Helena Drive in Brentwood, Los Angeles, in early 1962.

1962 Monroe returned to the public eye in the spring. She received a "World Film Favorite" Golden Globe Award and began to shoot a film for Fox, *Something's Got to Give*, a remake of *My Favorite Wife* (1940). It was to be co-produced by MMP, directed by George Cukor and to co-star Dean Martin and Cyd Charisse. Days before filming began, Monroe caught sinusitis. Despite medical advice to postpone the production, Fox began it as planned in late April.

Monroe was too sick to work for most of the next six weeks, but despite confirmations by multiple doctors, the studio pressured her by alleging publicly that she was faking it. On May 19, she took a break to sing "Happy Birthday, Mr. President" on stage at President John F. Kennedy's early birthday celebration at Madison Square Garden in New York. She drew attention with her costume: a beige, skintight dress covered in rhinestones, which made her appear nude. Monroe's trip to New York caused even more irritation for Fox executives, who had wanted her to cancel it.

Monroe next filmed a scene for *"Something's Got to Give"* in which she swam naked in a swimming pool. To generate advanced publicity, the press was invited to take photographs; these were later published in *Life*. This was the first time that a major star had posed nude at the height of their career. When she was again on sick leave for several days, Fox decided that it could not afford to have another film running behind schedule when it was already struggling with the rising costs of *Cleopatra* (1963). On June 7, Fox fired Monroe and sued her for $750,000 in damages. She was replaced by Lee Remick, but after Martin refused to make the film with anyone other than Monroe, Fox sued him as well and shut down the production. The studio blamed Monroe for the film's demise and began spreading negative publicity about her, even alleging that she was mentally disturbed.

Fox soon regretted its decision and reopened negotiations with Monroe later in June; a settlement about a new contract, including recommencing *Something's Got to Give* and a starring role in the black comedy *What a Way to Go!* (1964), was reached later that summer. She was also planning on starring in a biopic of Jean Harlow. To repair her public image, Monroe engaged in several publicity ventures, including interviews for *Life* and *Cosmopolitan* and her first photo shoot for *Vogue*. For *Vogue*, she and photographer Bert Stern collaborated for two series of photographs, one a standard fashion editorial and another of her posing nude, which were published posthumously with the title *The Last Sitting*.

Mimesis Stage 2 for Marilyn Monroe – The Alleged Affair with President John F. Kennedy

It is alleged that Marilyn Monroe and President John F. Kennedy had an affair that lasted for years. While there is uncertain speculation around the exact date the pair met, historians verify that JFK met Marilyn for the first time in 1954, a decade prior to her infamously sensual 'Happy Birthday' retention for the President. They were introduced by 'Rat Pack' actor Peter Lawson, JFK's brother-in-law. Both Marilyn and the Kennedys were long-time friends with Peter Lawford, a short-lived member of Frank Sinatra's Rat Pack who was married to Patricia, one of the Kennedys' many sisters. However, it wasn't until early in 1962 when they were both staying in Bing Crosby's Palm Springs house where many believe the affair first began.

In a 2001 biography by Donald Spoto, Marilyn's masseur, Ralph Roberts claims to have spoken to both JFK and Marilyn on a phone call when she rang to ask for advice on giving a massage. Susan Strasberg, the daughter of Marilyn's acting coach Lee Strasberg, also affirms the affair, claiming that it was on this night JFK had invited the actress to perform at his birthday gala. Marilyn felt "It was O.K. to sleep with a charismatic president. Marilyn loved the secrecy and the drama of it, but Kennedy was not the kind of man she wanted to spend her life with, and she made that very clear," Susan wrote.

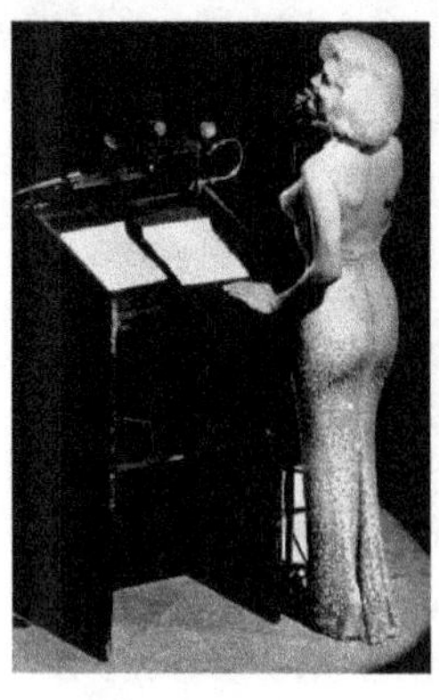

Fast forward a few months to May of 1962, Marilyn took the stage in a nearly-naked Bob Mackie dress (which Kim Kardashian wore to this year's Met Gala), for a performance that would be burned into many's memories for years to come thanks to its slightly sexual undertones.

Following the performance, JFK thanked Marilyn, stating "I can now retire from politics after having Happy Birthday sung to me in such a sweet and wholesome way".

Biographer James Spada reports that JFK "passed her off to his brother", Robert F. Kennedy (aka Bobby) when he "grew tired" of her, before adding "it was pretty clear that Marilyn had had sexual relations with both Bobby and Jack".[484]

Three months later, Monroe would be dead at the age of just 36 from what official accounts have long claimed to be an accidental overdose. Yet, much as the alleged affair between the US President and the most famous woman on earth continues to intrigue, there is far more concrete information regarding the affair Monroe had with his younger brother, Bobby Kennedy, who, at that time, was serving as the Attorney General of the United States. A man whose behavior plays a far more significant role in the last day of Marilyn's life, and her untimely death.

The Kennedy's relationship with Marilyn became extremely complex. The FBI had long been keeping a close surveillance on Marilyn, who was previously married to the playwright Arthur Miller. The FBI considered Miller a potential Communist during the McCarthy investigations into 'Un-American' activities during the 50s, Marilyn's intimate relationship with the Kennedys, plus her own opinions against the USA's stockpiling of nuclear weapons, caused the FBI to worry enough to create a "105" file on her – a number defined as alluding to anyone who had political views which might not align with those of the FBI.

Although there has never been any proven evidence that Bobby or John ever revealed state secrets to Marilyn, the relationship and her premature death were more than enough to cause the FBI concern and to feed the conspiracy theorists' rumors about her death for decades to come. [485]

The Final Mimesis for Marilyn Monroe – Her Death and Funeral [486]

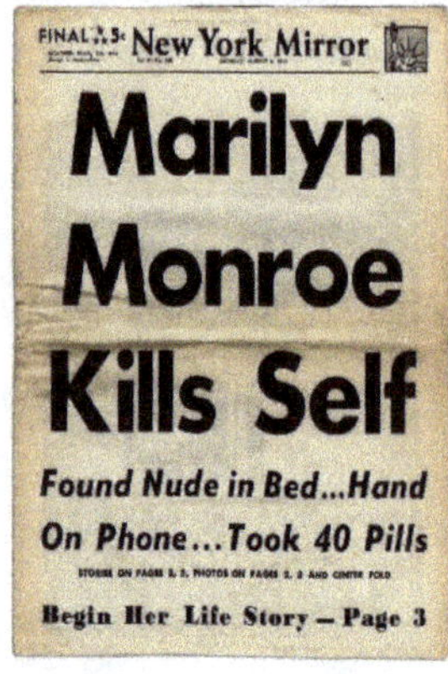

While there are a number of theories about the death of Marilyn Monroe, the official cause of her death is suicide.

During her final months, Monroe lived at 12305 Fifth Helena Drive in the Brentwood neighborhood of Los Angeles. Her housekeeper, Eunice Murray, was staying overnight at the home on the evening of August 4, 1962. Murray woke at 3:00 a.m. on August 5 and sensed that something was wrong. She saw light from under Monroe's bedroom door, but was unable to get a response and found the door locked. Murray then called Monroe's psychiatrist, Ralph Greenson, who arrived at the house shortly after and broke into the bedroom through a window to find Monroe dead in her bed. Monroe's physician, Hyman Engelberg, arrived at around 3:50 am and pronounced her dead. At 4:25 a.m., the Los Angeles Police Department was notified.

Monroe died between 8:30 p.m. and 10:30 p.m. on August 4; the toxicology report showed that the cause of death was acute barbiturate poisoning. She had 8 mg% (milligrams per 100 milliliters of solution) chloral hydrate and 4.5 mg% of pentobarbital (Nembutal) in her blood, and 13 mg% of pentobarbital in her liver. Empty medicine bottles were found next to her bed. The possibility that Monroe had accidentally overdosed was ruled out because the dosages found in her body were several times the lethal limit.

The Los Angeles County Coroner's Office was assisted in their investigation by the Los Angeles Suicide Prevention Team, who had expert knowledge on suicide. Monroe's doctors stated that she had been "prone to severe fears and frequent depressions" with "abrupt and unpredictable mood changes", and had overdosed several times in the past, possibly intentionally. Due to these facts and the lack of any indication of foul play, deputy coroner Thomas Noguchi classified her death as a probable suicide.

Monroe's sudden death was front-page news in the United States and Europe. According to Lois Banner, "it's said that the suicide rate in Los Angeles doubled the month after she died; the circulation rate of most newspapers expanded that month", and the *Chicago Tribune* reported that they had received hundreds of phone calls from members of the public requesting information about her death. French artist Jean Cocteau commented that her death "should serve as a terrible lesson to all those whose chief occupation consists of spying on and tormenting film stars", her former co-star Laurence Olivier deemed her "the complete victim of ballyhoo and sensation", and *Bus Stop* director Joshua Logan said that she was "one of the most unappreciated people in the world".

Her funeral, held at the Westwood Village Memorial Park Cemetery on August 8, was private and attended by only her closest associates. The service was arranged by Joe DiMaggio, Monroe's half-sister Berniece Baker Miracle, and Monroe's business manager Inez Melson. Hundreds of spectators crowded the streets around the cemetery. Monroe was later entombed at Crypt No. 24 at the Corridor of Memories.

In the following decades, several conspiracy theories, including murder and accidental overdose, have been introduced to contradict suicide as the cause of Monroe's death. The speculation that Monroe had been murdered first gained mainstream attention with the publication of Norman Mailer's *Marilyn: A Biography* in 1973, and in the following years became widespread enough for the Los Angeles County District Attorney John Van de Kamp to conduct a "threshold investigation" in 1982 to see whether a criminal investigation should be opened. No evidence of foul play was found

The one thing about dying young is that one does not have opportunity to engage the reflection stage of their lived experiences up to the end of their lived potential. That does not mean an individual does not reflect at intervals along their younger adult years; however, they eliminate the lived experiences that were cut short.

Monroe's crypt at Westwood Village Memorial Park Cemetery in Westwood Village

Mimesis of Life Summary for Marilyn Monroe, aka Norma Jeane Mortensen

While Marilyn Monroe developed into a brilliant and talented actress, an astute and smart businesswoman, she can be considered the female version of a tragic hero / heroine. Her reality was different than many of the roles she played on screen, the dumb blonde bombshell. However, relationship stability was elusive to Marilyn. The irony is that, according to the dialogue in the extensive history of text devoted to her life, what she seemed to need most was love. It also appears there was a mysterious irony to Marilyn. In researching and reading about her life, it is not quite clear if she was being used by men or if she was using men.

Suicide is the 12th leading cause of death in the United States, according to the Centers for Disease Control and Prevention. It is defined as the act of killing oneself. [487]

It is a mystery to many, why Marilyn Monroe would take her own life. There are key points in the state of mind of an individual and their propensity to kill themselves:

Key Points

- Stress-diathesis theories of suicide propose a key role for stressors in precipitating suicide in individuals who possess the diathesis (predisposition) for suicide.

- The overall level of life stress is associated with the risk of suicide.

- The type of stressors that increase the risk of suicide varies with the characteristics of individuals, such as age and sex.

- For example, the suicides of younger people are more often precipitated by interpersonal conflicts, whereas the suicides of older people are more often precipitated by chronic stressors such as medical illnesses.

There is a relationship between suicide and stress. The publicity given to suicides, especially suicides by celebrities, has been shown to lead to an increase in the suicide rate in the following days, especially among those of the same age and sex as the celebrity.[488] Coincidentally, Marilyn's sudden death was worldwide front-page news in the United States and Europe. According to Lois Banner, "it's said that the suicide rate in Los Angeles doubled the month after she died; the circulation rate of most newspapers expanded that month". [489]

Life stressors and suicide are related. Stress-diathesis models of suicidal behavior explain the stress/suicide relationship. Stress-diathesis refers to the relationship between a stressor (i.e., an event that causes stress) and a long-term vulnerability or predisposition to suicide (i.e., the diathesis). A diathesis is a long-term factor that increases the vulnerability of individuals to suicide. Diathesis confers a vulnerability that is then acted upon by life stress. The stress and the diathesis may also interact. Diathesis may predispose people to the occurrence of stressful life events, but also the experience of stressful life events may have a detrimental impact on the diathesis. Marilyn's mother was subject to mental illness. Marilyn's childhood was unstable. Marilyn's intimate relationships throughout her life did not seen to have any long-term stability. However, Marilyn was vulnerable in her search for long term stability in her love life. Add to this the stress of Hollywood, movie roles, movie production, the media and the shallow existence and lack of substantial relationships in Hollywood (and in life), makes one wonder, about Marilyn's preparation to deal with challenges in life, in the long term. [490]

Some of the people who knew Marilyn responded to her death with bitterness, blaming the pressures of Hollywood. Others lamented that she was shocked, depressed, and bewildered.

The following comments speak to the esteem with which Marilyn's peers held her.

> Joshua Logan, the director, said: "She was one of the most unappreciated people in the world."

> In Hollywood, Clark Gable's widow went to mass and prayed for the dead actress. In Italy,

> Sophia Loren broke into tears.

> In London, Sir Laurence Olivier said she was "the complete victim of ballyhoo and sensation,"

> The poet Jean Cocteau said in France: "Marilyn Monroe's tragic death should serve as a terrible lesson to all those whose chief occupation consists of spying on and tormenting film stars. Some of these reporters even spied on her from helicopters hovering over her house. That is scandalous."

At his estate in Woodbury, Conn., Arthur Miller, Miss Monroe's third husband, was asked if he had any comment. He declined to comment, "I don't, really," the playwright said.

Miss Monroe's second husband, Joe DiMaggio, the former baseball star, was unavailable for comment.

But her first husband, James E. Dougherty, a policeman, was informed of her death while he was patrolling the North Hollywood area. "I'm sorry," he said quietly.

Others, even the show business associates she had worked with recently, could not say much more.

George Axelrod, who wrote the script for the "Seven Year Itch," said he was stunned when he learned of the news in Paris.

Susan Strasberg, a close acquaintance of Miss Monroe, was speechless for several moments in Rome; then she said: "She was an extremely talented woman who was just beginning to do the things she wanted to do. She wanted to work in the theatre and--I can't talk anymore."

Miss Strasberg's parents, Lee and Paula Strasberg, directors of Actors Studio, where Miss Monroe had studied, were expecting Miss Monroe in New York this week-end. "Now it is all at an end," the Strasbergs said. "We hope that her death will stir sympathy and understanding for a sensitive artist and woman who gave joy and pleasure to the world."

"She was the only famous actress launched on sex appeal who redeemed sex with a sense of humor," Allessandro Blasseti, an Italian director, said in Rome. "The American cinema is now left with only the smile of Audrey Hepburn." Her talent as a comedienne--as much as her beauty--was often noted yesterday, and many said it was a pity that her beauty overshadowed everything else in the minds of most moviegoers.

Such talent and temperament as Miss Monroe possessed were not always easy to work with, some directors and performers conceded.

One character actress who appeared in "Bus Stop" recalled how the star was so often late and how, one day, she muffed a line twenty-seven times, to the consternation of the whole cast. "Josh Logan came over to me in the corner and said, 'Persuade her, humor her,'" the character actress recalled. "I said, 'Outside of saying her own line, what the hell do you want me to do?' "Everybody on the set--technicians, directors, actors--were standing around waiting for her to do her work; finally I went over to her, grabbed her by the shoulders and said, 'Look, either we get it right this time or I'm walking out of the picture.' Marilyn got it on the twenty-eighth try," the character actress said.

Billy Wilder, while admitting it had been taxing to direct Miss Monroe in the "Seven Year Itch" and "Some Like It Hot," said that it was nevertheless "worth a week's torment to get those three luminous minutes on the screen." [491]

CHAPTER 2

The Connection between the Three-Fold Mimesis of Life and the Environment

This chapter explores environmental factors that influence Mimesis construction. An ever-present dilemma permeates throughout the lived experiences of all human beings. All of what people will accomplish will become meaningless to them when they die. However, that does not mean their contribution will not have meaning to their family, other individuals, the society, or the world. Humans live with the thought that the earth can be destroyed at any time if a meteor crashed to earth or if countries entered into a nuclear war. Some think this phenomenon makes them more motivated to accomplish their goals, to make their mark on the world. Some think this phenomenon makes any contribution or life experience meaningless. Does that mean people should give up? Or, does that mean people should take action to counter the potential devastation that hypothetically humans will encounter"; encounter as a result of their own doing. If you think there is potential for negative phenomena to occur, the logical actions to take are those you believe will circumvent or remedy any hardship or disaster that may take place. [492] Some people learn how to handle the phenomena they encounter in their lived experiences and others falter, helplessly, to the destructive phenomena, that confronts them. For countries to have nuclear weapons is ridiculous and only demonstrates the human inability to collaborate and resolve differences. Volume I of "*the Three-Fold Mimesis of Life*" refers to the *Time Factor of Mimesis* and the paradox in human nature that is constructive and destructive. All of the many marvelous and magnificent advances humans have made the architecture, the priceless art, the scientific and medical advances, and the advances in technology; all potentially destroyed in seconds/minutes with one nuclear explosion. This fact alone highlights and emphasizes the fact that human Mimesis worldwide needs reconstruction. It also indicates the frailties, weakness, in humans, even and especially, in world leaders. Weapons and instruments of mass destruction to some indicate power. The truth is, realistically, they indicate "stupidity". Weapons of mass destruction reveal a latent hidden subconscious disregard for life and safety, even a suicidal tendency from a societal perspective.

The American democratic capitalistic individualistic system influences the Mimesis and Lived experiences of every American. The American political environment is valuable to some and disastrous for others. The psychological theories of Piaget and Vygotsky give valid reference to the environmental influence on development. However, the influence the American democratic capitalistic and individualistic system has on Black and minority Americans is significantly different from the influence it has on White Americans. Both Martin Luther King and Billy Graham were good men, ministers, Christians who preached the gospel of God and Jesus Christ, yet Martin Luther King was assassinated and Billy Graham died of old age. This Volume III explores to the how lived experiences shape and influence the Mimesis of humans. The environment has a considerable influence on Mimesis construction. Different individuals encounter different lived experiences and respond to those experiences in different ways. Does the government or society have any responsibility in your Mimesis construction? Environment might influence early Mimesis influence but the responsibility for your Mimesis development is yours. The American society has a significant influence over the socialization process of its citizens. The environment is sometimes a positive influential factor in the lived experiences humans encounter and sometimes it is a challenging influential factor. In either case, individuals have responsibility in the life choices they make. The environment in which an individual is exposed is often a determinant factor in the experiences they encounter. However, the individual does have agency over the life choices they make. Environment has a significant influence on human Mimesis. Lived experiences shaped by a dysfunctional environment present a significant moral dilemma when making life choices. Volume IV of *"the Three-Fold Mimesis of Life"* discusses *"moral dilemma"* in more depth. However, it is common knowledge that America has a significant population of racist, Nazis and deplorable people who hate and discriminate against African Americans, Jews, Hispanics, Asians, LGQBT individuals, non-Christians and Muslims. America has been a racist country for over 400 years, since White culture came to America in the 17th century. Settlers from England landed on the shores of America's Plymouth Rock then proceeded to integrate into America without regard for the culture or rights of the Native Americans. White culture has stained America's reputation with hypocrisy, claiming to be a free and equal country for all its citizens. The Constitution of the United States and religious philosophy (the Holy Christian Bible) sets the standard for moral ethical behavior; both reinforce the notion that all humans are created equal. Jesus stated the second most important commandment is "to love your fellow human as you do yourself. The reality of racism in America is significant because it affects the Mimesis of every American. Racism creates an artificial screen in the way people relate. People notice difference. They pretend not to notice difference, and the denial of difference is artificial reality. Conflict and hatred based on God given natural differences is a human deficiency and shortcoming, a human flaw. Difference is a good thing. Hatred is a bad thing. Minorities have been experiencing racism for centuries, while a significant number of White Americans strive to sustain racism. Those who challenge the deplorable existence of racism (Black and White) face an ongoing moral dilemma. Despite all of the decent Americans who believe in being fair, both minority and White Americans, the truth is that if America, and the powers that be, wanted racism eliminated and wanted a fair America then racism would be eliminated and America would be fair. That is the bottom line truth. The confusion in this American dilemma influences the Three-Fold Mimesis of every American. The institution of the American government, the office of the President, the Congress, the Senate and the Supreme Court can eradicate the practice of racism and discrimination overnight, if they make the right choice in the moral dilemma they face. The laws of the land grant equality for every American citizen, yet America allows racism and hate behaviors to exist. That is the moral dilemma. Why does America wage war on terrorist groups like ISIS and Al Qaeda and allow the Ku Klux Klan and Neo-Nazis and other hate and racist groups, destructive to America and humanity, to exist?

The irony, dilemma and the dichotomies in the way America discriminates between people and how individuals respond to their different environmental circumstances is explored by comparing the lived experiences of the following individuals. Just as important is how these individuals responded to their lived experiences in Stage 2 Mimesis. How the Stage 2 Mimesis determines the Stage 3 Mimesis for each of the following high-profile individuals is noteworthy. Not only do these comparisons reveal the individual's Mimesis construction but also the reader will gain insight into the society, and the environment, in which these individuals interacted.

Dr. Martin Luther King, Jr.	and	Billy Graham
Barack Obama	and	Donald Trump
Muhammad Ali	and	Richard Nixon
Oprah Winfrey	and	Queen Elizabeth II
Stanley "Tookie" Williams	and	Malcolm X
Jay-Z	and	Tupac Shakur
	and Elvis Presley	
Beyonce	and	Marilyn Monroe

Donald Trump and Queen Elizabeth II are the only individuals profiled who were born into a family of wealth. They started their life with a fortunate/advantaged social location status. Queen Elizabeth through her life has maintained the love and respect of her people. Comparatively, many Americans despise Donald Trump. Some like him. Most, who support him, do so out of selfish interest, rather than sentiment for him as a person. As a psychologist, I would hypothesize that even those who support Donald Trump do so for selfish interest and otherwise would have no interest in a relationship with him. Trump does have a significant following of people in America, many of whom themselves are of questionable character. While associates of Queen Elizabeth II speak highly of her.

Numerous associates of Donald Trump reveal his character. Money does not buy character. Money only makes an individual more of what they already are. A good person with money will do good things. A bad person with money will do bad things.

Global warming/climate change is an environmental dilemma that factors in the American Mimesis. The greatest scientific minds in the world predict that global warming/climate change is a threat to humans. Consistently, America and the world are experiencing effects of climate change / global warming … high temperatures, hurricanes, tornadoes, floods, fires, and natural disasters that climate scientist say is Nature's response to global warming. The mindset of American and world leadership does not respond to this crisis consistently with the threat global warming represents. In general, the same narrow-minded mentality and ignorance that perpetuates inequality, greed, racism, prejudice, and White supremacy is the same mentality that fails to give global warming/climate change the urgent attention it requires.

American greed is a primary inhibitor in the threats to nature and the inequalities that create and maintain the divisions and conflicts in America. Greed in America has become a source of moral vice to a devoted supporter of capitalism. Greed significantly affects economic inequality, corporate behavior, and public trust in ways that are detrimental to society, in general. There are schools of thought that believe the Western system of capitalism promotes greed and stratifies society in ways that create conflict and inequality. [493]

"America has an economic system set up to create the kind of mess we've seen recently," says social psychologist Tim Kasser, PhD, of Knox College in Galesburg, Ill. "Our form of capitalism encourages materialistic values, and the research shows that people high on materialism ... are more likely to engage in unethical business behaviors and manipulate people for their own purposes."

"In fact, American corporate capitalism—the highly competitive economic system embraced by the United States as well as England, Australia and Canada—encourages materialism more than other forms of capitalism", according to a study by Hebrew University of Jerusalem psychologist Shalom Schwartz, PhD.

Greed contributes to global warming through corporate profit motives that lead to overconsumption, pollution, and a resistance to sustainable practices, as well as through the high emissions from the lifestyles of the wealthiest individuals. This is evident in corporate lobbying to weaken environmental regulations, a short-term focus on profits over long-term sustainability, and the disproportionately large carbon footprint of the ultra-wealthy. Greed also drives resource exploitation, like deforestation for profitable industries, which exacerbates climate change. [494]

According to United States Senator Bernie Sanders of Vermont. *"Our economic crisis isn't inflation, it's corporate greed and the GOP will only make that worse"*.[495] Evaluating the confidence levels in the past presidential Administrations regarding the confidence in

Administrations, results indicate that international confidence favors democratic policies.[496] This is not a statement of endorsement for any political party. It merely indicates the policies that are most favorable to the national and international community.

A question to ask, is there any difference in how people viewed the environmental tone of the United States of America an when comparing Presidential Administrations? If there is a difference, did that cause your response to how you viewed your lived experiences to change?

Historically, the economy has been the major factor driving who gets elected to office. The economy is 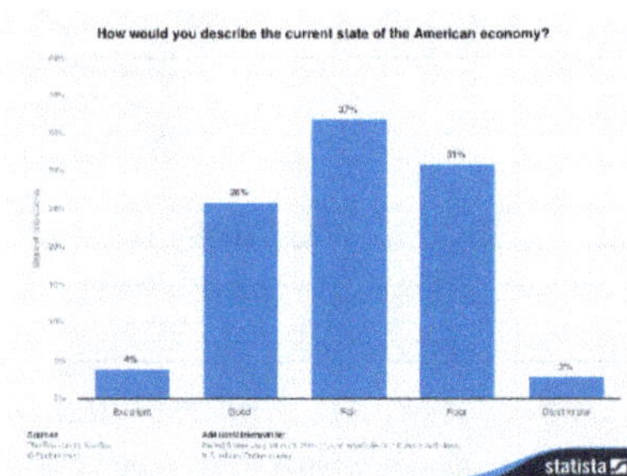 a primary controller in the American environmental tone and psychology. The economy also is a significant factor in the lifestyles people lead that determines their decisions. The economy environment factors significantly in Mimesis construction. A good economic environment garners Americans satisfaction. A bad economic environment creates American dissatisfaction. These different economic environments have a different impact on how Americans construct their Mimesis. Based on opinion data regarding the 2025 economic environment Americans are dissatisfied with the economy. [497] The impact of the economy affects both national and international interactions and policies, between countries and individuals.

The graphs below indicate public confidence levels for each administration (1999-2005), [498] based on international and national data.

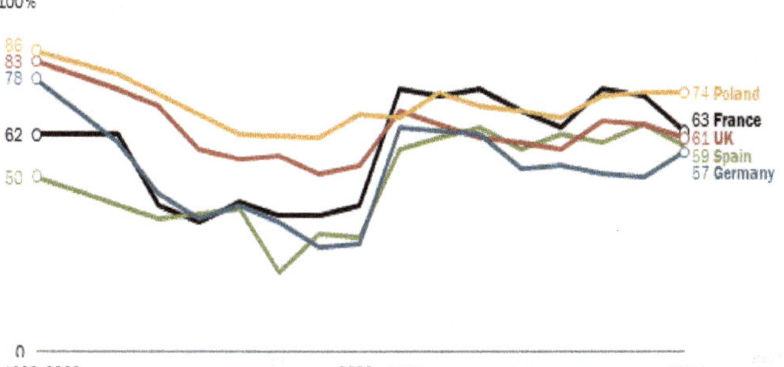

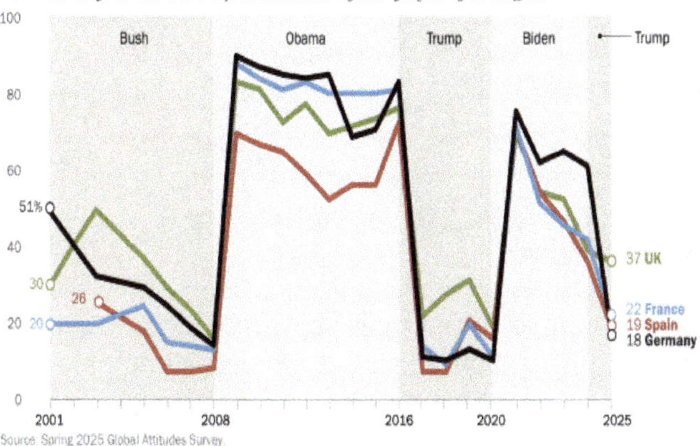

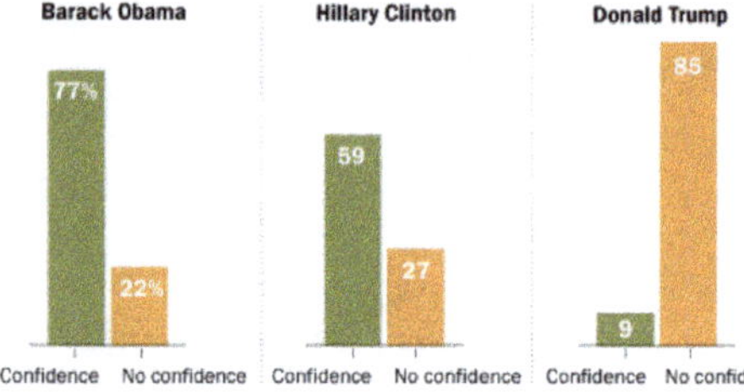
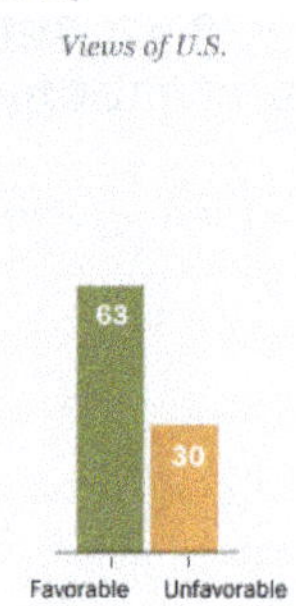

Overall economic assessments are little changed as Republicans and Democrats continue to diverge

*% who say economic conditions in the country today are **excellent/good***

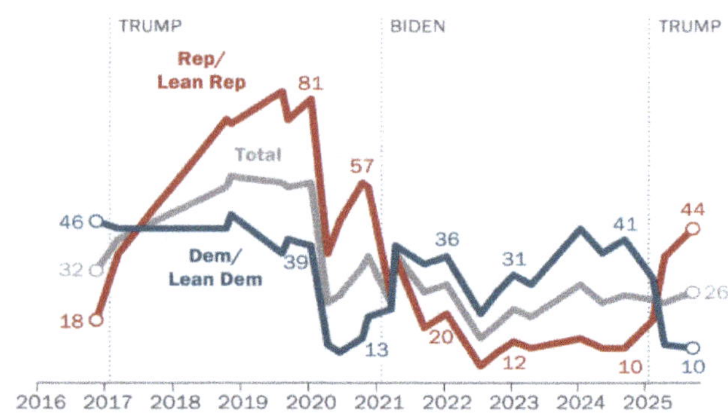

Multiple recent polls show that most Americans are pessimistic about the U.S. economy, citing persistent concerns over inflation and a weakening job market. However, public opinion is sharply divided along partisan lines, with Republicans expressing significantly more optimism than Democrats.

Scholars say government statistics cannot and do not, inaccurately assess the lived experience of the masses of the American people. Politics plays a larger role in shaping perceptions more than in presenting reality. In other words, the government statistics are not in touch with the lived experiences of the masses of the population or they lie. One possible reason is because when accumulating information on the economy, such a large disparity exist between the top 5% and the bottom 95% of the people that the economic activity of the top 5% skews the over statistical analysis of the economic condition of the country. [499] The following Gallup poll data give information on the opinions of the public.

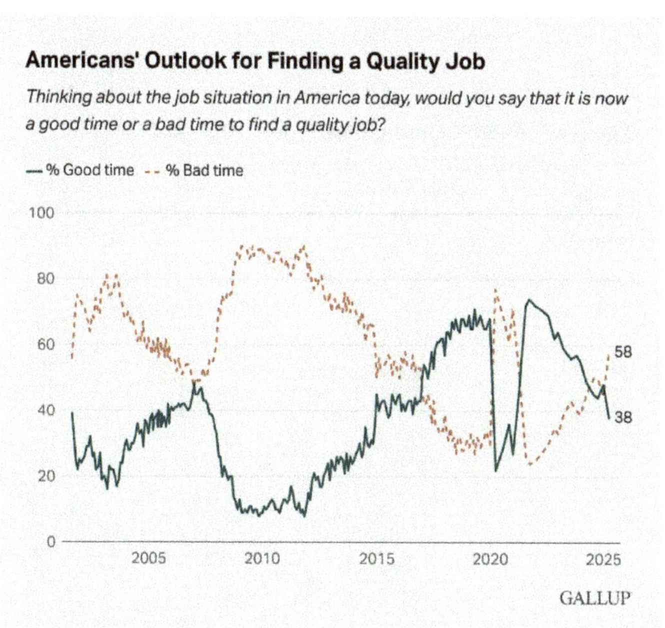

Americans' Current Financial Situation, 2001-2025

How would you rate your financial situation today — as excellent, good, only fair or poor?

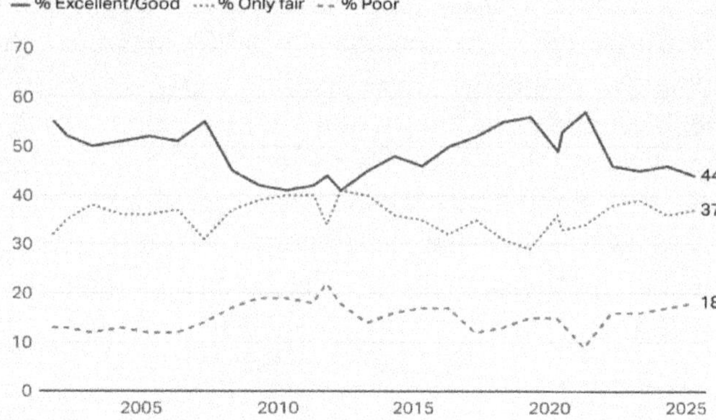

2001-2003 figures are selected trend, based on surveys conducted closest to April each year.

GALLUP

Gallup's Economic Confidence Index, 2020-2025

The Gallup Economic Confidence Index summarizes Americans' assessments of current economic conditions (% excellent or good minus % poor) and economic outlook (% getting better minus % getting worse). It has a theoretical range of -100 to +100.

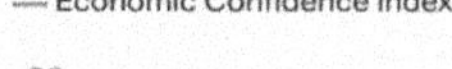

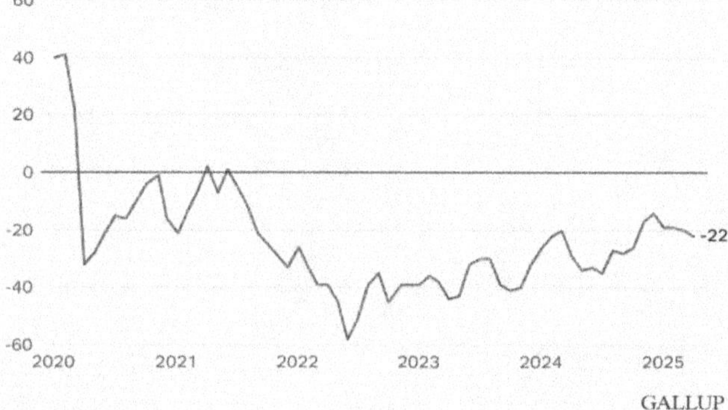

GALLUP

The political environment and administration overseeing the country sets the tone and stage for the issues individuals confront in the construction of their Mimesis and the lived experiences they will encounter. Stereotypically, republican administrations favor the interests of corporations, the rich and wealthy, and a capitalistic leadership orientation. Democrats tend to favor people and policies that provide social services for the citizens of the country. The facts are, however, that neither administration has made significant strides in closing the economic or discrimination inequalities, institutionalized in America. American policies have a tendency to benefit the rich and the wealthy to the detriment of the working and middle classes when either party is in office. Economics is a significant factor in the construction of Mimesis. Americans reflect their sentiments in research focused on how Americans rate the U.S. economy. Commonly, ratings and opinions follow along partisan lines.[500]

Average Family Wealth, by Race and Ethnicity, 1963–2022

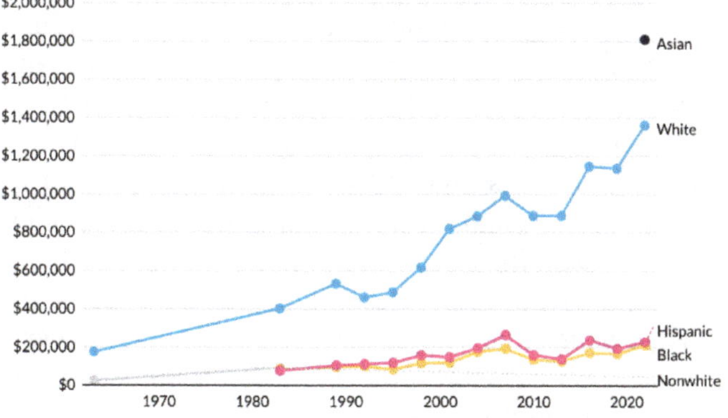

Source: Urban Institute calculations from the Survey of Financial Characteristics of Consumers 1962, the Survey of Changes in Family Finances 1963, and the Survey of Consumer Finances 1983–2022.

Notes: 2022 dollars. Until 1983, the surveys categorized all people of color as "nonwhite." The Survey of Consumer Finances began disaggregating data for Black and Hispanic families starting in 1983 and for Asian families starting in 2022. We used inflation adjustment factors from *Changes in U.S. Family Finances from 2019 to 2022: Evidence from the Survey of Consumer Finances*. No comparable data are available between 1963 and 1983.

URBAN · INSTITUTE

In addition to the issue of economic inequality, when combined with racism and discrimination, the inequalities in American society factor into how individuals construct their Mimesis.[501] The following charts provide information on the disparities in the economic structure in America. Race and Racism are correlating variables in the economics of the American system. The percentage of Americans considered "rich" varies. The top 1% of households own approximately 30% of the nation's wealth and have a net worth of about $38 million on average. Another measure of wealth places the top 1% at a minimum net worth of $13.7 million. On the other hand, a 2024 survey by Money US News.com found that only 2% of Americans identify as being in the "upper class". Nevertheless, based on wealth share, the top 1% of American households own nearly one-third of the nation's wealth.[502]

Poverty rates vary significantly by demographic group. For instance, in 2023, the poverty rate for American Indian and Alaska Native populations was 21.2%, the highest among racial or ethnic groups, compared to 7.7% for the White, non-Hispanic population. Poverty rates are consistently higher for racial and ethnic minorities in the United States, with Native Americans and Black Americans facing the highest rates, though rates for both groups saw historical lows in 2022. In 2023, the poverty rate for Black individuals was 15.4%, a slight increase from the previous year, while Hispanics also had a higher poverty rate than non-Hispanic whites. These disparities persist across age groups and are higher in rural areas, according to data from the USDA. [503] Economics and economic inequality are major factors in Mimesis construction.[504]

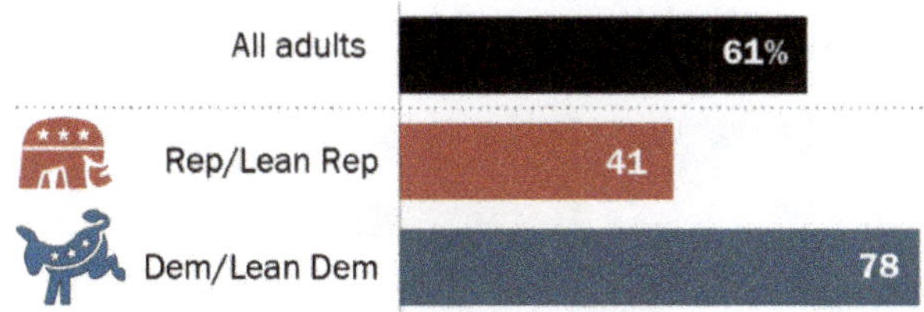

A majority of Americans say there's too much economic inequality in the U.S …

% saying there's too much economic inequality in the country these days

… but relatively few see it as a top policy priority for the federal government

% saying each of the following should be a top priority for the federal government to address

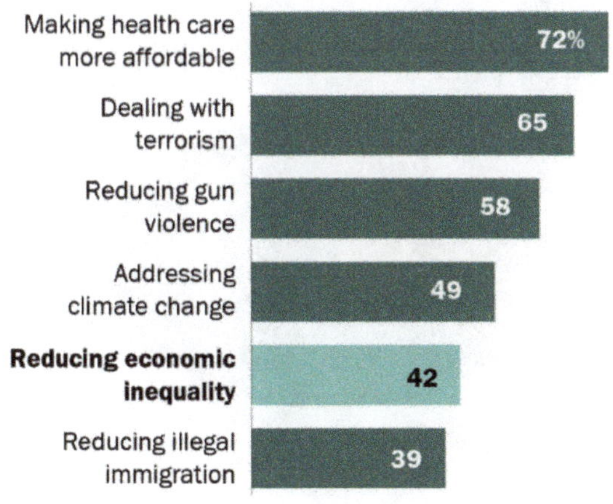

Source: Survey of U.S. adults conducted Sept. 16-29, 2019.
"Most Americans Say There Is Too Much Economic Inequality in the U.S., but Fewer Than Half Call It a Top Priority"

PEW RESEARCH CENTER

Most Americans who say there's too much inequality say addressing it requires significant changes to the economic system

Among those who say there is too much economic inequality, % saying that, in order to address economic inequality, the U.S. economic system ...

	Requires only minor changes	Requires major changes	Needs to be completely rebuilt
All adults	19	67	14
Rep/Lean Rep	36	50	12
Dem/Lean Dem	11	74	14

Note: Share of respondents who didn't offer an answer not shown.
Source: Survey of U.S. adults conducted Sept. 16-29, 2019.
"Most Americans Say There Is Too Much Economic Inequality in the U.S., but Fewer Than Half Call It a Top Priority"

PEW RESEARCH CENTER

Most Americans say there's too much inequality in the U.S.

% saying there is _____ economic inequality in the country these days

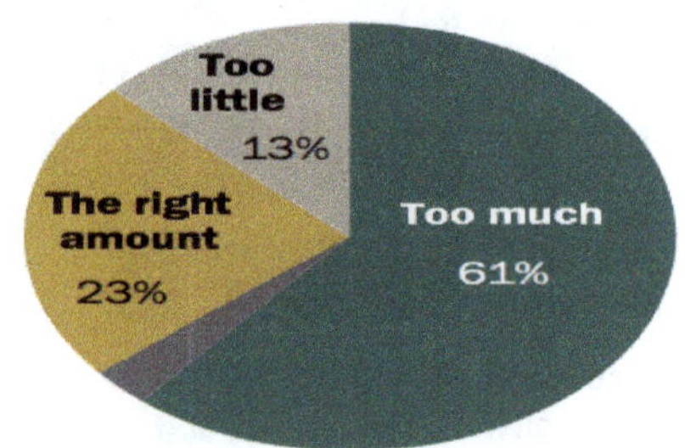

Note: Share of respondents who didn't offer an answer shown but not labeled.
Source: Survey of U.S. adults conducted Sept. 16-29, 2019.
"Most Americans Say There Is Too Much Economic Inequality in the U.S., but Fewer Than Half Call It a Top Priority"

PEW RESEARCH CENTER

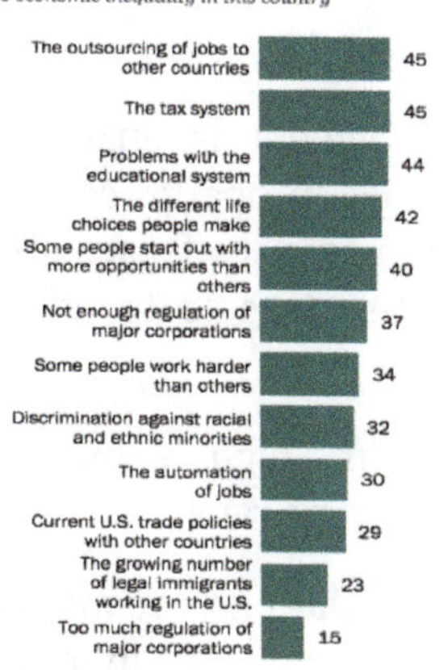

No consensus on major contributors to economic inequality

% saying each of the following contributes a great deal to economic inequality in this country

Source: Survey of U.S. adults conducted Sept. 16-29, 2019. "Most Americans Say There Is Too Much Economic Inequality in the U.S., but Fewer Than Half Call It a Top Priority"

PEW RESEARCH CENTER

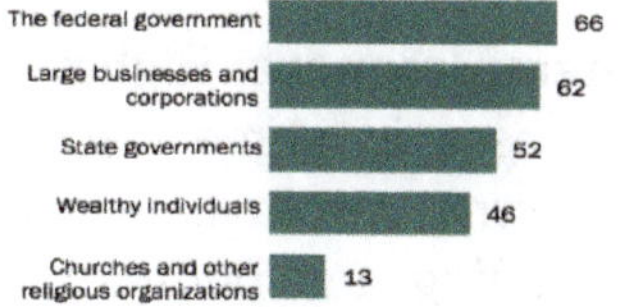

Most say federal government and large corporations should have a lot of responsibility in reducing inequality

Among those who say there is too much economic inequality, % saying each of the following should have a lot of responsibility in reducing inequality in the country

Source: Survey of U.S. adults conducted Sept. 16-29, 2019. "Most Americans Say There Is Too Much Economic Inequality in the U.S., but Fewer Than Half Call It a Top Priority"

PEW RESEARCH CENTER

Across income groups, large shares say the government shouldn't raise taxes on people like them to deal with inequality

Among those who say there is too much economic inequality, % saying that, in order to address economic inequality in this country, the government should ...

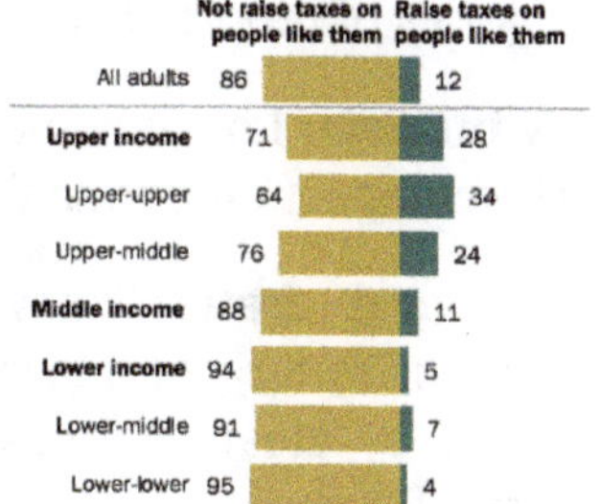

Note: Share of respondents who didn't offer an answer not shown. Family incomes are adjusted for differences in purchasing power by geographic region and for household size. Middle income is defined as two-thirds to double the median annual income for the survey sample. Lower income falls below that range, upper income falls above it. Lower-lower is less than half, lower-middle is half to two-thirds, upper-middle is two to three, and upper-upper is more than three times the median annual income for the survey sample. Source: Survey of U.S. adults conducted Sept. 16-29, 2019. "Most Americans Say There Is Too Much Economic Inequality in the U.S., but Fewer Than Half Call It a Top Priority"

PEW RESEARCH CENTER

While the majority of Americans say the government should not raise taxes to address inequality, it is ironic that the group who support raising taxes the most, are the wealthy. This could indicate that the wealth class acknowledge economic inequality, and its detriment to America but only a few are fair enough to admit it. [505]

The economic environment is a significant factor affecting crime, particularly in periods of unemployment and inequality. Both are linked to higher crime rates. Economic downturns often lead to increased property and violent crimes, as financial pressure can drive individuals to commit crimes and reduce the resources available for prevention. [506]

How the economy influences crime [507]

Unemployment: Higher unemployment is linked to increases in crime rates, especially property crimes. Economic stress can lead to a rise in offenses like shoplifting and burglary as people struggle to afford necessities.

Economic inequality: Areas with high economic inequality often experience higher crime rates.

Recessions and downturns: During economic downturns, there is often a sharp increase in most categories of reported crime.

Low income: Low income has a statistically significant positive impact on criminal activity.

Theft and fraud: Thieves may exploit economic conditions by targeting businesses that have cut security costs or by stealing items to resell due to increased demand for cheaper goods.

Inflation: Rising inflation and a higher cost of living can increase crimes like shoplifting and break-ins, as people look for ways to afford essentials like food and gas.

The relationship between the economy and crime is complex. While economic hardship can increase crime, crime can also negatively impact the economy. High crime rates can reduce economic growth and deter investment. Conversely, a reduction in violent crime can lead to significant economic benefits, such as budget savings, higher revenues, and personal income gains.

CHAPTER 3

Comparative Mimesis

Dr. Martin Luther King, Jr.
and
Reverend Billy Graham

Born: Michael King, Jr.
January 15, 1929
Atlanta, Georgia
Died: April 4, 1968
Memphis, Tennessee
Died by: Assassination by gunshot
Resting Place: Martin Luther King, Jr. National Historical Park
Spouse: Coretta Scott (m: 1953)
Children: (4) Yolanda
Martin III
Dexter
Bernice
Education: Morehouse College
Crozer Theological Seminary (BDIV)
Boston University (PhD)
Occupation: Baptist Minister, Civil Rights Leader

Born: William Franklin Graham, Jr.
November 7, 1918
Charlotte, North Carolina
Died: February 21, 2018 (99)
Montreal, North Carolina
Natural Causes
Resting Place: Billy Graham Library
Religion: Christianity (Evangelical Protestantism)
Spouse: Ruth Bell (m: 1943-2007)
Children: (5) Franklin Graham,
Anne Graham-Lotz,
Gigi Graham,
Ned Graham,
Ruth Graham
Denomination: Southern Baptist,
Education: Florida Bible

We are exploring the comparison between Dr. King and Rev. Graham because they are both ministers of God. Both Good men were honorable American citizens. However, the political American democratic capitalistic individualistic system responded to Dr. Martin Luther King in a very different way than it did to Reverend Billy Graham, even though both were devoted Christian ministers, devoted family men, and devoted their lives to champion Christian causes. Dr. Martin Luther King was a Baptist minister, a civil rights activist, and a leader in the Southern Christian Leadership Conference (SCLC). Dr. King was the most visible spokesperson and leader in the civil rights movement from 1955 until his assassination in 1968. He approached his crusade for civil rights through nonviolence and civil protest. Inspired by Mahatma Gandhi and Jesus, Dr. King expressed his Christian beliefs through nonviolent activism. It is a generally accepted fact that peace and harmony are favorable to war and conflict. If this is true, then why did Billy Graham, revered by White culture, and Dr. Martin Luther King, Jr., revered by White and Black cultures, experience different outcomes to their Mimesis?

Rev. Graham was a prominent evangelist and an ordained Southern Baptist minister who was internationally well known. Billy Graham and Dr. King developed a close friendship, as both were Christian ministers. Rev. Graham repudiated racial segregation and insisted on racial integration for his revivals and crusades. He invited Dr. King to preach jointly at a revival in New York City in 1957.[508] So, why did the American democratic capitalistic individualistic system respond to Billy Graham different from America's response to Dr. Martin Luther King Jr?

Why was Billy Graham such a revered figure to American Presidents and the religious evangelical movement in America and Dr. Martin Luther King, a man of non-violence, was scorned, brutalized and jailed by White racist then murdered, demonstrating for the rights and dignity of all humans to be treated equal? They both believed in the same things. Both in their own way did the work of God. One incident that might explain the dichotomy in the perception White society has of Billy Graham verses that of Dr. King is the experience Dr. King had while in the Birmingham, Alabama jail. In April 1963, the SCLC began a campaign against racial segregation and economic injustice in Birmingham, Alabama. The Birmingham campaign deployed nonviolent tactics. Black people in Birmingham, organizing with the SCLC, occupied public spaces with marches and sit-ins, openly violating discriminating and unjust laws. Dr. King and other demonstrators were arrested and jailed. While in jail, Dr. King penned a letter, known as "*Letter from Birmingham City Jail*" and "*The Negro Is Your Brother*." The letter was a plea to other clergymen. Among them were several White ministers and Reverend Billy Graham. The content of the letter stated, "people have a moral responsibility to break unjust laws and to take direct action rather than waiting potentially forever for justice to come through the courts. Injustice anywhere is a threat to justice everywhere. " White clergy, including Billy Graham, believed that social injustices existed but argued that the battle against racial segregation should be fought solely in the racist court system, not the streets. They also felt that Dr. King should temper his protest against racism, discrimination, and unfair treatment against Black Americans. As a result, White clergy, including Billy Graham, distanced themselves from Dr. King, failing to stand up for a just cause. In this case, one can argue that the non-support by Christian clergy was a subtle act of racism, in itself. White Christians and Black Christians had a different Mimesis even on the principles they both believed in, or professed to believe in. Even decent White people are reluctant to support equal rights and fight racism. This is the very reason racism exists in America, because the so-called *"good White people"*, allow racism to exist. Would they take the same position if White people were discriminated against, beaten, jailed, and killed? Consider that the United States went to war against England for *"taxation without representation"*. Unfair taxation caused the colonists to go to war.

The FBI , under the directive of Attorney General Robert F. Kennedy and J. Edgar Hoover, conducted surveillance on Dr. King and wiretapped his phone calls. That is certainly not how White people thought during the prelude to the Revolutionary War when they were victims. The irony is that when the colonists were taxed without representation and treated unfairly by the British, they went to war, the Revolutionary War. The colonists were only taxed unfairly, and they held the Boston Tea Party, sabotaging an English ship, throwing

Tea overboard. The only explanation is that the American democratic, capitalistic, individualistic system is racist. This is an example of the challenge confronting Black and minority people in America in order to gain fair treatment. The manner in which White America practices democracy is racist. African Americans believed with absolute certainty that Dr. Martin Luther King, Jr. was not a threat to America. Whites believed Dr. King was a threat to America. The fact is that Dr. King's non-violent protest was met with White violence. White authorities perceived a threat from his presence, his peaceful demonstrations, and his speeches citing love between people and equality between the races. Based on this reality, White people concluded Dr. King was an enemy of America, a threat. What does that say about White culture?

This is how White authorities responded to a peaceful Black demonstration against inequalities, and unfair treatment.

The truth is Dr. King was more American and Christian in his beliefs, position, and Mimesis than most White culture individuals. Minorities in America have to contend with this environment. Despite the challenges, Dr. King faced in his fight for civil rights head on. After his assassination, he became a revered figure in American history. Almost every major city had streets or expressways named for him. America declared a national holiday in his honor. An entire month (February) was devoted to honor Black history, all due to the legacy of Dr. King. The Stage 3 Mimesis of how others viewed Dr. King, after his death, was with the utmost reverence, even among a substantial White population. While Billy Graham was a revered man, he never achieved the notoriety and honor bestowed upon Dr. King. The Mimesis in the life of both men, when compared, is a statement about the hypocrisy of the American democratic capitalistic individualistic system. Billy Graham was afforded White privilege, while Dr. King experienced White racism. Examples of the reverence both men held in the aftermath of their Stage 3 Mimesis is shown in the photos below.

Led by Dr. King the 1963 march on Washington "was the largest gathering for civil rights of its time. An estimated 250,000 people attended the March on Washington for Jobs and Freedom on August 28, 1963, arriving in Washington, D.C. by planes, trains, cars, and buses from all over the country."[509]

Rev. Graham addressing Stadium crowd

Dr. King addressing a crowd.

Rev. Graham addressing a crowd.

April 7, 1968 Crowd of mourners in Harlem, New York gather in mourning and respect to Dr. King

Mourners of Dr. King in Atlanta

The national monument to Dr. Martin Luther King, Jr. erected in the nation's capital is a great honor bestowed upon Dr. King. A recognition of what he truly means to America and a testament of the country about what America should stand for. This honor is comparable to that bestowed up on George Washington (The Washington monument), Abraham Lincoln (The Lincoln memorial) and Thomas Jefferson (The Jefferson memorial).

Here is the question. America builds a National Monument Statue to Dr. Martin Luther King, Jr. and America removes the statues and monuments of the Southern Civil War racist personalities in America; a clear sign acknowledging the beliefs of the American Constitution and equality for all Americans is the right thing to establish. So why is America still racist? Why do American leaders and politicians allow blatant racism to exist? Laws can be legislated. The personal beliefs of human beings cannot be legislated. Personal beliefs of human beings are socialized and learned. Actions and behaviors can be legislated.

Billy Graham, evangelist pastor and counselor to presidents, died at age 99 of natural causes. Reverend Graham lived to the ripe old age of 99 years. Dr. King was assassinated at the youthful age of 39 years old.

Billy Graham with the look of Reflection …

Dr. King with the look of reflection

American Presidents honored and respected Billy Graham

Billy Graham lies in State in the Capitol Rotunda.

Why was Billy Graham revered without controversy and Dr. Martin Luther King, Jr. was revered with controversy? The environment the societal situation … Both were products of their environment and Christian heritage. Billy Graham was a product of the White America and Dr. King was a product of Black and minority America. The dark side of America created Dr. King. The White side of America created Billy Graham.

The environment weighs heavy on Mimesis. Dr. King's widow, Coretta Scott King laid in repose in the rotunda of the Georgia Capitol in Atlanta, when she passed away in 2006. It is characteristic of a great man to have a great woman by his side.[510] When Dr. King passed away, the Governor of Georgia, Lester Maddox refused Dr. Martin Luther King, Jr. the privilege of a state funeral with his body lying in state in the capitol rotunda. Maddox, then-governor of Georgia in 1968. Maddox considered King an "enemy of the country" and had stationed 64 riot-helmeted state troopers at the steps of the state capitol in Atlanta to protect state property. He also initially refused to allow the state flag lowered at half-staff, but was compelled to do so when told that the lowering was a federal mandate.[511] The point is that times and the environment are factors in the construction of human Mimesis. Coretta King had the honor refused to Dr. King. She laid in state at the Georgia Capital. She deserved the honor but so did Dr. King. The racist Governor of Georgia, Lester Maddox was responding to his own Mimesis, socialization and the environment that socialized and taught him.

Both Dr. King and Rev. Graham were great men, great Americans and great Christians. Yet Dr. King confronted different life experiences than Rev. Graham. The environment in America was catalyst for the life experiences of both men. What can be said about America and American culture based on an examination of the Mimesis of Dr. King and Rev. Graham? Rev. Billy Graham is dead and buried. Dr. King is dead and buried. Billy Graham died in 2018 (99 years old). Dr. King Died in 1968 (39 years old).

Grave sites of Dr. King (left) and Reverend Billy Graham (right)

An individual's life Mimesis is often impacted by the norms, ethics and morals of the society in which they live. While both Dr. King and Reverend Graham were both Christian, ethical and moral individuals, the society and environment responded to them differently. In this case, the American society and environment in which Dr. King lived was infested with immoral and unethical people, racists. While Reverend Graham was accepted by this society, not because he was immoral or unethical but because he was White and while he spoke against racism, he was careful not to offend White racist and for the most part did not venture in to or embrace the negative and immoral elements of racism, prejudice and discrimination.

Dr. Ronald Barnes

Muhammad Ali
and
Richard Nixon
(37th President of the United States)

Born:	Cassius Marcellus Clay
	January 17, 1942
	Louisville, Kentucky
Died:	June 3, 2016
	Scottsdale, Arizona
Burial:	Cave Hill Cemetery
	Louisville, Place
Monuments:	Muhammed Ali Center
	Muhammed Ali Mural,
	Los Angeles
Nationality:	African-American
Education:	Central High School
	(1958)
Spouses:	Sonji Roi (m: 1964, div: 1966); Belinda Boyd (m: 1967, div: 1977); Veronica Porche (m: 1977, div: 1986); Yolanda Williams (m: 1986)
Children: (9)	
Parents:	Cassius Marcellus Clay, Sr.
	Odessa Grady Clay
Nicknames:	The Greatest
	The Peoples Champion
	The Louisville Lip
Height:	6' 3"
Weight	Heavyweight
Total fights:	61
Wins:	56
Wins by KO:	37
Losses:	5

37th President of the United States
January 20, 1969 – August 9, 1974
Vice President of the United States
January 20, 1953 – January 20, 1961
United States Senator from California
December 1, 1950- January 1, 1953
United States House of Representatives
January 3, 1947- November 30, 1950

Born:	Richard Milhous Nixon
	January 9, 1913
	Yorba Linda, California
Died:	April 22, 1994
	New York City, NY
Buried:	Richard Nixon Presidential Library and Museum
Political Party:	Republican
Spouse:	Pat Ryan (m: 1940, died: 1993)
Children: (2)	Tricia – Julie
Parents:	Francis A. Nixon
	Hannah Milhous
Education:	Whittier College (BA)
	Duke University (LLB)
Occupation:	Politician, Lawyer, Author
Military Service:	U.S. Navy
	1942-1945 (active)
	1946-1966 (inactive)
Rank:	Commander
	Served in WWII

- Muhammed Ali and Richard Nixon represent a juxtaposition to the American dream and an outlier to the American democratic capitalistic individualistic system. Muhammed Ali, a Black man, was born as Cassius Marcellus Clay. One of the responses Black people had to White racism was to get rid of their "slave names", replacing them, with names considered more appropriate to Black culture and identity. This is why Cassius Marcellus Clay, Jr. changed his name to Muhammed Ali. Many Black people re-named themselves, influenced by this ideology during Ali's era. Parents gave their children names at birth that reflected their Black identity and African heritage. This is a statement that Black people embraced their heritage with pride in the face of White cultural efforts to demean Black culture. It is also a response to the discriminatory American democratic capitalistic individualistic system. A system that has historically excluded Blacks from the mainstream of American politics and economy.

Many consider Muhammed Ali the greatest boxer of all time. At the age of 18, he won a gold medal in the 1980 Rome Olympics. Upon his return home to the U.S., Ali, then known as Cassius Clay, became seriously distraught when he and a friend were refused service at a "whites-only" restaurant and got into a fight with a white gang when they left. Returning from Rome, Italy, an Olympic gold medal winner, becoming a hero representing America then experiencing racism confronted Ali with an American reality; America is a racist country or at the least America harbors too many racists. Too many White people are racist. With that realization, he threw his gold medal into the Ohio River, according to the story.

President John Kennedy's 1960 inauguration speech was historical. "Ask not what your country can do for you but what you can do for your country." However, what does one do when your country has no appreciation for what you do for your country? The realization that he was representing a White America that cared nothing for him could be the reason Ali threw his gold medal in the Ohio River. He viewed it as a meaningless symbol of "being used" by a country that does not care about him or about Black people. This was a realization that shaped Muhammed Ali's Stage 2 Mimesis.

That is a concern probably in the conscious of minority veterans who return home from war and cannot get a job. Inequality is a primary concern motivating the professional life of Muhammed Ali, Dr. Martin Luther King, Mahatma Gandhi and others who believe in humanity. One can hypothesize that the practice of the American democratic capitalistic individualistic system holds veterans in the same regard. They go to war thousands of miles away from their families, risk their lives and cannot get a job when they return home. There are exceptions but that is a common scenario. Consider the restaurant experience in Ali's life to be a catalyst that set him on the path to question the values of the American democratic capitalistic individualistic system, his becoming a member of the Nation of Islam as a minister, his refusal to join the army and his being admired by millions of people throughout the world. Many White people hated Ali. He made the comment that Black people come to his fights to see him win. White people come to see him lose. No matter because they all buy tickets to put their butts in the seats. His refusal to join the army did cause him hardship. Initially, classified as 4F, unfit for duty, he was reclassified 1A, fit for active duty, at the height of his career. Being the heavyweight champion at the time, he was stripped of his title and fought a court battle for three years before he was declared not guilty by the Supreme Court of the United States. Despite his three-year layoff, Ali returned to his boxing profession and regained the heavyweight title. From that point on, Americans respected, admired, and loved Ali, not only as a boxer but also as a man. Ali challenged the American democratic, capitalistic, individualistic system and won. Ali left a rich legacy, despite his early racial and political conflicts. He left millions of admiring fans who loved him not only for his skill in the boxing ring but also just as much for the giving qualities he possessed as a human being. Ali's stage three Mimesis found him loved and respected by both Black and White people worldwide.

Richard Milhous Nixon, a White man, a member of the Republican Party, served as the 37th president of the United States from 1969 until 1974. Nixon previously served as the 36th vice president from 1953 to 1961, under President Dwight D. Eisenhower. Nixon rose to national prominence as a congressional representative senator from California and vice president of the United States under Eisenhower. After winning a first and second term in the White House, Nixon withdrew the U.S. involvement in the unpopular Vietnam War. He achieved détente with the Soviet Union and China, and established the Environmental Protection Agency (EPA). Unfortunately, during his second term election, Nixon was involved in a criminal scandal meant to undermine the democratic presidential campaign, the Watergate scandal. The Nixon administration's continual attempts to cover up its involvement in the June 17, 1972, break-in of the Democratic National Committee headquarters caused him to become the only president in history to resign from office. Embarrassed and shamed, Vice President Gerald Ford succeeded Nixon and pardoned him. Nixon was accomplished in international affairs. Congressional peers considered him a success story in a troubled era, one who steered a sensible anti-Communist course against the destructive overzealous excessiveness of McCarthyism. However, "Nixon, both as a man and as a statesman, has been excessively maligned for his faults and inadequately recognized for his virtues." Nixon left a legacy of mistrust in government. In surveys of historians and political scientists, Nixon is generally ranked as a below-average president.[512] However, during his time serving America and while in office, Nixon was responsible for some significant accomplishments.

The irony in the public juxtaposing perspective on both Ali and Nixon is ironically American. The White public hated Ali in his early career when he adopted the Islamic faith. The White Public loved and respected Nixon in his early political career. The Public considered Nixon an astute politician. Later in life, Ali was loved and revered by people in all walks of life. Nixon, on the other hand, was seen as a pariah to the Republican Party, a political outcast. Muhammad Ali and Richard Nixon, ironically, can be thought of as "Trading Places".

Queen Elizabeth
and
Oprah Winfrey

Queen·of·the·United·Kingdom·and·
other·Commonwealth·realms¶
Reign:·February·6,·1952 – September·
8,·2022¶
Coronation:→June·2,·1953¶
Born:→Princess·Elizabeth·of·York¶
→   Elizabeth·Alexandra·Mary¶
    April·21,·1926¶
    Mayfair,·London,·England¶
Died: September·8,·2022¶
    Balmoral·Castle,·
    Aberdeenshire,·Scotland¶
Burial: September·19,·2022¶
    King·George·VI·Memorial·
    Chapel,·St.·George·Chapel,·
    Windsor·Castle¶
Spouse:·Prince·Philip,·Duke·of·
    Edinburg¶
    (m:·1947,·died:·(2021)¶
Children:·(4)·Charles·III¶
             Anne,·Princess·Royal¶
             Prince·Andrew,·Duke·
             of·York¶
             Prince·Edward,·Duke·
             of·Edinburgh¶
Parents: →   →   George·VI¶
     →   →   Elizabeth·Bowes-Lyon¶
Religion: →   Protestant¶

Born:→Oprah·Gail·Winfrey¶
   →   January·29,·1954¶
   →   Kosciusko,·Mississippi¶
¶
Education:Tennessee·State·
University¶
¶
Occupation:→Television·
    Presenter,·Actress,·
    Television·Producer,·Media·
    Proprietor,·Philanthropist,·
    Author¶
¶
Chairwoman·and·CEO·of·Harpo·
    Productions¶
¶
Political·Party: →   ·Independent¶
¶
Partner: →   Stedman·Graham¶
    →   →   (1966-Present)¶
¶
Website:·Oprah.com.¶

Oprah Winfrey and Queen Elizabeth are a perfect example of individuals who experienced a completely different early childhoods. However, they both wound up to become Queens in their own right and among their respective subjects; Elizabeth, the Queen of England and outlying territories, and Oprah, the Queen of Media.

During the reign of her grandfather's (King George VI) reign, Elizabeth was third in the line of succession to the British throne, behind her uncle Edward and her father. Although her birth generated public interest, she was not expected to become queen, as Edward was still young and likely to marry and have children of his own, who would precede Elizabeth in the line of succession. When her grandfather died in 1936 and her uncle succeeded as Edward VIII, she became second in line to the throne, after her father. Later that year, Edward abdicated, after his proposed marriage to divorced socialite Wallis Simpson provoked a constitutional crisis. Consequently, Elizabeth's father became king, taking the regnal name George VI. Since Elizabeth had no brothers, she became heir presumptive. If her parents had subsequently had a son, he would have been heir apparent and above her in the line of succession, the policy determined by the male-preference primogeniture in effect at the time.

Elizabeth received private tutoring in constitutional history from Henry Marten, Vice-Provost of Eton College, and learned French from a succession of native-speaking governesses. A Girl Guides company, the 1st Buckingham Palace Company, was formed specifically so she could socialize with girls her age. Later, she became as a Sea Ranger.[513] Elizabeth's early life was privileged and strictly controlled.

Oprah, on the other hand, experienced a challenging childhood. She was born in poverty and shuffled between living with her mother and father. Abused as a teenager, Oprah possessed the amazing quality to overcome adversity, dysfunction, and negative life experiences. She became the homecoming queen at her high school. She started early in the media business. In this regard, like Queen Elizabeth, Oprah realized her career direction early in her life. She graduated from college from Tennessee State University in 1986. Today, the only people who do not know Oprah Winfrey are those who have been hibernating for the last 30 years. Oprah is truly a rare phenomenon as an individual. Despite her own early hardships, she has exemplified an individual who has a deep caring for others and has put her money where her sentiment lies. Her philanthropic endeavors are abundant. During her reign as "Queen of the talk show circuit" (she was a Queen who reigned over the Kings), her personality resonated with men and women throughout America. Like Queen Elizabeth, her viewers loved her. According to reports, the show averages an estimated 7, 14, and 15–20 million viewers a day in the United States. Reports also range from 26 million and 42 million a week (5.2 million and 8.4 million a day). [514]

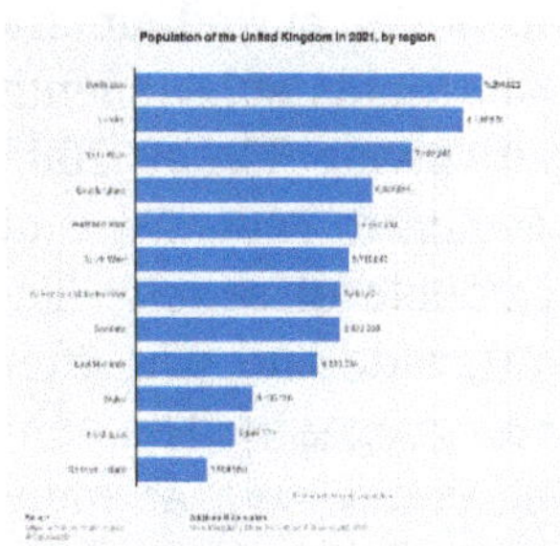

The population of the United Kingdom was estimated to have been over 67 million in 2021, with almost 9.3 million of these people living in South East England. London had the next highest population, at 8.8 million people, followed by the North West at 7.4 million. [515]

The statistics above include the entire United Kingdom. The population of England proper was 56.5 million people in 2021, compared with 53.1 million people ten years earlier in 2011. Compared with 1971 the population of England has grown by approximately ten million people.[516] Oprah had a viewership of almost one-half the population of England. Oprah's viewership of 20 million viewers a day vs the population of England 56 million people. The above statistics only include Oprah's viewership in the United States. The show aired on most ABC-owned stations in the United States except KTRK-TV, but CBS-affiliate KHOU carried the show for the entire run. Other stations through CBS Television Distribution, successor to King World carried her show, CTV in most Canadian markets, Diva Universal in Malaysia, TV3 in Ireland, GNT in Brazil, national TV3 in Sweden, Network Ten in Australia, La7d in Italy, MBC 4 in the Arab world, Metro TV in Indonesia, FARSI1 in Iran, and in the Netherlands on RTL4. In the United Kingdom. A number of different channels hosted *The Oprah Winfrey Show*. Channel 4 first broadcast the series on Monday October 3, 1988, The BBC & Sky One acquired the rights and started broadcasting the series from 9 January 1995 which meant at time during 1995 the show went out on 3 different channel. Five other networks picked up the terrestrial rights from early 1998. Rights subsequently *The Oprah Winfrey Show* went to Living TV by 2002, followed by ITV2 in 2006, and then to Diva TV, until rights went to TLC for the last couple of series. The show aired in 149 countries worldwide and was often renamed and dubbed into other languages.[517] The point is that Oprah Winfrey very well could have as much influence worldwide as the Queen of England. However, the primary point is the extraordinary Mimesis of both

Queens who reached phenomenal status and respect in their lives. Both, Queen Elizabeth and Oprah Winfrey, received a maximum of love and respect from their respective subjects (audiences) and the Mimesis of both Queens give substance that Mimesis in some cases is a yellow brick road to follow that requires strategic individual agency and decision-making. For others Mimesis is constructed for them. All they have to do is stay on the yellow brick road.

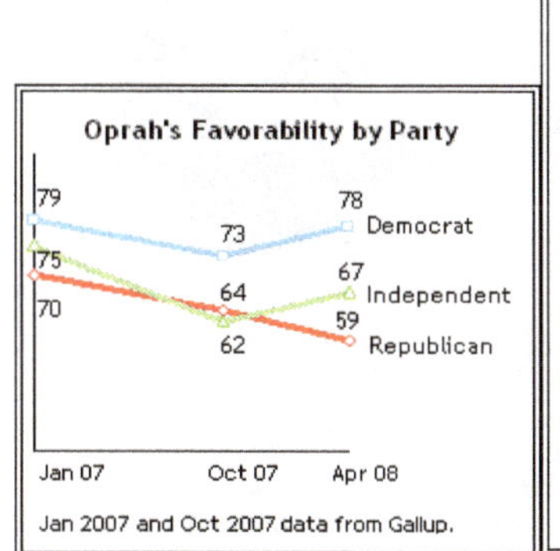

	Fav %	Unfav %	DK/Can't Rate %
Total	68	21	11=100
Men	55	31	14=100
Women	79	14	7=100
18-34	76	16	8=100
35-49	66	25	9=100
50-64	62	29	9=100
65+	67	18	15=100
College grad	66	26	8=100
Some college	73	19	8=100
HS or less	67	21	12=100
Republican	58	32	10=100
Democrat	78	16	6=100
Independent	66	23	11=100

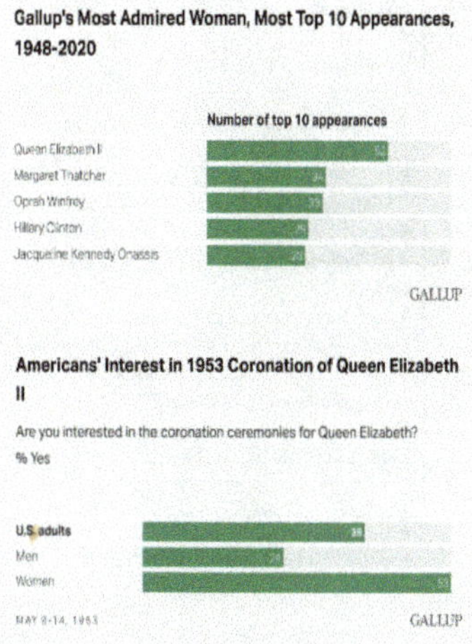

Both Oprah Winfrey and Queen Elizabeth are held in high regard. Even Americans admire the Queen of England. Data on Republicans admiration for Oprah Winfrey is the lowest. That is no surprise because Republicans are perceived as racists and misogynous. [518]

Malcom X
and
Stanley "Tookie" Williams

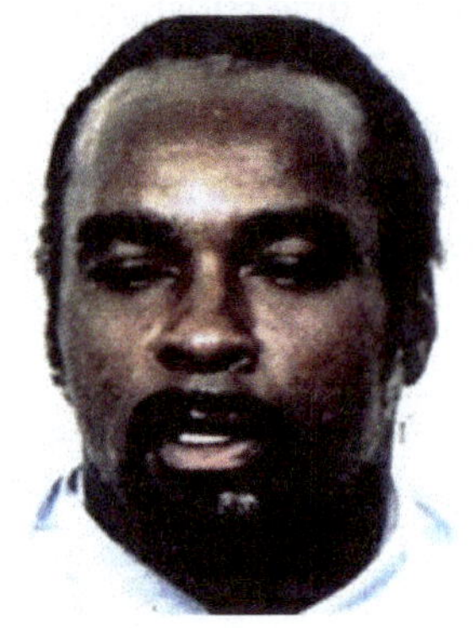

Born: Malcolm Little
May 19, 1925
Omaha, Nebraska

Died: February 21, 1965
New York City, NY

Cause of Death: Assassination by gunshot

Resting Place: Ferncliff Cemetary

AKA: Malik el-Shabazz

Occupations: Minister, Civil Rights activist
Organizations: Nation of Islam, Muslim Mosque, Inc., Organization of Afro-American Unity

Movement: Black Nationalism, Pan-Africanism, Islamism

Spouse: Betty Shabazz (m: 1958)

Children: (6)

Parents: Louise Helen Norton

Born: Stanley Williams III
December 29, 1953
Shreveport, Louisana

Died: December 13, 2005
San Quentin State Prison
San Quentin California

Cause of Death: Execution by lethal injection

Occupation: Gangster

Spouse: Bonnie Williams-Taylor (m: 1981)

Children: (3)

Affiliation: West Side Crips Street Gang

Convictions: First Degree Murder with special circumstances (4 counts) Robbery (2 counts)

Criminal Penalty: Death

Victims: (4)

Neither Malcolm X nor Tookie Williams died of natural causes. Both were killed. Malcolm was killed by an assassin and Tookie was electrocuted by the state of California. Malcom X, born as Malcolm Little was assassinated by an individual or individuals. Details of the assassination of Malcom X are uncertain. What is discerning is the historical racial discord and racism over centuries and during the modern era of the civil rights struggles (approximately 1955 to 1980 beginning when Ms. Rosa Parks, a black woman, refused to ride in the back of the bus, in compliance with White racist policies in Birmingham Alabama[519]). Still in this 22nd century, America has a significant racist population, allowed to have voice. During the civil rights era Malcom X, Dr. Martin Luther King, Jr., innocent individuals, were all assassinated, including Medgar Evers, President John F. Kennedy, and Senator Robert Kennedy. There is speculation that all perpetrators committing the murders claimed innocence. There is doubt regarding their guilt. Speculation points to a conspiracy in each of the killings. The point is that to have so many leaders partial to civil rights and equality killed during the same period of time makes one wonder about the legitimacy of American Conspiracy theories surrounding these incidents.

Tookie Williams was executed by lethal injection by the criminal justice system. Both Malcolm X and Tookie Williams engaged in criminal activity during their Stage 2 Mimesis. While Malcolm committed non-violent crimes (gambling, robbery, and drug dealing) Tookie, on the other hand, committed violent crimes (drug dealing, robbery and murder). Unfortunately, for Tookie, the crimes of murder he committed were his death sentence. Both men were, from all accounts, rehabilitated in prison. Malcolm X, then known as Malcolm Little, became

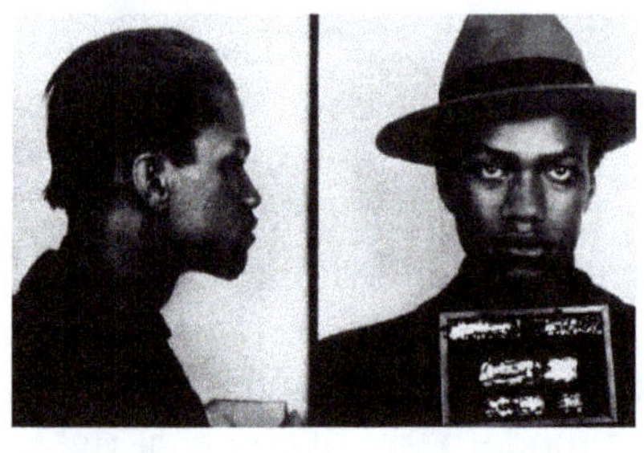

influenced by the religion of Islam under the philosophy and guidance of Elijah Muhammed. Malcolm X embraced the Islamic teachings and religion and became a major force in the growth of Islam in the United States. Malcolm was responsible for recruiting Muhammed Ali into the Islamic religion. While Malcolm's speeches did advocate a self-defense philosophy unlike his contemporary Dr. Martin Luther King, Jr. whose philosophy advocated non-violence. By all accounts, Malcolm rehabilitated in prison and in his post-prison years became an advocate for justice and equal rights.

Tookie Williams was also rehabilitated in prison. Upon reflecting on his life, Tookie came to realize the "error of his ways". He took on the cause of advocating against gangs and gang violence. Tookie wrote a number of books sending the message to kids to live a productive and crime free life. Tookie displayed sincere remorse for his crimes. However, when an individual confronts the fact they will pay for their crimes with their life that does cause one to seriously reflect on how their Mimesis was constructed. In the case of Tookie, it was evident that if were to do it over again, he would make different decisions. The state of California was not forgiving with Tookie. The state of California executed Tookie Williams by lethal injection on December 13, 2005.

Malcolm X on the other hand, while he was fully repentant of the crimes he committed in his earlier years, his life was still embroiled in controversy and conflict. Malcolm was a man of principle. There is a phenomenon about people who repent. Repentant smokers become unforgiving about people who smoke. The same with repentant drug users. They abhor drug users who have not stopped using drugs. Normally, they disassociate from drug users to prevent relapse. Alcoholics likewise. Malcolm having developed a higher moral and ethical character was unable to forgive the lack of ethical and moral standing he discovered in his leader, the Honorable Elijah Muhammed. When Malcolm discovered Elijah Muhammed fathered children with underage girls, he broke with the Elijah Muhammed led sect of the Nation of Islam. He also began to speak negatively about Elijah. The confusion in Malcolm's murder is that he incurred the wrath of the Federal Government (the FBI) with his self-defense rhetoric. He also incurred the wrath of the Nation of Islam with his criticism of its leader Elijah Muhammed. Either the FBI or the Nation of Islam could have killed Malcolm. To date the record states that Thomas Hagan a former member of the Nation of Islam was convicted for assassinating Malcolm X in 1965. For a period, he also went by the name Talmadge X Hayer, and his chosen Islamic name is Mujahid Abdul Halim. [520]

While there was sentiment to spare the life of Stanley "Tookie" Williams, there was also a clear and convincing case to give him the death penalty. He murdered four people. He did repent and by all accounts rehabilitated. Many people argued in behalf of sparing his life. Converting Tookie's sentence to life in prison could have been a significant benefit to the youth of America. He could have had a convincing voice in giving America's youth positive influence. However, the very real argument of: Why spare his life when the people he murdered are dead? Governor Schwarzenegger accepted the latter agreement.

Both Tookie Williams and Malcolm amassed a significant following based on the good works they accomplished through their rehabilitation and calling to contribute to society. The photo below shows the hundreds of people waiting in line to view the remains of Malcolm X.

Malcom X – Stage 3 Mimesis

The construction of ones Mimesis often occurs randomly during the Stage 2 adolescent developmental process. The phenomena individuals encounter and respond to have an accumulative effect on one's life experiences and Mimesis. An individual needs to understand as early as possible that they have agency in their developmental process. As agents in their Mimesis development individuals should understand they are agents in their Mimesis construction and it is important for them to be cognizant in constructing their Mimesis of Life as soon as possible. It is an advantage when the child has parents or caregivers who socialized positive concepts of Mimesis construction into the child's developmental process. Mimesis Construction is having a mentality of aforethought in the decisions you make and the behavior you adopt. The concept of Mimesis construction develops interest and agency in developing the individual's cognition and behavioral responses to lived experiences; such that they respond to positive phenomena and reject negative phenomena they encounter. **Malcom X – Stage 3 Mimesis**

One difference between Malcolm and Tookie in their final Mimesis is that Malcolm still has influence in society. There is a book and movie on his life. Civil rights organizations keep his philosophy and memory alive. For the most part, the movement to commute Tookie's death sentence is dead also.

Jay-Z
and
Tupac Shakur
and
Elvis Presley

Born: Shawn Corey Carter December 4, 1969 New York City, NY **Aka:** The Carter Administration Jigga, Hova, El Presidente **Occupations:** Rapper-Songwriter-record producer-entrepreneur-record executive-media proprietor **Organizations:** Shawn Carter Foundation **Title:** Founder of 40/40 club; Roc Nation; Rocawear; Reform Alliance **Spouse:** Beyonce **Children** (3) **Website:** lifeandtimes.com	**Born:** Lesane Parish Crooks June 16, 1971 New York City **Died:** September 13, 1996; Las Vegas, NV. **Cause of death:** Drive by homicide (gunshot) **Aka:** 2Pac; Tupac; Makaveli; MC; New York **Occupations:** Rapper; songwriter; actor; **Spouse:** Keisha Morris (m: 1995, annulled: 1996) **Parents:** Afeni Shakur Billy Garland **Website:** www.2pac.com	**Born:** Elis Aron Presley January 8, 1935 Tupelo, MS. **Died:** August 6, 1977; Memphis, TN. **Cause of Death:** Cardiac arrest due to drugs **Resting Place:** Graceland, Memphis **Occupations:** Singer; Actor **Military Service:** US Army, 1958-1960 **Rank:** Sergeant **Spouse:** Priscilla Beaulieu **Children** Lisa Marie **Aka:** Elvis; King of Rock N' Roll

All three artist are inductees into the Rock n' Roll Hall of Fame. All three artist are loved by millions of fans. All three are excellent entertainers. All three were rich. Among the three only Jay-Z is alive. Tupac and Elvis both died prematurely. A study concluded that those individuals who gained some kind of fame died at 77.2 years of age on average. Compare this to the average lifespan in the US of 78.5 years for creative-types, 81.7 for professionals and 83 for business leaders and politicians. [521]

There is one significant difference between Jay-Z, Tupac and Elvis. Tupac and Elvis were a rapper / a singer. They primarily focused on their craft. They had others manage their business affairs. In the case of Tupac, it was Suge Knight. In the case of Elvis, it was Colonel Tom Parker. Other individuals played a significant role in managing not only their business but also their performance itinerary. The people who managed Tupac and Elvis were compensated based on the earnings of Tupac and Elvis. The more money the entertainer made, the more money the manager made. Many entertainers kept grueling exhausting performance schedules. However, in the case of Jay-Z, he was not only a performer but he was also a student of his craft. He learned the business of music and entertainment. He was able to diversify his revenue opportunities. He was not only economically dependent on performance, which can be grueling and exhausting. Jay-Z not only managed his business but he manages his life. Tupac and Elvis to some degree had their life managed for them. Jay-Z is smart. The phenomena an individual encounters in their lived experience and how the individual responds to the phenomena they encounter, is what determines their The Mimesis of Life. To a significant extent, Tupac and Elvis relinquished some control over their Mimesis construction. On the other hand, Jay-Z, for the most part, controlled his own Mimesis. Tupac died at 25 years old. Elvis died at 42 years old. Both died while in their prime productive years. Jay-Z is now 56 years old (as of 2025) and a billionaire.

All three, Jay-Z, Tupac and Elvis grew up in disadvantaged environments. Sometimes the experience of being poor and experiencing poverty is a motivator that stimulates the individuals drive to succeed. Therefore, one has to evaluate the difference in the Mimesis construction of Jay-Z, Tupac and Elvis. Jay-Z was not a "choir boy" during his youth. He sold drugs and engage in criminal activity. The street environment exposed Jay-Z to potential danger, violence and situations that could have very well endangered his life early in his youth. However, he managed to escape the trap of life threatening situations. Tupac and Elvis obviously did not. Both Tupac and Elvis died long before the average age of death for celebrities, 77.2 years.

Beyonce Knowles Carter
and
Marilyn Monroe

Born: Beyonce Giselle Knowles
September 4, 1981
Houston, Texas
Aka: Harmonies by the Hive; Queen B
Occupations: Singer, Songwriter, dancer, actress, record producer, businesswoman, director
Spouse: Jay-Z
Children: (3)
Parents: Matthew Knowles
Tina Lawson
Relatives: Solange Knowles (sister)
Angela Beyince (cousin)
Nixon Alexander Knowles
(half-brother)
Formerly of: Destiny's Child singing group
Website: beyonce.com

Born: Norma Jeane Mortensen
June 1, 1926
Los Angeles, California
Died: August 4. 1962

Cause of Death;   Barbiturate
Overdose
Burial Place: Westwood Village
Memorial Park
Cemetery
Aka: Norma Jeane Baker
Occupation: Actress, Model, Singer
Spouses: James Dougerty
(m:1942; div: 1946)

Joe Dimaggio
(m: 1954; div: 1955)

Arthur Miller
(m: 1956; Div: 1961)

Parent: Gladys Pearl Baker
(mother)
Relatives: Berniece Baker (half-sister)
Website: marilynmonroe.com

Both Beyonce and Marilyn are and were beautiful and talented women. They had different environmental and social experiences during their Stage 1 Mimesis developmental process. All theories of childhood development advance the influence of positive caregiving in stage 1 of Mimesis construction, the early formative stage.

Beyonce's early childhood development experience was with a stable home life, a loving mother, father, and siblings, all of whom bonded in a stable loving home environment. Instability influenced Marilyn's childhood. She live in several foster homes and abandoned by her mother. Her mother had mental problems and she did not have the presence of a father in her life. Her foster caregiver (male) abused Marilyn in her youth. One can argue that Hollywood gave Marilyn an environment to escape from her childhood memories and opportunity to become other personas that replaced the reality of her childhood experiences and memories.

The human mind is a unique and astonishing part of the human being. The mind can be as creative as the human imagination. Individuals who struggles to grasp reality or who want to escape their reality, but practically can only generate various concepts and theories that have their limitations. "Identifying boundaries of applicability is essential. If the boundaries and limits are not well defined, unrealistic concepts and theories may turn into perceived dogmas, leaving the individual with illusions of misunderstanding. Concepts and theories cannot fully describe the ultimate reality due to the inaccessibility to all the elements of emergent reality, and due to the inherent unknowability of all that remains undiscovered and misunderstood. Thus, some disconnect from reality is inevitable and humans are caught between illusion and reality. The fundamental problem of illusions seizing the individual's awareness is the resulting reluctance to see things as they are and to be seen without illusions."[522]

Beyonce has a clarity that separates entertainment and "show business" from real life. She seemed to distinguish between the roles of entertainment and being a wife, mother, sister, daughter and friend. As an entertainer, Beyonce belongs to her fans. As a human being off stage Beyonce belongs to her family and friends. She is able to balance and distinguish between the two personas.

Marilyn on the other hand had a difficult childhood. It can be argued that Marilyn's solace was not in her childhood memories but in the life, she was living as a movie star. The accolade she received from fans and men filled a void of insecurity in Marilyn that her childhood neglected. Whereas Beyonce could leave Sasha Fierce on the stage or on the movie set, and go home with Beyonce, Marilyn, on the other hand, took Marilyn everywhere she went. Marilyn did not have an ability to separate the movie star Marilyn from the person Marilyn, and quite possibly, she did not want to.

Dr. Ronald Barnes

Beyonce's Alter Ego "Sasha Fierce"

Beyonce

Sasha Fierce can escape
from Beyonce and Beyonce
can escape from Sasha
Fierce.

Dr. Ronald Barnes

Marilyn

And Marilyn

The real Marilyn became Movie Star Marilyn. Marilyn did not escape from Movie Star Marilyn, and maybe she did not want to.

End Notes

1

Muhammad Ali -"This is your Life". Television Show.
Youtube. Retrieved from:
https://www.youtube.com/watch?V=ZWZOBX1vE7A

2

Disis, Jill (2018). How Oprah build Oprah Inc. CNN Business.
Retrieved from:
https://money.cnn.com/2018/01/09/media/oprah-
winfrey-career-
history/index.html#:~:text=The%20late%20movie%20critic
%20Roger,potential%20earnings%20on%20a%20napkin.

3

Yacobi, B. (2013). The Human Dilemma Life Between Illusion
and Reality Journal of Philosophy of Life Vol.3, No.3
(September 2013):202-211. Retrieved from:
https://www.philosophyoflife.org/jpl201312.pdf;
https://www.philosophyoflife.org/201312.html

4

Philip Matthew Stinson, Sr., J.D, Ph.D., John Liederbach,
Ph.D., Steven P. Lab, Ph.D., Steven L. Brewer, Jr., Ph.D.
POLICE INTEGRITY LOST: A STUDY OF LAW
ENFORCEMENT OFFICERS ARRESTED. Retrieved from:
https://www.ojp.gov/pdffiles1/nij/grants/249850.pdf
David Weisburd and Rosann Greenspan with Edwin E.
Hamilton, Hubert Williams, and Kellie A. Bryant (2000).
National Institute of Justice. Retrieved from:
https://www.ojp.gov/pdffiles1/nij/181312.pdf

EMILEE GREEN AND ORLEANA PENEFF| (2022). An Overview of Police Use of Force Policies and Research. Illinois Criminal Justice Information Authority. Retrieved from: https://icjia.illinois.gov/researchhub/articles/an-overview-of-police-use-of-force-policies-and-research

Degue, S., Fowler, K. A., & Calkins, C. (2016). Deaths Due to Use of Lethal Force by Law Enforcement: Findings From the National Violent Death Reporting System, 17 U.S. States, 2009-2012. *American journal of preventive medicine*, *51*(5 Suppl 3), S173–S187. Https://doi.org/10.1016/j.amepre.2016.08.027. Retrieved from: https://www.ncbi.nlm.nih.gov/pmc/articles/PMC6080222/

David Landau and Rosalind Dixon (). Abusive Judicial Review: Courts Against Democracy. Retrieved from: https://lawreview.law.ucdavis.edu/issues/53/3/53-3_Landau_Dixon.pdf

5

(2023). Prison Abolition. *The Marshall Project*. Retrieved from: https://www.themarshallproject.org/records/4766-prison-abolition

NINE PERSPECTIVES FOR PRISON ABOLITIONISTS. *INSTEAD OF PRISONS: A HANDBOOK FOR ABOLITIONISTS* Retrieved from: https://www.prisonpolicy.org/scans/instead_of_prisons/nine_perspectives.shtml

Law, Victoria (2022). Rethinking Incaraceration. *Harvard Radcliffe Institute*. Retrieved from: https://www.radcliffe.harvard.edu/news-and-ideas/rethinking-incarceration

6

Westbrook, Dmtri (2014). Opinion Editorial: Why is it that so Many White People Fear Black Men?
Westbrook, Dmitri C. (2014) "Opinion Editorial: Why is it that so Many White People Fear Black Men?," College Student Affairs Leadership: Vol. 1: Iss. 2, Article 4. Available at: https://scholarworks.gvsu.edu/csal/vol1/iss2/4 ; https://scholarworks.gvsu.edu/cgi/viewcontent.cgi?Article=1015&context=csal

Litwack, L. F. (1998). The White Man's Fear of the Educated Negro: How the Negro Was Fitted for His Natural and Logical Calling. *The Journal of Blacks in Higher Education*, *20*, 100–108. Https://doi.org/10.2307/2999249. Retrieved from: https://www.jstor.org/stable/2999249

Brown, Karen (2021). The Fear Black Employees Carry. *Harvard Business Review.* Retrieved from: https://hbr.org/2021/04/the-fear-black-employees-carry

7

Tanya de Sousa and Meghan Henry (2024). The 2024 Annual Homelessness Assessment Report (AHAR) to Congress. *U.S. Department of Housing and Urban Development (HUD).* Https://www.huduser.gov/portal/sites/default/files/pdf/2024-AHAR-Part-1.pdf

8

Gould-Ellen, Ingrid (1997) - Welcome Neighbors? New evidence on the possibility of stable racial integration. *Brookings Institute.* Retrieved from: https://www.brookings.edu/articles/welcome-neighbors-new-evidence-on-the-possibility-of-stable-racial-integration/

9

Yacobi, B. (2013). The Human Dilemma Life Between Illusion and Reality Journal of Philosophy of Life Vol.3, No.3 (September 2013):202-211. Retrieved from:

https://www.philosophyoflife.org/jpl201312.pdf;
https://www.philosophyoflife.org/201312.html

10

Frady, Marshall (2005). *Martin Luther King, Jr: A Life*. Pp. 12–15. ISBN 978-0-14-303648-7.

11

Blake, John. (2013). *How MLK became an angry black man*. Retrieved from:
https://www.cnn.com/2013/04/16/us/king-birmingham-jail-letter-anniversary/

12

Downing, Frederick L. (1986). *To See the Promised Land: The Faith Pilgrimage of Martin*

13

The King Center (2018). About Dr. King. Retrieved from:
http://www.thekingcenter.org

14

The King Center (2018). About Dr. King. Retrieved from:
http://www.thekingcenter.org/about-dr-king

15

Martin Luther King, Jr. (1968). "i've Been to the Mountaintop" Speech. Retrieved from:
https://www.americanrhetoric.com/speeches/mlkivebeentothemountaintop.htm

16

U.S. Office of Personnel Management. What are the Federal holidays? Https://www.opm.gov/frequently-asked-questions/pay-and-leave-faq/pay-administration/what-are-federal-holidays/

17

Sabourin, Rachelle (2014). 20 Martin Luther King Jr.
Monuments Around the World You Didn't Know Existed.
Retrieved from:
https://www.complex.com/style/2014/01/martin-luther-king-jr-monuments/

18

Dr. King explains the war in Vietnam was undermining the
fight for social justice by breeding insensitivity to the
suffering of South Asians and dulling America's collective
conscience...
Youtube. Martin Luther King Jr.: "My dream has turned into a
nightmare". Retrieved from:
https://www.youtube.com/watch?V=shhjykpwb8k

19

Muhammed Ali Biography. Retrieved from:
https://biography.jrank.org/pages/2728/Ali-Muhammad.html

20

Rhoden, William C. (June 20, 2013). "In Ali's Voice From the
Past, a Stand for the Ages". *The New York Times*.

21

Eig, Jonathan (2017). *Ali: A Life: Shortlisted for the William Hill
Sports Book of the Year 2017*. Simon &
Schuster. ISBN 9781471155963.

22

Skinner, Majorie, (2013). Not So Fast: Remembering the trials
of Muhammad Ali.. Portland Mercury. Retrieved December
27, 2013. Retrieved from:
https://www.portlandmercury.com/portland/not-so-fast/Content?Oid=10883366

23

Rhoden, William, C. (2013). In Ali's Voice from the Past, a Stand for the Ages. *New York Times*. Retrieved from: https://www.nytimes.com/2013/06/21/sports/in-alis-voice-from-the-past-a-stand-for-the-ages.html

24

Hauser, Thomas (2004). Muhammad Ali: His Life and Times. London: Robson Books. ISBN 978-1-86105-738-9. OCLC 56645513.

Kandel, Elmo (April 1, 2006). "Boxing Legend – Muhammad Ali". *Article Click*. Elmo Kandel. Archived from the original on June 11, 2008. Retrieved March 9, 2009.

25

Muhammad Ali -"This is your Life". Television Show. Youtube. Retrieved from: https://www.youtube.com/watch?V=ZWZOBX1vE7A

26

Morine, Hannah (2016). A Tribute to Muhammad Ali: The Athlete, Philanthropist And Legend". Odyssey. June 6, 2016. Retrieved from: https://www.theodysseyonline.com/tribute-muhammad-ali-athlete-philanthropist-legend

27

Biography.com (2018). Muhammad Ali Biography, Athlete, Philanthropist, Boxer (1942–2016). Biography.com. January 18, 2018. Retrieved from: https://www.biography.com/people/muhammad-ali-9181165

28

Levin, Josh (2016). The Time Muhammad Ali Stopped a Man from Leaping to His Death
In January 1981, the champ talked a man down from a ninth-floor ledge. JUNE 04, 20163:23 AM. Retrieved from:

https://slate.com/culture/2016/06/the-time-muhammad-ali-stopped-a-man-from-leaping-to-his-death.html

29

National Constitution Center (2012). Muhammad Ali 2012 Liberty Medal Ceremony. National Constitution Center. Retrieved January 17, 2018. Retrieved from: https://constitutioncenter.org/calendar/muhammad-ali-2012-liberty-medal-ceremony

30

National Constitution Center (2012). Muhammad Ali 2012 Liberty Medal Ceremony. National Constitution Center. Retrieved January 17, 2018. Retrieved from: https://constitutioncenter.org/calendar/muhammad-ali-2012-liberty-medal-ceremony

31

Bulman, May (June 5, 2016). "Muhammad Ali dead: Michael J Fox pays tribute to fellow Parkinson's disease sufferer and their 'common fight'". *The Independent*. Retrieved September 4, 2016. Https://www.independent.co.uk/news/people/muhammad-ali-dead-michael-j-fox-tribute-parkinsons-disease-common-fight-a7066416.html

32

Miller, Davis (September 12, 1993). "Still Larger Than Life – To Millions, Muhammad Ali Will Always Be the Champ". *The Seattle Times*. Retrieved August 5, 2009.

Hauser, Thomas (June 15, 1992). *Muhammad Ali: His Life and Times*. Simon and Schuster. ISBN 978-0-671-77971-9.

Ali, Hana Yasmeen (2013). Ali, Muhammad; *The Soul of a Butterfly*. Simon & Schuster.

Spears, Marc J. (September 14, 1999). "Ali: The Greatest of 20th century; Show stops when the champ arrives for awards dinner". *The Courier-Journal.*

33

Wilson, Stan (2012). Muhammad Ali returns to the Olympic stage, once again, in London
CNN. Updated 0550 GMT (1350 HKT) July 28, 2012. Retrieved from:
https://edition.cnn.com/2012/07/27/sport/olympics-muhammad-ali/index.html

34

Wilstein, Steve, Associated Press, "Retton, Hammill most popular American athletes in United States: poll"; *The Daily Gazette*, May 17, 1993.

35

Quittner, Joshua (June 14, 1999). "Ali—Time 100 People of the Century". *Time.*

36

"Sports Illustrated honors world's greatest athletes". *CNN. December 3, 1999.*

37

BBC News (1999). Ali crowned Sportsman of Century. Monday, 13 December, 1999, 08:16 GMT. Retrieved from: http://news.bbc.co.uk/1/hi/sport/561352.stm

38

Spears, Marc J. (September 14, 1999). "Ali: The Greatest of 20th century; Show stops when the champ arrives for awards dinner". *The Courier-Journal.*

39

SI Wire "SI dedicates Sportsman of the Year Legacy Award to Muhammad Ali", Sports Illustrated, September 25, 2015.

Retrieved September 13, 2015. Retrieved from: https://www.si.com/sports-illustrated-sportsman-year-legacy-award-renamed-for-muhammad-ali

40

Office of the Press Secretary (November 9, 2005). "Citations for Recipients of the 2005 Presidential Medal of Freedom". Washington D.C., U.S.: The White House, George W. Bush. Retrieved June 6, 2016. Retrieved from: https://georgewbush-whitehouse.archives.gov/news/releases/2005/11/20051109-10.html

41

HISTORY.COM EDITORS (2018). Muhammad Ali. History, ORIGINAL DEC 16, 2009. RETRIEVED FROM: HTTPS://WWW.HISTORY.COM/TOPICS/BLACK-HISTORY/MUHAMMAD-ALI

42

Kingworld (2004). OPRAH WINFREY SIGNS WITH KING WORLD PRODUCTIONS FOR NEW THREE-YEAR CONTRACT TO CONTINUE AS HOST AND PRODUCER OF "THE OPRAH WINFREY SHOW" THROUGH 2010-2011. Retrieved from: https://web.archive.org/web/20070210090815/http://www.kingworld.com/release/oprah_winfrey.html

43

Miller, Matthew (May 6, 2009). "The Wealthiest Black Americans". *Forbes*. Retrieved August 26, 2010. Retrieved from: https://www.forbes.com/2009/05/06/richest-black-americans-busienss-billionaires-richest-black-americans.html#9d62617956e7

44

Nsehe, Mfonobong (2015). "The Black Billionaires 2015". *Forbes*. Retrieved from: https://www.forbes.com/sites/mfonobongnsehe/2015/03/02/the-black-billionaires-2015/#29dda03c1636

45

"The most influential US liberals: 1–20". The Daily Telegraph. London. October 31, 2007. Retrieved May 20, 2010. Retrieved from: https://www.telegraph.co.uk/news/worldnews/1435442/The-most-influential-US-liberals-1-20.html

46

Mowbray, Nicole (March 2, 2003). "Oprah's path to power". *The Guardian*. UK. Retrieved August 25, 2008. Retrieved from: https://www.theguardian.com/media/2003/mar/02/pressandpublishing.usnews1

47

Mowbray, Nicole (March 2, 2003). "Oprah's path to power". The Guardian. UK. Retrieved August 25, 2008.
Oprah Winfrey. Forbes Special Report: The World's Billionaires (2006). October 2006. Retrieved August 25, 2008.

48

Oprah Winfrey. *Forbes Special Report: The World's Billionaires (2006)*. October 2006. Retrieved August 25, 2008. Retrieved from: https://www.forbes.com/lists/2006/10/O0ZT.html

49

"Oprah Winfrey Biography and Interview". Achievement.org. American Academy of Achievement. Winfrey has said in interviews that 'my name had been chosen from the Bible. My Aunt Ida had chosen the name, but nobody really knew how to spell it, so it went down as "Orpah" on my birth certificate, but people didn't

know how to pronounce it, so they put the "P" before the "R" in every place else other than the birth certificate. On the birth certificate it is Orpah, but then it got translated to Oprah, so here we are.'
"Oprah Winfrey in Melbourne for Australian tour 2015 spreads a message of love, reveals lost child". News.com.au. Retrieved September 25, 2017.
"Oprah Winfrey signs with King World Productions for new three-year contract to continue as host and producer of "The Oprah Winfrey Show" through 2010–2011" (Press release). King World Productions. August 4, 2004. Archived from the original on February 10, 2007. Retrieved September 24, 2009.
"Oprah Winfrey". Biography. Retrieved March 5, 2022.
Oswald, Brad (January 26, 2010). "Yes, she's Queen of all Media, but to Discovery, she's Life itself". Winnipeg Free Press. Retrieved August 22, 2014.
Denenberg, Dennis; Roscoe, Lorraine (September 1, 2016). 50 American Heroes Every Kid Should Meet (2nd Revised ed.). Millbrook Press. ISBN 9781512413298.
Miller, Matthew (May 6, 2009). "The Wealthiest Black Americans". Forbes. Retrieved August 26, 2010.
"Oprah Winfrey buys $14 million ski chalet in Colorado". The Telegraph. February 4, 2016.
"Biography.com". Biography.com. Archived from the original on January 13, 2010. Retrieved August 26, 2010.
"Oprah Winfrey Debuts as First African-American On businessweek's Annual Ranking of 'Americas Top Philanthropists'" (Press release). Urban Mecca. November 19, 2004. Archived from the original on November 20, 2004. Retrieved August 25, 2008.
Meldrum Henley-on-Klip, Andrew (January 3, 2007). "'Their story is my story' Oprah opens $40m school for South African girls". The Guardian. UK. Retrieved March 4, 2007.
"The most influential US liberals: 1–20". The Daily Telegraph. London. October 31, 2007. Archived *from the original on January 10, 2022. Retrieved May 20, 2010.*

50

Mowbray, N. (2003). Oprah's path to power. *The Guardian*. Retrieved from: https://www.theguardian.com/media/2003/mar/02/pressandpublishing.usnews1

51

Smolenyak, Megan Smolenyak (November–December 2008). "The quest for Obama's Irish roots". *Ancestry*. **26** (6): 46–47, 49. ISSN 1075-475X. Retrieved December 20, 2011. Retrieved from: https://books.google.com/books?Id=itgeaaaambaj&pg=PA46#v=onepage&q&f=false

52

Ochieng, Philip (November 1, 2004). "From home squared to the US Senate: how Barack Obama was lost and found". *The eastafrican*. Nairobi. Archived from the original on September 27, 2007. Retrieved from: https://web.archive.org/web/20070927223905/http://www.nationmedia.com/eastafrican/01112004/Features/PA2-11.html

53

Ripley, Amanda (April 9, 2008). "The story of Barack Obama's mother". *Time*. Retrieved April 9, 2007.

54

"Keeping Hope Alive: Barack Obama Puts Family First". The Oprah Winfrey Show. October 18, 2006. Retrieved June 24, 2008. Retrieved from: http://www.oprah.com/world/keeping-hope-alive/10

55

Karl, Jonathan (May 25, 2012). "Obama and his pot-smoking "choom gang"". ABC News. Retrieved May 25, 2012. Retrieved from:

https://abcnews.go.com/blogs/politics/2012/05/obama-and-his-pot-smoking-choom-gang/

56

Scott, Janny (July 30, 2007). "Obama's account of New York often differs from what others say". *The New York Times*. P. B1. Retrieved July 31, 2007. Retrieved from: https://www.nytimes.com/2007/10/30/us/politics/30obama.html

57

Horsley, Scott (July 9, 2008). "Obama's Early Brush with Financial Markets". NPR. Retrieved July 17, 2017. Retrieved from: https://www.npr.org/templates/story/story.php?Storyid=92337754

58

Obama (2006), pp. 327–332. See also: Brown, Sarah (December 7, 2005). "Obama '85 masters balancing act". The Daily Princetonian. Archived from the original on February 20, 2009. Retrieved February 9, 2009. Retrieved from: https://web.archive.org/web/20090220165725/http://www.dailyprincetonian.com/2005/12/07/14049/

59

Fornek, Scott (October 3, 2007). "Michelle Obama: 'He Swept Me Off My Feet'". Chicago Sun-Times. Archived from the original on January 18, 2010. Retrieved April 28, 2008. Retrieved from: https://www.webcitation.org/5msgzdbmo?Url=http://www.suntimes.com/news/politics/obama/585261,CST-NWS-wedding03.stng

60

Martin, Jonathan (July 4, 2008). "Born on the 4th of July". Politico. Archived from the original on July 10, 2008. Retrieved July 10, 2008. Retrieved from:

61

"Obamas choose private Sidwell Friends School". International Herald Tribune. November 22, 2008. Archived from the original on January 29, 2009. Retrieved July 2, 2015. Retrieved from:
https://web.archive.org/web/20090129194323/http://iht.com/articles/ap/2008/11/22/america/Obama-School.php

62

"American President: Barack Obama". Miller Center of Public Affairs, University of Virginia. 2009. Archived from the original on January 23, 2009. Retrieved January 23, 2009. Religion: Christian. Retrieved from:
https://web.archive.org/web/20090123091100/http://millercenter.org/academic/americanpresident/obama

63

Miller, Lisa (July 18, 2008). "Finding his faith". Newsweek. Archived from the original on February 6, 2010. Retrieved February 4, 2010. He is now a Christian, having been baptized in the early 1990s at Trinity United Church of Christ in Chicago. Retrieved from:
https://www.newsweek.com/cover-story-barack-obamas-christian-journey-92611

64

Pulliam, Sarah; Olsen, Ted (January 23, 2008). "Q&A: Barack Obama". *Christianity Today.* Retrieved January 4, 2013. Retrieved from:
https://www.christianitytoday.com/ct/2008/januaryweb-only/104-32.0.html?Start=2

65

Charles Babington; Darlene Superville (September 28, 2010). "Obama 'Christian By Choice': President Responds To Questioner". Huffpost. Associated Press. Archived from the original on May 11, 2011. Retrieved from:
https://web.archive.org/web/20111126115630/http://www

.huffingtonpost.com:80/2010/09/28/obama-christian-by-choice_n_742124.html

66

"Obama's church choice likely to be scrutinized". MSNBC. Associated Press. November 17, 2008. Retrieved January 20, 2009. Retrieved from:

67

Parker, Ashley. "As the Obamas Celebrate Christmas, Rituals of Faith Become Less Visible," The New York Times, December 28, 2013. Retrieved January 15, 2017. Retrieved from: https://www.nytimes.com/2013/12/29/us/as-the-obamas-celebrate-christmas-rituals-of-faith-stay-on-the-sidelines.html

68

Gilgoff, Dan. "TIME Report, White House Reaction Raise More Questions About Obama's Church Hunt," U.S. News & World Report, June 30, 2009. Retrieved January 15, 2017. Retrieved from: https://www.usnews.com/news/blogs/god-and-country/2009/06/30/time-report-white-house-reaction-raise-more-questions-about-obamas-church-hunt

69

""First Lady: We Use Sundays For Naps If We're Not Going To Church", CBS DC, April 22, 2014. Retrieved January 15, 2017. Retrieved from: https://washington.cbslocal.com/2014/04/22/first-lady-we-use-sundays-for-naps-if-were-not-going-to-church/

70

Sentinel News Wire (December 29, 2018). Gallup Poll Names Barack and Michelle Obama Most Admired Man and Woman of 2018. *Gallup News*. Retrieved from: https://lasentinel.net/gallup-poll-names-barack-and-michelle-obama-most-admired-man-and-woman-of-2018.html

71

Sentinel News Wire (December 29, 2018). Gallup Poll Names Barack and Michelle Obama Most Admired Man and Woman of 2018. *Gallup News.* Retrieved from: https://lasentinel.net/gallup-poll-names-barack-and-michelle-obama-most-admired-man-and-woman-of-2018.html

72

Reyes, B.J. (February 8, 2007). "Punahou left lasting impression on Obama". *Honolulu Star-Bulletin.* Retrieved February 10, 2007. *As a teenager, Obama went to parties and sometimes sought out gatherings on military bases or at the University of Hawaii that were attended mostly by blacks.*
Elliott, Philip (November 21, 2007). "Obama gets blunt with N.H. students". The Boston Globe. *Associated Press. P. 8A. Archived from the original on April 7, 2012.* Retrieved May 18, 2012.
Karl, Jonathan (May 25, 2012). "Obama and his pot-smoking "choom gang"". *ABC News.* Retrieved May 25, 2012.
Obama, Barack (2004) [1995]. Dreams from My Father: A Story of Race and Inheritance. *Pp. 93–94.* ISBN 978-0-307-39412-5. Retrieved June 3, 2016.
Maraniss, David (2012). Barack Obama: The Story. *Pages with "choom gang".* ISBN 978-1-4391-6753-3. Retrieved June 3, 2016. For analysis of the political impact of the quote and Obama's more recent admission that he smoked marijuana as a teenager ("When I was a kid, I inhaled"), see:
Seelye, Katharine Q. (October 24, 2006). "Obama offers more variations from the norm". *The New York Times. P. A21.* Retrieved October 29, 2006.
Romano, Lois (January 3, 2007). "Effect of Obama's candor remains to be seen". *The Washington Post. P. A1.* Retrieved January 14, 2007.
"FRONTLINE The Choice 2012". *PBS. October 9, 2012.* Retrieved October 29, 2012.

73

Wan, William; Clement, Scott (November 18, 2016). "Most of the world doesn't actually see America the way Trump said it did". *The Washington Post*. Retrieved February 8, 2021.

74

Andrew Finstuen, **Anne Blue Wills** and **Grant Wacker (2017).** *Billy Graham American Pilgrim*. Oxford University Press. ISBN: 9780190683528.

75

Wikepedia (2023). Evangelicalism. Retrieved from: https://en.wikipedia.org/wiki/Evangelicalism

76

"Who led Billy Graham to Christ..." Archives, Billy Graham Center, Wheaton College. Archived from the original on May 13, 2011. Retrieved May 12, 2011. Retrieved from: http://archive.wikiwix.com/cache/20110513224056/http://www.wheaton.edu/bgc/archives/faq/13.htm

77

Gibbs, Nancy; Ostling, Richard N. (November 15, 1993). "God's Billy Pulpit". *Time*. Retrieved November 7, 2011.

78

Schier, H. Edward (2013). "Civil Rights Movement". The Battle of the Three Wills: As It Relates to Good & Evil. ISBN 978-1-4817-5876-5.

Miller, Steven P. (2009). Billy Graham and the Rise of the Republican South. University of Pennsylvania Press. ISBN 978-0-8122-4151-8.

79

Wikipedia (2023). Billy Graham. Retrieved from: https://en.wikipedia.org/wiki/Billy_Graham

80

Wacker, G. (2018). How an aging Billy Graham approached his own death. *Washington Post.* Retrieved from: Https://www.washingtonpost.com/news/acts-of-faith/wp/2018/02/21/how-an-aging-billy-graham-approached-his-own-death/

81

Staff, journalnow. "Billy Graham has brain shunt adjusted". *Winston-Salem Journal.* Retrieved February 22, 2018. Retrieved from: https://journalnow.com/news/state_region/billy-graham-has-brain-shunt-adjusted/article_b1919452-0c66-560d-8e15-a283bfe48a7a.html

Wacker, G. (2018). How an aging Billy Graham approached his own death. *Washington Post.* Retrieved from: Https://www.washingtonpost.com/news/acts-of-faith/wp/2018/02/21/how-an-aging-billy-graham-approached-his-own-death/

82

"A Family at Cross-Purposes". The Washington Post. December 13, 2006. Retrieved August 18, 2007.
" "Graham's wife in coma, close to death; both will be buried at library". The Herald. June 14, 2007. Retrieved February 28, 2018.

83

"A Family at Cross-Purposes". The Washington Post. December 13, 2006. Retrieved August 18, 2007. Retrieved from: https://www.washingtonpost.com/wp-dyn/content/article/2006/12/12/AR2006121201338.html

84

Goodey, Emma (21 December 2015), "Queen Elizabeth the Queen Mother", The Royal Family, Royal Household, archived from the original on 7 May 2016,

retrieved 18 April 2016. Retrieved from:
https://www.royal.uk/queen-elizabeth-queen-mother

85

Fisher, Connie (20 April 1947), "A speech by the Queen on
her 21st birthday", *The Royal Family*, Royal
Household, archived from the original on 3 January 2017,
retrieved 18 April 2016. Retrieved from:
https://www.royal.uk/21st-birthday-speech-21-april-1947

86

Edwards, Phil (31 October 2000), "The Real Prince
Philip", Channel 4, archived from the original on 9 February
2010, retrieved 23 September 2009. Retrieved from:
https://web.archive.org/web/20100209095416/http://www
.channel4.com/history/microsites/R/real_lives/prince_phili
p_t.html;
https://www.telegraph.co.uk/news/uknews/1400208/Philip
-the-one-constant-through-her-life.html :

Brandreth, Gyles Daubeney, (2004). Philip and Elizabeth:
Portrait of a Marriage. Archives.
Https://archive.org/details/philipelizabeth0000bran

Davies, Caroline (20 April 2006), "Philip, the one constant
through her life", The Daily Telegraph,
London, archived from the original on 9 January 2022,
retrieved 23 September 2009. Retrieved from:
https://www.telegraph.co.uk/news/uknews/1400208/Philip
-the-one-constant-through-her-life.html

87

Hoey, Brian (2002). Her Majesty : fifty regal years. Archives.
Retrieved from:
https://archive.org/details/hermajestyfiftyr0000hoey_y9q3

88

Lacey, Robert *(2002), Royal: Her Majesty Queen Elizabeth II, Little, Brown,* ISBN 0-316-85940-0

89

Brandreth, Gyles Daubeney, (2004). Philip and Elizabeth: Portrait of a Marriage. Archives. Https://archive.org/details/philipelizabeth0000bran

90

Hoey, Brian (2022), Her Majesty Queen Elizabeth II: Platinum Jubilee Celebration: 70 Years: 1952–2022, Rizzoli, ISBN 978-1-84165-939-8

91

Bradford, Sarah (2012), Queen Elizabeth II: Her Life in Our Times, Penguin, ISBN 978-0-670-91911-6
Bradford, Sarah *(2002), Elizabeth: A Biography of Her Majesty the Queen (2nd ed.), Penguin,* ISBN 978-0-14-193333-7
Bradford, Sarah (2012), Queen Elizabeth II: Her Life in Our Times, Penguin, ISBN 978-0-670-91911-6
Pimlott, Ben *(2001), The Queen: Elizabeth II and the Monarchy, harpercollins,* ISBN 0-00-255494-1
Bond, Jennie (2006). Elizabeth : eighty glorious years. Archives. Retrieved from: https://archive.org/details/elizabetheightyg0000bond

92

Pimlott, Ben *(2001), The Queen: Elizabeth II and the Monarchy, harpercollins,* ISBN 0-00-255494-1

93

"Queen's 'fantasy assassin' jailed", BBC News, 14 September 1981, archived from the original on 28 July 2011, retrieved 21 June 2010. Retrieved from: http://news.bbc.co.uk/onthisday/hi/dates/stories/september/14/newsid_2516000/2516713.stm

Mcneilly, Hamish (1 March 2018), "Intelligence documents confirm assassination attempt on Queen Elizabeth in New Zealand", *The Sydney Morning Herald*, archived from the original on 26 June 2019, retrieved 1 March 2018. Retrieved from: http://news.bbc.co.uk/onthisday/hi/dates/stories/septemb er/14/newsid_2516000/2516713.stm
Ainge Roy, Eleanor (13 January 2018), "'Damn ... I missed': the incredible story of the day the Queen was nearly shot", *The Guardian*, archived from the original on 1 March 2018, retrieved 1 March 2018. Retrieved from: https://www.theguardian.com/uk-news/2018/jan/13/queen-elizabeth-assassination-attempt-new-zealand-1981

94

Lacey, Robert *(2002), Royal: Her Majesty Queen Elizabeth II, Little, Brown,* ISBN 0-316-85940-0

95

Bogert, Carroll R. (13 October 1986), "Queen Elizabeth II Arrives In Peking for 6-Day Visit", The Washington Post, ISSN 0190-8286, retrieved 12 October 2022. Retrieved from: https://www.washingtonpost.com/archive/politics/1986/1 0/13/queen-elizabeth-ii-arrives-in-peking-for-6-day-visit/60fd4c89-992c-4399-ae6a-3e38f15f7aad/

96

"Elizabeth Set to Beat Victoria's Record as Longest Reigning Monarch in British History", huffpost, 6 September 2014, archived from the original on 26 September 2014,

Modh, Shrikant (11 September 2015), "The Longest Reigning Monarch Queen Elizabeth II", Philately News, archived from the original on 1 December 2017,

Weiss, Hedy (24 August 2017), "Enthralling 'Audience' puts Britain's queen in room with politicians", Chicago Sun-Times, archived from the original on 26 March 2022,
"Queen Elizabeth II is now world's oldest monarch", *The Hindu, 24 January 2015, archived from the original on 2 January 2020,*
Rayner, Gordon (23 January 2015), "Queen becomes world's oldest monarch following death of King Abdullah of Saudi Arabia", *The Daily Telegraph, archived from the original on 10 January 2022,*
"Thailand's King Bhumibol Adulyadej dies at 88", *BBC News, 13 October 2016, archived from the original on 13 October 2016,*
Addley, Esther (13 October 2016), "Queen Elizabeth II is longest-reigning living monarch after Thai king's death", *The Guardian, archived from the original on 23 April 2022,*
"Queen Elizabeth II will be the world's oldest head of state if Robert Mugabe is toppled", *MSN, 14 November 2017, archived from the original on 15 November 2017,*
Rayner, Gordon (29 January 2017), "The Blue Sapphire Jubilee: Queen will not celebrate 65th anniversary but instead sit in 'quiet contemplation' remembering father's death", *The Daily Telegraph, archived from the original on 10 January 2022,*
"Queen and Prince Philip portraits released to mark 70th anniversary", *The Guardian, Press Association, 20 November 2017, archived from the original on 20 November 2017,*
Bilefsky, Dan (2 August 2017), "Prince Philip Makes His Last Solo Appearance, After 65 Years in the Public Eye", *The New York Times, archived from the original on 25 December 2007,*

97

"Prince Philip: The Queen says his death has 'left a huge void' – Duke of York", BBC News, 11 April 2021, archived from the original on 8 September 2022, Retrieved from: https://www.bbc.com/news/uk-56710086

98

"Man admits treason after breaking into grounds of Windsor Castle with crossbow 'to kill Queen'", Sky News, 3 February

2023, retrieved 3 February 2023. Retrieved from:
https://news.sky.com/story/man-admits-trying-to-harm-queen-after-being-caught-in-grounds-of-windsor-castle-with-a-crossbow-12802059

99

"Our structure", *Church of Scotland, 22 February 2010*, archived *from the original on 25 January 2020*, "Queen meets Pope Francis at the Vatican", *BBC News, 3 April 2014*, archived *from the original on 28 May 2017*, retrieved 28 March 2017

100

"Queen's doctors concerned for her health – palace", BBC News, 8 September 2022, archived from the original on 8 September 2022, retrieved 8 September 2022

Davies, Caroline (8 September 2022), "Queen under medical supervision at Balmoral after doctors' concerns", The Guardian, archived from the original on 8 September 2022, retrieved 8 September 2022

"Queen under medical supervision as doctors are concerned for her health. Prince Charles, Camilla and Prince William are currently travelling to Balmoral, Clarence House and Kensington Palace said", Sky News, 8 September 2022, archived from the original on 8 September 2022, retrieved 8 September 2022

Shaw, Neil (8 September 2022), "Duke of York, Princess Anne and Prince Edward all called to Queen's side", Plymouth Live, archived from the original on 8 September 2022, retrieved 8 September 2022

Coughlan, Sean (29 September 2022), "Queen's cause of death given as 'old age' on death certificate", BBC News, archived from the original on 1 October 2022, retrieved 29 September 2022

Prynn, Jonathan (9 September 2022), "Queen died 'with Charles and Anne by side as other royals dashed to Balmoral'", Evening Standard, archived from the original on 9 September 2022, retrieved 17 October 2022

"Queen Elizabeth II has died", BBC News, 8 September 2022, archived from the original on 8 September 2022, retrieved 8 September 2022
Kottasová, Ivana; Picheta, Rob; Foster, Max; Said-Moorhouse, Lauren (8 September 2022), "Queen Elizabeth II dies at 96", CNN, archived from the original on 8 September 2022, retrieved 8 September 2022

"Operation Unicorn: what happens after the Queen's death in Scotland?", The Guardian, 8 September 2022, archived from the original on 8 September 2022, retrieved 4 October 2022

"Operation Unicorn", Not "London Bridge": The Codename For Queen's Death", NDTV.com, Agence France-Presse, 8 September 2022, archived from the original on 21 September 2022, retrieved 4 October 2022

Silver, Christopher (13 September 2022), "Elizabeth, the last Queen of Scots?", Prospect, archived from the original on 13 September 2022, retrieved 26 September 2022

"Queen Elizabeth died of 'old age', death certificate says", The Guardian, 29 September 2022, archived from the original on 4 December 2022, retrieved 8 December 2022

101

"Queen 'will do her job for life'", BBC News, 19 April 2006, archived from the original on 8 December 2008, retrieved 4 February 2007. Retrieved from: http://news.bbc.co.uk/2/hi/uk_news/4921120.stm
Shawcross, William (2002), Queen and Country, mcclelland & Stewart, ISBN 0-7710-8056-5

Fisher, Connie (25 December 2000), "Christmas Broadcast 2000", *The Royal Family, Royal Household, archived from the original on 7 May 2016, retrieved 18 April 2016.* Retrieved from: https://www.royal.uk/christmas-broadcast-2000

102

"About The Patron's Lunch", The Patron's Lunch, 5 September 2014, archived from the original on 17 March 2016, retrieved 28 April 2016. Retrieved from: http://www.thepatronslunch.com/about-2
Hodge, Kate (11 June 2012), "The Queen has done more for charity than any other monarch in history", The Guardian, archived from the original on 22 February 2021, retrieved 25 February 2021. Retrieved from: https://www.theguardian.com/voluntary-sector-network/2012/jun/11/queen-charitable-support

"80 facts about The Queen", Royal Household, archived from the original on 21 March 2009, retrieved 20 June 2010. Retrieved from: https://web.archive.org/web/20090321215851/http://www.royal.gov.uk/latestnewsanddiary/Factfiles/80factsabouttheq ueen.aspx
Bush, Karen (2007), Everything Dogs Expect You to Know, London: New Holland, ISBN 978-1-84537-954-4.

Pierce, Andrew (1 October 2007), "Hug for Queen Elizabeth's first corgi", The Daily Telegraph, archived from the original on 10 January 2022, retrieved 21 September 2012. Https://www.telegraph.co.uk/news/uknews/1564705/Hug-for-Queen-Elizabeths-first-corgi.html

Delacourt, Susan (25 May 2012), "When the Queen is your boss", Toronto Star, archived from the original on 7 March 2013, retrieved 27 May 2012. Https://www.thestar.com/news/world/royals/2012/05/25/when_the_queen_is_your_boss.html

103

Elston, Laura PA Court Reporter (2022). How Much Does the Royal Family Cost? A Breakdown of the Key Figures. *THE PRESS ASSOCIATION.* Retrieved from: https://www.bloomberg.com/news/articles/2022-06-29/how-much-does-the-royal-family-cost-a-breakdown-of-the-key-figures?Leadsource=uverify%20wall

Shehadi, Sebastian (2022). How much money does the monarchy bring to the UK? Some £1.7bn a year...*Investment Monitor.* Retrieved from: https://www.investmentmonitor.ai/features/how-much-money-does-the-monarchy-bring-to-the-uk/#:~:text=The%20Accounts%20for%20the%20Sovereign,from%20the%20previous%2012%20months.

104

Richard Nixon's Genealogy. Retrieved from: https://www.archives.com/genealogy/president-nixon.html

105

Aitken, Jonathan (1996). Nixon: A Life. Washington, D.C.: Regnery Publishing. ISBN 978-0-89526-720-7.

106

Nixon Presidential Library and Museum. Retrieved from: https://web.archive.org/web/20131021225424/http://www.nixonlibrary.gov/index.php

107

Nixon Presidential Library and Museum. Retrieved from: https://web.archive.org/web/20131021225424/http://www.nixonlibrary.gov/index.php

108

Ambrose, Stephen E. (1989). Nixon: The Triumph of a Politician 1962–1972. Vol. II. New York: Simon & Schuster. ISBN 978-0-671-72506-8.

Office of the Federal Register (1999). "New Actions To Prevent Illnesses And Accidents". *Public Papers of the Presidents of the United States, Richard Nixon, 1971. National Archives and Records Service. General Services Administration*. ISBN 978-0-16-058863-1.

"Statement on Signing the National Sickle Cell Anemia Control Act". *The American Presidency Project. University of California, Santa Barbara. May 16, 1972.*

Wailoo, Keith (2001). Dying in the City of the Blues: Sickle Cell Anemia and the Politics of Race and Health. *University of North Carolina Press. P. 165*. ISBN 978-0-8078-4896-8.

Boger, John Charles (2005). School Resegregation: Must the South Turn Back?. Chapel Hill, N.C.: University of North Carolina Press. ISBN 978-0-8078-5613-0.

109

Ambrose, Stephen E. (1989). Nixon: The Triumph of a Politician 1962–1972. Vol. II. New York: Simon & Schuster. ISBN 978-0-671-72506-8.

Office of the Federal Register (1999). "New Actions To Prevent Illnesses And Accidents". *Public Papers of the Presidents of the United States, Richard Nixon, 1971. National Archives and Records Service. General Services Administration*. ISBN 978-0-16-058863-1.

"Statement on Signing the National Sickle Cell Anemia Control Act". *The American Presidency Project. University of California, Santa Barbara. May 16, 1972.*

Wailoo, Keith (2001). Dying in the City of the Blues: Sickle Cell Anemia and the Politics of Race and Health. *University of North Carolina Press. P. 165*. ISBN 978-0-8078-4896-8.

Boger, John Charles (2005). School Resegregation: Must the South Turn Back?. Chapel Hill, N.C.: University of North Carolina Press. ISBN 978-0-8078-5613-0.

110

Small, Melvin, ed. (2011). *A Companion to Richard M. Nixon.* Oxford: Wiley-Blackwell. ISBN 978-1-4443-3017-5 Olson, Keith W. "Watergate", pp. 481–496.

Rottinghaus, Brandon; Vaughn, Justin S. (February 19, 2018). "How Does Trump Stack Up Against the Best—and Worst—Presidents?". *The New York Times.* Archived *from the original on March 5, 2018.* Retrieved March 6, 2018.

"Presidential Historians Survey 2017". *C-Span.* Archived *from the original on March 1, 2017.* Retrieved May 14, 2018.*Retrieved from:* https://www.c-span.org/presidentsurvey2017/?Page=overall

"Siena's 6th Presidential Expert Poll 1982–2018". *Siena College Research Institute. February 13, 2019.* Archived *from the original on July 19, 2019.* Retrieved July 19, 2019. *Retrieved from:* https://scri.siena.edu/2019/02/13/sienas-6th-presidential-expert-poll-1982-2018/

111

Perry, Bruce (1991). Malcolm: The Life of a Man Who Changed Black America. *Barrytown, New York: Station Hill.* ISBN 978-0-88268-103-0.

Lomax, Louis E. *(1963). When the Word Is Given: A Report on Elijah Muhammad, Malcolm X, and the Black Muslim World. Cleveland: World Publishing.* OCLC 1071204.

112

Perry, Bruce (1991). Malcolm: The Life of a Man Who Changed Black America. *Barrytown, New York: Station Hill.* ISBN 978-0-88268-103-0.

Lomax, Louis E. *(1963). When the Word Is Given: A Report on Elijah Muhammad, Malcolm X, and the Black Muslim World. Cleveland: World Publishing.* OCLC 1071204.

113

Dozier, Vickki (February 21, 2015). "How Malcolm X's murder rippled through his hometown". Lansing State Journal. Lansing, Michigan. Retrieved from:
https://www.lansingstatejournal.com/story/news/local/2015/02/20/malcolm-xs-murder-rippled-hometown/23769113/

Perry, Bruce (1991). Malcolm: The Life of a Man Who Changed Black America. Barrytown, New York: Station Hill. ISBN 978-0-88268-103-0. Retrieved from:
Https://archive.org/details/malcolmlifeofman00perr

114

Perry, Bruce (1991). Malcolm: The Life of a Man Who Changed Black America. Barrytown, New York: Station Hill. ISBN 978-0-88268-103-0. Retrieved from:
https://archive.org/details/malcolmlifeofman00perr

115

Marable, Manning *(2011).* Malcolm X: A Life of Reinvention. *New York: Viking.* ISBN 978-0-670-02220-5. *Retrieved from:*
https://en.wikipedia.org/wiki/Malcolm_X:_A_Life_of_Reinvention

Marable, Manning (2009). "Rediscovering Malcolm's Life: A Historian's Adventures in Living History". In Marable, Manning; Aidi, Hishaam D (eds.). Black Routes to Islam. New York: Palgrave Macmillan. ISBN 978-1-4039-8400-5.

116

Marable, Manning (2011). Malcolm X: A Life of Reinvention. New York: Viking. ISBN 978-0-670-02220-5.

Malcolm X; Haley, Alex (1992) [1965]. The Autobiography of Malcolm X. New York: One World. ISBN 978-0-345-37671-8. Citations in this article refer to this edition, of the many that have been published.

Lord, Lewis; Thornton, Jeannye; Bodipo-Memba, Alejandro (November 15, 1992). "The Legacy of Malcolm X". U.S. News & World Report. P. 5. Archived from the original on January 14, 2012. Retrieved March 20, 2018. Retrieved from: https://web.archive.org/web/20120114124627/http://www.usnews.com/usnews/culture/articles/921123/archive_018698.htm

117

Natambu, Kofi (2002). The Life and Work of Malcolm X. Indianapolis: Alpha Books. ISBN 978-0-02-864218-5.

Malcolm X; Haley, Alex (1992) [1965]. The Autobiography of Malcolm X. New York: One World. ISBN 978-0-345-37671-8.

Marable, Manning (2011). Malcolm X: A Life of Reinvention. New York: Viking. ISBN 978-0-670-02220-5.

118

"Timeline of Malcolm X's Life". PBS. Archived from the original on November 9, 2020. Retrieved December 31, 2020. Retrieved from: https://www.pbs.org/wgbh/americanexperience/features/malcolmx-timeline-malcolm-xs-life/

119

Natambu, Kofi (2002). *The Life and Work of Malcolm X.* Indianapolis: Alpha Books. ISBN 978-0-02-864218-5.

Perry, Bruce (1991). *Malcolm: The Life of a Man Who Changed Black America*. Barrytown, New York: Station Hill. ISBN 978-0-88268-103-0.

120

Natambu, Kofi (2002). *The Life and Work of Malcolm X*. Indianapolis: Alpha Books. ISBN 978-0-02-864218-5.

Perry, Bruce (1991). *Malcolm: The Life of a Man Who Changed Black America*. Barrytown, New York: Station Hill. ISBN 978-0-88268-103-0.

121

Natambu, Kofi (2002). *The Life and Work of Malcolm X*. Indianapolis: Alpha Books. ISBN 978-0-02-864218-5.

Perry, Bruce (1991). *Malcolm: The Life of a Man Who Changed Black America*. Barrytown, New York: Station Hill. ISBN 978-0-88268-103-0.

Malcolm X; Haley, Alex (1992) [1965]. The Autobiography of Malcolm X. New York: One World. ISBN 978-0-345-37671-8.

122

Marable, Manning (2011). *Malcolm X: A Life of Reinvention*. New York: Viking. ISBN 978-0-670-02220-5.

Natambu, Kofi (2002). *The Life and Work of Malcolm X*. Indianapolis: Alpha Books. ISBN 978-0-02-864218-5.

123

Marable, Manning (2011). *Malcolm X: A Life of Reinvention*. New York: Viking. ISBN 978-0-670-02220-5.

124

Natambu, Kofi (2002). *The Life and Work of Malcolm X*. Indianapolis: Alpha Books. ISBN 978-0-02-864218-5.

125

Marable, Manning (2011). *Malcolm X: A Life of Reinvention.* New York: Viking. ISBN 978-0-670-02220-5.

Perry, Bruce (1991). *Malcolm: The Life of a Man Who Changed Black America.* Barrytown, New York: Station Hill. ISBN 978-0-88268-103-0.

126

Norbert Sachser,Sylvia Kaiser,and Michael B. Hennessy (2013). Behavioural profiles are shaped by social experience: when, how and why. Philos Trans R Soc Lond B Biol Sci. 2013 May 19; 368(1618): 20120344.
Doi: 10.1098/rstb.2012.0344. Retrieved from: https://www.ncbi.nlm.nih.gov/pmc/articles/PMC3638447/

127

Marable, Manning (2011). *Malcolm X: A Life of Reinvention.* New York: Viking. ISBN 978-0-670-02220-5.

128

Marable, Manning (2011). *Malcolm X: A Life of Reinvention.* New York: Viking. ISBN 978-0-670-02220-5.

Perry, Bruce (1991). *Malcolm: The Life of a Man Who Changed Black America.* Barrytown, New York: Station Hill. ISBN 978-0-88268-103-0.

130

Marable, Manning (2011). *Malcolm X: A Life of Reinvention.* New York: Viking. ISBN 978-0-670-02220-5.

Perry, Bruce (1991). *Malcolm: The Life of a Man Who Changed Black America.* Barrytown, New York: Station Hill. ISBN 978-0-88268-103-0

131

Lomax, Louis E. (1963). *When the Word Is Given: A Report on Elijah Muhammad, Malcolm X, and the Black Muslim World.* Cleveland: World Publishing. OCLC 1071204.

Natambu, Kofi (2002). *The Life and Work of Malcolm X.* Indianapolis: Alpha Books. ISBN 978-0-02-864218-5.

Marable, Manning (2011). *Malcolm X: A Life of Reinvention.* New York: Viking. ISBN 978-0-670-02220-5.

132

Lomax, Louis E. (1963). *When the Word Is Given: A Report on Elijah Muhammad, Malcolm X, and the Black Muslim World.* Cleveland: World Publishing. OCLC 1071204

Natambu, Kofi (2002). *The Life and Work of Malcolm X.* Indianapolis: Alpha Books. ISBN 978-0-02-864218-5.

Cone, James H. (1991). *Martin & Malcolm & America: A Dream or a Nightmare.* Maryknoll, New York: Orbis Books. ISBN 978-0-88344-721-5.

West, Cornel (1984). "The Paradox of the Afro-American Rebellion". In Sayres, Sohnya; Stephanson, Anders; Aronowitz, Stanley; Jameson, Fredric (eds.). *The 60s Without Apology.* Minneapolis: University of Minnesota Press. P. 51. ISBN 978-0-8166-1336-6.

133

Moore, R. Laurence (1987). *Religious Outsiders and the Making of Americans.* Oxford University Press. ISBN 978-0-19-536399-9.

Lomax, Louis E. (1963). *When the Word Is Given: A Report on Elijah Muhammad, Malcolm X, and the Black Muslim World.* Cleveland: World Publishing. OCLC 1071204.

Norwood, Stephen H.; Pollack, Eunice G. (2020). "White Devils, Satanic Jews: The Nation of Islam From Fard to Farrakhan". *Modern Judaism - A Journal of Jewish Ideas and Experience*. 40 (2): 137–168. Doi:10.1093/mj/kjaa006 – via Oxford University Press.

Pollack, Eunice G. (2013). *Racializing Antisemitism: Black Militants, Jews, and Israel 1950-present* (PDF). Vidal Sassoon International Center for the Study of Antisemitism, Henrew University of Israel.

134

Cone, James H. (1991). *Martin & Malcolm & America: A Dream or a Nightmare*. Maryknoll, New York: Orbis Books. ISBN 978-0-88344-721-5.

Marable, Manning (2011). *Malcolm X: A Life of Reinvention*. New York: Viking. ISBN 978-0-670-02220-5.

135

Natambu, Kofi (2002). *The Life and Work of Malcolm X*. Indianapolis: Alpha Books. ISBN 978-0-02-864218-5.

Remnick, David (1999) [1998]. *King of the World: Muhammed Ali and the Rise of an American Hero*. New York: Vintage Books. P. 165. ISBN 978-0-375-70229-7.

Ali, Muhammad (2004). *The Soul of a Butterfly: Reflections on Life's Journey*. With Hana Yasmeen Ali. New York: Simon & Schuster. ISBN 978-0-7432-5569-1.

136

Marable, Manning (2011). *Malcolm X: A Life of Reinvention*. New York: Viking. ISBN 978-0-670-02220-5.

Marsh, Clifton E. (2000) [1996]. *The Lost-Found Nation of Islam in America*. Lanham, Maryland: Scarecrow Press. ISBN 978-1-57886-008-1.

137

Branch, Taylor (1998). *Pillar of Fire: America in the King Years, 1963–65*. New York: Simon & Schuster. ISBN 978-0-684-80819-2.
Marable, Manning (2011). *Malcolm X: A Life of Reinvention*. New York: Viking. ISBN 978-0-670-02220-5.

138

Perry, Bruce (1991). *Malcolm: The Life of a Man Who Changed Black America*. Barrytown, New York: Station Hill. ISBN 978-0-88268-103-0.

"Malcolm X Exposes Elijah Muhammad". *Youtube*. Retrieved August 24, 2022. Retrieved from: https://www.youtube.com/watch?V=obdzhg3qsim

139

"Malcolm X Scores U.S. and Kennedy". *The New York Times*. December 2, 1963. P. 21. Retrieved June 19, 2018.

Perry, Bruce (1991). *Malcolm: The Life of a Man Who Changed Black America*. Barrytown, New York: Station Hill. ISBN 978-0-88268-103-0.

140

Perry, Bruce (1991). *Malcolm: The Life of a Man Who Changed Black America*. Barrytown, New York: Station Hill. ISBN 978-0-88268-103-0.

141

Handler, M. S. (March 9, 1964). "Malcolm X Splits with Muhammad". *The New York Times*. P. 1. Retrieved June 19, 2018.

142

Austin, David (Fall 2007). "All Roads Led to Montreal: Black Power, the Caribbean and the Black Radical Tradition in

Canada". *Journal of African American History*. **92** (4): 516–539. Doi:10.1086/jaahv92n4p516. S2CID 140509880

Oloruntoba-Oju, Omotayo (December 2012). "Pan Africanism, Myth and History in African and Caribbean Drama". *Journal of Pan African Studies*. **5** (8): 190 ff.

143

Marable, Manning (2011). *Malcolm X: A Life of Reinvention*. New York: Viking. ISBN 978-0-670-02220-5.

Perry, Bruce (1991). *Malcolm: The Life of a Man Who Changed Black America*. Barrytown, New York: Station Hill. ISBN 978-0-88268-103-0.

144

Malcolm X, *Autobiography*, pp. 388–393; quote from pp. 390–391.

145

Perry, Bruce (1991). *Malcolm: The Life of a Man Who Changed Black America*. Barrytown, New York: Station Hill. ISBN 978-0-88268-103-0.

146

Kondo, Zak A. (1993). *Conspiracys: Unravelling the Assassination of Malcolm X*. Washington, D.C.: Nubia Press. OCLC 28837295.

147

Karim, Benjamin (1992). *Remembering Malcolm*. With Peter Skutches and David Gallen. New York: Carroll & Graf. ISBN 978-0-88184-881-6.

Evanzz, Karl (1992). *The Judas Factor: The Plot to Kill Malcolm X*. New York: Thunder's Mouth Press. ISBN 978-1-56025-049-4.

Kihss, Peter (February 22, 1965). "Malcolm X Shot to Death at Rally Here". *The New York Times*. P. 1. Retrieved June 19, 2018.

Marable, Manning (2011). *Malcolm X: A Life of Reinvention*. New York: Viking. ISBN 978-0-670-02220-5.

Perry, Bruce (1991). *Malcolm: The Life of a Man Who Changed Black America*. Barrytown, New York: Station Hill. ISBN 978-0-88268-103-0.

Evanzz, Karl (1992). *The Judas Factor: The Plot to Kill Malcolm X*. New York: Thunder's Mouth Press. ISBN 978-1-56025-049-4.

148

Davis, Ossie (February 27, 1965). "Malcolm X's Eulogy". The Official Website of Malcolm X. Retrieved August 9, 2016. Retrieved from: https://www.malcolmx.com/eulogy/

149

Rickford, Russell J. (2003). *Betty Shabazz: A Remarkable Story of Survival and Faith Before and After Malcolm X*. Naperville, Illinois: Sourcebooks. ISBN 978-1-4022-0171-4.

150

King, Martin Luther Jr. (February 26, 1965). "Telegram from Martin Luther King Jr. To Betty al-Shabazz". The Martin Luther King Jr. Research and Education Institute. Archived from the original on February 1, 2016. Retrieved May 28, 2018.

151

Decaro, Louis A. (1996). *On the Side of My People: A Religious Life of Malcolm X*. New York: New York University Press. ISBN 978-0-8147-1864-3.

152

Rickford, Russell J. (2003). *Betty Shabazz: A Remarkable Story of Survival and Faith Before and After Malcolm X*. Naperville, Illinois: Sourcebooks. ISBN 978-1-4022-0171-4.
"Malcolm X". *The New York Times*. February 22, 1965. P. 20.

Evanzz, Karl (1992). *The Judas Factor: The Plot to Kill Malcolm X*. New York: Thunder's Mouth Press. ISBN 978-1-56025-049-4.

Kenworthy, E. W. (February 26, 1965). "Malcolm Called a Martyr Abroad". *The New York Times*. P. 15.

"How World Saw Malcolm X's Death" (PDF). *New York Amsterdam News*. March 13, 1965.

"How World Saw Malcolm X's Death" (PDF). *New York Amsterdam News*. March 13, 1965. Retrieved from: https://www.alkalimat.org/brothermalcolm/Timothy_Johnson-Malcolm_X_A_Comprehensive_Annotated_Bibliography-1986-3.pdf

King, Martin Luther Jr. (March 13, 1965). "The Nightmare of Violence" (PDF). *New York Amsterdam News*.

153

Jeremiah Unterman (2017). *Justice for All: How the Jewish Bible Revolutionized Ethics*. University of Nebraska Press. P. 109. ISBN 978-0827612709. The modern definition of "to repent," according to the *Oxford English Dictionary*, is "To review one's actions and feel contrition or regret for something one has done or omitted to do; (esp. In religious contexts) to acknowledge the sinfulness of one's past action or conduct by showing sincere remorse and undertaking to reform in the future."

154

Perry, Bruce (1991). Malcolm: The Life of a Man Who Changed Black America. Barrytown, New York: Station Hill. ISBN 978-0-88268-103-0.

155

Perry, Bruce (1991). *Malcolm: The Life of a Man Who Changed Black America.* Barrytown, New York: Station Hill. ISBN 978-0-88268-103-0.

156

Gray, Paul (June 8, 1998). "Required Reading: Nonfiction Books". *Time.* Retrieved March 28, 2016.

157

Asante, Molefi Kete (2002). *100 Greatest African Americans: A Biographical Encyclopedia.* Amherst, New York: Prometheus Books. P. 333. ISBN 978-1-57392-963-9.

Marable, Manning; Frazier, Nishani; mcmillian, John Campbell (2003). *Freedom on My Mind: The Columbia Documentary History of the African American Experience.* New York: Columbia University Press. P. 251. ISBN 978-0-231-10890-4.

Salley, Columbus (1999). *The Black 100: A Ranking of the Most Influential African-Americans, Past and Present.* New York: Citadel Press. P. 88. ISBN 978-0-8065-2048-3.

Nasr, Seyyed Hossein (2002). *The Heart of Islam: Enduring Values for Humanity.* New York: harpercollins. P. 97. ISBN 978-0-06-073064-2.

Perry, Bruce (1991). *Malcolm: The Life of a Man Who Changed Black America.* Barrytown, New York: Station Hill. ISBN 978-0-88268-103-0.

Turner, Richard Brent (2004). "Islam in the African-American Experience". In Bobo, Jacqueline; Hudley, Cynthia; Michel,

Claudine (eds.). *The Black Studies Reader*. New York: Routledge. P. 445. ISBN 978-0-415-94554-7.

Cone, James H. (1991). *Martin & Malcolm & America: A Dream or a Nightmare*. Maryknoll, New York: Orbis Books. ISBN 978-0-88344-721-5.

West, Cornel (1984). "The Paradox of the Afro-American Rebellion". In Sayres, Sohnya; Stephanson, Anders; Aronowitz, Stanley; Jameson, Fredric (eds.). *The 60s Without Apology*. Minneapolis: University of Minnesota Press. P. 51. ISBN 978-0-8166-1336-6.

Marable, Manning (2009). "Rediscovering Malcolm's Life: A Historian's Adventures in Living History". In Marable, Manning; Aidi, Hishaam D (eds.). *Black Routes to Islam*. New York: Palgrave Macmillan. ISBN 978-1-4039-8400-5.

Sales, William W. (1994). *From Civil Rights to Black Liberation: Malcolm X and the Organization of Afro-American Unity*. Boston: South End Press. ISBN 978-0-89608-480-3.

Woodard, Komozi (1999). *A Nation Within a Nation: Amiri Baraka (leroi Jones) & Black Power Politics*. Chapel Hill, North Carolina: University of North Carolina Press. P. 62. ISBN 978-0-8078-4761-9.

Haley, William "Epilogue", *The Autobiography of Malcolm X*, p. 471.

Gray, Paul (June 8, 1998). "Required Reading: Nonfiction Books". *Time*. Retrieved March 28, 2016.

Millere, Mauricelm-Lei (2021). *Malcolm X and The Organization of Afro-American Unity: African American Defense League (A2DL – OAAU)*. Online: Kindle Books. P. 5. ASIN B097YR2SBH.

Young, Paul (March 30, 2014). "Real Life Inspirations Behind Some of the Best Comic Book Villains". *Screen Rant.*

Eells, Josh (February 18, 2018). "The 'Black Panther' Revolution". *Rolling Stone.* Archived from the original on February 25, 2018. Retrieved March 2, 2018.

Ramos, Dino-Ray; N'Duka, Amanda (January 9, 2019). "New Hollywood Podcast: Michael B. Jordan Talks How 'Black Panther' Shifted Hollywood's Idea Of Representation". *Deadline Hollywood.* Retrieved October 2, 2019.

158

"National Register of Historic Places – Nebraska, Douglas County". National Register of
Historic Places. Retrieved October 2, 2014.

159

"Malcolm X Homesite". Michigan Historical Markers. Archived from the original on August 5, 2020. Retrieved June 20, 2018.

160

Rickford, Russell J. (2003). *Betty Shabazz: A Remarkable Story of Survival and Faith Before and After Malcolm X.* Naperville, Illinois: Sourcebooks. ISBN 978-1-4022-0171-4.

161

Hunt, Lori Bona (February 26, 1991). "Malcolm X's Widow Sees Signs of Hope". *Milwaukee Journal.*

Lee, Felicia R. (May 15, 1993). "Newark Students, Both Good and Bad, Make Do". *The New York Times.* Retrieved June 19, 2018.
Witkowsky, Kathy (Spring 2000). "A Day in the Life". *National crosstalk.* Retrieved October 2,

Shabazz Public School Academy. Retrieved February 27, 2023.

Belvin, Brent (October 6, 2004). *Master's Thesis: Malcolm X Liberation University: An Experiment in Independent Black Education* (Thesis). North Carolina State University. Retrieved October 2, 2014. Retrieved from: https://repository.lib.ncsu.edu/handle/1840.16/563

162

Flynn, Pat (January 7, 1996). "Big Crowd Welcomes New Library Warmly". *The San Diego Union-Tribune.*

Valencia Park/Malcolm X Library. Retrieved from: https://www.sandiego.gov/public-library/locations/valencia-park-malcolm-x-library

163

NPR Special Series (2005). Timeline – Tookie's Path to Death. *The Execution of Stanley Tookie Williams.* Retrieved from: https://www.npr.org/templates/story/story.php?Storyid=5047269

164

"A Conversation with Death Row Prisoner Stanley Tookie Williams from his San Quentin Cell". *Democracy Now!.* November 30, 2005. Archived from the original on November 15, 2007. Retrieved September 10, 2009. Retrieved from: http://www.democracynow.org/article.pl?Sid=05%2F11%2F30%2F153247

165

NPR Special Series (2005). Timeline – Tookie's Path to Death. *The Execution of Stanley Tookie Williams.* Retrieved from:

https://www.npr.org/templates/story/story.php?Storyid=5047269

166

Morain, Dan (June 11, 1989). "Death Row Violence Part of Gang Power Struggle, San Quentin Officials Say". *Los Angeles Times*. Retrieved February 9, 2020. Retrieved from: https://www.latimes.com/archives/la-xpm-1989-06-11-mn-3235-story.html

167

People v. Williams - Cal Sup Ct (April 11, 1988). Retrieved from: http://online.ceb.com/calcases/C3/44C3d1127.htm

168

Egelko, Bob (December 7, 2005). "A QUESTION OF EVIDENCE Stanley Tookie Williams' best hope for clemency may depend more on raising doubt about his guilt than on his redemption". San Francisco Chronicle. Retrieved from: https://www.sfgate.com/news/article/A-QUESTION-OF-EVIDENCE-Stanley-Tookie-Williams-2590472.php

169

Executed Inmate Summary – Stanley Williams California Department of Corrections and Rehabilitation. Retrieved from: https://www.cdcr.ca.gov/capital-punishment/inmates-executed-1978-to-present/executed-inmate-summary-stanley-williams/

170

"Stanley Tookie Williams: I Want the World to Remember Me for My "Redemptive Transition"". *Democracy Now!*. December 13, 2005. Retrieved from: https://www.democracynow.org/2005/12/13/stanley_tookie_williams_i_want_the

171

Sahagun, Louis (December 20, 2005). "A Public Goodbye for Williams". *The Los Angeles Times*. Retrieved July 14, 2009. Retrieved from: https://www.latimes.com/archives/la-xpm-2005-dec-20-me-williams20-story.html
Richardson, Lisa (December 21, 2005). "Funeral Service Celebrates Williams' Conversion From Violence to Peace". *The Los Angeles Times*. Retrieved from: https://www.latimes.com/archives/la-xpm-2005-dec-21-me-williams21-story.html
"Tookie Williams Is Executed". *Www.cbsnews.com*. Retrieved February 21, 2020. Retrieved from: https://www.cbsnews.com/news/tookie-williams-is-executed-13-12-2005/

172

Stanley "Tookie" Williams (2005). Stanley "Tookie" Williams. Simon & Schuster. Retrieved from: https://www.simonandschuster.com/authors/Stanley-Tookie-Williams/43384768#:~:text=Stanley%20Tookie%20Williams%2C%20activist%20and,He%20was%20executed%20in%202005.

173

Sheehey, Maeve (June 30, 2021). "Trump debuts at 41st in C-SPAN presidential rankings". *Politico*. Retrieved from: https://www.politico.com/news/2021/06/30/trump-cspan-president-ranking-497184

"American Presidents: Greatest and Worst". Siena College Research Institute. June 22, 2022. Retrieved July 11, 2022. Retrieved from: https://scri.siena.edu/2022/06/22/american-presidents-greatest-and-worst/

174

Ashford, Grace (February 27, 2019). "Michael Cohen Says Trump Told Him to Threaten Schools Not to Release

Grades". *The New York Times*. Retrieved June 9, 2019.
Retrieved from:
https://www.nytimes.com/2019/02/27/us/politics/trump-school-grades.html
Kranish, Michael; Fisher, Marc (2017) [2016]. *Trump Revealed: The Definitive Biography of the 45th President*. Simon & Schuster. ISBN 978-1-5011-5652-6.
Viser, Matt (August 28, 2015). "Even in college, Donald Trump was brash". *The Boston Globe*. Retrieved May 28, 2018.
Montopoli, Brian (April 29, 2011). "Donald Trump avoided Vietnam with deferments, records show". *CBS News*. Retrieved July 17, 2015. Retrieved from:
https://www.cbsnews.com/news/donald-trump-avoided-vietnam-with-deferments-records-show/
Eder, Steve; Philipps, Dave (August 1, 2016). "Donald Trump's Draft Deferments: Four for College, One for Bad Feet". *The New York Times*. Retrieved August 2, 2016. Retrieved from:
https://www.nytimes.com/2016/08/02/us/politics/donald-trump-draft-record.html

175

Barron, James (September 5, 2016). "Overlooked Influences on Donald Trump: A Famous Minister and His Church". *The New York Times*. Retrieved October 13, 2016.
Scott, Eugene (August 28, 2015). "Church says Donald Trump is not an 'active member'". *CNN*. Retrieved September 14, 2022.

Jenkins, Jack; Mwaura, Maina (October 23, 2020). "Exclusive: Trump, confirmed a Presbyterian, now identifies as 'non-denominational Christian'". Religion News Service. Archived from the original on October 24, 2020..
Peters, Jeremy W.; Haberman, Maggie (October 31, 2019). "Paula White, Trump's Personal Pastor, Joins the White House". *The New York Times*..

176

The Editorial Board (2017). President Trump Craves Loyalty, but Offers None, New York Times. Retrieved from: https://www.nytimes.com/2017/05/12/opinion/president-trump-craves-loyalty-but-offers-none.html

Kruse, M. (2018). I need Loyalty. *Politico Magazine*. Retrieved from: https://www.politico.com/magazine/story/2018/03/06/donald-trump-loyalty-staff-217227/

Reuters Staff (2017). Comey says Trump told him, 'I need loyalty. I expect loyalty'. *Reuters*. Retrieved from: https://www.reuters.com/article/us-usa-trump-russia-comey-loyalty-iduskbn18y2qj

Milbank, Dana (2017). Trump demands loyalty but does not give it. Washington Post. Retrieved from: https://www.ctnewsonline.com/opinion/article_0b3b882a-70d0-11e7-9103-7b27a7c88c87.html

177

Greenberg, Jonathan (April 20, 2018). "Trump lied to me about his wealth to get onto the Forbes 400. Here are the tapes". *The Washington Post.*.

178

Stump, Scott (October 26, 2015). "Donald Trump: My dad gave me 'a small loan' of $1 million to get started". *CNBC.*.

Barstow, David; Craig, Susanne; Buettner, Russ (October 2, 2018). "11 Takeaways From The Times's Investigation into Trump's Wealth". *The New York Times.*.

Barstow, David; Craig, Susanne; Buettner, Russ (October 2, 2018). "Trump Engaged in Suspect Tax Schemes as He Reaped Riches From His Father". *The New York Times*..

"From the Tower to the White House". *The Economist.* February 20, 2016. Retrieved February 29, 2016. Mr Trump's performance has been mediocre compared with the stockmarket and property in New York.

Swanson, Ana (February 29, 2016). "The myth and the reality of Donald Trump's business empire". The Washington Post..

Alexander, Dan; Peterson-Whithorn, Chase (October 2, 2018). "How Trump Is Trying—And Failing—To Get Rich Off His Presidency". *Forbes.*

179

Buettner, Russ; Craig, Susanne; mcintire, Mike (September 27, 2020). "Long-concealed Records Show Trump's Chronic Losses And Years Of Tax Avoidance". *The New York Times.*

180

Buettner, Russ; Craig, Susanne (May 7, 2019). "Decade in the Red: Trump Tax Figures Show Over \$1 Billion in Business Losses". *The New York Times*. Retrieved May 8, 2019.

Friedersdorf, Conor (May 8, 2019). "The Secret That Was Hiding in Trump's Taxes". *The Atlantic.*

181

Alexander, Dan (October 16, 2020). "Donald Trump Has at Least \$1 Billion in Debt, More Than Twice The Amount He Suggested". *Forbes.*

182

Pullig, Chris (June 2008). "What is Brand Equity and What Does the Branding Concept Mean to You?" (PDF). *Baylor.edu.* Baylor University.

Röwekamp, Josephine (May 2010). "Under one umbrella? Step 3 in brand development: Brand architecture" (PDF). *Kleiner und bold gmbh*. KU Gesundheitsmanagement.
Erdem, Tülin (1 August 1998). "An Empirical Analysis of Umbrella Branding". *Journal of Marketing Research*. 35 (3): 339–351. Doi:10.2307/3152032. JSTOR 3152032.

183

Mahler, Jonathan; Flegenheimer, Matt (June 20, 2016). "What Donald Trump Learned From Joseph mccarthy's Right-Hand Man". *The New York Times*. Retrieved May 26, 2020.
Kranish, Michael; O'Harrow, Robert Jr. (January 23, 2016). "Inside the government's racial bias case against Donald Trump's company, and how he fought it". *The Washington Post*.

"Donald Trump: Three decades, 4,095 lawsuits". *USA Today*. Archived from the original on April 25, 2022.
Brenner, Marie (June 28, 2017). "How Donald Trump and Roy Cohn's Ruthless Symbiosis Changed America". *Vanity Fair*.

Smith, Allan (December 8, 2017). "Trump's long and winding history with Deutsche Bank could now be at the center of Robert Mueller's investigation". *Business Insider*.
Flitter, Emily (July 17, 2016). "Art of the spin: Trump bankers question his portrayal of financial comeback". *Reuters*.

184

Rich, Frank (April 30, 2018). "The Original Donald Trump". *New York*. Retrieved May 8, 2018.
Kessler, Glenn (March 3, 2016). "Trump's false claim he built his empire with a 'small loan' from his father". *The Washington Post*.

Kranish, Michael; Fisher, Marc (2017) [2016]. *Trump Revealed: The Definitive Biography of the 45th President*. Simon & Schuster. ISBN 978-1-5011-5652-6.
Geist, William E. (April 8, 1984). "The Expanding Empire of Donald Trump". *The New York Times*.

185

"Company News; Trump's Plaza Hotel Bankruptcy Plan Approved". *The New York Times*. Reuters. December 12, 1992.:
https://www.nytimes.com/1992/12/12/business/company-news-trump-s-plaza-hotel-bankruptcy-plan-approved.html

Stout, David; Gilpin, Kenneth N. (April 12, 1995). "Trump Is Selling Plaza Hotel To Saudi and Asian Investors". *The New York Times*..

186

Bagli, Charles V. (June 1, 2005). "Trump Group Selling West Side Parcel for $1.8 billion". *The New York Times*..

187

Kranish, Michael; Fisher, Marc (2017) [2016]. *Trump Revealed: The Definitive Biography of the 45th President*. Simon & Schuster. ISBN 978-1-5011-5652-6.

188

Tully, Shawn (March 10, 2016). "How Donald Trump Made Millions Off His Biggest Business Failure". *Fortune*..

Mcquade, Dan (August 16, 2015). "The Truth About the Rise and Fall of Donald Trump's Atlantic City Empire". *Philadelphia*..

189

Garcia, Ahiza (December 29, 2016). "Trump's 17 golf courses teed up: Everything you need to know". *CNN Money*..

190

Anthony, Zane; Sanders, Kathryn; Fahrenthold, David A. (April 13, 2018). "Whatever happened to Trump neckties? They're over. So is most of Trump's merchandising empire". *The Washington Post.* Retrieved September 29, 2021. Retrieved from: https://www.washingtonpost.com/politics/whatever-happened-to-trump-ties-theyre-over-so-is-most-of-trumps-merchandising-empire/2018/04/13/2c32378a-369c-11e8-acd5-35eac230e514_story.html

191

Morris, David Z. (September 24, 2017). "Donald Trump Fought the NFL Once Before. He Got Crushed". *Fortune..*

192

Kessler, Glenn (August 11, 2016). "Too good to check: Sean Hannity's tale of a Trump rescue". *The Washington Post.* Retrieved March 14, 2019. Retrieved from: https://www.washingtonpost.com/news/fact-checker/wp/2016/08/11/too-good-to-check-sean-hannitys-tale-of-a-trump-rescue/

193

Solnik, Claude (September 15, 2016). "Taking a peek at Trump's (foundation) tax returns". *Long Island Business News.* Retrieved September 30, 2021.

194

Barstow, David; Craig, Susanne; Buettner, Russ (October 2, 2018). "Trump Engaged in Suspect Tax Schemes as He Reaped Riches From His Father". *The New York Times..*

195

Puente, Maria (June 29, 2015). "NBC to Donald Trump: You're fired". *USA Today.*

Rutenberg, Jim (June 22, 2002). "Three Beauty Pageants Leaving CBS for NBC". *The New York Times.*

196

Barbaro, Michael (May 19, 2011). "New York Attorney General Is Investigating Trump's For-Profit School". *The New York Times.*
197

Eder, Steve (November 18, 2016). "Donald Trump Agrees to Pay $25 Million in Trump University Settlement". *The New York Times.*

198

Cillizza, Chris; Fahrenthold, David A. (September 15, 2016). "Meet the reporter who's giving Donald Trump fits". *The Washington Post..*

Bradner, Eric; Frehse, Rob (September 14, 2016). "NY attorney general is investigating Trump Foundation practices". *CNN..*

199

Jacobs, Ben (December 24, 2016). "Donald Trump to dissolve his charitable foundation after mounting complaints". *The Guardian..*

200

Katersky, Aron (November 7, 2019). "President Donald Trump ordered to pay $2M to collection of nonprofits as part of civil lawsuit". *ABC News..*

201

Mccauley, Dana (April 29, 2016). "This is the woman who made Donald Trump a household name". *Newscomau.* Archived from the original on November 4, 2018..

Shnayerson, Michael (January 2, 1988). "Inside Ivana's Role in Donald Trump's Empire". *Vanity Fair.* Archived from the original on December 29, 2020.

202

Ransom, Jan (2019). *Trump Will Not Apologize for Calling for Death Penalty Over Central Park Five. New York Times.* Retrieved from:

https://www.nytimes.com/2019/06/18/nyregion/central-park-five-trump.html

Laughland, Oliver. (2016). Donald Trump and the Central Park Five: the racially Charged rise of a demagogue. The Guardian. Retrieved from: https://www.theguardian.com/us-news/2016/feb/17/central-park-five-donald-trump-jogger-rape-case-new-york

Lopez, German (2020). Donald Trump's long history of racism, from the 1970s to 2020. Vox. Retrieved from: https://www.vox.com/2016/7/25/12270880/donald-trump-racist-racism-history

203

Ian Haney López (Trump's Racism Isn't Just Racism, It's a Strategy. **University of California, Berkeley. Retrieved from:** https://belonging.berkeley.edu/trumps-racism-isnt-just-racism-its-strategy

204

Lopez, German (2020). Donald Trump's long history of racism, from the 1970s to 2020. Vox. Retrieved from: https://www.vox.com/2016/7/25/12270880/donald-trump-racist-racism-history

Lopez, German (2020). The lowest moment of Donald Trump's press conference. *Vox.* Retrieved from: https://www.vox.com/identities/2017/2/16/14642184/trump-congressional-black-caucus-racism

205

Lopez, German (2020). The lowest moment of Donald Trump's press conference. *Vox*. Retrieved from: https://www.vox.com/identities/2017/2/16/14642184/trump-congressional-black-caucus-racism

206

Ransom, Jan (2019). *Trump Will Not Apologize for Calling for Death Penalty Over Central Park Five. New York Times.* Retrieved from: https://www.nytimes.com/2019/06/18/nyregion/central-park-five-trump.html

Laughland, Oliver. (2016). Donald Trump and the Central Park Five: the racially Charged rise of a demagogue. The Guardian. Retrieved from: https://www.theguardian.com/us-news/2016/feb/17/central-park-five-donald-trump-jogger-rape-case-new-york

Lopez, German (2020). Donald Trump's long history of racism, from the 1970s to 2020. Vox. Retrieved from: https://www.vox.com/2016/7/25/12270880/donald-trump-racist-racism-history
Lopez, German (2020). The lowest moment of Donald Trump's press conference. *Vox*. Retrieved from: https://www.vox.com/identities/2017/2/16/14642184/trump-congressional-black-caucus-racism

207

Ransom, Jan (2019). *Trump Will Not Apologize for Calling for Death Penalty Over Central Park Five. New York Times.* Retrieved from: https://www.nytimes.com/2019/06/18/nyregion/central-park-five-trump.html

208

Putterman, Samantha (2019). Says Donald Trump scored a 73 on an IQ test administered to him while in high school at New York Military Academy. Politifact: The Poynter Institute. Retrieved from: https://www.politifact.com/factchecks/2019/may/14/viral-image/social-media-post-sharing-newspaper-story-trump-ha/

209

CEO: eqworks Coaching & Training For Leaders Gimmack, Phillip (2016). Donald Trump's emotional intelligence - let's take a look... HRZONE. Retrieved from: https://www.hrzone.com/lead/future/donald-trumps-emotional-intelligence-lets-take-a-look

210

Becket, Stefan (2023). Timeline: Donald Trump, Stormy Daniels and the $130,000 payment to buy her silence. CBS News. Retrieved from: https://www.cbsnews.com/news/donald-trump-stormy-daniels-investigation-timeline-manhattan-district-attorney/

Gregorian, Dareh (2021). National Enquirer publisher fined $187,500 for Trump hush money payment. CBS news. Retrieved from: https://www.nbcnews.com/politics/donald-trump/national-enquirer-publisher-pay-187-500-fine-trump-hush-money-n1269370

211

Chen, Shawna (2023). Timeline: The probe into Trump's alleged hush money payment to Stormy Daniels. AXIOS. Retrieved from: https://www.axios.com/2023/03/18/trump-stormy-daniels-payment-probe

212

Politics (2023). New York's probe of Trump's involvement in hush-money case, explained. PBS. Retrieved from:

https://www.pbs.org/newshour/politics/new-yorks-probe-of-trumps-involvement-in-hush-money-case-explained

213

Santucci, John (July 28, 2015). "Donald Trump's Ex-Wife Ivana Disavows Old 'Rape' Allegation". *ABC News*. Archived from the original on April 27, 2020. Retrieved May 17, 2020. I referred to this as a 'rape,' but I do not want my words to be interpreted in a literal or criminal sense. Retrieved from: https://abcnews.go.com/Politics/donald-trumps-wife-ivana-disavows-rape-allegation/story?Id=32732204

214

Carmon, Irin (October 13, 2016). "The Allegations Women Have Made Against Donald Trump". *NBC News*. Archived from the original on October 15, 2016..

215

Ransom, Jan (November 4, 2019). "E. Jean Carroll, Who Accused Trump of Rape, Sues Him for Defamation". *The New York Times*. Archived from the original on November 30, 2019..

216

Del Valle, Lauren (2023). Jury finds Donald Trump sexually abused E. Jean Carroll in civil case, awards her $5 million. *CNN Politics*. Retrieved from: Retrieved from: https://www.cnn.com/2023/05/09/politics/e-jean-carroll-trump-lawsuit-battery-defamation-verdict/index.html

217

Jacobs, Shayna; Fahrenthold, David (November 12, 2021). "Former 'Apprentice' contestant Summer Zervos ends defamation lawsuit against Trump". *Washington Post*.

218

Vagianos, Alanna (March 13, 2019). "Trump Accuser Alva Johnson Says Her Goal Is To Get 'Justice For The Other 20 Plus Women'". *Huffpost*. Archived from the original on March 30, 2019.

219

Twohey, Megan; Barbaro, Michael (October 12, 2016). "Two Women Say Donald Trump Touched Them Inappropriately". *The New York Times*. Archived from the original on October 13, 2016.

220

Tumulty, Karen (October 14, 2016). "Woman says Trump reached under her skirt and groped her in early 1990s". *The Washington Post*. Archived from the original on October 14, 2016..

221

Reilly, Mollie; Stein, Sam (October 13, 2016). "Trump Faces Another Accusation—This Time, He Looked Up Models' Skirts". *The Huffington Post*. Archived from the original on March 31, 2019..

222

Redden, Molly (October 15, 2016). "Donald Trump 'grabbed me and went for the lips', says ninth accuser". *The Guardian*. Archived from the original on October 15, 2016..

223

Jackson, Hallie; Johnson, Alex (October 13, 2016). "Miss USA Contestant Details Unwanted Encounters With Trump". *NBC News*. Archived from the original on October 13, 2016..

224

Osborne, Lucy (September 17, 2020). "Donald Trump accused of sexual assault by former model Amy Dorris". *The Guardian*.

225

Redden, Molly (October 20, 2016). "Tenth woman accuses Donald Trump of sexual misconduct". *The Guardian*. Archived from the original on October 20, 2016..

226

Rupar, Aron (October 9, 2019). "Trump faces a new allegation of sexually assaulting a woman at Mar-a-Lago". *Vox*..

227

Kurtzleben, Danielle (October 13, 2016). "A List Of The Accusations About Trump's Alleged Inappropriate Sexual Conduct". NPR. Archived from the original on October 13, 2016..

228

Twohey, Megan; Barbaro, Michael (October 12, 2016). "Two Women Say Donald Trump Touched Them Inappropriately". *The New York Times*. Archived from the original on October 13, 2016..

229

Kurtzleben, Danielle (October 13, 2016). "A List Of The Accusations About Trump's Alleged Inappropriate Sexual Conduct". NPR. Archived from the original on October 13, 2016..

230

Oppenheim, Maya (December 10, 2017). "Former Fox News anchor claims Donald Trump tried to kiss her in a lift". *The Independent*. Archived from the original on December 11, 2017.

231

Flores, Reena (October 22, 2016). "Another Donald Trump accuser comes out with charge of sexual misconduct". *CBS News*. Archived from the original on October 22, 2016.

232

Mathis, Ben (October 27, 2016). "Today's Trump Apocalypse Watch: Miss Finland edition". *Slate*. Archived from the original on November 8, 2016

233

Lyle, Josh (October 12, 2016). "Miss Washington 2013 says Donald Trump groped her". Seattle, Washington: KING-TV. Archived from the original on October 13, 2016.

234

Steinbuch, Yaron (October 12, 2016). "Former teen beauty queens: Trump barged in on us changing". *New York Post*. Archived from the original on October 13, 2016.

235

Kurtzleben, Danielle (October 13, 2016). "A List Of The Accusations About Trump's Alleged Inappropriate Sexual Conduct". NPR. Archived from the original on October 13, 2016.

236

Helderman, Rosalind; Reinhard, Beth (July 17, 2019). "Behind the scenes the night Trump partied at Mar-a-Lago with Jeffrey Epstein and NFL cheerleaders". *The Washington Post*. Archived from the original on July 20, 2019.

Steib, Matt (July 17, 2019). "NBC Obtained Trump–Epstein Footage After Trump Kissed an Anchor Without Consent". *New York*. Archived from the original on July 18, 2019.

237

Harper, Shaun (October 8, 2016). "Many Men Talk Like Donald Trump in Private. And Only Other Men Can Stop Them". *The Washington Post*. Archived from the original on October 14, 2016.

"It's not just the powerful". *The Economist*. October 13, 2016. Archived from the original on October 16, 2016.

Taylor, Jessica (October 7, 2016). "'You Can Do Anything': In 2005 Tape, Trump Brags About Groping, Kissing Women". NPR. Archived from the original on October 13, 2016.

Mahdawi, Arwa (October 15, 2016). "This is what rape culture looks like—in the words of Donald Trump". *The Guardian*. Archived from the original on October 18, 2016.

Collins, Nancy (October 13, 2016). "Donald Trump Talks Family, Women in Unearthed Transcript: "When I Come Home and Dinner's Not Ready, I Go Through the Roof"". *The Hollywood Reporter*. Archived from the original on October 15, 2016.

238

"Transcript: Donald Trump's Speech Responding To Assault Accusations". NPR. October 13, 2016. Archived from the original on October 24, 2016.

239

Gillin, Joshua (August 24, 2015). "Bush says Trump was a Democrat longer than a Republican 'in the last decade'". *Politifact*.

240

Oreskes, Michael (September 2, 1987). "Trump Gives a Vague Hint of Candidacy". *The New York Times*.

241

Meacham, Jon (2016). *Destiny and Power: The American Odyssey of George Herbert Walker Bush*. Random House Publishing Group. P. 326. ISBN 9780812979473.

242

Johnson, Glen. "Donald Trump eyeing a run at the White House". *Standard-Speaker*. Hazleton, Pennsylvania.

243

Bobic, Igor; Stein, Sam (February 22, 2017). "How CPAC Helped Launch Donald Trump's Political Career". *Huffpost*.

244

Preston, Mark; Silverleib, Alan (February 3, 2012). "Trump endorses Romney". *CNN*.

245

Cillizza, Chris (June 14, 2016). "This Harvard study is a powerful indictment of the media's role in Donald Trump's rise". *The Washington Post*

246

Flitter, Emily; Oliphant, James (August 28, 2015). "Best president ever! How Trump's love of hyperbole could backfire". *Reuters*

247

Finnegan, Michael (September 25, 2016). "Scope of Trump's falsehoods unprecedented for a modern presidential candidate". *Los Angeles Times*.

248

Graham, David A. (May 13, 2016). "The Lie of Trump's 'Self-Funding' Campaign". *The Atlantic*.

Reeve, Elspeth (October 27, 2015). "How Donald Trump Evolved From a Joke to an Almost Serious Candidate". *The New Republic*.

Nussbaum, Matthew (May 3, 2016). "RNC Chairman: Trump is our nominee". *Politico*.
"2016 General Election: Trump vs. Clinton". *Huffpost*. Archived from the original on October 2, 2016.
"US presidential debate: Trump won't commit to accept election result". *BBC News*. October 20, 2016.

249

Borger, Julian (October 26, 2021). "Republicans closely resemble autocratic parties in Hungary and Turkey – study". *The Guardian*.

250

Edwards, Jason A. (2018). "Make America Great Again: Donald Trump and Redefining the U.S. Role in the World". *Communication Quarterly*. **66** (2): 176. Doi:10.1080/01463373.2018.1438485. ISSN 0146-3373. S2CID 149040989. On the campaign trail, Trump repeatedly called North Atlantic Treaty Organization (NATO) 'obsolete'.
(2020) "Trump's promises before and after the election". *BBC*. September 19, 2017. Retrieved from: https://www.bbc.com/news/world-us-canada-37982000

251

Bierman, Noah (August 22, 2016). "Donald Trump helps bring far-right media's edgier elements into the mainstream". *Los Angeles Times*.

Weigel, David (August 20, 2016). "'Racialists' are cheered by Trump's latest strategy". *The Washington Post*.

Pierce, Matt (September 20, 2020). "Q&A: What is President Trump's relationship with far-right and white supremacist groups?". *Los Angeles Times*.

252

Diamond, Jeremy; Frates, Chris (July 22, 2015). "Donald Trump's 92-page financial disclosure released". *CNN*.
Isidore, Chris; Sahadi, Jeanne (February 26, 2016). "Trump says he can't release tax returns because of audits". *CNN*.

Gresko, Jessica (February 22, 2021). "Supreme Court won't halt turnover of Trump's tax records". *Associated Press*.

253

Eder, Steve; Twohey, Megan (October 10, 2016). "Donald Trump Acknowledges Not Paying Federal Income Taxes for Years". *The New York Times*.

254

Desilver, Drew (December 20, 2016). "Trump's victory another example of how Electoral College wins are bigger than popular vote ones". *Pew Research Center*.
Crockett, Zachary (November 11, 2016). "Donald Trump will be the only US president ever with no political or military experience". *Vox*.

255

Przybyla, Heidi M.; Schouten, Fredreka (January 21, 2017). "At 2.6 million strong, Women's Marches crush expectations". USA Today.

Logan, Brian; Sanchez, Chris (November 10, 2016). "Protests against Donald Trump break out nationwide". Business Insider.

256

Rosenberg, Matthew (July 6, 2017). "Trump Misleads on Russian Meddling: Why 17 Intelligence Agencies Don't Need to Agree". *The New York Times*.
Sanger, David E. (January 6, 2017). "Putin Ordered 'Influence Campaign' Aimed at U.S. Election, Report Says". *The New York Times*.

Berman, Russell (March 20, 2017). "It's Official: The FBI Is Investigating Trump's Links to Russia". *The Atlantic*.

257

Venook, Jeremy (August 9, 2017). "Trump's Interests vs. America's, Dubai Edition". The Atlantic.

"Donald Trump: A list of potential conflicts of interest". BBC. April 18, 2017. Retrieved from: https://www.bbc.com/news/world-us-canada-38069298

Den, Erica; Polantz, Katelyn (August 17, 2020). "Appeals court lets emoluments lawsuit against Trump proceed". CNN.

258

Dam, Andrew (2021). Trump will have the worst jobs record in modern U.S. history. It's not just the pandemic. Washington Post Business. Retrieved from: https://www.washingtonpost.com/business/2021/01/08/trump-jobs-record/

259

Dam, Andrew (2021). Trump will have the worst jobs record in modern U.S. history. It's not just the pandemic. Washington Post Business. Retrieved from: https://www.washingtonpost.com/business/2021/01/08/trump-jobs-record/

260

Bliss, Laura (November 16, 2020). "How Trump's $1 Trillion Infrastructure Pledge Added Up". Bloomberg News.

Dam, Andrew Van (January 8, 2021). "Trump will have the worst jobs record in modern U.S. history. It's not just the pandemic"

261

Pearle, Lauren (February 5, 2019). "Trump administration admits thousands more migrant families may have been separated than estimated". *ABC News.*
Domonoske, Camila; Gonzales, Richard (June 19, 2018). "What We Know: Family Separation And 'Zero Tolerance' At The Border". *NPR.*

262

Calamur, Krishnadev (July 16, 2018). "Trump Sides With the Kremlin, Against the U.S. Government". *The Atlantic.*

263

Gramlich, John (January 13, 2021). "How Trump compares with other recent presidents in appointing federal judges". *Pew Research Center.*
Phillip, Abby; Barnes, Robert; O'Keefe, Ed (February 8, 2017). "Supreme Court nominee Gorsuch says Trump's attacks on judiciary are 'demoralizing'". *The Washington Post.*

264

CDC (2023). Data Tracker. *Centers for Disease Control and Prevention.* Retrieved from: https://covid.cdc.gov/covid-data-tracker/#datatracker-home

265

United States military casualties of war. Retrieved from: https://en.wikipedia.org/wiki/United_States_military_casualties_of_war

266

Stone, Will (2021). The U.S. Battles Coronavirus, But is it Fair to compare pandemic to a War? *NPR.* Retrieved from: https://www.npr.org/sections/health-shots/2021/02/03/962811921/the-u-s-battles-coronavirus-but-is-it-fair-to-compare-pandemic-to-a-war#:~:text=Press-,Comparing%20Death%20Tolls%20From%20COVID%2D19%20To%20Past%20Wars%20Is,killed%20more%20Americans%20than%20WWII.

267

Hein, Alexandria (January 31, 2020). "Coronavirus declared public health emergency in US". *Fox News*. Retrieved from: https://www.foxnews.com/health/coronavirus-declared-public-health-emergency-in-us

268

"Trump deliberately played down virus, Woodward book says". BBC News. Retrieved from: https://www.bbc.com/news/world-us-canada-54094559

269

Watson, Kathryn (April 3, 2020). "A timeline of what Trump has said on coronavirus". *CBS News*. Retrieved from: https://www.cbsnews.com/news/timeline-president-donald-trump-changing-statements-on-coronavirus/

270

Allen, Arthur; mcgraw, Meridith (March 5, 2020). "Trump gets a fact check on coronavirus vaccines – from his own officials". *Politico*.

271

Liptak, Kevin (March 13, 2020). "Trump declares national emergency – and denies responsibility for coronavirus testing failures". *CNN*

272

Baumgaertner, Emily; Rainey, James (April 2, 2020). "Trump administration ended pandemic early-warning program to detect coronaviruses". *Los Angeles Times*.

273

Shear, Michael D.; Weiland, Noah; Lipton, Eric; Haberman, Maggie; Sanger, David E. (July 18, 2020). "Inside Trump's Failure: The Rush to Abandon Leadership Role on the Virus". *The New York Times*.

274

Berenson, Tessa (March 30, 2020). "'He's Walking the Tightrope.' How Donald Trump Is Getting Out His Message on Coronavirus". *Time*.

Georgiou, Aristos (March 19, 2020). "WHO expert condemns language stigmatizing coronavirus after Trump repeatedly calls it the "Chinese virus"". *Newsweek*

"Coronavirus: Outcry after Trump suggests injecting disinfectant as treatment". *BBC News*. April 24, Retrieved from: https://www.bbc.com/news/world-us-canada-52407177

275

Lemire, Jonathan (April 9, 2020). "As pandemic deepens, Trump cycles through targets to blame". *AP News*.

276

Acosta, Jim; Liptak, Kevin; Westwood, Sarah (May 29, 2020). "As US deaths top 100,000, Trump's coronavirus task force is curtailed". *CNN*

Liptak, Kevin (May 6, 2020). "In reversal, Trump says task force will continue 'indefinitely' – eyes vaccine czar". *CNN*.

277

Cohen, Zachary; Hansler, Jennifer; Atwood, Kylie; Salama, Vivian; Murray, Sara (July 7, 2020). "Trump administration begins formal withdrawal from World Health Organization". *CNN*.

"Coronavirus: Trump moves to pull US out of World Health Organization". *BBC News*. July 7, 2020. Retrieved from: https://www.bbc.com/news/world-us-canada-53327906

278

Higgins-Dunn, Noah (July 14, 2020). "Trump says U.S. would have half the number of coronavirus cases if it did half the testing". *CNBC*.

Bump, Philip (July 23, 2020). "Trump is right that with lower testing, we record fewer cases. That's already happening". *The Washington Post*.

Gumbrecht, Jamie; Gupta, Sanjay; Valencia, Nick (September 18, 2020). "Controversial coronavirus testing guidance came from HHS and didn't go through CDC scientific review, sources say". *CNN*.

Valencia, Nick; Murray, Sara; Holmes, Kristen (August 26, 2020). "CDC was pressured 'from the top down' to change coronavirus testing guidance, official says". *CNN*.

279

Wilson, Jason (April 17, 2020). "The rightwing groups behind wave of protests against Covid-19 restrictions". *The Guardian*.

Shear, Michael D.; Mervosh, Sarah (April 17, 2020). "Trump Encourages Protest Against Governors Who Have Imposed Virus Restrictions". *The New York Times*.

Chalfant, Morgan; Samuels, Brett (April 20, 2020). "Trump support for protests threatens to undermine social distancing rules". *The Hill*.

Kumar, Anita (April 18, 2020). "Trump's unspoken factor on reopening the economy: Politics". *Politico*.

280

Danner, Chas (July 11, 2020). "99 Days Later, Trump Finally Wears a Face Mask in Public". *New York*.

Blake, Aron (June 25, 2020). "Trump's dumbfounding refusal to encourage wearing masks". *The Washington Post*.

Danner, Chas (July 11, 2020). "99 Days Later, Trump Finally Wears a Face Mask in Public". *New York*.

281

Rabin, Roni Caryn; Cameron, Chris (July 5, 2020). "Trump Falsely Claims '99 Percent' of Virus Cases Are 'Totally Harmless'". *The New York Times*.

Sprunt, Barbara (July 7, 2020). "Trump Pledges To 'Pressure' Governors To Reopen Schools Despite Health Concerns". *NPR*.

282

Mcginley, Laurie; Johnson, Carolyn Y.; Dawsey, Josh (August 22, 2020). "Trump without evidence accuses 'deep state' at FDA of slow-walking coronavirus vaccines and treatments". *The Washington Post*.

Lafraniere, Sharon; Weiland, Noah; Shear, Michael D. (September 12, 2020). "Trump Pressed for Plasma Therapy. Officials Worry, Is an Unvetted Vaccine Next?"

Sun, Lena H. (September 12, 2020). "Trump officials seek greater control over CDC reports on coronavirus". *The Washington Post*.

283

Olorunnipa, Toluse; Dawsey, Josh (October 5, 2020). "Trump returns to White House, downplaying virus that hospitalized him and turned West Wing into a 'ghost town'". *The Washington Post*.

Weiland, Noah; Haberman, Maggie; Mazzetti, Mark; Karni, Annie (February 11, 2021). "Trump Was Sicker Than Acknowledged With Covid-19". *The New York Times*.

284

Ben Protess, Alan Feuer and Danny Hakim (2023). Donald Trump Faces Several Investigations. Here's Where They Stand. NY Times. Retrieved from: https://www.nytimes.com/article/trump-investigations-civil-criminal.html

Ollstein, Alice Miranda (April 14, 2020). "Trump halts funding to World Health Organization". *Politico*.

285

Protess, Ben, Feuer, Alan and Hakim, Danny (2023). Donald Trump Faces Several Investigations. Here's Where They Stand. New York Times. Retrieved from: https://www.nytimes.com/article/trump-investigations-civil-criminal.html

286

MICHAEL R. SISAK, COLLEEN LONG and WILL WEISSERT (2023). AP sources: Trump facing at least 1 felony charge in NY case. AP News. Retrieved from: https://apnews.com/article/trump-indictment-new-york-hush-money-election-488c76cf92269e2c258d5203a6e981a1

287

Nicholas Wu and Kyle Cheney (2022). The Jan. 6 panel had cooled focus on GOP lawmakers. Then Brooks happened. *Yahoo. News*. Retrieved from: https://www.yahoo.com/news/jan-6-panel-had-cooled-224112437.html

288

Kara Scannell (2022). E. Jean Carroll sues Trump for battery and defamation as lookback window for adult sex abuse survivors' suits opens in New York. *CNN*. Retrieved from: https://www.cnn.com/2022/11/24/politics/e-jean-carroll-trump-battery-defamation-lawsuit/index.html

289

Bump, Philip (September 25, 2019). "Trump wanted Russia's main geopolitical adversary to help undermine the Russian interference story". *The Washington Post*.

Cohen, Marshall; Polantz, Katelyn; Shortell, David; Kupperman, Tammy; Callahan, Michael (September 26, 2019). "Whistleblower says White House tried to cover up Trump's abuse of power". *CNN*.

290

Bump, Philip (September 25, 2019). "Trump wanted Russia's main geopolitical adversary to help undermine the Russian interference story". *The Washington Post*.

Fandos, Nicholas (September 24, 2019). "Nancy Pelosi Announces Formal Impeachment Inquiry of Trump". *The New York Times*.

Cohen, Marshall; Polantz, Katelyn; Shortell, David; Kupperman, Tammy; Callahan, Michael (September 26, 2019). "Whistleblower says White House tried to cover up Trump's abuse of power". *CNN*.

Forgey, Quint (September 24, 2019). "Trump changes story on withholding Ukraine aid". *Politico*.

Santucci, John; Mallin, Alexander; Thomas, Pierre; Faulders, Katherine (September 25, 2019). "Trump urged Ukraine to work with Barr and Giuliani to probe Biden: Call transcript". *ABC News*.

291

Herb, Jeremy; Mattingly, Phil; Raju, Manu; Fox, Lauren (January 31, 2020). "Senate impeachment trial: Wednesday acquittal vote scheduled after effort to have witnesses fails". *CNN*.

292

Naylor, Brian (January 11, 2021). "Impeachment Resolution Cites Trump's 'Incitement' of Capitol Insurrection". *NPR*.

Fandos, Nicholas (January 13, 2021). "Trump Impeached for Inciting Insurrection". *The New York Times*.

Blake, Aron (January 13, 2021). "Trump's second impeachment is the most bipartisan one in history". *The Washington Post.*
Levine, Sam; Gambino, Lauren (February 13, 2021). "Donald Trump acquitted in impeachment trial". *The Guardian.*

293

BENNIE G. THOMPSON, LIZ CHENEY, ZOE LOFGREN, ADAM B. SCHIFF, PETE AGUILAR, STEPHANIE N. MURPHY, JAMIE RASKIN, ELAINE G. LURIA ADAM KINZINGER (2022). F I NAL REPO R T OF THE SELECT COMMITTEE TO INVESTIGATE THE JANUARY 6TH ATTACK ON THE UNITED STATES CAPITOL. *United States House of Representatives.* Retrieved from: https://www.govinfo.gov/content/pkg/GPO-J6-REPORT/pdf/GPO-J6-REPORT.pdf

294

Cillizza, Chris (2021). 11 Trump associates have now been charged with crimes. 11! *The Point. CNN Politics.* Retrieved from: https://www.cnn.com/2021/07/21/politics/tom-barrack-trump-arrested/index.html

295

The Guardian Staff (2023). The legal problems still overshadowing Fox News after its Dominion settlement. The Guardian. Retrieved from: https://www.theguardian.com/media/2023/apr/19/the-legal-problems-still-overshadowing-fox-news-after-its-dominion-settlement

Bauder, David; Chase, Randall; and Mulvihill, Geoff (2023). Fox, Dominion reach $787M settlement over election claims. AP News. Retrieved from: https://apnews.com/article/fox-news-dominion-lawsuit-trial-trump-2020-0ac71f75acfacc52ea80b3e747fb0afe

296

Knowles, David (2023). Why did Tucker Carlson leave Fox News? Here's what we know. Yahoo! News. Retrieved from: https://news.yahoo.com/why-did-tucker-carlson-leave-fox-news-heres-what-we-know-230800125.html#:~:text=While%20the%20exact%20reason%20for,have%20been%20a%20central%20factor.&text=Here's%20a%20look%20back%20at,events%20that%20preceded%20Monday's%20announcement.

297

Office of Public Affairs (2023). Jury Convicts Four Leaders of the Proud Boys of Seditious Conspiracy Related to U.S. Capitol Breach: All Defendants Convicted of Multiple Felonies. *Department of Justice. Press Release No. 23-519.* Retrieved from: https://www.justice.gov/opa/pr/jury-convicts-four-leaders-proud-boys-seditious-conspiracy-related-us-capitol-breach

298

Kunzelman, Michael (2023). Proud Boys' Tarrio guilty of Jan. 6 seditious conspiracy. Associated press. Retrieved from: https://apnews.com/article/jan-6-enrique-tarrio-seditious-conspiracy-trial-f8738f17552cda21eef6d89504da2a0e

299

Chozick, Amy (September 29, 2018). "Why Trump Will Win a Second Term". *The New York Times*.
Parnes, Amie (April 28, 2018). "Trump's love-hate relationship with the press". *The Hill*.

Cillizza, Chris (June 14, 2016). "This Harvard study is a powerful indictment of the media's role in Donald Trump's rise". *The Washington Post*. Retrieved from: https://www.washingtonpost.com/news/the-fix/wp/2016/06/14/this-harvard-study-is-a-powerful-indictment-of-the-medias-role-in-donald-trumps-rise/

Thomsen, Jacqueline (May 22, 2018). "'60 Minutes' correspondent: Trump said he attacks the press so no one believes negative coverage"

Darcy, Oliver (November 12, 2020). "Judge dismisses Trump campaign's lawsuit against CNN". *CNN*.

Grynbaum, Michael M. (December 30, 2019). "After Another Year of Trump Attacks, 'Ominous Signs' for the American Press". *The New York Times*.

Wise, Justin (March 8, 2020). "Trump escalates fight against press with libel lawsuits". *The Hill*.

Klasfeld, Adam (March 9, 2021). "Judge Throws Out Trump Campaign's Defamation Lawsuit Against New York Times Over Russia 'Quid Pro Quo' Op-Ed". *Law and Crime*.

300

Dale, Daniel (June 5, 2019). "Donald Trump has now said more than 5,000 false things as president". *Toronto Star*.

Factcheck (2015). The 'King of Whoppers': Donald Trump. Retrieved from: https://www.factcheck.org/2015/12/the-king-of-whoppers-donald-trump/

301

Glenn Kessler, Salvador Rizzo and Meg Kelly (2021). Trump's false or misleading. Washington Post. Retrieved from: https://www.washingtonpost.com/politics/2021/01/24/trumps-false-or-misleading-claims-total-30573-over-four-years/

302

MEGAN BRENAN (2019). Trump Seen Marginally as Decisive Leader, but Not Honest. Gallup. Retrieved from: https://news.gallup.com/poll/260495/trump-seen-marginally-decisive-leader-not-honest.aspx

303

MEGAN BRENAN (2019). Trump Seen Marginally as Decisive Leader, but Not Honest. Gallup. Retrieved from: https://news.gallup.com/poll/260495/trump-seen-marginally-decisive-leader-not-honest.aspx

304

Gallup (2021). Presidential Approval Ratings for Donald Trump. Retrieved from: https://news.gallup.com/poll/203198/presidential-approval-ratings-donald-trump.aspx

305

Gerhard Peters (2021). "Presidential Job Approval Ratings Following the First 100 Days." The American Presidency Project. Ed. John T. Woolley and Gerhard Peters. Santa Barbara, CA: University of California. 1999-2021. Retrieved from:

https://www.presidency.ucsb.edu/statistics/data/presidential-job-approval-ratings

306

Shepard, Steven (2017). Poll: Voters see Trump as reckless, not honest. Politico. Retrieved from: https://www.politico.eu/article/donald-trump-poll-voters-see-trump-as-reckless-not-honest/

307

Von Hoffman, Nicholas (March 1988). "The Snarling Death of Roy M. Cohn". *Life*. New York City: Time, Inc.

308

Novak, Analisa (2023). Sen. Elizabeth Warren on Trump Indictment: "No one is above the law, not even a former president". CBS News. Retrieved from: https://www.cbsnews.com/news/trump-indictment-news-elizabeth-warren-no-one-is-above-the-law-former-president/

309

Buford, Larry (2022). Words of the Week – Chickens Coming Home to Roost! Retrieved from: https://lasentinel.net/words-of-the-week-chickens-coming-home-to-roost.html

310

Geller, Wendy (2023). Donald Trump Mistakes Picture of Rape Accuser E. Jean Carroll For Marla Maples: 'That's My Wife'. Yahoo! Life. Retrieved from: https://www.yahoo.com/lifestyle/donald-trump-mistakes-picture-rape-023418436.html

311

Carroll, E. Jean (June 21, 2019). "Donald Trump Assaulted Me, But He's Not Alone on My List of Hideous Men". *The Cut*. Retrieved June 21, 2019. Donald Trump assaulted me in a Bergdorf Goodman dressing room 23 years ago. But he's not alone on the list of awful men in my life. Retrieved from: https://www.thecut.com/2019/06/donald-trump-assault-e-jean-carroll-other-hideous-men.html

312

EVAN B CULTURE (2017). "Jay Z Is The Greatest Rapper of All Time Even If He's Not Your Favorite". *Respect My Region*. July 28, 2017. Retrieved from: https://www.respectmyregion.com/jay-z-greatest-rapper-time-even-hes-not-favorite/

313

Holland, Fahiemah Al-Ali,Frank (December 10, 2020). "Billionaire Jay-Z becomes the latest cultural influencer to launch his own cannabis brand". *CNBC*.

O'Malley Greenburg, Zach (June 3, 2019). "Artist, Icon, Billionaire: How Jay-Z Created His $1 Billion Fortune". *Forbes*.

314

Bloomberg, Michael (April 18, 2013). "Jay Z: The World's 100 Most Influential People". *Time*. ISSN 0040-781X

Arnold, Chuck (May 12, 2021). "Jay-Z leads Rock & Roll Hall of Fame inductees — among some head-scratchers". *New York Post*.

315

Adaso, Henry. How Well Do You Know Jay-Z? Archived March 4, 2016, at the Wayback Machine About.com.

316

Birchmeier, Jason. Jay-Z Biography. Allmusic. Retrieved from: https://www.allmusic.com/artist/jay-z-mn0000224257/biography

317

Koroma, Salima (May 15, 2009). "Industry Insider Reveals "Secret War" Between LL Cool J and Jay-Z". Hiphopdx.

318

Reid, Shaheem (February 27, 2002). "Where's The Love? Jay-Z Disses Grammys Again". MTV News.

319

"Jay-Z Chart History – Billboard". *Www.billboard.com*. Retrieved from: https://www.billboard.com/artist/jay-z/chart-history/hsi/

320

Jones, Steve (November 7, 2000). "Jay-Z's rap dominates". *USA Today*. Gannett Company, Inc.

321

"The #7 Biggest Moment: Jay-Z & Nas Squash Beef". *XXL Magazine*. February 6, 2008.Retrieved from: https://www.xxlmag.com/the-7-biggest-moment-jay-z-nas-squash-beef/

Reid, Shaheem (December 12, 2001). "Mobb Deep Strike Back at Jay-Z on Infamy". MTV.

322

Grein, Paul (February 29, 2012). "Week Ending Feb. 26, 2012. Albums: Half of the Top 10 | Chart Watch (NEW) – Yahoo Music". Music.yahoo.com.
Andrews, Travis M. (March 20, 2019). "Jay-Z, a speech by Sen. Robert F. Kennedy and 'Schoolhouse Rock!' among recordings deemed classics by Library of Congress". *The Washington Post*.

323

Andrews, Travis M. (March 20, 2019). "Jay-Z, a speech by Sen. Robert F. Kennedy and 'Schoolhouse Rock!' among recordings deemed classics by Library of Congress". *The Washington Post*.

324

Anderson, Kyle (August 24, 2009). "A Young Jay-Z Describes His Early Influences". MTV News.

325

"Jay-Z's Business Portfolio". KSFM. May 18, 2010. Retrieved from:
https://web.archive.org/web/20160306221018/http://ksfm.cbslocal.com/2010/05/18/jay-zs-business-portfolio/

326

"Iconix to Buy Rocawear, Jay-Z's Clothing Line". *The New York Times*. March 7, 2007. Retrieved from:
https://www.nytimes.com/2007/03/07/business/07clothes.html

"Jay-Z: Down To 98 Problems Yet?". MTV. February 7, 2007. Retrieved from:
https://web.archive.org/web/20070309153953/http://www.mtv.co.uk/channel/mtvuk/07032007/jay_z_down_to_98_problems_yet

327

Rooney, Kyle (July 29, 2016). "Jay Z promotes Reebok". *HNHH*.

328

Emily Smith and Ian Mohr (November 10, 2014). "Jay Z drops $200 million for stake in champagne company". Page Six.

Sarah Spickernell. "How much is Jay-Z worth? Rapper adds luxury champagne brand Armand de Brignac to personal empire with purchase from Sovereign Brands". City A.M.

329

Courtney Connley (February 2, 2015). "Jay Z Makes $56 Million Bid to Buy Music Streaming Company". Black Enterprise.

330

"With $20M In The Bank, jetsmarter Is Building The Uber Of The Skies". *Techcrunch*. Retrieved from: https://techcrunch.com/2015/07/23/with-20m-in-the-bank-jetsmarter-is-building-the-uber-of-the-skies/

331

"Jay-Z Stepping Down As Def Jam President/CEO". *MTV*. Retrieved from: https://www.mtv.com/news/qm66bk/jay-z-stepping-down-as-def-jam-presidentceo

"Jay Z | Jay-jay Z Acquires Independent German Label". Contactmusic.com. April 4, 2011. Retrieved from: https://www.contactmusic.com/jay-z/news/jay-jay-z-acquires-independent-german-label_1211060

332

Perpetua, Matthew (April 6, 2011). "Jay-Z Launches New Pop Culture Site Life + Times". *Rolling Stone*.

333

Brooks, Matt (September 26, 2011). "The Washington Post – Jay-Z: Brooklyn Nets to debut at Barclays Center in 2012". *The Washington Post*.

"Report: Jay-Z to drop Nets ownership stake, become player agent". SI.com. Retrieved from: https://web.archive.org/web/20130411194142/http://nba.si.com/2013/04/09/jay-z-brooklyn-nets-nba-agent/

334

Ozanian, Mike (September 17, 2013). "Jay Z Set To Get $1.5 Million For His Barclays Center Stake". *Forbes*.

335

Goble, Corban (April 2, 2013). "Jay-Z Starts Roc Nation Sports Agency, Signs Yankees Player Robinson Canó". *Pitchforkmedia*.

336

Stutz, Howard (August 28, 2008). "40/40 Club closing to make way for Palazzo sports book". Casino City Times.

"Will Smith, Jay-Z back beauty line". CNN. May 18, 2005. Retrieved from: https://money.cnn.com/2005/05/18/news/newsmakers/cosmetics/index.htm

"Jay-Z Bringing His 40/40 Club To Airports". *MTV News*. *Retrieved from:* https://web.archive.org/web/20101204053543/http://www.mtv.com/news/articles/1653340/20101201/jay_z.jhtml
Greenburg, Zack O'Malley. "Inside Jay Z's Cohiba Comador Cigar
Venture". *Forbes*. Https://www.forbes.com/sites/zackomalleygreenburg/2014/04/16/inside-jay-zs-cohiba-comador-cigar-venture/?Sh=45414a615f4a
"Roc Nation Teams With Brooklyn's Long Island University to Open Music, Sports & Entertainment School". *Complex*. Retrieved from: https://www.complex.com/music/2020/08/roc-nation-long-island-university-partner-music-sports-entertainment-school

337

Tauber, Michelle (October 25, 2004). "The Good Life". *People*.

Ehrich Dowd, Kathy; Clehane, Diane; Helling, Steve (April 22, 2008). "Beyoncé and Jay-Z File Signed Marriage License". *People*.

Owoseje, Toyin (June 18, 2012). "Beyoncé Buys Jay-Z $40m Private Jet for Father's Day". *International Business Times*. Newsweek Media Group.

Kaufman, Gil (January 13, 2010). "Jay-Z And Beyoncé Named Top-Earning Couple in Entertainment". MTV News.

France, Lisa Respers; Melas, Chloe. "Beyoncé and Jay Z welcome twins". CNN.

338

Wessler, Mike (2022). Updated charts provide insights on racial disparities, correctional control, jail suicides, and more: New data visualizations expose the harms of mass incarceration. *Prison Policy Initiative*. Retrieved from: https://www.prisonpolicy.org/blog/2022/05/19/updated_c harts/#:~:text=Racial%20disparities%20in%20the%20crimin al%20legal%20system&text=The%20system%20of%20mass %20incarceration,people%20in%20jails%20and%20prisons.

339

Okwerekwu, Ike (May 5, 2019). "Tupac: The Greatest Inspirational Hip Hop Artist". *Music For Inspiration*.

340

Planas, Antonio (April 7, 2011). "FBI outlines parallels in Notorious B.I.G., Tupac slayings". *Las Vegas Review-Journal*.

341

"Notorious B.I.G., Tupac Shakur To Be Inducted Into Hip-Hop Hall Of Fame". *BET*. December 30, 2006. Retrieved from: https://web.archive.org/web/20061230051113/http://ww w.bet.com/Music/Archives/BET.com%2B-%2bnotorious%2BB.I.G._%2btupac%2bshakur%2bto%2bbe% 2binducted%2binto%2bhip-Hop%2bhall%2bof%2bfame%2B152.htm

"The Best Selling Tupac Albums of All Time". *2paclegacy.net.* August 4, 2019. Retrieved from: https://2paclegacy.net/the-best-selling-tupac-albums-of-all-time/

342

Walker, Charles F. (February 26, 2014). "Tupac Shakur and Tupac Amaru" Retrieved from: https://charlesfwalker.com/tupac-shakur-tupac-amaru/

Scott, Cathy (October 2, 1996). "22-year-old arrested in Tupac Shakur killing". *Las Vegas Sun.*

Bass, Debra D. (September 4, 1997). "Book chronicling Shakur murder set to hit stores". *Las Vegas Sun.*

343

"Rare Interview With Tupac's Biological Father". Power 107.5. December 30, 2013. Retrieved from: https://mycolumbuspower.com/2916523/rare-interview-with-tupacs-biological-father-video/
"Afeni Shakur" (PDF). 2Pac Legacy. Retrieved from: https://web.archive.org/web/20080409074113/http://www .2paclegacy.com/images/assets/bio_afeni_shakur/afeni_sha kur_biography.pdf;

Sullivan, Randall (January 3, 2003). *Labyrinth: A Detective Investigates the Murders of Tupac Shakur and Notorious B.I.G., the Implication of Death Row Records' Suge Knight, and the Origins of the Los Angeles Police Scandal.* New York City: Grove Press. ISBN 0-8021-3971-X.

Martin, Douglas (June 3, 2011). "Elmer G. Pratt, Jailed Panther Leader, Dies at 63". *The New York Times.*

Shakur, Assata (1987). *An Autobiography of Assata Shakur.* Lennox S. Hinds (foreword). Lawrence Hill Books. ISBN 0-88208-221-3.

344

Lewis, John (September 6, 2016). "Tupac Was Here". *Baltimore Magazine.*

King, Jamilah (November 15, 2012). "Art and Activism in Charm City: Five Baltimore Collectives That Are Facing Race". *Colorlines.* ARC.

Case, Wesley (March 31, 2017). "Tupac Shakur in Baltimore: Friends, teachers remember the birth of an artist". *The Baltimore Sun.*

Bastfield, Darrin Keith (2002). *Back in the Day: My Life and Times with Tupac Shakur.* Da Capo Press. P. 5. ISBN 978-0-345-44775-3.
Golus, Carrie (December 28, 2006). *Tupac Shakur.* Lerner Publications. ISBN 9780822566090.

345

Chung, James (February 25, 2020). "These Were Tupac's Startling Last Words". *SPIN.*

346

Brown, Preezy (November 12, 2016). "How '2Pacalypse Now' Marked The Birth Of A Rap Revolutionary". *Vibe.*

347

Westhoff, Ben (September 12, 2016). "How Tupac and B.I.G. went from friends to deadly rivals". *Vice.com.*

348

Philips, Chuck (September 13, 2012). "Tupac Shakur Interview 1995". *The Chuck Philips Post.*
Philips, Chuck (October 25, 1995). "Tupac Shakur: 'I am not a gangster'". *Los Angeles Times.*

349

Anderson, Joel (October 30, 2019). "The Moment Tupac and Biggie Went From Friends to Enemies". *Slate Magazine*.

350

Parker, Derrick; Diehl, Matt (2007). *Notorious C.O.P.: The Inside Story of the Tupac, Biggie, and Jam Master Jay Investigations from the NYPD's First "Hip-Hop Cop"*. New York: St. Martin's Griffin. Pp. 113–116. ISBN 9781429907781

351

Phillips, Chuck (July 31, 2003). "As Associates Fall, Is 'Suge' Knight Next?". *Los Angeles Times*.

"Maxwell, Tupac Top Soul Train Awards". E! Online. March 7, 1997. Retrieved from: https://www.eonline.com/news/34166/maxwell_tupac_top_soul_train_awards Huey, Steve (n.d.). "2Pac – *All Eyez on Me*". *Allmusic*.

Williams, Stereo (June 4, 2016). "Tupac's 'Hit 'Em Up': The Most Savage Diss Track Ever Turns 20". *The Daily Beast*.

352

Williams, Stereo (February 3, 2019). "John Singleton on That Tupac AIDS Test: 'That Was a Joke!'". *The Daily Beast*.

Powell, Kevin (February 14, 2021). "Revisit Tupac's April 1995 Cover Story: 'READY TO LIVE'". *VIBE.com*.

Tate, Greg (June 26, 2001). "Sex & Negrocity by Greg Tate". Villagevoice.com.

Markman, Rob (May 30, 2013). "Tupac Would Have 'Outshined' 'Menace II Society,' Director Admits". MTV.

Tinsley, Justin (March 22, 2019). "A look back at 'Above the Rim' on its 25th anniversary". *Andscape.*

Rodriguez, Jason (September 2011). "Pit of snakes". *XXL Magazine.*

353

Perez-Pena, Richard (December 2, 1994). "Wounded Rapper Gets Mixed Verdict In Sex-Abuse Case". *The New York Times.* Gladwell, Malcolm (December 2, 1994). "Rapper Shakur guilty of sex abuse, not guilty of sodomy and gun charges". *The Washington Post.*

354

Perez-Pena, Richard (December 2, 1994). "Wounded Rapper Gets Mixed Verdict In Sex-Abuse Case". *The New York Times.* ISSN 0362-4331

James, George (February 8, 1995). "Rapper Faces Prison Term For Sex Abuse". *The New York Times.* P. B1.

Bruck, Connie (June 29, 1997). "The Takedown of Tupac". *The New Yorker.*

"Doe v. Shakur (civil case)". *Casetext.* January 22, 1996. Retrieved from: https://casetext.com/case/jane-doe-plaintiff-v-tupac-a-shakur-and-charles-l-fuller-defendants?__cf_chl_f_tk=r9pasmbxdbk.xirwih.zgwssvpy1rw 9up1.2e4khbui-1642425136-0-ganycgznct0

355

"Tupac believed his rape case was connected to his Quad Studios shooting". *XXL.* June 5, 2014. Retrieved from: https://www.xxlmag.com/tupac-thought-rape-case-connected-quad-studio-shooting/

356

Au, Wagner James (December 11, 1996). "Yo, Niccolo!". *Salon*. San Francisco, California: Salon Media Group Inc. Retrieved from: https://archive.ph/20070929103156/http://archive.salon.com/media/media2961211.html
357

Philips, Chuck (October 25, 1995). "Tupac Shakur: 'I am not a gangster'". *Los Angeles Times*. Retrieved from: https://www.latimes.com/local/la-me-tupac-qa-story.html

358

Smothers, Ronald (November 2, 1993). "Rapper Charged in Shootings of Off-Duty Officers". *The New York Times*. ISSN 0362-4331

Butler, Rhett (May 28, 2020). "Redo '93: Tupac Shakur's Shootout With Police Proves Power To People". *The Source*.

359

Samaha, Albert (October 28, 2013). "James Rosemond, Hip-Hop Manager Tied to Tupac Shooting, Gets Life Sentence for Drug Trafficking". *Village Voice*. New York City.
Anderson, Joel (February 14, 2020). "Slow Burn Season 3, Episode 1: Against the World". *Slate Magazine*.
Gelder, Lawrence Van (December 3, 1994). "Rapper, Shot and Convicted, Leaves Hospital for Secret Site". *The New York Times*. ISSN 0362-4331
Anderson, Joel (February 14, 2020). "Slow Burn Season 3, Episode 1: Against the World". *Slate Magazine*.

360

Stewart, Alison (March 18, 2008). "What Did Sean 'Puffy' Combs Know?". Npr.org.

Samaha, Albert (October 28, 2013). "James Rosemond, Hip-Hop Manager Tied to Tupac Shooting, Gets Life Sentence for Drug Trafficking". *Village Voice*. New York City.
Rodriguez, Jayson. "Game Manager Jimmy Rosemond Recalls Events The Night Tupac Was Shot, Says Session Was 'All Business'". *MTV News*.
Watkins, Greg (June 15, 2011). "Exclusive: Jimmy Henchman Associate Admits to Role in Robbery/Shooting of Tupac; Apologizes To Pac & B.I.G.'s Mothers". *Allhiphop.com*.

KTLA News (July 13, 2012). "Convicted Killer Confesses to Shooting West Coast Rapper Tupac Shakur". *The Courant*.

361

Pareles, Jon (September 14, 1996). "Tupac Shakur, 25, Rap Performer Who Personified Violence, Dies". *The New York Times*

362

"Rapper Tupac Shakur to face assault charge". *Ocala Star-Banner*. September 9, 1994. Retrieved from: https://news.google.com/newspapers?Nid=1988&dat=1994 1101&id=n0aoaaaaibaj&pg=3900,36494

Gonzalez, Victor (May 10, 2012). "TUPAC'S TEMPER: FIVE GREATEST FREAKOUTS, FROM MTV TO JAIL TIME". *Miami New Times*.

363

"Rapper Tupac Shakur charged". UPI. May 6, 1994. Retrieved from: https://www.upi.com/Archives/1994/05/06/Rapper-Tupac-Shakur-charged/3414768196800/

364

"Settlement in Rapper's Trial for Boy's Death". *San Francisco Chronicle*. November 8, 1995. Retrieved from: https://www.sfgate.com/news/article/PAGE-ONE-Settlement-in-Rapper-s-Trial-For-3019996.php

---

"Marin slaying case against rapper opens". *San Francisco Chronicle*. Retrieved from: https://www.sfgate.com/news/article/Marin-slaying-case-against-rapper-opens-3122665.php

365

Miller, Matt; Rahimi, Gobi M. (September 6, 2016). "I Spent Six Days Protecting Tupac on His Deathbed". *Esquire*. New York City: Hearst Magazines.

O'Neal, Sean (August 30, 2011). "Yes, the Outlawz smoked Tupac's ashes". *The A.V. Club*.

"Tupac's life after death". Smh.com.au. September 13, 2006.

Koch, Ed (October 24, 1997). "Tupac Shakur's Death Certificate Details". *Numberonestars*. Las Vegas Sun. "Detailed information on the fatal shooting" . *Alleyezonme*. Retrieved from: https://web.archive.org/web/20080514151716/http://www.alleyezonme.com/info/96shooting.html

366

O'Neal, Sean (August 30, 2011). "Yes, the Outlawz smoked Tupac's ashes". *The A.V. Club*.

367

Philips, Chuck (September 7, 2002). "Who killed Tupac Shakur?: Part 2". *Los Angeles Times*. Los Angeles, California. Leland, John (October 7, 2002). "New Theories Stir Speculation On Rap Deaths". *The New York Times*. "Unsealed FBI Report on Tupac Shakur". Vault.fbi.gov. Retrieved from: "Unsealed FBI Report on Tupac Shakur". Vault.fbi.gov. "FBI files on Tupac Shakur murder show he received death threats from Jewish gang". *Haaretz*. Haaretz Service. April 14, 2011. Retrieved from:

https://www.haaretz.com/jewish/2011-04-14/ty-article/fbi-
files-on-tupac-shakur-murder-show-he-received-death-
threats-from-jewish-gang/0000017f-f5c3-d318-afff-
f7e3913c0000

368

Reeves, Mosi (September 13, 2016). "8 Ways Tupac Shakur
Changed the World". *Rolling Stone.*

Okwerekwu, Ike (May 5, 2019). "Tupac: The Greatest
Inspirational Hip Hop Artist". *Music For Inspiration.* Retrieved
from: https://medium.com/music-for-inspiration/tupac-the-
greatest-inspirational-hip-hop-artist-7118f02747ed

Espinoza, Joshua (September 25, 2020). "Vice Presidential
Nominee Kamala Harris Names 2Pac as the 'Best Rapper
Alive'". *Complex.*

"The 50 Most Influential Rappers of All
Time". *BET.* Retrieved from:
https://archive.ph/20140530203134/http://www.bet.com/
music/photos/2011/09/50-most-influential-
rappers.html%23!2011-topic-tu-pac-crop
369

Brown, Peter Harry; Broeske, Pat H. (1997). *Down at the End
of Lonely Street: The Life and Death of Elvis Presley.*
Signet. ISBN 978-0-451-19094-9.

370

Guralnick, Peter (1994). *Last Train to Memphis: The Rise of
Elvis Presley.* Little, Brown. ISBN 978-0-316-33225-5.

Guralnick, Peter; Jorgensen, Ernst (1999). *Elvis Day by Day:
The Definitive Record of His Life and Music.*
Ballantine. ISBN 978-0-345-42089-3.

371

Kamphoefner, Walter D (2010). ""Elvis and Other Germans: Some Reflections and Modest Proposals on the Study of German-American Ethnicity" (2009)". In Kluge, Cora Lee (ed.). *Paths Crossing: Essays in German-American Studies*. Peter Lang. ISBN 978-3-0343-0221-0.

Dundy, Elaine (2004). *Elvis and Gladys* (2nd ed.). University Press of Mississippi. ISBN 978-1-57806-634-6.

Guralnick, Peter; Jorgensen, Ernst (1999). *Elvis Day by Day: The Definitive Record of His Life and Music*.
Ballantine. ISBN 978-0-345-42089-3.

Keough, Riley [@rileykeough] (July 19, 2017). "I had one great grandma who was creek and one who was full blood Cherokee" (Tweet).

372

Dundy, Elaine (2004). *Elvis and Gladys* (2nd ed.). University Press of Mississippi. ISBN 978-1-57806-634-6.

Guralnick, Peter (1994). *Last Train to Memphis: The Rise of Elvis Presley*. Little, Brown. ISBN 978-0-316-33225-5.

373

Dundy, Elaine (2004). *Elvis and Gladys* (2nd ed.). University Press of Mississippi. ISBN 978-1-57806-634-6.

Guralnick, Peter (1994). *Last Train to Memphis: The Rise of Elvis Presley*. Little, Brown. ISBN 978-0-316-33225-5.

374

Guralnick, Peter (1994). *Last Train to Memphis: The Rise of Elvis Presley*. Little, Brown. ISBN 978-0-316-33225-5.

375

Guralnick, Peter (1994). *Last Train to Memphis: The Rise of Elvis Presley*. Little,

Brown. ISBN 978-0-316-33225-5.

Stanley, David; Coffey, Frank (1998). *The Elvis Encyclopedia*. Virgin Books. ISBN 978-0-7535-0293-8.

Matthew-Walker, Robert (1979). *Elvis Presley. A Study in Music*. Midas Books. ISBN 978-0-85936-162-0.

Bertrand, Michael T (2000). *Race, Rock, and Elvis*. University of Illinois Press. ISBN 978-0-252-02586-0.

Jorgensen, Ernst (1998). *Elvis Presley – A Life in Music: The Complete Recording Sessions*. St Martin's Press. ISBN 978-0-312-18572-5.

376

Guralnick, Peter (1994). *Last Train to Memphis: The Rise of Elvis Presley*. Little,
Brown. ISBN 978-0-316-33225-5.

Stanley, David; Coffey, Frank (1998). *The Elvis Encyclopedia*. Virgin Books. ISBN 978-0-7535-0293-8.

Matthew-Walker, Robert (1979). *Elvis Presley. A Study in Music*. Midas Books. ISBN 978-0-85936-162-0.

Bertrand, Michael T (2000). *Race, Rock, and Elvis*. University of Illinois Press. ISBN 978-0-252-02586-0.

Jorgensen, Ernst (1998). *Elvis Presley – A Life in Music: The Complete Recording Sessions*. St Martin's Press. ISBN 978-0-312-18572-5.

377

Guralnick, Peter (1994). *Last Train to Memphis: The Rise of Elvis Presley*. Little, Brown. ISBN 978-0-316-33225-5.

Stanley, David; Coffey, Frank (1998). *The Elvis Encyclopedia.* Virgin Books. ISBN 978-0-7535-0293-8.

Matthew-Walker, Robert (1979). *Elvis Presley. A Study in Music.* Midas Books. ISBN 978-0-85936-162-0.

Bertrand, Michael T (2000). *Race, Rock, and Elvis.* University of Illinois Press. ISBN 978-0-252-02586-0.

Jorgensen, Ernst (1998). *Elvis Presley – A Life in Music: The Complete Recording Sessions.* St Martin's Press. ISBN 978-0-312-18572-5.

378

Guralnick, Peter (1994). *Last Train to Memphis: The Rise of Elvis Presley.* Little, Brown. ISBN 978-0-316-33225-5.

Brown. ISBN 978-0-316-33225-5.

Stanley, David; Coffey, Frank (1998). *The Elvis Encyclopedia.* Virgin Books. ISBN 978-0-7535-0293-8.

Matthew-Walker, Robert (1979). *Elvis Presley. A Study in Music.* Midas Books. ISBN 978-0-85936-162-0.
Bertrand, Michael T (2000). *Race, Rock, and Elvis.* University of Illinois Press. ISBN 978-0-252-02586-0.

Jorgensen, Ernst (1998). *Elvis Presley – A Life in Music: The Complete Recording Sessions.* St Martin's Press. ISBN 978-0-312-18572-5.

379

Guralnick, Peter (1994). *Last Train to Memphis: The Rise of Elvis Presley.* Little, Brown. ISBN 978-0-316-33225-5.

380

Guralnick, Peter (1994). *Last Train to Memphis: The Rise of Elvis Presley.* Little, Brown. ISBN 978-0-316-33225-5.

381

Guralnick, Peter (1994). *Last Train to Memphis: The Rise of Elvis Presley*. Little, Brown. ISBN 978-0-316-33225-5.

382

Guralnick, Peter (1994). *Last Train to Memphis: The Rise of Elvis Presley*. Little, Brown. ISBN 978-0-316-33225-5.

383

Miller, Madison (March 23, 2021). "Elvis Presley: How the King of Rock 'n' Roll Developed His Signature Dance Moves". *Outsider*.

Guralnick, Peter (1994). *Last Train to Memphis: The Rise of Elvis Presley*. Little, Brown. ISBN 978-0-316-33225-5.

384

Guralnick, Peter (1994). *Last Train to Memphis: The Rise of Elvis Presley*. Little, Brown. ISBN 978-0-316-33225-5.

385

Guralnick, Peter (1994). *Last Train to Memphis: The Rise of Elvis Presley*. Little,
Brown. ISBN 978-0-316-33225-5.

386

Guralnick, Peter (1994). *Last Train to Memphis: The Rise of Elvis Presley*. Little,
Brown. ISBN 978-0-316-33225-5.

387

Guralnick, Peter (1994). *Last Train to Memphis: The Rise of Elvis Presley*. Little,
Brown. ISBN 978-0-316-33225-5.

388

Guralnick, Peter (1994). *Last Train to Memphis: The Rise of Elvis Presley*. Little,
Brown. ISBN 978-0-316-33225-5.

389

Guralnick, Peter; Jorgensen, Ernst (1999). *Elvis Day by Day: The Definitive Record of His Life and Music.*
Ballantine. ISBN 978-0-345-42089-3.

Guralnick, Peter (1994). *Last Train to Memphis: The Rise of Elvis Presley*. Little,
Brown. ISBN 978-0-316-33225-5.

Stanley, David; Coffey, Frank (1998). *The Elvis Encyclopedia.*
Virgin Books. ISBN 978-0-7535-0293-8.

390

Fensch, Thomas (2001). *The FBI Files on Elvis Presley*. New
Century Books. ISBN 978-0-930751-03-6.

Koch, Ed; Manning, Mary; Toplikar, Dave (May 15, 2008). "Showtime: How Sin City evolved into 'The Entertainment Capital of the World'". *Las Vegas Sun.*

Guralnick, Peter; Jorgensen, Ernst (1999). *Elvis Day by Day: The Definitive Record of His Life and Music.*
Ballantine. ISBN 978-0-345-42089-3.

Guralnick, Peter (1994). *Last Train to Memphis: The Rise of Elvis Presley*. Little,
Brown. ISBN 978-0-316-33225-5.

391

Gould, Jack (June 6, 1956). "TV: New Phenomenon – Elvis Presley Rises to Fame as Vocalist Who Is Virtuoso of Hootchy-Kootchy". Retrieved from:
http://graphics8.nytimes.com/packages/pdf/archives/elvis-presley-on-milton-berle-show-06-06-1956.pdf

Fensch, Thomas (2001). *The FBI Files on Elvis Presley*. New Century Books. ISBN 978-0-930751-03-6.

Koch, Ed; Manning, Mary; Toplikar, Dave (May 15, 2008). "Showtime: How Sin City evolved into 'The Entertainment Capital of the World'". *Las Vegas Sun*.

Guralnick, Peter; Jorgensen, Ernst (1999). *Elvis Day by Day: The Definitive Record of His Life and Music*. Ballantine. ISBN 978-0-345-42089-3.

Guralnick, Peter (1994). *Last Train to Memphis: The Rise of Elvis Presley*. Little, Brown. ISBN 978-0-316-33225-5.

392

Austen, Jake (2005). *TV-A-Go-Go: Rock on TV from American Bandstand to American Idol*. Chicago Review Press. ISBN 978-1-55652-572-8.
393

Keogh, Pamela Clarke (2004). *Elvis Presley: The Man, The Life, The Legend*. Simon & Schuster. ISBN 978-0-7434-5603-6.

394

Guralnick, Peter; Jorgensen, Ernst (1999). *Elvis Day by Day: The Definitive Record of His Life and Music*. Ballantine. ISBN 978-0-345-42089-3.

Jorgensen, Ernst (1998). *Elvis Presley – A Life in Music: The Complete Recording Sessions*. St Martin's Press. ISBN 978-0-312-18572-5.

395

Austen, Jake (2005). *TV-A-Go-Go: Rock on TV from American Bandstand to American Idol*. Chicago Review Press. ISBN 978-1-55652-572-8.

Edgerton, Gary R. (2007). *The Columbia History of American Television*. Columbia University Press. ISBN 978-0-231-12165-1.

Victor, Adam (2008). *The Elvis Encyclopedia*. Overlook Duckworth. ISBN 978-1-58567-598-2.
Guralnick, Peter (1994). *Last Train to Memphis: The Rise of Elvis Presley*. Little,
Brown. ISBN 978-0-316-33225-5.

396

Moore, Scotty; Dickerson, James (1997). *That's Alright, Elvis*. Schirmer Books. ISBN 978-0-02-864599-5.

Marsh, Dave (1980). "Elvis Presley". In Marsh, Dave; Swenson, John (eds.). *The Rolling Stone Record Guide* (2nd ed.). Virgin. ISBN 978-0-907080-00-8.

Austen, Jake (2005). *TV-A-Go-Go: Rock on TV from American Bandstand to American Idol*. Chicago Review Press. ISBN 978-1-55652-572-8.

Edgerton, Gary R. (2007). *The Columbia History of American Television*. Columbia University Press. ISBN 978-0-231-12165-1.

Victor, Adam (2008). *The Elvis Encyclopedia*. Overlook Duckworth. ISBN 978-1-58567-598-2.
Gould, Jack (June 6, 1956). "TV: New Phenomenon – Elvis Presley Rises to Fame as Vocalist Who Is Virtuoso of Hootchy-Kootchy". Retrieved from:
http://graphics8.nytimes.com/packages/pdf/archives/elvis-presley-on-milton-berle-show-06-06-1956.pdf

Fensch, Thomas (2001). *The FBI Files on Elvis Presley*. New Century Books. ISBN 978-0-930751-03-6.

Koch, Ed; Manning, Mary; Toplikar, Dave (May 15, 2008). "Showtime: How Sin City evolved into 'The Entertainment Capital of the World'". *Las Vegas Sun*.

Guralnick, Peter; Jorgensen, Ernst (1999). *Elvis Day by Day: The Definitive Record of His Life and Music*. Ballantine. ISBN 978-0-345-42089-3.

Guralnick, Peter (1994). *Last Train to Memphis: The Rise of Elvis Presley*. Little, Brown. ISBN 978-0-316-33225-5.

Stanley, David; Coffey, Frank (1998). *The Elvis Encyclopedia*. Virgin Books. ISBN 978-0-7535-0293-8.

Stanley, David; Coffey, Frank (1998). *The Elvis Encyclopedia*. Virgin Books. ISBN 978-0-7535-0293-8.

Matthew-Walker, Robert (1979). *Elvis Presley. A Study in Music*. Midas Books. ISBN 978-0-85936-162-0.

Bertrand, Michael T (2000). *Race, Rock, and Elvis*. University of Illinois Press. ISBN 978-0-252-02586-0.

Jorgensen, Ernst (1998). *Elvis Presley – A Life in Music: The Complete Recording Sessions*. St Martin's Press. ISBN 978-0-312-18572-5.

397

Victor, Adam (2008). *The Elvis Encyclopedia*. Overlook Duckworth. ISBN 978-1-58567-598-2.

398

Presley, Elvis Aron; DD 214: Armed Forces of the United States Report of Transfer or Discharge. US Department of Defense. March 5, 1960.

Clayton, Dick; Heard, James (2003). *Elvis: By Those Who Knew Him Best*. Virgin Publishing. ISBN 978-0-7535-0835-0.

Guralnick, Peter (1999). *Careless Love: The Unmaking of Elvis Presley*. Back Bay Books. ISBN 978-0-316-33297-2.

399

Presley, Elvis Aron; DD 214: Armed Forces of the United States Report of Transfer or Discharge. US Department of Defense. March 5, 1960.

400

Guralnick, Peter (1994). *Last Train to Memphis: The Rise of Elvis Presley*. Little,
Brown. ISBN 978-0-316-33225-5.

401

Jeffrey, Joyann. "Priscilla Presley and Elvis Presley's relationship story, in their own words". *TODAY.com*.

Marcus, Greil (1982). *Mystery Train: Images of America in Rock 'n' Roll Music* (Revised ed.). E.P. Dutton. ISBN 978-0-525-47708-2.

Jeffrey, Joyann. "Priscilla Presley and Elvis Presley's relationship story, in their own words". *TODAY.com*.

Jorgensen, Ernst (1998). *Elvis Presley – A Life in Music: The Complete Recording Sessions*. St Martin's Press. ISBN 978-0-312-18572-5.

Guralnick, Peter; Jorgensen, Ernst (1999). *Elvis Day by Day: The Definitive Record of His Life and Music*.
Ballantine. ISBN 978-0-345-42089-3.

Guralnick, Peter (1994). *Last Train to Memphis: The Rise of Elvis Presley*. Little,
Brown. ISBN 978-0-316-33225-5.

402

Slaughter, Todd; Anne E. Nixon (2004). *The Elvis Archives.* Omnibus Press. ISBN 978-1-84449-380-7.

Matthew-Walker, Robert (1979). *Elvis Presley. A Study in Music.* Midas Books. ISBN 978-0-85936-162-0.

Marcus, Greil (1982). *Mystery Train: Images of America in Rock 'n' Roll Music* (Revised ed.). E.P. Dutton. ISBN 978-0-525-47708-2.

Jorgensen, Ernst (1998). *Elvis Presley – A Life in Music: The Complete Recording Sessions.* St Martin's Press. ISBN 978-0-312-18572-5.

Robertson, John (2004). *Elvis Presley: The Complete Guide to His Music.* Omnibus Press. ISBN 978-1-84449-711-9.

Presley, Elvis Aron; DD 214: Armed Forces of the United States Report of Transfer or Discharge. US Department of Defense. March 5, 1960.

Clayton, Dick; Heard, James (2003). Elvis: By Those Who Knew Him Best. Virgin Publishing. ISBN 978-0-7535-0835-0.

Guralnick, Peter (1999). Careless Love: The Unmaking of Elvis Presley. Back Bay Books. ISBN 978-0-316-33297-2.

403

Guralnick, Peter (1999). Careless Love: The Unmaking of Elvis Presley. Back Bay Books. ISBN 978-0-316-33297-2.

404

Ponce de Leon, Charles L. (2007). *Fortunate Son: The Life of Elvis Presley.* Macmillan. ISBN 978-0-8090-1641-9.

405

Marsh, Dave (2004). ""Elvis Presley"". In Brackett, Nathan; Hoard, Christian (eds.). *The New Rolling Stone Album Guide* (4th ed.). Simon & Schuster. ISBN 978-0-7432-0169-8.

Guralnick, Peter (1999). Careless Love: The Unmaking of Elvis Presley. Back Bay Books. ISBN 978-0-316-33297-2.

Victor, Adam (2008). *The Elvis Encyclopedia*. Overlook Duckworth. ISBN 978-1-58567-598-2.

406

Kubernick, Harvey (2008). *The Complete '68 Comeback Special*. CD Booklet RCA/BMG. UPC 88697306262.

Guralnick, Peter (1999). Careless Love: The Unmaking of Elvis Presley. Back Bay Books. ISBN 978-0-316-33297-2.

407

Hopkins, Jerry (2007). *Elvis – The Biography*. Plexus. ISBN 978-0-85965-391-6.

Guralnick, Peter (1999). *Careless Love: The Unmaking of Elvis Presley*. Back Bay Books. ISBN 978-0-316-33297-2.
408

Kubernick, Harvey (2008). *The Complete '68 Comeback Special*. CD Booklet RCA/BMG. UPC 88697306262.
409

Marsh, Dave (1980). "Elvis Presley". In Marsh, Dave; Swenson, John (eds.). *The Rolling Stone Record Guide* (2nd ed.). Virgin. ISBN 978-0-907080-00-8.

Jorgensen, Ernst (1998). *Elvis Presley – A Life in Music: The Complete Recording Sessions*. St Martin's Press. ISBN 978-0-312-18572-5.

410

Guralnick, Peter (1999). Careless Love: The Unmaking of Elvis Presley. Back Bay Books. ISBN 978-0-316-33297-2.

Guralnick, Peter; Jorgensen, Ernst (1999). *Elvis Day by Day: The Definitive Record of His Life and Music*. Ballantine. ISBN 978-0-345-42089-3.

Jorgensen, Ernst (1998). *Elvis Presley – A Life in Music: The Complete Recording Sessions*. St Martin's Press. ISBN 978-0-312-18572-5.

411

Guralnick, Peter (1999). Careless Love: The Unmaking of Elvis Presley. Back Bay Books. ISBN 978-0-316-33297-2.

Guralnick, Peter; Jorgensen, Ernst (1999). *Elvis Day by Day: The Definitive Record of His Life and Music*. Ballantine. ISBN 978-0-345-42089-3.

Jorgensen, Ernst (1998). *Elvis Presley – A Life in Music: The Complete Recording Sessions*. St Martin's Press. ISBN 978-0-312-18572-5.

Moyer, Susan M. (2002). *Elvis: The King Remembered*. Sports Publishing LLC. ISBN 978-1-58261-558-5.
412

Stein, Ruthe (August 3, 1997). "Girls! Girls! Girls!". *San Francisco Chronicle*. Retrieved December 29, 2009.

413

Hopkins, Jerry (2007). *Elvis – The Biography*. Plexus. ISBN 978-0-85965-391-6.

Stanley, David; Coffey, Frank (1998). *The Elvis Encyclopedia*. Virgin Books. ISBN 978-0-7535-0293-8.

414

Stanley, David; Coffey, Frank (1998). *The Elvis Encyclopedia*. Virgin Books. ISBN 978-0-7535-0293-8.

Robertson, John (2004). *Elvis Presley: The Complete Guide to His Music*. Omnibus Press. ISBN 978-1-84449-711-9.

415

The Beatles (2000). *The Beatles Anthology*. Chronicle Books. ISBN 978-0-8118-2684-6.

Guralnick, Peter (1999). *Careless Love: The Unmaking of Elvis Presley*. Back Bay Books. ISBN 978-0-316-33297-2.

Jorgensen, Ernst (1998). *Elvis Presley – A Life in Music: The Complete Recording Sessions*. St Martin's Press. ISBN 978-0-312-18572-5.

416

Stanley, David; Coffey, Frank (1998). *The Elvis Encyclopedia*. Virgin Books. ISBN 978-0-7535-0293-8.

Robertson, John (2004). *Elvis Presley: The Complete Guide to His Music*. Omnibus Press. ISBN 978-1-84449-711-9.

417

Guralnick, Peter (1999). *Careless Love: The Unmaking of Elvis Presley*. Back Bay Books. ISBN 978-0-316-33297-2.

Williamson, Joel (2015). *Elvis Presley: A Southern Life*. Oxford University Press. ISBN 978-0-19-986317-4.

Marsh, Stefanie (December 21, 2015). "Did Elvis indoctrinate me? Probably – but I don't see it as a bad thing". *The Times*

Hopkins, Jerry (2007). *Elvis – The Biography*. Plexus. ISBN 978-0-85965-391-6.

Keogh, Pamela Clarke (2004). *Elvis Presley: The Man, The Life, The Legend*. Simon & Schuster. ISBN 978-0-7434-5603-6.

418

Guralnick, Peter; Jorgensen, Ernst (1999). *Elvis Day by Day: The Definitive Record of His Life and Music*. Ballantine. ISBN 978-0-345-42089-3.
Higginbotham, Alan (August 11, 2002). "Doctor Feelgood". *The Observer*. Retrieved December 29, 2009. Retrieved from: https://www.theguardian.com/theobserver/2002/aug/11/features.magazine27
Keogh, Pamela Clarke (2004). *Elvis Presley: The Man, The Life, The Legend*. Simon & Schuster. ISBN 978-0-7434-5603-6.

419

Guralnick, Peter (1999). *Careless Love: The Unmaking of Elvis Presley*. Back Bay Books. ISBN 978-0-316-33297-2.
Hopkins, Jerry (1986). *Elvis: The Final Years*. Berkley. ISBN 978-0-425-08999-6.

420

Guralnick, Peter (1999). *Careless Love: The Unmaking of Elvis Presley*. Back Bay Books. ISBN 978-0-316-33297-2.
Hopkins, Jerry (1986). *Elvis: The Final Years*. Berkley. ISBN 978-0-425-08999-6.

421

Stanley, David; Coffey, Frank (1998). *The Elvis Encyclopedia*. Virgin Books. ISBN 978-0-7535-0293-8.
Guralnick, Peter (1999). *Careless Love: The Unmaking of Elvis Presley*. Back Bay Books. ISBN 978-0-316-33297-2.

422

Guralnick, Peter; Jorgensen, Ernst (1999). *Elvis Day by Day: The Definitive Record of His Life and Music*. Ballantine. ISBN 978-0-345-42089-3.

Guralnick, Peter (1999). *Careless Love: The Unmaking of Elvis Presley*. Back Bay Books. ISBN 978-0-316-33297-2.

423

Marsh, Dave (1989). *The Heart of Rock & Soul: The 1001 Greatest Singles Ever Made*. Penguin Books. ISBN 978-0-14-012108-7.

424

Victor, Adam (2008). *The Elvis Encyclopedia*. Overlook Duckworth. ISBN 978-1-58567-598-2.

425

Scherman, Tony (August 16, 2006). "Elvis Dies". *American Heritage*
Guralnick, Peter (1999). *Careless Love: The Unmaking of Elvis Presley*. Back Bay Books. ISBN 978-0-316-33297-2.

426

Guralnick, Peter (1999). *Careless Love: The Unmaking of Elvis Presley*. Back Bay Books. ISBN 978-0-316-33297-2.

427

Stanley, David; Coffey, Frank (1998). *The Elvis Encyclopedia*. Virgin Books. ISBN 978-0-7535-0293-8.

Humphries, Patrick (2003). *Elvis the No. 1 Hits: The Secret History of the Classics*. Andrews mcmeel Publishing. ISBN 978-0-7407-3803-6.

Higginbotham, Alan (August 11, 2002). "Doctor Feelgood". *The Observer*

428

Alden, Ginger (2014). *Elvis & Ginger: Elvis Presley's Fiancée and Last Love Finally Tells her Story*. New York: Berkeley Publishing. ISBN 978-1-101-61613-0.

429

Woolley, John T.; Peters, Gerhard (August 17, 1977). "Jimmy
Carter: Death of Elvis Presley Statement by the
President". *American Presidency Project*. University of
California, Santa Barbara.
Hopkins, Jerry (2007). *Elvis – The Biography*.
Plexus. ISBN 978-0-85965-391-6.
Guralnick, Peter (1999). *Careless Love: The Unmaking of Elvis
Presley*. Back Bay Books. ISBN 978-0-316-33297-2.
Victor, Adam (2008). *The Elvis Encyclopedia*. Overlook
Duckworth. ISBN 978-1-58567-598-2.

430

Matthew-Walker, Robert (1979). *Elvis Presley. A Study in
Music*. Midas Books. ISBN 978-0-85936-162-0.
Warwick, Neil; Kutner, Jon; Brown, Tony (2004). *The
Complete Book of the British Charts: Singles & Albums* (3rd ed.).
Omnibus Press. ISBN 978-1-84449-058-5.
Guralnick, Peter (1999). *Careless Love: The Unmaking of Elvis
Presley*. Back Bay Books. ISBN 978-0-316-33297-2.

431

Baden, Michael M.; Hennessee, Judith Adler
(1990). *Unnatural Death: Confessions of a Medical Examiner*.
Ballantine. ISBN 978-0-8041-0599-6.
Ramsland, Katherine (2010). ""Cyril Wecht: Forensic
Pathologist – Coverup for a King"". Trutv.
Guralnick, Peter (1999). *Careless Love: The Unmaking of Elvis
Presley*. Back Bay Books. ISBN 978-0-316-33297-2.

432

Baden, Michael M.; Hennessee, Judith Adler
(1990). *Unnatural Death: Confessions of a Medical Examiner*.
Ballantine. ISBN 978-0-8041-0599-6.
Ramsland, Katherine (2010). ""Cyril Wecht: Forensic
Pathologist – Coverup for a King"". Trutv.

Higginbotham, Alan (August 11, 2002). "Doctor Feelgood". *The Observer*.

433

Tennant, Forest (June 2013). "Elvis Presley: Head Trauma, Autoimmunity, Pain, and Early Death". *Practical Pain Management*.
Higginbotham, Alan (August 11, 2002). "Doctor Feelgood". *The Observer*.
Williamson, Joel (2015). *Elvis Presley: A Southern Life*. Oxford University Press. ISBN 978-0-19-986317-4.
Wertheimer, Neil (1997). *Total Health for Men*. Rodale Press.

434

Lott, Eric; Uebel, Michael (1997). ""All the King's Men: Elvis Impersonators and White Working-Class Masculinity"". In Stecopoulos, Harry (ed.). *Race and the Subject of Masculinities*. Duke University Press. ISBN 978-0-8223-1966-5.

Doss, Erika Lee (1999). *Elvis Culture: Fans, Faith, and Image*. University of Kansas Press. ISBN 978-0-7006-0948-2.

Keogh, Pamela Clarke (2004). *Elvis Presley: The Man, The Life, The Legend*. Simon & Schuster. ISBN 978-0-7434-5603-6.

Victor, Adam (2008). *The Elvis Encyclopedia*. Overlook Duckworth. ISBN 978-1-58567-598-2.

435

Victor, Adam (2008). *The Elvis Encyclopedia*. Overlook Duckworth. ISBN 978-1-58567-598-2.

Whitburn, Joel (2010). *The Billboard Book of Top 40 Hits* (9th ed.). Billboard Books. ISBN 978-0-8230-8554-5.

436

Victor, Adam (2008). *The Elvis Encyclopedia*. Overlook Duckworth. ISBN 978-1-58567-598-2.

Whitburn, Joel (2010). *The Billboard Book of Top 40 Hits* (9th ed.). Billboard Books. ISBN 978-0-8230-8554-5.

437

Milly, Jenna (August 26, 2002). "A Hunka-Hunka Fried Peanut Butter". *CNN*.
Martin, Douglas (June 5, 2000). "Mary Jenkins Langston, 78, Cook for Presley". *The New York Times*.

438

Kerlinger, Charlie (2022). Elvis Presley: King Of Rock And Roll And Hollywood Walk Of Fame Star. Retrieved from: https://www.benvaughn.com/elvis-presley-king-of-rock-and-roll-and-hollywood-walk-of-fame-star/

439

Chan, Melissa (2017). Elvis Presley Died 40 Years Ago. Here's Why Some People Think He's Still Alive. *Time*. Https://time.com/4897819/elvis-presley-alive-conspiracy-theories/

Lusher, A. (2017). Why are people so convinced Elvis is still alive? The bizarre world of 'the King's truth seekers'. Https://www.the-independent.com/arts-entertainment/music/features/elvis-presley-alive-sightings-seen-spotted-working-in-graceland-groundsman-82nd-birthday-proof-king-of-rock-n-roll-faked-his-own-death-dead-on-toilet-dna-evidence-autopsy-biopsy-not-in-the-a7895261.html

440

"Beyoncé's star formation: from Destiny's Child to Queen Bey". *The Guardian*. June 27, 2016. Retrieved from: https://www.theguardian.com/music/2016/jun/27/beyonce-star-formation-destinys-child-queen-bey-tour

441

"Beyoncé's Style Evolution: See Photos". *Billboard*. June 24, 2022. Retrieved from: https://www.billboard.com/photos/beyonces-style-evolution-see-photos-1235105288/1-beyonce-2000-style-evolution-billboard-1240/

442

Trust, Gary (July 5, 2022). "Beyonce Joins Paul mccartney & Michael Jackson for This Hot 100 Milestone — As a Solo Artist & With a Group". *Billboard*.

443

Cooper, Brittney. "Beyoncé: Time 100 Women of the Year – 2014: Beyoncé Knowles-Carter". *Time*.

"Artist of the Decade". *Billboard*. March 12, 2013. Retrieved from: https://www.billboard.com/music/music-news/artists-of-the-decade-266420/

444

"Beyoncé Knowles' Biography". Fox News Channel. April 15, 2008. Retrieved from: http://www.foxnews.com/story/0%2C2933%2C204978%2C00.html?Spage=fnc%2Fentertainment%2Fbeyonce

Dhillon, Georgina (October 3, 2012). "Beyoncé Knowles: A Creole Queen". *Kreol International Magazine*. UK: Rila Publications.

Khanna, Nikki (2011). *Biracial in America: Forming and Performing Racial Identity*. Vermont: Lexington Books. P. 63. ISBN 978-0-7391-4574-6.

445

Cherese Cartlidge (May 17, 2012). *Beyoncé*. Greenhaven Publishing LLC. P. 14. ISBN 978-1-4205-0966-3.

Janice Arenofsky (2009). *Beyoncé Knowles: A Biography*. ABC-CLIO. P. 2. ISBN 978-0-313-35914-9.

"Beyoncé Knowles: Biography – Part 1". *People*. Retrieved from:
https://web.archive.org/web/20080307175108/http://www.foxnews.com/story/0,2933,204978,00.html?Spage=fnc%2Fentertainment%2Fbeyonce

446

"Beyoncé Knowles: Biography – Part 1". *People*. Retrieved from:
https://web.archive.org/web/20080307175108/http://www.foxnews.com/story/0,2933,204978,00.html?Spage=fnc%2Fentertainment%2Fbeyonce

447

Tyrangiel, Josh (June 13, 2003). "Destiny's Adult". *Time*.

Kaufman, Gil (June 13, 2005). "Destiny's Child's Long Road To Fame (The Song Isn't Called "Survivor" For Nothing)". MTV News.

448

"Beyoncé Knowles' Biography". Fox News Channel. April 15, 2008. Retrieved from:
http://www.foxnews.com/story/0%2C2933%2C204978%2C00.html?Spage=fnc%2Fentertainment%2Fbeyonce

449

Dekel-Daks, Tal (January 29, 2013). "Ten Things About ... Destiny's Child". *Digital Spy*. Retrieved from:
https://www.digitalspy.com/showbiz/10-things-about/a454691/ten-things-about-destinys-child/

450

Kaufman, Gil (June 13, 2005). "Destiny's Child's Long Road To Fame (The Song Isn't Called "Survivor" For Nothing)". MTV News.
"The Best Man – Original Soundtrack".
Allmusic. Archived from the original on October 27, 2021.
Farley, Christopher John (January 15, 2001). "Music: Call Of The Child". *Time*. Retrieved from:
https://web.archive.org/web/20071130020409/http://www w.time.com/time/magazine/article/0,9171,998976,00.html

451

Kaufman, Gil (June 13, 2005). "Destiny's Child's Long Road To Fame (The Song Isn't Called "Survivor" For Nothing)". MTV News.
"Beyoncé: 'I was depressed at 19'". Contact Music. December 1, 2008. Retrieved from:
https://www.contactmusic.com/beyonce-knowles/news/beyonce-i-was-depressed-at-19_1088171
"Beyoncé Knowles Opens Up About Depression". *Female First*. CBS Interactive Inc. December 18, 2006. Retrieved from:
https://www.femalefirst.co.uk/celebrity/Beyonce+Knowles-12915.html

452

Basham, David (January 18, 2001). "Beyoncé To Star In "Carmen" Remake". MTV News. Retrieved from:
https://www.mtv.com/news/lcpbxf/beyonc-to-star-in-carmen-remake#:~:text=Destiny's%20Child%20frontwoman%20Bey onc%C3%A9%20Knowles,by%20French%20composer%20G eorges%20Bizet.

453

Chandler, D. L. (April 5, 2011). "Jay-Z And Beyoncé Celebrate Three Years Of Wedded Bliss". MTV Rapfix. Viacom. Retrieved from:

https://web.archive.org/web/20110408000429/http://rapfi
x.mtv.com/2011/04/05/jay-z-and-beyonce-celebrate-three-
years-of-wedded-bliss/
"Beyoncé Knowles: Dangerously in Love". *The Guardian*.
June 26, 2003.

454

Martens, Todd (November 28, 2003). "'Stand Up' Ends 'Baby
Boy' Reign". *Billboard*.
Patel, Joseph (February 4, 2004). "Beyoncé Wins Most,
Outkast Shine, 50 Cent Shut Out at Grammys". MTV News.

455

Patel, Joseph (January 28, 2004). "Beyoncé, Alicia Keys And
Missy Elliott Plan Spring Tour". MTV News.
Alexis, Nadeska (October 16, 2012). "Beyoncé To Perform at
Super Bowl XLVII Halftime Show". MTV News.
"Gold and Platinum – Destiny's Child". Recording Industry
Association of America (RIAA).

456

Welch, Andy (May 22, 2014). "Destiny's Child reunite on new
Michelle Williams song 'Say Yes' – listen". *NME*.

Cohen, Jonathan (June 15, 2005). "Destiny's Child To Split
After Fall Tour". *Billboard*.

"Destiny's Child Debuts World Children's Day at mcdonald's
Anthem" (Press release). Los Angeles. PR Newswire.
November 15, 2005.

"Beyoncé and Solange Knowles Become First Sisters to Land
No. 1 Albums". Etonline.com. Retrieved from:
https://www.etonline.com/music/199983_beyonce_and_sol
ange_knowles_become_first_sisters_to_have_number_1_alb
ums

457

Hasty, Katie (September 13, 2006). "Beyoncé's *B-Day* Makes Big Bow at No. 1". *Billboard.*

"Beyoncé – Irreplaceable". Australian-charts.com. Archived from the original on July 7, 2012.

"Green Light the next single". Sony BMG Music Entertainment (UK). July 27, 2007.

"49th Annual Grammy Awards Winners List". Grammy Awards.

"*B'Day* (Deluxe Edition) – Beyoncé". Allmusic. Retrieved from: https://www.allmusic.com/album/release/bday-deluxe-edition-mr0002778311

Whitfield, Deanne (October 27, 2007). "Malaysia's loss is Indonesia's gain: Beyoncé Knowles to play Jakarta". *The Jakarta Post.*

458

"I Am ... Sasha Fierce". Allmusic. Archived from the original on October 27, 2021. Retrieved from: https://www.allmusic.com/album/i-amsasha-fierce-mw0000801448

Jonathan, Cohen (November 26, 2008). "Beyoncé Starts 'Fierce' Atop Album Chart". *Billboard.*

"Don Omar: The Reggaeton Starts Plugs In For Digital Sales With 'idon' And An iphone App". *Billboard.* Vol. 121, no. 16. April 25, 2009. P. 41. ISSN 0006-2510.

Crawford, Trish (January 23, 2009). "Beyoncé's single an anthem for women". *Toronto Star.*

Nero, Mark Edward. "2009 BET Awards". About.com.

Casserly, Meghan (December 10, 2012). "Beyoncé's $50 Million Pepsi Deal Takes Creative Cues From Jay-Z". *Forbes*.

Masterson, Lawrie (April 12, 2009). "Is Beyoncé Beyond Her Best?". *The Daily Telegraph*.

Harling, Danielle (January 5, 2007). "Beyoncé Donates Movie Salary To Drug Treatment Centers". Black Entertainment Television.

Kaufman, Gil (January 16, 2009). "Beyoncé To Sing For Obamas' First Dance at Inaugural Ball". MTV News.

Lewis, Hilary (April 25, 2009). "Box Office Preview: Audience *Obsessed* With Beyoncé". *Business Insider*.

Wigler, Josh (June 6, 2010). "2010 MTV Movie Awards: Complete Winners List". MTV News.

Donahue, Ann (December 20, 2009). "Beyoncé, Taylor Swift, Peas Lead Grammy Award Nominations". *Billboard*.

Lamb, Bill. "Beyoncé Tied With Lauryn Hill For Most Grammy Nominations in a Single Year by a Female Artist". About.com.

Trust, Gary (March 15, 2010). "Lady Gaga, Beyoncé Match Mariah's Record". *Billboard*.

Sperling, Daniel (July 30, 2011). "Beyoncé: 'Career break saved my sanity'". *Digital Spy*.

Knowles, Beyoncé. "Eat, Play, Love". *Essence*.

Crosley, Hillary (February 26, 2010). "Beyoncé Says She 'Killed' Sasha Fierce". MTV News.

Johnson, Caitlin A. (December 13, 2006). "Beyoncé On Love, Depression, and Reality". *CBS News*.

459

"Beyoncé to Headline Glastonbury Festival" (Press release). Columbia Records. February 10, 2011. Retrieved from: https://www.prnewswire.com/news-releases/beyonce-to-headline-glastonbury-festival-115756999.html

Phillips, Sarah (June 28, 2011). "Beyoncé headlining at Glastonbury was a great girl power moment". *The Guardian*. London.

Dillon, Nancy (May 2, 2012). "Beyoncé set to win a writing award from the New York Association of Black Journalists". *Daily News*.

"Beyoncé To Perform '4 Intimate Nights With Beyoncé' At New York's Roseland Ballroom". Beyoncé's Official Website. August 5, 2011.

Grein, Paul (July 2, 2014). "Chart Watch: Ed Sheeran's Transatlantic #1". Yahoo! Music.

Makarechi, Kia (May 25, 2012). "Beyoncé, Revel: Singer's Atlantic City Concerts Mark First Return To Stage Since Blue Ivy Carter Was Born". *Huffpost*.

Prance, Sam (February 5, 2011). "Beyoncé Breaks Spotify Record as '4' Hits a Billion Streams". MTV.

Garibaldi, Christina (January 11, 2013). "Destiny's Child Drop New Single 'Nuclear'". MTV News.

Richards, Chris (January 10, 2013). "Beyoncé to sing 'The Star-Spangled Banner' at inauguration". *The Washington Post*.

Acuna, Kirsten (January 23, 2013). "HBO Wasn't 'Crazy in Love' With Beyoncé Co-Directing Her Documentary". *Business Insider.*

460

Ramsay, Jennifer. "Beyoncé Shatters itunes Store Records With 828,773 Albums Sold in Just Three Days". Apple.

Caulfield, Keith (December 17, 2013). "It's Official: Beyoncé Makes History With Fifth No. 1 Album". *Billboard.*

"Beyoncé announces 2014 UK and Ireland tour taking in O2 Arena and more". *Metro.* UK. December 11, 2013.

Malkin, Marc (April 2013). "Beyoncé Covering Amy Winehouse for The Great Gatsby". E News. Montgomery, James (May 31, 2012). "Beyoncé Cast As Queen Tara in 3-D Animated Film 'Epic'". MTV News.

Sisario, Ben (December 16, 2013). "Beyoncé Rejects Tradition for Social Media's Power". *The New York Times.*

Makarechi, Kia (December 18, 2013). "Beyoncé's Album Sales Cross 1 Million in itunes". *Huffpost.*

Mackay, Emily (December 16, 2013). "Beyoncé – Beyoncé". *NME.* Retrieved from: https://www.nme.com/reviews/reviews-beyonce-15005-316828

Trust, Gary (February 5, 2014). "Katy Perry Tops Hot 100, Beyoncé Bounds to No. 2". *Billboard.*

Grow, Kory (August 7, 2014). "Beyoncé to Receive MTV Video Vanguard Award, Perform at vmas". *Rolling Stone.*

Copsey, Rob (March 6, 2015). "Beyoncé revealed as most-streamed female artist by women". Official Charts Company.

"Kanye West storms Grammy stage, rants about Beck's surprise album of the year win". Fox News Channel. February 9, 2015. Retrieved from: https://web.archive.org/web/20150209113458/http://www.foxnews.com/entertainment/2015/02/09/kanye-west-storms-grammy-stage-over-beck-surprise-grammy-win/

461

Kreps, Daniel (February 6, 2016). "Watch Beyoncé's Surprise New Video For 'Formation'". *Rolling Stone.*

Waddell, Ray (February 8, 2016). "Beyoncé to Embark on 'Formation' Stadium Tour". *Billboard.*

"Beyoncé sends political message with Super Bowl halftime performance of new single, "Formation"". *CBS News.* Retrieved from: https://www.cbsnews.com/news/super-bowl-50-beyonce-single-formation-police-brutality-black-lives-matter-coldplay-bruno-mars/

"amas 2016: See the Full List of Winners". *Billboard.* November 20, 2016. Retrieved from: https://www.billboard.com/music/awards/amas-2016-winners-list-7581457/

Caulfield, Keith (May 1, 2016). "Beyoncé Earns Sixth No. 1 Album on Billboard 200 Chart With 'Lemonade'". *Billboard.* Retrieved from: https://www.billboard.com/pro/beyonce-earns-sixth-no-1-album-on-billboard-200-chart-with-lemonade/

Rys, Dan (April 25, 2017). "Beyonce's 'Lemonade' Was the World's Best-Selling Album in 2016". *Variety.* Retrieved from: https://variety.com/2017/music/news/beyonce-lemonade-drake-one-dance-best-selling-2016-1202395667/

Herbert, Geoff (December 5, 2016). "Time Person of the Year: 2016 finalists revealed – who should win?". *Syracuse.com*.

Vaglanos, Alanna (January 4, 2017). "For The First Time Ever, A Black Woman Will Be Headlining Coachella". *Huffpost*. AOL.

Blair, Olivia (February 13, 2017). "Grammy Awards 2017: Beyoncé tearful as Adele dedicates Album of the Year win to Lemonade". *The Independent*.
Trust, Gary (December 11, 2017). "Ed Sheeran & Beyonce's 'Perfect' Tops Billboard Hot 100". *Billboard*.

Exposito, Suzy (April 15, 2018). "Beychella: Beyonce Schools Festivalgoers in Her Triumphant Return". *Rolling Stone*. New York City.

"Beyoncé and Jay-Z leave their hearts on stage and gave us Everything". *Timeslive*. Retrieved from: https://www.elle.com/fashion/celebrity-style/a25378332/beyonces-global-citizen-outfits-africa/

462

Weingarten, Christopher R. (April 17, 2019). "Beyoncé's 'Homecoming': 5 Things We Learned About Her Coachella Triumph". *The New York Times*.

Aswad, Jem; Halperin, Shirley (April 19, 2019). "Beyonce's Netflix Deal Worth a Whopping $60 Million". *Variety*.

Lesnick, Silas (April 25, 2017). "Disney Movie Release Schedule Gets a Major Update". *Comingsoon.net*.

Gonzales, Erica (January 24, 2019). "Beyoncé Is Singing "Can You Feel the Love Tonight" in the Lion King Remake". *Harper Bazzar*.

Strauss, Matthew (July 9, 2019). "Beyoncé Releasing New Song "Spirit" Tonight, Curates Lion King Album". *Pitchfork Media*.

Strauss, Matthew (July 9, 2019). "Beyoncé Releasing New Song "Spirit" Tonight, Curates Lion King Album". *Pitchfork Media*.

Kreps, Daniel (June 19, 2020). "Beyoncé Drops Surprise New Song 'Black Parade' on Juneteenth". *Rolling Stone*.

Romack, Coco (June 23, 2020). "Beyoncé Just Dropped A Powerful A Capella Rendition Of 'Black Parade'". *MTV News*.

Spangler, Todd (June 28, 2020). "Beyoncé Visual Album 'Black Is King' Coming to Disney Plus". *Variety*.

Daly, Rhian (March 15, 2021). "Beyoncé breaks record for most Grammy wins by a female artist or any singer". *NME*.

Triscari, Caleb (September 5, 2021). "Beyoncé contributes new song 'Be Alive' to Will Smith's 'King Richard' film". *NME*.

Bahr, Sarah (February 8, 2022). "Beyoncé Scores Her First Oscar Nomination". *The New York Times*. ISSN 0362-4331

463

Bloom, Madison (June 20, 2022). "Listen to Beyoncé's New Song "Break My Soul"". *Pitchfork*.

Sisario, Ben (June 16, 2022). "Beyoncé Announces New Album 'Renaissance,' Out Next Month". *The New York Times*.

Caulfield, Keith (August 7, 2022). "Beyonce's 'Renaissance' Bows at No. 1 on Billboard 200 With Year's Biggest Debut By a Woman". *Billboard*.

"Beyoncé is criticised for using an offensive lyric on her Renaissance album". *BBC News*.
Snapes, Laura (January 22, 2023). "Beyoncé makes controversial live return at exclusive Dubai concert". *The Guardian*.

Skinner, Tom; tomskinner (January 23, 2023). "Beyoncé faces backlash for performing private show in Dubai". *Rolling Stone UK*.

Aswad, Jem (February 1, 2023). "Beyoncé Announces 'Renaissance' Stadium Tour Dates". *Variety*. Penske Media Corporation. Retrieved from: https://variety.com/2023/music/news/beyonce-renaissance-world-tour-1235508233/

464

Caldwell, Rebecca. "Beyoncé Knowles admire "Tina Turner is someone that I admire". *Quotefancy*. Retrieved from: https://quotefancy.com/quote/1277761/Beyonc-Knowles-Tina-Turner-is-someone-that-I-admire-because-she-made-her-strength

Watson, Margeaux (August 29, 2006). "Influences: Beyoncé". *Entertainment Weekly*.
Caldwell, Rebecca (July 21, 2001). "Destiny's Child". *The Globe and Mail*. Toronto, Ontario, Canada: The Woodbridge Company. P. R1.

Frere-Jones, Sasha (April 3, 2006). "Mariah Carey's record-breaking career". *The New Yorker*.
Arenofsky, Janice (2009). *Beyoncé Knowles: A Biography*. Greenwood Press. P. 80. ISBN 978-0-313-35914-9.

Watson, Margeaux (August 29, 2006). "Influences: Beyoncé". *Entertainment Weekly*.

Bickel, Britt (April 6, 2012). "Beyoncé Shares Personal Family Photos, Thanks Sade On New Website". CBS Radio.

Gibson, Cristina & Ashley Fultz (January 14, 2011). "Which Famous Friend's B-Day Did Jay-Z and Beyoncé Celebrate?". E!.

Bain, Becky (May 18, 2013). "Beyoncé Pays Tribute To Donna Summer: "She Was An Honest And Gifted Singer"". *Idolator.*

Watson, Margeaux (August 29, 2006). "Influences: Beyoncé". *Entertainment Weekly.*

Wikipedia (2025). Cultural Impact of Beyonce. Https://en.wikipedia.org/wiki/Cultural_impact_of_Beyonc%C3%A9

465

"Beyoncé, Top Stars Tip Their Hats to Michael Jackson". *People. June 27, 2009*
"One-on-one with the great Beyoncé transcript". *Yahoo!. October 11, 2011. Archived from* the original *on July 14, 2014.*
 "Michael Jackson returns to stage". *BBC News. November 16, 2006.* Archived *from the original on October 27, 2021.*
Caldwell, Rebecca. "Beyoncé Knowles admire "Tina Turner is someone that I admire". *Quotefancy.* Archived *from the original on October 27, 2021.*
Watson, Margeaux (August 29, 2006). "Influences: Beyoncé". *Entertainment Weekly.* Archived *from the original on January 7, 2007.*
Caldwell, Rebecca (July 21, 2001). "Destiny's Child". The Globe and Mail. *Toronto, Ontario, Canada:* The Woodbridge Company. *P. R1.* Archived *from the original on October 27, 2021.*
"Beyonce: 'I Always Wanted To Be Just Like Whitney Houston'". *Essence.*

Arenofsky, Janice (2009). Beyoncé Knowles: A Biography. Greenwood Press. *P. 80.* ISBN 978-0-313-35914-9.
"Beyonce inspired by Madonna". Business Standard. *December 24, 2013.* Archived *from the original on October 27, 2021.*
"The 50 Best R&B Albums of the '90s". Complex. Archived *from the original on October 27, 2021. Frere-Jones, Sasha (April 3, 2006).* "Mariah Carey's record-breaking career". *The New Yorker.* Archived *from the original on October 27, 2021.*
August 30, Margeaux Watson Updated; EDT, 2006 at 04:00 AM. "Beyonce: What influences my music". *EW.com.*
Admin (January 13, 2021). "Beyoncé". *Stylectory.*
"Beyoncé". *Teachrock.*
"Janet Jackson comeback: 7 pop stars she influenced". *HELLO!. May 16, 2016.*
Chan, Stephanie (October 31, 2014). "Beyonce Dresses Up as Janet Jackson for Halloween". *The Hollywood Reporter.*
"Exclusive: Beyoncé Talks Prince: 'I Was So Scared!'". Giant. *Radio One. June 7, 2010.* Archived *from the original on June 16, 2010.*
Retrieved May 20, 2019. (July 2018). "10 celebridades que son grandes fanáticas de otras celebridades". *E! Online.* Archived *from the original on October 27, 2021.*
Bickel, Britt (April 6, 2012). "Beyoncé Shares Personal Family Photos, Thanks Sade On New Website". CBS Radio. *Archived from* the original *on April 13, 2012.*
Bain, Becky (May 18, 2013). "Beyoncé Pays Tribute To Donna Summer: "She Was An Honest And Gifted Singer"". Idolator. Archived *from the original on October 27, 2021.*
Gibson, Cristina & Ashley Fultz (January 14, 2011). "Which Famous Friend's B-Day Did Jay-Z and Beyoncé Celebrate?". E!. Archived *from the original on August 5, 2011.*

466

"When Did Beyoncé and Jay-Z Start Dating?". *Capital FM.* Retrieved from:

https://web.archive.org/web/20180521130800/http://ww
w.capitalfm.com/artists/beyonce-knowles/photos/jay-z-
relationship-best-moments/dating/

Chandler, D.L. "Jay-Z and Beyoncé Celebrate Three Years of
Wedded Bliss". MTV Rapfix.

Helling, Steve (April 22, 2008). "Beyoncé and Jay-Z File
Signed Marriage License". *People*.

Lee, Youyoung (June 3, 2013). "Beyoncé, Jay-Z Go On Date
in New York, Watch *Iron Man 3*". *Huffpost*.

"Beyoncé documentary describing 'pain and trauma' of
miscarriage airs on BBC – News – TV & Radio". *The
Independent*. Retrieved from:
https://web.archive.org/web/20130331011153/http://ww
w.independent.co.uk/arts-entertainment/tv/news/beyonc-
documentary-describing-pain-and-trauma-of-miscarriage-
airs-on-bbc-8495450.html

Bailey, Alyssa (April 6, 2018). "Jay-Z on Overcoming
Cheating: Beyoncé 'Knew I'm Not the Worst of What i've
Done'". *Elle*. New York City: Hachette Filipacchi
Media. Retrieved from:
https://www.elle.com/culture/celebrities/a19700877/jay-z-
on-cheating-on-beyonce-david-letterman-interview/

Bernstein, Nina (January 9, 2012). "After Beyoncé Gives
Birth, Patients Protest Celebrity Security at Lenox Hill
Hospital". *The New York Times*

Smith, Catharine (August 29, 2011). "Beyoncé Pregnancy:
New Twitter Record Set At MTV vmas". *Huffpost*.

467

BBC (2017). Jay-Z admits to cheating on Beyonce and says music was their 'therapy'. *Bbcnewsbeat*. Retrieved from: https://www.bbc.com/news/newsbeat-42177522

Koimoi.com Team (2023). When Jay Z Confessed To Cheating On His Wife, Beyonce & Said: "In My Case, It's Deep, Then All The Things Happen There: Infidelity..." *Hollywood News*. Retrieved from: https://www.koimoi.com/hollywood-news/when-jay-z-confessed-to-cheating-on-his-wife-beyonce-said-in-my-case-its-deep-then-all-the-things-happen-there-infidelity/

Bailey, Alyssa (April 6, 2018). "Jay-Z on Overcoming Cheating: Beyoncé 'Knew I'm Not the Worst of What i've Done'". *Elle*. New York City: Hachette Filipacchi Media. Retrieved from: https://www.elle.com/culture/celebrities/a19700877/jay-z-on-cheating-on-beyonce-david-letterman-interview/

Pareles, Jon (April 25, 2016). "Review: Beyoncé Makes 'Lemonade' Out of Marital Strife". *The New York Times*.

468

Bergin, Allen E., (1994). Psychology and Repentance. BYU Speeches. Retrieved from: https://speeches.byu.edu/talks/allen-e-bergin/psychology-repentance/

469

Stritof, Sheri Causes and Risks of Why Married People Cheat. Verywell Mind. Retrieved from: https://www.verywellmind.com/why-married-people-cheat-2300656#:~:text=Why%20do%20people%20cheat%3F,%2C%20%20sexual%20desire%2C%20and%20circumstance.

470

Tabik, M. (2019). Psychological functions of repentance according to Islamic sources. *Journal of Islamic Psychology*, 4(9), 5-28. Retrieved from: http://psychology.riqh.ac.ir/article_13133.html?Lang=en#:~:text=Based%20on%20semantic%20functions%20of,)%20%E2%80%9Cincreased%20divinity%20development%E2%80%9D.

471

Forgiveness. A Guide to Psychology and its Practice. Retrieved from: https://www.guidetopsychology.com/forgive.htm

472

"Beyoncé's star formation: from Destiny's Child to Queen Bey". *The Guardian*. Retrieved from: https://www.theguardian.com/music/2016/jun/27/beyonce-star-formation-destinys-child-queen-bey-tour

Grady, Constance (August 15, 2022). "How Beyoncé turned herself into a pop god". *Vox*.

"Her Highness". *The New Yorker*. February 20, 2013. Retrieved from: https://www.newyorker.com/culture/culture-desk/her-highness

Fram, Eric (November 20, 2018). "Turning the Tables: Your List Of The 21st Century's Most Influential Women Musicians". NPR.

Smith, Caspar (November 29, 2009). "Beyoncé: artist of the decade". *The Guardian*.

Cooper, Leonie (December 3, 2019). "10 Artists Who Defined The Decade: The 2010s". *NME*.
"Paul Flynn talks to Beyoncé | Music". *The Guardian*. March 9, 2021. Retrieved from:

https://www.theguardian.com/music/2006/aug/18/urban.popandrock

"Michael Eric Dyson Says "Beyoncé Snatched the Crown From Michael Jackson"". *Okayplayer*. February 18, 2019.

Menza, Kaitlin (December 12, 2014). "One Year Later: How Beyoncé's Surprise Album Ended Up Changing the Music Industry Forever". *Marie Claire*.

Cox, Jamieson (April 25, 2016). "Beyoncé's 'visual album' Lemonade sets a new standard for pop storytelling". *The Verge*.

Smith, Da'Shan (June 2, 2019). "Surprise Albums: 17 Drops That Shocked The Music World | udiscover". *Udiscover Music*.

Atherton, Ben (January 13, 2012). "CSIRO unveils bootylicious Beyoncé fly". ABC News (Australia).

Sommers, Kat. "The Rise of the Visual Album: How 'Lemonade' Stacks Up". *BBC America*. Archived from the original on October 27, 2021.

473

Hertel, Howard; Heff, Don (August 6, 1962). "Marilyn Monroe Dies; Pills Blamed". *Los Angeles Times*.

Chapman, Gary (2001). "Marilyn Monroe". In Browne, Ray B.; Browne, Pat (eds.). *The Guide to United States Popular Culture*. University of Wisconsin Press. ISBN 978-0-87972-821-2.

474

Spoto 2001, p. 88, for first meeting in 1944; Banner 2012, p. 72, for mother telling Monroe of sister in 1938.

Spoto 2001, p. 9 for the exact year when divorce was finalized; Banner 2012, p. 20; Leaming 1998, pp. 52–53.

Banner, Lois (2012). *Marilyn: The Passion and the Paradox.* Bloomsbury. ISBN 978-1-4088-3133-5. Retrieved from: https://archive.org/details/marilynpassionpa0000bann

475

Churchwell, Sarah (2004). *The Many Lives of Marilyn Monroe.* Granta Books. ISBN 978-0-312-42565-4.

Keslassy, Elsa (April 4, 2022). "Marilyn Monroe's Biological Father Revealed in Documentary 'Marilyn, Her Final Secret'". *Variety.*

Anagnoson, Alex (October 2, 2022). "The Truth About Marilyn Monroe's Siblings". *Nicki Swift.*

476

Spoto, Donald (2001). *Marilyn Monroe: The Biography.* Cooper Square Press. ISBN 978-0-8154-1183-3. Retrieved from: https://archive.org/details/marilynmonroe00dona

477

Spoto, Donald (2001). *Marilyn Monroe: The Biography.* Cooper Square Press. ISBN 978-0-8154-1183-3. Retrieved from: https://archive.org/details/marilynmonroe00dona

478

Banner, Lois (2012). *Marilyn: The Passion and the Paradox.* Bloomsbury. ISBN 978-1-4088-3133-5

479

Spoto, Donald (2001). *Marilyn Monroe: The Biography.* Cooper Square Press. ISBN 978-0-8154-1183-3. Retrieved from: https://archive.org/details/marilynmonroe00dona

"Inside Marilyn Monroe's Family Tree". November 17, 2020. Retrieved from: https://www.biography.com/actors/marilyn-monroe-family-genealogy

Anagnoson, Alex (October 2, 2022). "The Truth About Marilyn Monroe's Siblings". *Nicki Swift.*

Banner, Lois (2012). *Marilyn: The Passion and the Paradox.* Bloomsbury. ISBN 978-1-4088-3133-5. Retrieved from: https://archive.org/details/marilynpassionpa0000bann

480

Banner, Lois (2012). *Marilyn: The Passion and the Paradox.* Bloomsbury. ISBN 978-1-4088-3133-5. Https://archive.org/details/marilynpassionpa0000bann

Spoto, Donald (2001). *Marilyn Monroe: The Biography.* Cooper Square Press. ISBN 978-0-8154-1183-3. Retrieved from: https://archive.org/details/marilynmonroe00dona/page/n9/mode/2up

Churchwell, Sarah (2004). *The Many Lives of Marilyn Monroe.* Granta Books. ISBN 978-0-312-42565-4.
Summers, Anthony (1985). *Goddess: The Secret Lives of Marilyn Monroe.* Victor Gollancz Ltd. ISBN 978-0-575-03641-3.

481

Banner, Lois (2012). *Marilyn: The Passion and the Paradox.* Bloomsbury. ISBN 978-1-4088-3133-5. Https://archive.org/details/marilynpassionpa0000bann

Spoto, Donald (2001). *Marilyn Monroe: The Biography.* Cooper Square Press. ISBN 978-0-8154-1183-3. Retrieved from: https://archive.org/details/marilynmonroe00dona/page/n9/mode/2up

Churchwell, Sarah (2004). *The Many Lives of Marilyn Monroe*. Granta Books. ISBN 978-0-312-42565-4.

Summers, Anthony (1985). *Goddess: The Secret Lives of Marilyn Monroe*. Victor Gollancz Ltd. ISBN 978-0-575-03641-3.

482

Banner, Lois (2012). *Marilyn: The Passion and the Paradox*. Bloomsbury. ISBN 978-1-4088-3133-5. Https://archive.org/details/marilynpassionpa0000bann

Spoto, Donald (2001). *Marilyn Monroe: The Biography*. Cooper Square Press. ISBN 978-0-8154-1183-3. Retrieved from: https://archive.org/details/marilynmonroe00dona/page/n9/mode/2up

Churchwell, Sarah (2004). *The Many Lives of Marilyn Monroe*. Granta Books. ISBN 978-0-312-42565-4.

Summers, Anthony (1985). *Goddess: The Secret Lives of Marilyn Monroe*. Victor Gollancz Ltd. ISBN 978-0-575-03641-3.

482

Banner, Lois (2012). *Marilyn: The Passion and the Paradox*. Bloomsbury. ISBN 978-1-4088-3133-5. Https://archive.org/details/marilynpassionpa0000bann

Spoto, Donald (2001). *Marilyn Monroe: The Biography*. Cooper Square Press. ISBN 978-0-8154-1183-3. Retrieved from: https://archive.org/details/marilynmonroe00dona/page/n9/mode/2up

Churchwell, Sarah (2004). *The Many Lives of Marilyn Monroe*. Granta Books. ISBN 978-0-312-42565-4.

Summers, Anthony (1985). *Goddess: The Secret Lives of Marilyn Monroe*. Victor Gollancz Ltd. ISBN 978-0-575-03641-3.

483

Waxman, Olivia, B. (2018). How Did Marilyn Monroe Get Her Name? This Photo Reveals the Story. *Time*. Retrieved from: https://time.com/5368339/marilyn-monroe-real-name-story/

"How Did Marilyn Monroe Get Her Name? This Photo Reveals the Story". *Time*. Retrieved from: https://time.com/5368339/marilyn-monroe-real-name-story/

484

Gilchrist, Ava (2001). Here's What 'Blonde' Get's Right (And Wrong) About Marilyn Monroe & JFK's Relationship. *Marie Claire*. Retrieved from: https://www.marieclaire.com.au/marilyn-monroe-jfk-relationship

Crossan, Bob (2022). Blonde: The true story of Marilyn Monroe and the Kennedy brothers. *Luxury London Entertainment*. Retrieved from: https://luxurylondon.co.uk/culture/entertainment/marilyn-monroe-jfk-bobby-kennedy-blonde-netflix/

485

Crossan, Bob (2022). Blonde: The true story of Marilyn Monroe and the Kennedy brothers. *Luxury London Entertainment*. Retrieved from: https://luxurylondon.co.uk/culture/entertainment/marilyn-monroe-jfk-bobby-kennedy-blonde-netflix/

Gilchrist, Ava (2001). Here's What 'Blonde' Get's Right (And Wrong) About Marilyn Monroe & JFK's Relationship. *Marie Claire*. Retrieved from: https://www.marieclaire.com.au/marilyn-monroe-jfk-relationship

486

Banner, Lois (2012). *Marilyn: The Passion and the Paradox.* Bloomsbury. ISBN 978-1-4088-3133-5. Https://archive.org/details/marilynpassionpa0000bann

Spoto, Donald (2001). *Marilyn Monroe: The Biography*. Cooper Square Press. ISBN 978-0-8154-1183-3. Retrieved from: https://archive.org/details/marilynmonroe00dona/page/n9/mode/2up

Churchwell, Sarah (2004). *The Many Lives of Marilyn Monroe.* Granta Books. ISBN 978-0-312-42565-4.

Summers, Anthony (1985). *Goddess: The Secret Lives of Marilyn Monroe.* Victor Gollancz Ltd. ISBN 978-0-575-03641-3.

487

APA (). Suicide and suicide prevention. The American Psychological Association. Retrieved from: https://www.apa.org/topics/suicide

488

Lester, D., Gunn, J. F. (2016). Chapter 32- Psychology of Suicide. *Science Direct, Stress: Concepts, Cognition, Emotion, and Behavior, Handbook of Stress Series Volume 1 2016, Pages 267-272.* Retrieved from: https://www.sciencedirect.com/science/article/pii/B9780128009512000327 ; https://reader.elsevier.com/reader/sd/pii/B9780128009512

000327?Token=FBCA4840194EF0C5DB867C3D01C99E535
E31D6593E31FB85A0ED7F4148F53888C4404B2473388327
20E187C8F36CA15A&originregion=us-east-
1&origincreation=20230425021111

489

Banner, Lois (2012). *Marilyn: The Passion and the Paradox*.
Bloomsbury. ISBN 978-1-4088-3133-5.
Https://archive.org/details/marilynpassionpa0000bann

490

Lester, D., Gunn, J. F. (2016). Chapter 32- Psychology of
Suicide. *Science Direct, Stress: Concepts, Cognition, Emotion,
and Behavior, Handbook of Stress Series Volume 1
2016, Pages 267-272*. Retrieved from:
https://www.sciencedirect.com/science/article/pii/B97801
28009512000327 ;
https://reader.elsevier.com/reader/sd/pii/B9780128009512
000327?Token=FBCA4840194EF0C5DB867C3D01C99E535
E31D6593E31FB85A0ED7F4148F53888C4404B2473388327
20E187C8F36CA15A&originregion=us-east-
1&origincreation=20230425021111

491

"Brilliant Stardom and Personal Tragedy Punctuated the Life
of Marilyn Monroe". *The New York Times*. August 6, 1962.
Retrieved from:
https://archive.nytimes.com/www.nytimes.com/books/98/
11/22/specials/monroe-obit2.html

492

Ben G. Yacobi (2013). The Human Dilemma Life Between
Illusion and Reality. Journal of Philosophy of Life Vol.3, No.3
(September 2013):202-211 [Essay]. Retrieved from:
Http://www.philosophyoflife.org/jpl201312.pdf

493

Azar, Beth (2009). How greed outstripped need: American culture set us up for the economic fall, psychologists say. *American Psychological Association, January, 2009, (40) 1,* https://www.apa.org/monitor/2009/01/consumerism#:~:text=14,Jerusalem%20psychologist%20Shalom%20Schwartz%2C%20phd.

494

Jean-Pierre, T. (2021). Greed Will Continue to Drive Climate Change. *Medium.* Https://medium.com/age-of-awareness/greed-will-continue-to-drive-climate-change-4ec8702b818d

495

Sanders, Bernie (2022). Our economic crisis isn't inflation, it's corporate greed and the GOP will only make that worse. Https://www.sanders.senate.gov/op-eds/our-economic-crisis-isnt-inflation-its-corporate-greed-and-the-gop-will-only-make-that-worse/

496

RICHARD WIKE,JACOB POUSHTER,LAURA SILVERANDJANELL FETTEROLF (2025). U.S. Image Declines in Many Nations Amid Low Confidence in Trump. Pew Research Center. Https://www.pewresearch.org/global/2025/06/11/us-image-declines-in-many-nations-amid-low-confidence-in-trump/

RICHARD WIKEANDJACOB POUSHTER (2016). America's international image. Pew Research Center. Https://www.pewresearch.org/global/2016/06/28/americas-international-image/

497

Statistica (2025). How would you describe the current state of the American economy?

Https://www.statista.com/statistics/1318216/americans-views-current-state-economy/

498

RICHARD WIKE,JACOB POUSHTER,LAURA SILVERANDJANELL FETTEROLF (2025). U.S. Image Declines in Many Nations Amid Low Confidence in Trump. Pew Research Center. Https://www.pewresearch.org/global/2025/06/11/us-image-declines-in-many-nations-amid-low-confidence-in-trump/

RICHARD WIKEANDJACOB POUSHTER (2016). America's international image. Pew Research Center. Https://www.pewresearch.org/global/2016/06/28/americas-international-image/

499

Christina Pazzanese (2025). Economy is doing OK. So why are Americans so pessimistic about their prospects? *The Harvard Gazette*. Https://news.harvard.edu/gazette/story/2025/09/economy-is-doing-ok-so-why-are-americans-so-pessimistic-about-their-prospects/

Copeland, J. (2025). Most Americans continue to rate the U.S. economy negatively as partisan gap widens. Pew Research Center. Https://www.pewresearch.org/short-reads/2025/10/03/most-americans-continue-to-rate-the-us-economy-negatively-as-partisan-gap-widens/#:~:text=Most%20Americans%20continue%20to%20Orate,28%20among%203%2C445%20U.S.%20adults.

Saad, Lydia (2025). Americans' Economic, Financial Expectations Sink in April. Gallup. Https://news.gallup.com/poll/659630/americans-economic-financial-expectations-sink-april.aspx#:~:text=The%20bar%20chart%20titled%20%22Americans,76%25%20over%20the%20same%20period.

500

Copeland, J. (2025). Most Americans continue to rate the U.S. economy negatively as partisan gap widens. Pew Research Center. Https://www.pewresearch.org/short-reads/2025/10/03/most-americans-continue-to-rate-the-us-economy-negatively-as-partisan-gap-widens/#:~:text=Most%20Americans%20continue%20to%20rate,28%20among%203%2C445%20U.S.%20adults.

501

Staff (2024). Nine Charts about Wealth Inequality in America. *Capital One Foundation, as part of Urban's Financial Well-Being Data Hub.* Https://apps.urban.org/features/wealth-inequality-charts/

502

Brenan, Megan (2024). Steady 54% of Americans Identify as Middle Class: More Republicans, fewer Democrats identify as working class and lower class. Gallup. Https://news.gallup.com/poll/645281/steady-americans-identify-middle-class.aspx

503

Shrider, Em (2023). Poverty Rate for the Black Population Fell Below Pre-Pandemic Levels. *United States Census Bureau.* Https://www.census.gov/library/stories/2023/09/black-poverty-rate.html#:~:text=Poverty%20rates%20in%202022%20were,poverty%20(ratio%20of%201.5).

504

JULIANA MENASCE HOROWITZ, RUTH IGIELNIK AND RAKESH KOCHHAR (2020). Most Americans Say There Is Too Much Economic Inequality in the U.S., but Fewer Than Half Call It a Top Priority: Democrats and Republicans differ on whether addressing economic inequality requires major changes to the economic system. Pew Research Center. Https://www.pewresearch.org/social-trends/2020/01/09/most-americans-say-there-is-too-much-economic-inequality-in-the-u-s-but-fewer-than-half-call-it-a-top-priority/ ;

Https://www.pewresearch.org/social-trends/2020/01/09/views-of-economic-inequality/

Https://www.pewresearch.org/social-trends/2020/01/09/what-americans-see-as-contributors-to-economic-inequality/

Https://www.pewresearch.org/social-trends/2020/01/09/views-on-reducing-economic-inequality/

505

JULIANA MENASCE HOROWITZ, RUTH IGIELNIK AND RAKESH KOCHHAR (2020). Most Americans Say There Is Too Much Economic Inequality in the U.S., but Fewer Than Half Call It a Top Priority: Democrats and Republicans differ on whether addressing economic inequality requires major changes to the economic system. Pew Research Center. Https://www.pewresearch.org/social-trends/2020/01/09/views-on-reducing-economic-inequality/

506

NCJRS Virtual Library (1976). ECONOMIC CRISES AND CRIME - CORRELATIONS BETWEEN THE STATE OF THE ECONOMY, DEVIANCE AND THE CONTROL OF DEVIANCE. *U. S. Department of Justice. NCJ Number: 35597.* Https://www.ojp.gov/ncjrs/virtual-library/abstracts/economic-crises-and-crime-correlations-between-state-economy#:~:text=RESEARCH%20FINDINGS%20ARE%20AS%20FOLLOWS,SHARPLY%20IN%20PERIODS%20ECONOMIC%20DISTRESS.

507

Itskovich, E. (2024). Economic Inequality, Relative Deprivation, and Crime: An Individual-Level Examination. Justice Quarterly, 42(4), 637–658. Https://doi.org/10.1080/07418825.2024.2435859 ; https://www.tandfonline.com/doi/full/10.1080/07418825.2024.2435859#abstract

Karpavicius, T., Stavytskyy, A., Giedraitis, V. R., Ulvidienė, E., Kharlamova, G., & Kavaliauskaite, B. (2024). What Determines the Crime Rate? A Macroeconomic Case Study. *Economies, 12*(9), 250. Https://doi.org/10.3390/economies12090250 ; https://www.mdpi.com/2227-7099/12/9/250#:~:text=The%20relationship%20between%20economic%20inequality%20and%20crime,higher%20crime%20rates%20(Widyastaman%20and%20Hartono%202022).

NCJRS Virtual Library (1976). ECONOMIC CRISES AND CRIME - CORRELATIONS BETWEEN THE STATE OF THE ECONOMY, DEVIANCE AND THE CONTROL OF DEVIANCE. *U. S. Department of Justice. NCJ Number: 35597.* Https://www.ojp.gov/ncjrs/virtual-library/abstracts/economic-crises-and-crime-correlations-between-state-economy#:~:text=RESEARCH%20FINDINGS%20ARE%20A

S%20FOLLOWS,SHARPLY%20IN%20PERIODS%20ECONO
MIC%20DISTRESS

508

Ellis, Carl. (2018). "Preaching Redemption Amidst Racism:
Remembering Billy Graham". *Christianity Today.*
Retrieved March 3, 2018. Retrieved from:
https://www.christianitytoday.com/edstetzer/2018/februar
y/advocate-for-all-remembering-billy-graham.html

509

March on Washington for Jobs and Freedom. National Park
Service. Retrieved from:
https://www.nps.gov/articles/march-on-washington.htm

510

(2006). King to lie in repose in Georgia Capitol
Funeral for widow of civil rights leader scheduled for
Tuesday. Retrieved from:
http://www.cnn.com/2006/US/02/02/king.funeral/

511

Suggs, Donnell (2018). The Georgia Governor Who Refused
To Attend MLK's Funeral
Retrieved from: https://mlk.wabe.org/georgia-governor-
refused-attend-mlks-funeral/
Https://en.wikipedia.org/wiki/Assassination_of_Martin_Lut
her_King_Jr.
Funeral of Martin L. King Jr. Retrieved from:
https://en.wikipedia.org/wiki/Funeral_of_Martin_Luther_Ki
ng_Jr.#:~:text=A%20state%20funeral%20or%20lying,Atlanta
%20to%20protect%20state%20property.

512

Black, Conrad *(2007).* Richard M. Nixon: A Life in Full. *New
York: Public Affairs Books.* ISBN 978-1-58648-519-1.

FARRELL, JOHN A. (2017). The Year Nixon Fell Apart
The year was 1970, and the paranoid, stressed president
starting drinking, stealing away from the White House and,
eventually, going after his enemies. Retrieved from:
 Https://www.politico.com/magazine/story/2017/03/john-
farrell-nixon-book-excerpt-214954

513

Bond, Jennie (2006), *Elizabeth: Eighty Glorious Years*, Carlton
Publishing Group, ISBN 1-84442-260-7

Lacey, Robert (2002), *Royal: Her Majesty Queen Elizabeth II*,
Little, Brown, ISBN 0-316-85940-0

Marr, Andrew (2011), *The Diamond Queen: Elizabeth II and
Her People*, Macmillan, ISBN 978-0-230-74852-1

Pimlott, Ben (2001), *The Queen: Elizabeth II and the Monarchy*,
harpercollins, ISBN 0-00-255494-1

514

"Oprah Winfrey – The Many Faces of Oprah". New York TV
Show Tickets Inc. Retrieved from:
https://web.archive.org/web/20100831022714/http://www
.nytix.com/tvshows/Archive/oprahwinfrey/oprahwinfrey.ht
ml

"Oprah Winfrey queen of a declining empire – daytime
TV". *The Christian Science Monitor*. November 22, 2009.
Retrieved from:
https://www.csmonitor.com/USA/2009/1122/p02s01-
usgn.html

Stelter, Brian; Carter, Bill (November 19, 2009). "Oprah
Winfrey to End Her Talk Show". *The New York
Times*. Retrieved from:
https://archive.nytimes.com/mediadecoder.blogs.nytimes.co
m/2009/11/19/oprah-winfrey-to-end-her-talk-show/

515

Statista (2021). Population of the United Kingdom in 2021.
Retrieved from:
https://www.statista.com/statistics/294729/uk-population-
by-
region/#:~:text=Population%20of%20the%20UK%202021%
2C%20by%20region&text=The%20population%20of%20the
%20United,North%20West%20at%207.4%20million.

516

Statista (2021). The Population of England from 1971 to
2021. Retrieved from:
https://www.statista.com/statistics/975956/population-of-
england/#:~:text=The%20population%20of%20England%20
was,by%20approximately%20ten%20million%20people.

517

"The Oprah Winfrey Show". CTV.ca. September 25,
2003. Retrieved from:
https://web.archive.org/web/20070528093333/http://www
.ctv.ca/servlet/articlenews/show/ctvshows/20030925/Opr
ah-bio/20061017/

"Global Distribution List of The Oprah Winfrey Show".
Oprah.com. March 29, 2011. Retrieved from:
https://www.oprah.com/pressroom/global-distribution-list-
of-the-oprah-winfrey-show

518

(2008). Opinion of Oprah More Politicized, Gore's Ratings Improve. *Pew Research Center.* Https://www.pewresearch.org/politics/2008/05/14/opinion-of-oprah-more-politicized-gores-ratings-improve/#:~:text=Table%20of%20Contents-,Table%20of%20Contents,as%20last%20January%20(79%25)

Brenan, Megan (2022). Gallup Vault: Queen Elizabeth Resonated Across the Pond. *Gallup.* Https://news.gallup.com/vault/401282/gallup-vault-queen-elizabeth-resonated-across-pond.aspx

Vanessa Williamson and Isabella Gelfand (2019). Trump and racism: What do the data say? Brookings. Https://www.brookings.edu/articles/trump-and-racism-what-do-the-data-say/

Brian F. Schaffner (2025). Follow the Racist? The Consequences of Trump's Expressions of Prejudice for Mass Rhetoric. *Newhouse Professor of Civic Studies Department of Political Science & Tisch College Tufts University.* Https://www.ashford.zone/images/2018/09/followtheracist_v2.pdf

BRIAN F. SCHAFFNER, MATTHEW MACWILLIAMS and TATISHE NTETA (). Understanding White Polarization in the 2016 Vote for President: The Sobering Role of Racism and Sexism. *POLITICAL SCIENCE QUARTERLY | Volume 133 Number 1 2018 | www.psqonline.org# 2018 Academy of Political Science.* DOI: 10.1002/polq.12737; https://onlinelibrary.wiley.com/doi/epdf/10.1002/polq.12737

Marc Hooghe, and Ruth Dassonneville (2018). Explaining the Trump Vote: The Effect of Racist Resentment and Anti-Immigrant Sentiments. *Cambridge University, American Political Science Association, 2018.*

Doi:10.1017/S1049096518000367 ;
https://www.cambridge.org/core/services/aop-cambridge-core/content/view/537A8ABA46783791BFF4E2E36B90C0BE/s1049096518000367a.pdf/explaining_the_trump_vote_the_effect_of_racist_resentment_and_antiimmigrant_sentiments.pdf

519

History, Art & Archives. The Civil Rights Movement and the Second Reconstruction, 1945—1968, *The United States House of Representatives*. Retrieved from:
https://history.house.gov/Exhibitions-and-Publications/BAIC/Historical-Essays/Keeping-the-Faith/Civil-Rights-Movement/

520

Andy Newmann, John Eligon: *Killer of Malcolm X Is Granted Parole* Archived 2020-10-24 at the Wayback Machine. *The New York Times*, March 20, 2010. Retrieved from:
https://www.nytimes.com/2010/03/20/nyregion/20parole.html

James Fanelli: *Quiet Life of an X Assassin* Archived 2013-05-07 at the Wayback Machine. *New York Post*, May 18, 2008. Retrieved from:
https://nypost.com/2008/05/18/quiet-life-of-an-x-assassin/

David J. Garrow: *Does Anyone Care Who Killed Malcolm X?* Archived 2020-10-24 at the Wayback Machine. *The New York Times*, February 21, 1993. Retrieved from:
https://www.nytimes.com/1993/02/21/opinion/does-anyone-care-who-killed-malcolm-x.html

521

Besant, Alexander (2013). Celebrities tend to die earlier than the average person, study says. The World, Lifestyle. Retrieved from: https://theworld.org/stories/2013-04-18/celebrities-tend-die-earlier-average-person-study-says

---

522

Ben G. Yacobi (2013). The Human Dilemma Life Between Illusion and Reality. Journal of Philosophy of Life Vol.3, No.3 (September 2013):202-211 [Essay]. Retrieved from: Http://www.philosophyoflife.org/jpl201312.pdf